1st edition 2024

ISBN Paperback 979-8-9892342-5-7

ISBN Ebook 979-8-9892342-6-4

Dark Tides

The Crown of the Seven Realms Series

Book III

CONTENT WARNING

Ahoy, Darling Readers!

Before you dive into the wild, untamed waters of this literary adventure, your Captain has a few words of warning for you. This isn't a pleasure cruise, savvy? It's a journey filled with risqué rendezvous, swashbuckling skirmishes, and storms of the heart that'll make even the saltiest sea dog blush.

Sexually Explicit Scenes: Batten down the hatches, brave adventurers! We're charting a course straight into the steamy, saucy, and sometimes downright naughty waters of passion. Prepare yourselves for scenes that'll make a mermaid sing and a Kraken blush. If you're faint of heart or prefer your tales as tame as a landlubber's bath water, you might want to abandon ship now.

This treasure trove is brimming with the following and more:

Spanking, breath play, edging, degradation, rope play, domination, explicit sex, voyeurism, anal play, sex toys, oral play, choking, spitting, cum play, virgin sex, rough sex, power play, orgasm denial, face-fucking, dual penetration, blood and gore, and a whole bounty of other carnal delights that'd make even Blackbeard himself raise an eyebrow.

Violence: Avast, dear readers! This is no pleasure cruise through calm waters. Expect to encounter bloody battles, vicious brawls, and enough brutality to make a shark wince. If your stomach is as delicate as a ship's figurehead, you best steer clear. There are torture, mutilation, and interrogation scenes that'll make you want to walk the plank.

Sensitive Topics: Life on the high seas isn't always smooth sailing, and the characters navigate treacherous emotional waters. We're dealing with mental maelstroms, traumatic tempests, and heartaches that cut deeper than a dagger. It's raw, it's real, and it's as honest as a pirate's promise. But if these turbulent tides hit too close to home—no shame in dropping anchor and taking a breather.

So here's the deal, my dear crew: your well-being is the most precious booty of all. If the seas get too rough, close the book, grab a drink, chat with your mates, or parley with a trusted confidant. You come first, you scurvy dog! Feel free to skip, skim, or sail past any parts that threaten to sink your spirits.

Now, if you're still with me, hoist the colors, don your eyepatch (or remove your garments, no judgment on this ship), and prepare to set sail! It will be a wild ride filled with adventure, passion, and a dash of the forbidden.

Fair winds and following seas (or not, you chart your own course),

Your Captain, The Author with the Most(est) Booty,

A.L. Hampton

CAPTAINS
HAVEN
SIREN
GUARDED
WATERS
SERRAPHATIC
COVE
UNDINITE
PALACE
POOLS
OF
REFLECTION
SELK
SHOR

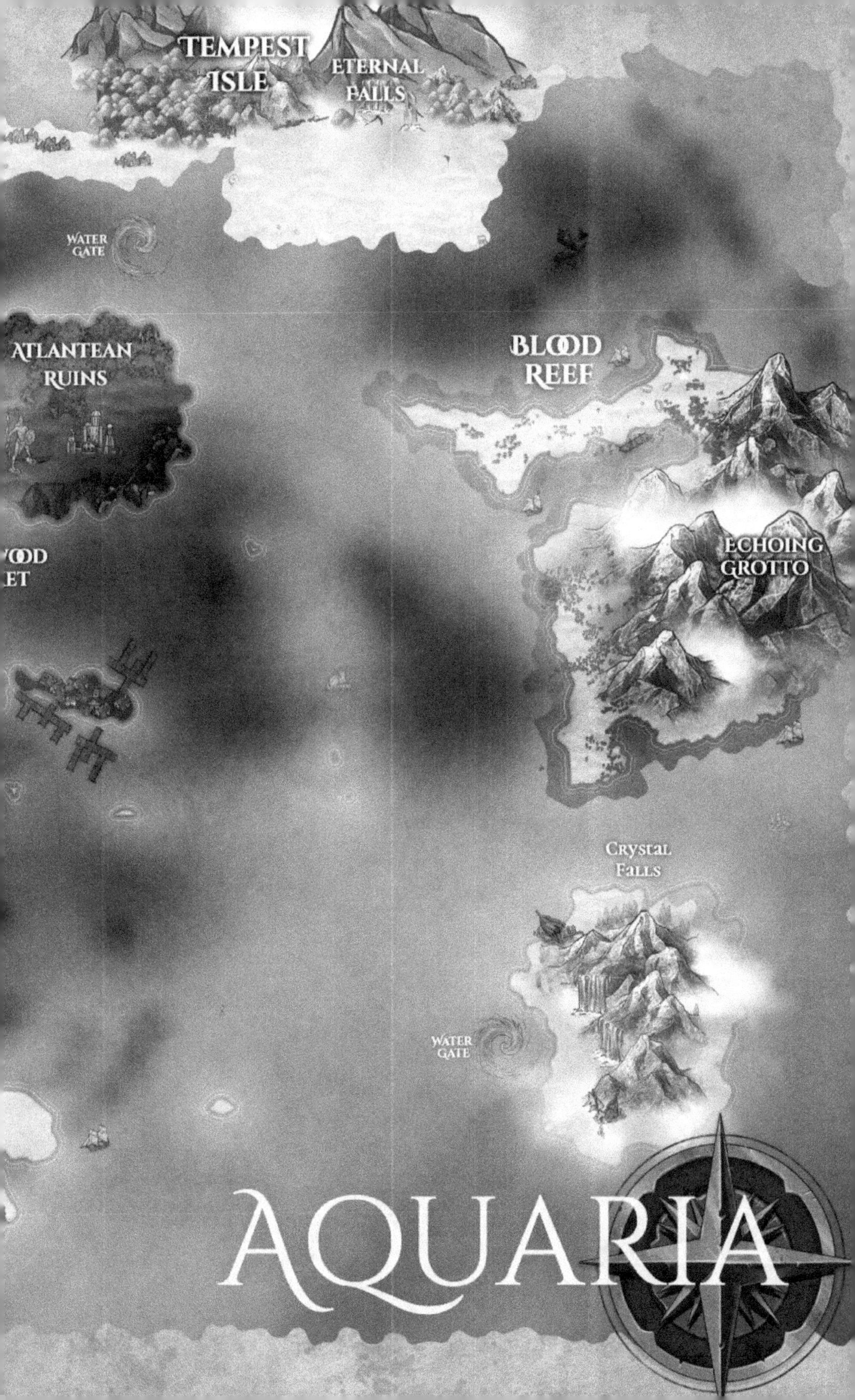

TEMPEST ISLE
ETERNAL FALLS
WATER GATE
ATLANTEAN RUINS
BLOOD REEF
ECHOING GROTTO
WOOD ET
Crystal Falls
WATER GATE
AQUARIA

AQUARIA

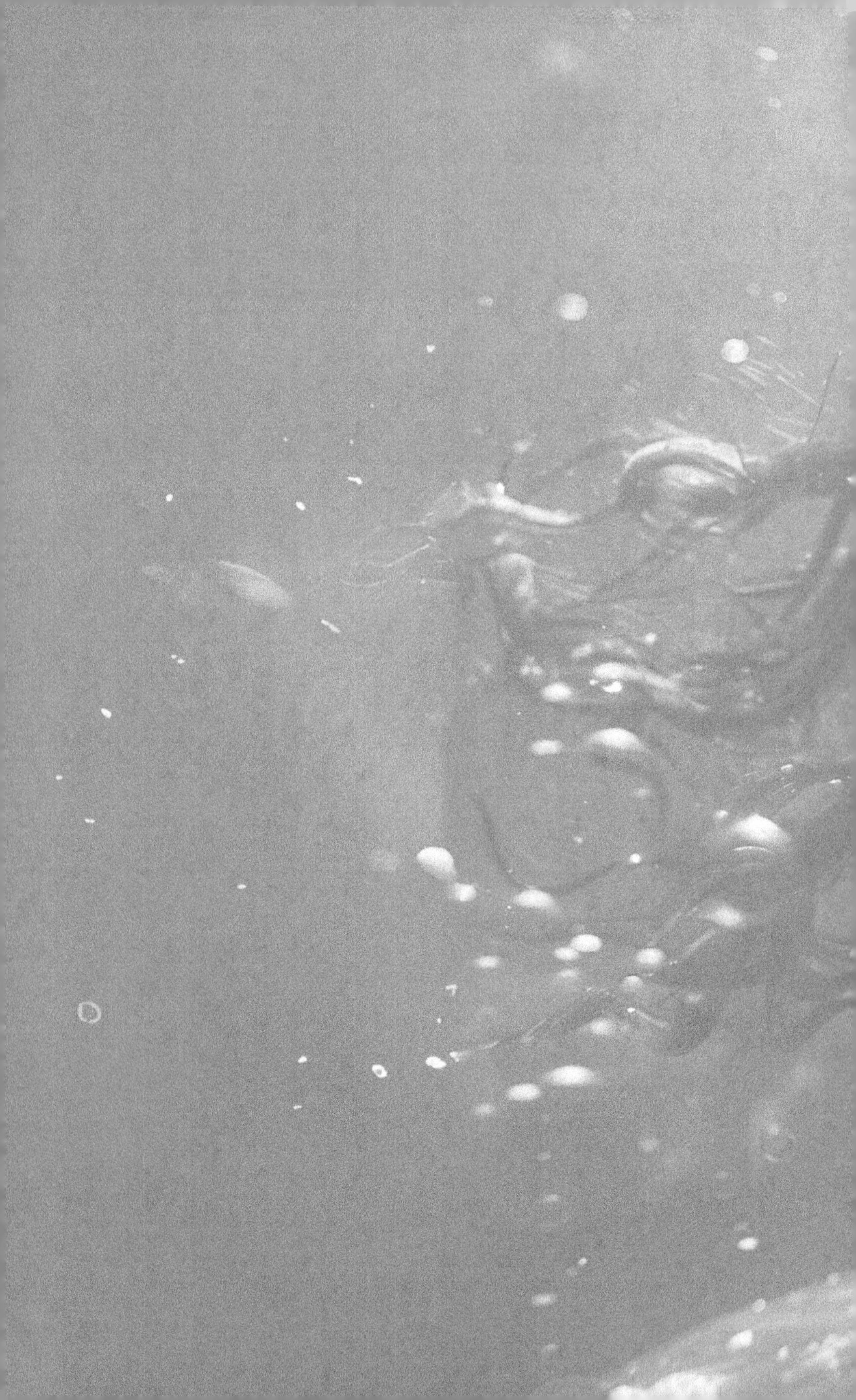

DANICA

1

The sharp cold of steel against my throat jolts my senses awake, and I struggle to keep my vision from blurring into oblivion. Before me stands a burly pirate, a scar slashing from his temple to his jawline, his eyes glinting with suspicion and curiosity.

"Well, well, what do we have 'ere?" he growls, pressing the blade further.

Rhyland and Erik are passed out beside me, their unmoving forms a stark reminder of the witch's cruelty. I fear she may have drained them, too, or worse.

Here I am, stuck in this absurd situation, my heart beating fast. And why, you ask? Because apparently, Captain Barbossa's long-lost brother, decided to park his pirate booty right in my way, making it impossible for me to check on my guys.

Could this situation get any more ridiculous?

Honestly, I feel like I'm in a bad parody of *"The Goonies,"* except instead of searching for treasure, I'm trying to navigate this labyrinth of lunacy. My mind is spinning fast, desperately trying to understand how we managed to land ourselves in this predicament.

I take a deep breath, trying to calm my racing heart and gather my thoughts. "Look, I know this seems strange," I manage to say, my voice strained but steadier than I feel. "We mean you no harm, I swear."

The pirate chuckles with a rough, gravelly voice that echoes across the deck. "Mean us no harm, eh? You must think we're daft." He bellows to his crewmates, "Seize 'em, lads!"

Before I can react, other pirates surround us, grabbing hold of Rhyland and Erik's unconscious bodies and binding them with thick ropes. I'm yanked off my feet, a cry of pain escaping me as my body protests the rough handling. My arms are tied tightly behind my back, the ropes biting into my skin.

Dragged through the ship, the salt air stings my neck wound, my head feels like it's about to explode, and the constant sway of the deck beneath me exacerbates my nausea. I'm shoved into a dank, dimly lit hold in the ship's bowels, the walls slick with moisture and the air thick with the smell of salt and decay.

My brilliant plan to conjure a portal to the safety of my apartment? Yeah, that worked out spectacularly.

Instead of sipping coffee in my cozy living room, we're now standing on a pirate ship, of all places. Bravo, me! I've really outdone myself this time. The portal must've detoured through the land of "let's make things as complicated as possible" before unceremoniously dumping us here. So, now the million-dollar question is: whose ship is this, and how in the world did my portal misfire so epically?

I swear, if this is the universe's idea of a practical joke, I'm not laughing.

As I struggle to make sense of our predicament, the scar-faced pirate looms over me, his breath hot and stinky. "Arr, ye better start talkin'. What brings ye to our ship, and why shouldn't we be tossin' ye to the sharks?"

I manage to lift my head, meeting his gaze through my exhaustion. "A misfire," I admit, forcing the words out. "I tried to open a portal to safety, but something went wrong. We landed here by mistake."

The pirate narrows his eyes, suspicion mixing with a hint of intrigue. "Ye expect me to believe that, do ye?"

"It's the truth," I state as my head swims. "We're trying to stop a war that threatens all realms."

"Portals don't exist, lass—haven't for a long time. Now, tell me," he snarls, leaning closer, "what sorcery ye wield?"

Wonderful. Time for another round of "Explain Yourself to the Otherworlders." You'd think the universe could just hang up a big fat neon sign saying, "Savior Incoming," and save me the trouble.

A murmur runs through the gathered pirates, uncertainty and fear flickering in their eyes. The door to the hold swings open at that moment, and a tall figure steps inside. He exudes authority and commands immediate respect from the pirates.

"What's the meanin' of this?" the man asks, his gaze sweeping over us.

The scar-faced pirate straightens, clearly addressing his superior. "Found these intruders, Cap'n. They claim to have no idea how they got 'ere and speak of some war—some great danger."

The man steps closer, his sea-green eyes settling on me. "Explain yourself," he demands.

"Look, Captain," I sigh, my words heavy with exhaustion, "I'm here to find the Aquanite Stone. There's a big bad who's trying to break through the realms, and it's up to me to stop him and save all your asses."

The Captain raises an eyebrow, "What are ye going on about, lass? What stone? And who?"

I open my mouth to give him a snarky response, but suddenly, the world starts spinning like a top. My vision blurs, and I sway unsteadily. I blink rapidly, trying to clear the spots dancing before my eyes, but it's useless. My body's decided it's had enough, and it's staging a revolt.

"Please... just listen," I whisper, my voice fading as my strength wanes.

The floor rushes up to meet me, and I dimly wonder if this is how it ends—passing out at the feet of a pirate captain. Not exactly the heroic move I had in mind.

Just before I lose consciousness, I hear the Captain bark out an order, his voice cutting through the haze. "Get the lass some medical attention, now! Move yer lazy hides!"

As the darkness claims me, I can't help but think that maybe, just maybe, I've found an unexpected ally in this mess of a situation. Or perhaps I'm just delirious from exhaustion and the lack of decent food in this floating prison.

Either way, it looks like my fate is in the hands of a pirate crew now. I just hope they're more competent than they look.

I wake slowly, the chill sinking into my bones as I come to—dizzy and disoriented. My surroundings swim into view—dank, dimly lit, and damp. The harsh smell of salt and mildew permeates the air. I look down and see the ropes binding my wrists rough and tight, chafing my already raw skin.

I'm in some makeshift cell, surrounded by steel bars and one cell door—locked.

Panic surges in my chest. I glance down to find my daggers missing.

What the hell?

Quickly scanning the area, I spot them resting on a barrel outside my cell.

I try to summon them, hoping the rune magic will teleport my trusty pointy pals into my hands. Instead, they unceremoniously clatter to the ground.

Rude.

I heave a frustrated sigh and give it another go. This time, they actually make it to my hands by some miracle.

I waste no time and start sawing away at the rope with the dagger. It's a bitch to do, but with a bit of finesse, some awkward maneuvering, and what feels like a goddamn eternity, the ropes finally decide to cooperate and fray, setting me free at last.

Just doing that alone has my body weak, drained from the witch's magic and the blood loss.

I quickly sheath them back on my hips.

My thoughts go to Rhyland and Erik.

Where are they?

Are they okay? I can't bear the thought of them being hurt—or worse.

"Rhyland..." I reach through our mental tether. I feel he's close, but he doesn't answer.

Anxiety gnaws at me as time passes, each second stretching into eternity. The occasional creak of the ship's hull, the sway of the ocean, and the distant murmur of voices add to my growing unease.

My thoughts drift to Lucian and the fate that awaits him. We left him behind, and now I can't shake the sickening feeling of what Azrael might do to him. The knot in my throat tightens, threatening to choke me with the weight of my fears.

What if he uses Lucian to attempt the sacrifice?

I need to get back to the Mortal Realm—fast. Every second we spend here is another second Lucian is at the mercy of that twisted asshole.

I have to believe, really believe, that we'll find a way to make things right and rescue his snarky ass.

We're obviously in Aquaria, and the weight of responsibility presses down on me, urging me to find the Aquanite Stone and end this nightmare.

But—I can't let Lucian down. I won't. I'll find a way back to him, no matter what it takes.

I can't feel my powers—that wellspring of energy usually bubbling just below the surface is eerily absent. I try to summon my fire, but not even a spark flickers to life.

What the hell did that witch do to me?

I close my eyes, trying to center myself and focus on anything but my predicament. We need to convince these pirates to help us. Moretemis's threat looms larger with each passing second.

The door creaks open just then, and a sliver of light cuts through the darkness. The tall figure from before—the Captain—steps inside, his presence casting an oppressive shadow.

"Awake at last," he remarks, his tone too neutral to be comforting. "Ye have some explainin' to do."

Disorientation floods through me as I try to gauge how long I've been unconscious. My head throbs mercilessly, each pulse sending a fresh wave of dizziness.

Slowly, I attempt to sit up, but the movement sends my head spinning even more violently. I grit my teeth against the nausea rising in my throat.

Come on, Dani, get it together. You can't afford to be weak right now. Rhyland and Erik need you. Lucian needs you. The realms need you.

With a deep breath, I force myself to focus past the pain and dizziness—one step at a time. First, assess the situation. Then, find a way out of this mess. I hope I haven't been out for too long. Every moment counts, and I can't let this setback cost us everything.

"How long—?"

"A day." The Captain quickly answers. "Now, answer me."

I lift my head, meeting his piercing gaze with what little strength I have left. "There's so much to explain. Something terrible is coming."

The Captain's eyes widen as he notices my hands, free from their bonds. "How in the blazes did you get your hands untied, lass? What kind of witchcraft are you playing at?"

I resist the urge to roll my eyes, even as the room spins around me. "It's a long story, Captain, and one I don't have the energy to tell right now. But please—just listen to me."

He crouches down to my level, his eyes searching mine. "And why should I trust a single word you say? Strangers appear outta nowhere on me ship, and you expect me to believe you ain't a threat?"

"Because we were trying to protect everyone," I say, my voice cracking with emotion. "We're fighting to keep a dark force from entering our worlds. We must stop it, or everyone—including you—will suffer."

The Captain studies me, the skepticism in his eyes wavering just slightly.

I take a deep breath, trying to steady myself and gather my thoughts. "I know this all sounds crazy. But I swear to you, it's all true. I need the stone to stop it."

The Captain strokes his beard, his expression thoughtful. "And what, exactly, does this have to do with me and my crew, lass? We're pirates, not heroes. We don't go around saving the world from ancient evils."

I can't help but laugh at that, even as the action sends a fresh wave of dizziness washing over me. "Believe me, Captain, I'm no hero either. I'm just a girl caught up in something bigger than herself. But, like it or not, we're all in this together now—if the darkness succeeds, it won't matter if you're a pirate, queen, or lowly deckhand. All our asses are doomed."

The Captain is silent for a long moment, his eyes searching mine as if trying to gauge the truth of my words. "I'll consider yer words. You'll remain here until I decide what to do with you."

He stands and heads for the door, leaving me hopeful we can still turn this around.

"Wait, where are my friends?"

The Captain looks over his shoulder, "They've been detained."

Shit. What will they do to Erik and Rhyland? My thoughts spin out of control.

The door slams shut with a resounding thud, trapping me back in the darkness of the ship's hold. But a little thing like this won't keep this girl down for long.

As exhaustion tugs at my eyelids, I can't help but smirk at the thought of these so-called pirates, thinking they can hold me captive. They clearly haven't met the right kind of stubborn yet.

A frustrated sigh escapes my lips. As soon as my power decides to grace me with its presence again, these pirates are in for a rude awakening. They have no idea what kind of force they're dealing with.

Reaching out with everything I have, I call to Rhyland through our bond. *"Rhyland...talk to me..."*

At first, nothing but an eerie silence hangs heavy in the air. But then, like a flickering candle flame, I feel the barest whisper of his presence brushing against my consciousness. He's there, somewhere close, and he's trying to connect back to me. Relief washes over me, knowing he's still fighting, even in his drained state courtesy of that wretched witch.

If I can find a way to recharge and tap into that inner wellspring of power again, maybe I can escape this dank hellhole and find Rhyland—get Lucian. And then, God help anyone who gets between me and saving the realms.

A part of me clings to the hope that the Captain might listen to reason and grant us a chance at freedom. I *really* don't want things to get ugly.

Exhaustion is weighing me down like an anchor, demanding I give in and catch some shut-eye. As much as I'd love to fight it, my body's screaming at me for more sleep. So I'm surrendering, letting my eyes drift closed as I desperately cling to that tiny flicker of a chance we can wiggle out of this pirate pickle.

DANICA

2

I jolt awake as the ship takes a severe dip and dive, flinging me from my cot onto the stale, cold floorboards. Shouts erupt above me as the crew yells commands.

"Close the sails!"

"Cap'n on the helm!"

One pirate laughs maniacally, "Bring on the storm!"

The door bursts open, and a young pirate swaggers in. He's lean but muscular, with sun-kissed skin and a mop of tousled brown hair. His eyes sparkle with a hint of mischief beneath the red bandana tied around his forehead. Rings adorn his fingers as he approaches my cell door.

"Cap'n orders to move you to his chambers, lass. We're under the Dark Tides, and this area of the ship likes to flood."

Dark Tides? What the hell is that? Before I can voice my confusion, water bursts in through the side of the hull, icy and unforgiving. It begins to rise at my feet, sending shivers through my already exhausted body.

"Hurry," I command, trying to mask the tremor in my voice.

The pirate fumbles with the keys, dropping them as the ship pitches forward again. I'm slammed back into the far wall, the air rushing from my lungs as the pirate tumbles.

The waters rise quickly as he dives under to find the keys he dropped. He comes up empty-handed, his face etched with frustration as the waters continue to climb. Panic seizes my chest, a cold fist squeezing my heart.

No, no, no, I will *not* drown on a *freaking* pirate ship!

He dives down again, disappearing beneath the dark surface. Seconds stretch into an eternity as I wait, the water now lapping at my shoulders. Cold seeps into my bones, draining what little energy I have left. Fear claws at my throat, threatening to drag me under before the water has a chance.

In this cell with no keys, I am a sitting fucking duck!

"Dani... What's wrong, baby?" Rhyland's voice booms into my headspace, jolting me out of my spiral of despair.

Finally! Relief wars with my fear as I realize he's here—in my mind, our bond is as strong as ever.

"Oh, you know, just enjoying some quality 'me time' in the luxurious accommodations of this fine pirate vessel," I quip, my voice dripping with sarcasm despite the rising water in the ship's hull. *"It's like a spa day, really. Nothing quite like the refreshing sensation of nearly drowning to make a girl feel alive."*

Rhyland's voice crashes into my mind like a tidal wave, equal parts relief and frustration. *"Dani, what the hell is going on? Are you okay? I can feel your fear, making me want to tear this ship apart with my bare hands."*

I can't help but smile, my protective Viking. *"Peachy!"*

Let's let sarcasm fuel my resolve because causing him more fear will only add to mine—no need to turn this into a goddamn fear-fest.

Rhyland's growl of frustration rumbles through our bond. *"Fuck, I can't get to you. They've got me and Erik locked up tight."*

I quickly shut him down and focus on not dying.

Just when I think he's lost forever, the pirate resurfaces, gasping for air. "The keys, lass—in your cell; get 'em!"

Shit!

Without wasting a moment, I suck in a lungful of air and dive down. The cold water zaps me of more energy, like a thousand icy needles piercing my skin. I open my eyes, but I can't see a damn thing. It's blurry, dark, and dank. I swim to the floor and start feeling around for anything, my fingers numb and clumsy. My lungs already burn, screaming for air, and I'm forced to head back up.

I burst through the surface, gasping and sputtering, the hold nearly full.

"Hurry up, lass, or I'm leaving ye!" the pirate shouts, strained and annoyed.

I gulp down another breath and dive back under. I swim further back toward the wall, my movements sluggish and heavy. I can barely swim, weakened.

Again, I feel around the floor, desperation fueling my search. Suddenly, my eyes snag a faint glint of something metal. I swim toward it quickly, my heart pounding in my ears. I grab the keys, the cold metal biting into my palm, and swiftly swim back up.

"Got 'em!" I gasp, holding the keys triumphantly above the water.

"Good, now open the door, lass. Quickly." The pirate's voice is tight and impatient, barely audible above the rushing water and the pounding of my own heart.

I suck in a desperate breath and plunge back into the icy depths, my lungs already burning from the exertion. The water engulfs me, its inky darkness pressing in from all sides, disorienting and terrifying. I force my eyes open, ignoring the sting of the salt, and swim frantically toward the cell door.

My numb fingers fumble with the keys, the metal slippery and elusive in my grasp. I want to scream in frustration, but I can't afford to waste what little air I have left. Every second counts, and I feel my strength ebbing away with each passing moment.

Finally, by some miracle, I manage to slide the key into the lock. I twist it with all my might, my muscles straining against the water's resistance. For one heart-stopping moment, I fear it won't turn, that I'll be trapped here, doomed to a watery grave. But then, with a click that reverberates through my bones, the lock gives way.

I shove against the door, desperation fueling my efforts. But it's like trying to move a mountain, the water's pressure holding it firmly in place. My lungs are on fire now, screaming for air, black spots dancing at the edges of my vision. I can't give up now, not when I'm so close.

With a final, furious burst of strength, I wrench the door open just enough to squeeze through. I kick off the floor, propelling myself upward, my arms and legs pumping with the last of my energy. The surface seems impossibly far away, a shimmering mirage I can never quite reach.

But I refuse to surrender, refuse to let this be my end. I claw through the water, every fiber of my being focused on that precious pocket of air above me. Just a little further, just a few more strokes...

I break the surface with a gasping, spluttering cry, my starved lungs greedily sucking in the damp, musty air of the flooding hold. I cling to the edge of the cell, my body shaking uncontrollably from cold and exhaustion. But I'm alive, and that's all that matters.

The pirate grabs my arm, his grip like a vice, hauling me through the opening. "Come on, lass, we're not out of this yet!"

I can only nod, too spent to speak, and let him drag me forward into the churning waters. The fight isn't over, not by a long shot. But I'll be damned if I let this storm, or these pirates, be the end of me.

Together, we fight through the flooded corridor, the water churning around us like an angry beast. My muscles burn with exhaustion, and my body is heavy as lead. But the pirate's iron grip keeps me moving, keeps me fighting.

Finally, we reach the stairs leading to the upper deck. I cling to the railing, my breath coming in ragged gasps as I haul myself up, step by agonizing step. The storm rages above us, the wind howling like a vengeful spirit. But even as the rain lashes my face and the ship pitches beneath my feet, I've never been so grateful to feel the sting of the elements.

We burst onto the deck, the pirate's arm still locked around me. I collapse against him, shivering and spent, my energy utterly drained. But I'm alive. Against all odds, I'm still breathing.

And now, I have to find a way to keep it that way.

The pirate slams the steel hatch shut, the clang reverberating through the storm-tossed ship. "Up ye go, lass," he grunts, his rough hand clamping around my arm as he hauls me to my feet.

I stagger, my legs barely cooperating after the ordeal. The deck pitches beneath me, and I nearly faceplant right there, but I'll be damned if I let these pirates see me as some swooning damsel. I grit my teeth and force myself to take in my surroundings.

Pirates swarm the deck like ants, their shouts barely audible over the howling wind and crashing waves. They scurry up rigging and haul on ropes, desperately trying to keep the massive ship from capsizing. And massive it is—this behemoth makes a regular Galleon look like a bathtub toy.

"Oh, fantastic," I mutter under my breath. "I've been kidnapped by the *compensating* pirates."

My sarcasm is short-lived, though, as the ship pitches forward violently. I go flying, slamming into a stack of barrels with a bone-jarring thud. Pain explodes through my shoulder, white-hot and searing. I barely have time to catch my breath before a monstrous wave crests over the ship's side, drenching me in icy seawater and ripping me away from my precarious perch.

I tumble across the deck, scrabbling for purchase on the slick boards. My fingers find a rope lashed to the ship's wall, and I cling to it like a lifeline, the rough fibers biting into my palms. The storm rages around me, the wind a thousand icy knives slicing at my skin. Salt spray stings my eyes, blurring my vision.

"Come on!" The pirate appears through the chaos, his hand outstretched.

I hesitate for a split second, instinct warring with the need to survive. But another wave slams into the ship, the deck bucking like an enraged beast, and I know I don't have a choice.

I lunge for his hand, my fingers locking around his wrist. He hauls me up, and then we're running, slipping and sliding across the treacherous deck. I glimpse at an ornate door looming ahead, the wood dark and heavy—the Captain's quarters.

But even as we stumble toward that promise of safety, I can't shake the feeling that I'm leaping from the frying pan straight into the fire. These pirates may have saved me from drowning, but something tells me they're not the type to do favors for free.

We burst through the door into the Captain's quarters, the pirate slamming it shut behind us with a resounding bang. The sudden absence of wind and rain is almost deafening, the muffled sounds of the raging storm now a distant roar.

I stagger forward, my legs finally giving out as I collapse onto a nearby sofa. The plush velvet feels almost obscene against my salt-stiffened clothes, but I'm too exhausted to care. I focus on catching my breath, on slowing the frantic pounding of my heart.

The pirate looms over me, his dark eyes unreadable in the flickering lamplight. "You will stay here until the Cap'n can speak with you."

I nod, too drained to argue. But as he turns to leave, a sudden surge of gratitude pushes past my fatigue. "Thank you..." I rasp out, my tongue thick and clumsy with salt and dehydration.

He pauses, his hand on the doorknob, and looks back at me. Surprise flickers across his face as if he's not used to hearing those words.

"What is your name?" I ask, the question tumbling out before I can stop it.

A ghost of a smile tugs at the corner of his mouth. "Finn," he says after a moment. "Finn Blackwell."

"Well, Finn Blackwell," I say, mustering a weak grin, "I owe you one. You know, for the whole 'saving my life' thing."

He shrugs, the gesture somehow both nonchalant and self-conscious. "Just doin' me job, lass. Can't have ye drownin' before the Cap'n's had a word, now can we?"

I snort the sound somewhere between a laugh and a cough. "Heaven forbid."

Finn shakes his head, a glimmer of amusement in his eyes. "Rest up, lass. Somethin' tells me you'll be needin' your strength."

With that, he slips out the door, leaving me alone with my thoughts and the muffled roar of the storm. I sink back into the sofa, my eyes drifting shut as exhaustion claims me again.

But even as I slip into a fitful doze, Finn's words echo in my mind. He's right—I will need every ounce of strength and wit to navigate the treacherous waters I've found myself in.

Because something tells me that this is just the beginning of a very long, very dangerous journey, and if I want to make it out alive, I'll have to be ready for anything these pirates—and the cruel, capricious sea—can throw at me.

My thoughts drift back to Rhyland. *"I'm okay,"* I inform him. *"I'm in the Captain's Quarters."*

Whatever these pirates want, I'll be ready. I'll keep my wits sharp and my eyes sharper. Not a chance in hell I'm becoming anyone's pawn or plaything.

Because when the time comes, I'll be ready to turn the tables and show them just what this "lass" is made of.

"I need to fucking get to you—now. I can feel your weakness. I need to heal you."

"I know." I'm so damn tired I can barely keep our mental conversation going. *"Let me speak with the Captain."*

That's the last thing I manage to say before my eyes close and darkness sweeps me away.

RHYLAND

3

I pace the cell like a caged animal, my frustration and anger building with every goddamn step. The fact that these piece of shit pirates have the balls to keep us separated is a huge fucking mistake. They have no idea who they're messing with, and when I get out of here, they'll learn the hard way.

"She's safe," I grunt to Erik, who looks like he's seconds away from going apeshit.

I feel you, brother. Being trapped in this tiny, dank cell is enough to drive anyone out of their fucking mind.

Erik and I just woke up not that long ago. Dani's fear pulled me out of that witch's coma. Once I was awake and coherent, I woke Erik's ass up.

Erik was going through all my emotions with me, my fear, my panic as I relayed to him what was happening to Dani—nearly drowning on this cursed fucking ship. With me not being able to do a damn thing to help her.

The worst part is the weakness that's settled into my bones. I've felt drained since we went through that portal and passed out. That witch did something to me like nothing I've ever experienced before, and it's trickled down to Erik, too. My magic is gone—can't use my telekinesis. It's like Amara and her magic-draining bullshit all over again.

How long this will last, I have no fucking clue. Did the witch permanently curse us? The thought chills my spine, but I refuse to let it show. I have to stay strong, for Dani's sake, if nothing else.

"I'm glad the Little Huntress is well and safe," Erik mumbles from what I can only imagine is a piss-soaked floor. The stench here is enough to make my eyes water, and the constant rocking of the ship isn't helping matters.

Where they have us on this god-forsaken ship is a mystery. All I know is it's a small room with a cell that we're caged in like animals. The storm earlier finally stopped, but the thrashing and tossing us around like ragdolls has drained me more than I already feel.

I can't stop wondering how the fuck we ended up here. I would've thought Dani would conjure a portal to her apartment, maybe, or somewhere safe—not our next goddamn destination with Lucian captured and drained by those fucking witches, and now we're prisoners on a pirate ship in the middle of god fucking knows where.

Something must've happened while she conjured the portal. I know she was weak and just as drained. It would make sense why the misfire.

"So, assuming we're in Aquaria," Erik starts, his voice rough with exhaustion, "What the hell do we know?"

I shake my head, trying to clear the fog from my mind. "A lot—and it's crawling with pirates."

I tell Erik what we all learned of this realm—filled with merfolk, pirates, and other creatures. There's also the grand Undinite Palace, where the merfolk Queen rules. Somewhere in this realm lies the ruins of an ancient civilization called Atlantis, which may hold crucial clues to our quest.

"But navigating this treacherous realm won't be easy, especially with us locked up and magic-drained by that fucking witch."

"Sounds delightful," Erik observes with his usual stoicism. "Clearly, we were unprepared for such a task. Dani was weak and barely opened the portal enough for our escape."

"I know." I sigh and lean against the wall, the damp wood creaking with the sway of the ship.

"Lucian—" Erik starts.

I hold up my hand to stop him as my mind races back to Lucian and how we—how *I*—fucking abandoned him. He told me to get Dani to safety, but the guilt is weighing on me more now. I've already lost one brother to my own goddamn stupidity, and now, if I lose Lucian too, what the hell kind of man—brother— does that make me?

As if reading my mind, "Rhyland, you did what you had to do. Lucian understood that. He wanted you to protect Dani, and that's exactly what you did. We'll find him, brother. We'll get him back and make those witches pay for what they've done."

Erik is always the one to spout wisdom and grace, trying to settle my nerves—he knows damn well the guilt is eating me alive and that I'll go into a headspace that's not pleasant for any bastard around me.

"We know Azrael and how he works. He will use Lucian as bait," Erik says.

I couldn't agree more. The same way he used me to get Dani to come running.

The door opens, and a tall man walks in, wearing a tricorn hat with a rugged beard and savage sea-green eyes. "Ah, I see ye both have woken up."

I lunge at the bars, a feral snarl ripping from my throat, my fangs extending, ready to tear into the bastard. "Let me out of this fucking cell, now. Who the hell are you? And what have you done with my girl, you piece of shit?"

The man stumbles back, his eyes growing wide with fear as he takes in the sight of my elongated canines, the predatory gleam in my gaze. "What in blazin' hells are ye?" he stammers, his voice trembling like a leaf in a hurricane.

It's clear as day that these pirates have never seen our kind, never come face to face with the supernatural fury of a vampire on the warpath.

Good. I'll use that to my advantage, use it to scare these assholes so bad they'll be shitting themselves for a week.

I lean forward, my lips peeling back in a snarl more animal than man. "I'm your worst fucking nightmare, asshole," I growl. "I'm the monster that's going to tear you apart piece by fucking piece unless you tell me where my girl is. Right. Fucking. Now."

The Captain straightens himself, erasing his fear, "I'm the Captain of this ship, and I'll be the one askin' the questions here. Speakin' of yer girl, I've got 'er up in me cabin for some... questionin'." He lets the innuendo hang in the air, a cruel smile on his lips.

Rage boils inside me, and I rattle the bars, my voice a menacing growl. "You lay one fucking finger on her, and I swear to all the *gods*, I will rip you apart piece by piece. I will make you beg for death before I'm done with you, you son of a bitch."

The Captain stands there, shaking his head. "I don't take kindly to threats," he hisses.

Erik stands by my side, his eyes cold and his voice laced with menace. "We don't want to harm anyone unnecessarily. We are here to help the realms from an impending doom. The girl you have is valuable—important. Harm her, and not only will

I allow my brother to end your miserable existence, but I will take great pleasure in dismembering your corpse until not even your own mother could recognize you."

The captain's eyes widen slightly, but he quickly regains his composure. He leans back against the wall, crossing his arms over his chest. "Saving the realms, you say? And what exactly is this great calamity that threatens us all?"

I rattle the bars again, my patience wearing thin. "Let us out, give me my girl," I growl, my fangs glinting in the dim light, "and maybe we will tell you."

But the captain isn't ready to let it go. He cocks his head to the side, studying us with a calculating gaze. "No, I don't think so," he says slowly, a smirk playing at the corners of his mouth. "If there's some grand danger out there, I reckon I have a right to know about it. Especially if you plan on dragging my ship and crew into the middle of it."

I let out a low, menacing snarl, my claws digging into the metal of the bars. "I won't ask again," I hiss. "Let us out, or I'll paint this whole fucking ship red with your blood."

The captain's smirk widens, and he pushes off the wall with a casual grace. "You're in no position to be making demands, boy," he drawls, his hand dropping to the pistol at his hip. "But I'm a reasonable man. Tell me more about this 'saving the realms' business, and maybe we can come to an arrangement."

Erik leans forward, his hand resting on the bars, "You are treading on thin ice, Captain," he warns, his tone as cold as the ocean's depths. "The world's fate hangs in the balance, and you would waste time with petty games and power plays?"

The captain's eyes narrow, and for a moment, I see a flicker of something dangerous in his gaze. But then it's gone, replaced by a mask of false joviality.

"Petty games?" he chuckles, shaking his head. "Oh, I assure you, this is no game. But if you want my help, you'll have to give me more than vague warnings and empty threats."

I open my mouth to tell him exactly where he can shove his help, but Erik cuts me off with a sharp look.

"Very well," he says, his voice tight. "The short version is this: an ancient evil has awakened, a being of immense power and malevolence. It will consume the realms if left unchecked, leaving nothing but death and destruction in its wake."

The captain's eyebrows shoot up, and he blows a low whistle. "Well, ain't that just a right cheery bedtime story," he drawls. "And let me guess, you lot are the only ones who can stop it?"

I bare my fangs at him, my patience at its limit. "We're the only ones with a fucking chance," I snarl. "And if you don't start cooperating, I'll ensure you live just long enough to see the world burn."

DANICA

4

"Wake up, lass!" the Captain's gruff voice rudely yanks me from my less-than-peaceful slumber.

I jolt upright, immediately regretting every life choice that led me to this moment, as a pounding headache threatens to split my skull in two. Through bleary eyes, I watch as the Captain sheds his soaked coat and disappears behind a changing screen.

The storm seems to have passed. The ship is steady, and I don't hear any howling winds outside.

I gingerly massage my temples, trying to ease the throbbing pain. This migraine is sucking the life out of me faster than a vampire at a blood drive, and my stomach is staging a mutiny, demanding sustenance.

I inhale sharply, my face contorting in pain as I gingerly touch the burning wound on my neck. "Ssss... ahh! Damn it!" I hiss through clenched teeth.

Azrael, you sadistic bastard. I swear, the next time I see you, I will make you suffer in more ways than one.

I take a shaky breath, trying to compose myself. "Please tell me you have something to drink on this floating tub," I rasp, my voice as rough as sandpaper.

"There's rum," the Captain replies, his vague gesture toward a table with a decanter and cups doing little to inspire confidence.

I can't stop the eye roll that follows. "Wow, rum. How original—got anything that won't make me go blind? Like, I don't know, water?"

The Captain emerges from behind the screen, looking annoyingly refreshed in dry clothes. He strides over, grabs a flask, and practically shoves it into my hands. "Here. Drink."

I eagerly grab the flask, practically inhaling the cool, crisp water. It's like liquid ambrosia, and I gulp it down like I've just crossed a desert. Water dribbles down my chin as I surface for air, only to dive back in for more.

"Easy there, lass. I'd rather not have you redecorating my quarters with your stomach contents," the Captain barks, his tone heavy with irritation.

Suitably chastised, I cap the flask and hand it back, trying to catch my breath. "Thanks," I mutter, my voice still a bit breathless.

The Captain fixes me with a penetrating stare, his eyes narrowing. "Alright, lass. I'm willin' to listen. But don't be givin' me that vague 'we need your help' nonsense again."

I finally get a look at the Captain. He epitomizes a rugged seafarer with his crisp white shirt open just enough to reveal an impressively hairy chest. His sea-green eyes are sharp enough to cut through any salty mist, and coupled with that burly beard and chiseled features—he's like the poster boy for "Handsome Middle-Aged Pirates Monthly."

I bet he has a waiting list of mermaids dying to braid that shoulder-length brown hair. He probably thinks he's God's gift to the Seven Seas or something.

I meet the Captain's gaze head-on, mustering my most confident facade. "I've already told you the deal, but if you want me to play the part of a repeating parrot, then sure, I'll squawk it out for you one more time."

I take a deep breath, trying to channel my usual confidence and sass, but it comes out shaky. "Look, we're on a mission to stop the big bad from turning the realms into his playground of destruction," I explain, filling him in on my role, my powers, and the crown's significance. "You know, the usual 'chosen one' gig. If we don't step up and save the day, we're all pretty much screwed. Happy now?"

The Captain stares at me like I've just sprouted a second head, his expression a mix of disbelief and exasperation. "You've got a real way with words, don't ye, lass?"

I flash him a grin. "What can I say, Captain? I've got a gift. But seriously, I know it sounds like something out of a bad fantasy novel, but I swear to you, it's all true. And whether you like it or not, you and your crew are now smack dab in the middle of it."

"And who's this *we* you keep mentioning?" the Captain asks, crossing his arms over his chest.

"Dani—it's *such* a pleasure to meet you," I say with a mock curtsy. "My partners in crime are Rhyland and Erik—the two you've captured somewhere on this ship. We are not exactly locals, if you catch my drift."

The Captain scoffs. "No kiddin'. But that still doesn't explain why I should give a rat's ass about yer little heroic quest." He narrows his eyes, studying me intently. "And while we're on the subject, how the hell did you get on my ship in the first place?

"We are from the Mortal Realm," I begin, my voice steady despite the nerves fluttering in my stomach. "I accidentally conjured a portal here. Well, sort of. We were planning to come to Aquaria anyway, just... not right this second."

The Captain raises an eyebrow. "The Mortal Realm, you say? And you just happened to conjure a portal that dropped you onto my ship? Forgive me if I find that a bit hard to swallow, lass."

"Believe me, Captain, it wasn't exactly a pleasure cruise for us either. One minute, I'm conjuring a portal to my apartment; the next, we're taking an unexpected dip in the ocean and getting hauled aboard your floating funhouse."

His lips twitch as if he's fighting back a smile. "You've got a sharp tongue on ya, lass. But that still doesn't explain why I should give a damn about your little quest."

"Because, Captain, our quest isn't just about us. It's about the fate of all the realms, including Aquaria. There's a darkness coming, an evil that threatens to consume everything in its path. And if we don't find a way to stop it, to fulfill our mission, then none of us will be safe. Not even the great Captain..."

I pause, realizing I still don't know his name. "What do they call you, anyway? Captain Scurvy? Admiral Barnacle-Beard?"

"You're a cheeky one—the name's Captain Gideon Sterling. And I'll have you know, I keep my beard meticulously groomed."

I can't help but grin at that, feeling a flicker of hope. If he's willing to banter with me, maybe there's a chance he'll hear me out after all.

"Captain Sterling, then. Look, I know this all sounds crazy. Portals, dark prophecies, ancient evils threatening to destroy the world. But I swear to you, it's all true. And whether you like it or not, you and your crew are now a part of it."

"Hold on, are you talking about the Sea Witch?" Gideon asks, his brow furrowed with concern. "That wretched wench is going to be the death of us all, mark me words."

I scoff. "Oh, come on. A Sea Witch? What's next? You'll tell me there are Krakens and Sea Monsters, too?"

Gideon fixes me with a look that suggests I've just committed the ultimate faux pas, like insulting his mother or questioning his pirate prowess. "Aye, lass. Those beasties be among us, and they're a right pain in the arse, let me tell ye."

I shake my head. Looks like I owe Disney an apology. Who would've thought that *Ursula,* the sassy sea witch extraordinaire, was more than just a cartoon character?

I mean, really? After all the supernatural shenanigans I've been through, am I surprised that sea monsters and sea witches are a thing? Come on, girl. It's time to embrace the weird and accept that anything is possible in this crazy world of ours.

But as Gideon's words sink in, my amusement quickly fades, replaced by a growing sense of unease. I swallow hard, my face turning serious as the gravity of our predicament hits me like a ton of bricks.

Note to self: never, *ever* discredit the existence of anything, no matter how bizarre or seemingly fictional. If you can dream it up, it's probably out there somewhere, waiting to make your life much more interesting.

I launch into my umpteenth recitation of the tale, detailing the Dark Prophecy and my unfortunate role in this cosmic catastrophe. It's like a well-worn script at this point, but I try to inject some enthusiasm into my voice.

As I speak, I can see the Captain's expression shifting from skepticism to something closer to disbelief. He looks at me like I've just asked him to swallow a bucket of nails, his face contorting as if trying to digest battery acid.

"Let me get this straight," his voice flat. "Yer some *chosen one*—an angel—destined to save the world from an ancient evil that wants to destroy everythin'? And you expect me to just take yer word for it and risk my crew's lives on some half-baked quest?"

I bristle at his tone, my frustration rising. "I know it sounds crazy, Captain. Believe me, I didn't ask for this either. But the fact remains if we don't do something and don't find a way to stop Moretemis, then everything we know and love will be lost."

Oh, how I wish I could whip out my supernatural party trick and be like, "Bam! There you have it, Captain. Proof that I'm not just some delusional damsel spouting nonsense."

But nooo, my powers have decided to take an extended vacation without bothering to send a postcard. Typical. The one time I actually need them to make a point, they're nowhere to be found.

His eyes narrow at the mention of Moretemis, a flicker of recognition passing over his face. "*Moretemis?* The Shadow Lord? Yer tellin' me he's real?"

I nod, "Oh, he's real alright. And he's not just coming. He's practically knocking on our door with a battering ram. The prophecy's got the whole 'epic final battle' thing down pat—light versus darkness, good versus evil, yada yada."

I lean in, resting my elbows on my knees. "But here's the deal, Captain. You thought you could sail through life, avoiding all this? Tough luck! Whether we like it or not, we're all guests at this shindig now."

The Captain leans back in his chair, his expression troubled. "I've heard the stories, the whispers in the dark. But I always thought they were just that—stories. Tales to scare children and keep sailors in line."

I shake my head, my voice urgent. "They're not just stories. They're warnings, glimpses of what's to come if we don't act. And right now, you and your crew may be the only thing between us and total destruction."

Oh, I'm not just laying it on thick—I'm slathering it on like a baker frosting a wedding cake! Desperate times call for desperate measures, right? If a little extra drama is necessary to get Captain Oblivious here to wake up and smell the impending doom, then hand me a metaphorical piping bag and watch me work my magic. He needs to see this prophecy for the cosmic-level, world-altering, can't-just-stick-your-head-in-the-sand-and-ignore-it situation that it is!

"Look, it's the truth. This darkness is coming and won't stop for a pirate parley. It's up to me and my friends to end it, or we're all doomed."

The Captain gulps his drink, eyes assessing me with a new intensity. "And you think my crew and I can help you stop this great evil, do ye?"

I shrug. "Honestly? I think we need all the help we can get. You seem like a nice guy, and who better to ask than a Pirate with a penchant for justice?"

Gideon strokes his beard, a thoughtful expression on his face. "You've got a silver tongue, lass. I'll give you that. But this is no small thing yer askin'."

I nod, understanding his hesitation. "I get it, Captain. You've got your ship to run and your crew to look after. But think about it this way—if we fail, if this darkness takes over, there won't be any more ships to captain or seas to sail. It'll be game over for all of us."

The Captain is silent momentarily, his gaze distant as if weighing the world's fate on his shoulders. Finally, he sighs, his shoulders slumping in resignation.

"I must be out of my goddamn mind," he mutters, more to himself than to me. "But I can't just sit back and do nothin', not if what yer saying is true."

He fixes me with a hard stare, his voice deadly serious. "But let's get one thing straight, lass. I'm not doing this for you or some mystical prophecy. I'm doing it for my crew, for the people I've sworn to protect. And if at any point I think you're leading us astray or putting my men in unnecessary danger, I won't hesitate to kill you and your friends."

I nod, understanding the weight of his words. "I wouldn't expect anything less. But I promise you, I will do everything in my power to ensure we succeed, to make sure we all come out of this alive and victorious."

The Captain grunts a noncommittal sound that could mean anything. But I take it as a sign of agreement, a glimmer of hope in the darkness.

Finally, he gives a curt nod as if coming to a decision. "Captain Gideon Sterling, at your service," he says, suggesting that 'service' is a relative term. "Welcome aboard The Seraph—we're among the most respected pirate crews on the high seas."

DANICA

5

I can't help but raise an eyebrow at that. "Respected pirates? Isn't that kind of an oxymoron?"

Gideon shoots me a look that could wither a lesser person. "Watch it, lass. We've got a code. We're not mindless savages like some of the other scallywags out there."

I hold up my hands in a placating gesture. "Sorry. I'm just trying to wrap my head around all of this. Sea witches, sea monsters, honorable pirates... it's a lot to take in."

Gideon's expression softens a fraction. "Aye, I suppose it is. But you'd best get used to it, lass. If you're sailing with us, you'll need to learn the lay of the land—or the sea, as it were."

"Other scallywags?" I ask, my curiosity piqued despite the circumstances.

The Captain heaves a long-suffering sigh. "Aye, there's no shortage of pirate factions in these waters. You've got the Crimson Brotherhood, a charming bunch who'd sooner bathe in your blood than say hello. And the Serpent Skulls? Sneaky bastards, the lot of them."

I take in this information, my mind whirling. "And where do you and your merry band of misfits fit into this delightful pirate hierarchy?"

Captain Sterling puffs out his chest, a glimmer of pride in his eyes. "We're the Silver Tide. We fight for justice and honor, protecting the innocent from the scum of the seas. Pirates with principles, you might say."

What are the odds of landing on *the one* pirate ship with a moral compass in a literal sea of scoundrels? It's like the universe finally decided to throw me a bone. Either that or the crown took over once that witch bitch drained me like a cheap-ass battery.

I just need to rest and recharge.

"So, any other colorful characters I should know in this delightful pirate soap opera?"

Gideon chuckles. "Well, there's the Azure Rovers. They're a different breed altogether—Captain Seaborn and I go way back. They're more interested in chasing legends and lost treasures than plundering and pillaging. They're not quite as bloodthirsty as the others, but make no mistake—they're still pirates, through and through."

I lean back on the sofa, my brain whirring like an overclocked computer trying to process this avalanche of new information. It's a lot to take in, but I know that navigating this tangled web of pirate politics will be crucial to our survival. It's like navigating a minefield while blindfolded and juggling chainsaws—one wrong step, and we're all fish food.

The Captain's eyes narrow. He gestures to my crown, a glint of curiosity in his gaze. "Is that the fancy crown ye being talkin' about?"

Struggling with my hair and the headpiece as they have now become a knot of bullshit on top of my head, I explain the crown's functions and stones, watching as his expression shifts from intrigue to calculating.

"That's quite the piece of jewelry. Mind if I take a closer look?" he asks, his tone too casual for my liking.

Typical pirate.

I shake my head, "No can do, Captain. This thing is stuck on my head tighter than a barnacle on a whale's backside."

Captain Gideon Sterling is the embodiment of every pirate fantasy—ruggedly handsome and with an air of confidence that borders on cocky. A small scar on his face only adds to his handsome features. But beneath that devil-may-care exterior lies a sharp mind, a loyal heart, and a fierce determination to protect his crew and ship.

"Dani, I'm losing my goddamn mind here. What the hell is going on?" Rhyland growls. His frustration and desperation pulses through our bond like a living thing.

"I know, me too." I shoot back, my nerves frayed to the breaking point. *"I think I've managed to convince Captain Blackbeard wannabe to lend us a hand. Turns out, a little sass and a lot of attitude go a long way with these pirate types."*

Rhyland's response is a string of curses, *"I don't give a flying fuck about his help. Tell that son of a bitch to release me, or I swear, he's going to be my first meal as soon as I sink my teeth into his scurvy-ridden ass."*

I roll my eyes, even though Rhyland can't see me. *"Charming as ever, aren't you, babe? Look, let me handle this. We need the Captain's cooperation if we're going to get out of this mess in one piece."*

I return my attention to the Captain, plastering on my most winning smile. "So, about my friends. Any chance you could, you know, let them out of their cages? I promise they're housebroken. Mostly."

The Captain eyes me skeptically; his weathered face creases with suspicion. "Not until ye've been fed and properly clothed, lass. I take care of my own, and now that you're one of us, it is my responsibility to see to yer needs."

I can't help but snort at that, my eyebrows climbing toward my hairline. "One of you? I don't recall signing up for the pirate life, Captain. And as for my needs, well... let's say I'm a little more high-maintenance than your average wench."

The Captain's lips twitch as if he's fighting back a smile. "Aye, that much be clear, lass. But the fact remains, ye are on my ship now, which makes ye my concern. So, ye'll eat, ye'll dress, and then we'll see about freeing yer companions. Savvy?"

I let out a long-suffering sigh, realizing that resistance is futile. "Alright, alright. You win, Captain Jack. But let's get one thing straight: as for the wardrobe situation...I'm not exactly the 'yo-ho-ho and a bottle of rum' type. So, if you could rustle up something that doesn't scream 'wench of the seven seas,' I'd be eternally grateful."

The Captain chuckles, a deep, rumbling sound that fills the cabin. "It's Captain *Sterling*. I'll see what I can do. But ye best be warned—life on the high seas ain't for the faint of heart. Ye'll need to toughen up if ye hope to survive."

Obviously, my pirate pun went straight over his head.

I flash him a grin, "I'm tougher than I look. And trust me, I've survived worse than a few pirates and a little ocean spray."

Captain Sterling rises from his seat, strides to the door, and bellows for one of his crew.

Finn appears—the young handsome lad who saved my drowning ass, snapping to attention. "Yes, Cap'n?"

"Finn, tell Barnaby to send up some grub from the galley," the Captain orders.

"Aye, aye, Cap'n!" Finn disappears, off to relay the message.

Gideon returns to his seat, fixing me with a pointed look. "Once you eat and dress," his tone leaves no room for argument. "Then we can talk more about this... quest of yours. But if you ask me, our best bet is to get an audience with the Queen. She'll know what to do."

I nod eagerly, my stomach growling in anticipation. I'm so hungry I could devour an entire feast for Queen Undine herself. I've read about her in the book, how she rules over the aquatic realm with an iron fist and a heart of gold. Or something like that.

But before I jump to conclusions, let's not forget the little surprise party the Fae realm threw. Talk about a plot twist; even M. Night Shyamalan didn't see coming! How nothing was as written in the Fae Book.

Who knows if she is even the Queen anymore?

It's almost as if the universe is trying to tell me something. Like, "Hey, Dani! You know those books you've been treating like your personal supernatural Wikipedia? Yeah, about that... it might not be entirely accurate."

But in all seriousness, I need to put on my detective hat and start separating fact from fiction—time to dust off the cobwebs and figure out which parts of the book are still relevant and which parts belong in the "ancient history" section.

Gideon regards me for a moment, his expression unreadable. "These *friends* of yours... what's a girl like you doing with them?"

"Rhyland, the big, broody Viking guy? He's my mate. And the silver fox, Erik? That's his brother—but don't worry—they only bite if you ask nicely." I flash a cheeky grin, trying to lighten the mood.

The Captain's eyebrows shoot up, but to his credit, he doesn't look too shocked. "Well, that's a new one. I'm just surprised to see a nice girl like yerself caught up with those creatures."

I shrug, trying to play it cool. "Things have changed in our world—they're good guys, I promise. A little rough around the edges, but who isn't in this day and age?"

Gideon nods slowly as if processing this new information. "So, uh, do they... bite with those fangs of theirs?" Gideon asks, his face all worried-like.

"Only if you're into that sort of thing and you ask nicely," I say with a grin. Gideon looks relieved for a second until I add, "Or if you royally piss them off real good—then it's a free-for-all." I shrug.

Gideon raises an eyebrow, half-relieved, half on edge. "Aye, thanks for that. Just what I needed to hear."

As if on cue, there's a knock at the door. Finn enters, carrying a tray laden with steaming dishes. The smell of hot food makes my mouth water and my stomach growl even louder.

"Ah, perfect timing," the Captain says, gesturing for Finn to set the tray on the table. "Dig in, lass. You're going to need your strength for what's to come."

I don't need to be told twice. I practically lunge for the tray, which holds some seafood chowder. It smells delicious, so I grab a hunk of bread, dip it in the chowder, and tear it into it like a starving wolf. The flavors explode on my tongue—rich, hearty, and oh-so-satisfying.

I pause mid-bite, a piece of bread dangling precariously from my mouth as I catch Gideon and Finn's intense stares. They're looking at me like I'm a particularly challenging riddle they're trying to decipher. I swallow the bread, nearly choking, and shoot them a sheepish grin.

"What can I say? I've never been one for table manners," I quip, wiping my mouth with the back of my hand. "I like food."

Gideon's eyes glint with something that might be amusement or possibly indigestion. It's hard to tell with him. "It's refreshing to see a woman—a lady such as yerself— who doesn't hide her appetites," he remarks, his tone laced with a hint of innuendo.

I nearly snort into my chowder. Is he seriously trying to flirt with me right now? While I'm shoveling food into my face like a starving bear?

Points for boldness, I suppose.

Finn, who's been watching this exchange with a smirk, chimes in. "Aye, lass. It's a rare sight to see a woman enjoy her vittles with such... enthusiasm. Most ladies would be worried about maintaining their figure, but you? You dive right in, like a true seafarer."

I raise an eyebrow. "Well, Finn, when you've been through the kind of shit I have, you learn to appreciate the simple things in life. Like a good meal and not giving a damn what anyone thinks about your table manners."

Finn's eyes widen before he throws his head back and laughs, the sound rich and genuine. "Ha! I like your spirit, lass. You'd fit right in with the crew, I reckon. We could use more straight-shooters like you around here."

I shrug, my grin turning sly. "What can I say? I'm a woman of many talents. Eating like a starved bear just happens to be one of them. But don't get too excited, pirate. I'm spoken for, and my man's the jealous type."

Finn holds up his hands in mock surrender, his eyes twinkling with amusement. "Aye, I gathered as much. I've heard the way that Viking speaks of you. I may be a pirate, but I'm not stupid enough to poach another man's treasure."

I chuckle at that. "Smart man. Rhyland's not the type to share, and trust me, you don't want to be on his bad side."

Finn nods, his expression turning serious for a moment. "Noted, lass. But just so you know, if you ever need a friend or an ally on this ship, you can count on me. Pirate's honor."

I smile at him, genuinely touched by the offer. "Thanks, Finn. I appreciate that. And who knows? Maybe we can swap stories sometime. I bet you've got some wild tales to tell."

Finn's grin returns, wide and mischievous. "Oh, you have no idea, lass. Stick around, and I'll regale you with adventures that'll make your hair curl."

I laugh, shaking my head. "I'll hold you to that, Finn."

As I turn back to my chowder, I can't help but feel a sense of camaraderie with Finn. Sure, he's a pirate, but something about his easy humor and quick wit puts me at ease.

My headache is starting to fade, thanks to the water and food I've managed to shovel into my mouth.

But let's be honest, I still feel like complete and utter shit, like my magical mojo has been sucked dry by a gang of power-hungry leeches.

It's as if that inner wellspring of power has just fucked off to Tahiti, leaving me high and dry with nothing but a metaphorical "wish you were here" postcard. I swear, if that wretched witch has somehow managed to zap away my abilities or curse me with some bullshit power-leeching hex, I'm going to be royally pissed.

It's bad enough that I'm stuck on this floating wooden prison, surrounded by pirates who probably haven't seen a soap bar in decades.

If my superpowers don't decide to make a triumphant comeback soon, we'll all be sitting ducks—and not the cute, fluffy kind. More like the "oh shit, we're screwed" variety.

"Oh, and about that Broody Viking—that *mate* of yours," Gideon says casually, pausing at the door. "He doesn't like me."

I roll my eyes, "He doesn't like anyone. Don't take it personally."

"Aye, lass. I'll send Izabelle to ye, to fetch some proper garments."

I nod, returning to the food in front of me. Just as he's about to duck out, "Oh, and Captain..." He stops, turning to face me with a raised eyebrow. "Just a friendly word of advice—keeping that Viking of mine locked up for too long might not be the wisest course of action. Unless, of course, you're eager to discover the consequences firsthand." I warn.

The Captain regards me with a mixture of amusement and exasperation. "Is that a threat, lass? Or merely a bit of friendly counsel?"

I shrug. "Take it however you like, Captain. But let's just say that my man has a bit of a temper when it comes to being separated from his beloved. And trust me, you don't want to be on the receiving end of that particular brand of Viking fury."

The Captain chuckles, shaking his head. "Ye be a bold one, lass. I'll give ye that. But I'll not be cowed by idle threats, not on me own ship."

"They're not idle threats, Captain. More like... strongly worded suggestions. After all, I wouldn't want you to explain to your crew why their beloved Captain suddenly sprouted a few extra holes in his neck. Might be a bit of a damper on morale, don't you think?"

The Captain's eyes narrow, but I can see a glimmer of respect in his gaze. "Aye, ye make a fair point, lass. I'll take yer 'suggestions' under advisement. But mark my words—if that Viking of yours steps out of line, he'll have more to worry about than a few extra nights in the brig."

I grin, "Duly noted, Captain. But something tells me that you and Rhyland might have more in common than you think. After all, you both have a flair for the dramatic and a penchant for making threats you may or may not be able to back up."

The Captain snorts, a wry smile tugging at the corners of his mouth. "Ye've got a sharp tongue on ye, lass. Best be careful how ye wield it. Not everyone takes kindly to a lass with a wit as quick as her blade."

I wink, my grin turning impish. "Oh, don't worry about me. I've been dealing with men who can't handle a woman with a mind of her own for longer than I care to remember. It's all part of my charm."

The Captain shakes his head, a look of resignation on his face. "Heaven help us all, then. I've got a feeling that life on the high seas just got a whole lot more interesting with ye aboard, lass."

And with that, he turns and strides out of the room, leaving me to my thoughts and my half-eaten meal.

My mind wanders back to Lucian, and I can't help but feel a tsunami of worry. I'm betting my last magical penny that Azrael and his coven of bitchy witches are holding him hostage— using him as a bargaining chip in their twisted little game. After all, it's no secret that they're after Rhyland for their jacked-up ritual.

And let's be honest, Azrael loves to bargain like a sleazy used car salesman on crack. He's probably sitting there, rubbing his hands together and cackling with glee at the thought of having Lucian as his prized possession.

I just hope Lucian doesn't push his luck too far with his captors. We all know how much he loves to run that smart mouth of his, spewing out witty one-liners and sarcastic quips like it's his job.

But in this case, his usual tactic of "if you can't dazzle them with your brilliance, baffle them with your bullshit" might land him in even deeper shit.

LUCIAN

6

Okay, let's see here. I'm tied to a chair, my head feels like it's been used as a punching bag by a gang of angry midgets, and my mouth is drier than a nun's cooch.

I blink, trying to clear the fog from my brain, but it's like navigating through pea soup.

Where the hell am I?

I'm not sure what the hell is going on, but I know one thing for sure: I'm thirsty as fuck. Like, "I'd sell my left nut for a sip of water," thirsty. And to make matters worse, I'm tied to a chair in some swanky gothic mansion that looks like it was ripped straight out of a Tim Burton wet dream.

I mean, don't get me wrong, I can appreciate a good aesthetic. But this? This is just overkill.

But I digress. The real issue here is that I have no fucking clue where I am or how I got here. It's like my brain's been put through a blender set to "puree," and all that's left are a few chunky bits of memory floating around in a sea of confusion.

Enter tall, dark, and brooding, accompanied by a blonde bombshell who looks like she just stepped out of a Victoria's Secret catalog. Seriously, this chick is all legs and lips. Long, golden hair cascades down her back, and her bright green eyes are fixed on me with an intensity that makes me squirm.

"Ah, I see you're awake," the man says, with a sinister glee that makes my skin crawl. "Now the real fun begins."

I lick my lips, trying to regain some moisture in my mouth. "Look, buddy, I don't know who you are or what your deal is, but I'm gonna need you to untie me, like yesterday."

The man chuckles, a sound about as comforting as a razor blade in my underwear. "Oh, I don't think so. We have some questions for you first."

I raise an eyebrow. "Questions? What kind of questions? Like, 'What's your favorite color?' or 'How many licks does it take to get to the center of a Tootsie Pop'?"

Blondie steps forward, her lips curving into a smirk. "More like, 'who are you' and 'what do you remember'?"

I blink. "Who I am?" I think about that briefly, and my mind draws a blank. *What the hell?* It's like someone hit the delete button on my memories, and now I'm left with nothing but a vague sense of confusion and a thirst that just won't quit.

"Lady, I don't have a fucking clue. As for what I remember..." I trail off, searching my brain for anything but coming up empty. "I got nothing. It's like someone took a giant eraser to my mental chalkboard."

The man leans down, his eyes boring into me. "You mean to tell me you have no recollection of your identity, your past, or why you're here?"

I meet his gaze, unflinching. "That's what I'm saying—Tall, Dark, and Ominous. I'm drawing a complete blank. I don't know who I am, where I am, or why I feel like I could drain a lake and still be thirsty."

They both exchange another look, and I can tell something's wrong. They start arguing in hushed tones, but I can still make out bits and pieces.

"Paige," the man hisses, his voice low and dangerous. "You took too much."

Blondie, who I'm guessing is Paige, rolls her eyes. "Oh, please, Azrael. I did exactly what you asked. It's not my fault if he's got a mind like a steel trap."

Azrael? Paige? What the fuck kind of names are those?

"Fix it," Azrael demands, his tone leaving no room for argument.

"I can't just 'fix it,' you imbecile," Paige snarls, her hands curling into fists at her sides. "It's not like I have a magic wand to wave around and make everything better."

I watch them go back and forth, my confusion growing every second. I have no idea what they're talking about, but I get the distinct impression that I'm royally fucked.

"Um, excuse me," I pipe up, drawing their attention back to me. "Hi, yeah, still tied up over here. And also, still thirsty as fuck. Any chance we could take a little break from the cryptic bullshit and get me a drink?"

Paige's eyes widen, and she turns to Azrael with a look of alarm. "He doesn't even know *what* he is," she whispers, but my ears pick up on it clear as day.

What I am? What the hell is that supposed to mean?

Azrael shrugs, a sinister smile playing at the corners of his mouth. "Well, then. This should be interesting."

He steps closer, looming over me like a shadow. "Tell me, Lucian. How badly do you want that drink?"

I swallow hard—my throat feels like it's lined with sandpaper. "Pretty fucking badly, if I'm being honest."

Azrael's smile widens, and something about it makes my blood run cold. "Well, then. Let's see what we can do about that, shall we?"

He turns to Paige, and there's a glint in his eye that I really don't like. "Bring in the girl."

Girl? What girl? What the fuck is going on here?

But before I can ask, Paige is gone, and Azrael is circling me like a shark who has just caught the scent of blood.

"You know, Lucian," he says, his voice a low purr. "I think we're going to have a lot of fun together, you and I."

Somehow, I seriously fucking doubt that.

The door opens again, and Paige returns, dragging a young woman behind her. The girl looks terrified, her eyes wide and her body trembling. She can't be more than twenty, with long, dark hair and pale skin marred by tears and smudged makeup.

"What the hell is this?" I demand, my eyes darting between Azrael, Paige, and the girl. "What are you doing?"

Azrael smiles, and it's a smile that makes me want to piss myself a little. "Why, we're getting you that drink you wanted so badly, of course."

He nods to Paige, who shoves the girl forward. She stumbles and falls to her knees in front of me, and the scent of her fear is so thick I can almost taste it.

Wait, what? Taste it? What the fuck is wrong with me?

I panic; my heart should be beating out of my chest, but I feel nothing. No heartbeat?

"I don't want this," I say, my voice shaking. "I don't want to hurt her."

Azrael laughs. The sound chills me to the bone. "Oh, but you do, Lucian. You just don't know it yet."

He leans down, his face inches from mine. "You're a vampire, you idiot. And right now, that thirst you're feeling? It's not for water, beer, or any other mortal drink. It's for *blood*."

I feel like I've been punched in the gut. A vampire? Me? No, that's impossible. Vampires aren't real. They're just stories, myths, Hollywood bullshit.

Even as I think about it, I can feel the hunger gnawing at my insides, the burning in my throat screaming for something to quench it.

I feel a strange sensation in my mouth. It's like a pressure building, a painful and exhilarating ache. My gums throb, and I run my tongue over my teeth to soothe the discomfort.

And that's when I feel them—fangs.

They elongate, pushing through my gums like twin daggers. Sharp and deadly, they scrape against my tongue. It's an alien but strangely familiar feeling—like a long-forgotten memory suddenly snapping into focus.

"No," I whisper, shaking my head. "No, I won't do it. I won't hurt her."

Paige sighs, rolling her eyes. "Oh, for fuck's sake. Stop being such a pussy and just drink already."

She grabs the girl by the hair, yanking her head back and exposing her throat. The girl whimpers, and the sound is like a knife to my gut.

"I can't," I say, my voice breaking. "Please, don't make me do this."

Azrael's hand is on my shoulder, his grip like a vice. "You can, and you will. You're a monster, Lucian. A predator. This is what you are made for."

He leans in closer, his breath hot against my ear. "Now, drink. Before I rip her throat out myself and force-feed you like a baby bird."

Hunger is rising in me now, a tidal wave of need that threatens to drown me. I can hear the girl's heartbeat, the rush of blood beneath her skin, and it's calling to me like a siren song.

"I'm sorry," I whisper, "I'm so fucking sorry."

And then I lunge forward, my fangs sinking into her throat. She screams, but the sound is drowned out by the roaring in my ears, the flavor explosion on my tongue.

Her blood hits my tongue like liquid ecstasy, a symphony of flavors exploding in my mouth. It's sweeter than the finest wine, richer than dark chocolate—more intoxicating than any drug. Every gulp sends waves of pleasure coursing through my body, lighting up every nerve ending like a fucking Christmas tree.

I can feel her life force flowing into me, warm and vibrant, filling the hollow emptiness inside. It's better than sex, better than anything I've ever experienced—I think? Each heartbeat pushes more of that crimson ambrosia into my mouth, and I'm lost in the primal rhythm of feed, swallow, repeat.

Her fear, her essence, her very life—I'm consuming it all, and holy fuck, it's like mainlining pure power. I can feel her getting weaker as I get stronger, her heartbeat slowing while my body surges with stolen vitality. It's horrifying and beautiful and absolutely fucking addictive.

The monster inside me purrs with satisfaction, demanding more, always more. The other part of me is screaming to stop, but it's like trying to hold back a tsunami with a paper umbrella. I'm too far gone, too lost in the primal ecstasy of the feed.

This is what I am now. A predator. A monster. A fucking vampire high on the ultimate rush, and god help me, but I never want it to end.

DANICA

7

I'm just polishing off the last morsels of my meal when the door swings open, and a woman who can only be Izabelle walks in. She strolls into the room with the self-assured air of someone who knows she's the top dog in this floating den of masculinity.

Izabelle is a vision, with caramel-colored skin a few shades deeper than mine and mesmerizing turquoise eyes that seem to see right through me. Her long, lustrous hair cascades down her back in a deep, rich brown waterfall, the color of dark chocolate mixed with hints of cinnamon. She's got a figure that would make a grown man weep, her curvaceous body barely restrained by the provocative, pirate-inspired ensemble she's sporting.

A snug, off-the-shoulder top with flowing sleeves highlights her generous cleavage, while form-fitting, high-waisted trousers cling to her hips like a lover's embrace. Knee-high boots and a belt with a shimmering silver buckle round out the look, giving her an aura of peril and seduction.

But the instant her gaze meets mine, it's evident that Izabelle isn't here to play nice. She hurls a bundle of clothes at me with a look of pure contempt. Her voice is laced with scorn as she speaks.

"The Captain says ye need clothes. Put these on and be quick about it. I don't have all day to play dress-up with the likes of *you*."

I snatch the clothes out of the air, my heart pounding with anger and disbelief at her hostile demeanor. I open my mouth to retort, but Izabelle cuts me off before I can get a word in edgewise.

"Let me make one thing *crystal* clear, wench. I'm the *only* woman on this ship and intend to keep it that way. These men? They're *mine*, every single one of them, and

I won't have some scrawny little harlot coming in and stealing their attention away from where it belongs."

I can practically taste the jealousy radiating off of Izabelle, her bitterness and resentment crashing over me like a tidal wave of pure, unadulterated envy. It doesn't take a genius to read between the lines of her little speech—when she says these men are "hers," I'm pretty sure she's not talking about a spiritual friendship bracelet situation.

The realization hits me, leaving me gasping for air as my eyes widen in shock. Holy shit, she's sleeping with the entire crew! I mean, I know pirates aren't exactly known for their moral fortitude, but damn. That's a level of promiscuity that even I, with my sordid history of questionable life choices, find hard to wrap my head around.

I feel a strange mixture of disgust and pity swirling in my stomach as I try to imagine the kind of life Izabelle must have led to end up in this position. I mean, what could drive a woman to seek validation and power through sex with a bunch of unwashed, unruly pirates? It's like a twisted version of "The Bachelorette," except she's handing out STDs instead of roses.

But even as I'm reeling from this revelation, a small part of me can't help but feel a twinge of sympathy for Izabelle. Don't get me wrong—I still think she's a raging bitch with a severe case of territorial instincts.

But I don't have time to dwell on Izabelle's tragic backstory. I've got bigger fish to fry—like figuring out how the hell I'm going to survive on this floating den of iniquity.

"Steal their attention? Please. I'm not interested in your floating orgy. I've got my own man, and trust me, he's *more* than enough to keep me satisfied."

Izabelle's eyes blaze with fury, and she takes a menacing step toward me. "You'd better watch yer mouth, you little tramp. I've gutted wenches for less than the filth ye be spewing."

I refuse to back down, meeting her gaze with a bold smirk. "Aren't you just a peach? But it's a hard pass on the whole 'being gutted' thing. I'm rather fond of my internal organs, you know."

Izabelle looks like she's about to explode with rage, but she takes a deep breath, visibly struggling to control her temper. "Just put on the damn clothes and stay out of my way. And if I catch you sniffin' around my men? You'll wish you never set foot on this ship."

With that, she whirls around and storms out of the room, slamming the door behind her with enough force to make the walls shudder.

I stare after her for a moment, my heart racing with adrenaline and disbelief. Holy hell, what have I gotten myself into? I've barely been on this ship for a day, and I've already made an enemy with the resident pirate prostitute.

I glance down at the clothes in my hands, wrinkling my nose at their musty odor.

I'm pretty sure these things are practically marinated in pirate jizz. Just hand me a black light, and I'll make my case with glowing, unsavory proof.

But beggars can't be choosers, and right now, I'm definitely in the begging category.

With a heavy sigh, I peel off my salt-crusted leathers and wipe myself off the best I can. I can already feel a scratchy rash taking hold on parts that shall not be named. I go to put on my new outfit, and isn't that just freaking great—it's an exact copycat of Izabelle the Pirate Whore's getup.

I start with the off-the-shoulder blouse, made of flowy white fabric that feels surprisingly soft against my skin. As I pull it on, I realize that the neckline is so low that it's practically an invitation for my girls to break free. The only thing keeping them tucked in is a simple tie in the front.

Next up is the tight leather corset, which looks like it was designed by someone who has a serious grudge against the female respiratory system. I struggle to get it on, cursing as I try to figure out how the hell I'm supposed to lace this thing up without dislocating a shoulder.

After what feels like an eternity of tugging, pulling, and some creative contortionism, I finally manage to get the corset on and sinched. And holy mother of cleavage, my rack is nearly spilling out—like I'm trying to smuggle a pair of cantaloupes onto the ship!

I'm not exactly lacking in the chest department—I've always been blessed with a decent set of sweater puppies that could stop traffic. But this corset is taking my already ample assets to a whole new level of 'in-your-face!'

I wriggle into the high-waisted leather pants, which are very comfortable, and damn, do they make my ass look good.

I can't help but think that no matter where I go, I always find myself in outfits that belong on the more risqué side of the tracks. It's like the universe conspires to ensure I'm always one wardrobe malfunction away from a full-blown scandal.

I slip on the thigh-high boots and fasten the silver-studded belt around my waist, finishing my new ensemble. As I slide my daggers into the belt on each side, I glimpse myself in the mirror and nearly do a double-take. Holy mother of all things scandalous, I look like I'm about to star in *"Pirates of the Caribbean: After Dark Edition"!*

I gape at my reflection, my eyes wide with shock and amusement.

I can just imagine the field day Izabelle and the rest of the crew will have with this. I can practically hear the lewd comments and wolf whistles already. Just what I need—a bunch of horny pirates leering at me like I'm the catch of the day.

I let out an exasperated groan. I mean, really? These are my options? It's like choosing between the lesser of three fashion evils.

On one hand, I could rock this absurd getup and risk looking like a reject from a low-budget pirate porn. On the other, I could stick with my crusty, salt-encrusted leathers and spend the day itching and scratching like a flea-ridden dog. Or, I could say, "screw it," and go au naturel, giving these horny pirates an eyeful they'll never forget.

I snort at the thought, shaking my head. As tempting as it might be to scandalize the crew with my birthday suit, I'd rather not put on an impromptu strip show. I've got standards, even if they are buried beneath layers of snark and sarcasm—not to mention, Rhyland would have my ass bent over the first rum barrel, punishing me for even considering it.

I try to comb out the knots in my salt-crusted hair the best I can with my fingers, and it's like snagging a fishing lure. I give up and try to fluff it up over the girls the best I can, hoping that the whole "just rolled out of the sea" look is in style on this floating fashion disaster.

Just as I'm coming out from behind the changing wall, in walks Captain Sterling, and I'm already bracing myself for his inevitable "appreciation of the female form" in this damn costume.

But before I can even open my mouth to deliver a preemptive snark attack, my eyes land on Rhyland and Erik, who are coming in behind the Captain. And just like that, all thoughts of witty comebacks fly right out of my head.

I don't hesitate. I launch myself at Rhyland like a heat-seeking missile, throwing my arms around his neck and clinging to him like a koala on a eucalyptus tree. I bury my face in his neck, inhaling his scent like it's the sweetest perfume, and I swear I could stay like this forever.

"Rhyland," I breathe against his neck.

Rhyland's arms come around me, holding me tight, and I feel like I can finally breathe again. He's here. He's real. And for a moment, everything else fades away—the ship, the pirates, my ridiculous outfit. It's just me and him, and nothing else matters.

I pull back just enough to look up at him, my eyes searching his face for any sign of injury or distress. "Are you okay? Did they hurt you? I swear, if anyone laid a finger on you, I'll—"

Rhyland cuts me off with a chuckle, his hand coming up to cup my cheek. "I'm fine, baby. I promise. I'm just so fucking glad you're safe and that I can hold you in my arms again."

I lean into his touch, my eyes fluttering closed momentarily as I savor the feeling of his skin against mine. It's like a balm to my frayed nerves, a reminder that we're together despite everything we've been through.

"I was worried after we entered here; you weren't moving, and..." I trail off, the words sticking in my throat as the memory of Rhyland's lifeless form flashes through my mind.

Rhyland quickly settles my nerves, his voice low and reassuring, with a hint of his usual alpha male swagger. "I'm fine, sweetheart. Just zapped of everything."

I nod. I know the feeling.

I quickly kiss Rhyland, needing to feel his lips on mine—but with an audience watching, a full-on make-out session will have to wait.

I reluctantly untangle myself from Rhyland's embrace and turn to face my stoic, silver-haired vampire. He's standing a few feet away, his posture rigid and his expression unreadable.

"Little Huntress," he says, his tone formal and sweet. "I am relieved to see you unharmed."

I close the distance between us and wrap my arms around his waist, hugging him tight. "I'm glad you're okay too, Erik. You had me worried there for a minute."

The Captain clears his throat, drawing our attention back to him. "Alright, now that ye lot are back together, let's have a little parley—savvy?"

Rhyland turns to face him, his body tensing like a coiled spring. I can feel the anger radiating off of him in waves, and I know this isn't going to be pretty.

"First off," Rhyland growls, his voice low and dangerous, "you wanna explain why the hell you let my girl almost fucking drown on this floating piece of shit?"

I wince at the harshness of his words, but I can't say I blame him. I mean, I'm pretty pissed off about the whole almost-drowning thing myself.

The Captain holds up his hands in a placating gesture, but a glint of amusement in his eye makes me want to smack the smirk right off his handsome face. "Now, now, mate. No need to get yer knickers in a twist. The lass is fine, ain't she?"

Rhyland takes a step forward, his fists clenched at his sides. "That's not the fucking point," he snarls. "She's not just some piece of cargo you can toss around."

"We were under the Dark Tides, mate. I knew what must be done to ensure she didn't kick the bucket." The Captian retorts.

I place a hand on Rhyland's arm to calm him down before he does something stupid. Like, oh, I don't know, punching the Captain in his smug face.

"Rhyland," I murmur, my voice soft but firm. "It's okay. I'm fine. Let's just hear what he has to say."

Rhyland looks down at me, his eyes blazing with fury. For a moment, I think he will ignore me and go off on the Captain anyway. But then he takes a deep breath, his shoulders sagging slightly as he nods.

"Fine," he grits out. "But I swear, if anything happens to her on this fucking ship, I'll hold you personally responsible and rip your goddamn throat out."

The Captain nods, his expression turning serious for once. "Fair enough, mate. I give ye my word. No harm will come to the Lass while she's under my protection."

I resist the urge to snort at that. *Protection?* More like imprisonment. But I keep my mouth shut, not wanting to antagonize the situation any further.

I step forward. "Alright, Captain, fill us in. What's the deal with these Dark Tides you keep yammering on about?"

The Captain heaves a sigh that could rival the wind in his sails, his eyes going distant like he's reliving some nautical nightmare. "Aye, lass, the Dark Tides be a curse upon these waters, a blight on the very soul of the sea. They strike without warning, pullin' pirates and sailors alike down to the briny depths, claimin' their souls for the Sea Witch's twisted collection."

My eyebrows shoot up so high they practically merge with my hairline. Collecting souls? Well, if that doesn't sound like Moretemis's particular brand of bullshit, I don't know what does.

I glance at Rhyland and Erik—their faces light up as they've just had a major "Aha!" moment. I would bet my left ass cheek she's holding the last shard of the Soul Stone.

"'Tis all part of the Sea Witch's curse, ye see," the Captain continues. "She seeks to punish those who dare to sail her waters, draggin' them down to a watery grave as payment for their transgressions."

I can't help but roll my eyes at the dramatics. "Okay, hold up. What waters are we talking about here? Is there a specific area we need to avoid, or is *Ursula* just snacking on souls willy-nilly?"

Gideon frowns, his confusion written all over his face, "Ursula?" The name going straight over his head. "Nay, love—Calypso"

I blink, my brain taking a moment to catch up with the Captain's words. "Calypso?" I repeat. "What, like the music? Don't tell me we're dealing with a sea witch who's into steel drums and reggae."

The Captain's frown deepens—a vein throbbing in his forehead. "Nay, lass, not the music. Calypso be the name of the Sea Witch herself, the one who cursed these waters and claimed the souls of countless sailors."

The Captain shakes his head, continuing, "And it is all of 'em, love—all the seas. It takes a good ship, a sturdy crew, and a Cap'n with nerves of steel to sail through the Dark Tides and keep the ship afloat."

He puffs out his chest like a preening peacock. Excellent, just what we need. A pirate with an ego the size of the seven seas.

As much as I want to take the wind out of his sails (pun totally intended), I know we need all the information we can get if we're going to navigate these cursed waters and make it out alive.

My mind is already whirling with plans and possibilities. If Moretemis—Calypso—Soul Stone—is responsible for the Dark Tides, we will need all the help we can get to navigate them and emerge in one piece.

"Now," the Captain continues, clasping his hands behind his back and rocking on his heels. "About that little matter of helpin' ye lot with this quest of yers."

RHYLAND

8

I finally start to calm down, the rage simmering beneath the surface as I take a deep breath and try to focus on the task. But then I get a good look at Dani, and I nearly choke on my tongue.

Christ, this woman... The way she looks in anything she puts on, it's enough to drive a man fucking crazy.

Seriously, she could be wearing a goddamn potato sack and still manage to look like a walking wet dream. It's like her body was specifically designed to make my blood run hot and my thoughts turn sinful.

That damn pirate wench outfit is going to undo me. The way it hugs her curves, barely containing her luscious breasts and hinting at the treasures beneath... Fuck me, it's taking every ounce of my self-control not to throw her over my shoulder, find the nearest empty room, and show her exactly what she does to me.

She looks fucking edible, and suddenly I've got a thing for pirate wenches. I don't want anyone else to see her like this. She's mine, and I'll be damned if I let these filthy bastards lay their eyes on what belongs to me.

I mentally growl. *"Do you have to look so sexy in everything you put on? I don't want you prancing around in that, tempting all these horny fucking pirates. Can't you, I don't know, put on something else?"*

Dani sighs, her voice echoing in my head with that sassy tone that always drives me crazy. *"Oh, sure, let me just pop on over to the nearest Pirate Wench Boutique and pick up something a little more modest. I'm sure they have a lovely selection of floor-length gowns and turtlenecks."*

Did that bastard Captain purposely give her this outfit to wear? So he can fucking ogle what's mine, like the pervy son of a bitch he is?

I swear, if I catch him eyeing her curves or undressing her with his filthy gaze, I'll rip his goddamn eyes out. No one gets to feast on the sight of my woman but me.

My little angel has no idea what she's doing to me right—

"Aye, I see Izabelle brought ye some clothes—ye clean up nicely." The Captain praises with a wink.

This son of a bitch.

I growl under my breath, my hands itching to reach out and cover her up, shielding her from his lustful gaze—I know the crew will have a hay day. But I know Dani can handle herself, and the last thing I want to do is make her feel like I don't trust her or not give her credit for handling herself.

The Captain breaks through my thoughts, motioning for us to sit down, "We're making our way to Captain's Haven," his says with false cheer. "There, we can dock and find suitable quarters for you to freshen up. And with some luck, we might even be able to arrange a meeting with the Queen herself to help find ye stone ye need."

Dani perks up at that. "Queen Undine, correct?"

The Captain looks at her momentarily. His brow furrows in confusion. "Nay, lass," he says slowly, like talking to a particularly dim-witted child. "Queen Undine died ages ago. Queen Cordelia rules now."

Dani's face falls, but she quickly recovers, her expression curious. "I see," she says with a bit of sadness. "And how do we go about getting an audience with her?"

Dani and I both studied our asses off on the book of Aquaria, and I see why she's so fucking defeated; nothing is as it seems from those dusty old tomes—same with the book of the Fae. It makes sense, though, since those books were written centuries ago, and with the realms shut off, well, no shit, nothing is as it was written.

The information is outdated as hell, and now we're stuck in this goddamn place with no real clue what to expect.

The only good thing about it is that it gives Dani a waypoint.

The Captain chuckles, shaking his head. "It's not that simple, lass. The Queen is a bit of a stickler and doesn't take kindly to entertaining guests. But there is a way."

He pauses for a moment, letting the suspense build like the fucking drama queen he is. "You'll have to speak with someone from Serraphatic Cove," his voice low and conspiratorial.

Dani frowns, her nose wrinkling in confusion. "What is that, and why do we need to go there?"

The Captain's eyes glint with amusement. "Serraphatic Cove is the island of the merfolk," he explains, his voice taking on a dreamy quality. "It's only there that ye can speak with one of them and possibly be granted an audience with the Queen. It's rare, but sometimes it works."

I feel a surge of hope rising in my chest, but I quickly tamp it down. I've been around long enough to know that nothing is ever as easy as it seems, especially when dealing with the supernatural."And what's the catch? There's always a catch with these things."

The Captain grins, his gold tooth glinting in the lamplight. "Ah, you're a sharp one, ain't ya? The catch is, ye'll have to prove yourselves worthy of the merfolk's attention. And that's no easy feat, let me tell ye."

Dani throws up her hands. "I knew it," she sighs, shaking her head in disbelief. "There's always a catch with you supernatural types. It's never a simple 'Hey, can we talk to your leader?' It's always 'prove your worth' this and 'retrieve a mystical artifact' that."

Dani tenses beside me, her hand gripping mine tightly. I give her a reassuring squeeze, but I know my girl is not about to let this one slide.

"Okay, let me guess," her voice laced with enough sarcasm to sink a ship. "We'll have to go on an underwater scavenger hunt, right? Maybe find Ariel's long-lost treasure or Sebastian's secret stash of Jamaican rum?"

The Captain blinks at her. "Who's Ariel?" his voice laced with genuine bewilderment.

Dani rolls her eyes. "Never mind. The point is, we've been through this song and dance before. And let me tell you, Captain, it's getting a little old."

Her eyes narrow on the Captain."But hey, if that's what it takes to get an audience with her Royal Fishiness, then fine. We'll jump through their hoops and play their little games. But remember, Captain—We're here to save the world and do whatever it takes to make that happen."

The Captain nods slowly, his expression turning serious. "Aye, lass," his voice low and gruff. "I can see that. And I respect it. But the merfolk are a proud people who don't take kindly to outsiders. If you want their help, you'll have to earn it."

Erik, the stoic bastard, takes in all this information with his usual look of complete and utter boredom. Typical of my brother.

It's like nothing fazes him, no matter how crazy or convoluted the situation gets. He stands there, his expression as blank as a goddamn slate, as if he's listening to someone recite the phonebook instead of unraveling ancient secrets and navigating treacherous realms.

But I know better than to let his bored act fool me. Deep down, I know he's processing every detail, analyzing every angle, and formulating a plan. He's a fucking mastermind, always ten steps ahead, even if he looks like he couldn't give a rat's ass about what's going on around him.

I trust him with my life, and I know he's got our best interests at heart, even if he doesn't always show it. That's our brotherly bond, an unspoken understanding transcending any momentary annoyance or frustration.

"Alright, Captain," my voice steady. "Cut the bullshit and tell us straight. What must we do to prove ourselves worthy to these fish folk? We're not here to play fucking games. We've got shit to do and people to save, so lay it out for us."

The Captain's grin widens, and he leans forward in his seat, his eyes glinting with mischief. "They like shiny things, booty of such—"

"Why did I not see *that* coming?" Dani's sarcasm is at an all-time high now. "What kind of gadgets, gizmos, and plenty are we talking about here, Captain?" Her tone as sweet as poisoned honey. "Something special, or just any old whoozits and whatzits galore from a sunken pirate ship treasure?"

The Captain blinks at her, clearly not getting the reference. "I... I'm not sure what you mean by *whoozits* and *whatzits*, lass. But I can assure you, the artifact we seek is no mere trinket."

Dani sighs, her shoulders slumping in defeat. "Of course not. Alright, so what is this oh-so-special thingamabob we're supposed to retrieve?"

The Captain's eyes glint with excitement. "It's called the Siren's Lyre and said to be hidden deep within the Coral Caverns on Serraphatic Cove. Legend has it that the merfolk used it to communicate with the gods themselves and that it holds the key to unlocking their deepest secrets."

Dani raises an eyebrow, her interest piqued. "The Siren's Lyre? Like, a musical instrument?"

The Captain nods, a grin spreading across his face. "Aye, love. But not just any musical instrument. The Siren's Lyre is said to have the power to control the tides and summon somthin' of great power at the wielder's biddin'."

Dani's eyes widen, "Okay, that's... that's pretty impressive. But let me guess—it's guarded by a terrifying sea monster or ancient curse, right?"

The Captain chuckles, shaking his head. "Not quite, lass. Traps and puzzles guard the Siren's Lyre, each more fiendishly clever than the last. It's said that only the most cunning and resourceful of adventurers can hope to retrieve it."

Dani nods, her expression thoughtful. "Traps and puzzles, huh? Well, I guess that's better than a giant squid or a Kraken."

I can feel Dani's excitement about this shooting through our bond. She fucking lives for this type of shit. Solving puzzles, riddles, and cracking codes—it's like her goddamn lifeblood.

The Captain grins, "Aye, lass, that it is. But I have faith in you and yer crew."

Dani sighs, "Alright, priority check." She locks eyes with me, "Step one: Head back to our world. Step two: Snag Lucian. Because there's no way in hell I'm playing 'Under the Sea' scavenger hunt while that nutjob has Lucian."

She's right. I already feel like a fucking asshole for abandoning Lucian, and Dani's inner remorse is shooting through our bond like a goddamn live wire. She hates abandonment with a passion and would never have done it herself. But she was weak and barely able to stay conscious. She would've fought tooth and nail to save Lucian, even if it meant sacrificing herself.

That's just the kind of person she is—loyal to a fault and willing to put everything on the line for the people she cares about. It's one of the many reasons I love her so damn much, even if it scares the shit out of me sometimes.

But something about the Captain's story isn't sitting right with me. It's like a puzzle piece is still missing, a crucial detail he's intentionally keeping from us. And I'll be damned if I'm going to let him lead us into some trap or wild goose chase without getting the whole picture.

Why would the merfolk, with all their power and knowledge of the sea, need us to retrieve this artifact? What's the real reason behind this supposed quest? I don't particularly appreciate being kept in the dark, especially when the stakes are this high.

I won't let Dani's guilt and my sense of failure cloud my judgment. We need to keep our wits about us and approach this with a healthy dose of skepticism. The last thing we need is to get caught up in some political shitstorm or ancient feud that has nothing to do with us.

"Hold up, something doesn't add up here," I interject. "If this artifact is so damn important to the merfolk, why can't they just swim down there and retrieve it themselves? Why do they need us to play fetch for them?"

I narrow my eyes on the Captain's face for any hint of deception. "This whole thing seems fishy as fuck, no pun intended. What aren't you telling us?"

Beside me, I can sense Dani's mind working overtime, trying to piece together the puzzle. I know she's just as skeptical as I am; her analytical brain searches for the missing pieces.

"There's got to be more to this story," I press on, my tone growing insistent. "Some reason why the merfolk haven't fetched it themselves. So why don't you cut the cryptic bullshit and give us the full picture, Captain?"

The door swings open, and a young man wearing a red bandana barges in. "Cap'n, we be reachin' the port. We need ye on the helm," he announces, his voice urgent.

The Captain rises and heads to the door, "Aye—We'll finish this discussion when we make landfall."

DANICA

9

As we make our way off the ship and onto the docks of Captain's Haven, a sense of relief washes over me. Don't get me wrong, I love a good adventure as much as the next girl, but there's something to be said for the feeling of solid ground beneath your feet after being cooped up on a floating wooden death trap for days.

The water lapping gently against the shore is a shade of blue so vivid and clear it's as if someone took a giant bottle of Windex to the ocean. And the sand? It's so white and pristine like pure sugar cane was dumped onto the beach and left as is.

As much as I'd love to kick off my boots and bury my toes in that soft, inviting sand, we have more pressing matters to attend to. Like, you know, rescuing Lucian from the clutches of a psychotic vampire king-wannabe and saving the world from total destruction. Just another day in my crazy, chaotic life.

I can't shake the thought of what Lucian is enduring; guilt suffocates me. As usual, Rhyland picks up on my emotions and laces his fingers with mine. He gazes into my eyes with those piercing blues, and without uttering a word, he gets it. He knows exactly how I feel.

Rhyland, Erik, and I had a quick huddle before disembarking the ship. We're all in the same predicament—our powers are gone, and we feel weaker than ever.

I'm starting to freak out about what that witch did to us. Is this voodoo mojo permanent, or what?

I've gotten used to my magic—feeling that untapped power buzzing inside me. I've come to depend on it; it's part of me now. Without it, I feel exposed and adrift.

My new dumpster fire of a mission? Figuring out how the hell we're going to score an audience with the Water Queen and somehow track down this... Siren's Lyre.

The dull ache and burning sensation in my neck is a constant reminder of Azrael and his shitty bite. I've been trying my best to ignore it, to push through the pain and focus on the task at hand, but it's getting harder and harder to do so.

As if reading my mind, Rhyland leans close, his breath hot against my ear. "I plan to remedy that as soon as we are alone, Angel," he murmurs, his voice low and full of promise.

I shiver at his words, my body responding instinctively to his nearness. It never ceases to amaze me how in tune Rhyland is with me, how he always seems to know exactly what I'm feeling and what I need.

Is our bond getting stronger? Or is he just that damn good at reading me? Either way, I can't deny the thrill that runs through me at the thought of being alone with him, of feeling his hands on my skin—his lips on my neck.

That steamy public bathroom tryst at Playful Pint is still playing on a loop in my head, and my hormones are going haywire at the mere thought of some alone time with Rhyland. This man will forever and always be my kryptonite, my Achilles' heel, my—*I can't even think straight when he's around*— weakness.

"Right this way." The Captain navigates through the sea of sailors and pirates. "Finn! Purge the hold."

"Aye, aye, Cap'n." Finn acknowledges and heads toward the back of the ship.

Yeah, Finn. Purge the hold—the one I almost freaking drowned in.

As we make our way through Captain's Haven, I marvel at the sheer variety of sights, sounds, and smells that assault my senses. The air is thick with the scent of Caribean spices and roasting meats, and everywhere I look, vendors are hawking their wares and sailors stumbling drunkenly from tavern to tavern.

The day's heat is already starting to become known, and I can feel the sweat trickling down my neck as we weave through the crowds of sailors, merchants, and ne'er-do-wells that throng the docks.

Palm trees blanket the island, making it feel like a slice of tropical paradise.

We pass by a bustling shipyard where burly men with muscles the size of my head hammer away at half-built vessels, their sweat glistening in the hot sun. The heat is so intense it's like walking through a sauna fully clothed, and I can feel the fabric of my shirt sticking to my skin in all sorts of uncomfortable places.

"Aye, here we are," the Captain says, stopping and turning to face us with a flourish. "Welcome to the Loot and Booty Inn."

The building looks like it's barely held together with spit, prayers, and a whole lot of wishful thinking.

I raise an eyebrow at the name. "The Loot and Booty Inn?" I repeat, with sarcasm.

Gee, that's subtle. What's next, the Plunder and Pillage Pub? The Rape and Ravage Resort?

As we step inside, I'm immediately assaulted by the smells of stale beer, sweat, and something that reeks suspiciously like week-old fish. The common room is dimly lit and smoky, with a long wooden bar running along one wall and a smattering of tables and chairs filling the rest of the space. The clientele looks like a who's who of the pirate world, with rough-looking men and women in various states of inebriation and undress lounging about, eyeing us with curiosity and suspicion.

But what really catches my eye is the woman behind the bar—a buxom redhead with a face full of freckles and a smile that could charm the gold right out of a pirate's pocket. She's wearing a tight-fitting corset that looks like it's about to burst at the seams and a short skirt that barely qualifies as a suggestion.

"Aye, here." Gideon flips a bag of coins to Rhyland. Rhyland snags it midair. "This ought to cover the room and board."

"Thanks," Rhyland mutters.

"Clean yerselves up and meet me at the Salty Siren Tavern. There's a boutique around the corner where ye can find some fresh clothes to change into."

I catch Erik scanning the area with his usual stoic intensity, his sharp eyes taking in every detail of our surroundings. But even he can't disguise the hint of sordid disgust that flickers across his face as he takes in the dilapidated building and its colorful clientele.

"Little One," his voice as stoic and formal as ever, even in the face of such squalor. "Please tell me I am not expected to dress up like a pirate to blend in with this... colorful crowd."

I snort at his words, a grin spreading across my face as I imagine the ever-serious Erik decked out in full pirate regalia, complete with an eye patch and a parrot on his shoulder.

"When in Rome, big guy," I quip. "Or, in this case, when in Aquaria, do as the pirates do."

Erik's eyes narrow, and I can practically see the gears turning in his head as he tries to devise a way to avoid playing dress-up.

As we approach the bar to check in, I see the woman's eyes light up with interest at the sight of Rhyland and Erik. She leans forward, her cleavage practically spilling out of her top like a pair of overripe melons, and purrs, "Well, hello there, handsomes. What can I do for you, *fine* gentlemen, today?"

She addresses them like I'm not even here.

I watch with a mixture of morbid fascination and gag-inducing revulsion as the redheaded barmaid throws herself at Rhyland; her attempts at seduction are about as subtle as a sledgehammer to the face. I've seen more restrained performances from a drunken tavern wench on Dollar Draft night.

I'm seething inside right now at this thirsty skank brazenly hurling herself at my man right in front of my face. I can practically taste her desperation, and it's making me gag.

Girl, please.

Before I can unleash my verbal smackdown, Rhyland steps forward, his hand resting possessively on the small of my back. "We need two rooms for the night. And I would appreciate it if you kept your eyes and flirting to yourself, sweetheart."

The barmaid pouts, her lower lip jutting out like a petulant child. "Aw, don't be like that, sugar," she simpers, batting her eyelashes so hard I'm surprised they don't fly right the fuck off her face. "I was just being friendly."

I can't help but let out a derisive snort. "Friendly? Is that what you call throwing yourself at taken men these days?" I ask, "Where I come from, we have a different word for it. It's called *desperate.*"

The barmaid's eyes narrow to slits, and for a moment, I think she might try to go for my jugular. But apparently, even she has some sense of self-preservation because instead, she tosses two keys onto the bar with a huff.

"Rooms 3 and 4, up the stairs and to the left," she sneers, her voice colder than a frost giant's ballsack. "Enjoy your stay—if you can."

I flash her a sweet smile, swiping the keys off the bar. "Oh, we will, sweetie. And thanks for the warm welcome. It's always *so* lovely to know the staff here is so... accommodating."

With that, I turn on my heel and sashay up the stairs, putting a little extra sway in my hips just to drive home the point. Rhyland follows close behind, his presence a solid wall of muscle and agitation.

As we make our way down the narrow hallway to our rooms, I hear Erik's amused chuckle echoing behind us as he heads off to his accommodations.

"You know, Little Huntress," he calls out, amused, "one of these days, that sharp tongue of yours will land you in hot water."

I shrug, a wicked grin spreading across my face. "What can I say, Erik? It's a gift. And besides, someone's got to keep these thirsty wenches in line. Lord knows Rhyland's too much of a gentleman to do it himself."

Rhyland shakes his head. "What?" utterly confused.

I ignore him and head for the door to our room.

A small smile plays at the corners of his mouth. "You're going to be the death of me, woman," his voice low and rough with affection. "I put that bar wench in her place, didn't I?"

I roll my eyes. "Yeah, calling her 'sweetheart' really drove home the point, Casanova," I huff.

Erik laughs, his eyes twinkling with amusement. "I'll leave you to handle this one, brother. I feel you'll need all the luck you can get."

I unlock the door and step inside, ready to wash off the journey's grime and maybe stir up a little trouble. Rhyland's voice stops me.

"What was I supposed to say, hmm?" he snaps, his tone all alpha as he closes the door behind him. "Did you want me to grab her by the throat and stake my claim on you on the counter in front of everyone like some kind of territorial beast?"

I feel my cheeks flushing hot at the thought of his hands on her—touching another female—but I refuse to back down. "Oh, I don't know, Rhyland," I drawl. "Maybe something a *little* more forceful than 'keep your flirting to yourself, *sweetheart*.' I mean, really? That's the best you could come up with?"

Rhyland's eyes narrow, and I can see the muscle in his jaw ticking with frustration. "For fuck's sake, Dani, what do you want from me? I shut her down, didn't I? I made it clear that I wasn't interested in her pathetic attempts at seduction."

I know he's right, but I can't shake the irrational surge of jealousy coursing through my veins. It's like nothing I've ever experienced before, and I can't help but wonder if it has something to do with our bond.

I remember Rhyland telling me that he could smell Faderyn's lust, and now I'm starting to think that maybe, just maybe, I'm experiencing something similar.

The thought sends a shiver down my spine, and I can feel my body responding to Rhyland's nearness—thrilling and terrifying.

But I'll be damned if I let Rhyland see how much this affects me. So, instead, I plaster a sassy smirk on my face and cross my arms over my chest.

"Yeah, well, maybe next time you could try something a little more direct," I quip, my voice as sharp as a blade. "Like, 'sorry, but I'm already spoken for by a badass brunette who could kick your ass six ways to Sunday.' That ought to get the message across."

Rhyland's lips twitch, a wicked glint in his eye as he fights back a smirk. "Just like that, huh?" he drawls, his voice low and teasing. "Is that what you want to hear, Angel? You want me to wax poetic about how fucking perfect you are, how you're the only woman who could ever make me feel this way?"

He leans in closer, his breath hot against my ear as he whispers, "You want me to tell you how I'm going to worship every inch of your body, how I'm going to make you come so hard you see stars? How I will claim you, over and over again, until there's no doubt in your mind that you belong to me, body and soul?"

I shiver at his words, my pulse racing and my core clenching with a fierce rush of desire. He's always had a way with words, knowing what to say to set my blood on fire and turn my thoughts to mush.

I step closer to him, my eyes locked on his as I trail a finger down his chest. "Oh, I don't know, Rhy-Pie. I think I might need a little more convincing. You know, just to make sure the message *really* sinks in."

Rhyland's eyes darken with desire, his hands coming to rest on my hips as he pulls me flush against him. "Is that a fucking challenge, Angel? Because you know I never back down from a challenge."

"Mayb—" Rhyland cuts me off as his lips crash into mine, the kiss intense and possessive. I melt into him, my fingers tangling in his hair as I pour all my jealousy and frustration into the searing embrace.

Rhyland, true to his alpha nature, seizes me by my nape—grabbing a handful of my hair, his touch firm and demanding. Our kiss deepens, our tongues battling for control in a dance as old as time.

A gasp escapes me as he tugs my hair, pulling just enough to send goosebumps across my flesh. "Jealous, baby?" he growls, flashing that infuriatingly sexy smirk, dimple and all.

I'm not one to succumb to jealousy, but something primal stirs within me at the thought of another saucy sea wench casting her eyes on him. "No," I lie, trying to keep my cool.

"You're a horrid liar, Angel," he murmurs against my lips, his voice husky and low.

He nips at my bottom lip, his teeth grazing the sensitive skin and sending sparks of pleasure racing straight to my clit. "What do you say, baby? You want me to stop talking and start demonstrating just how fucking crazy you make me?"

I can only whimper in response, my body arching into his touch as I surrender myself to the intensity of his passion. I know that he's going to do just that—showing me, with every touch, every kiss, every thrust of his hips, just how thoroughly and completely I own his heart.

Rhyland's strong hands grip my ass, pulling me close as he effortlessly hoists me up. Instinct takes over as my legs wrap around his waist, our tongues dancing in a ferocious, sensual rhythm. Our kiss is raw—intense, and all we can think about is devouring each other. We've come close to losing each other—*again*, and the thought has us teetering on the brink of despair.

With a groan, Rhyland slams me down onto the nearby vanity. The impact sends trinkets and knick-knacks tumbling to the floor, but we're beyond caring. He wraps one hand around my throat, his grip firm and possessive, while the other yanks my hair back. He breaks our kiss, leaving me panting for more. "You've got nothing to be jealous of, Angel," he rumbles, his voice low and rough. "You're the only thing I see in this world. The only thing I crave." He thrusts his cock against my core, making me gasp. "And the only thing that makes me this fucking hard and desperate for more."

I moan against his lips, desperately needing the sensation of his mouth on mine. His breath fills me and gives me life. I can't breathe without this man, and I never want to.

He stares into my eyes with an intensity that sets me on fire. "I don't give a shit about anyone else, about any other female on this fucking planet or any other. You're it for me, baby. You're my fucking world, my reason for breathing, my everything."

I can feel the truth of his words resonating through our bond, the sheer depth of his emotions crashing over me like a tidal wave. It's overwhelming and all-consuming, and I find myself drowning in the intensity of his love.

"I need you to trust in us—in this thing between us. Because I sure as fuck ain't ever letting you go, not in this lifetime or any other."

He pulls me closer, his forehead resting against mine as he takes a shuddering breath. "You're mine, Dani. Mine to love, mine to cherish, mine to protect. And I'll be damned if I let anything or anyone come between us, even your own fucking doubts."

I know he's mirroring what I did in Luminara, showing him that he's all I see—all I want. But the green-eyed monster still gnaws at my insides—wondering if there's a way to turn it off.

"I'll worship every inch of your body," he promises, his hands sliding up my sides to cup my breasts, his thumbs teasing my nipples into aching peaks. "You're mine," he whispers against my ear, sending electrical shocks through my body. "And I will prove it to you. I'll willingly devote every fucking moment, every damn second, proving that you're the only woman I want, the only one I can't get enough of," Rhyland states, his hands exploring my body with a possessive hunger.

He sucks on my pulse point in my neck. "I'll mark myself on your skin, your heart, your very essence, day after day, kissing you and keeping myself buried deep inside you until you never question anything ever again."

He's already marked my soul—my heart. My entire being.

His words are filthy, provocative, and so fucking arousing that I can feel the evidence of my desire soaking through my pants. I'm lost in a haze of lust and love, my body trembling with the force of my need for him.

"I'll never stop choosing you—never stop fighting for you, never stop loving you with every beat of my heart," he vows, his voice rough with emotion. "You're my goddamn addiction, Dani. My reason for existing. And I'll spend the rest of my life making sure you never doubt that for a single fucking moment."

Oh, for crying out loud, someone put me out of my misery! My Viking just went full Shakespeare on my ass, waxing poetic and baring his soul like he's auditioning for a romance novel, and what do I do? I turn into a gushing mess.

Seriously, my underwear might as well have taken a dip in Lake Horny.

I just had to be a complete idiot and let my jealousy get the better of me for no damn reason. I'm basically the poster child for Irrational Relationship Insecurities Anonymous.

An emotional whiplash meets self-inflicted embarrassment—the gift that keeps on giving.

His lips claim mine in a bruising kiss, his tongue delving deep as he pours every ounce of his love and hunger into the kiss.

Rhyland's eyes flash with a combination of possessiveness and desperation as he reaches for the lace of my corset, his fingers fumbling with the delicate fabric in his haste to free me from its confines. With a sharp tug, the corset snaps, the sound of tearing fabric mingling with my gasp of relief.

Finally, I can breathe—no longer feeling like a fashionable torture device is slowly suffocating me.

But I don't have much time to revel in my newfound oxygen supply before Rhyland's lips are crashing down on mine, his kiss a passionate blend of want and frustration. Our tongues tangle and dance, our teeth knocking together in our haste to devour each other.

I rip at the buckles of his pants, desperate to free the hard length of him from the confines of his trousers. And when my hands finally make contact with his bare skin—soft velvet wrapped in hard steel—he groans, his hands tugging at my pants as I writhe and shimmy, desperate to be rid of the constricting fabric.

I'm practically squirming with need, my body arching up to meet his.

Finally free, I spread my legs, my core aching for the feel of him filling me up. "I want you..." I moan, my voice a mixture of need and desperation. "I need you inside me. Now."

Rhyland's gaze softens momentarily as he dips his head to capture my lips in a gentle kiss. "You have no idea how much I need you, too, Angel," he murmurs against my mouth. But the soft moment is fleeting as his eyes darken with a primal hunger that sends shivers of anticipation racing through my veins.

He takes my hardened nipple into his hot mouth, his tongue flicking and teeth nipping, which has me squirming beneath him and begging for more. "You're so fucking beautiful, baby," he groans, his voice rough with desire. "I could spend an eternity worshipping this perfect body."

His lips and teeth move to my other nipple, lavishing attention and sucking gently, and I'm a wiggling mess, desperate for release. "Rhy, please," I beg, my voice hoarse with need.

There's a feral gleam in his eyes as he aligns himself with my entrance, his gaze never breaking from mine as he thrusts into me with a force that steals my breath. I cry out, my back arching off the vanity as he fills me to the hilt.

"That *begging*, baby..." he growls, his teeth clenched tightly. There's a warning in his tone, a dark promise. "How can I fucking resist it when you sound so goddamn desperate for my cock?"

Rhyland's hips stutter as he pulls out almost entirely, only to slam back into me, the force of the impact sending a wave of pleasure crashing through me. The vanity creaks and groans with each harsh thrust, the sound of wood slamming into the wall as Rhyland loses himself in the rhythm of our bodies.

"Keep making those sweet little moans, Angel," he rumbles, his hand tightening possessively on my hip, fingers digging into my flesh. "Keep begging me to fuck you, to take you hard and claim you... Fuck, they're a siren's call straight to my cock."

"Yes..." I gasp, my voice little more than a raspy plea as I arch my back, urging him to go deeper, harder. "Fuck... R-Rhyland. Your cock... It feels...so...damn...good."

My words are jumbled, my brain unable to form coherent sentences as pleasure spikes through me. It's like every nerve ending is lit up like the Fourth of July, my body buzzing with a high that makes my head spin.

That draws another primal growl from him, the sound reverberating through me like a strike of thunder. It's clear that my words have only fueled the fire burning within him, stoking the flames of his desire until they rage out of control.

Rhyland's eyes, dark azure pools, smolder with lust, love, and something wilder, more primal. It's like looking into the depths of a storm, where a tempest of emotions rages, threatening to sweep me away.

I bet poor Erik, who is in the next room, wishes he had earplugs. But let's be real, it's not exactly a state secret that Rhyland and I go at it like a couple of lovestruck teenagers.

"*Christ*, baby. You're insatiable, aren't you?" he growls, his body pounding into mine with primal urgency. "You're so wet, clenching around me, milking me with your sweet cunt."

Rhyland and that filthy *mouth*—and fuck, if that doesn't send me over the edge.

LUCIAN

10

I sit here, my mind reeling as I stare at the lifeless body of the girl at my feet. Her once vibrant eyes are now vacant, staring into oblivion. I didn't mean to kill her, but the moment her blood touched my tongue, I was lost in a frenzy of hunger and desire. The taste was intoxicating, and I couldn't stop myself.

What the hell have I become?

Azrael circles me like a shark, his eyes gleaming with a twisted sense of satisfaction. "This is what you are, Lucian. A predator. A killer. Embrace it."

I clench my fists, anger and confusion battling for dominance within me. "Listen, you discount Dracula. I don't know what kind of sick game you're playing, but I'm not interested in being your personal murder puppet."

Azrael chuckles, with condescension. "Oh, but you don't have a choice, my dear Lucian. You see, you're nothing more than a bargaining chip. We're waiting for your little friends to come to rescue you, and then the real fun begins."

I narrow my eyes, trying to make sense of his words. "Friends? What friends? And what the hell do you want with me anyway?"

Azrael leans in close, his breath cold against my skin. "I have plans for you, Lucian. I will mold you into my villain, a weapon to unleash upon the world—daming your soul to feed my master. And your friends? They'll be walking straight into a trap."

Paige, the blonde bombshell with a permanent scowl, interrupts our little chat. "Azrael, a word."

They step away, but my heightened senses allow me to hear every word of their conversation.

Paige's voice is laced with doubt. "What makes you so certain they will return for him?"

Azrael's reply is confident and sinister. "I'm counting on Dani's bleeding heart to rescue her friend. She won't be able to resist playing the hero. Then we spring the trap."

Paige scoffs. "I wouldn't be so sure. The curse I put on them might make things a bit more complicated. Those bastards won't be able to use their powers—"

"What do you mean?" Azrael's tone turns sharp.

Paige's voice is defensive. "I did what I could, okay? I tried to stop her from opening the portal, but they got away—*as you saw*—before I could finish the spell. I don't know how long it will hold."

I feel trapped in a bad soap opera with no script as they continue arguing. Powers? Curses? Friends, I can't remember. It's all too much.

I twist in my seat, trying to loosen the ropes that bind me. Come on, super strength, don't fail me now. I mean, seriously, if I'm supposed to be this badass vampire, why can't I break free from these glorified twine strings? It's like being held captive by a kindergartener's art project.

I clear my throat, interrupting their little spat. "Hey, Dumb and Dumber, mind cluing me in on what the hell you're yapping about? Because right now, I'm more lost than a blind man in a maze, and you two are about as helpful as a screen door on a submarine. So, how about we take a little break from the evil scheming and fill me in on the details?"

Azrael glares at Paige, his eyes burning with frustration. "You couldn't, I don't know, erase his smart-ass mouth while you were busy fucking around in his head?" Azrael smooths back his hair in a show of frustration. "It's like listening to an annoying child."

Paige scoffs. "Doesn't work that way. You can't just erase a person's personality like you're hitting the delete button. I could only erase certain aspects of his memory, not the fundamental essence of who he is."

Azrael turns to me, his eyes narrowing. "You want to know what's going on? Fine. Your so-called friends abandoned you and left you here with us. And now, we will use you as bait to lure them back. Once they're here, let's just say they won't be leaving anytime soon."

Paige rolls her eyes. "Don't be so fucking dramatic, Azrael. We still have work to do. The curse won't hold forever, and we need to be ready."

I feel a surge of anger course through my veins. "Listen up, you Fuckwad, I don't belong to anyone. And if I do have friends out there, I'm pretty sure they're smart enough to see through your little bullshit. I mean, seriously, 'spring the trap'? What is this, a Looney Tunes cartoon? Will you paint a tunnel on a wall next and hope they run into it?" I laugh. "What's next, a monologue about your evil plan while stroking a cat?"

I'm just getting warmed up with this dickhead, trying to act like he's the lovechild of Dr. Evil and a hemorrhoid. I mean, seriously, who the fuck does he think he is, with his little "no one is leaving this place" speech?

"Ooh—ooh, let me guess, you're also going to tell me that I have to choose between joining you or dying, right? Newsflash, buddy, I've seen this movie before, and spoiler alert: the good guys always win. So why don't you take your discount Sanderson Sister over there and return to the drawing board? Because if this is your A-game, I'd hate to see your B-material."

Paige laughs—a harsh and grating sound. "We'll see about that, *pretty boy*. In the meantime, get used to your new life as Azrael's pet monster."

As they leave me alone with my thoughts and the dead girl at my feet, I can't help but wonder what twisted path I've stumbled upon—it's like I'm trapped in a nightmare I can't wake up from. But one thing's for damn sure: I'm not going down without a fight.

If Azrael thinks he can turn me into his puppet of darkness, he's got another thing coming. And by "thing," I mean my foot up his ass. Sideways. I may be confused as a chameleon in a kaleidoscope, but I'll be damned if I let some glorified edge lord and his bitchy sidekick pull my strings like a marionette at a fucked-up demonic children's party.

I'm the master of my own destiny, the captain of my soul, and the only one allowed to screw up my life with bad decisions and questionable judgment calls.

The world returns to me in a dizzying rush as I'm jolted awake by insistent hands shaking my shoulders. My eyes flutter open, and I find myself staring into the faces of two stunningly beautiful women. One has vibrant, hot pink bubblegum hair that looks like it could light up a room, a nose ring in her left nostril, and rich chocolate brown eyes, while the other sports a wild mane of rain-bow-streaked locks—her eyes—electric blue.

"Who the hell are—" I start, but Bubblegum Girl quickly silences me with a finger to her lips.

"Shhhh! We're getting you out of here," she whispers, her voice sweet and urgent.

I blink, trying to clear the fog from my mind. "Do I know you?"

Rainbow Brite smirks, her eyes glinting with mischief. "Yes, you idiot. You don't remember us?"

"Nope. Nada. Apparently, my brain has been wiped cleaner than a porn star's ass crack after a bleaching session."

The two girls exchange a look of confusion and concern before frantically working on the ropes that bind me to the chair.

"I think they're cursed, Emily. I can't get them off," Bubblegum Girl says, her delicate fingers struggling against the unyielding knots. 'We need to hurry. I don't know how long my spell will last."

Spell? So she's a witch, too? Great, just great. It's like I've stumbled into a live-action remake of *Hocus Pocus*, except instead of Bette Midler and her fabulous hair, I'm stuck with these two.

What fucking time era am I in? Is this the Middle Ages, where people are burning witches at the stake and everyone's got a bad case of the plague? Or is this some futuristic, neo-pagan dystopia where technology and sorcery have merged into an unholy alliance?

I half-expect Gandalf to come strolling around the corner, smoking his pipe and muttering about hobbits and rings of power.

Beam me up, Scotty. There's no intelligent life down here, just a bunch of witchy shit and a whole lot of what-the-fuckery.

"By all means, take your time, ladies. It's not like Tweedle Dee and Tweedle Dumber are right around the corner." I dramatically gasp, "Oh wait, they fuck-ing are." I whisper. "I can hear them talking in the next room." My words drip with sarcasm, masking the growing sense of unease in the pit of my stomach.

"Shit!" Emily hisses, her rainbow hair flying as she ducks behind me. "Let me give it a go." She tugs at the ropes, frustration etched in her furrowed brow. "Fuck! They've got some witchy crap on them. These damn things won't budge."

"Oh, a potty mouth. I like you already, sweetheart. You kiss your mother with that mouth? Wait, scratch that. I don't want to know what you do with your mother. That's a whole different kind of family therapy that I'm not equipped to handle."

She looks at me, over my shoulder, her rainbow hair falling into her eyes. "You know...you sure do seem calm and unhelpful for being tied up. Is this like a kink for you or something?"

I smirk, "Oh, you have no idea, sweetheart. The things I could show you..."

Emily scoffs, rolling her eyes. "Yeah, I'll pass on the BDSM 101 lesson, thanks—I prefer my partners with a pulse."

She yanks at the ropes again, her frustration mounting. "Fucking hell, these things are tighter than a nun's asshole. What did they do, dip them in super glue?"

I chuckle at her vocabulary, "Maybe if you ask nicely, they'll untie themselves."

Emily shoots me a withering glare. "Oh, haha. Very funny, Mr. Comedian. Why don't you put that mouth of yours to good use and help me figure out how to get you free? Or would you rather sit there and crack jokes until Azrael returns to finish the job?"

I grin, my mind diving straight into the gutter. "I mean, I could think of a few other uses for my mouth, but I don't think now's the time or place..."

Emily groans, shaking her head in exasperation. "For fuck's sake, do you ever stop? I swear, it's like talking to a horny teenager. A *really* old, really annoying horny teenager."

She tugs at the ropes one last time, her fingers slipping. "Son of a bitch! These damn things are impossible!"

Bubblegum Girl gently touches Emily's shoulder, her voice soothing. "Em, maybe we should try something else? We're running out of time."

Emily sighs, her shoulders slumping. "Yeah, you're right. But I swear to god, if this asshole makes one more innuendo, I'm going to gag him with his own *dick*."

My eyebrows shoot up, my grin turning lecherous. "Promises, promises..."

Emily tugs at the ropes again, "Come on, you piece of shit knots," she mutters under her breath. "Untie, damn it!"

Suddenly, an invisible force emanates from Emily's hands, crackling the air with energy like a static shock on steroids. The ropes unravel as if commanded by an unseen power, slithering to the ground like serpents retreating from a charmer's flute.

Bubblegum Girl gasps, her pink hair seeming pale compared to the shock on her face. "How the hell did you do that?"

Emily stares at her hands, her eyes wide with disbelief and wonder. "I... I don't know."

I spring to my feet, rubbing my chafed wrists. "Right, so what's the plan, ladies? Are we gonna stand around here waiting for the gruesome twosome to return, or are we getting out of Dodge? Because as much as I love the ambiance of this place, I'd rather not stick around for the encore performance of 'Torture: The Musical.'"

I pause, my eyes darting between Emily and her hands, trying to process the mind-bending telekinetic badassery I just witnessed. "But seriously, Rainbow Brite, that was some impressive shit. I mean, I've seen some weird things in my time, like a midget wrestling a grizzly bear while wearing a tutu, but untying ropes with your mind? That's a whole new level of fucked up. If you could do that with bras, you'd be every teenage boy's wet dream come true. Hell, you'd be my wet dream come true."

Emily shoots me a withering glare that could shrivel a man's balls at fifty paces, but I can see the hint of a smirk tugging at her lips, betraying her amusement. "Really? That's where your mind goes? Teenage boys and bras? You're such a pig."

I shrug, a grin spreading across my face. "What can I say? I'm a man of simple tastes. And by simple, I mean perverted."

Bubblegum Girl clears her throat, her expression of amusement and impatience. "As much as I hate to interrupt this fascinating discussion, we *really* should get moving. I don't think Azrael and Paige will be too thrilled when they realize their prisoner has flown the coop."

I nod, my face turning serious for a moment. "Bubblegum Girl is right. We need to make like a tree and get the fuck out—"

As if summoned by my words, Azrael and Paige burst into the room, their faces twisted with rage. "Well, well, well, if it isn't the two *bitches* who helped set the trap," Paige sneers, with malice. "You witches are going to pay for all their deaths."

Uh-oh. What did these two do?

The tension in the air is palpable as Paige begins to chant in an ancient, guttural language that sounds like a mixture of nails on a chalkboard and a dying cat's last meow. Suddenly, with a roar, a ring of fire erupts around us, the flames leaping and dancing like a pack of starving, rabid wolves.

The heat is unbearable, searing my skin and singeing my hair, making it feel like I'm being roasted alive in the depths of Hell's own kitchen. Rivers of sweat pour down my face, stinging my eyes and blurring my vision as I squint through the inferno, trying to discern whether this is just a vivid, alcohol-induced nightmare or if I'm actually about to become a crispy, vampire-flavored snack.

"Uhhh, now what the fuck do we do?" I manage to choke out, my voice barely audible over the deafening roar of the flames. "I don't suppose either of you has a fire extinguisher hidden in your ass? Or maybe a magical 'get out of hellfire free' card? Because I'm pretty sure my vampire healing factor doesn't cover 'death by supernatural barbecue.'"

Azrael prowls around the fire's perimeter like a predator stalking its prey, his features contorted to make him look like a demented, constipated gargoyle. "No one is leaving this place," he snarls. "You will all burn, your ashes scattered to the winds, your souls forever trapped in the depths of my master's darkest, most nightmarish realm."

But Bubblegum Girl, her neon pink locks shimmering like a beacon of hope amid the chaos, refuses to be cowed by Azrael's threats. "Emily, take my hand!" she shouts, her words laced with a desperate, unyielding determination.

Without hesitation, Emily reaches out, their fingers intertwining in unity and strength, their hands clasped together like a lifeline during the storm.

Together, they begin to chant in a haunting melody that seems to resonate with the very fabric of reality. As their words grow in power, the flames start to flicker and retreat as if cowering before their combined might, the once-threatening ring of fire now little more than a sputtering candle.

Seizing the moment, Azrael lunges for Bubblegum Girl. His hands outstretched like claws, his face a mask of pure, rage. I react on instinct, launching myself at him and wrapping my arms around his neck in a vise-like grip, my muscles straining with the effort. I may not know who these girls are, but they're here to help me, and I'll be damned if I let this bastard lay a finger on them.

"Sorry, pal," I grunt, my breath hot against his ear. "But I'm afraid I can't let you touch the merchandise. These ladies are under my protection now, and you know what they say: never touch a man's bubblicious babes."

Azrael thrashes against my hold, his elbows slamming into my ribs with bruising force, each blow sending shockwaves of pain through my body. I grit my teeth, refusing to relinquish my grasp, my determination fueled by a desperate need to protect these strangers who risked everything to save me.

"Is that all you got?" I taunt, my voice strained with the effort of keeping him restrained. "I've had grandmas' hit harder than you. And they were dead at the time."

Out of the corner of my eye, I glimpse Paige. Her face contorted into a grotesque mask of hatred. Her eyes blaze with a manic, hellish light as she unleashes a torrent of flames toward Emily and Bubblegum Girl, the searing heat of the inferno palpable even from across the room.

But Emily, in a stunning display of selfless bravery, leaps in front of her friend, her hands raised before her as if to shield them both from the onslaught. Her vibrant, rainbow-hued hair whips around her face in a dazzling kaleidoscope of color, starkly contrasting the sinister, angry red of the flames bearing down upon her. And then, to the shock and disbelief of everyone present, the fire bounces off an invisible barrier surrounding Emily, dissipating into nothingness as they meet her unwavering resolve. It's as if she's encased in a bubble of pure, indomitable willpower, forming an impenetrable shield against Paige's malicious onslaught.

Bubblegum Girl stares at Emily, her jaw hanging open in a perfect "O" of astonishment, her eyes wide with disbelief. It's clear that even she, with all her magical knowledge and experience, has never witnessed anything quite like this before.

"What the hell are you? What have you done?!" Paige screeches, her voice shrill and laced with fear and unease.

And then, in a moment that will be forever seared into my memory (and not just because of the third-degree burns), Emily goes full-on Human Torch, her hands thrusting outward as she unleashes a blistering torrent of flames directly at Paige. It's like watching a scene from a Michael Bay movie on steroids, except instead of Megan Fox, we've got a pissed-off Rainbow Brite with the power to shoot fire from her fingertips.

Paige is engulfed in flames in a matter of seconds, her agonized screams reverberating through the room. The stench of burning flesh and hair fills the air, making me wonder if this is what KFC smells like in the ninth circle of Hell.

As the flames die down, leaving behind only a smoldering, unrecognizable husk that was once Paige, Emily stares at her hands in shock and disbelief. "I... I didn't know I could do that," she whispers, her voice trembling with awe and fear.

Meanwhile, Azrael continues to struggle against my unrelenting grip. His movements grow weaker by the second, and his breath comes in ragged gasps.

"Nooo, goddammit." he gurgles through my choke hold.

I bear down, my muscles straining with the effort, and drive him to the ground, the impact jarring my bones. In a last-ditch attempt to break free, he tries to flip me off him, his body writhing beneath me like a snake caught in a trap. But I tighten my hold, my molars cracking from the sheer force, my arms locked around his neck like a noose.

"Shh, shh, it's okay," I whisper, with mock sympathy. "Just go to sleep, big guy. I promise, when you wake up, you'll be in a better place—like hell, for example."

Then, with a sickening snap, Azrael goes limp in my arms, his body as lifeless as a rag doll.

The room falls silent, save for the heavy panting of the three of us, the echoes of the battle still ringing in our ears. Rainbow Brite and Bubblegum Girl stare at me, their expressions of awe and horror. I release Azrael's lifeless body, my hands shaking as the reality of what I've done sinks in, the weight of his death settling on my shoulders like a physical burden.

"Deaths?" I ask, my voice hoarse, my throat raw from the smoke and the screaming. "Who's death's? What the hell did you two do to piss off Tweedledee and Tweedledum so badly? Did you steal their matching set of 'I'm with stupid' t-shirts?"

Bubblegum Girl shakes her head, her pink locks bouncing with the movement. "It's a long story, and we don't have time to explain. We need to get the hell out of here before Azrael wakes up and reinforcements arrive."

Ok, so he's not dead. Right. Vampire.

I nod, pushing myself to my feet, my legs trembling beneath me as the adrenaline wears off. My body aches, and my mind reels with questions, but I know she's right. We need to put as much distance between ourselves and this nightmare and find a place to regroup and plan our next move.

"Alright, let's blow this popsicle stand," I say, cracking my neck and stretching my arms above my head. "But for the record, I expect a full explanation later. And maybe a foot rub. I've had a hell of a day."

As we flee the castle, the weight of the unknown hangs heavy on my shoulders, the darkness of the night pressing in on us from all sides. Who are these girls, and what have they done to incur the wrath of those psychopaths?

"So," I pant, glancing sideways at my new companions as we pile into their car, which looks like it's seen better days. The upholstery is torn, the dashboard is cracked, and the whole thing smells like a mix of stale cigarettes and desperation. It beats walking—or running—or being burned alive by a fire-wielding psychopath. "Anyone up for a celebratory round of tequila shots? First round's on me. And by 'on me,' I mean 'stolen from the nearest liquor store,' because let's face it, I'm probably broke, right?"

Emily rolls her eyes. "Seriously? We just narrowly escaped being barbecued by a couple of supernatural nutjobs, and you're thinking about tequila?"

I shrug, flashing her my most charming grin. "What can I say? I have my priorities straight. Besides, after the night we've had, I think we've earned a little liquid courage. And maybe some nachos—*Definitely* nachos."

DANICA

11

After Rhyland thoroughly pillaged my village and left me a satisfied, panting mess, we finally scrubbed off layers of salt, grime, and who knows what else in the tub (seriously, I don't even want to think about what kind of funky pirate cooties we might have picked up on that ship. I finally got to wash my hair. And let me tell you, after my day, that little luxury felt like pure heaven.

The best part? I can still hide my crown with a mere thought, so at least that little parlor trick still works in my favor.

Small victories.

Rhyland finally took care of Azrael's nasty bite by giving me his blood. And, of course, he needed his dose of SPF to keep his strength up.

We didn't have any fancy tools to draw blood for Erik, so we went old school—sliced my hand open and filled a glass the savage way. Rhyland patched me up again, though he hated every second of it.

"You honor me, Little One," Erik said, then glanced at Rhyland. "And you, brother."

Rhyland, as expected, brushed it off with a casual, "Don't mention it."

Once we were all squeaky clean and smelling like something other than the wrong end of a Kraken, we headed to the Buccaneer's Wardrobe to pick out some fresh threads. Because, let's face it, if we're going to be stuck in this realm, we might as well look the part.

Rhyland, Erik, and I spent the whole time going back and forth about Lucian, and we all know deep down in our gut that Azrael is holding him hostage. That piece of shit is probably banking on us coming back to rescue Lucian so that he can spring some trap and catch us all in one fell swoop. The joke's on him because we're not going down without a fight.

With some intel about their brotherly bond, Rhyland also put my mind at ease—he'd feel it if Lucian died. It's all tied to their connection through their Maker.

We're going to get Lucian back, come hell or high water. But how are we going to do that? That's the million-dollar question.

It's not like we can just portal back to the Mortal Realm and bust down Azrael's door, especially not with our powers and magic on the fritz thanks to that witch's curse. Seriously, how long is this going to last? Does it have an expiration date, or are we just supposed to stumble around like a bunch of normies until we figure out how to lift it?

We finally arrive at the Salty Siren Tavern—Rhyland—all eye candy in his pirate getup. *Holy hell, my man cleans up nicely.* That crisp white shirt, those high-waisted leather pants, the skull buckle at his waist? I'm pretty sure I started drooling the moment he put this on.

That teasing glimpse of ink peeking out from his shirt's open collar... I mean, holy ship. If we weren't on a quest to interrogate Captain Barbosa's long lost cousin—I mean, Gideon, I'd be seriously considering saying, "Screw it, let's ditch this joint, head back to our pirate pleasure den, and set sail for round two.

As for me, I managed to snag the best outfit they had for a woman that didn't involve a gown and a parasol. Because let's be honest, I'm not about to go gallivanting around the high seas looking like I'm ready for a fancy tea party on the Titanic. No. Instead, I scored a pair of brown leather pants that fit like they were painted on (in the best way possible) and a flowy white shirt that's just low-cut enough to be sexy without screaming, "Ahoy, mateys, check out the goods!"

At least the girls aren't on a mission to touch the sky and being hoisted to the max.

Of course, Rhyland couldn't keep his paws to himself, fiddling with the drawstring like a kid with a new toy. I finally had to slap his hands away before he undid all my hard work. A nice leather wrap around my waist to hold my trusty daggers finishes the look.

And Erik? The silver fox can rock the pirate look like nobody's business. He wore the same white shirt and leather pants combo as Rhyland, but with his shoulder-length silver hair and brooding demeanor, he looks like he has just stepped out of a romance novel. A really, really good romance novel.

So here we are, all decked out in our matching pirate getups, sashaying into the Tavern like we're the hottest new crew in town. And get this—the place is practically a carbon copy of the Playful Pint back home, just with a few more eye patches and peg legs thrown in for that authentic pirate ambiance.

I spot Gideon lurking at a table in the back, and we start strutting over, ready to scheme up our next move and maybe toss back a few pints of grog—rum—whatever swill these pirates are knocking back.

If there's one thing this insane rollercoaster of an adventure has drilled into my head, it's that sometimes you've just gotta say, "screw it," embrace the chaos, and enjoy the wild ride. Even if said ride involves cursed magic, hostage situations, and more swashbuckling than a pirate impersonator contest at a rum-soaked pirate festival.

"Well, matey's," Gideon drawls, his eyes twinkling with amusement as he takes in our new attire. "Ye clean up nicely, I must say. Lookin' right sharp, the lot of ye."

The captain gives an approving nod, clearly impressed by the transformation. "Now that yer properly outfitted, ye'll blend in better with the crowd here. Fewer suspicious glances thrown yer way, I reckon."

I can't help but let a smirk sneak across my face as I smooth down the front of my leather pants. "What can I say? Impressing people is our thing."

Gideon chuckles and waves us over. "Come on, let's have a round of rum and a game of cards."

We gather around the table, and a voluptuous waitress with a mane of blonde locks sashays over, plunking mugs of rum in front of us. I whiff the amber liquid and nearly choke on the spot.

"Whew," I cough, eyes watering just a bit. "That's some serious stuff."

Gideon grins, taking a hearty swig from his mug. "Aye, that it is, lass. But it'll put some hair on your chest."

I roll my eyes at his display of bravado but take a cautious sip anyway. The rum sears its way down, setting my belly ablaze and giving me a delightful little buzz.

"So, what's the game?" I ask, raising an eyebrow at the deck of cards in the center of the table.

"Black poker, five cards," Gideon replies, his fingers deftly shuffling the deck. "Ye know how to play, lass?"

I shrug, a confident smirk tugging at my lips. "I think I can figure it out."

Gideon nods, handing out stacks of coins to Rhyland, Erik, and me. "Consider this a loan," he says with a wink. "Ye'll pay me back in full, of course."

I snort, my fingers closing around the cool metal. "Of course."

Gideon launches into a rapid-fire rundown of the game. I tune in just enough to catch the basics: Poker. We're talking five cards, bets placed, and the best hand wins. Bluffing's key; you've got to know when to fold or go all in.

As he drones on, I analyze the rules in my head, my brain working overtime. Really, this is just a glorified exercise in probability and psychology—a fancy game of numbers and reading people.

It's just another puzzle to solve, and I'm a pro at cracking codes. Bring it on.

As the game starts, I scope out the other pirates at the table. To my left, there's this grizzled old sea dog with an eye patch and a gnarly scar running down his weathered cheek. He goes by Will.

Finn, the Captain's trusty right-hand man, raises his mug in my direction, a playful glint in his eye. "Look at you, lass. All gussied up and ready to take on the world. Or at least, ready to take on a few drunk pirates in a game of chance."

I flash him a confident grin. "Thanks, Finn. Hope you're ready to lose?"

Finn chuckles, shaking his head. "Oh, I'd like to see you try."

Next to the Captain is this young, cocky pirate with a mop of curly black hair and a gold hoop earring. He keeps trying to catch my eye, his gaze drifting south to the displayed goods. Please, buddy. Eyes up here.

And then there's Izabelle, with her flowing brown locks and tits practically spilling out of her top. Those piercing turquoise eyes of hers are boring into my very soul. She's circling the table like a damn shark, her fingers trailing over Gideon's shoulders like she owns the man. And the way she's eyeing me? It's pure disdain.

If looks could kill, I'd be pushing up daisies by now. But you know what? Two can play at this bitch's game. I'll be damned if I let some pirate wench get under my skin. She can take those nasty looks and shove 'em where the sun don't shine, for all I care.

Bring it on, you two-bit hussy. Let's dance.

"Well, well, well," she sneers. "If it isn't the little landlubber who thinks she can play with the big boys."

I flash Izabelle a smile, my fingers idly fiddling with the coins before me. "Izabelle," I purr. "Always a pleasure to see your charming face. I see you're still keeping these sailor boys on a tight leash."

She narrows her eyes at me, her lips curling into a sneer. "Well, someone has to keep them in line," she retorts, her gaze flicking pointedly to my cleavage. "Wouldn't want them getting distracted by any... loose cargo."

Oh, this bitch did not just go there.

I lean forward, giving her a deliberate eyeful of my assets. "Honey, if you're worried about loose cargo, maybe you should check your own *deck*," I smirk. "Seems like a few things might have shifted during your last *voyage* if you know what I mean."

"Aye, and ye best be keeping yer hands off 'em, wench. They're mine."

"For the love of Neptune, Izabelle, mind yer tits!" Finn spits, already glaring daggers at her.

I can practically hear her teeth grinding from here. Oh, this is just too much fun. I do so love ruffling the feathers of insecure skanks.

"What is this about?" Rhyland's voice floats into my mind.

I can sense his unease through our bond, the way his protective instincts are flaring up in the face of this unexpected development.

"Nothing, just a jealous harpy who thinks I'm out to steal her pirate orgy," I fire back into his mind, rolling my eyes for good measure.

Rhyland scoffs beside me, shaking his head. He knows damn well I can handle myself, so he just leans back and lets me handle it. He's got that look on his face, probably remembering how I handled Amara and her brand of bullshit.

Erik's eyes dart back and forth between Izabelle and me, a smirk playing at the corners of his mouth like he's desperately trying to hold in a laugh. He knows I won't just sit back and take shit from anyone, especially not some skanky pirate whore.

"I'm not interested in your men," I laugh, shaking my head in disbelief. "Maybe if you spent less time worrying about me and more time working on your own charm and wit, you wouldn't have to resort to petty intimidation tactics to keep your crew in line."

Izabelle looks like she's about to explode, her face turning an alarming shade of purple. I can practically see the steam coming out of her ears as she struggles to respond coherently.

"Enough, Izabelle," Gideon orders. "The lass is our guest. Treat her with respect."

Izabelle looks like she wants to argue but thinks better of it. With a final glare in my direction, she huffs, crossing her arms over her chest.

Game, set, and match, bitch. Better luck next time.

A couple of hours, a shitload of rum, and a whole lot of me wiping the floor with these so-called pirates later, I'm sitting pretty in the winner's circle and feeling damn good about my buzz. We've been yapping about this Siren's Lyre thing and why the Merfolk can't just swim in and grab it themselves.

These fishy folks have been trying to get their fins on this magical trinket for generations, hoping to use its power to boost their magical mojo. The thing is guarded by crazy puzzles and traps that have stumped them for ages.

This sea goddess Lyria gave the Siren's Lyre to the Merfolk's ancestors and pumped it with some seriously potent juju. But Lyria, being the crafty goddess she was, wanted to ensure no one could waltz in and snatch it. So, she set up this whole gauntlet of trials where the trinket is hidden.

These trials are designed to be impossible for any sea critter to solve. Apparently, you need some unique set of skills and qualities.

So, the Merfolk have been swimming in circles for centuries, trying to crack this code but coming up empty-handed every time. It's like the world's most frustrating underwater escape room.

I look at Gideon skeptically. "And what, Captian, makes you think I'm the key to snagging this little bauble?"

"Aye, lass. You said so yerself. You've got that fancy light magic mojo going on—Chosen One and all that jazz. So, why the hell not?" Gideon shrugs like it's the most obvious thing since rum and bad decisions.

I can't help but roll my eyes. "Oh, sure. Because being the 'Chosen One' automatically means I'm some magical lockpick for ancient underwater puzzles, right?"

Gideon chuckles, shaking his head. "You've gotta admit, it's a hell of a coincidence, love. The Merfolk have been trying to crack this thing for generations, and then you show up, destined and shit. Ye need a reason to meet with the Queen—here is your shot."

I guess there's only one way to find out.

I excuse myself from the table because my bladder is about to stage a mutiny if I don't hit the head soon. All that rum's gone to my kidneys, and they're unhappy about it.

As I'm weaving my way through the crowded tavern, the rum decides to sucker punch me right in the equilibrium. Suddenly, I'm a dizzy dame, stumbling around. I have to stop and grab onto a chair to keep from face-planting on the sticky floor.

Holy hell, that's some potent pirate juice.

After taking a moment to remember which way is up, I finally make it to the ladies' room and take care of business. Sweet relief. I feel much lighter and less wobbly as I return to the table.

On my way, I spot this gypsy-looking woman tucked back in a small room in the corner of the tavern with a spread of tarot cards in front of her. She's got that mysterious, fortune-teller vibe—long, flowing skirts, jangly bracelets, and a scarf wrapped around her head. Her eyes are lined with kohl, making them look even more intense as they lock onto mine.

She crooks a finger at me, beckoning me to her table with a knowing smile. It's like she's been waiting for me—like she knew I'd be stumbling by at this moment.

Part of me wants to keep walking, ignore her, and return to the game. But there's something about her—something that pulls at me like a magnet. Before I know it, my feet move, carrying me closer to her table and whatever secrets she might hold.

I guess I'm about to get my fortune told, whether I like it or not. Here's hoping the cards are kind and that this isn't just some rum-fueled hallucination.

As I stroll up to the gypsy's table, the heady aroma of incense and spices wraps around me like a sensual caress, making my head spin even more than the copious amounts of rum I've already guzzled down. The woman's eyes pierce through me, and I can't help but shiver as I plop down in the seat across from her, my legs sprawling out in front of me.

It's not exactly the picture of grace and poise, but with all this rum sloshing around in my system—being a proper lady? She has pretty much packed her bags and caught the first flight out of here.

Before I can even open my mouth to speak, she's on her feet and moving towards the door with a swiftness that belies her age. The lock clicks into place with an ominous finality, and I can't help but raise an eyebrow at her sudden need for privacy.

"Well," I drawl, folding my arms over my chest. "Looks like we've officially entered the 'serious business' zone."

I've never been one to buy into tarot cards, fortune tellings, or any of that ho-cus-pocus. I'm a science girl—I deal with facts, equations, and hard evidence. So, you can bet I'm eyeing her with more skepticism than a cat at bath time.

The gypsy stares at me, her expression inscrutable. " I am Nixie, and I sense a great destiny about you, child," her voice low and throaty. "But also great danger."

I can't help but snort at that, my lips twisting into a wry grin. "Tell me something I don't know," I quip. "Danger is pretty much my middle name at this point."

She ignores my sarcasm, her eyes never leaving mine. "You seek answers," her voice becoming mystical. "About your power—it's lost."

I bolt upright, my buzz evaporating fast—my heart pounding in my chest, "How the hell do you..."

She waves a hand dismissively as if my question is of no consequence. "The cards whisper secrets to those who know how to listen."

"Can you fix me?" a glimmer of hope in my voice. Maybe this Gypsy—Nixie can shed some light on why *my* light has decided to take an extended leave of absence, leaving me high and dry while it sips margaritas on some cosmic beach.

"I shall try."

I lean forward, my elbows resting on the table as I fix her with a determined stare. "Alright, then," my voice low and serious. "Let's hear what they have to say."

The gypsy nods, her fingers deftly shuffling the worn deck of tarot cards. The soft swish of paper against paper fills the air like a whispered promise. She lays them out on the table, her eyes fluttering closed as she begins to chant in a language I don't understand.

The gypsy's fingers deftly flip over the first card, and I can't help but lean in for a closer look. "The Lovers," she announces, tapping the card with a knowing smile. "Your past, present, and future—your mate. A Viking vampire, fierce and loyal. Your destiny."

I nearly choke on my spit at her words, my eyes bugging out of my head like a cartoon character. "Ummm...wow," I sputter. "How do you know—?

The gypsy chuckles, her eyes twinkling with amusement. "The cards, my dear. They reveal all."

I narrow my eyes at her, not entirely convinced. But before I press further, she's already moving on to the next card like she didn't just drop a major truth bomb on my ass.

"The Tower," she declares, laying down a card that looks like some sort of medieval 9/11. "Trials and tribulations, magic and Fae. You've faced them all and emerged stronger for it."

I can't help but nod, a rueful smile tugging at my lips. "You can say that again," I mutter, thinking back on all the crazy shit Rhyland and I have been through. "But I'm not sure if 'stronger' is the right word. More like 'barely hanging on by a thread.'"

The gypsy clucks her tongue, shaking her head. "Ah, but you underestimate yourself, my dear. The fact that you're still standing here after all you've endured? That takes a strength that few possess."

I can feel my cheeks heating up at her words. "Yeah, well, I had help," I mumble, thinking of Rhyland, Lucian Erik, and all the others who have stood by my side.

Nixie smiles, her eyes knowing. "Of course you did. No one can face such trials alone. But your inner strength allowed you to accept that help and trust in others even when the world seemed darkest."

I swallow hard, feeling a lump forming in my throat. She's right, of course. As much as I like to play the tough, independent badass, I know I wouldn't have made it this far without the people who have become my family.

I can feel the sting of tears pricking at the corners of my eyes as I think of all the people who have become like family to me on this wild ride. Axilya, Faderyn, even the snarky bastard Lucian—I miss them all so damn much it feels like there's a gaping hole in my chest.

Nixie must sense my sudden melancholy because she reaches out and pats my hand in a gesture of comfort. "The bonds of friendship and love are never truly broken, my dear," she says softly. "Even when distance separates us, those connections remain."

I sniffle a bit, nodding my head in agreement. "Yeah, I know," I mutter, swiping at my eyes with the back of my hand. "Doesn't make it suck any less, though."

Nixie chuckles, her eyes twinkling with understanding. "Indeed it does not. But take heart, for the cards have more to reveal."

RHYLAND

12

I lean back, nursing my drink. A smirk tugs at my lips as I replay the scene from earlier—Dani verbally bitch-slapping Izabelle, putting that jealous bitch in her place. Fuck, it was hot as hell watching my girl assert herself like that, all fiery confidence and take-no-shit attitude.

Not that I'm surprised. Dani throws off sex appeal like it's breathing. She's got curves that could make a grown man weep and a confidence that's sexy as sin. But it's not just her body that gets me going—it's her mind that floors me. The way she picked up on poker like it was nothing, wiping the deck with seasoned players despite never having played before. That analytical brain of hers, always working, always cracking shit and solving puzzles... It's sexy as hell.

The memory of her jealousy still echoes in my mind. Seeing her all fired up over that redheaded barmaid was a thing of beauty. It's a sign that our bond is growing stronger—she's feeling it with every fiber of her being.

I had no problem reassuring her, no hesitation in reminding her that she's the only one I see, the only one I crave. She's all I want, all I can think about. Every fiber of my being is attuned to her; every beat of my heart is in sync with hers.

Dani's not usually the jealous type. She's too confident, too self-assured to let something like that get under her skin. But this bond between us, this unbreakable tie that binds our souls together... it's going to intensify everything she feels, everything she is.

She will be even more possessive and fiercely protective of what's hers. And fuck, if that doesn't just light a fire in my veins.

My fierce, fearless Angel claimed me, body and soul. And I've claimed her right back. We belong to each other, now and forever. And anyone who tries to come between us... Well, let's just say they'll learn the hard way what happens when you fuck with a man's mate.

Erik grunts from his seat to my left. "I'm curious, brother... what of this Siren's Lyre? Aren't Merfolk Sirens?"

Erik never stops analyzing and looking for angles others might miss. He's got a tactical mind that won't quit, always working to identify potential threats and figure out how to neutralize them.

It's like he's got a supercomputer in his head, constantly processing data and spitting out strategies. He sees patterns and connections that the rest of us couldn't hope to grasp, and he uses that knowledge to stay one step ahead of the game.

I pause, considering the question. The book didn't describe the Merfolk that way but mentioned Sirens. Curiosity piqued, I turn to Captain Gideon, who's busy laughing and bantering with his crew.

"Gideon," I call out, waiting for him to look up from his rum. "What of Sirens? Do they exist?"

The captain takes a swig, his eyes gleaming with mischief. "Aye, they do, lad. The Merfolk have been at odds with 'em for centuries—the Sirens, also known as Water Nymphs."

Well, fuck me sideways. Water Nymphs? This just keeps getting better. I raise an eyebrow, leaning forward. "So what's the story there?"

Gideon chuckles, a wicked grin spreading across his face. "Ye ever heard tales of sailors being lured to their doom by a pretty face and a sweet song? That be the Sirens' doing, mate."

He takes another gulp of rum, savoring the burn. "Ye see, these Water Nymphs, they be sexual creatures, blessed by Poseidon himself with the power to trap men's minds and hearts. They sing, and the poor bastards are powerless to resist, followin' blindly to their watery graves, grinnin' like fools the whole way."

I feel a shiver run down my spine at his words. Mind control and sex appeal? Sounds like a damn dangerous combination.

The captain leans back, his expression turning sly. "Legend has it that a single kiss from a Siren can make ye forget yer own name, make ye willing to do anything, be anything they desire. They'll lure ye into the water with promises of pleasure beyond yer wildest dreams... and once they have ye, well. Let's just say there ain't no coming back from that, lad."

I whistle lowly, my mind reeling with the implications. "So what, they're like some kind of sex demons?"

Gideon laughs, loud and booming. "Aye, in a manner of speaking. But make no mistake, mate—they're dangerous. Many a sailor has met his end in the arms of a Siren, too lost in lust to realize he's drowning."

He shakes his head, a hint of warning in his eyes. "The Merfolk, they see the Sirens as a threat, a blight on their kind. They've been trying to wipe 'em out for generations to protect the innocent from falling prey to their wiles. But the Sirens, they're a wily bunch. Always seem to find a way to survive, to keep on seducing poor bastards to their doom."

I sit back, my mind reeling. Fucking hell. As if this quest wasn't complicated enough already, now we've got to worry about supernatural seductresses trying to sex us to death?

"So what do we do?" I ask, looking between Erik and Gideon. "How do we fight something like that?"

The Captain shrugs, his expression grim. "Ye don't, lad. Best ye can hope for is to avoid 'em altogether. Stick to the shallows, steer clear of their huntin' grounds."

I glance at Erik, seeing my concern mirrored in his steely gaze. We're going to have to be on our guard every fucking second if we want to make it out of this realm with our souls intact.

But then again, I think with a smirk, if anyone can resist the wiles of a Siren, it's me. After all, I've already got the most desirable woman in the world warming my dick. What's a water nymph compared to my Angel?

I shift in my seat, my pants suddenly feeling too tight.

Down boy, I mentally berate my eager cock. Now's not the time for a fucking boner.

Still, as Gideon launches into another bawdy tale of sailors falling prey to the Sirens' charms, I can't shake the feeling that we're in for one hell of a ride.

And not necessarily the fun kind—

The tavern doors slam open, and every head in the place snaps around to see who's ballsy enough to make an entrance like that. And holy shit, the man who strides in is enough to answer that question.

This guy's got an aura like a goddamn thunderstorm, all dark and menacing like he's about to rain down lightning and destruction on anyone who looks at him wrong. He's built like a fucking tank, all bulging muscles and violence, with shoulder-length red hair that makes him look like some deranged Viking berserker.

And his eyes... those eyes are sharp and calculating, sweeping over the room like he's sizing up his next meal. Like he's just daring someone, anyone, to step up and challenge him so that he can rip their fucking head off and use it as a goddamn soup bowl.

The whole place goes silent as the grave the moment he walks in, everyone frozen in place like mice caught in a serpent's gaze. You can practically hear the collective intake of breath, the sheer terror that ripples through the crowd at the sight of this beast of a man.

I swear, the guy looks like he eats children for breakfast and picks his teeth with their tiny bones. Like he'd snap your neck as soon as he looks at you and then return to chugging his ale like nothing happened.

"Gideon," he booms, his voice carrying an edge of malicious delight. "How long has it been?"

I glance over at the Captain; hell, he looks like he's about to blow a blood vessel. Anger is etched into his face, and he's gripping his mug so tight I'm surprised it hasn't shattered.

"Bloodbane," he says through clenched teeth.

This is not a man to be fucked with, that's for damn sure. Not unless you want to end up as a red smear on the tavern floor, your last memory, the sound of his laughter as he grinds your skull beneath his boot.

He starts moving towards our table, the crowd parting like the Red Sea. Izabelle jumps up to block his path, all bristling defiance and bared teeth.

"What the hell do you want?" she snarls, staring at the man like another barroom brawler. "That's far enough. You know the rules; you can't touch us here—this is common land."

"Enough, Izabelle," Gideon snaps, his voice cracking with tension. "Stay out of this."

Bloodbane smirks, eyeing Izabelle like she is an annoying gnat to be swatted aside. The rest of the pirates at our table don't need to be told twice. They scatter like cockroaches, tripping over each other in their haste to get clear, leaving just me, Erik, and Gideon to face the scrutiny of this asshole.

Bloodbane's gaze lands on me and Erik, and I meet it head-on, refusing to be cowed by this overgrown bastard. There's something in his blood-red eyes, a hunger beyond mere bloodlust or battle-fury. It's like he can see straight into my fucking soul—like he knows something I don't.

"I was sent here by the Sea Witch—word travels fast in Aquaria," he drawls, his tone full of malice. "Something..." he sniffs the air in my direction, "smells...different."

Beside me, Erik's wound tighter than a fucking spring, his muscles locked and ready for action. I can feel the power rolling off him in waves, barely held in check by sheer force of will.

"And she has a right to know who enters her realm," Bloodbane continues, his gaze never leaving ours.

Well, fuck. It's clear as day that this asshole is in the Sea Witch's pocket. And it's equally clear that she's caught wind of our presence here.

Gideon clears his throat, trying to draw Bloodbane's attention. "What ye be on about, Bloodbane?"

But the red-haired bastard ignores him completely, focusing solely on me and Erik. As he stalks closer, I catch a whiff of his scent—brine and blood and something sharper, like the crackle of ozone before a storm.

"Can't say I've ever seen the likes of ye two," he muses, his eyes narrowing. "Tell me, with who do you sail?"

"They're with me crew, Bloodbane," Gideon warns, his voice low and dangerous. "Back off."

But Bloodbane laughs, a harsh, grating sound that sets my teeth on edge. "You don't give the orders here, Captain," he sneers. "The Sea Witch does. And she wants to know about these two."

He takes another step forward, his hand drifting towards the wicked-looking blade at his hip. "So I'll ask again," he growls. "Who are they, and what are they doing in Aquaria?"

I glance at Erik, seeing my grim determination mirrored in his eyes. We both know we can't let this fucker get his hands on us, can't let him drag us before the Sea Witch.

But we also know we're in a tight spot here. We're outnumbered and out-weaponed, and starting a brawl in the middle of the tavern will only draw more attention to ourselves.

Fuck. Fuck fuck fuck.

I take a deep breath, my mind racing as I devise a plan. We need to find Dani, get out of here, and regroup somewhere safe.

But first, we need to deal with this red-haired bastard and his goons.

Bloodbane takes another step toward Gideon, his eyes glittering with cruel amusement. "So why don't you be a good little sailor and tell me what I want to know?" he asks, with false sweetness. "Unless you'd rather see your precious crew decorating the bottom of the ocean."

I glance around, my heart sinking as I take in the sheer number of Bloodbane's men. There's at least twenty of the fuckers, all armed to the teeth and leering at us like we're their next meal. Compared to Gideon's handful of crew members, it's like pitting a pack of wolves against a couple of fucking lapdogs.

I repeat the mantra in my head, over and over, like a desperate prayer.

I can't lose control.

Don't lose control.

Don't fucking lose control.

I clench my fists, my nails digging into my palms hard enough to draw blood. I need to stay calm, need to keep my shit together. Because if I let go, if I unleash the beast inside me...

It won't be pretty.

My bad side, the part of me that revels in blood and violence and destruction... it's always there, lurking just beneath the surface. And right now, it's howling for release.

But I can't let it out—can't let it take control. Because if I do, if I give in to that primal, savage fury...

There's no telling what I'll do.

I might tear this whole fucking Tavern apart, might rip every last one of these pirates to shreds in my blind, unthinking rage.

No, I need to hold it together—I need to stay focused, stay sharp.

So I clench my jaw, take a deep, shuddering breath, and force myself to be still—to push down the beast, to lock it away behind a wall of iron will.

Gideon's face goes white with fury, his fists clenching at his sides. But he doesn't make a move, doesn't say a word. He knows he's outmatched here, knows that Bloodbane could cut through his men. "Yer breaking the code, Bloodbane. Ye know ye can't do—"

"Fuck the code. I will do whatever I damn well please." Bloodbane snarls.

I silently pray to any deity that might be listening, begging them to keep Dani away a bit longer.

Why she hasn't returned to the table is either a blessing or something happened to her, and now I'm all kinds of fucked up. But I don't sense her fear—I would know if she was in trouble.

Bloodbane is in our faces, his breath hot and rank against my skin. "Time's up, boys," he snarls, his hand closing around the hilt of his blade. "You can either come with me quietly, or I can drag you to the Sea Witch in pieces. Your choice."

"I think there's something else you bastards would prefer—something the Sea Witch would really want," Izabelle interrupts.

We all stare at her, confusion and suspicion written across our faces.

"Go on..." Bloodbane demands, his eyes narrowing to dangerous slits.

"There's a female here. She's got some kind of power," Izabelle continues, a sly smile playing at the corners of her mouth.

"Don't—" Finn starts, but one of Bloodbane's goons stops him with a knife to his throat.

"Izabelle—" Gideon warns, his voice low and urgent. But before he can say anything else, Bloodbane is in his face, looming over him like a thundercloud.

"Go on, lass," Bloodbane growls, his attention fixed solely on Izabelle. "Tell me more about this... powerful female."

Izabelle smirks, a wicked gleam in her eye. "Curvy little brunette thing—I think you bastards would be much more interested in what she's got to offer."

She jerks her head towards the back of the tavern, where Dani disappeared moments ago. My heart clenches in my chest, and I feel a low, menacing growl building in the back of my throat.

Oh, fuck no. This bitch did not just sell out my girl.

Rage explodes through my veins like a goddamn wildfire. I can't believe what I'm hearing. This treacherous cunt just threw Dani to the wolves. And for what? Because she's jealous?

My hands ball into fists, claws digging into my palms. It takes every ounce of self-control not to lunge across the table and rip Izabelle's throat out.

I catch Erik's eye, seeing my own fury and disbelief mirrored in his gaze. We both know what this means.

I give Erik a slight, almost imperceptible nod. He returns it, his face grim and his eyes hard as flint.

We're ready. Ready to fight, ready to kill. Ready to do whatever it takes to keep Dani safe.

"Go find her." Bloodbane nods to one of his crew. "And bring her to me."

I bare my fangs in a deadly snarl. "You won't fucking touch her."

Beside me, Erik bares his fangs.

I see a flash of fear in Bloodbane's eyes for a split second, quickly replaced by pure, unadulterated hatred. "And there it is," he sneers. "What have we here, boys?"

"Dani—" before I can even warn her, Bloodbane moves.

And then it's just fucking chaos.

DANICA

13

Nixie turns over the next card, and I lean forward eagerly, my heartache momentarily forgotten. "The Emperor," she intones, tapping the stern-looking figure on the throne. "Your vampire has a hidden power, a legacy waiting to be unleashed. Lightning courses through his veins, the blood of a powerful ancestor."

I bolt upright, curiosity burning hot. This is the third time someone's gotten cryptic about Rhyland's supposed "hidden ancestor" and mysterious powers, and I'm tired of being left in the dark.

"But what—?"

"The Hierophant," she says, cutting me off and turning over a card with an old man in robes. "To find his true heritage is to find the answer."

"Well, that's about as clear as mud," I snap. "What ancestor, who—?"

"Patience, my dear," her voice soft and soothing. "The answers will come in due time." The gypsy gives me that same enigmatic smile.

I huff in frustration. "Due time, my ass," I mutter. "I've got a mate with a mysterious past, supernatural baddies on my tail, and powers locked up tight. I don't have time to wait for the universe to get its shit together."

Nixie sighs, shaking her head. "You young people, always so impatient," she mutters, but there's amusement in her eye.

"Can't you give me a hint, at least? A name, a place, something to go on?"

She shakes her head, her expression serious. "To give you too much too soon would rob you of the journey," she says solemnly. "The discovery of one's heritage, of the power that flows through one's veins, is a sacred thing. It cannot be rushed or forced."

This makes me wonder how much Rhyland knows about his past and heritage. He's given me the SparkNotes version of his mortal life, but what about the prequel?

My brain is now in full-on sleuth mode. Unraveling the mystery of someone's past, their lineage? That's catnip for my curious mind.

I mean, it's my job description back home.

But given Rhyland's past, I suspect a simple blood sample in my lab won't cut it. This will require a full-on deep dive into the supernatural world—time to channel my inner Scooby-Doo and crack this case wide open.

We're talking about a guy who's been around for centuries, seen empires rise and fall, and probably has more secrets than the CIA.

Does Rhyland share the same fate as me, clueless about his real parents?

If so, Rhyland and I are fated with the same messed-up history—just in different periods. The universe really has a sick sense of humor.

I collapse back into my seat, my mind reeling with questions. Before I can start firing them off, the gypsy is already shifting gears to the present.

"The High Priestess," she announces, and I perk up at the sight of the veiled lady between the pillars. "You have immense power within you, but it is blocked, trapped behind a wall of magic."

I nod vigorously. "Yes!" I exclaim. "That witch bitch put the whammy on me, and now I'm about as magical as a potato. Can you fix it?"

The gypsy shakes her head, a knowing smile playing at her mouth. "The Hermit," she says, flipping over a card with an old man holding a lantern. "You must dig within yourself, find the light that ignited your journey. Believe in it, and it will reawaken."

I take a deep breath, trying to focus through the haze of alcohol and cryptic bullshit. Could it really be that simple? Just click my heels three times and say, "I believe in me," and poof—powers restored?

Before I can voice my skepticism, the gypsy is already moving on, her voice taking on a spooky quality that makes the hairs on my neck stand up.

"The Wheel of Fortune," she whispers, laying down a card depicting various creatures clinging to a spinning wheel. "Dragons, darkness, death... Loss. Crossing times and realms. Your path is fraught with danger, child."

I feel my heart do acrobatics as a cold sweat breaks out on my forehead.

When I think I've seen and heard it all, the universe throws fire-breathing lizards into the mix. Who knows where or when I'll run into one of those scaly beasts, but this gypsy's track record is spot-on so far.

The word 'loss' sticks in my throat. I'm afraid to ask, my curiosity battling with my sense of self-preservation. Do I even want to know? I've already lost Adrian, and that wound is still raw.

So I stick to what's essential—the here and now. I can't afford to dwell on the unknown, or I'll drive myself crazy. Time to focus on the present and tackle the future when it rears its ugly head.

"You know, don't you?" I ask, my voice barely above a whisper. "Who I am—What I'm meant to do?"

The gypsy's eyes bore into mine, ancient and knowing. "You are the Sun," she says, turning over another card to reveal a radiant sun shining on a child riding a white horse. "A bringer of light, a catalyst for change."

Suddenly, Rhyland's voice floats inside my head, and all hell breaks loose outside the tavern. I sober up quickly when I hear shouts and crashes echoing through the walls, and I'm on my feet in a flash, ready to investigate.

But the gypsy's hand shoots out, clamping down on my wrist with an iron grip. "Sit," she commands. "You must stay here, where it is safe."

I stare at her incredulously. "Are you out of your damn mind?" I hiss, yanking my arm free. "Something is going down out there, and you expect me just to sit here?"

Nixie's eyes narrow, and for a moment, I swear I see flames dancing in their depths. "No," her voice low and serious. "You are too important, child. Too vital to the fate of the realms. Whatever is happening out there, it is not for you to face. Not yet."

I feel my frustration bubbling up like a volcano, the rum and the gypsy's cryptic bullshit making my head feel like it's about to explode. I open my mouth to argue.

Nixie's hand slams down on the table, making me jump as she lays out the final card with a dramatic flourish. I feel a chill run down my spine as I take in the image—a horned, demonic figure looming over two cowering, chained souls.

"Heed my words, child," the gypsy whispers, her voice urgent. "The shadows are coming, hungry for the light that shines within your Viking. They seek to snuff out his flame, to claim him as their own."

I feel my blood turn to ice, a sense of dread settling in the pit of my stomach.

My nightmares come rushing back, hitting me like a freight train—Rhyland lost to the Darkness—Moretemis—Seraphina's warning pulsing in my head like a strobe light.

RHYLAND

14

The red-haired bastard lunges at me with a roar, his fist connecting with my jaw with enough force to snap a mortal's neck. But I'm no mortal, and I've taken more brutal hits from toddlers.

I retaliate with a snarl, my fist slamming into his gut and doubling him over. I follow up with a knee to his face, feeling the satisfying crunch of cartilage.

But Bloodbane is tough, and he's back on his feet instantly, his eyes blazing with fury. He comes at me again, this time with a wicked-looking dagger.

I dodge the first swipe, feeling the blade whistle past my ear. But the second one catches me across the ribs, opening up a shallow gash that starts oozing blood.

Fuck. That's going to slow me down.

My anger skyrockets, a white-hot fury burning through my veins. I need to get to Dani, find her, and make sure she's safe. But this asshole, this fucking Bloodbane, is in my way.

I try to reach for my telekinesis, to slam the fucker against the wall and hold him there until I can rip his throat out, but there's nothing. Still cut off from my abilities, leaving me with only my brute strength.

But I don't need my powers to deal with this piece of shit. I've got centuries of Viking combat training and rage that could level mountains coursing through my veins.

I roar, which shakes the very foundations of the tavern. And then I'm on him, tackling him to the ground with enough force to crack the floorboards beneath us.

My fists are a blur as I rain down blows on his ugly face, feeling his bones shatter and splinter beneath my knuckles. The wet, meaty sound of flesh splitting open fills my ears, and I can feel his blood splattering against my skin, hot and sticky.

But I don't stop. I can't stop. Not until this fucker is a broken, bloody ruin beneath me. Not until I've made him pay for every second he's kept me from getting to Dani.

The realization hits me like a punch to the gut, stealing the breath from my lungs. The attack on us—the tavern, Bloodbane, and his goons... sent by the Sea Witch. Just how much does she already know, and what will she do?

Panic claws at my throat, a sickening knot of fear and dread that threatens to undo me.

I lose myself in the violence, in its pure, primal rush. I'm a man possessed, a berserker lost in the throes of battle-rage. There's nothing but the pounding of my fists, the crunch of bone, and the coppery scent of blood in my nostrils.

There are too many of them, and they keep coming, wave after wave of Bloodbane's goons pouring through the door.

I can feel myself starting to tire, my muscles screaming in protest as I keep swinging and fighting. Bloodbane is a mess beneath me, his face a ruin of shattered bone and pulped flesh, but still he struggles, still he tries to sink his blade into my flesh.

Bloodbane reaches for my throat, digging his meaty hands in, choking me as I continue to rain punches.

I bare my fangs, ready to rip his fucking throat out and be done with this prick, but before I can strike, something hard smashes into the back of my skull. The impact sends me sprawling off Bloodbane and onto the floor.

Sunovabitch!

Stars burst in my vision, and everything spins. The room tilts and sways, but through the haze, I see Bloodbane scrambling to his feet, seizing the opportunity to run for it.

My head throbs, and then I feel a firm hand clamp down on my arm, hauling me up.

It's Erik, his face grim. "Enough," he shouts over the roar of the chaos around us. "We need to leave. Now."

Fuck playing it smart. Fuck regrouping and plotting and scheming. The only thing that matters now is blood, hot and wet and gushing down my throat as I unleash hell on these bastards who dared to fuck with what's mine.

Control snapped—now all I want is *blood*.

I'm moving, a blur of speed and savagery, as I tear through Bloodbane's goons like a whirlwind of death.

I don't think, don't hesitate, don't hold back. I let my vampire instincts take over completely, unleashing the beast within to wreak bloody havoc.

My fangs sink into throats, tearing through flesh and muscle, the coppery taste of blood flooding my mouth. My claws rip through bone and sinew like they're made of paper, splattering blood and viscera across the walls, the floor, my face, hands, and clothes. The scent of it, thick and heavy, fills my nostrils, but I barely notice. All I can focus on is the savage joy of the kill, the primal rush of rending my enemies limb from limb.

I haven't fed like this since the Werewolf massacre back home. When I took out half of Marcus's pack—draining them until nothing was left but husks.

The memory of that night flashes through my mind, vivid and bloody. The scent of fear was thick in the air, the sound of screams and snarls echoing through the forest. The savage joy of the hunt, of the kill, of feeling my enemies' life force flowing into me with every frenzied gulp.

It was a slaughter, a bloodbath of epic proportions. I tore through those wolves like they were nothing—like they were less than nothing. I reveled in their terror, pain, and knowledge that I was the apex predator, the monster that even monsters feared.

It was glorious and terrifying, and it was everything I am, everything I was made to be.

A killer. A destroyer. A fucking force of nature.

And now, as I tear through Bloodbane's men with the same ruthless efficiency and savage glee, I feel that old bloodlust rising inside me once again.

It's like a drug, like the sweetest ambrosia. The more I kill, the more I need to kill. The more blood I spill, the more I crave.

It's a vicious cycle, a never-ending spiral of death and destruction. And some dark, twisted part of me loves every fucking second of it.

Screams fill the air, high and shrill and full of terror, as the patrons and pirates witness the slaughter unfolding around them. They've never seen brutality like this, never witnessed such raw, unbridled savagery. To their mortal eyes, it must seem like the end of days, like hell itself has opened up to swallow them whole.

But I don't care. Let them scream.

All I see is red; all I can taste is the coppery tang of blood on my tongue. I'm lost in the frenzy, the savage joy of the kill, and nothing else matters.

Dimly, I'm aware of Erik joining the fray, his sword glinting in the lantern lights. We move together like a well-oiled machine, a duo of death and destruction that leaves nothing but broken bodies and shattered bones in our wake.

Gideon and Izabelle are there, too, their swords flashing as they cut down any fucker stupid enough to get in their way. But they're just background noise, barely registering in my blood-soaked haze.

There's a feeling deep in my gut, something primal and urgent, like a siren's call. It's a sickening sensation, a twist of pain and dread that lashes at my insides like a whip.

But I ignore it, push it down, and lock it away. I can't afford to be distracted, not now, not when I'm lost in the throes of bloodlust and savage fury.

DANICA

15

The door explodes inward, splinters flying like deadly confetti. I barely register the ugly mug barreling towards me before my hands reach for my daggers, muscle memory taking over as adrenaline surges through my veins.

"Yer comin' with me, wench," he snarls, his breath reeking of cheap ale and poor life choices.

Oh, hell no.

I see Nixie fleeing the room, her skirts billowing behind her. I don't blame her—this is about to get ugly.

I don't hesitate. I react. I use the table as a launchpad, propelling myself into a double kick that would make any action hero proud. My legs whirl around like lethal pinwheels, sending this jerk flying like a sack of potatoes.

He slams into the wall with a satisfying thud, his body crumpling. But I'm not finished. I grab the wooden chair and bring it down on his head with all my force, the wood shattering as he weakly tries to shield himself.

But this brute is resilient. He drags himself to his feet, his sword sliding out with a sinister rasp. I can see the fury smoldering in his eyes, the promise of retribution etched into every line of his ugly mug.

That's when I get a good look at his face, and holy shit, it's like something out of a horror movie. This dude is built like a brick, with a mane of red hair that looks like it hasn't seen a comb in years. But it's his eyes that catch my attention—they're red and swollen like someone used his face as a punching bag.

Come and get it, you overgrown oaf. I've got a blade in each hand and a point to prove, and I'll be damned if I'm going to let this numbskull take me down without a fight.

Let's dance, asshole.

The pirate's sword slices through the air with a deadly whistle. I bring my daggers up just in time. The sound of metal clashing against metal is like music to my ears, a sweet symphony of "fuck you, not today."

The force of the blow rattles my teeth and sends shockwaves up my arms, but I'm not about to flinch. I grit my teeth and shove him back with everything I've got. He goes flying like a rag doll, slamming into the wall with a satisfying thud for a second time.

I take a moment to catch my breath, but the stench of stale sweat and cheap booze rolling off this guy is enough to make me want to hurl. But I don't have time to dwell on his questionable hygiene because he's already back on his feet and coming at me again.

"Stop fightin', bitch," the pirate snarls, spittle flying from his lips. "Ye won't win with me."

I can't help but laugh, the sound harsh and mocking. "Oh, buddy," I drawl, twirling my daggers. "You have no idea who you're fucking with."

He lunges, his sword flashing in a deadly arc. I dodge to the side, feeling the rush of air as the blade misses me by inches. I lash out with my daggers, the razor-sharp edges slicing through his sleeve and drawing blood.

He roars in pain and anger, charging at me like a raging bull. I sidestep his clumsy attack, my foot lashing out to catch him behind the knee. He stumbles, his sword clattering to the ground as he falls.

But he's not done yet. He rolls to his feet with surprising agility, his fists clenched and ready. I barely have time to brace myself before he's on me, his meaty hands grabbing for my throat.

I ram my knee into his balls, a wicked grin spreading across my face as he crumples. His face turns a delightful shade of purple that clashes horribly with his ginger hair.

But this bastard is made of sterner stuff. He's back on his feet before I can catch my breath, his meaty paws knocking my daggers out of my hands. His fingers wrap around my throat like a vice, squeezing the life out of me with a sadistic gleam in his eye.

I can feel my lungs screaming for air and my vision blurs. My head feels like it's about to explode as this asshole cuts off my air supply. I gather every last shred of strength, channeling my inner warrior princess, and drive my knee into his nuts again.

But apparently, this guy's balls are made of steel. He grunts like a pig and squeezes even harder, his fingers digging into my flesh like hot pokers. I can feel my consciousness starting to slip away, my body going limp as my brain screams for oxygen.

I am not going to let this overgrown ape choke me out without a fight.

I summon all my strength, channeling all those hours of training with Rhyland and Erik. With a burst of adrenaline-fueled fury, I slam my hands down on his forearms. The shock of the blow loosens his grip just enough for me to wiggle free, gasping for air like a fish out of water.

I don't hesitate. I dive for my daggers like a woman possessed, my fingers closing around the hilts just as he lunges for me again.

The world narrows to the frenzied dance of combat; my senses are heightened to a razor's edge as I fight on pure instinct and muscle memory. I'm forced to rely on my skill and determination without my powers to aid me.

The pirate is relentless, his attacks coming fast and furious, each backed by a strength born of desperation and greed. I can see it in his eyes—the hunger for whatever bounty he thinks he can claim by capturing me.

I duck and weave, my daggers flashing in the dim light as I parry his blows and strike back with my own. The clash of steel on steel echoes through the room, mingling with our grunts of exertion and the frantic pounding of my own heart.

Sweat stings my eyes, and my lungs burn with each ragged breath, but I push through the pain and fatigue, knowing that to falter now would be to forfeit my life. I can feel the adrenaline surging through my veins, a wild, reckless energy that lends strength to my limbs and speed to my reflexes.

But even with all my skill and determination, I can feel myself starting to falter. The pirate is stronger than me and has the advantage of brute force. Each blow I block sends shockwaves up my arms, and I can feel my grip on my daggers starting to weaken.

He sees his opening and lunges forward, his sword arcing towards my throat in a deadly slash. I twist to the side, but I'm a fraction of a second too slow. The blade bites into my shoulder, sending a white-hot bolt of agony lancing through my body.

I cry out, my dagger falling from my nerveless fingers as I stagger back, my vision blurring with pain. The pirate presses his advantage, his fist slamming into my face, once—twice—three times in rapid succession.

I feel my nose break, the crunch of cartilage, and the warm gush of blood filling my mouth. My head snaps back with each blow, stars exploding behind my eyelids as my brain rattles around in my skull.

The world tilts and spins, and my knees give out beneath me. I hit the ground hard, the impact driving the air from my lungs. I try to push myself up to keep fighting, but my arms are like jelly, and my muscles refuse to obey my commands.

The last thing I see before the darkness claims me is the pirate's boot, his foot drawing back in preparation for a final, vicious kick. And then there's nothing but the taste of blood and the sound of my ragged breathing as I slip into unconsciousness, the gypsy's ominous warning still ringing in my ears.

RHYLAND

16

"R etreat!" someone bellows, his voice thick with pain and fear. "Every man for himself!"

And just like that, the tide turns. What's left of Bloodbane's crew scramble over each other in their haste to get to the doors, their faces pale with terror as they flee for their lives.

I let out a roar of pure, savage fury, ready to give chase. But before I can move, Erik's hand clamps down on my shoulder, his grip like iron.

"Let them go," Erik growls, his voice low and deadly. "We have more important things to worry about."

For a moment, I want to argue, want to tear my arm from his grasp and go after those fleeing bastards. But then... Dani. And just like that, the rage drains out of me, replaced by a cold, implacable fury that burns in my veins like ice.

I burst into the back room, my heart pounding. The scent of Dani's blood hits me like a punch to the gut, and I freeze, my eyes widening in horror.

The room is a disaster. Chairs and tables are overturned, smashed to kindling. And there, on the floor, is a pool of blood.

Dani's blood.

Her daggers lay scattered on the floor, a stark reminder of the fight she put up.

I reach out instinctively, my voice a raw growl. *"Baby, where are you? Talk to me..."*

But there's nothing. No answer. She's hurt and in a bad way.

For a moment, I can't move, can't breathe. It's like the world has stopped turning. And then the rage hits me, a tidal wave of fury and desperation that threatens to drown me.

I let out a scream that's half agony, half rage, and slam my fists into the wall with all my strength. Wood splinters and cracks beneath my hands, but I barely feel it. All I can feel is the sickening dread, the gut-wrenching fear for my mate.

Erik is instantly by my side, his face draining of color as he enters the scene. He knows what this means and knows that Dani is gone—taken.

I burst out of the tavern, my heart pounding like a war drum. The hot, musty air slaps me in the face, but I barely feel it. All I can think about is Dani, my angel, my heart, my fucking soul.

I cast out my senses, searching for any trace of her, any hint of her presence. And there, on the edge of my consciousness, I feel her—she is close.

I latch onto it like a drowning man latching onto a rope, and then I'm running, my feet pounding against the sand as I race towards the docks.

The bright moon casts an eerie glow over the water, illuminating the scene before me. And there, pulling away from the docks is a massive ship with blood-red flags hoisted high.

No. No, no, no.

FUCK!

They have her. Those fucking bastards have my girl, and they're taking her away from me.

But I won't let them. I won't let them take her, not now, not ever.

I run faster, my feet flying over the sand like I'm running on air. I can hear Erik behind me, his feet pounding against the sand as he tries to keep up.

But I don't slow down, don't hesitate. I just keep running, my eyes locked on that fucking ship like it's the only thing in the world that matters.

Because it is, Dani is on that ship, and I won't rest or stop until I have her back in my arms where she belongs.

I reach the end of the docks just as the massive Galleon begins to pull away, the water churning beneath its hull. For a heart-stopping moment, I think I'm too late, that I've lost her forever.

But then I spot it—a small rowboat tied to the dock, bobbing gently in the water.

I don't even think. I leap into the boat; my only thought is getting to that ship and tearing it apart plank by fucking plank if I have to. Erik is right behind me, his face set with grim determination.

"Lads!" It's Gideon, clutching his side as he staggers towards us, his shirt dark with blood. "Ye won't catch 'em in that little cockleshell."

I snarl, slamming my fist against the side of the boat hard enough to send splinters flying. He's right, damn him. This pathetic excuse for a vessel will never catch that ship, not in a thousand years.

I turn to Gideon, my eyes blazing. "Then we take your ship," I growl, my voice low and deadly. "Now."

Gideon meets my gaze, his own eyes glinting with fierce approval. "Aye," he agrees, spitting a glob of blood onto the dock. "Let's be on our way, then."

Erik and I scramble out of the dinghy, meeting with Gideon on the shore. The old pirate captain straightens up, his voice booming across the docks.

"Finn! Ye mangy cur, where are ye?"

Finn appears momentarily, his face a mask of confusion and concern. "Cap'n? What's all this, then?"

"We're setting sail," Gideon snaps. "Get the ship ready, and be quick about it."

Finn gapes at him, his eyes wide with disbelief. "Cap'n, have ye lost yer bloody mind? We can't go after the Crimson Brotherhood. It's suicide!"

I take a step forward, ready to tear the insubordinate little shit limb from limb, but Gideon beats me to it. He rounds on Finn, his face thunderous, his eyes flashing.

"They have the girl, ye idiot! Ye'll do as yer Cap'n commands, boy," he snarls. "Or ye'll answer to me. Now move yer arse, before I kick it from here to the Mermaid's Cove."

Finn's eyes widen, "Fuck." he shakes his head as a look of anger crosses his features. He swallows hard, his throat bobbing, and nods. "Aye, Cap'n," a hint of sadness in his tone. "We'll have her ready to sail in two shakes."

"See that ye do," Gideon growls before returning to Erik and me. "Come on, lads. Let's get ye armed and ready. We've got a damsel to save and a sea witch to gut from stem to stern."

I nod, my jaw clenched tight. Every instinct I have is screaming at me to just leap into the fucking water and swim after that ship—to tear it apart with my bare hands until I have Dani safe in my arms again.

She's powerless right now, and if I had to guess, is hurt pretty badly since she's gone silent on me.

But as much as it kills me, I know Gideon's right. We need a ship of our own, need the speed and the firepower and a crew of ruthless sons of bitches at our backs. So I follow him up the gangplank, my heart pounding like a war drum and my blood singing with the promise of the violence to come.

Hold on, baby. Just hold the fuck on. I'm coming for you, and I'm bringing hell with me.

Those bastards have no idea what's about to hit them, no clue about the world of pain they just brought down on their own heads.

They think they can take what's mine? They think they can lay a hand on my mate and just fucking sail away into the sunset?

They've got another thing coming. I'll hunt them to the ends of this fucking realm if I have to, through hell and high water and everything in between.

And when I catch them... when I finally lay my hands on the filthy bastard that dared to touch my girl...

There won't be enough left of him to feed the fish.

That's a promise sworn on in my honor as a Viking, warrior, her man, and mate.

I'm coming for you, Angel.

And God help anyone who gets in my fucking way.

LUCIAN

17

I lounge on the couch, sipping from a blood bag like it's a Capri Sun. Don't get me wrong, I'm grateful for the sustenance, but there's something about the plastic aftertaste that just doesn't quite hit the spot like a warm, willing neck. But beggars can't be choosers, I guess. Or, in this case, vampires can't be choosers.

I learned my lesson real quick when the blood called to me like an addict, and I attempted to attack both Emily and Sable in a fit of hunger-fueled desperation. It's like my brain short-circuits, and all I can think about is sinking my fangs into their soft, warm flesh and gulping down that sweet nectar of life.

But Emily, with her freaky witch powers that I still don't fully understand, just holds up a hand like she's some kind of supernatural traffic cop, and suddenly I'm knocked on my ass, feeling like my head is about to explode into a million tiny pieces. It's like the worst migraine you can imagine, multiplied by a thousand, with a side of 'fuck you, vampire boy.'

And the worst part? Emily just keeps me in that state of mind-numbing agony until I'm reduced to a screaming bitch on the floor, begging for mercy. It's humiliating, really. Here I am, a big bad vampire who's probably seen and done some seriously fucked up shit in my long undead life, and I'm brought to my knees by a tiny slip of a witch with a chip on her shoulder.

But I guess I can't really blame her. I did try to snack on her and her bestie like they were walking, talking juice boxes. So, we came to a compromise. I drink from plastic sippy straws like a goddamn toddler, and the girls get to keep their necks hole-free and their hearts beating. It's a win-win, except for my dignity, which has pretty much been shredded to pieces at this point.

I smirk at the two witches who have been playing nursemaid to me for the past couple of days. "You know, I gotta hand it to you ladies. You sure know how to show a guy a good time. Blood bags, memory loss, and a crash course in supernatural politics. It's like a fucked-up version of a spa day."

Emily rolls her eyes. "Yeah, well, consider yourself lucky, *fangboy*. If it weren't for the fact that we need you in one piece, I would've let you starve. Or maybe I would've just fed you to the neighbor's chihuahua. God knows that little fucker could use a chew toy."

I clutch my chest in mock horror. "Oh, Emily, you wound me! And here I thought we were building a beautiful friendship based on mutual snark and a shared love of inappropriate humor. I'm hurt, truly."

Emily scoffs, and I can practically hear her eyes rolling in their sockets. It's like her default setting is 'unimpressed with Lucian's bullshit.'

So far, I've learned that vampires are out of the coffin now. Like, we're not just lurking in the shadows anymore, waiting to pounce on unsuspecting virgins and dramatic teenagers. Nope, we're out and proud, walking among the humans like another minority group fighting for our rights.

But I guess that's just the way the world works now. Vampires, witches, werewolves... we're all just one big, happy, dysfunctional family like the Addams Family, but with more blood and less quirky charm.

And speaking of family, I've got two brothers out there somewhere—Brothers by blood, or I guess, by venom. I don't remember Jack shit about them, but according to Emily and Sable, they're pretty badass. I mean, they'd have to be to put up with my amnesiac ass.

This Dani chick is the key to this prophecy: the chosen one, the savior of the supernatural world, the whole nine yards.

Also, can we talk about the "no sunlight" situation? Emily and Sable keep this apartment blacked out like it's perpetually Halloween. I mean, I get it; they're trying to keep me from bursting into flames like a fucking marshmallow at a campfire—but come on.

This Dani girl is the only one who can give me access to the sun, which sucks ass—because she's missing.

I wonder what other surprises this brave new world has in store for me. Maybe I'll find out that fairies are real, and they're all just a bunch of glitter-covered assholes with a penchant for mischief. Or perhaps I'll discover that dragons are a thing, and they're just really grumpy lizards with a hoarding problem.

Who the fuck knows?

All I know is that I'm along for the ride, whether I like it or not. And if I'm gonna be a part of this supernatural soap opera, I might as well embrace the chaos and have some fun with it.

But first, I need to figure out who the hell I am and what my role is in this whole clusterfuck of a situation. Because right now, I feel like I'm just a supporting character in someone else's story, and I'll be damned if I'm gonna let that stand

"Why do you keep me around?" I ask, my tone equal parts frustrated and curious. "I mean, I can't remember jack shit. Not my friends, my family, my vampire past... it's all just one big, gaping hole in my memory. I'm like a walking, talking amnesiac with fangs. But apparently, I'm essential for some reason that you haven't fully explained yet. So what gives?"

Emily sighs like she's explaining something to a particularly dense child. "Because... you're important to Danica, to your brothers. You sacrificed yourself for her, you dumbass. That's why we couldn't just leave you to rot with those sadistic assholes."

I raise an eyebrow, trying to place this 'Danica' chick in my mind, but it comes up empty. It's like remembering a dream after you've woken up—the harder you try to grasp the details, the more they slip away. "So, out of the kindness of your heart for your *friend,* you risked your neck to rescue me? Don't get me wrong, I'm grateful, but that seems like a lot of trouble for someone you barely know."

Emily's expression softens just a fraction. "Look, Lucian... I know this is all really confusing for you right now. But trust me when I say that you're important. Not just to Danica, but to the fate of the whole fucking world. I know that sounds like some cheesy fantasy novel bullshit, but it's true. Whether you remember it or not, you're a key player in this prophecy."

I nod, feeling a strange sense of determination welling up inside me. "Alright, Rainbow Brite. You've convinced me. I may not know who the fuck I am or what the hell is going on, but if you say I'm important, then I guess I'll just have to take your word for it. But if I end up saving the world and not getting laid as a reward, I'm gonna be pissed."

Emily rolls her eyes again. "God, you're such a fucking horndog. Is that all you think about? Getting laid?"

I grin, waggling my eyebrows suggestively. "Hey, a man's gotta have his priorities straight. And right now, my priorities are remembering who I am, saving the world, and getting some sweet, sweet vampire lovin'. Not necessarily in that order."

Bless her heart, Sable tries to play peacemaker. "Guys, come on. We've got bigger problems to worry about than Lucian's need to get laid. Azrael is still out there and may find another powerful vampire to complete their freaky ritual."

I nod, taking another sip of blood. "Right, right. The prophecy, the stones, the crown, yadda yadda yadda. It's all starting to come back to me now. Oh wait, no, it's not. Because that bitch Paige went all 'Eternal Sunshine of the Spotless Mind' on my ass and erased my entire fucking life story."

Emily sighs, pinching the bridge of her nose. "Look, I know this is a lot to take in. But we don't have time for a pity party. We need to find a way to get your memories back—and fast. Because if Azrael manages to get the witch covens on his side, we're all screwed. And not in a fun way."

I raise an eyebrow, a slow grin spreading across my face. "Witch covens, huh? Tell me more, tell me more. Like, do they wear pointy hats and ride broomsticks? Or is that just a stereotype perpetuated by the patriarchy to keep powerful women down?"

Sable shakes her head. "No, Lucian, it's not like that. Covens are just groups of witches who work together to amplify their power. They're all over the world, and some are incredibly strong. If Azrael can convince them to join him, it could tip the scales in his favor."

Emily nods grimly. "Sable's right. If Azrael can get the witch covens on his side, we're fucked. Like, royally fucked. We're talking end-of-the-world, fire-and-brimstone, dogs-and-cats-living-together kind of fucked."

I lean back and prop my feet on the coffee table, "Alright, let me see if I've got this straight. We're facing off against a shadow demon who probably has a severe case of 'I'm the baddest motherfucker in the room' syndrome, his psycho boyfriend Azrael, who I'm guessing is the brains behind this whole operation and potentially covens of super-powered witches who may or may not be on their side in this whole 'end of the world' scenario. Oh, and apparently, I'm somehow part of this entire shitshow, even though I can't remember a goddamn thing about it.

"And to top it all off, we've got our supposed savior, this Dani girl; who's the key to stopping all of this, but she's nowhere to be found? Sounds like a typical soap opera to me."

Emily throws a pillow at my head, which I deftly dodge. "This isn't a joke, asshole. We need a plan, and we need it now. Because if we don't stop Azrael, there won't be a world left to save."

I hold up my hands in surrender, the empty blood bag dangling from my fingers. "Alright, alright, I get it. Serious business, end of the world, blah blah blah. But can we at least order a pizza first? All this talk of prophecies and covens is making me hungry. And not for blood, for once."

After devouring an entire pizza like a ravenous beast and enduring hours of witchy woo-woo bullshit, I finally threw in the towel. Seriously, if I had to listen to one more incantation or drink another foul-tasting potion, I was going to lose my goddamn mind. I mean, I appreciate Emily and Sable trying to help me recover my memories, but there's only so much magical mumbo-jumbo a guy can take before he starts to question his sanity.

Emily and Sable tried their best. They threw everything but the kitchen sink at me—I half-expected them to start sacrificing small animals and dancing naked under the moonlight. But despite all their valiant efforts and hours of chanting until I thought my ears would bleed, we got nowhere. Nada. Zilch.

So, I finally called it quits before they could suggest something really crazy, like a magical enema or a lobotomy. I may be desperate to remember who I am, but I draw the line at anything involving my ass or my brain matter.

Or do I draw the line at anything near my ass?

I quickly shake the thought from my mind and continue watching episode after episode of this cooking show. I'm totally invested at this point. I'm twenty episodes deep and rooting for the underdog chef who keeps getting yelled at by that angry British dude. I guess I relate to the whole "trying to prove yourself against impossible odds" thing.

Suddenly, I sense a disturbance in the force. And no, I'm not talking about that weird noise your aunt makes after eating too many bean burritos. I'm talking about the kind of disturbance that makes your nether regions stand at attention, and your eyes pop out of your head like a cartoon character on Viagra.

That's right, folks. I'm talking about moaning. Sweet, sweet, passionate moaning. The kind of moaning that could make even the most celibate monk consider breaking his vows and joining the dark side.

I spring into action like a horny gazelle. My reflexes fine-tuned from years of... well, I don't really know, do I? Amnesia's a bitch like that. But who cares about the past when the present serves up such a delectable auditory feast?

I mute the TV faster than you can say, "Bow chicka, wow, wow," because no one needs the dulcet tones of Gordon Ramsay screaming about undercooked scallops when there's real-life porn happening just a few feet away.

The unmistakable sounds of moaning and a gasp could make even the most jaded porn star stand up and take notice. Oh, it's on like Donkey Kong, my friends.

My mind races with possibilities. Could it be? Are Emily and Sable getting their lesbian freak on right under my nose? Or is this some elaborate prank designed to test the limits of my vampiric hearing and my ability to resist temptation?

I may be an amnesiac, but I'm still a red-blooded male. And the thought of two smoking hot witches going at it like rabbits in heat is enough to make even the most disciplined vampire lose his cool.

But I'm a gentleman, damn it. And a gentleman doesn't go barging into other people's sexy times uninvited... Who the fuck am I kidding? I'm no gentleman. I'm a horny, amnesiac vampire with the impulse control of a toddler on a sugar high.

But I can't just barge in there, no matter how much my dick is begging me to. Emily would have my fucking balls on a silver platter if I snooped. So, I do what any civilized, sexually frustrated male would do in this situation—I run to the door.

LUCIAN

18

I'm standing here, my ears turned up to eleven, biting my knuckle to muffle the sounds of my excitement. I reach for the door handle with trembling fingers, turning the knob with the stealth of a ninja on Xanax. I crack the door open just a sliver, just enough to get a tantalizing glimpse of the sapphic shenanigans going down on the other side.

And holy mother of fuck, what a view it is. Sable, spread out like a goddamn buffet of creamy skin and wanton desire. Her legs are parted like the Red Sea, inviting Emily to dive in and taste the forbidden fruit. And Emily, oh Emily, she's knelt between those silky thighs like a supplicant at the altar of pussy.

Her tongue is doing things that would make even the most seasoned porn star blush. She laps and swirls and flicks like she's trying to win a fucking gold medal in clit licking. And Sable, sweet, innocent Sable, she's coming undone like a spool of thread, all breathy moans and desperate whimpers.

"Come for me, little witch," Emily purrs, her voice heavy with seduction. "Give it to me, baby."

And just like that, my cock is harder than a fucking diamond, straining against the confines of my jeans like it's trying to break free and join the party. I'm so turned on it's almost painful, my balls aching with the need for release.

I watch, transfixed, as Emily plunges two fingers deep into Sable's slick heat, pumping them in and out like a piston in a sex machine. Her mouth never leaves Sable's clit, sucking and teasing and driving her to the brink of insanity.

"Yes, yes, oh...fuck!" Sable cries out, her voice sharp and desperate, like a sinner begging for salvation.

"Yeah, you like that, my dirty little witch?" Emily growls, her words muffled by the press of Sable's pussy against her lips. "You like getting finger-fucked, don't you?"

I can't help it. My hand drifts down to my crotch, rubbing the aching bulge of my cock through my jeans. I bite my lip to stifle a moan, my hips rocking forward of their own accord, seeking friction, seeking relief.

And then Sable is coming, her body convulsing like she's being electrocuted by pleasure. Her cries fill the room, a symphony of ecstasy that makes my balls tighten and my cock throb. I'm so fucking close, just from watching, just from imagining.

But it's not over yet. Oh no, not by a long shot. It's Sable's turn to take control, flipping Emily onto her back and descending on her like a starving woman at a feast. She takes Emily's nipple into her mouth, sucking and biting and teasing until Emily is writhing beneath her, a slave to her own desire.

When did I unzip my pants?

Standing there, cock in my hand, jerking it—I bite my lip to silence any sound that might escape as my breaths quicken.

"My turn to make you scream," Sable whispers, her fingers finding Emily's clit and rubbing in slow, torturous circles. "I'm gonna make you squirt all over this room."

Holy mother of all that is sinful and depraved! I let out an involuntary moan as I continue to stroke my... ego. Yeah, let's go with ego. Suddenly, the joyous sounds of lesbian love-making come to a screeching halt, replaced by the unmistakable sound of a very pissed-off witch realizing they have an uninvited audience.

Fuck me sideways with a silver dildo. I've really stepped in it this time.

Before I can even think about tucking Little Lucian back into his coffin, the door flies open with enough force to blow Emily's hair back like she's in a goddamn shampoo commercial. And let me tell you, if looks could kill, I'd be deader than disco.

"What the actual fuck, Lucian?!" Emily screeches, her voice hitting a pitch that could shatter glass and my fragile masculinity in one fell swoop.

I freeze, my hand still wrapped around my cock, my face a mask of guilt and terror. I try to stammer out an excuse, but my brain has short-circuited, fried by the sheer magnitude of my horniness and the depth of my shame.

"I, uh... I heard noises, and I thought maybe you were, uh..."

Emily's hands are on her hips, her nipples hard and glistening with Sable's saliva. "You thought we were what, exactly? Having a tea party? Playing patty-cake? Please, do enlighten us, you perverted little shit."

Oh shit, I'm so fucked. I'm about to have my balls hexed off by a pissed-off lesbian witch, and I can't even bring myself to care because, hot damn, that was the hottest thing I've ever witnessed.

Alright, brain, time to unfuck yourself. I somehow manage to stuff my cock back into my pants, like shoving Play-Doh into a tiny container. There we go—crisis averted.

But then Sable, ever the voice of reason, tries to intervene. "Emily, let's just take a deep breath and relax, okay? There's no harm..."

Emily surprises us both. She takes a deep, calming breath, her perfect breasts rising and falling with the motion, her face softening as curiosity takes over. I'm frozen, unsure of what's about to happen next, but damn, I'm intrigued.

"Emily, my love, what do you say we invite him to join our little party?" Sable's eyes sparkle with mischief and my brain misfires.

Oh, FUCK...hell yes. Yes, please.

And just like that, dick reinflated.

Emily lets go of the door and saunters to the bed—clearly an invitation.

It looks like all that stress and bullshit we've been through has led to the promise of a witch threesome.

Sable grins, her eyes locking with mine. "I've always wondered what it would be like to be with a vampire. What do you say, Lucian? Care to join us? We promise not to bite... much."

Sweet baby Jesus, that's it. Sign me up. I silently thank every god and deity I can think of as I step into the room, my cock throbbing for release.

When was the last time I got laid? Fuck if I know.

I'm nervous as hell, but I try to channel my inner badass.

"Come to the bed, big boy." Sable purrs, her voice like velvet.

Big boy? Fuck yes, I'm your big boy.

My feet move of their own accord, and I find myself standing at the foot of the bed, my anxiety and excitement going through the roof.

Sable doesn't waste a second. She pounces on me like a sexy cougar, her hands already working my pants down. With a swift tug, she yanks, and my cock springs free like a jack-in-the-box. It bounces off my abs, leaving a trail of pre-cum in its wake.

"Mmm, just as I thought. *Big boy*, indeed." Sable wraps her hand around my length, giving me a few strokes, and damn, her hand feels good. I'm not small, and I'm very proud of Little Lucian.

Sable takes me into her mouth without warning, and it's like I've died and gone to heaven. "Oh, fuck me sideways and call me a believer. That feels in-fucking-credible," I groan, my head falling back in sheer bliss, my eyes rolling back so far I can almost see my brain.

Emily slides up behind Sable, hands on her hips. "Get on your knees, baby. I want to eat your sweet pussy while you suck his cock."

I watch as Sable gets on her knees, mouth still wrapped around me, Emily kneeling behind her, sucking her clit, and eating her ass like it's her favorite meal.

Is this real life?

Someone pinch me because I must be dreaming. Or dead. Or both.

Sable moans around my cock, the vibrations nearly sending me over the edge.

Fuck, fuck, fuckity fuck.

I close my eyes, focusing on not blowing my load too soon. Must... resist... the urge... to paint... her face... like a Jackson Pollock masterpiece...

"Make me choke, Lucian," Sable purrs, sweet eyes looking up at me.

I grin wickedly. Oh, she wants to play rough? I can do rough. I grab her bubblegum pink hair, gripping tight as I thrust my cock deep into her throat, making her gag like a freshman at a frat party.

I pull back, "Shit, sorry. You okay?"

Sable, the badass bitch, just wants more "No, I like it—do it again. Don't be shy."

I grin and pull her hair, guiding her head back onto my cock, and thrust hard into her throat, picking up a steady, relentless rhythm. Fuck yes, I'll do it again. And again. And again. I can feel her throat clenching around me like a vise grip, and it takes everything in me not to lose it.

Emily reaches for something on the bedside table and straps on a massive dildo, thick and veiny, like something out of a bad dragon fever dream.

"Jesus, Christ! Are you, for real, gonna...that behemoth....in there?" My voice cracks like a teenage boy's, unable to form a cohesive sentence.

I've seen some impressive equipment in my day (I think), but this? This is like the Godzilla of dongs, the Moby Dick of... well, you know. Someone better call Guinness World Records 'cause we're about to witness a miracle of human anatomy right here!

Sable, the cock-sucking goddess, moans in response, eyes rolling back in her head "Mmm-hmm," is all she says, and damn, the sight of her taking me in, eyes glazed over with lust has me ready to blow like a goddamn geyser.

Emily positions herself behind Sable, taking a moment to admire the view. "Ohhh, such a pretty little pussy, all ready to take my fat dick," Emily purrs.

Sable moans, throat vibrating around my cock like a damn Xbox controller. Emily starts to move, slipping the monster cock inside Sable, her hips snapping as she fucks with long, deep strokes like she's trying to rearrange her internal organs.

"More, baby, give me more!" Sable cries out, body arching back like a bow-string.

Emily's hands grip Sable's hips tight enough to leave bruises. Then, she looks at me, a devilish glint in her eye that makes my balls want to retreat into my body. "Lucian, why the hell are you not spit-roasting this filthy little witch like the pig she is?"

Those words are my undoing. I grab Sable's hair with both hands and thrust my cock deep into her warm, wet mouth. Hearing those words is like a switch being flipped in my brain. I'm no longer concerned about her comfort or well-being. She wants it rough, and I'm going to give it to her like the fucking animal I am.

I snap, hips pistoning like a man possessed, and my lust takes over. "That's it, you filthy little cock socket. Take every inch like the cum-hungry slut you are. Choke on my dick like it's your last fucking meal."

Sable pops off my cock, "Yes, keep talking dirty."

I growl, treating her mouth like my personal fleshlight. "Fuck, I bet you could suck the chrome off a trailer hitch, couldn't you, you dirty girl?"

I grip her hair tighter, slamming into her throat.

Emily continues her assault on Sable's pussy, standing up behind her to get the perfect angle, like a porn star pro. Sable moans and screams around my cock, but I shut her up by pushing deeper, her throat now my own personal fuck toy.

"There ya go, baby." Emily's words are like a whip, cracking through the air. "You gonna be a dirty little fuck doll?"

"Yes!" Sable manages to scream around my cock, the vibrations nearly making me see stars

"Mmm...yeah, you are." Emily slams into Sable harder, the sound of skin slapping together filling the room like a round of applause.

Hearing their filthy words is like pouring gasoline on the fire in my veins. I grip Sable's hair tighter, pounding my cock down her throat like it's my sole purpose in life, while Emily fucks her from behind like a rabid animal.

Drool and foam gather around Sable's lips, creating a slick, wet hole for me to fuck with wild abandon, her drool dripping in long strings down to the floor. God, I'm choking the shit out of her, and I don't even care. The sight of her spit running down my thighs is so goddamn hot; I have to slow down so I don't blow my load down her throat like a firehose.

I pull out real quick, "Spit on it."

Sable complies, spit running down my cock like a waterfall. Fuck, I love a good sloppy blowjob. Nothing beats the feeling of a warm, wet mouth worshipping your cock like it's a goddamn religious artifact.

I ease off the throttle, frantically racking my brain for something, anything, to stave off the impending jizz-pocalypse. Reciting the periodic table? Nah, too fucking nerdy. Imagining Rosie O'Donnell in a thong? Blech, gross, but not quite vomit-inducing enough. Picturing Mitch McConnell's ballsack? Okay, that's definitely a one-way ticket to Limp Dicksville, but even that nightmarish image isn't doing the trick right now.

And then, like a big fuck you from the porn gods, a stunning brunette with golden eyes pops into my head; her skin is sun-kissed and flawless like an airbrushed magazine cover.

Where the hell did she come from? And why is she invading my thoughts while I'm balls-deep in Witch Barbie's mouth?

My balls are tightening like a python's grip, and Little Lucian is ready to erupt like Mount Vesuvius. I've got no clue who this mystery girl is or why she seems so familiar, but I can't get her out of my head to save my damn life (or my load, for that matter).

I open my eyes and focus on Sable sucking my cock like a Hoover, looking up at Emily, slamming a massive dildo into Sable. I'm trying to focus on the live-action porno playing out right in front of me, hoping it'll be enough to push Mystery Girl out of my head. But it's like trying to ignore an elephant in the room, or in this case, a sexy, golden-eyed elephant trampling all over my brain.

"Ohh, my dirty witch is creamy. That's it, baby. I'm gonna milk this pussy like a fucking dairy farm." Emily's dirty talk is like a porno soundtrack.

Christ on a cracker, this is like the best fucking thing to ever happen to me (or at least, the best thing I can remember happening to me, which admittedly isn't much).

But even with all this grade-A spank bank material right in front of me, I can't stop thinking about those golden eyes and that perfect, kissable skin. Who is she? Why does she seem so familiar? She must be someone from my past (or at least, the part of my past that's been wiped cleaner than a fucking Etch A Sketch).

When I thought my life couldn't get any more screwed up, the universe decides to throw me a curve ball in the form of a phantom fantasy girl. It's like the powers that be are saying, "Hey Lucian, we know you're balls deep in the middle of a fucking epic threesome, but here's a mystery chick to mindfuck you even more. You're welcome, asshole."

I can't take it anymore. With a grunt and a thrust, I explode like a goddamn geyser, my cum rocketing down Sable's throat like a surface-to-air missile. She squirms and gags, but I hold her steady, making damn sure she swallows every last drop like it's the antidote to a poison she just drank.

"Fuuuuuck yes, drink that shit down like mother's milk, you nasty little semen demon. Ungh, fuck!"

"LUCIAN!" I nearly jump out of my skin, falling off the couch in a tangle of limbs and a flying pizza box. I look around, disoriented, and see Sable and Emily staring at me with confusion, amusement, and annoyance.

It was a dream—a messed-up fever dream that my brain decided to conjure up. I quickly scramble to my feet, brushing pizza crumbs off my chest and trying to play it cool (spoiler alert: I'm failing miserably).

Emily, looking annoyed, "You ate all the damn pizza? We leave for thirty minutes, and you manage to inhale an entire pizza like some black hole with a tapeworm?"

Sable, giggling and eyeing me, "Looks like someone was having a nice little dream." Her eyes twinkle with mischief. "Secret's out, Lucian. We heard what you were saying in your sleep. My, my, you have quite a vocabulary, don't you? Semen Demon, huh?"

I stammer, embarrassed. "Uh... sorry. I was hungry. You know how it is, you start eating, and then suddenly, the whole pizza is gone, and you're left wondering what the hell just happened, like some food-induced blackout."

I am internally screaming, trying to shake the image of the dream out of my head. This is so damn embarrassing. My brain decided to take a vacation without telling the rest of me. And now I'm standing here trying to play it off like I didn't just have the most vivid, messed-up dream of my entire afterlife.

Emily rolls her eyes. "Hungry for what, exactly? Because from what we heard, it sure as hell wasn't pizza you were craving."

Sable giggles, "Yeah, unless that's some kind of new pizza topping I've never heard of."

I sigh, rubbing my temples. "Can we please just pretend like this never happened? I'm begging you, I'll do anything. I'll buy you both a pony if you let me live this down."

Emily smirks, "A pony? What are we, twelve? If you really want us to forget about your little sleep-talking session, about us no less—you'll have to do better than that."

Sable nods in agreement, "Yeah, I'm thinking more of a lifetime supply of chocolate and a foot massage whenever we want."

I sigh, resigned to my fate. "Fine, fine, whatever. I'll buy you all the chocolate in the world and rub your feet until my hands fall off. Just please, for the love of all that is holy, never mention this again."

Emily and Sable exchange a look. "Deal. But know that we'll never let you live this down. You're officially the pervert of the group now."

The girls leave and go to bed, and I flop back down on the couch.

I still can't shake the image of that mystery brunette. It's like she's burned into my retinas, haunting me.

Frustration consumes me. I swear, if this is some cosmic joke, I'm not laughing. The universe needs to quit messing with me and give me some answers before I lose what's left of my already messed-up mind.

I groan, rubbing my temples. My brain is stuck on this chick like a broken record. Those golden eyes, that sun-kissed skin—it's like she's haunting me, taunting me from the depths of my psyche.

I sigh heavily as I try to calm down. I take a few deep breaths and attempt to will myself back into submission. But Little Lucian is having none of it.

I mean, can you really blame me? After that wet dream, it's a goddamn miracle I haven't painted the ceiling yet. I let out a shaky breath, frustrated as hell. Part of me wants to say screw it, spank the monkey in shame—consequences be damned. But the tiny rational part of my brain that's still functioning knows that's a terrible fucking idea.

So, with a heavy heart, I try to ignore it and focus on the cooking show still droning on in the background.

But it's no use. I can only think about the mystery brunette.

Fuck, I need a drink. Or ten. Maybe if I get blackout drunk, I'll forget about this dream girl for a little while. One can only hope.

DANICA

19

I wake up to a world of pain, my face feeling like it's been used as a punching bag by a heavyweight champion. That red-haired bastard really did a number on me. As I slowly sit up, gingerly touching my face, I realize my nose is definitely broken. I feel like I've been run over by a truck, backed up on, and then run over again for good measure.

Defeated and disoriented, I survey my surroundings. I'm in a room on a ship, but it's unlike any ship's quarters I've ever seen. The room is surprisingly spacious, with ornate wooden panels lining the walls. A large, intricately carved desk sits in the corner, its surface covered with maps, charts, and various navigational instruments. The bed I'm sitting on is a grand four-poster affair draped with rich, velvety curtains in deep shades of red and gold. Plush carpets cover the floor. It's all opulent and luxurious, a far cry from what I would expect on a pirate ship.

Suddenly, the door swings open, and in walks the red-haired asshole himself, a smug grin plastered across his face. "Well, well, well, look who's finally come 'round," he drawls, his voice dripping with mock concern. "Three days—You took quite a beating there, lass."

Three days?

I jump up from the bed, ready to give him a piece of my mind, but immediately regret it as the room starts spinning like a carnival ride. I stumble, grabbing onto the bedpost for support.

"Sit down," he barks, his tone sharp. "Yer in no condition to be movin' about just yet."

I shoot him a nasty glare, my anger rising. "Yeah, well, your face is killing me. Whoever pummeled it must've taken pride in their work because you're rocking that Pug look hard. Did you pay extra for that, or was it a special 'beat me senseless' discount?"

He huffs and begins to pour himself a drink.

"Who are you, and what do you want with me?" I seethe, with contempt.

He only smirks, like he's enjoying some private joke at my expense. "Captain Bloodbane at yer service," he says with a mock bow. "Ye be sailin' with the Crimson Brotherhood now, lass."

Oh, yeah, that just clears everything right up, doesn't it? He finally parks his ass in a chair, leaning forward like he's about to share some juicy gossip.

"Now, let's get down to business, shall we?" he says, his eyes gleaming with malice and amusement that makes my skin crawl. "I've got big plans for ye, lass. It seems the sea witch has caught wind of yer arrival, and she's just dyin' to have a little chat with ye."

I feel my blood turn to ice at the mention of the sea witch. Well, shit. This can't be good.

"She's put a nice bounty on ye, and I intend to deliver." he finishes.

I have no idea what this crazy bastard has in store for me, but one thing's for damn sure—I'm not going down without a fight. I may be bruised and battered, but I'm far from broken. If this red-haired asshole thinks he can use me as a pawn in his twisted little game of chess, he's got another thing coming.

I lean forward, meeting his gaze with a defiant glare of my own. "Listen up, Captain Douchebag, I don't know what kind of sick, twisted plan you've got cooking up in that pea-sized brain of yours, but let me make one thing crystal clear: I'm nobody's puppet—you want to dance with the sea witch? Be my guest. But leave me out of it."

He laughs, the sound grating on my nerves. "Ye don't have a choice, lass. The sea witch wants ye, and what the sea witch wants, the sea witch gets."

I instinctively reach out to Rhyland through our bond, my mind desperately seeking his comforting presence. The moment his voice rumbles inside my head, I jolt a little, the whiplash of his immediate response catching me off guard.

"Thank the gods... Where are you? Are you okay?" His words are laced with consern, and I can feel the tension radiating through our connection.

I almost melt at the sound of his voice. The relief of still having him with me, even if not physically, is overwhelming. *"I'm on a ship with this Bloodbane asshole,"*

I spit back, my anger and frustration boiling over. *"No clue where we are, nautically speaking."*

"Okay, just hold on, baby. I'm right behind you. I'm with Gideon, and we're coming to get you. Just hang in there, sweetheart." His words are a lifeline, a promise of salvation in this hellish situation.

Thank Jesus! It's about damn time. I thought I'd have to stage a one-woman jailbreak on this floating cesspool.

"What's taking so long? I've been knocked out for three days, Rhyland. Three. Days." I push back, my frustration getting the better of me. I know it's not his fault, but damn it, I hate being the damsel in distress.

Rhyland sounds weary, like he's been running on fumes and caffeine for the past seventy-two hours. *"We've had nothing but issues keeping up with Bloodbane's ship, baby. I think the sea witch knows we're coming and is messing with the tides just to screw with us."*

Oh, well, that's just great. Not only do I have to deal with Captain Asshat and his merry band of dickwads, but now the sea witch is hell-bent on keeping me on course—sticking her crusty tentacles in the way.

I sigh, my anger deflating like a popped balloon. I know he's doing everything he can, and it's unfair of me to take my frustrations out on him. *"I'm scared...I don't know what this witch wants with me, but I doubt it's for a tea party and girl talk."*

"I know, baby. But you're strong, stronger than you even know. You can handle whatever that sea hag throws at you. And I'll be there soon, I swear it. I love you, Dani. More than anything in this world or any other."

I feel tears prickling at the corners of my eyes, but I blink them back. I can't afford to fall apart now, not when I need to be strong. *"I love you too, Rhyland. Now hurry up and get your sexy Viking ass over here before I have to start cracking skulls on my own."*

Rhyland chuckles, the sound warm and comforting even through the bond. *"That's my girl."*

"So, lass, what'll it be? You going to come nicely, or do I need to chain ye to the bed until we arrive at Blood Reef?" The captain's words are a harsh reminder of my current predicament.

Blood Reef? Where the hell is that?

"He's taking me to Blood Reef, Rhyland," I quickly shoot down the bond, my mind racing with the implications of this new information.

I can feel Rhyland's anger and determination surging through our connection, a palpable force threatening to consume me. *"I am going to rip that motherfucker apart for laying a finger on you. Just hold on.*

I take a deep breath, trying to steady myself. I know Rhyland will move heaven and earth to find me, but I also know I can't just sit here and wait for rescue like some damsel in distress. I have to find a way to fight back, to buy time until help arrives.

I look up at Bloodbane, my eyes narrowing with defiance. "I'll come nicely. But if you think for one second that I'm going to make this easy for you, you've got another thing coming, asshole."

The captain smirks, his eyes glinting with cruel amusement. "We'll see about that, lass. We'll see."

"Where the hell is this Blood Reef?" I ask, trying to keep the fear out of my voice. I've never heard of the place, but if it's where Bloodbane is taking me, I doubt it's some tropical paradise with fruity cocktails and cabana boys.

Bloodbane grins, the expression more predatory than amused. "It be another day or two's sail from here, lass. Blood Reef is a hidden an' treacherous place, surrounded by jagged rocks an' fierce currents that make it near-impenetrable to those who don't know the safe passages."

He leans forward, his eyes glinting with a cruel sort of glee. "It be the perfect hideout for pirates, smugglers, an' other unsavory types. The waters 'round the reef have an eerie red hue..." The captain's voice drops to a conspiratorial whisper. "Legend has it that the red tinge be the blood of all the poor souls who met their end on them jagged rocks. The reef claims lives like a thirsty beast, always lurkin', waitin' for its next victim."

I try to push down the rising sense of dread in my gut. Blood Reef sounds like the pirate equivalent of a supervillain's secret lair. And if it's as hard to get to as he claims, Rhyland will have a hell of a time trying to rescue me.

"Once we reach the reef," Bloodbane continues, "we'll make our way to the hidden cove known as Pirate's Haven. It be a bustlin' den of thieves an' cutthroats where anythin' can be bought or sold for the right price." He gives me a knowing look.

"An' at the heart of it all lies the Blood Reef Black Market, a wretched hive of scum an' villainy where the most notorious pirates in all the realm come to trade their ill-gotten gains."

I swallow hard, my mouth suddenly dry. This just keeps getting better and better. Not only am I being dragged to some godforsaken pirate stronghold, but I'm also going to be paraded through a black market like a prize heifer at the county fair.

But I'll be damned if I'm going to let this bastard see me sweat. "Sounds like a real charming place. I can't wait to see the tourist brochures. 'Come to Blood Reef, where the water's red and the pirates are plenty!'"

Bloodbane throws his head back and laughs, "Oh, you've got spirit, lass. I'll give ye that. But trust me, by the time the sea witch is done with ye, you'll be beggin' for the sweet release of death."

I clench my jaw. *Like hell I will.*

With that, he leaves me, bolting the door behind him like he's locking up a prized possession. I let out a breath I didn't realize I was holding, the air rushing out of me like a deflating balloon. I lunge for the window, my heart pounding in my chest, hoping against hope that I'll see anything that will give me a clue as to where the hell we are. But all I see is an endless expanse of black seas, stretching out as far as the eye can see.

My face hurts—my body weak. I start to panic as I realize that my powers are still nowhere to be found.

I spot a glass pitcher with water on the table and make a beeline for it, chugging it down like it's the elixir of life. As the cool liquid slides down my throat, the gypsy's message comes back to me. She said my powers weren't stolen, only blocked, and I had to believe in myself to get them back.

I scoff, rolling my eyes. *It can't be that simple, can it?*

What choice do I have, though? I trudge back to the bed and plop down, crossing my legs in a meditation pose. I close my eyes, trying to block out the throbbing pain in my face and the constant rocking of the ship. I focus on my powers and how they first manifested when Rhyland awoke them with his love and devotion. I think about how it feels when that wellspring of energy sits just below the surface, waiting for me to tap into it.

But as I sit here, trying to will my powers back into existence, I realize something is missing. It's not just about Rhyland or the love we share. It's about me, about who

I am at my core. I've been so focused on everyone else—on Rhyland, the prophecy, saving the realms—that I've forgotten to focus on myself.

I take a deep breath, letting it out slowly as I dig deep. I think about all the challenges I've faced and all the obstacles I've overcome. I think about the strength and resilience that have gotten me this far, the sheer stubborn determination that refuses to let me give up.

Focusing on that inner fire, I feel a flicker of something deep inside me. It's small at first, barely noticeable, but it grows as I nurture it with my thoughts and emotions. I think about my love for Rhyland and the unbreakable bond we share. I think about my friends, newfound family, and everyone counting on me to succeed.

But most of all, I think about myself—about the fierce, sassy, take-no-shit woman I am. I am Danica Pierce, and some witch-bitch will not take away what I am at my core.

As that thought crystallizes in my mind, I feel a sudden rush of energy, like a dam bursting inside me. My powers come roaring back to life, flooding my veins like liquid fire. The cabin is suddenly awash in a blinding golden light emanating from my skin.

My body, which had felt so weak just moments before, thrums with energy. I feel alive, every nerve ending firing with renewed purpose. It's like I've been plugged into a cosmic power source, my batteries recharged and ready to take on the world.

I open my eyes, a slow smile spreading across my face as I feel the familiar hum of power coursing through me. Oh, it is on now. Captain Bloodbane and his crew have no idea what they're in for.

I jump up and head for the door, ready to unleash holy hell on these bastards, but something stops me. I glimpse myself in the mirror hanging on the wall, and I can't help but stare at the sight that greets me.

I watch, transfixed, as my body weaves itself back together, like a tapestry of flesh and bone being stitched back into place by an invisible needle. It's like watching a time-lapse video of a flower blooming in reverse, the damage and bruising giving way to new life and vitality.

My nose, which had been throbbing with pain just moments before, instantly heals, the bones shifting and realigning with a sickening crack that would have made me cringe if it didn't feel so damn good. It's like someone hit the reset button on my face, erasing all evidence of the beating I took at the hands of this asshole.

The bruises that mottled my skin, turning it a sickening shade of purple and blue, fade away like watercolors in the rain. It's like watching a masterpiece painted in reverse, the colors bleeding away to reveal the unblemished canvas beneath.

I can't help but reach up and touch my face, half-expecting to feel the swelling and tenderness still there. But my skin is smooth and cool.

It's the most surreal thing I've ever experienced, and that's saying something, considering the crazy stuff I've seen since meeting Rhyland. But this? I've always wondered how the Atherite stone would work on me—this is some next-level healing mojo, and I'm here for it. I can't help but giggle, the sound bubbling up from my throat like champagne.

Feeling rejuvenated and looking like a million bucks again, I stride towards the door, ready to bust out of this floating prison and give Captain Asshat a piece of my mind. I stop short, my hand hovering over the handle as I hear my name being called. It's faint, like a whisper on the wind, but I'd know that voice anywhere.

At first, I think I'm losing my mind, that the stress of being kidnapped and beaten has finally pushed me over the edge. But then I hear it again, a little louder this time, and I know it's not just in my head.

Suddenly, a searing pain rips through my gut, doubling me over like the Hulk has sucker-punched me. It feels like someone's reached inside me and started playing tug-of-war with my intestines. I grit my teeth, trying to breathe through the agony, but it's like trying to inhale through a straw.

What fresh hell is this? Is this some fucked-up side effect from my powers coming back online? If so, I want a goddamn refund.

The pain lashes at me like a whip, tearing through my insides. I collapse to the floor, writhing in pain as the sensation of being torn in two intensifies. It's like my body is trying to rip itself apart from the inside out, and all I can do is scream.

"Stop, stop, stop, please stop!" I chant through gritted teeth. My eyes squeezed shut against the blinding agony.

And then, as if things couldn't get any weirder, a portal rips open above my head. But this one's different from the ones I've conjured. It's like a swirling energy vortex, shimmering and pulsing with an otherworldly light. I can't see what's on the other side, but I can feel it calling me, beckoning me to step through.

The pain ratchets up, and I scream again, my body writhing on the floor. It's like my insides are being liquefied and sucked out through a straw.

"Danica, what's wrong?" Rhyland's voice echoes through our bond. His concern is palpable even through the haze of agony. I can feel him trying to soothe me to counteract the pain that's ripping me apart.

"I—I don't k-know..." I manage to push through my mind, my words barely coherent through the pain.

The vortex swirls faster, the colors blending in a dizzying kaleidoscope. The pain is so intense now that I can barely stand, but somehow, I manage to stagger to my feet, swaying like a drunk after a three-day bender.

"There's a portal... I have to go."

"No! Danica, don't. Stay where you are." Rhyland's voice is desperate, pleading, but I can barely hear him over the roaring in my ears.

I know I should listen to him, that jumping through a mysterious portal while being held captive on a pirate ship is probably the dumbest thing I could do. But the pain is too much, the pull too intense. It's like the portal is calling to me, demanding that I step through, and I'm powerless to resist.

"I'm sorry..."

And then, before I can talk myself out of it, I jump, hurling myself into the swirling vortex of light and color.

"Danica!!" Rhyland's anguished scream is the last thing I hear before the world disappears in a blinding flash of white.

20

G one—just...gone.

The second I feel Dani slip away, it's like a fucking piece of me is torn out, leaving a ragged, gaping hole where my heart used to be. I can't feel her anymore, can't hear her voice in my head, or sense her presence.

I let out a roar of pure, raw rage, the sound ripping from my throat like the snarl of a wounded beast. I have no goddamn clue where she is now, no fucking idea what realm or dimension she's been dragged to. It's just like in the Whispering Woods all over again when she was yanked away from me and hauled off to Atheria.

Is that where she is now? Has she been summoned there again, pulled across the veil by some unseen force?

But then, why was she in so much pain?

"Hold fast, ye mangy dogs! Keep her steady!"

Captain Gideon's shout cuts through my thoughts, dragging me back to the harsh reality of the present. I'm standing on the deck of Sterling's ship, my hands gripping the rough, salt-stained rope that runs along the vessel's side. The sky above is a roiling mass of black clouds, shot through with blinding lightning flashes. The wind screams like a banshee, whipping the sails and driving sheets of icy rain across the deck like damn needles.

But the real danger is the waves. They tower over the ship like goddamn mountains, massive walls of dark water that smash into us with the force of a fucking avalanche. Each impact sends shudders running through the deck beneath my feet, making the timbers groan and creak like they're about to splinter apart.

I'm drenched to the bone, my clothes plastered to my skin, my hair a matted mess—soaked. The taste of salt is heavy on my tongue, mixed with the coppery sting of blood where I've bitten my lip to shreds.

All around me, the crew is scrambling to keep this floating deathtrap from capsizing, their faces tight with fear and grim determination. They cling to the rigging like rats on a sinking ship, bellowing to each other as they fight to reef the sails and batten down the hatches.

"Secure those fucking lines, ye pox-ridden whoresons!" one of the mates roars, his voice barely audible over the shrieking wind. "Heave, damn yer hides! Heave like yer balls are on fire!"

But even as they fight and strain every muscle and sinew to keep the ship on course, I can see the terror in their eyes. They know, just like I fucking do, that this ain't no regular storm. This is the handiwork of that sea bitch, a twisted force of nature that wants nothing more than to suck us down to a watery grave.

As if to hammer that point home, a massive wave crashes over the bow, sending a wall of bone-chilling water slamming into the deck. I hear shrieks, the sound of men being swept overboard and dragged into the churning depths. One poor fucker goes cartwheeling past me, his eyes bulging with horror as he claws desperately for something to grab onto. But there ain't shit to hold, nothing to save him from the gnashing jaws of the sea. He vanishes beneath the waves; his scream is cut off like someone flipped a switch.

"Damn ye, ye black-hearted bitch!" Captain Sterling roars from his place at the helm, his face a mask of fury and defiance. "Ye'll not take me ship, d'ye hear? Ye'll not have me crew!"

He wrestles with the wheel, his muscles straining as he keeps the ship pointed into the wind. But it's a losing battle, and we all know it. The Sea Witch's power is too strong, and her hold over the elements is too powerful.

Another wave slams into the ship's side like a massive, watery fist, the impact shuddering through the deck and rattling my bones. I lose my grip on the salt-crusted rope, my fingers numb and clumsy from the biting cold. My feet slip and slide on the slick, pitching deck, scrabbling for purchase as the world tilts and heaves around me.

For a heart-stopping, gut-clenching moment, I'm certain I'm about to go over. I can see it in my mind's eye, can feel the icy, black waters closing over my head as the hungry depths swallow me whole. I'll sink like a stone, dragged down into the lightless abyss to join the bloated, fish-gnawed corpses of the poor sods who the sea has already claimed.

Just as I'm about to pitch headfirst over the railing, a strong hand clamps down on my arm like a vice. I'm yanked back from the brink with enough force to make my shoulder scream in protest, my feet scrambling to find solid footing on the heaving deck.

I look up, blinking, stinging salt water from my eyes, to see Erik looming over me like a drowned rat. His silver hair is plastered to his skull in dark, snaky tendrils, his chiseled features twisted into a mask of grim determination. The howling wind snatches at his clothes, making the sodden fabric snap and flutter like a tattered banner.

"On your feet, brother," his voice barely audible over the shrieking gale. "We're not dead yet, and I am not about to let this bitch of a storm claim us now."

I nod, my jaw clenched so tight I feel my teeth grinding together. The taste of salt and blood is thick on my tongue, the copper-bright tang of it mingling with the acrid burn of bile at the back of my throat. My muscles scream in protest as I haul myself upright, every fiber aching with the strain of fighting against the storm's fury.

But Erik is right. We're not dead, not yet. And as long as there's a single spark of life left in my battered, beaten body, I won't let this fucking tempest win.

The storm rages on for what feels like a fucking eternity, each minute stretching out into an endless nightmare of howling wind and crashing waves. By the time the tides finally settle and the clouds break apart to reveal the sun, I'm so goddamn exhausted I can barely stand.

I collapse onto the deck, my chest heaving. My muscles are screaming, my lungs burning from fighting against the relentless onslaught of the sea.

This has been our reality ever since we set sail. Every day, a new battle against the Dark Tides threatens to drag us down into the Sea Witch's clutches. But Gideon and his ship have held firm, refusing to bow to the bitch's fury.

I glance up as the captain approaches, his face grim beneath his salt-stained beard. "Aye, mate," he growls, his voice rough with exhaustion. "We've been blown off course again, set adrift by that wretched hag's black magic. But never fear, I'll set us right."

"They are heading to Blood Reef," I choke out, my throat raw and aching. "That bastard Bloodbane."

Gideon pales for a moment, his weathered face going slack with shock. But he quickly rights himself, squaring his shoulders and setting his jaw. "Aye," he says, then turns on his heel and strides away, barking orders to his battered crew.

But even as he goes, I can feel the icy claws of despair sinking into my gut because Dani's not on Bloodbane's ship anymore, not even in this realm. I can feel it in my bones, the sickening certainty that she's been ripped away from me once again, dragged through some portal to God knows where.

And I have no clue what to do, how to get her back, or even if we should still chase after that traitorous prick Bloodbane.

Erik helps me to my feet, his legs unsteady beneath him. His silver eyes are as cold and hard as ever, his jaw set with grim determination. "You alright, brother?"

I nod, then stand on wobbly legs, the deck shifting beneath my feet. "Dani," I rasp out, my voice barely above a whisper. "She... she went through a portal. I felt it, felt her agony as it ripped through me like a blade. It was just like before when she was taken to Atheria."

Erik's eyes widen, a flicker of shock and dread passing over his stoic features. "Atheria?" he echoes, his voice tight with disbelief. "Again?"

I shake my head, my gut twisting with fear and frustration. "I don't know," I admit, the words bitter on my tongue. "This... this felt different, somehow. Like she was being pulled somewhere else, somewhere even further away."

Before Erik can respond, a familiar figure slinks into view. Izabelle's tight outfit clings to her curves, her dark hair hanging in wild, dripping tangles around her face.

It takes every ounce of self-control I have not to lunge at her, to wrap my hands around her slender throat and squeeze until her lying tongue turns black and her treacherous eyes bulge from their sockets.

I nearly did that when we boarded the ship and found her hiding among the crew. The only thing that stayed my hand was Gideon's intervention, his fierce insistence that we needed every able-bodied pirate we could get if we had a chance of weathering Bloodbane and his crew.

But now, with Dani gone and my heart shattered, I can feel the leash on my rage fraying with every passing second.

"The fuck do you want, you two-faced bitch?" I snarl.

Izabelle smirks, her full lips curving in a wicked, taunting smile. "Ooh, someone's got a fiery spirit!" she coos, her words as smooth as silk and just as deceptive. "Now, is that any way to address a fine lady such as meself? The Captain's requestin' the pleasure of your company, along with that charmin' companion of yours," her voice a compelling mix of arrogance and allure. "Best not be keepin' him waitin', my dears. Savvy?"

I step forward, my hands balling into fists at my sides. "You're no lady," I growl, my voice low and deadly. "You're a backstabbing cunt who sold out my mate because you're a jealous bitch and to save your own hide."

Izabelle's eyes flash with anger, her smug facade cracking momentarily. But she quickly regains her composure, tossing her head and letting out a throaty little laugh. "Psh, don't be givin' me that injured pride act, sailor'," she scoffs, her hand cutting through the air with a dismissive flourish. "You and I both know you'd have done the exact same thing if our roles were reversed, so let's not pretend otherwise, eh?"

I open my mouth to tell her exactly where she can shove her assumptions, but Erik cuts me off with a sharp look. "Enough," his voice cold and hard as steel. "We have no time for these petty squabbles. Izabelle, you said we were wanted in the captain's quarters?"

The pirate whore nods, her smirk widening. "Aye, that's the truth of it, me fine, strapping lad," she purrs, her gaze unabashedly roaming over Erik's chiseled physique, desire smoldering in her eyes. "The Captain's given his orders, and he wants to lay eyes on the both of you. Now."

"Go fuck yourself," I tell her.

Izabelle's smirk widens, her eyes glittering with malicious amusement. But she saunters away without another word, her hips swaying in a way that makes me want to retch.

We enter Gideon's quarters, freshly cleaned and dressed in dry clothes. The captain offers us rum, and I down two glasses before refilling a third. The burn of the alcohol is a welcome distraction from the icy knot of fear and rage in my gut.

Erik sits quietly beside me, nursing his glass with a grim expression. He hasn't said a word since we left the deck, but I can feel the tension radiating off him.

Gideon clears his throat, explaining the significance of Blood Reef and how it's notorious as a hub for illegal trade and underhanded dealings. The perfect place for a traitorous fuck like Bloodbane to offload valuable merchandise.

Like my mate—My Angel.

I tighten my grip on the glass, "She's gone," I grit out, the words tasting like ash. "Dani. She... she went through some portal. I felt it, felt her agony as it ripped through me like a knife to the heart."

Gideon's brow furrows in confusion. "A portal?" he echoes, leaning forward. "To where? And why?"

I shake my head, frustration and helplessness warring in my chest. "I don't know," I admit bitterly. "All I know is that she's not on his ship anymore or in this realm. She's... somewhere else entirely."

Gideon sits back, stroking his beard. "Well, that certainly complicates matters," he muses. "If the lass isn't even in Aquaria anymore, chasing after Bloodbane might be naught but a wild goose chase."

I nod stiffly. As much as it galls me to admit it, the captain is right. We could waste precious time and resources pursuing a dead end without knowing where Dani is or how to get to her.

But the thought of just sitting on my ass and waiting, of doing nothing while my mate is out there somewhere, alone and in pain... it's enough to make my blood boil.

Erik must sense my growing agitation because he leans forward and places a calming hand on my shoulder. "Brother," he says softly. "I know it's hard, but we must be smart about this. We can't help Danica if we go off half-cocked and get ourselves killed."

I take a deep breath, forcing myself to unclench my jaw and loosen my grip on the glass. He's right, damn him. As much as every fiber of my being is screaming at me to act, I know that rushing in blind is a surefire way to get us all killed.

And that won't do Dani any good at all.

I take another swig of rum, letting the burn ground me in the present. I turn to Gideon, "We wait," I say, the words tasting like bile. "As much as it kills me to say it... we wait. Dani is strong, and our bond is unbreakable. She'll find her way back to me, one way or another. And when she does..."

I let the sentence hang, the unspoken promise of violence and retribution heavy in the air.

Gideon nods, his eyes glinting with understanding and approval. "Aye," he says, raising his glass in a silent toast. "We wait. And we make damn sure we're ready for whatever storm is brewing on the horizon."

I nod, clinking my glass against his before downing the contents in one long, burning swallow. The rum sears a fiery path down my throat, but it's nothing compared to the inferno raging in my heart.

I can't lose myself this time. I have to stay strong and keep my head on straight.

Come back to me, baby, I think fiercely, my eyes slipping closed as I send the thought out into the ether across the vast expanse of realms and dimensions that separate us.

DANICA

21

I slam onto the hard floor like a sack of potatoes, the impact reverberating through my bones. Pain radiates through every inch of my body, and for a moment, I'm sure I've broken something important, like my spine or my dignity.

I lay there, gasping for air, trying to will the world to stop spinning.

What the hell was that?

One minute I'm on Captain Douchbag's ship, the next, I'm being sucked through a portal like Alice down the rabbit hole, only instead of Wonderland, I've ended up in hell.

Nausea rolls through me in waves, and I swallow hard, fighting the urge to puke.

Once my breathing is under control, I look around, trying to get my bearings.

Holy shit, I'm in my apartment.

How did I get here? I slowly stand, my head spinning. I'm about to start questioning my sanity when I hear the front door open, and in walks Lucian, carrying groceries like he's just returned from a Sunday stroll.

I stand there, stunned, my mouth hanging open. It takes me a moment to remember how to speak. "Lucian?"

Even to my own ears, I sound unsure, like I'm not entirely convinced he's really there.

How did he get free? How long have I been gone?

He glances up at me, and the grocery bag slips from his hands, spilling its contents all over the floor. Milk splatters everywhere, and I'm pretty sure I hear the crunch of broken eggs. But Lucian doesn't seem to notice; his eyes lock on me like he's seeing a ghost.

"How?" is all I manage to get out before he's on me in a blur of motion, moving so fast I can barely track him. The next thing I know, my back is against the wall, and he's all up in my personal space, his face inches from mine.

"You..." he breathes, his voice barely above a whisper. He's looking at me like I'm some enigma he can't quite figure out—like a puzzle missing a few pieces.

Finally gathering my wits, I snap, "Yes, it's me, you idiot. Now back up and explain to me how—"

But he cuts me off, burying his face in my neck and inhaling deeply, his lips barely grazing my skin. "Why do you smell so good? You smell like..." He takes another deep breath, his nose skimming along my collarbone. "Like caramel candy, like Willy Wonka's chocolate factory, like..." He licks up my neck, and I can't suppress the shiver that runs through me. "Like I want to eat you alive."

I push at his chest to create distance between us, but it's like trying to move a brick wall. "Lucian, get off me. What the hell is wrong with you?" I demand, my voice sharp with annoyance.

"I smell something else—familiar, like a part of me, somehow. Are you mine?"

I look at him like he's lost his damn mind. He's smelling his blood, the unwanted parasite still coursing through my veins. "Yeah, jackass, it's *your* blood. Remember?" I snap, rolling my eyes. "And no, I'm not yours. I'm Rhyland's—your brother. Ring any bells?"

He shakes his head and chuckles, the sound dark and dangerous. "Nope. Sure don't. My memory's been wiped cleaner than a baby's ass, and right now, I don't give a flying fuck about any of that. All I want is to taste you, Dream Girl."

His fangs slide out, sharp and gleaming, and his brown eyes glaze with hunger. *Oh, shit.*

That witch wiped Lucian's memory. Fabulous—just wonderful. As if dealing with Lucian on a regular basis wasn't enough of a pain in the ass, now I've got to deal with an amnesiac version of him? This is just peachy, really. I'm sure this will end well for everyone involved.

This is a whole new level of fucked up.

He's still got me pressed up against the wall, his body molded to mine in a way that's far too intimate for my liking. I can't blast his ass across the room, not without my blood in his system, so I need to talk him down—to get through to him somehow.

"Okay, okay... let's take a step back and talk—you don't remember anything?" I ask, trying to keep my voice calm and even. "You don't know who I am?"

"You've been sneakily starring in all my naughty dreams—my private backstage fantasies." His big brown puppy dog eyes meet mine. "And let's just skip the chit-chat, Dream Girl. What I *really* want is to sample every delectable inch of you, get up close and personal with that sweet neck of yours, and drink until I've had my fill."

His words send a bolt of fear through me, but there's something else, too—something I really don't want to examine too closely. Lucian fantasizing and dreaming about me is just what I need.

Great, he's got a death wish and is dragging me along for the ride.

Now he's looking at me like I'm a feast laid out just for him, his eyes dark with hunger and desire.

I try to push him away again, but it's like trying to move a mountain. "Lucian, please, you don't want to do this. This isn't you," I plead, my voice trembling despite my efforts to keep it steady.

But he's not listening. His lips trail down my neck, his fangs grazing my skin. "Just one little nibble...it's all I need, beautiful."

For the love of all that is *HOLY.* Maybe one bite will be okay; that way, he's protected from my light, and then I can blast him into next fucking week. I shouldn't even consider this, but Lucian is far gone and isn't budging.

Rhyland is going to kill me. And then resurrect me just to kill me again.

I shudder, and then, with a gentleness that catches me completely off guard, he sinks his fangs into my neck, piercing my skin like it's made of butter. I gasp, my hands fisting in his shirt as a tidal wave of sensation crashes over me. This is wrong on so many levels, like, we're talking "invading Russia in the winter" levels of wrong here. But it's Lucian; he needs my blood so I don't accidentally fry him like a chicken nugget with my powers. Still, this isn't right. He shouldn't be doing this, and I sure as hell shouldn't be allowing it.

But here we are, in a situation that's about as comfortable as a cactus in a Speedo, and I'm letting him drink from me like I'm a walking, talking juice box. I mean, I get it; he's not in his right mind, and I don't want to hurt him. I feel like I'm in some twisted vampire soap opera, and I'm the unwitting heroine who's about to get swept off her feet by the smart-ass, amnesiac vampire brother to my mate.

UGH.

I stand still, just waiting for him to get enough to return to his senses. But then I feel his venom seep into my bloodstream, and knowing Lucian and how *generous* he is, he's giving me a triple dose, the bastard. I can feel it seeping in, spreading through my veins like wildfire—my body instantly limp, my knees and legs giving out under my weight. But Lucian only holds me tighter against him, cradling me like I'm something precious, something to be cherished.

My mind is screaming at me to push him away, to put an end to this before it goes any further—my body betrays me. The sensation of his fangs in my neck, the feeling of his lips on my skin... it's doing things to me that I don't want to think about. Damn vampire venom, turning me into a puddle of goo when I should be focused on getting out of this situation.

My body ignites, heat coursing through my veins as my core tightens—courtesy of his venom. It's like I've just been injected with a supercharged dose of desire. My arousal skyrockets, and I can't help but reach up, tangling my fingers in his hair and curling it around my hand, practically begging him to keep going.

He moans into my neck, the vibration shooting down my spine like an electric current. *"Sweet merciful chimichangas, you taste like heaven dipped in sunshine and a tall glass of lemonade— I can smell your arousal—I can't freaking stop,"* he groans, his voice bouncing around my brain like a pinball on a sugar high.

I can't move, trapped like a fly in a spider's web under the onslaught of his bite, his venom turning my limbs to jelly. His teeth sink deeper, and he pulls harder at my blood, drinking me down like I'm the finest vintage. My hands fall to my sides, useless and limp, as he continues to hold me to him, his body molded to mine.

I can feel him getting hard, his dick pressing against my stomach as he grinds into me, his hips moving in a slow, sensual rhythm that makes me want to scream. This is wrong, so wrong, but my body doesn't seem to care, responding to his touch like a flower turning towards the sun.

I try to gather my thoughts, to focus on anything but the pleasure coursing through me, but it's like trying to catch smoke with my bare hands.

I can't seem to make myself move or find the strength to push him away—I'm frozen in place, caught between the horror of what's happening and the undeniable pleasure of his bite. I'm pretty sure this is what going mad feels like, and I'm not a fan.

Then my vision darkens, like the lights going out at the end of a terrible play. My body grows weaker with each pull on my neck, and I'm entirely limp in his arms now. He holds me up, cradling my head with one hand and wrapping his strong arm around my back, trapping me against him.

He's taking too much.

"Lucian..." I whisper, or at least I think I do. My voice is barely a breath as my body is being drained dry. "S-stop." That's all I can manage, and it's about as effective as yelling at a hurricane to calm down.

He doesn't stop. If anything, his grip tightens, and he sucks harder, like he's trying to draw every last drop of me into him. His moaning grows more intense, vibrating against my skin, and I know he's completely lost to the bloodlust. He doesn't recognize me, doesn't realize why my blood is driving him crazy, and now my fear is kicking into overdrive. My brain is screaming at me to fight, to run—to do anything to get away, but my body isn't listening. It's like I'm a puppet, and the strings have been cut.

"Luc-ian...p-please," I try one last time, but my eyes flutter shut, and I feel the darkness taking over. I'm teetering on the brink of unconsciousness, my heartbeat slowing in my ears like a dying drumbeat. My body's failing me, and all I can do is pray that something snaps him out of this before it's too late.

I fall into the black oblivion, my eyes shutting as I can only pray for a miracle. I don't know how long I drift in that abyss, but the next sensation piercing the darkness is the taste of sweet and bitter copper on my tongue. Slowly, I open my eyes to find Lucian staring down at me, worry and fear etched in his big brown eyes. His wrist is pressed against my mouth, and the realization hits me like a freight train.

"I'm sorry," he whispers with regret in his eyes.

Oh, no... no... no. Not again. As his blood drips down my throat, I can feel my strength slowly returning, the darkness receding with each swallow. But my body still isn't listening to anything my brain is trying to tell it.

Lucian's eyes soften with relief. He rips his wrist away from my mouth. Before I can muster the energy to say anything, his lips crash into mine, kissing me with wild abandon.

It's a kiss that demands everything and offers no room for argument.

It's overwhelming, the blend of our blood still fresh on his lips, the residual power of his venom coursing through my veins, making everything feel heightened, more intense. His hands are everywhere, cradling my head, gripping my waist, pulling me closer as if he's afraid I'll disappear if he lets go.

His tongue, soft, spongy, and warm, slowly flicks against mine, and I can't help but respond, thrusting back with need—the venom still a massive factor in my body's betrayal. Each stroke of his tongue against mine sends shivers down my spine, igniting a fire within me that makes it impossible not to kiss him back, matching his rhythm with increasing fervor.

His actions become urgent as if he can hear my thoughts, and his fierce possessiveness borders on feral. And yet, beneath it all, there's a gentleness, a softness that speaks of something deeper, something more.

Just then, he jerkingly rears back like a puppet on a string, his neck twisting to the side with a sickening crack that churns my stomach. He slumps to the floor, and I follow, my legs and limbs useless.

My blood trickles down my neck in a sticky stream, a dreadful reminder of what just happened.

"Danica!" a voice I'd know anywhere screeches from the other side of the room. "Jesus fuck, I'm so sorry."

Emily rushes over, helping me off the floor with Sable on my other side. They practically carry me to the couch, where I slump down like a ragdoll. Sable dashes to the kitchen and returns quickly, pressing a wet dish towel to my neck.

I crane my neck around Emily to get a look at Lucian's lifeless body sprawled on the floor. "Is he... dead?" I croak.

I know I shouldn't be worried about that asshat right now, but I can't help it. I don't want him dead, even if he did try to drain me.

"Hell no. Just taking a nice long timeout," Emily snaps. "Shit, girl. I'm so fucking sorry he did that to you. I didn't think it would actually work."

Sable chimes in, her voice a mixture of 'no shit' and awe. "It worked, Emily."

I look back and forth between them, my confusion and annoyance growing by the second. "*What* worked? What the hell are you two talking about?"

Emily gives me a look that's a cross between sheepish and 'please don't kill me.' "We sort of... summoned you here. With a spell."

I blink. Once. Twice. Three times. "You did *what* now?"

"We summoned you," Sable explains, her voice gentle like talking to a spooked horse. "We were trying to find a way to get you back—we had no idea where you went, so we found this spell—"

"And you thought, hey, let's just give it a whirl and see what happens?" I ask, my tone sharp, with venom. "Did it not occur to you that maybe, just maybe, fucking with magic you don't understand could be a bad idea?"

Emily rolls her eyes. "Oh, don't give me that shit. We were trying to help you. And it worked, didn't it? You're here, aren't you?"

I let out a humorless laugh. "Yeah, I'm here. And so is Lucian, who just tried to turn me into a fucking Bloody Mary—Thanks for that, by the way."

Sable winces, her face a picture of guilt. "We didn't know that would happen, Dani. Lucian was gone, and we didn't think..."

I sigh, the anger draining from me as quickly as it came. I know they were trying to help, even if their methods were questionable at best. The fact that she got me out of Bloodbane's bullshit is a relief. "I know, Sable. I'm sorry. I'm just... I'm fucking exhausted, and this whole situation is just..."

"Fucked up?" Emily supplies helpfully.

"Yeah. Fucked up. Do you have any idea what that damn summons did to me? It felt like someone was trying to rip my insides out through my ass. Not exactly a pleasant experience, let me tell you."

Emily and Sable exchange a look of 'Oh shit.' Emily drops to her knees in front of me, her expression of guilt and apology. "I'm sorry, hun. We just thought..." She struggles for a moment, trying to find the right words. "Look, I'm new to this whole witchy shit, okay? We had no idea where you jetted off to. We were worried, and I-I don't know...I thought having you here could help with Lucian's issues—I'm tired of babysitting the vampire toddler."

I raise an eyebrow at her, clearly conveying how unimpressed I am with her explanation. "So, let me get this straight. You thought you'd just, what, summon me here like a friggin genie in a bottle, get me to fix Lucian's scrambled egg brain? Did it not occur to you that maybe, just maybe, I might have some objections to being yanked across dimensions like a goddamn yo-yo?"

Sable winces, "We didn't think it through—"

"Wait. What do you mean you're new to this witchy shit?" I snap, glaring pointedly at her. "Emily, you're no witch. Sable, yes. But you? Since when did you decide to enroll in the Hogwarts School of Witchcraft and Wizardry?"

They both exchange a look, "That's the other thing we summoned you here for..."

"So, let me see if I understand this." I lean back, trying to make sense of the wild story Emily and Sable have dropped on me. "You guys rescued Lucian from Azrael and Paige, and in the middle of all this chaos, Emily suddenly turned into Supergirl—with fire powers and who knows what else?"

Emily grins, clearly enjoying her newfound abilities. "Yep, pretty much. Who knew that biting the dust would come with such kickass perks?"

I roll my eyes but can't hide my intrigue. "And how exactly did this magical transformation happen?"

Sable clears her throat, her voice steady. "I've been doing some digging and talked to my Grandma. She believes you somehow siphoned all the witch's magic into Emily."

The memory of that night rushes back like a tidal wave. Emily, dead on the grass, her body a charred mess, and the haunting screams of the witches I roasted still echoing in my head. "So you're telling me that when I brought Emily back from the dead, she absorbed the powers of those witches?"

Sable nods, sipping her coffee. "Precisely. Normally, when a witch dies, her power returns to the Earth, creating a balance. But when you resurrected Emily, their powers went into her instead of dispersing back to the Earth. It's kind of like a supernatural shortcut. At least, that's my theory."

I sit here, my mind reeling as I process this bombshell. "This is insane. I thought witches were just humans with the power of chanting."

Sable shakes her head, a patient smile on her face. "It's more than that," she clarifies. "Power runs through bloodlines. No one can create witches; it has to be through a direct descendant of one of the original witch lines."

I gulp my coffee, the sweet caffeine jumping through my veins. "So, Emily then is a descendant of some long-lost witch?" I ask, my brow furrowing as I attempt to piece together this puzzle.

Sable shrugs, her expression thoughtful. "That is still up for debate—her situation is different as you brought her back from death. We don't know what to make of it."

I lean back on the couch, my mind whirring with possibilities. "Okay, so Emily died. I brought her back to life, and now she has powers that rival Sabrina, the Teenage Witch. And we have no idea if she's related to any witches or if this is just some freaky side effect of resurrection?"

Sable nods, her eyes sparkling with excitement and uncertainty. "That's the gist of it. It's uncharted territory, Dani. We're in the realm of the unknown here."

I shake my head, my eyes wide. "This is some next-level shit."

Emily, who's been uncharacteristically quiet during this exchange, finally pipes up. "Tell me about it. I'm still trying to wrap my head around the fact that I can start fires with my mind. It's like I'm living in a damn X-Men movie."

I turn to her, a grin spreading across my face. "Hey, at least you got a cool origin story from it. Not everyone can say they died and came back with witchy superpowers."

Emily rolls her eyes, but I can see the hint of a smile tugging at her lips. "Yeah, well, I could have done without the whole 'dying' part. That shit was not fun."

I reach over and squeeze her hand, my heart clenching at the memory of her lifeless body. "I know, Em. I'm just glad you're here, powers or no powers."

She squeezes back, her eyes shining with unshed tears. "Me too."

We sit here for a moment, the weight of everything hanging in the air between us. Finally, I break the silence, "Alright, so we've got a lot to figure out. Emily's powers, Lucian's memory, and let's not forget that I need to return to Aquaria and Rhyland."

The thought of Rhyland sends a pang of longing through my heart. I miss him more than I ever thought possible, and being here while he's in Aquaria makes me want to scream. I need to figure out Lucian and get back to Rhyland—like yesterday.

I glance down at Lucian, who's still out cold on the floor. He looks almost peaceful, like a sleeping baby vampire. "How long is he going to be napping like that?"

Emily shrugs. "Takes about a few hours, give or take."

I raise an eyebrow, curious about how she knows that little tidbit. If I had to guess, it's not the first time she's had to put Lucian in a supernatural time-out. I make a mental note to ask her about that when we're not knee-deep in interdimensional drama.

"We should use this time to come up with a plan. Lucian's memory loss is a big issue, and we need to figure out how to fix it." Sable pauses, "We've tried everything to uncurse him, but nothing works. That bitch did a number on him, and I'm not sure if it's reversible."

"I can try something," I offer, my mind racing with possibilities. "Maybe I can tap into my angel powers and uncurse his brain. It's a shot in the dark but worth a try."

Emily raises an eyebrow, clearly intrigued. "Your angel power? You think you can act like some celestial brain surgeon?"

I shrug, trying to sound more confident than I feel. "Why not? I've got this whole light and creation gig going on. Maybe I can give his scrambled egg brain a little reboot."

LUCIAN

22

U gh, fucking hell. I awake, groaning and rubbing my neck. Emily and her witch bullshit, snapping my neck again like it's her favorite party trick. The last time she pulled this shit was when I tried to take a little sip from Sable's delectable neck. Not my finest moment, I'll admit, but come on! I'm learning.

Speaking of which, my eyes snap open faster than a bear trap, and I'm hit with the memory of almost draining that walking, talking honey pot with the golden eyes. I sit up, and lo and behold, there she is—Dream Girl—staring at me like a puzzle wrapped in a mystery wrapped in a chimichanga.

Emily glares daggers. "Welcome back to the land of the living, you *ass!* Don't even think about trying that shit again, or I swear to all that is unholy, I will shove your shriveled little balls so far up your ass you'll be coughing up sperm for a month. Got it, Deadboy?"

"Well, hello to you too, sunshine. It is always a pleasure to wake up to your dulcet tones and colorful threats." I grin cheekily. "You sure know how to make a vamp feel all warm and fuzzy inside. Oh wait... that's just the sensation of my balls retreating in terror. Silly me."

I turn my attention back to the honey-gold-eyed goddess, putting on my most charming smile. "Sorry about that, sweetcheeks. But can you really blame a guy for being tempted? Your blood... it's like the nectar of the gods. It's like you were made just for me..."

She sighs, pinching the bridge of her nose like she's about to lose her shit. "My blood calls to *all* vamps, you idiot. So no, I'm not your personal blood bag, and I sure as hell wasn't made for you."

Well, fuck me sideways. I must look confused as hell, like I've got a goddamn dick shoved up my ass because Sable jumps in to save the day. "Lucian, this is Dani. The one we've been telling you about."

Oh, shit. Shit, shit, shit.

Holy mother of plot twists, Batman! She's the super-powered savior chick, and I just tried to Hoover her like a fucking Dust Buster.

I was like a vampire version of Cookie Monster when she went all ragdoll in my arms. Let me tell you, her blood is like nothing else (at least, nothing my amnesia-riddled brain can recall).

Imagine chugging a glass of liquid lightning mixed with the finest aged whiskey, and you might come close to the mind-blowing flavor explosion that is Dani's hemoglobin elixir. I swear, I'd fight through a horde of rabid chihuahuas to get another sip of that divine nectar.

In my bloodlust haze, she mumbled something about my blood being inside her. Has she been sipping on my sauce before?

I don't know what the hell that's all about, but my entire circulatory system is screaming, "Dani, Dani, Dani!" like a lovesick groupie.

Christ on a cracker, I wish I could remember how all this vampire voodoo works.

And oh, oh, let's not forget her super blood. My brain clicks into overdrive. I practically leap to my feet and make a beeline for the windows. With the flair of a Vegas showman, I fling the curtains open, letting the sunlight pour in. I tilt my head back, arms outstretched, like I'm in some dramatic Broadway musical. "Ahhhh... there it is," I sigh, soaking up the rays like a sun-deprived plant.

The girls all scoff at my antics as I return to my seat. I run a hand through my golden hair, trying to process this clusterfuck of information. "So, let me see if I understand. You're the chosen one, the big kahuna, the supernatural savior... and I just tried to slurp you up like a fucking Go-Gurt?"

Smooth move, Lucian. Real smooth.

Dani quirks an eyebrow, a smirk playing on her lips. "Oh, don't worry, Count Drac-u-la-di-da. I'm sure we can find a way to jog your rusty old memory."

I shake my head, a shit-eating grin spreading across my face. "We've got some sort of freaky blood-bond mojo going on? Like, you're the Buffy to my Spike, the Bill to my Sookie?"

"Please. You're not nearly cool enough to be Spike or Bill. If anything, you're more like the lovechild of Damon Salvatore and a rabid chihuahua—all bark, no bite, and annoying as hell."

I gasp, clutching my chest like I've just been shot. "Ouch, baby! You really know how to hurt a guy. But let's be real here—Damon and Elena? Total endgame material. You sure you want to open that can of worms?"

I lean in closer, waggling my eyebrows suggestively. "Because I seem to recall a certain steamy little moment between us. Care to refresh my memory, or should I start writing my own version of Fifty Shades of Bloodsucking?"

Oh man, the way she kissed me back? Her tongue danced in my mouth while her fingers clutched me like I was the last taco on Earth! I swear, I was harder than a superhero's resolve. Just thinking about those soft lips and her mouth? Yeah, it's definitely giving me a little chub!

The look on her face is priceless. I can't tell if she's about to shit a brick or if she's just really, really constipated."You okay there, Dani-girl?" I ask, fighting back a grin.

She glares at me, her cheeks flushing a delightful shade of red. "Shut up, Lucian. I'm fine. Just... thinking."

"Thinking? Is that what we're calling it now?" I smirk. "Because from where I'm standing, it looks more like you're about to pop a vein trying to squeeze out a stubborn turd."

She punches me in the arm hard enough to make me wince. "You're disgusting, you know that? Why do I even put up with you?"

I grin, rubbing my arm where she hit me. "Because I'm charming, witty, and devastatingly handsome? Oh, and let's not forget my sparkling personality."

"More like annoying, immature, and a giant pain in my ass. Seriously, Lucian, do you ever take anything seriously?"

I wink. "Care to shed some light on that little blood bombshell? Because I'm pretty pissed off, I don't remember sipping from a neck as delectable as yours."

Dani sighs, clearly annoyed. "It's a long story; frankly, I don't have the time or *crayons* to explain it to you right now. Let's just say that we've got a bit of a... complicated history. One that involves some blood-sharing and your brain becoming Swiss cheese."

"It obviously didn't work," Emily says to my side, sighing out of frustration.

I turn to her, a grin spreading across my face. "Oh, so you guys already gave my noggin a good old-fashioned shake-and-bake, huh?"

Emily scoffs. "No shit, Sherlock. While you were busy catching some z's, we tried to jumpstart your old fart memory. But apparently, even magic has limits when it comes to fixing stupid."

"Ooh, sick burn, Sabrina," I quip. "But seriously, what's the deal? I thought you witches were all-powerful and whatnot—and you...the savior of the multiverse."

Dani lets out a huff of exhaustion. "We tried to heal you, but this damn stone has a mind of its own and apparently has a prejudice against your kind."

My eyes take in Dani's fancy headgear, and BAM! It's like a mental laxative—all that magical mumbo-jumbo Sable and Emily were spewing about the crown's bling comes flooding back faster than Taco Tuesday's revenge.

"Hold up, hold up," I say, pointing at the bedazzled headpiece. "Isn't that the tiara with all the infinity stones or some shit? The one that's supposed to give you superpowers and make you the ultimate magical girl?"

Dani groans, clearly not impressed by my references. "They're not *infinity stones*, you dumbass. They're ancient elemental gems that grant the wearer control over different aspects of reality."

I raise an eyebrow, intrigued. "Oh, so you're saying I'm too much of a bad boy even for ancient magical artifacts? I'm flattered."

"More like too much of a pain in the ass. The stone probably took one look at your twisted excuse for a brain and decided it wanted no part of it."

"Ouch, babe. You really know how to make a guy feel special," I say, placing a hand over my heart. "But hey, I'm not one to hold a grudge, especially not against a rock. I mean, who am I to judge? I've been stoned plenty of times myself. At least, I think."

Emily groans, rubbing her temples. "For fuck's sake, Lucian. Can you take anything seriously for once in your undead life?"

I shrug. "Life's too short to be serious all the time. Oh wait, I guess that doesn't really apply to me anymore, does it? Perks of being a creature of the night and all that jazz."

Dani sighs, shaking her head like an exasperated teacher dealing with an over-enthusiastic but clueless student. "Look, the point is, we tried to help you, but it didn't work. So, we'll have to find another way to get your memories back. But we don't have time to sit here and use you as a science experiment. I need to get back to Rhyland—to Aquaria."

My ears practically do a backflip at that. *Aquaria?* Oh yeah, that's like the magical water Disneyland that Emily and Sable yammered on about during their 'saving the world' TED Talk. "Wait a sec," I say, finally clocking her outfit, "is that why you're dressed like a sexy pirate wench?" I bite my lip, trying and failing to keep the shit-eating grin off my face. "Because if so, my entire collection of inappropriate spank bank material just upgraded to 'sexy pirate wench' edition."

Emily and Sable both scoff at my lewd comment.

"Unfuckingbelievable," Dani snaps. "The world is on the brink of collapsing, and your mind is firmly planted in the gutter? Just when I thought you couldn't get any worse. I much prefer the version of you with memories—at least *that* Lucian had some self-control."

She gestures to her outfit, exasperation dripping from every word. "This getup isn't for your personal *spank bank*, okay? It's to blend in with the crowd in Aquaria. You know, the realm I need to return to to prevent *the* actual apocalypse? But sure, let's ogle and make inappropriate comments instead. That helps."

Sable jumps in, her sweet voice adding a touch of reason to the chaos. "Everyone, let's just take a deep breath. Dani, you're right—we need to focus. Lucian, control yourself. We have a lot at stake here."

I hold my hands up in surrender. "Alright, alright. Lay it on me, ladies. What's the game plan?"

Dani stays silent for a long moment, the gears turning in her pretty little head. After what feels like an eternity of waiting for her to solve world hunger or some shit, she finally speaks up. "I'll go back and take Lucian with me."

Emily, in all her bitchy glory, "Thank fucking god. I can't babysit this overgrown man-child anymore."

"Are you sure that's wise? Bringing him along in his current state?" Sable asks, voicing her concerns.

I mull it over for a second. Is it a good idea to hop dimensions or realms or whatever the fuck they're called when I can barely remember my own name? Then again, it beats sitting around here twiddling my thumbs while surrounded by two sexy witches, one of whom is just itching to snip my balls off at the first opportunity. Plus, it means more one-on-one time with Little Miss Honey Pot over there.

I flash Dani a grin. "Hey, I'm game if you are, sweetcheeks. A little interdimensional road trip sounds like just the thing to jog my memory. And if not, well, at least I'll have some eye candy to keep me company along the way."

Emily makes a gagging noise. "Gross. Can you keep it in your pants for, like, five seconds?"

I smirk. "Sorry, babe. When you're packing heat like I am, it's hard to always keep the safety on."

Sable shakes her head, looking like she's questioning every life choice that led her to this moment. "Dani, are you absolutely certain about this? We don't know what kind of trouble he could cause in Aquaria."

Dani sighs, rubbing her temples. "I don't have a choice. We need all the help we can get, and like it or not, Lucian's a powerful ally. I'll just have to keep a close eye on him and make sure he doesn't do anything too stupid."

"Moi? Stupid? Never. I'm the picture of grace and decorum."

Emily snorts. "Yeah, if grace and decorum got shit-faced and had a baby with poor decision-making skills."

Dani laughs, then focuses back on me. "How about you shut the hell up and focus on not getting us killed in Aquaria? Do you think you can handle that, champ?"

I give her a cheeky salute, my hand snapping to my forehead with all the precision of a drunk soldier. "Aye, aye, captain. One steaming hot order of 'not fucking things up' coming right up. Served with a side of 'I'll do my best, but no promises.'"

I pause, a mischievous grin spreading across my face. "But just for the record, if you ever want to use that crown to, you know, play out some fantasies... I'm totally down. We could have our own little roleplay adventure."

RHYLAND

23

I stand at the ship's railing, my eyes fixed on the horizon, where the dark blue waters stretch out endlessly. The sea is deceptively calm now, contrasting with the howling storm that nearly tore us apart hours before. In the distance, I can make out an island's lush, green outline, its jungle-covered slopes rising from the waves like the back of some ancient, slumbering beast.

"We be right above the Atlantean Ruins," Gideon says beside me, his voice low and gruff. "And headin' smack dab in the middle of Siren-guarded waters."

"Great, just what we need right now," I growl, with sarcasm. "Can't you get us back on course, away from these Siren-infested waters?"

Gideon shakes his head, pointing to the tattered remnants of our sails. "Aye, lad, once we fix our sails. That bitch of a storm did a number on 'em, and we can't go anywhere until they be mended."

Erik, perched on a barrel to my left, speaks up. "And how long will these repairs take, Captain?"

"About an hour, give or take," Gideon replies, scratching his beard. "I got me crew workin' double-time to get 'em replaced. Once that's done, we'll be on our merry way, puttin' these cursed waters behind us."

I turn back to the railing, my eyes scanning the deep blue waters. Despite the danger lurking beneath the surface, I can't deny this place's raw, wild beauty. It stirs something deep within me, old memories of my Viking days spent sailing the seas in search of new lands and discoveries.

My gaze is drawn to the island in the distance. "What's that place?" I ask, curiosity getting the better of me.

Gideon steps beside me, his weathered face creasing with awe and unease. "That be Tempest Isle, mate. A right treacherous place, shrouded in mystery and danger."

I feel a chill run down my spine at his words. "And the Sirens?" I ask, my voice tight. "What's their role in all this?"

Gideon's face darkens. "They be the guardians of the isle, lad. Tempest Isle be their domain, and they don't take kindly to trespassers. They use their songs to lure ships onto the rocks, then drag the survivors down to their watery grave."

"What more can you tell us of this island, Captain?" Erik asks.

Gideon's expression darkens further. "Legend has it the isle be cursed, haunted by the restless spirits of long-dead explorers and treasure hunters. They say it be home to untold treasures, riches beyond yer wildest dreams. But no one who's ever set foot on its shores has lived to tell the tale."

I feel a stirring of old memories at his words. The thrill of the unknown, the rush of adrenaline that came with each new horizon...

I shake my head, trying to clear the cobwebs of nostalgia from my mind. "What kind of treasures are we talking about here, Captain? And why has no one ever made it back alive?"

Gideon leans in, "They say the island be home to a great temple, lad. A place of ancient power and forgotten magic. Within its walls, there be said to lie a treasure beyond compare, a relic of the old gods themselves."

I feel a prickling sense of unease. "And the reason no one's ever made it back?"

Gideon's face twists into a grimace. "The jungle, lad. They say it be alive, a sentient thing with a will of its own. It plays tricks on the mind, shows ye things that can't be real. And then there be the creatures that lurk within its depths, beasts of legend and nightmare that hunt and devour any who dare to trespass on their domain."

I stare at him, soaking in his words, and it dawns on me that this may be the place we need to investigate.

Captain Sterling claps me on the back before striding off towards the helm. Izabelle slinks along beside him, her hips swaying with each step, a wicked glint in her eye as she shoots me a sly wink.

I shake my head, my lip curling in disgust as I turn my attention back to Erik. Our eyes lock, silver on blue, and I can practically see the gears turning behind his stoic facade.

What if the stone is there, hidden away on that island like some kind of twisted treasure hunt?

But we can't know for sure, not until Dani returns from wherever she's been taken. She's the key to all of this, the one with the power to sense the stones and guide us to them.

Erik must see the determination in my gaze because he shakes his head. "Brother, I know that look," he warns. "You're not seriously considering setting foot on that island, are you?"

I shrug. "What if it's there, Erik? What if the stone we need is hidden away on Tempest Isle, just waiting for us to claim it?"

He frowns. "It's possible," he admits reluctantly. "But it's also incredibly dangerous. You heard what the captain said about the horrors that lurk on that island. Is it really worth the risk?"

I lean forward, my eyes intense and my voice low. "We know firsthand what forbidden areas mean in a realm, Erik. Dani figured that out before any of us, back in Luminara, when she sensed the Faerite stone hidden away in that Hidden Valley."

He nods slowly, his expression thoughtful. "True. But that was different, Rhyland. We had Dani with us then to guide us and keep us safe. Without her..."

He trails off, his eyes clouding with worry and uncertainty.

"I'm not saying we go in blind, brother. I know we need to wait for Dani." I grasp his shoulder, looking into his silver eyes, "It's just a stepping stone, and it might point us to where we need to look."

Dani will claw her way back to me, come hell or high water. No force in this world or any other can keep us apart for long, and if I know my fierce little Angel, she'll fight like a demon to get back to where she belongs—right here, by my side.

But the not knowing, the uncertainty of where she is or what she's going throug h... it's eating me alive. Is she hurt? Is she scared? Is she calling out for me, wondering why I'm not there to protect her—to keep her safe?

The thought of it is enough to make me want to roar with frustration, to tear the whole world apart until I find her and bring her back to me.

But I can't do that; I can't let myself spiral into that pit of despair and helplessness. I have to hold on to hope, to the unshakable faith that our bond is stronger than any distance, any obstacle that tries to come between us.

Because that's what you do when you love someone with every fiber of your being—when they're the very air you breathe and the beat of your immortal heart. You believe in them, in the strength of your connection and the power of your love.

You trust this is just another challenge to overcome, another trial to endure. It's not the end of your story but just another chapter in the epic saga of your love.

And I do believe in her, in us. I believe in it with every ounce of my soul, every last shred of my being.

So I'll wait for her, as long as it takes. I'll hold on to the memory of her smile, the sound of her laughter, the feel of her skin against mine. I'll let those memories be my anchor, my guiding light in the darkness, until she finds her way back to me.

Because she will come back—she has to.

Erik nods, "Agreed."

Hours later, after I've downed my dose of Dani's blood like a fucking junkie getting his fix, we're finally ready to set sail back toward Captain's Haven to wait for my mate's return.

In her infinite wisdom, Dani insisted that Erik and I keep vials of her blood on us at all times, just in case of emergencies. And fuck me sideways, she was right. She's off in some other goddamn realm, doing God knows what, while Erik and I are stuck here with our thumbs up our asses, waiting for her to come back.

But thank fuck she was smart enough to think ahead, to learn from our past mistakes, and make sure we'd be prepared for situations like this. It's just one more reason why she's the most incredible woman in all the realms.

The silver-colored sails billow overhead, straining against the wind as the ship surges forward, cutting through the waves like a knife. The salty spray stings my face, tang, sharp, and bracing on my tongue as I take a deep, lungful breath of ocean air.

I'm standing at the very point of the ship, the wind whipping through my hair and tugging at my clothes as we race across the open sea. Behind me, I can hear the rhythmic rasp of Erik's whetstone against his blade, the sound as familiar and comforting as a lullaby.

Gideon is at the helm, his weathered hands steady on the wheel as he guides us through the choppy waters. But something catches my eye behind him, a flicker of movement that has me squinting against the sun's glare.

I leap up onto the rigging, and there, on the horizon, I see it—a line of ships, their black sails stark against the endless blue of the sky. And on those sails, a green serpent coiling out of a bleached white skull, the emblem stark and menacing.

"Captain!" I shout down from my perch, my voice cracking like a whip over the roar of the wind and the sea. "Behind you!"

Gideon spins around, his eyes widening as he sees the approaching ships. His face drains of color, and his skin goes pale beneath his tan.

"Hoist the other sails, ye scurvy dogs!" he bellows, his voice booming across the deck like a cannon shot. "We need more speed, and we need it now!"

I leap from the rigging, crouching on the deck before sprinting up to the helm, my boots pounding against the salt-stained wood.

"What the fuck is going on?" I demand, my voice low and urgent. "Who are they? Friends of yours?"

Gideon shakes his head, his expression grim. "Nay, lad. That be Captain Thalassia Viper and her Serpent Skulls. And trust me when I say, she be no friend of ours."

I clench my jaw, my hands balling into fists at my sides as I stare at the approaching ships, their black sails growing larger with every passing second. The wind howls in my ears, almost drowning out the frantic pounding of my heartbeat.

But beneath the fear, dread, and uncertainty, I feel something else stirring in my chest—a flicker of excitement, anticipation, and the thrill that comes with facing down a worthy foe.

I'm moving before I realize it, my boots pounding against the deck as I race to help hoist the other sails. The fucking pirates are moving like molasses, their fingers clumsy and slow on the rigging, and I know we don't have a second to waste.

I grab a rope, my muscles straining as I haul on it with all my strength. Beside me, Erik is doing the same, his face set in a grim mask of determination as we work together to get this floating tub of shit moving faster.

They're gaining on us, the sleek black vessels cutting through the waves like a pack of hungry wolves, their sails straining against the wind. I can see the glint of sunlight on metal and the flash of cannon ports being opened and primed for firing.

Fuck!

We're sitting ducks out here, our ass flapping in the breeze like a goddamn flag. What kind of water magic fuckery do these bastards have up their sleeves to be gaining on us so damn fast?

Gideon's voice cracks like a whip across the deck, sharp and urgent. "Load up the cannons, ye poxy bilge rats! Prepare to fire!"

The pirates scatter like rats, some diving below deck to man the cannons while others scramble up the rigging to the topside guns. I can hear the clang and clatter of cannonballs being loaded, the grunts and curses of men straining to haul the heavy iron spheres into place.

Gideon spins the helm hard to the right, the muscles in his arms bulging as he wrenches the ship in a stomach-churning turn. The deck tilts beneath my feet, and I go flying, my body slamming into a stack of barrels and crates with a bone-jarring thud.

I'm up again instantly, my reflexes as sharp as ever despite the ringing in my ears and the ache in my ribs. I can see the Serpent ships bearing down on us, their hulls painted with leering skulls and twisting serpents, their cannons aimed straight at our hearts.

And then, with a roar that shakes the very timbers of the ship, they open fire.

The air splits with the sound of cannon shots, the acrid stench of gunpowder filling my nostrils as the iron balls hurtle toward us like meteors from the heavens. I hear the splintering of wood and the screams of men as shrapnel rips through flesh and bone, and I drop to the deck on instinct, covering my head with my arms.

As much as it fucking galls me, wood is still a vampire's weakness, and I can't afford to be skewered like a goddamn pig on a spit.

So I grit my teeth and hug the blood-slicked planks, my ears ringing with the thunder of cannons and the howl of the wind. The ship shudders and groans around me, the wood creaking like the bones of some ancient, dying beast, and I know we're in for the fight of our fucking lives.

DANICA

24

The plan is set. Emily and Sable will play Hogwarts and help Emily level up her magical girl powers while Lucian and I take a little interdimensional road trip back to Aquaria. Apparently, my apartment is now Fort Knox, thanks to some hardcore protection spells that will fry any unwanted visitors like a bucket of extra crispy KFC.

But here's where things get a little wibbly-wobbly, timey-wimey. Turns out, my little jaunt in Aquaria was, in fact, five or so days in the mortal world, whereas my Luminara vacation had time speeding up like it was on a cocaine bender. Time here and time in Aquaria is linear.

Wrap your head around that shit.

Trying to make sense of the temporal shenanigans between these worlds is giving me a migraine worse than the one I get after listening to Lucian running his mouth. It's just another piece of the batshit crazy puzzle that is my life, and I'm starting to think I might need a PhD in quantum physics just to keep up.

"And Emily, if you ever pull that summoning shit again, I swear to every deity in existence, I will personally come back and haunt your ass. If you need me, find another way to reach out. Carrier pigeon, smoke signals, interpretive dance—I don't care. Just don't yank me across dimensions like a cosmic yo-yo. Capiche?"

Emily nods vigorously, her eyes wide with amusement and genuine understanding. "Cross my heart and hope to die, stick a needle in my eye—wait, no, fuck that. I've already died once, and it wasn't fun. But I promise, Dani. No more surprise summonings. Scout's honor."

I raise an eyebrow, "Em..." I warn.

She grins, "Fine, then. Witch's honor. Or is it Demon Hunter's honor now? I'm still figuring out the proper terminology for my new supernatural status."

I can't help but chuckle, shaking my head at her antics. Even amid all this chaos, Emily always finds a way to make me laugh. It's one of the things I love most about her.

"Just promise me, Em—no more magical kidnappings. I've got enough on my plate with the whole 'fate of the world' thing. I don't need to add 'surprise interdimensional travel' to my list of worries."

She nods again, this time with a more serious expression. "I promise. I'll find another way to reach you if I need you. No more portal-pulling or dimension-dragging. You have my word."

I smile, feeling a weight lift off my shoulders. "Thanks, Em."

We embrace, holding each other tight. I breathe in her familiar scent, lavender, and something uniquely Emily. It's a smell that always makes me feel safe, even in the craziest circumstances.

I pull away. "Alright, gang," I say, clapping my hands together. "Let's get this show on the road. We've got a world to save, memories to restore, and powers to master—just another day in the life of Dani and her merry band of misfits."

I focus on conjuring a portal, tapping into the power deep within me. It responds immediately—eager to fulfill my request. But I need a specific location, a direct path to Rhyland. If he's sailing with Gideon, I have no idea where he could be. So, I try a different approach. I concentrate on Rhyland himself—his chiseled features, Nordic blue eyes, commanding presence, and the love that binds us together. A shimmering gateway begins to materialize before me, rippling like water, glowing a brilliant blue.

Lucian gasps beside me, his eyes wide with awe. "Well, fuck me sideways and call me Gandalf! That's some serious Lord of the Rings shit right there, Honey Pot!"

"Shut up," I hiss, my brow furrowed in concentration. "I need to focus, and your constant yapping isn't helping." I close my eyes, pouring all my thoughts and emotions into the image of Rhyland. The portal shimmers more intensely, expanding in size. Opening my eyes, I'm greeted by a vast expanse of nothingness. "Okay, that's new," I mutter under my breath.

Lucian leans in, squinting at the void. "Uh, correct me if I'm wrong, but aren't portals supposed to lead somewhere? Because this looks like the entrance to my ex's soul—empty and devoid of any signs of life."

I glare at him, "You're not helping." But he's right. This isn't what I usually conjure. Still, there's no turning back now. I glance at Lucian, my voice filled with determination. "Let's go."

He grins, rubbing his hands together. "Alrighty then! Into the abyss we go! Hey, do you think they have chimichangas on the other side? Because I could really go for a chimichanga right about now."

I roll my eyes. "You're about to enter an unknown realm, and all you can think about is Mexican food?"

Lucian shrugs. "Interdimensional travel makes me hungry. Plus, we'll need our strength for whatever's waiting for us on the other side of this thing."

I hate to admit it, but he has a point. I take a deep breath, steeling myself for the unknown. "Okay, on the count of three. One... two..."

"THREE!" Lucian shouts, grabbing my hand and leaping into the portal with a whooping battle cry.

And just like that, we're hurtling through the shimmering gateway, the world we know disappearing behind us as we plunge into the mysterious depths of the void.

We then land on a slick, wet deck. The loud sounds of gunfire and cannon blasts assault my ears. I scramble to my feet, taking in the chaotic scene around me. It's like a war zone, with pirates rushing in every direction.

Suddenly, I hear a faint whistle, growing louder by the second. Before I can react, Lucian tackles me from behind, sending us both crashing to the deck. A cannonball whizzes over our heads, missing us by mere inches. It slams into the ship's side, creating a gaping hole, splinters of wood flying everywhere. The impact reverberates through my bones as I struggle to catch my breath.

"OH MY FUCK!" Lucian yells above me."Did we just stumble onto the set of *Pirates of the Caribbean*? Because this shit looks way too real to be a movie!"

I shove him off me, my heart racing. "No, you dumbass. This is Aquaria, and it looks like we've just crash-landed in the middle of a goddamn pirate battle royale."

Lucian's eyes light up with a manic gleam. "Well, blow me down! I always knew I was destined for a life of swashbuckling and plundering booty. Both literally and figuratively, if you catch my drift."

I shoot him a withering glare, ducking as another cannonball whistles past our heads. "Can you maybe save the innuendos for a time when we're not actively being shot at? Or is that too much to ask from that one-track mind of yours?"

My eyes scan the chaos for any sign of Rhyland. I can feel his broody presence, tantalizingly close. Just then, he comes sprinting from the ship's bow, his eyes fierce and alight with battle. Another cannon fires off to my right, and I cringe instinctively. Rhyland moves in a blur, his supernatural speed carrying him towards me. He wraps his arms around me, his embrace gentle and protective, as he ducks us to the deck. The cannonball screams past, missing my head by a hair's breadth, and slams into the ship's floorboards.

The sound is deafening, like a bomb detonating right beside us. The floor gives way beneath our bodies, and we plummet into the ship's lower hull, a tangle of limbs and splintered wood.

The stench of gunpowder and sweat fills my nostrils, mingling with the salty scent of the sea. My heart pounds against my ribcage, adrenaline coursing through my veins. I cling to Rhyland; his solid presence is the only thing keeping me grounded amid this insanity.

"Rhyland," I gasp, my voice barely audible over the chaos. "What the hell is going on?"

"Hi, Angel," Rhyland pants, trying to catch his breath as he looks down at me, his ocean-blue eyes swirling with relief and worry. "You have impeccable fucking timing, as always. Welcome back to the high seas, baby."

He kisses me then, fierce and passionate, even as we lay tangled in a heap at the bottom of the ship. The battle rages above us, the sounds of clashing swords and exploding cannons echoing through the wooden hull, but none of it matters. All that exists is the heat of Rhyland's lips on mine, the desperate hunger in his kiss, and the overwhelming love that consumes us both.

It's a kiss that says everything we can't put into words—the ache of our separation, the relief of being reunited, and the unshakable bond that ties our hearts together.

Rhyland's hands grip my waist, his fingers digging into my skin as he pulls me closer, molding my body to fit perfectly against his. Every trace of Lucian's kiss vanishes as Rhyland's hot mouth and soft tongue have me panting and moaning.

The kiss is short but intense, a brief stolen moment amidst the chaos surrounding us. When we finally break apart, we're both breathing hard, our chests heaving as we struggle to catch our breath. Rhyland rests his forehead against mine, his ocean-blue eyes boring into my own with a fierce intensity that makes my heart skip a beat.

"What the hell happened? Where did you go?" he asks, his voice rough with emotion. " I felt your pain—"

I reach up, cupping his face in my hands, my thumbs brushing over his bearded jaw. "I'm here now—it's a long story. I am okay."

He nods, his arms tightening around me, holding me close. "Okay. But I'm never letting you out of my sight again. You're stuck with me, baby."

I laugh, the sound mingling with the din of battle above us. "I wouldn't have it any other way."

"I love you, Angel," he whispers, his voice rough with emotion. "I fucking love you so much."

I smile, my heart swelling with adoration for this man who holds my soul in his hands. "I love you too. More than anything."

He grins that crooked, heart-stopping smile that never fails to make my knees weak.

Lucian's head suddenly pops up through the hole in the floor, looking down at us with concern and confusion. "Hey, are you—" He pauses mid-sentence, his eyes zeroing in on Rhyland. "Whoa, whoa, whoa. Who the fuck are you, tall, dark, and handsy? And why do you have your paws all over my sweet little Honey Pot?"

Rhyland looks at Lucian, his brow furrowed in confusion. "Lucian?" he then looks at me, growling, "You went to the Mortal realm? And why the fuck is he calling you Honey Pot? What the hell is he talking about, Dani?"

I sigh, rolling my eyes. "It's a lot to unpack." I grumble, "and one we definitely don't have time for right now, with the whole 'trying not to die' situation we've got going on here."

Lucian, being Lucian, isn't about to let it go that easily. "Uh, excuse me, but I think I deserve an explanation. I didn't just jump through a magical portal and land in the middle of Pirates: Douchebag Edition for shits and giggles, you know."

"Put a sock in it, Lucian. We don't have time for your little game of twenty questions right now."

Lucian's eyebrows shoot up, a smirk playing on his lips. "Oh, I get it—you must be the shitstick that Dani was talking about. Sorry, pal, but I don't share. Finder's keepers and all that shit."

Rhyland's eyes frown in confusion, then they flash angrily, a deep growl rumbling in his chest. "I'm going to fucking kill him—"

Another explosion rocks the ship, nearly knocking us off our feet and re-minding us of the more pressing matters."Guys, seriously? Can we put the dick-measuring contest on hold until we're not in imminent danger of being blown to bits?" I snap, my patience wearing thin.

Rhyland looks like he's about to argue, but I shoot him a glare that could melt steel. He sighs, relenting, but not before casting one last murderous look in Lucian's direction.

With that, Rhyland and I scramble through the debris, navigating the splin-tered remains of our unwanted resting spot as we make our way back topside. Lucian trails behind us, his smart-ass comments and suggestive looks making me want to chuck him overboard and let the sharks deal with him.

Just another day in the life of Dani Pierce, dimensional traveler and unwilling referee in the world's most screwed-up brotherly rivalry. Fuck my life sideways with a rusty spork.

As we emerge onto the deck, the chaos of battle engulfs us once more. Pirates clash with our crew, swords flashing and pistols firing. The air is thick with smoke and the coppery scent of blood, and I can't help but wonder how the hell I keep ending up in these situations.

Oh, right. Because the universe has a sick sense of humor and enjoys watching me navigate this clusterfuck of destiny, danger, and dick-measuring contests.

I grab a discarded sword from the deck, its weight feeling oddly comfortable in my hand. Rhyland and Lucian flank me, their weapons at the ready, and for a moment, I almost feel sorry for the poor bastards who are about to face our combined wrath.

Almost.

The deck is a blur of motion, pirates from both sides locked in a deadly dance of steel and blood.

I catch sight of the ships surrounding us, their black sails adorned with serpentine crests—too many to count. Our ship retaliates with a barrage of cannon fire, the broadside assault sending explosions of fire and smoke ripping through the enemy vessel. The force of the blast nearly knocks me off my feet, but Rhyland's strong arms keep me steady.

"These are the Serpent Skulls," he informs me, his voice barely audible over the din of battle. "And we're trying not to die or get our asses capsized."

I nod, my heart pounding in my chest. "Right, got it. Don't die, don't sink—sounds like a plan."

Erik appears beside us, his silver hair whipping in the wind, his face a mask of stoic determination. "Little Huntress," he greets me formally, even amid the battle. "It is good to see you and have you back, though I wish it were under better circumstances."

I grin. "Erik, it's always a pleasure. Have you kept Rhyland in one piece while I've been MIA?"

He almost smiles, but another explosion rocks the ship, and we're all thrown off balance.

I spot another sword abandoned on the deck, its blade catching the sun like a beacon of hope—because, boy, do I miss my daggers right about now. Without hesitation, I lunge for it, my fingers wrapping around the hilt just as an enemy pirate charges toward me, his eyes wild with bloodlust.

Our blades flash in the sunlight as I fight this ugly son of a bitch. The deck becomes a blur of motion and blood, the air thick with the stench of gunpowder and sweat. I lose myself in the rhythm of the fight, my power flowing through me like a current, guiding my every move.

I feel the familiar tingle that starts in my scalp, down to my fingertips, and spreads through my veins like liquid fire. Time seems to slow as I tap into my power, the world around me blurring as I slip into the slipstream. It's a sensation I'll never tire of—the way everything fades away, leaving only the crystal clarity of the moment. I move with fluid grace, my sword a blur of silver as I dodge the pirate's attack and counter with a swift strike. The blade finds its mark, and the pirate crumples to the deck, his blood staining the weathered wood.

God, I love this power. The thrill, the sheer exhilaration of bending time to my will. I don't think I'll ever get over it, the way it makes me feel invincible, untouchable.

I can't help but grin, the thrill of the fight coursing through my veins. Rhyland shoots me a look. His eyebrow raised in a silent question.

"What?" I shrug, my tone sarcastic. "A girl's gotta have her hobbies."

He shakes his head, a smile tugging at the corner of his mouth. "You're fucking incredible, you know that?"

And with that, I charge into the fray, my swords clashing against the blades of the Serpent Skulls who have boarded our ship. I let my instincts take over, my body moving in a deadly dance as I parry and thrust, the power within me surging to the surface.

But even with my abilities, the odds are stacked against us. The Serpent Skulls seem endless, their numbers far greater than ours. I lose sight of Rhyland and Erik in the chaos, my focus narrowing to the next opponent, the next strike.

Lucian, the love child of Jackie Chan and the Energizer Bunny hopped up on a lethal dose of snark and badassery, is taking on these pirates like they're nothing more than glorified punching bags—having the time of his fucking life doing it.

He's a whirlwind of flying fists and smart-ass quips, his fighting style a bizarre fusion of taekwondo and "I saw this in a movie once." He leaps into the air, defying gravity and common sense in equal measure, and lands a spinning kick that would make Chuck Norris weep with envy. The pirate on the receiving end of this ass-whooping collapses, his jaw making a sound like a gunshot as it shatters.

"Ooh, sorry about that, buddy!" Lucian cackles, sounding about as sincere as a used car salesman. "Looks like you'll be eating through a straw for a while. But hey, I hear the liquid diet is all the rage these days!"

Another pirate, apparently not one for learning from his comrades' mistakes, charges at Lucian with a sword that looks like it was last used to butter toast. Lucian dodges the blade with a fluidity that would make a ballerina jealous, then retaliates with a series of punches that turn the poor bastard's internal organs into pudding.

He follows up with an uppercut that sends the pirate airborne, his teeth making a delightful tinkling sound as they scatter across the deck. The unfortunate schmuck does a half-gainer over the railing; his screams are cut short as he belly-flops into the unforgiving sea.

"Ooh, I give that dive a solid 7.5," Lucian quips, dusting off his hands. "The splash was a little sloppy, but he gets bonus points for style."

But the fun's just getting started as a gaggle of pissed-off pirates surround our resident jester, their faces contorted with rage and the promise of imminent violence. Lucian grins, cracking his neck like he's about to sit down for a relaxing massage.

"You boys looking for a good time?" he asks with mock seduction. "Because I'm about to rock your world."

A symphony of broken bones and bruised egos follows as Lucian tears through the pirates like a kid on a sugar rush. He's all flying kicks and vicious elbows, his movements a blur of kinetic energy and chaos. One pirate gets a knee to the groin so hard his testicles probably relocate to his throat.

"Oof, right in the baby maker!" Lucian winces, his grin threatening to split his face in half. "Guess you won't be sowing your wild oats anytime soon, huh, champ?"

The few pirates still standing decide that discretion is the better part of valor and try to make a break for it, but Lucian's not about to let his new playmates go that easily. He chases after them, cackling like a hyena on nitrous oxide.

"Aww, leaving so soon?" he calls out. "But we were just getting to the good part!"

He catches one poor sap by the collar, then slams his face into the mast with enough force to leave a dent. The pirate slides to the deck, his nose a pulpy mess of blood and snot.

"Now that's what I call a face-lift," Lucian quips, admiring his handiwork. "You're welcome, by the way. I just improved your looks by a factor of ten."

As the last pirate crumples to the ground, Lucian stands amid the carnage, looking like a kid who just won a lifetime supply of candy. He turns to me, his eyes gleaming with mischief.

"WOOO! Who knew I had all those sick moves hidden up my sleeves? I sure as hell didn't!"

"I did—but apparently, your play-by-play commentary has leveled up from mildly annoying to full-blown 'dear God, please shut the fuck up.'"

Lucian grins. "Is it just me, or was that better than sex?" he asks, waggling his eyebrows suggestively. "I mean, not that I would know. I'm saving myself for marriage. Or at least for the next warm body that catches my eye."

I roll my eyes, wondering for the umpteenth time how the hell I got stuck with this lovable asshole as a companion—

And then, all hell breaks loose. A cannonball explodes mere feet away from me, the force of the blast slamming into my body like a sledgehammer. I go airborne, my balance shot to shit.

Time seems to slow down as I tumble towards the railing, my life flashing before my eyes. Well, not really. It's more like a highlight reel of all the times I've managed to cheat death. My luck has finally run out.

Lucian leaps into action, blurring towards me with his supernatural speed. But even he can't outrun gravity.

The impact of the railing knocks the air from my lungs, leaving me gasping. And then I'm tumbling, the world around me spinning in a dizzying kaleidoscope of blue and white. I hit the water with a splash, the icy embrace of the sea swallowing me whole.

Out of nowhere, a heavy barrel smashes into my chest and takes me down further. Just my luck—it's a powder keg. I feel myself sinking like a lead balloon, or more accurately, a lead balloon filled with dread and a spark of irritation. I finally manage to shove the damn keg off me. The clamor of the battle above fades, replaced by the muffled roar of the ocean and the relentless pounding of my heart.

It's like I've been yeeted into an alternate reality where all that exists is the bone-chilling cold, the oppressive darkness, and the searing ache in my lungs screaming, "Oxygen, please!"

Well, isn't this just a cherry on top of my *shit* sundae?

I sink deeper, the weight of my clothes and the force of the impact dragging me down into the depths. Panic claws at my throat, my mind screaming at me to fight, to swim, to do something. But my limbs feel heavy, my muscles refusing to cooperate.

After all the shit I've been through, all the battles I've fought and won, I'm going to die like this? Drowning in the middle of nowhere, with no one but the fish to witness my pathetic demise?

Hell no. I refuse to go out like this. I'm so done with this "drowning" bullshit. It's getting old fast. With a surge of determination and a mental "fuck you" to the universe, I force my arms and legs to move, kicking and clawing my way toward the surface.

The water resists me, trying to pull me back down into its annoyingly bright blue depths. It's like the ocean is mocking me. But I'm not having it. I won't let this overgrown puddle win.

My lungs scream for air. The edges of my vision blur, darkness creeping in like a hungry predator.

Something catches my eye as I give in to the inevitable. The water around me is crystal clear, the sunlight filtering in shimmering rays. And there, moving through the depths with otherworldly grace, is a figure that seems to have sprung straight from the pages of a fairy tale. Her hair is a billowing cloud of black smoke.

Holy shit, is that a mermaid?

I blink, my mind reeling with disbelief. I must be hallucinating, my oxygen-deprived brain conjuring up fantasies in my final moments. But before I can even process the thought, she's there, her face mere inches from mine. Her eyes are a startling shade of green, flecked with silver, that seems to shimmer in the underwater light. Her skin is smooth and pale, like the finest pearl plucked from the depths of the sea. Her tail is a sparkly silver.

She's the most beautiful creature I've ever seen, and for a moment, I forget all about the fact that I'm drowning.

She reaches out, her fingers brushing against my cheek with a gentleness that belies the strength I can see in her lithe form. Then she pulls me close, her lips pressing against mine in a kiss that sends shockwaves through my entire body.

Air flows into my lungs, sweet and life-giving, chasing away the burning ache that had consumed me moments before. My eyes widen in shock as I struggle to comprehend what's happening.

The mermaid pulls back, a smile playing on her lips. *"Welcome to Aquaria, land-dweller,"* she says, her voice whispering into my mind—like a siren's song, alluring and dangerous all at once. *"Someone would like to meet with you."*

I'm pretty sure my jaw is on the ocean floor now. I have so many questions and so many thoughts racing through my mind. Before I can voice any of them, she takes my hand and begins to swim, pulling me deeper into the mysteries of this strange and wondrous world beneath the waves.

RHYLAND

25

The Serpent Skulls just keep coming, their numbers seemingly endless as they swarm over the deck like a plague of fucking locusts. Our ship is barely holding together, the hull splintered and the sails in tatters as we fight for our lives amidst the chaos and carnage.

I let out a roar of fury as a pirate charges me, his cutlass flashing in the sunlight. I meet his blade with my own, the clang of steel on steel ringing out like a thunderclap. We trade blows back and forth, our swords clashing and sparking as we dance across the blood-slick deck.

But I'm done playing games. With a snarl, I lunge forward and sink my blade deep into the bastard's belly, the razor-sharp edge slicing through flesh and muscle like butter. I feel the hot gush of blood over my hand and hear the wet, tearing sound as I rip the sword free in a spray of crimson.

The pirate staggers back, his eyes wide with shock and agony. But I'm not finished with him yet. I grab him by the throat, my fingers digging into his flesh as I yank him close and sink my fangs into his neck. The coppery tang of his blood floods my mouth, hot and thick and pulsing with life. I drink deep, feeling the rush of power as it courses through my veins, making me stronger, faster, more deadly.

Behind me, I hear the ring of Erik's sword as he takes on three pirates at once, his blade flashing in a blur of silver. A head flies, bouncing across the deck in a spray of blood and brains. But the other two keep coming, their eyes wild with bloodlust and fury.

My focus wavers for a split second as movement catches my eye, drawing my gaze up to the helm. There, locked in a fierce duel with a female pirate, is Captain Sterling. The woman is a fucking force to be reckoned with, her blade flashing in a blur of silver as she matches the captain blow for blow.

She's good, damn good. Better than any pirate I've ever seen. Her movements are fluid and graceful, her sword an extension of her arm as she parries and thrusts with deadly precision.

Suddenly, she drops low, sweeping her leg out in a lightning-fast kick that takes the captain's feet out from under him. He goes down hard, his back slamming against the deck with a sickening crack.

But before the woman can press her advantage, Izabelle is there, materializing out of nowhere like a fucking ghost. Her cutlass is in her hands, the blade flashing in the sunlight as she hurls herself at the female pirate.

The two women clash in a whirlwind of steel and fury as they dance back and forth across the deck. Izabelle is a blur of motion, her cutlass slashing and swiping with deadly precision as she tries to drive the other woman back to protect her fallen captain.

But the female pirate is just as fast, just as skilled. She meets Izabelle's attacks with incredible, calculated grace, her sword darting in and out like a serpent's tongue as she probes for weaknesses, for openings to exploit.

"Sterling! You will not win this one. You are outnumbered, and ye will yield." the Serpent Skull woman yells. She must be the Captain Gideon spoke of—Captain Thalassia Viper.

A shot rings out, the crack of a pistol splitting the air. I feel the impact of the bullet slamming into my chest, the searing pain of it tearing through muscle and bone. I snarl in rage and pain, my vision going red around the edges as I charge forward, moving faster than the eye can follow.

I'm on the shooter in an instant, my hand closing around his throat like a vice. I feel the pop and snap of tendons and cartilage as I rip his throat out, the hot gush of blood splattering my face and chest. His body crumples to the deck, his eyes staring sightlessly at the sky.

Our ship shudders beneath my feet as another volley of cannon fire rips through the hull, its force sending shockwaves through the deck. I can feel the ship listing heavily to one side, the timbers groaning and creaking as they strain under the onslaught.

We can't take much more of this. We're being torn apart, piece by fucking piece.

I throw my head back and roar at the sky, my voice raw with anger and desperation. And then, deep inside me, I feel it. That raw, primal energy that's always been there, waiting just beneath the surface of my skin. I dig deep, reaching for it with every fiber of my being, every last shred of my will.

And it answers.

With a snarl, I thrust my palms out toward one of the enemy ships, channeling all my rage and power into a devastating blast. A pulse of telekinetic energy blasts from my hands, slamming into the side of the nearest enemy ship with the force of a wrecking ball.

The hull explodes inward, the wood splintering and cracking like an eggshell. Water gushes through the gaping hole, the ship listing heavily to one side as it begins to sink beneath the waves.

Fuck yes. A savage grin splits my face from ear to ear. *It's on now, you bastards.*

I blur to the other side of the ship, my hands already outstretched. Another blast of energy, another ship capsizing in a spray of shattered wood and churning foam.

I do it again and again, my body moving on pure instinct and adrenaline as I rain down destruction on our enemies like the fucking wrath of the gods. Ships sink and capsize all around us, the screams of dying men mingling with the roar of the waves and the boom of cannon fire.

Even as the enemy fleet crumbles beneath my onslaught, the deck of our ship is still swarming with Serpent Skull pirates, their blades flashing and their eyes wild.

I rush through them like a goddamn whirlwind, my hands a blur of motion as I snap necks and tear out throats, rip beating hearts from chests, and crush skulls like overripe fruit. The rage is a living thing inside me now, a beast that won't be sated until every last one of these fuckers is dead at my feet.

Because I'm done with this shit. I'm done with these pirate fucks and their games, done with the endless cycle of violence and death. All I want is my Angel, safe and sound in my arms once more.

And I'll tear the whole fucking world apart to make that happen if that's what it takes.

The battle had been long and brutal, a seemingly endless slog of blood, steel, and screaming fury. But finally, after what feels like an eternity of hacking, slashing, and spilling guts across the deck, we have them beaten. Captain Thalassia Viper, the bitch who led the attack, is jumping ship with the handful of pirates who managed to survive our onslaught. They pile into a rickety dinghy, their faces twisted with fear and defeat as they row frantically away from the carnage.

I stand here on the deck, my chest heaving and my sword dripping with blood, as I scan the chaos for any sign of my mate. Danica had been fighting alongside me, her blade flashing in a blur of silver as she cut down pirate after pirate with a fierce, feral grace. But now, as the smoke clears and the screams die away, I realize with a sinking feeling that she is nowhere to be seen.

"Danica!" my voice raw and hoarse from the hours of battle.

But there is no answer, no flash of chestnut hair or gleam of honey-gold eyes amidst the carnage.

Lucian's nowhere to be seen either. I reach out for him through our mental link, but it's like shouting into a fucking void. Nothing.

What the fuck? She was right here, fighting by my side. But in the heat of battle, with the blood pounding in my ears and the adrenaline surging through my veins, I lost track of her.

I reach out through our mental connection, my thoughts tinged with desperation and fear. *"Baby? Can you hear me? Where are you, Angel?"*

Nothing. No response, no flicker of her presence in my mind. Just a yawning, aching emptiness that makes my heart clench and my stomach twists with dread.

Goddammit! I can't lose her, not again.

I race to the ship's edge, my boots pounding against the blood-slick deck as I scan the churning waters below. The sea is littered with bodies, the floating corpses of pirates and sailors alike bobbing in the waves like macabre flotsam. But there is no sign of Danica, no flash of her vibrant, living presence amidst the death and destruction.

Without a second thought, I dive over the side, the icy water hitting my sweat-soaked skin like a slap to the face. I open my eyes, the salt stinging and burning as I scan the murky depths for any sign of my mate. But all I see are sinking ships and drifting debris, the remnants of the battle slowly settling to the bottom of the sea.

I surface with a gasp, my lungs burning and my heart pounding. "Danica!"

But there is no answer, no sign of her amidst the carnage. I start swimming frantically, my muscles exhausted as I haul myself from one floating corpse to the next, searching for any sign of her.

No. No. This can't be fucking happening, not again. I have just gotten her back, have just—

"Mate!" Gideon yells from the ship. "Ye best be gettin' out of the waters. The Sirens will be down there taking whatever souls they can find. Get out, now!"

I feel a chill run down my spine at his words, a prickling sense of unease that has nothing to do with the cold sea.

Sirens. Of course. As if we didn't have enough to worry about, with Danica missing the ship in tatters and the crew exhausted and bleeding.

But I don't have time to dwell on the new threat, and I don't have time to do anything but scan the churning waters for any sign of my mate. I squint against the sun's glare, my eyes straining to pick out any hint of movement or color amidst the bobbing corpses and drifting debris.

But there's nothing. No flash of chestnut hair, no gleam of honey-gold eyes. Just an endless expanse of blue-green water, broken only by the occasional splash of crimson blood or the pale, bloated flesh of the dead.

I feel my heart sink, a cold, leaden weight settling in the pit of my stomach as the reality of the situation crashes over me like a tidal wave. Danica is gone, vanished without a trace in the chaos of the battle. And now, with the threat of the Sirens lurking beneath the waves, I have no real option than to get the hell out of these Siren-invested waters.

The real question—how the fuck am I going to get back on the goddamn ship now? I'm treading water in the middle of a sea of corpses, my muscles burning with exhaustion and my mind reeling.

Suddenly, a figure bursts out of the water beside me, the splash of their emergence sending ripples cascading across the surface. My heart leaps into my throat, hope, fear, and desperate longing all tangled together in a knot of raw emotion.

I squint against the sun's glare, my eyes straining to make out the details of the figure bobbing in the waves. And then I see it—a flash of chestnut hair and a gleam of honey-gold eyes.

My heart stops, my breath catching, "Dani!"

I start swimming towards her, my arms churning through the water with a strength born of pure, unadulterated desperation. My muscles scream in protest, my lungs burning with the effort of propelling myself through the churning sea.

But I don't care; I don't even feel the pain or the fatigue. All I can think about is getting to my mate, wrapping her in my arms, and never letting her go again.

As I draw closer, though, something starts to feel off. Dani's face is different; her features are too perfect, too symmetrical. And her smile—it's not the warm, loving grin I know so well, but something colder, more predatory.

"Hello, handsome," her voice like honey, silk, and sin all wrapped up in one.

I feel my limbs go limp, my body suddenly heavy and sluggish in the water. It's like I'm moving through molasses; every stroke is an effort of will that drains the strength from my muscles and the air from my lungs.

Who the hell?

And then, like a bolt of lightning splitting the sky, the crack of gunfire shatters the spell. I hear Gideon's voice, rough and urgent, cutting through the haze of enchantment like a knife."Back off ye man eatin' bitch!"

I shake my head, the fog of the siren's song clearing from my mind as I realize the danger I'm in. The creature in front of me is not my angel. No, it's a monster, a demon of the sea that seeks to drag me down into the abyss and steal the very breath from my lungs.

I don't hesitate. I dive beneath the waves, my legs kicking and my arms paddling with a strength born of pure animal panic. I can hear the creature behind me and feel the brush of its fingers against my ankle as it tries to grab hold and drag me back.

But I'm faster, my body cutting through the water like a blade as I surge towards the ship. Above me, I can hear the sharp crack of Gideon's pistol, muffled and distorted by the water. The gunshots echo through the depths like a series of dull, distant thunderclaps, a reminder of the danger that lurks below.

And then, like a miracle, I hear Erik's voice calling out to me from above. I look up, my eyes locking with his as he leans over the railing, a coil of rope clutched in his hand.

"Grab on!" he yells, and I don't hesitate.

I lunge forward, my fingers closing around the rough, salt-crusted fibers of the rope as I start hauling myself up the side of the ship. My muscles scream in protest, my lungs burning with the effort of dragging my exhausted, waterlogged body out of the sea.

I clamber over the railing and onto the deck. I collapse in a heap, my chest heaving and my limbs trembling with exhaustion. The world spins around me, the colors too bright and the sounds too loud after the muffled darkness of the water.

But even as I lie there, gasping for breath and trying to steady the pounding of my heart, I can't shake the image of the Siren's face, the perfect replica of my mate's features twisted into something cold and alien and utterly terrifying.

And I know, with a sickening certainty that settles in the pit of my stomach like a lead weight, that this is just the beginning, that the horrors lurking beneath the waves are nothing compared to the trials that lie ahead.

DANICA

26

I marvel at the breathtaking beauty surrounding us as we glide through the water. It's like swimming through a living kaleidoscope, with schools of brightly colored fish darting past, their scales glinting in the filtered sunlight. Coral reefs stretch out before us, their vibrant hues a dazzling array of pinks, purples, and blues, each teeming with life.

But I can't shake the feeling that I'm way out of my depth—both literally and figuratively. I'm a long way from the surface and even further from the life I knew before all this interdimensional bullshit started. It's like I've been dropped into the middle of a Disney movie on acid.

Except instead of a singing crab and a lovable flounder, I've got a mysterious mermaid with a hidden agenda and a one-way ticket to the land of "what the actual fuck."

And the worst part? I didn't even get to sign a contract or negotiate my terms. Nope, I just got sucked into this mess like a piece of plankton in a whale's mouth, with no idea where I'm going or how I'm going to get back to the surface.

The mermaid is a vision of ethereal beauty and power. Her long, inky black hair flows behind her like a living shadow, contrasting sharply with the silvery scales covering her arms and chest. Her tail is a sleek, powerful appendage that propels her through the water with effortless grace. And those spikes along her back? They look like they were ripped straight from a shark's fin, giving her an air of danger.

She dives deeper, dragging me like a ragdoll caught in a riptide. My lungs start to burn, and panic rises in my chest. I pull away, trying to free my hand from her vise-like grip, but she ignores my protests.

When I think I'm about to black out, she whirls around and presses her lips to mine, breathing life into my starved lungs. *"We are almost there,"* she sing-songs into my head, her voice a haunting melody.

I decide to take advantage of this newfound mental connection. *"Where the hell are you taking me?"* I demand.

She looks over her shoulder and smiles, her eyes glinting with amusement and secrecy. *"You'll see,"* she replies cryptically, her tail flicking through the water.

Well, at least I know the Faerite stone is working its magic, allowing us to communicate telepathically. It's a small comfort in a sea of uncertainty, but I'll take what I can get at this point.

Suddenly, I see a shimmering pool ahead, its surface rippling with an otherworldly light. It's vertical, like a doorway standing upright in the middle of the ocean, and every instinct screams at me to swim away.

Before I can make a break for it, the mermaid tightens her grip and pulls me forward with a powerful kick of her tail.

"Relax," she whispers. And just like that, my body relaxes as if compelled.

What the hell?

We reach the shimmering pool, and she swims through it without hesitation, dragging me along.

As we pass through the shimmering veil, I feel a rush of energy coursing through my body. The water around us starts to churn and swirl, and for a moment, I'm convinced I'm about to be torn apart by the sheer force of it all.

The swirling sensation intensifies, and I feel my consciousness slip away.

Then, utter darkness.

I jolt awake, my mind spinning like a top. I slowly peel myself off the wet, slick stone, feeling like a piece of gum stuck to the bottom of a shoe. It takes me a moment to realize that I'm on solid ground. The last thing I remember is swimming under the sea like a discount Ariel and then going through some watery portal that made me feel like I was being flushed down the world's most giant toilet.

I look around, and my eyes nearly pop out of their sockets. Holy shit, this place is like nothing I've ever seen before. It's dark but hauntingly beautiful, like a gothic cathedral designed by Gomez Adams on a bender. Water surrounds me like a giant glass fishbowl, casting an eerie blue glow over everything.

As my eyes adjust to the dim light, I realize I am in some underground palace. The walls are adorned with intricate carvings of sea creatures and mythical beasts, their eyes seeming to follow me as I move. Bioluminescent plants and creatures cast a soft, otherworldly glow, making it feel like I've stumbled into a scene from Avatar.

"I've done what you have asked, your Majesty," a voice behind me says, snapping me out of my morbid reverie.

Your Majesty? Where the hell am I, the underwater kingdom of Atlantis? I turn around, half-expecting to see Poseidon himself, a talking crab, or a singing fish, but instead, I'm greeted by the sight of the most stunning creature I've ever seen.

There, lying in a pool of water like a gothic mermaid queen is a woman. Her skin is a rich, dark brown, like the color of black coffee, and her hair is styled in long, intricate dreadlocks that fall past her waist and move with a life of their own. Her eyes are a deep, soulful brown that seems to hold all the universe's secrets.

"Ah, Lorelei. Thank you kindly," the dark mermaid says, her voice like honey poured over razor blades. "You shall be richly rewarded."

Lorelei? Like the mythical siren who lured sailors to their doom with her enchanting voice? Oh, this keeps getting better and better.

I clear my throat, trying to find my voice amid all this insanity. "Uh, excuse me, your *Majesty*, but would you mind telling me what the actual *fuck* is going on here? Because last time I checked, I didn't sign up for a one-way ticket to Ursula's lair."

The dark mermaid smiles, her lips curling up in a way that makes me feel like I'm about to become her next meal. "Welcome to my domain, my dear," she says, her voice echoing like whispers of the sea in the vast cavern. "I've been waiting for your arrival."

Well, fuck me sideways with a rusty trident.

"Who the hell are you?" I ask, trying to keep my voice steady. My crown is buzzing like a nest of angry hornets, and I can practically taste the deception in the air, thick and cloying like molasses.

The dark mermaid slowly lifts herself out of the pool, her opalescent black tail slapping against the floor with a splash that echoes through the cavernous space. And then, in a moment that makes my heart stop and my jaw drop, her tail starts to shimmer and shift, morphing into a pair of smooth, toned legs that would make even the most seasoned supermodel weep with envy.

She stands there, her naked body on full display like some underwater burlesque show. I can't help but stare, my eyes tracing the curves of her figure and the intricate patterns of opalescent black scales that still cling to her skin like armor.

A male approaches from the shadows, wrapping her in a black robe adorned with intricate swirls of silver and gold. The fabric clings to her, accentuating her curves in an alluring and terrifying way.

"I am Calypso," she says, her voice is sweet that belies the danger lurking beneath the surface. "And I've been just itching to meet you..."

She looks at me expectantly, waiting for me to introduce myself.

I feel the blood drain from my face so fast you'd think I'd seen a ghost, my stomach twisting itself into a pretzel as the name Calypso—the Sea Witch—registers—the same psycho Gideon warned me about.

Great. Just great. Here I thought I'd dodged Bloodbane's whole "kidnap me and drag me to the Sea Witch" schtick, but nope! Apparently, all roads lead to her royal pain-in-the-ass-ness.

If I had to put money on it, I'd say she's planning to throw a massive wrench in my grand tour of this underwater wonderland.

Awesome.

I turn behind me, my heart pounding, and see Lorelei bobbing up and down in a pool of water like a demented mermaid Barbie. She's got a smirk plastered on her face that makes me want to slap it right off, but I manage to restrain myself. Barely.

"I'm so glad you've met my Siren," Calypso purrs, her eyes sparkling with mischief and malice. "I'm certain you'll meet plenty more now that you're my honored guest."

A Siren?

Oh, that's just great! So now I get to deal with two different species that look alike. It's good to know that my life just got even more complicated. Add that to the ever-growing list of "Things That Totally Could've Been Mentioned Earlier."

But Calypso? Now, she's a different kettle of fish—gotta be a mermaid. No shark-like fin cutting through her back, and she's rocking a pair of legs. Cue the endless stream of questions.

I straighten my spine, squaring my shoulders like I'm about to go into battle. Which, let's be real, I probably am.

"Listen, *Ursula*, as much as I appreciate the invitation to your little underwater soirée, I'm afraid I will have to decline. You see, I've got places to be, people to save, and a whole lot of interdimensional fuckery to sort out. So, if you don't mind, I'll be on my way."

I start to turn, half-expecting to be blasted into oblivion by some magical sea witch mojo. But to my surprise, Calypso smiles, her lips curling up in a way that makes my blood run cold.

"Oh, my precious dear," her voice smooth like the calm sea. "I'm afraid you're misunderstanding. You won't leave until I get what I desire from you."

Suddenly, the water in a nearby pool erupts like a geyser, and a man comes bursting through the surface with all the grace of a drunken swan. But it's not just any man—it's a Siren, complete with scales, shark fins, and a tail that looks like it could bitch-slap a great white shark into submission.

Clutched in his muscular arms like a sack of potatoes is another man, limp and lifeless. The Siren flops his cargo onto the floor with about as much care as a toddler with a rag doll, giving him a rough shove for good measure.

"Your Majesty, I also found this one—just off the wreckage of the ships. I thought you would like it."

I peer at the lifeless form on the ground, my heart sinking as I take in the familiar golden hair and lithe, muscular build.

Oh my god!

"Lucian!" I shout, my voice cracking with fear and rage. I drop to my knees beside him, my hands shaking as I search for any sign of life. But he's not breathing, his chest as still as a statue.

I whirl around to face the Siren asshole, my eyes blazing with a fury that could burn a forest. "What the hell did you do to him, you overgrown fish stick?" I snarl, my hands curling into fists at my sides.

But the Siren only smirks, his tail flicking lazily behind him like a cat toying with a mouse. "Thank you, Triton," Calypso purrs, her voice honeyed like the sweetest nectar. "Your services have been most appreciated, indeed."

Appreciated? Appreciated?!

She's acting like he just brought her a fucking fruit basket, not the lifeless body of my friend. I want to scream, to lash out, to tear this whole fucking palace apart with my bare hands.

But I can't. Because right now, the only thing that matters is Lucian. I turn back to him, "Lucian, you asshole," I whisper, my voice cracking like glass. "Don't you dare fucking die on me."

I start compressions, my hands shaking as I try to force life back into his lungs.

One, two, three, four, five. *Breathe, you stubborn son of a bitch.*

One, two, three, four, five. *Come on, Lucian.*

"Come on, you jerk," I mutter, my voice thick with unshed tears. "Don't die on me. Not like this. Not here."

But he remains still, his skin growing colder by the second. Tears blur my vision, hot and stinging as they roll down my cheeks. This can't be happening. This can't be real.

I feel a hand on my shoulder, cold and clammy like the touch of a corpse. I look up to see Calypso looming over me, her dark eyes glittering with a hunger that makes my skin crawl.

"Don't fret, my dear," her voice smooth like honey laced with poison. "He isn't dead. Not *yet*, anyway."

Just then, Lucian sputters and coughs, spewing out a veritable tsunami of seawater. I quickly roll him onto his side as he continues to hurl up what seems like the entire freakin ocean, rubbing his back in soothing circles and making shushing noises that probably do nothing at all to help.

"Oh, thank God," I mutter, relief washing over me like a tidal wave. I mean, I know it takes a lot to kill a vampire, but I'm still learning the ropes here. For all I know, these Sirens could have some secret vampire kryptonite up their scaly sleeves.

"Ughhh—" Lucian groans, his voice rough and raspy like he's been gargling with sandpaper. "What in the ever-loving *fuck* just happened?" He pushes himself up onto his hands and knees, retching up another gallon of seawater that splashes onto the floor in a truly disgusting display.

"Thanks for drowning me, you asshole." Lucian sputters and coughs.

It doesn't take a genius to figure out what went down. Lucian, being the noble fucking idiot that he is, must've dived in after me when I took my little unplanned swim. And like the poor, unsuspecting bastard he is, got snatched up by one of Calypso's goons, just like yours truly.

I take a deep breath, trying to steady my nerves and keep my breakfast from making a surprise reappearance. I push myself to my feet, my legs shaking.

My hands flame on as I meet Calypso's gaze, my eyes blazing with a defiance that borders on suicidal. "Alright, you overgrown tuna," I snarl. "What's your angle here? Why the hell did you drag us down here?"

Before I can blink, Calypso waves her hand, and a smoky cloud envelops my hands, snuffing out the flames like a candle in the wind. I stand there, stunned, my mouth hanging open.

"Not needed, little goddess."

My stomach plunges, my heart hammering like a jackhammer in my chest. Then I see it—a seashell necklace with a black stone embedded in it.

The Soul Stone. I knew it, I freakin' knew it!

Calypso's smile widens, her teeth glinting like pearls in the dim light. "Oh, my sweet little pawn, do you have no idea what storm you've stumbled into? But fret not. You'll learn soon enough."

She pauses momentarily, letting her words sink like a stone in my gut. "For now, let's just say that you two will be my honored guests for a spell. And if you cooperate, do as I ask, and fetch what I need, you'll be on your merry way."

"Whoa, whoa, whoa," Lucian says, holding his hands like he's trying to stop traffic. "Let me get this straight. You yank us out of our regularly scheduled lives, drag us down to your little underwater Barbie Dream House, and then expect us to run errands for you like a couple of well-trained poodles? Yeah, that's gonna be a hard pass from me."

I shoot him a look, silently begging him to shut his damn mouth before he gets us both turned into fish food. But Lucian, being the lovable dumbass that he is, grins at me like he's having the time of his life.

"What?" he asks, with enough mock innocence to choke a nun. "I'm just saying what we're all thinking. I mean, come on. Look at this place. It's like a cross between Aquaman's secret lair and a Bond villain's wet dream. I keep waiting for the sharks with frickin' laser beams attached to their heads to show up."

"Lucian," I warn, my voice low and deadly, like the calm before the shitstorm. "I swear to every god in every realm, if you don't shut your damn mouth, I will personally feed you to the nearest Kraken, piece by piece."

"Promises, promises," he smirks. "Keep talking dirty to me."

I roll my eyes. Calypso clears her throat, drawing our attention back. "If you two are quite finished," her voice like ice water down my spine. "Maybe we can get down to business, yes?"

"Just so you know, I can conjure a portal on a whim and leave this place anytime I want, so your whole 'keeping us here' bullshit? Yeah, that's not gonna fly, sister."

Calypso's eyes narrow into slits, her smile morphing into a predatory grin that makes the hairs on my neck stand up. "Oh, I wouldn't be so certain about that, dear."

Smoky tendrils whip out from the shadows, wrapping around Lucian like a python coiling around its prey. He lets out a strangled cry as the tendrils slam him against the wall with a sickening thud, his body writhing in their grasp.

Lucian's face contorts in agony, his eyes bulging as he gasps for air, the tendrils tightening around his throat like a noose. "You see, little goddess," Calypso purrs, her voice oozing with malice, "Lucian's soul is untethered—I could easily siphon his soul, along with that Silver Fox you hold so precious."

How in the seven hells does she know about Erik? What, does she have some magical stalker globe or something?

My blood turns to ice in my veins, my heart seizing in my chest. The Soul-Tie thing. Shit. I can't lose Lucian or Erik—not after everything we've been through, not after all the shit we've survived. Lucian's eyes lock with mine, wide and desperate, as he struggles against the shadows, his fingers scrabbling uselessly at the tendrils around his neck.

I know those shadows too well, the icy cold touch of their despair, the whispers of hopelessness that seep into your very bones. They're the same shadows Azrael wielded, the same shadows that nearly broke me before.

"All it takes to end one of your precious vampires is a simple decapitation or ripping out their hearts, and then... their souls belong to me." Her words send an icy shiver, washing over me with a sickening sense of déjà vu.

My mind flashes back to that night in the alley behind Karma. Adrian's lifeless body, his heart torn from his chest, the light fading from his eyes. The scene plays out like a horror movie on repeat, a stark reminder of how I failed him. My guilt rises in my throat—burning bile.

And now, here I am, face to face with a bitch who seems hell-bent on proving she can do the same damn thing. The thought of her getting her slimy tentacles on

Lucian, Erik, and anyone I care about... it's enough to make my blood boil, and my stomach churn.

"Dani..." Lucian chokes out, his face turning an alarming shade of red as he struggles for air.

I surrender my hands, my voice shaking. "Alright, alright," I say, words rushing out. "Just let him go. Please."

Calypso stares at me, her eyes boring into mine like she's trying to read my soul. Then, with a flick of her wrist, the shadows retreat, melting back into the darkness.

Lucian drops to the floor in a heap, gasping for air. "Ahhh...you fucking psycho!" he croaks, his voice like he's been gargling with razor blades and whiskey. "That's it. I want a goddamn refund for this underwater shit show. I didn't sign up for the hentai tentacle version of Finding fucking Nemo!"

Calypso smiles, a cruel, twisted thing that makes my skin crawl. "Dani, is it? Consider that a warning. Cross me, and I won't hesitate to tear apart everything and everyone you hold dear."

She leans forward, her face inches from mine, her breath hot. "You're in my world now, little girl. And in my world, there are no rules, no mercy. Only pain and suffering for those foolish enough to defy me."

I swallow hard, my throat dry as the desert. I know she's not bluffing—she has the power to make good on her threats. And the thought of losing Lucian, Erik, or anyone I care about... it's enough to make me want to vomit.

I take a deep breath, square my shoulders, and meet her gaze head-on, my eyes blazing with defiance.

"I get it," my voice steady despite the terror churning in my gut. "You're the big bad sea witch, and we're all just pawns in your little game. But let's get one thing straight. You may have the power to hurt the people I care about, but that doesn't mean I'm going to roll over and play dead."

I take a step forward. Chin lifted in a silent challenge. "You want me to retrieve this thing for you? Fine. I'll do it. But not because I'm afraid of you, and not because I give a fuck about your little power trip. I'll do it because I care about my friends and because I'm not going to let you hurt them."

Calypso's eyes flash with something that might be respect or pure bloodlust. "Bold words, Dani, but we'll see how long that bravado holds when you confront the horrors waiting for you."

She turns and glides away, her black robe billowing behind her like a cloud of ink in the water. "Rest now, little girl," she calls over her shoulder, her voice echoing through the chamber. "You will need your strength for what's coming."

And with that, she's gone, leaving me alone with Lucian and the sinking feeling that I've just signed my death warrant.

27

I'm in Lucian's face in a hot second, glaring at him. "You just had to go and follow me?" I snap.

The thought of Lucian being trapped down here with me, his soul at the mercy of this sea witch—It's bad enough that I'm tangled up in this mess, but the thought of Calypso being able to end his life with a snap of her fingers makes me sick to my stomach.

Lucian shrugs, his face sporting a grin so smug it could win awards. "Well, excuse me for trying to save your delicious ass—someone had to play hero before you became an all-you-can-eat buffet for Jaws and his fishy friends. Next time, I'll just let you audition for 'Titanic: The Sequel' all by yourself."

"Bravo, Lucian. Stellar performance. You only managed to drown yourself in the process. And let's not kid ourselves. It's not like we're any better off now. Your little stunt will get you killed—congrats on that one." I can feel the tears threatening to spill, so I quickly turn away, refusing to let him see me cry.

Breathe, just...breathe.

But it's no use. The fear is like a living thing inside me, clawing at my insides like a monster.

"We're stuck down here with a crazy fish lady, and your soul is on the line," my voice barely above a whisper. "If anything happens to you...I'll never forgive myself."

Lucian rolls his eyes. "Well, excuse the hell out of me for trying to save your cute little ass, Honey Pot! So, my heroic move sucked ass. My bad! And all this 'lost souls' crap you're rambling about? It's all Greek to me, Dream Girl. What kind of dick do you think I am? A premium-grade-A asshole with extra cheese? Besides, if I let you kick the bucket on my watch, those witchy wonder twins would never shut up about it. They'd probably drag your soggy ass back from the dead so they could murder me in technicolor while you watched with popcorn. So yeah, you're welcome for the impromptu lifeguard service, Baywatch."

I roll my eyes. His memory loss is cranking the chaos up to eleven. Before I can come up with a scathing retort, Rhyland's voice thunders into my head.

"Dani."

I keep my tone soothing, trying to calm the storm I can feel brewing in Rhyland's mind.

"Hey, babe, don't freak out. I was Siren-napped and was brought to Calypso's lair, but I'm not hurt. Lucian is here with me." I quickly respond, thanking every deity I can think of that I can still communicate with him in this underwater deathtrap.

"How the hell—" He stops, and I can feel his relief through our bond, knowing that I'm unharmed. But I can also sense his anger and hostility at the situation simmering beneath the surface. *"How can I get to you? Tell me what to do, and I'll fucking do it."*

I send a wave of calm through our connection, trying to soothe his rage. *"I know you would, babe, and I love you for that. But let's try to handle this without going all 'Poseidon's Wrath' on the entire ocean, okay? Calypso has the Soul Stone—she's threatened Lucian already, and...she needs me for some bullshit quest, so I'm going to see what she wants. In the meantime, stay put until I can find a way out of here. I don't need you charging in, guns blazing, and pissing her off."*

"Fuck—she does? You're certain it's the Soul Stone?" his tone uncertain. *"I don't fucking like this, Dani. You know I hate sitting on my ass while you're being held captive by some sea bitch."*

I think back to those freaky shadow wisps and how she nearly choked Lucian to death.

"Without a doubt! Just don't do anything stupid, Rhyland—I mean it. Trust me, okay?"

"I do trust you. That has nothing to do with this, Angel. And why the hell is Lucian down there with you? What happened with him—when you went back?"

"Cliffnotes version—Emily summoned me to the apartment. Plot twist: she's a witch now. Apparently, when you bring someone back from the dead at a witch massacre, you absorb their magical mojo, and now Em's got a shiny new set of witchy powers. They had staged a daring rescue mission for Lucian, who's now basically a toddler in a grown man's body, thanks to Azrael and that other witch bitch hitting the 'factory reset' button on his brain."

Rhyland is quiet for an eternity before finally responding, *"Oh. What the hell do you mean by 'factory reset' button?"*

"Lucian's memory is a blank slate—He doesn't remember anything about us, the mission, nada." I quip.

"You alright there, champ? You look like you're trying to hold in a fart that's got a vendetta against your intestines. Your face..." he circles his finger around his face, emphasizing his point, "has got 'constipated philosopher' written all over it. What's on your mind, sunshine?"

I scoff. "No, you dumbass. I'm talking with Rhyland."

He stares at me like I've just claimed to be the lovechild of Bigfoot and the Loch Ness Monster. I let out an exasperated sigh, realizing that I will have to reteach this walking, talking embodiment of a migraine everything from scratch, and the mere thought of it is already making my brain throb in protest.

My thoughts cut off as a male Siren glides into the room, like some water God.

He's tall, with long brown hair that looks like it was styled by a mermaid with a salon addiction, and dark eyes that could make even the most hardened criminal go weak in the knees. And his body—he's ripped like a Greek god, with abs you could grate cheese on. He's wearing flowy pants made from seaweed and wishful thinking, leaving his chiseled chest on full display.

As the siren approaches me, I find myself scuttling back like a crab on a hot beach. Ever the gallant hero, Lucian steps in front of me, his hands held out like he's trying to stop traffic. "Whoa, whoa, that's far enough, shark bait," his tone serious, with enough machismo to make Rambo look like a pussy.

The siren smirks like he's heard it all before. And then, he starts to hum. And holy shit, it is a sound that could make even the most tone-deaf person weep with joy. It's beautiful and eerie all at once.

I can feel my eyes glazing over, my body turning mush like I'm under some spell. Even Lucian, usually about as hypnotizable as a brick wall, looks ready to follow this guy into the depths of hell.

Then, just as quickly as it started, the humming stops. I shake my head, trying to clear the cobwebs from my brain. "It looks stunning on you," the Siren says, his voice like honey poured over gravel.

I blink, trying to figure out what the hell he's talking about. And that's when I feel it—a weight around my neck that wasn't there before. I reach up, and holy shit, there's a seashell necklace wrapped around my throat like a choker.

"What the hell?" I mutter, trying to yank the thing off. But it doesn't budge; the smooth, cold surface of the shell chokes me more like a noose. "What is this?" I demand, my voice rising in pitch. "Take it off." I cough, trying to get air.

The Siren smirks like he's getting a kick out of watching me struggle. "The more you try to remove it, the tighter it'll get. Unless you're into autoerotic asphyxiation, I suggest you leave it be," he says, his voice oozing with smugness. "Calypso's gift to you."

"Why? What the hell is this thing?" I growl, my hands balling into fists at my sides. The choker finally eases up, letting me breathe properly again.

"It's a tracker," he says, his eyes glinting with sadistic glee. "It's a precautionary measure."

With that, he spins on his heel and swags out of the room, leaving me standing there with my blood pressure skyrocketing. Great, now I'm some underwater pet with a goddamn tracking device.

I turn to Lucian, my eyes blazing with fury. "Well, isn't this just peachy?" I snarl. "Not only are we trapped down here with a bunch of fish-faced assholes, but now I've got this stupid necklace that turns me into a goddamn beacon."

Lucian shrugs, grinning. "Hey, look on the bright side. At least you'll always have a place to put your seashell collection."

I shoot him a glare that could freeze hell itself. Before I can retort, another Siren enters the room, a female with long, flowing hair the color of purple coral and eyes as blue as the deepest ocean.

"Calypso requests your presence at dinner," her voice like gentle waves. "You are to dress in the attire provided and join her in the dining hall to discuss your quest."

Fantastic. Sure, let's dress up and act like we're here by choice, not because we're prisoners in this underwater funhouse of horrors.

"Follow me," she says, clarifying that 'no' isn't an option.

I shoot Lucian a look, but he just shrugs and trots after her like an eager lapdog. I let out a heavy sigh, my shoulders sagging in resignation.

As soon as I am able, I'm burning this damn collar off.

As we make our way through the winding corridors, I can't help but marvel at the sheer beauty of it all. The walls are made of shimmering black pearls inlaid with glittering gemstones. Bioluminescent plants line the hallways, casting an eerie blue glow over everything.

But it's the view outside that takes my breath away. Through the glass dome, I can see the vast expanse of the ocean stretching out in every direction. Schools of brightly colored fish dart past, their scales glinting like precious jewels. In the distance, I can see the shadowy outline of a massive whale, its song echoing through the water like a beautiful symphony.

A pod of dolphins swims up, and the craziness suddenly melts. I'm pressing myself against the glass like an overexcited kid at the aquarium, my eyes wide with wonder.

Oh my god, they're so cute!

I've always been a total sucker for dolphins—they're such incredible creatures. Intelligent, playful, and affectionate. In high school, I was convinced my career path would be Marine Biology. But that all changed when I discovered I was adopted, leading me to choose genetics instead.

"Oh, hello there," I coo at the glass as if they can hear me. One of the dolphins swims closer and flips its fin at me, almost like it's waving. A pure and joyful laugh bubbles out of me. "Oh my god, did you see that?"

Lucian, just as captivated, is smooshed up against the glass right next to me, laughing and grinning like a fool.

"Ahem!" We both jump at the sound of the siren clearing her throat. "If you two are quite finished molesting the glass, perhaps you could follow me now."

Well, excuse us for having a moment of joy in this underwater prison. Rude much?

We finally reach a set of enormous double doors, their surface intricately carved with scenes of underwater life. The siren pushes them open, revealing a grand bedroom that seems to have been designed with human comfort in mind.

The room is a stunning blend of dark elegance and aquatic beauty. The walls are a deep, rich blue, reminiscent of the ocean's depths, adorned with intricate patterns that look like the currents themselves carved them. The floor is a polished black stone that seems to shimmer like the scales of a fish, and the ceiling is a masterpiece of swirling blues and greens, like the sea's surface on a stormy day.

The room's centerpiece is a massive bed, a frame made of what looks like driftwood, twisted and gnarled into an intricate headboard. The bedding is a lush, deep green, like the color of seaweed, with delicate, shimmering shells that catch the light like tiny stars.

On the other side of the room, there's a vanity table carved from a single piece of black coral. The mirror above it is framed with twisted, dark metal.

But perhaps the most stunning feature is the floor-to-ceiling windows that look out into the depths of the sea.

"You will bathe and dress for dinner. You will be meeting with Her Majesty," the female siren commands. "I will return in one hour to escort you."

It's all so formal, so civilized. This is not what I expected when I imagined meeting the Sea Witch. I had visions of some ancient, decrepit hag with a temper shorter than a sea urchin's spine, living in a lair that reeked of rotting kelp. Not this.

Lucian lets out a low whistle, his eyes bugging out. "Hot damn, this is some next-level bougie shit. So, who's calling dibs on the bath first? Or should we be good little eco-warriors and conserve water by doubling up?" He waggles his eyebrows at me, grinning.

I roll my eyes. "In your dreams, buddy. Ladies first, of course. And by ladies, I mean me, myself, and I."

I sashay into the bathing area, and holy mother of luxury, it's like stepping into a spa designed by Poseidon himself. The room is enormous, with a massive, onyx-colored clawfoot tub that looks carved out of a single, gigantic gemstone. The surface is so smooth and polished that I can practically see my reflection.

One wall is lined with mirrors stretching from floor to ceiling, each framed by eerie bioluminescent flowers. But the real showstopper is the open ceiling, topped with a glass dome that offers a breathtaking view of the open sea above.

I take in the mesmerizing dance of the waves and the shimmering play of light filtering through the water. "Wow," I breathe, the word slipping out in a reverent whisper.

I step closer to the tub, running my hand along the smooth, cool surface. The onyx is so dark it's almost hypnotic, like staring into the depths of a bottomless abyss.

"Careful, Honey Pot," Lucian's voice cuts through my reverie, his tone dripping with glee. "If you lean in too far, you might fall in and drown. And then who would I have to annoy the shit out of?"

I flip the bird over my shoulder. "*Har har*, very funny. Now, if you'll excuse me, I will take a nice, long, Lucian-free bath. Try not to break anything while I'm gone."

"Aww, come on. You don't need me to scrub those hard-to-reach places?" Lucian smirks, his eyebrows doing a suggestive little dance. "I'm a pro at washing hair, too. These magic fingers of mine have mad massage skills."

"Tempting, but I think I can manage to lather, rinse, and repeat all by myself, thanks." I give him a gentle shove towards the door, "Now, be a good little vampire and go entertain yourself while I enjoy some much-needed alone time with my new best friend, Mr. Bubble."

Lucian pouts exaggeratedly. "Fine, fine. I see how it is. Abandoning me in my hour of need. I'll just be out here, all alone, with nothing but my thoughts and the faint sound of splashing to keep me company."

With that, I give him one final nudge out the door and close it with a satisfying click.

First order of business—getting this stupid collar off. I'm nobody's pet, and I'll be damned if I let some sea witch treat me like a dog on a leash.

I reach up, my fingers closing around the smooth surface of the shell. I can feel my power stirring within me, a heat that starts in my belly and spreads outward, permeating my entire being with a warm, tingling sensation.

I focus on that feeling and the light that sits beneath my skin, waiting to be unleashed. My hands begin to glow, a soft, pulsing light that grows brighter with each passing second.

I can feel the heat building in my hands, a searing, almost painful sensation that makes me grit my teeth and clench my jaw.

But I don't let up, don't back down. I pour every ounce of my strength and determination into the task at hand, willing the collar to break, to shatter, to fucking disintegrate into dust.

And then, with a snap that seems to echo through the room, the collar falls away, clattering to the floor at my feet. With a sense of grim satisfaction, I watch it crumble and dissolve, turning to ash and blowing away on some unseen breeze.

I take a deep breath, feeling like a weight has been lifted off my shoulders.

I undress, peeling off my salt-encrusted clothes and letting them fall to the floor in a heap. The air is cool against my bare skin, raising goosebumps along my arms and legs. But as I sink into the steaming water, feeling it envelop me like a warm, soothing embrace, all the tension, fear, and exhaustion of the fucking day I've had starts to ease out.

For a moment, I forget our danger and the impossible task ahead. I let myself breathe and exist in this perfect, peaceful instant.

But, like all good things, it doesn't last. Reality comes crashing back in Lucian's voice, muffled by the closed door but still annoyingly audible.

"Hey, Dani...? You have people out here that say they need to help wash you? I swear to god, if you allow them in and not me, I'm gonna be very, very—"

I sink lower into the water, submerging myself completely to cut off his babbling.

It's going to be a long night.

RHYLAND

28

After hours of busting our asses, we finally managed to get a few sails up and running, just enough to get us out of these siren-infested waters and head towards Driftwood Market. Gideon tells me it's the safest place to regroup and lick our wounds—to patch up the ship and resupply while we wait for Dani.

And thank fuck for that because Gideon's ship took one hell of a beating in that battle. The hull is riddled with holes, the deck is slick with blood and gore, and the main sails and masts are blown to shit. But somehow, against all odds, the stubborn old girl never sank.

As we limp our way to Driftwood Market, I fill Gideon and Erik in on what I learned about Dani, how she's been captured by the Sea Witch—and Lucian is with her. I'm still pissed at the little shit for getting all territorial with her, memory wiped or not. Gonna have to stake my claim on her in front of his damn face until he gets the fucking message, or he's going to be getting his ass handed to him...again.

The thought of Dani down there, alone with Lucian, is enough to make my blood boil. I know my brother—know the kind of bullshit tactics he'll try to pull on her, especially after what I already saw.

I clench my fists at my sides, my nails digging into my palms hard enough to draw blood. I try to breathe through the rage and frustration, focusing on the steady rhythm of the waves and the salt spray on my face. But it's no use. The fury is like a living thing inside me, coiled and ready to strike at the slightest provocation.

"Brother, Lucian doesn't stand a chance." Erik's voice cuts through the haze of my anger. "I know that look, that fury you're holding."

I stare out at the horizon, my eyes narrowed against the glare of the setting sun. "I know that," I snarl. "But even with his memories gone, Lucian's still a fucking shit starter. And his blood still flows through her veins..."

I trail off, the words sticking in my throat like shards of glass. I hate the fact that this is even a goddamn issue—hate the thought of my own brother trying to stake a claim on my mate.

"I saw the look in his eye, Erik," my jaw clenched so tight my teeth grind together. "The way he was watching her like she was a fucking prize to be won. Like she belonged to him."

Erik sighs, a sound that's equal parts exasperation and amusement. "She will kick his ass before you can, brother. Mark my words."

I glance over at him, my eyebrows raised in surprise. Sure enough, there's a grin tugging at the corners of his mouth, a glint of mischief in his silver eyes. Despite everything, I feel a flicker of pride kindling in my chest.

Because he's right, my feisty little Angel is more than capable of putting Lucian in his place, of showing him exactly who he's dealing with. She's a force to be reckoned with, a fierce and fearless warrior who won't take shit from anyone, least of all my arrogant prick of a brother.

But that doesn't mean I won't have words with him myself the second I lay eyes on him again.

After an entire day of sailing, the sun finally dips below the horizon, painting the sky in shades of orange and pink before fading to a deep, inky blue. And there, rising out of the darkness like a beacon of light and life, is Driftwood Market.

From a distance, it looks like a floating city, a sprawling maze of rafts and small islands lashed with ropes and planks. Fires flicker and dance on the decks of the makeshift buildings, their warm glow casting long shadows across the water. Lanterns hang from every post and railing, their soft light mingling with the stars overhead to create an eerie and enchanting scene.

As we guide our battered ship toward the docks, I feel a sense of anticipation building in my chest. After the chaos and carnage of the battle with the Serpent Skulls, three days of hell through the Dark Tides, and the gut-wrenching fear and uncertainty of losing Dani, the sight of this vibrant, bustling hub of commerce and culture is like a balm to my battered soul.

The moment I step off the gangplank and onto the weathered planks of the dock, my senses are assaulted by a dizzying array of sights, sounds, and smells. The air is thick with the aroma of exotic spices and roasting meat, the tang of salt and brine mingling with the sweet scent of ripe fruit and fresh bread.

All around me, I hear the clink of coins changing hands, the rustle of fabric as bolts of shimmering silk and rich velvet are unfurled for inspection, the clatter of pottery, and the clang of metal on metal as blacksmiths and artisans ply their trade.

I let my gaze roam over the stalls and shops, taking in the dizzying array of displayed goods. There are barrels of spices in every rainbow color, their heady scents mingling in the air. There are baskets of fresh fruits and vegetables, their skins smooth and unblemished. There are racks of gleaming weapons and armor, their edges honed to a razor's sharpness.

But amidst the beauty and wonder, a sense of danger lurks beneath the surface. I can see it in the merchants' calculating eyes, how their hands hover near their weapons even as they smile and bargain. Cutthroats and thieves wait in the shadowed corners and narrow alleys, ready to relieve unwary travelers of their coins and lives.

Gideon leads us through the winding, chaotic planks of Driftwood Market, navigating the maze of stalls and shops with the ease of a man who's spent half his life in places like this. He guides us past the whorehouses, their doorways draped with gauzy curtains and the scent of perfume and sex heavy in the air. Past the merchants hawking their wares, their voices rising and falling in a cacophony of accents and languages as they try to lure in passing customers.

We don't have time to linger—I don't have the patience to stop and browse when my mate is being held captive for whatever this fucking sea bitch wants with her. So I keep my head down and my feet moving, following Gideon as he leads us to a dimly lit tavern near the edge of the market.

The moment we step inside, the noise and chaos of the market fade away, replaced by the low murmur of conversation and the clink of glasses. The air is thick with the scent of ale and sweat, the floorboards sticky beneath our boots as we weave our way through the crowd to an empty table in the back.

As we settle in, Gideon signals the barkeep for drinks. She quickly sets our drinks on the table and leaves with a wink. "Drink up, mates."

Gideon turns to me with a grim expression on his weathered face. "We be safe here, lads. This here market be common ground. It goes against the pirate code to attack here."

I clench my jaw, my fingers tightening around my mug as I level a hard stare at the captain. "Just like at Captain's Haven," I fire back.

Just the thought of that bastard Bloodbane and what he did back there, snatching Dani away from me like she was some fucking prize to be won, has me practicing breathing techniques like some goddamn meditative asshole.

Gideon flinches at my words, his face twisting with guilt and fury. "Aye, that scurvy dog broke the code, and he'll pay a steep price for that."

Beside me, Erik leans forward, his silver eyes glinting with a calculating light. "What price is that, Captain?"

Gideon takes a long swig of his ale, his gaze distant as he stares into the murky depths of his mug. "By attackin' on common ground, he's violated the most sacred of our laws," his voice low and grave. "The punishment for such a crime be harsh and unforgivin'."

He sets his mug down with a heavy thunk, his eyes meeting mine with a fierce intensity. "He'll be cast out, banished from every port and harbor in the realm. No ship will take him on. No other crew or initiate will sail under his command. And if he dares to show his face in Captain's Haven again..."

Gideon's hand drifts to the hilt of his sword, his fingers curling around the weathered leather. "He'll be fired upon on sight, his ship sunk to the depths, and his crew left to the mercy of the sea. That be the price of betrayal, lad. And it's a price that bastard will pay, mark my words."

I feel a grim sense of satisfaction, a flicker of vindictive pleasure at the thought of that traitorous fuck getting what he deserves. But it's a fleeting thing, quickly swallowed up by the all-consuming need to get Dani.

So I take a deep breath, forcing myself to unclench my fists and relax my jaw. I meet Gideon's gaze head-on, my eyes burning with a fierce, unyielding determination.

"Good," I growl. "But right now, all I give a damn about is getting my mate back and bringing her home where she belongs. I'll deal with that piece of shit Bloodbane later."

Because for all the hell he put my angel through, all the pain and fear he caused her... I'm going to make him pay. I'm going to make him suffer in ways he can't even fucking imagine until he's begging for the sweet release of death.

A group of pirates swagger in, all decked out in silver and blue colors. The captain, a tall fucker built like a goddamn brick shithouse with dark hair and piercing gray eyes, is sporting a tricorn hat like he's the king of the fucking sea. He scans our table, nodding at Gideon as he saunters over.

"Gideon, my man!" the man says, plopping down at our table like he fucking owns the place. "How's life been treating you, old timer?"

"Orion, ye scurvy dog! Haven't seen you in awhile. How be the winds treatin' ye, lad?" Gideon bellows, pouring our new guest a drink with a flourish. The rest of the crew descends on our table like a flock of seagulls.

"Can't complain, old man. Things have been pretty wild lately." He leans back, a lazy grin spreading across his face. "Heard The Viper attempted to take you down. That chick never learns, does she?"

"Rhyland, meet the one and only Captain Orion Seaborn of the Azure Rovers—a right proper mate o' mine." Gideon introduces us with a grin. I give the man a quick handshake, not in the mood for pleasantries.

"Aye, news be traveling faster than a greased pig 'round these parts! That bitch did try to stake her claim, but we sent her packing with her tail 'tween her legs." Gideon boasts, puffing out his chest.

"Gossip spreads like wildfire in these parts, old man." Orion laughs, taking a swig of his ale. "That bitch has been trying to raid our ships for years, but she never seems to get the message." He turns to me, curiosity gleaming in his gray eyes. "So, what brings you fine gentlemen here, if you don't mind me asking?"

I clench my jaw, not in the fucking mood to rehash this shit. Thankfully, Gideon steps in to answer.

"Ship repairs, of course. Viper had us lippin' in." Gideon explains. "And this lad, be a friend of mine, Orion—been sailing with us now. But, the Sea Witch has snatched the lad's lady herself. We be waitin' here, patchin' up our vessel 'fore we set sail to rescue the fair maiden."

Orion's eyes widen, "Calypso has your girl?" he sits back in his seat, "I'm sorry, man. Any friend of Gideon's is a friend of mine—Is there anything I can do to help?"

I drink my ale and ignore him. Erik, however, steps in, "We would be honored, Captain." he nods toward Orion.

Gideon takes a long swig of his ale, his weathered face grim as a tombstone. "Aye, which brings me to what I wanted to speak to ye about," his voice low and urgent like he's about to drop a fucking bombshell. "Calypso's gonna have yer lass retrieve the Siren's Lyre."

I feel my blood boil at his words, my fingers clenching around my mug so hard I'm surprised the thing doesn't shatter into a million pieces. Kidnapping my woman to be that sea witch's errand girl? It's enough to make me want to tear the whole goddamn ocean apart with my bare hands.

I'm going to need to get drunk for this. Really fucking drunk.

"Holy shit," Orion mutters, shaking his head. "Doesn't surprise me that crazy bitch would try to kidnap someone to do her dirty work." He gulps down his ale, then turns to me with a questioning look. "So, what's so special about your lady love that has the Sea Witch using her to collect such a sought-after artifact?"

I bristle at his words, not liking how he talks about Dani as if she's just some random chick. I know he's trying to help, but I'm pissed off and not in the mood for twenty fucking questions.

"Aye, the lass is special, Orion. And the Sea Witch has caught wind of it," Gideon chimes in, trying to diffuse the tension.

"What makes you believe that?" I growl, taking a long gulp of my ale. The shit tastes like ass, burning my throat and making my eyes water. But right now, I need that burn—need the dull haze of alcohol to take the edge off my rage before I do something I'll regret.

Gideon leans back in his chair. "Calypso's been wantin' to get her hands on that accursed thing for as long as anyone can remember. It's been an ongoin' battle 'tween her and the merfolk, a power struggle that's spanned centuries."

The table falls silent as the other pirates suddenly find their cards incredibly fascinating, their eyes glued to their hands like they hold the secrets of the universe. But I can tell they're listening, their ears practically perking up like a bunch of nosy fucking dogs, trying to catch every word of our conversation.

A sickening sense of dread settles in the pit of my stomach. Because if Calypso is willing to go to such lengths to get her hands on this goddamn Lyre...

Then there's no telling what she might do to Dani to make it happen. The thought of my angel in that sea witch's clutches, being forced to do her bidding...

"We know the lass's role and what she is—and I'm guessing Calypso does too," Gideon confirms, his voice grave. "And if that's the case, Calypso will do all she can to use Dani's gifts to get what she wants before she takes control."

Orion looks confused, his brow furrowed. "What do you mean? *What* is she, and what is her role?"

Gideon glances at me, seeking permission to unload the whole fucking prophecy and Dani's role in this shitstorm. I nod, not wanting to get into this entire thing myself. I'm too wound up, too ready to snap at the slightest provocation.

I close my eyes and reach out to her through our mental bond while Gideon and Erik fill in Orion. *"Baby, what the fuck is going on? I'm losing my goddamn mind here."*

A moment later, her voice is sassy and soothing all at once. *"She's having us meet with her for dinner to discuss something she needs,"* she says with sarcasm. *"You know, just your typical, civilized chat with a sea witch."*

I frown, my brows furrowing like I'm trying to solve a fucking riddle. A civilized dinner invitation? That doesn't sound like something you'd typically hear from a creature known for dragging sailors to their watery graves.

But it confirms what Gideon is saying. She needs Dani to fetch this damn thing, and she's playing nice... for now.

Orion leans back in his chair, his tone casual, like he's discussing the fucking weather. "That Lyre is said to be on Tempest Isle, man. But the damn place is blocked and swarmed with those Sirens."

Gideon shakes his head, his voice gruff. "Nay, lad. It be at Serraphatic Cove, or so the tales be tellin'."

Orion shrugs, a lazy grin spreading across his face. "Doesn't matter. If your lady is what you say she is, I feel things are about to change in this realm." He takes a long swig of his drink, his dark hair falling into his eyes as he plays his cards with easy confidence. "And that, my old friend, is something I am counting the days for."

I can't stop worrying about her even as I try to wrap my head around it. The whole Lucian thing is still nagging at me, a constant itch in the back of my mind that I can't fucking scratch.

"Has that asshole tried anything on you?"

I can feel her anxiety through the bond, a flicker of unease that makes my heart clench in my chest. But then her voice comes through again, solid and confident and full of that sassy wit that I love so damn much.

"Yeah, but I've got him handled," she says, and I can practically see the smirk on her face, the mischievous glint in her honey-gold eyes.

I feel a rush of pride at her words, a fierce, savage joy at the thought of my mate putting that arrogant prick in his place. But it's not enough, not nearly fucking enough to ease the rage and the fear and the gut-wrenching worry that's been eating me alive ever since she disappeared.

The barmaid returns with another round of drinks, and I slam them down in one go, the burn of the alcohol searing my throat. But I barely feel it; I am too focused on Dani's voice and the desperate, clawing need to have her back in my arms where she belongs.

"Good," I growl. *"Keep him alive, so when I see him again, I can kill him myself.*

"For whatever it's worth, "Orion pulls me out of my mental connection, "I'm here to help. Whatever ya need, lad."

I nod, "Thanks."

DANICA

29

I enter the dining hall, and my jaw nearly hits the floor. The room is a friggin' underwater paradise, with a long table stretching out before us like a damn runway, groaning under the weight of a seafood feast. Lobsters the size of small children, oysters that glisten as if polished by a battalion of pearl-obsessed elves, and fish that look like they were plucked straight from a damn rainbow.

At the head of this oceanic feast sits Calypso, resplendent in a gown of shimmering black scales; the front is daringly open, barely covering her assets. Her mermaid scales creep up her torso, catching the light like an array of glittering gems.

She flashes us a dazzling and terrifying smile, her teeth glinting like sharks in the soft light. "Ah, my honored guests," she purrs. "Please, take a seat. We have much to discuss."

As I scope out the room, I am immediately drawn to the gigantic floor-to-ceiling windows offering a jaw-dropping view of the underwater world. The vast expanse of the sea stretches before me, an endless canvas of deep, rich blues that seem to darken and intensify as dusk settles in. It's like being in a high-end aquarium, minus the screaming children and overpriced souvenirs.

Dining with the fishes?

The scene's beauty is almost enough to make me forget the gravity of my situation.

Almost.

I glance over at Lucian, who shrugs and plops his ass down in the nearest chair, sprawling out like he's the king of this underwater castle.

I let out a sigh that comes from the depths of my soul. This should be interesting.

I was scrubbed within an inch of my life by a bunch of handsy attendants—which was all kinds of awkward—combed through the tangled mess of my hair like it was nothing, shaved and trimmed me up in all my nether regions, and then stuffed me into a dress. I must admit that the gown is beautiful—black and sleek, with sequins that catch the light. It's got a slit up the left leg that goes on for miles, showing off a generous slice of skin. No shoes, though. Apparently, mermaids don't believe in footwear.

Not to be outdone, Lucian is decked out in an outfit that screams "underwater royalty." The bastard looks fresh as a damn daisy—like he just stepped out of some high-end Merman spa instead of being kidnapped and dragged to the bottom of the ocean.

His usually unruly golden blonde hair is now perfectly coiffed, slightly spiked in the front in a way that probably took an hour and a metric ton of hair gel to achieve.

The arrogant ass spent the entire time trying to charm the pants off me (figuratively speaking, since I was already in the gown) with his over-the-top flattery and cheesy one-liners. He continued about how stunning I looked and how he'd love to parade me around like some trophy girlfriend. But I shut down his advances like a boss, deflecting his flirtations. Not to mention sulking and pouting as I allowed the attendants to help me with my bath instead of him.

After chatting with Rhyland and trying to calm his Viking temper, which did jack shit for my Berserker Bae, I'm still dreading the moment I have to drop the bomb about Lucian biting me—nearly killing me—and then playing vampire nursemaid with his blood. Rhyland is going to shit a damn Viking longship when he hears about that.

And let's not even start on Lucian kissing me. Actually, on second thought, I'll just file that spicy little detail under "need-to-know basis" and call it a day.

"Yeah, so what's with the fancy getup and the whole 'trying to impress me' act?" I snap.

"I see you didn't take kindly to my necklace." Calypso notices.

I immediately grab my neck, glaring fiercely. "I'm not some pet you can just slap a collar on."

Calypso shrugs, "Very well, then. It was strictly for your safety. I meant no harm."

"Let's cut to the chase and tell me what this whole kidnapping bullshit is about. Not to mention, why the hell did you send that Bloodbane prick after me?"

Calypso smirks, sipping from a black goblet adorned with seashells and intricate designs."Patience, little guppy. Eat, please. You must be starving."

Come to think of it, I am starving. The mere mention of food makes my stomach growl like a caged beast. Attendants glide around the table, bearing trays laden with mouthwatering delicacies. I load up my plate with a lobster the size of my head, a heap of mussels, a couple of crab legs, and some other weird-looking dishes that smell like heaven.

I don't hesitate to dig in, tearing into the food like a starving animal. I need to keep my strength up, after all.

As I take my first bite of the lobster, an explosion of flavors bursts across my tongue. The meat is succulent and tender, with a subtle sweetness perfectly balanced by the rich, buttery sauce it's been bathed in.

Even as I savor the delicious flavors, my mind is racing, trying to figure out what Calypso wants from me and how the hell I will get out of this mess.

"Bloodbane is a loyal pirate to my needs, getting things done with hardly any payment. Once I heard of your arrival, I knew I needed to speak with you," her tone flat. "Anyhow, you vanished, and then suddenly you were back," She shrugs like she's discussing the weather, not my interdimensional field trip.

I stare at her, my brain doing mental gymnastics to keep up with this fishy fuckery. "Hold up, rewind, and freeze. How the hell did you know I was even here? Or left, for that matter? What, did you install an interdimensional LoJack on my ass when I wasn't looking?"

Lucian lets out a hearty laugh, his mouth half-full of whatever aquatic delicacy he's currently demolishing.

I'm half expecting her to pull out a crystal ball or reveal a network of spying clownfish. Because apparently, in this neon fever dream of an ocean, privacy is about as absolute as my chances of growing gills.

Then it dawns on me—the Soul Stone. Azrael always knew when I tore open a portal. Maybe Calypso's little trinket has the same party trick up its sleeve.

I lean forward, my eyes narrowing. "Do you know what that asshole did to me?" I bark. "I mean, seriously? Sending Captain Hook's rejected cousin to rough me up? That's your grand plan? What's next, hiring the Kraken as your personal Uber driver?"

My words drip with sarcasm thicker than tar on a beach. "If this is how you treat *guests*, I'd hate to see what you do to people you don't like. Do you feed them to the sharks, or is that too cliché for Your Royal Fishiness?"

Calypso flinches at my words. "I gave strict orders to bring you in unharmed."

I lean back in my chair, crossing my arms over my chest. "Well, obviously, he didn't get the memo. Next time you want to chat, try sending a fucking e-vite. Or hell, a singing telegram. Anything's better than your current 'kidnap first, ask questions later' policy."

"My apologies for how he treated you. I've been surrounding myself with pirates my whole life on Blood Reef—Bloodbane wasn't supposed to harm you—only deliver you to my doorstep."

Huh—lived her whole life surrounded by pirates, has she? What is she, the queen of Blood Reef? Where scallywags haul in souls to trade with this walking, talking soul slurper?

Give me a break.

Quickly changing topics, "Do you want to know what I desire?" Calypso asks, with a sickly sweet tone as she sips her drink.

I glance up from my plate, my eyes landing on a small fishbowl sitting next to her, filled with live fish darting around in a panic.

"Yes, by all means, let's drag this out all night. It's not like I'm being held here against my will or anything," I quip.

Calypso's lips curve into a smile that is cruel and sinister. She reaches into the fishbowl, plucking out a bright yellow fish, and tosses it into her mouth, swallowing it whole with a single, sickening slurp. I can't help but wonder if she just devoured Flounder, Ariel's loyal sidekick.

"Have you ever heard of the Siren's Lyre?"

I resist the urge to roll my eyes.

Seriously? That's what she's after?

The same damn thing Gideon told me to swipe to get in line to meet the Queen of this underwater shit show? It makes me wonder why Calypso thinks so highly of herself, like she's the goddamn ruler of the seven seas.

"Yeah, I've heard of it," I reply, with nonchalance as I crack a king crab leg in half, popping a flaky, tender piece into my mouth. I almost moan in bliss at the sweet and delicate taste.

Calypso fixes me with a piercing stare, her eyes boring into mine like she's trying to read my soul. "Do you know what it does?"

I take a moment to mull it over, recalling the info dump Gideon had given me. "Something about a long-lost sea goddess, Lyria, who handed the Siren's Lyre over to the Merfolk's ancestors and juiced it up with some potent mojo," I quip. "But it's hidden somewhere, and no one can get their hands on it."

Calypso's wide, predatory smile sends a chill down my spine. "Incorrect, little guppy. The Siren's Lyre is precisely what it sounds like. Lyria's gift was crafted for the Sirens—not the Merfolk. The tales from the land have been twisted into falsehoods, which doesn't surprise me, among other lies. But I know *you* can obtain it, and I need it."

I'm stuck between believing Gideon's version or trusting this sea witch's twisted tale. With a dramatic toss, I throw my crab leg down and lean back in my chair, crossing my arms over my chest. "And what makes you so sure I'm the one for the job? Last I checked, I'm not your personal treasure hunter."

Calypso rises from her seat, her movements fluid and graceful as she glides toward me. She leans close, her breath tickling my ear as she whispers, "I know who you are, Dani. The Savior, the *Chosen One*. The key to obtaining the Siren's Lyre lies within *reflections* of one's true nature, and you, my dear, have a soul that shines brighter than any treasure in the oceans."

I feel my heart skip a beat, a cold sweat breaking out on my neck.

Calypso pulls back, her eyes glittering with hunger and anticipation. "I can help you, Dani. I can help you obtain the Aquanite stone—the very stone you need to fulfill your destiny. Help me retrieve the Siren's Lyre, and I'll help you get it."

The room feels like it's spinning, the weight of her words crashing over me. I glance at Lucian, who's watching the exchange with confusion and concern.

I narrow my eyes, suspicion coiling in my gut like a serpent ready to strike. Why would Calypso, a loyal lackey of Moretemis, suddenly offer to help me find the Aquanite stone? Is this Siren's Lyre some metaphorical nuke designed to set off a chain reaction of catastrophic events that will bring this realm to its knees?

My mind races, piecing together the fragments of my destiny. I'm not just meant to find the stone; I'm supposed to be the glue that holds this whole damn realm together, the one who unites it against the forces of darkness.

Calypso starts muttering to herself, having what appears to be a heated debate with... well, herself. Lucian catches my eye and makes the universal 'cuckoo' gesture, twirling his finger beside his temple. I have to bite my lip to keep from laughing.

I lean forward, my elbows resting on the table as I fix Calypso with a steely gaze. "Thanks for the offer, but I think I'll pass. I can find the Aquanite stone alone without your help."

Calypso's eyes flash with a dangerous glint, her smile turning razor-sharp. "You're making a grave mistake, little goddess. I didn't say I'd help you *find* it; I said I'd help you *obtain* it. You'll stumble in the dark without my guidance, chasing shadows and dead ends."

I push back from the table, rising to my feet. "I'll take my chances. I've faced worse odds before and come out on top."

Lucian glances at me, his brow furrowed with concern. I give him a subtle nod, a silent reassurance that I know what I'm doing.

Calypso comes closer, her movements fluid and graceful as she stalks toward me, her gown shimmering like a thousand scales in the soft light. "You have no idea what you're up against, little girl. The forces at play here are far beyond your comprehension. Nothing is as it seems here—"

"Maybe so, but I've got something you don't: a fire in my belly and a stubborn streak a mile wide. I'll find the stone, unite the realm, and send you and Moretemis packing, with or without your help." I stand my ground, refusing to be intimidated by her posturing.

Calypso starts muttering again, locked in another heated argument with... herself? Thin air? Her imaginary friend?

Who the hell is she talking to?

Did she forget to take her mermaid meds this morning, or is she entirely off her rocker?

The tension in the room immediately cranks up, crackling like electricity in the air. Calypso's eyes glitter with malevolent rage as she hisses, "You forget what I am capable of doing."

Her shadow tentacles lash out in a flash, wrapping around Lucian's throat and hoisting him above the table. He gasps for breath, his face turning a sickly shade of purple as he claws at the tendrils, constricting his windpipe.

My anger surges—a white-hot fury that burns through my veins like lava. I've had enough of this bitch pushing us around like pawns on a chessboard. With a primal scream, I summon a ball of pure, blinding light and hurl it at Calypso's shadows. The tentacles recoil as if burned, dropping Lucian to the floor in a heap. He lands with a sickening thud, coughing and sputtering as he tries to suck air back into his lungs.

Calypso whirls on me, her eyes blazing with unholy fury. Her shadows surge forward, enveloping my torso in a suffocating embrace. I can feel the air being squeezed from my lungs, my ribs creaking under immense pressure."I don't want to fight you, Dani," she snarls. "I am only asking for your assistance. The tides need to be turned. Continue to defy me, and I'll act on my promise concerning your friends."

I struggle against the shadows, my vision blurring at the edges. Her cryptic talk is only confusing me more—with a last, desperate surge of strength, I close my eyes and reach deep within myself, tapping into the well of light that burns at my core. It explodes outward in a blinding beam, searing through the shadows. Calypso screams in rage and pain as her tendrils retreat, and I collapse to the floor, gasping for breath.

But the reprieve is short-lived. In a blur of motion too fast for my eyes to follow, Calypso is on Lucian, her hand plunging into his chest like a dagger. He lets out a strangled cry, his eyes wide with shock and agony as he falls to his knees, clutching at her arm in a futile attempt to dislodge it.

"I warned you."

DANICA

30

I can feel his pain—the searing agony of his heart nearly being torn from his body. The damn Faerite stone is working its twisted magic, forcing me to experience everything connected to the supernatural—it makes me want to fucking scream.

"No. No. NO! STOP!" I shout, hurling another beam of light at her. But she's too quick, dissipating into a cloud of shadows that swirls across the room like a tornado, mimicking Azrael's shadows. When she re-emerges, she's still got her hand buried in Lucian's chest around his heart, a twisted smile on her face.

I can feel the fight draining out of me, replaced by a sinking sense of despair. Lucian's pain shoots through me like a searing needle, a phantom agony that feels all too real. I clench my chest, gasping for breath as the ghostly sensation of his heart being ripped out courses through my body.

It's a pain I know all too well—a cruel reminder of the loss I've already suffered. Adrian's face flashes before my eyes, his anguished screams echoing in my mind. I can't lose Lucian, not like this. Not when I've already lost so much.

But fighting shadows is a losing battle, and I know it. Calypso's power is too great, and her mastery over the darkness is too complete. I'm like a flickering candle trying to hold back the tide of night, and I can feel myself being swallowed up by the inky blackness.

Still, I can't give up. I won't. Lucian is counting on me, and I'll be damned if I let him down. So I grit my teeth and push through the pain, forcing myself to stay standing even as my knees threaten to buckle.

"Alright, stop!" I choke out, my voice raw with emotion. "I'll fucking do it, goddamnit. Just let him go."

The words taste like ash in my mouth—a bitter surrender I know will haunt me for the rest of my days. But what choice do I have? I can't let Lucian die, not when I have the power to save him.

Even if it means making a deal with the devil herself.

Calypso's lips curve into a smile as genuine as a three-dollar bill. "Smart girl," she says with false sweetness.

She yanks her hand out of Lucian's chest with a sickening squelch, like she's pulling a boot out of thick mud. Her hand is covered in blood, dripping onto the floor in a macabre display. Lucian crumples to the ground, clutching his chest as he gasps for air.

"Fuck you, you psychotic cunt," Lucian wheezes, his voice strained with pain and anger. He staggers to his feet, still holding his chest, but the gaping hole that was there moments ago is already starting to close up, leaving only a bloody stain on his shirt as evidence of the trauma.

Calypso saunters to a trickling fountain at the back of the room as casually as if she's just finished a pleasant stroll in the park. She begins washing her hands, the water turning pink as it swirls in the basin. "Now then, shall we get back to the task at hand?" she asks, her tone as nonchalant as if she's discussing the weather rather than the fact that she just tried to rip out my friend's fucking heart.

I can feel my blood boiling with rage, my fists clenching at my sides as I struggle to keep my composure. This bitch is certifiably insane, with a side order of sadistic tendencies that would make even the most hardened serial killer blush.

But as much as I want to tear her limb from limb, I know I'm outmatched. She holds all the cards, and she knows it. If I want to get out of here alive, with Lucian in tow, I will have to play along with her twisted little game.

For now, at least.

Lucian shoots me a look that's equal parts pissed off and resigned, as if he knows exactly what I'm thinking. "Well, let's get this shit show on the road, then," he quips, "Wouldn't want to keep *Her Majesty* waiting."

I nod, taking a deep breath to steady myself. "Fine. What do I need to do?"

Calypso smiles—a cruel, twisted thing that makes my skin crawl. "I'm so glad you asked, my dear. Let's discuss the details over dessert, shall we?"

She gestures to the table, where a group of nervous-looking servants carries trays of what looks like sea-foam green pudding.

I exchange a glance with Lucian, who just shrugs and mouths, "What the fuck," before plastering a fake smile on his face and taking a seat at the table.

I follow suit, my stomach churning with fear and anticipation. Whatever Calypso has planned, I know it won't be good.

"First things first, you will have to collect a key at Serraphatic Cove. The key is crucial to obtaining the Siren's Lyre. Before obtaining the key, you must visit the Pools of Reflection to access the water gates throughout the realm."

My head is spinning like a damn top already. "Woah, slow down—wait a minute." I let out a deep, frustrated breath. "What key and pools of what now?"

Calypso lays it all out for me. First, I must obtain a key to unlock the area of the Siren's Lyre, which is essential to its super-secret hiding spot—the key is tucked away in some underwater cave off the shores of Serraphatic Cove.

Why make things easy, right?

Once I've got the key, I must go to Tempest Isle, where the Siren's Lyre is hidden in a dusty old tomb. Calypso makes sure to give me the full rundown of all the charming bullshit and challenges I'll face along the way.

Oh, and let's not forget about the Pools of Reflection. These magical little puddles are the golden tickets to accessing the underwater gates that can zip me around the realm like some aquatic subway system. They're the same gates that felt like I was being flushed down a giant toilet. Plus, they're the VIP passes to specific locations that only the truest of hearts can enter. Apparently, your soul needs to be as pure as driven snow to get this job done.

Lucian leans back in his chair, a grin spreading across his face. "Come on, Lara Croft, whaddaya say? Let's get this tomb-raiding shit started. I'll be the Jonah to your Lara, minus the whole 'getting captured and almost sacrificed' thing. I don't do damsel in distress, Honey Pot."

I look at him. "Hold your horses, Indiana Jones. We still don't know what *Ursula* here plans to do with this magical lyre once we hand it over."

I turn back to Calypso, fixing her with a pointed stare. "So, once I get this thing for you, what then? I'm not about to go on a wild goose chase for some ancient artifact without knowing what chaos it will unleash. What's your end game?"

Calypso smiles enigmatically like she's got a secret that she's dying to share but can't. "That is for me to know and for you to find out."

I feel my eye twitch, my patience wearing thin. "Listen, lady, I'm not a fan of surprises, especially when they involve potentially world-ending relics. For all I know, this Siren's Lyre could be a one-way ticket to Armageddon."

Calypso waves a dismissive hand like she's swatting away a pesky gnat. "I told you I could help you obtain the Aquanite Stone, Dani. Surely that's worth a little trust on your part?"

I narrow my eyes, suspicion coiling in my gut like a snake ready to strike. Something doesn't add up here. Why would Calypso, who's clearly in cahoots with Moretemis, suddenly be so eager to help me? It's like a vampire offering to donate blood—it just doesn't make sense.

Lucian seems to pick up on my unease, leaning forward with a serious expression that looks out of place on his usually cheerful face. "Let's cut the bullshit. You're not exactly known for your warm and fuzzy charitable side, so what's in it for you? I've got a sixth sense for this kind of shady business, and it's tingling like a *motherfucker* right now."

Calypso smiles, but her face looks like she's trying to solve a Rubik's Cube. "I—I... I'm..."

Calypso's either having a stroke or putting on one hell of a show. "My motivations are my own, and you'd do well not to question them. Suffice it to say, obtaining the Siren's Lyre is in both of our best interests. So, do we have a deal or not?"

Brilliant. Just what we need—a cryptic, crazy mermaid with an attitude problem. What's next, a riddle-spouting sphinx?

I exchange glances with Lucian, who shrugs and mumbles, "Your call, boss."

I lean forward, fixing Calypso with a hard stare. "Alright, before I sign on the dotted line, I need to know if there are any hidden clauses or fine print I should be aware of—any nasty surprises you'll spring on me later? And am I allowed to bring some backup, or is this a solo mission?"

I need to know if gathering Rhyland and Erik will interfere with this arrangement. The last thing I need is Calypso crying foul because I decided to even the odds a bit.

Calypso's grin widens. "No, you're free to use all the help you can get. In fact, I'll even have my Sirens assist you if you find yourself in need."

I hold up a hand, shaking my head vehemently. "Nope. No way. I want nothing to do with your fish sticks on steroids."

The thought of those creepy, singing seductresses makes me want to hurl.

Lucian snorts, barely containing a laugh. "Fish sticks? More like sushi with a side of seduction. I bet they'd love to get their fins on a prime specimen like myself." He waggles his eyebrows suggestively, and I resist smacking him upside the head.

"Focus, Casanova," I mutter, rolling my eyes. "We've got bigger fish to fry than your libido."

Calypso clears her throat, drawing our attention back to her. "As entertaining as this banter is, I have other important matters. So, do we have an agreement, Dani? You retrieve the Siren's Lyre, and I'll help you with the Aquanite Stone... as well as not harm your friends in the meantime. Simple as that."

I've got a million and one questions bouncing around in my head like a bunch of hyperactive ping-pong balls.

Like, what's the deal with Calypso's split personality? One minute she's all smiles and hospitality, the next she's going full-on psycho bitch. And what the hell does she need this magical trinket for anyway? Is she trying to accessorize her way to world domination?

But the question that has me scratching my head is about the whole mermaid and Siren anatomy thing. Last time I checked, these enchanted sea creatures were supposed to be all tails, no legs. So why are they strutting around on land like on an underwater catwalk?

"Okay, I've gotta ask," I blurt out, unable to contain my curiosity any longer. "What's with the legs? Aren't you guys supposed to be out there flipping your fins and making a splash? And while we're at it, what's the deal with this place?" I gesture wildly around the room. My arms stretched out like I'm trying to encompass the entire underwater lair.

Calypso fixes me with a stare that's equal parts amused and exasperated like she's trying to decipher whether to answer my questions or turn me into sushi. After a moment, she takes a delicate sip of her drink, "So many questions, little human." She leans back in her chair, a smirk playing at the corners of her lips. "We merfolk have always had the ability to walk on land and swim in the sea. It's part of our magic."

I take a bite of my dessert, which tastes like a heavenly pistachio pudding had a love child with ambrosia. "So, you guys can just swap out your tails for legs whenever you feel like it? That's pretty damn convenient."

For a split second, Calypso's expression shifts, a flicker of sadness passing over her features before she schools her face back into its usual resting bitch mode. "In a sense, yes," she replies, her tone guarded.

In a sense? Well, that's about as clear as the ocean's murky depths. Something smells fishy around here, and it's not just the seafood platter in front of me. She's holding back, keeping secrets.

But it looks like I won't get any more information from her. She's clamming up faster than a shell at low tide, and I know a dead end when I see one.

I take a deep breath, weighing my options. I'm not too fond of being Calypso's errand girl, but if it means getting one step closer to fulfilling my destiny and saving the realms, I'll do what I must.

"Fine," I say, my voice tight with resignation. "We'll get you the Siren's Lyre. But if this comes back to bite me in the ass, I'm coming for you, Calypso. And trust me, you don't want to see me when I'm pissed." My voice is firm with resolve. "I'm doing this on my terms. There will be no interference, no hidden agendas, and definitely no surprise appearances from your scaly entourage. Got it?"

She nods. "Now, shall we seal this agreement then?"

Confusion etched on my face, I watch as Calypso glides towards me. An attendant hands her something I can't quite make out. "I just need..." she starts before unceremoniously plucking a strand of my hair.

"Ouch!" I yelp, rubbing my scalp. "What the hell?"

She ignores me, weaving my hair into a bracelet of seashells and coral that glimmers in the dim light. It's stunning—like a miniature ocean—but I can't shake the feeling that there's more to this than meets the eye.

Calypso holds the bracelet aloft, her eyes gleaming with an otherworldly light. She starts chanting in a language that sounds like a cross between a lullaby and a curse, her voice rising and falling like the tides. The words hang in the air, pulsing with a strange, hypnotic energy that makes my skin crawl.

Oh, shit. What have I gotten myself into? It looks like my word alone isn't going to cut it with the sea witch.

"Uhhh—What's with the hocus pocus?" Lucian chimes in, his eyebrows raised skeptically. "Is this some kind of underwater pinky swear? Because if so, I want in on the action."

I shoot him a look that says, "Not helping." Before I can tell him to shut up, the bracelet starts glowing like a deep-sea rave. I can feel the magic building—a tingling of energy that dances along my skin like the brush of a thousand tiny electric eels.

Suddenly, the bracelet splits in two, each half shooting out to wrap around my wrist and Calypso's. The coral and shells fuse, forming a seamless band that feels cool and smooth against my skin, but I can't shake the feeling that I've just signed my soul away to the devil of the deep.

I can feel the magic of the pact settling into my bones, a tingle of power coursing through my veins like liquid nitrogen. It's a heady feeling—a rush of adrenaline mixed with something ancient and primal—but also terrifying in its intensity.

Calypso lowers her arms, a satisfied smile on her face. "It's done," her voice ringing with finality. "You are bound to our agreement, Dani. May the tides guide you to success."

"What the hell did I just agree to, exactly?" I ask, my voice laced with equal parts sarcasm and trepidation.

"Exactly what you said you do, and I am bound to what I promised you—it's called a Coral Pact," Calypso explains as if it's the most obvious thing in the world.

"Sure, because that clears everything up," I mutter, eyeing the bracelet like it might sprout teeth and bite me. "And what happens if one of us doesn't hold up our end of the bargain? Do we get fed to the sharks or something?"

Calypso laughs, a sound that's as beautiful as it is bone-chilling. "I wouldn't dream of breaking our pact, Dani. Now, shall we celebrate our agreement with a toast?"

I exchange a wary glance with Lucian, who shrugs and gives me a "Your funeral, babe" look.

I take a deep breath, trying to quell the unease churning in my gut. I've made my bed, and now I have to lie in it. I hope I haven't bitten off more than I can chew with this Coral Pact business.

She snaps her fingers, and a servant appears with a tray of shimmering, iridescent drinks. I eye them warily, not trusting anything from Calypso's hands.

On the other hand, Lucian grabs a glass and downs it in one gulp. "Whoa, that's got a kick to it! It's like mermaid farts mixed with the essence of a sea cucumber's ballsack."

I wrinkle my nose in disgust, pushing my own glass away. "I think I'll pass on the underwater absinthe, thanks."

Calypso shrugs, delicately sipping her drink. "Suit yourself. But remember, the clock is ticking. You have until the next full moon to bring me the Siren's Lyre. Don't disappoint me."

"Great," I say, standing up from the table, ready to get the fuck out of here. "If that's all, I think it's time we take our leave. There are places to go and relics to find; you know how it is."

Lucian also rises, stretching his arms above his head with a groan. "Yeah, I could use a real drink after all this excitement. Preferably something strong enough to make me forget about the whole 'almost getting my heart ripped out' thing."

Calypso waves a dismissive hand. "By all means, you may go."

And with that, I waste no time.

RHYLAND

31

The room spins around me as I down another mug of ale, the bitter liquid sloshing over my lips and dribbling down my chin. I'm drunk, really fucking drunk, and the world has taken on a hazy, dreamlike quality.

Beside me, Gideon, Orion, and Erik are laughing and cutting up, their voices loud and boisterous in the crowded tavern. We've been here for hours, drinking and bullshitting and trying to forget the clusterfuck of a situation we've found ourselves in.

The tavern is alive with raucous energy, the air thick with the scent of ale and sweat. Our table is littered with cards and coins, the remnants of my pathetic attempts at poker scattered before me like a fucking testament to my piss-poor gambling skills.

In the corner, a group of musicians belts out a sea shanty, their voices rising above the crowd's din. The melody is infectious, and soon enough, the bar patrons are on their feet, stomping and clapping along with the beat.

But even through the drunken haze, I can't stop thinking about Dani. Can't stop worrying about her, wondering if she's okay. It's like a constant ache in my chest, a dull, throbbing pain that no amount of alcohol can numb.

Suddenly, I feel a flicker of something at the edge of my consciousness. A presence, warm and familiar and achingly sweet. For a moment, I think it's just the booze fucking with me, conjuring up visions of my mate that aren't really there.

But then the tavern door swings open, and my heart stops dead in my chest.

Because there, standing in the doorway like a fucking vision, is Dani.

She's wearing a black dress that clings to every curve of her body, the fabric shimmering and sparkling in the dim light of the tavern. There's a slit running up the side of the skirt, so high that it leaves absolutely nothing to the imagination, and her feet are bare, the delicate arches of her soles and the slender curves of her toes almost more erotic than if she were completely naked.

She looks ethereal, enchanting, breathtaking. Like a fucking goddess come to earth. And for a moment, all I can do is stare, my mouth hanging open like a goddamn idiot.

I stumble to my feet, nearly falling on my ass in the process. "Baby...?" I slur, my voice thick and clumsy with alcohol. "Is that really you?"

She's in front of me now, her honey-gold eyes swirling with amusement and exasperation. Her sweet and intoxicating scent—honey, spice, and something uniquely hers—envelops me, making me reach out for her. My hands shake as I pull her close.

She's real. She's really fucking here.

"Are you drunk?" she snaps, her voice sharp and sassy.

I stagger back, my balance shot to hell as the room tilts. "No," I slur, my head wobbling from side to side like a dog trying to clear water from its ears. "Well, maybe a little." I hold up my fingers, squinting at them like I'm trying to solve a goddamn math problem. "How did you—?"

Before I finish the thought, she's shuffling me back to the table, her small hands firm on my shoulders as she pushes me down into my seat. I grab her by the hips, yanking her down onto my lap and burying my face in her neck, breathing in the sweet, familiar scent of her.

No way in hell I'm ever letting her go again. She's going to be stuck to me like a fucking barnacle from now on, whether she likes it or not.

She turns to face me, grabbing my bearded face between her palms. "Hey," she says softly, her eyes searching mine with concern and relief.

I lean in, capturing her lips in a sloppy, drunken kiss. I don't care who's watching, don't care about anything but the feel of her mouth on mine, the taste of her on my tongue. I moan into the kiss, my hands tightening on her hips as she mimics the sound.

"Hey, do you assholes fucking mind?" a voice cuts through the haze of lust and alcohol, sharp and sarcastic. "I'm about two seconds away from whipping my dick out and going to town right here on this table. Either take it to a room or start charging admission."

I pull back from the kiss, my eyes narrowing as I turn to glare at my little brother. He's lounging in his chair, a smirk on his face as he watches us with amusement and disgust.

"Put a cork in it, Lucian," Dani snaps. "Or do I need to find a muzzle for your smart mouth?"

"Actually, on second thought, keep going. I could use some new material for my spank bank. Just let me grab some popcorn first and maybe a raincoat. I have a feeling things are about to get messy."

I feel a growl building in my throat, my hands tightening on Dani's hips as I fight the urge to lunge across the table and wipe that smug fucking look off his face. But before I can do anything stupid, Erik stands up, his silver eyes warm as he hugs Dani.

"Little Huntress," he says softly, "It is so good to see you safe and well."

I feel a flicker of jealousy at the sight of another man touching my mate, even if it is my own brother. But I push it down, forcing myself to release my grip on Dani's waist so she can return the embrace.

Dani tightly hugs Erik. "Thank you, Erik. It's good to see you, too."

The second he releases her, I yank her back down onto my lap, my hand creeping up the slit of her dress to rub circles on the soft, smooth skin of her thigh. She shivers at the touch, her eyes fluttering closed for a moment before she takes a deep breath and turns to face the others.

I lean back in my chair, watching as Gideon leans forward, his eyes gleaming with curiosity beneath that ridiculous fucking tricorn hat of his. "Lass, 'tis a relief to see ye back and in one piece. But we be all dyin' to know what that sea witch Calypso did to ye and how ye managed to escape her clutches."

Izabelle scoffs, mumbling some shit under her breath and rolling her eyes. "Not all of us."

Dani shoots her a glare that could melt steel, ignoring her pathetic attempts at taunting.

"Captain Orion Seaborn, at your service." Orion holds out his hand, a friendly grin on his face that makes me want to punch him in his perfect fucking teeth.

Dani shakes his hand, her eyebrow raised. "New friend?" she asks Gideon, her tone laced with amusement.

"Aye, lass, this be an old friend. He's the Captain of the Azure Rovers I mentioned to ye about." Gideon nods, his voice gruff.

Dani nods in acknowledgment, a smirk playing at the corners of her lips. "Ah, yes. Gideon had nice things to say about you—sort of."

Orion's grin widens, his eyes fucking twinkling like he's Santa Claus or some shit. "Sort of?" He coughs, clearly taken by my angel's beauty and sass. I can see the red creeping up his neck, the fucker. He's not used to being in the presence of such a goddess. "Am I gonna have to beat the old man again for spreading false rumors?"

Dani smiles, her eyes dancing with mischief. "No, nothing like that. It's just that you're pirates, through and through." She shrugs like it's the most obvious thing in the world.

Orion grins, holding his hands up in mock surrender. "Well, in that case, Gideon, you are safe."

I've had enough of this flirty bullshit. I need to know what the fuck happened to my woman. "What the hell happened, Dani?" I growl, my patience wearing thinner than a fucking thread.

Dani holds up a hand—her sass dialed up to the level that makes me want to kiss that smart mouth of hers until she's breathless and begging. "I'll get to that, but first, I need a damn drink." She waves her hand like the queen she is summoning her subject, and I can't tear my eyes away from her face, even as I signal the barmaid.

Because the suspense is killing me, and I need to know what kind of fucked-up shit Calypso put her through. More importantly, I want to learn how to keep it from happening again.

The barmaid catches Dani's signal and acknowledges her request with a wave. Erik, ever the gentleman, slides his drink over to her with a nod of permission. Dani takes a deep pull, the liquid sloshing down her throat before she wipes her lips with the back of her hand. "Thanks," she says, her voice husky from the burn of the alcohol.

I know my woman. She won't spill until she's damn well ready. All I can do is sit back and wait for her to drop the bombshell I know is coming.

Erik looks over at Lucian, "Brother." and tilts his head in a show of brotherly love.

Ever the walking, talking embodiment of a shit-stained toilet bowl, Lucian waves dismissively, "Hey. Yeah, don't remember you either, dude. Sorry, my brain's been wiped cleaner than a porn star's asshole after an all-night gangbang. No offense."

Erik holds up his hand, "None taken. Just hope we can do something to get your memories back."

"That bitch did a number on all of us," Dani states. "Our hex might be gone, but I have a feeling your issue is a whole different shit show. One that even my magnificent self can't unfuck."

I brought it up to Dani in our back-and-forth mental conversations while she was down with Calypso that my powers had come back online. Naturally, she asked me how the hell I did it. I couldn't give her any real answer other than the fact that I was absolutely raging with those Serpent fuckers, and somehow, they just answered the call.

Lucian never misses an opportunity for innuendo and waves her off with a smirk, "Don't you worry, your pretty little head, Honey Pot. I'm fine with how I am right now, even if I don't remember shit. Tabula rasa, baby. It's like a fresh start but with more amnesia and less 'finding yourself' bullshit."

Dani stiffens in my lap, the bond funneling to her what I feel. Her body goes rigid with tension. My fingers gently caress her inner thigh's smooth, supple skin. The feel of her soft, warm flesh beneath my palm helps to calm the rage simmering inside me, grounding me in the moment. But I swear, if this smug bastard calls her *"Honey Pot"* one more fucking time, I'm going to snap and rip his goddamn tongue out.

I narrow my eyes at Lucian, "Tabula rasa, huh? More like tabula dumb-assa in your case, dipshit. Fresh start? You're still the same irritating prick, memories or not. The only difference is now you've got an excuse for being an even bigger pain in the ass."

Lucian, not one to back down from a challenge, leans forward with a grin like a fucking lunatic "Tabula dumb-assa? Oh, that's rich coming from a tight ass like you, Captain Broody McBroodington. You're just jealous that I get to start over with a clean slate while you're stuck with that giant stick up your ass."

He taps his temple, his grin widening, "See, the way I figure it, losing my memories is like hitting the jackpot. No more angsty flashbacks, no more guilt trips over shit I can't change. It's like a get out of jail free card but for my brain."

Erik exhales heavily beside me, his stoic demeanor briefly interrupted as he takes a long pull from his mug of ale. "It appears that even without your memories, you two persist in engaging in this inane, fucking bickering like a pair of petulant children."

Lucian winks, blowing me a mocking kiss, "You don't say? Well, I've got plenty of new ways to be a pain in his brooding, self-righteous ass." Nodding towards me. "It's a talent, really."

"Alrighty, boys, let's all take a deep breath and pop a chill pill, shall we? As much as I love watching this testosterone-fueled pissing contest, we've got more pressing matters to discuss," Dani says, with that signature sass.

I take a moment to compose myself, pressing a soft kiss to Dani's arm as I lean back in my chair.

I watch as Izabelle unwinds herself from Gideon like a fucking snake, sauntering toward Lucian with her tits practically spilling out of her dress. "Well, I find you just fascinating, lad," she purrs, planting her ass right on Lucian's lap and curling her arms around his neck like she's marking her territory. "Mind if I sit, Sailor?"

Lucian looks disgusted, and all the men at the table grumble—clearly not impressed with her cheap act.

Dani rolls her eyes so hard I'm surprised they don't fall out of her fucking head. "If it isn't the port's most popular porthole," she sneers, with disgust.

Izabelle glares at Dani, her face twisting into an ugly scowl. "What's the matter, landlubber? Jealous?"

Dani scoffs. "No, sweetheart, I just know my friend here has more standards than you have goals. News flash, bitch: he's not interested in whatever STDs you're peddling."

Izabelle stands up like she's about to throw down, but Dani keeps herself down on my lap, cool as a fucking cucumber. I wrap my arm around her waist, my fingers digging into her hip possessively.

"Sit the fuck down, Izabelle," Orion stands, blocking her path like a human wall. "Go be a good whore and scuttle back to whatever rat-infested bilge you crawled out of. I'm sure there's a line of drunken sailors just waiting to plunder your treasure chest."

"Fuck you, Seaborn." Izabelle spits as she turns and walks away.

Dani tries to hide her laugh. Lucian's just sitting there with a shit-eating grin on his face, clearly enjoying this fucking circus.

"Seaborn," Gideon growls, warning. "That be enough out of ye."

Orion plops his ass back down in his chair. He swipes his drink off the table, the glass scraping against the worn wood, and takes a long swig. The smirk on his face says he doesn't give two shits about Gideon's warning.

I can't help but admire the guy's balls, even if I want to punch him in his smug face. He's got that easy confidence from knowing he can handle whatever comes his way.

"Look, I know you're all bursting with questions," Dani says, her voice collected despite our simmering tension. "Let's address the elephant in the room—or should I say, the Sea Witch in the ocean."

I feel a flicker of dread at her words, a cold, creeping fear that crawls up my spine and settles in the pit of my stomach. But I force myself to listen, to focus on her words even as the alcohol and the lust and the fucking relief of having her back cloud my mind.

She tells us everything about Calypso's demands, the Siren's Lyre, and the impossible task ahead of us. With every word, I feel myself sobering up, the haze of drunkenness fading away to be replaced by a cold, brutal clarity.

"She just let you go?" I ask, my voice rough and skeptical. "Just like that?"

Dani nods, her eyes meeting mine. "For now," she says softly. "I have to hold up my end of the bargain."

I feel a prickling sense of unease run down my spine that has nothing to do with the alcohol still coursing through my system. Because if Calypso is willing to let Dani go, even temporarily...

Then there's no telling what kind of fucked up game she's playing or what kind of danger my mate might be walking into when the time comes.

"Wait, what bargain?" I ask, my voice low and rough.

Dani holds up her wrist and shows us all a bracelet that looks like a bunch of seashells. "Coral Pact," she says as if that explains everything.

Lucian, ever the fucking smart ass who never knows when to shut the fuck up, "Oh yeah, Little Miss Sunshine here made a deal with the sea-bitch herself, didn't you, Honey Pot? To get this magical Lyre thingy— All to save my magnificent, shapely ass from having my heart ripped out and used as a fucking paperweight. Because you're head over fins in love with me, admit it. I mean, who wouldn't be?" he gestures dramatically to himself. "I've got a feeling we're about to be in deeper shit than a whale's colonoscopy."

A growl builds in my throat, my hands squeezing Dani's hip. "She's not a fucking *Honey Pot*," I snarl, my eyes narrowing as I glare at my brother. "Stop calling her that."

Memory loss or not, this fucker needs to learn his goddamn place.

But Lucian grins, his eyes gleaming with mischief. "Ooh, did I hit a nerve, tough guy?" he taunts. "Struck too close to home? Because... damn," he licks his lips obscenely, "she tastes like fucking heaven, doesn't she? Sweet, like honey—addictive, better than any blood we've ever had. What's wrong, big guy? Pissed that I got a taste of your girl? Or just pissed that I can describe her better than you can?"

The table goes dead silent. Erik slowly rises from his chair, bracing for the shitstorm that's about to go down. Gideon and Orion swipe their mugs off the table and scoot back, their chairs screeching across the floor.

It hits me like a goddamn sledgehammer. The realization that Lucian would've needed Dani's blood to cross over with her. And from the way he's talking, the fucker took it straight from the source.

And I fucking snap!

RHYLAND

32

I feel Dani stiffen in my lap, her eyes wide with shock and worry. Before she can say anything, my fangs snap out; she's on her feet, scrambling away, as I stand, chair clattering to the floor behind me as I lunge across the table.

I grab Lucian by the front of his shirt, hauling him up until we're nose to nose. "Listen to me, you little shit," I snarl, my voice low and deadly. "Dani is mine. My mate, my love, my fucking reason for living. You don't get to talk about her like you know her—like she's yours. You understand me, you piece of shit? And if you even think about laying another finger on her, I will rip your fucking arm off and beat you to death with it."

Lucian's eyes widen momentarily, like he just realized he's poked a particularly pissed-off bear with a very short stick. A flicker of 'oh shit' crosses his face before he slaps on a smirk. "Whoa there, Hulk, let's not go all 'roid rage on me," he quips, despite the underlying hint of 'please don't fucking kill me.' "Take it easy, man. Breathe in, breathe out, do some fucking yoga or whatever it is you do to keep from tearing people's heads off."

But I can see the lie in his eyes, the hunger and the fucking possessiveness that mirrors my own. And I know, in this moment, that this is far from over.

Lucian may have forgotten who he is and the bond that ties Dani to me, but I sure as hell haven't.

And I will fight to my last fucking breath to keep her by my side, where she belongs.

Dani rushes up, her hand on my arm, "Alright, boys, that's enough! This macho pissing contest needs to end before someone loses an eye—or worse, ruin my dress." She turns to Lucian, fixing him with her best 'don't-test-me' glare. "Lucian, zip it before I find a creative way to make you." Then, she grabs my arm, tugging me towards her. "And you, Fangzilla, you're coming with me. We need to chat briefly before you decide to redecorate Lucian's face."

Stepping outside into the tropical, cool night air, I can't stop pacing, my body thrumming with anger and frustration. "He fucking bit you?" I snarl, my voice low and rough.

Dani flinches momentarily, her eyes wide and wary as she watches me. "Yes—but he didn't know—"

"I don't give a flying fuck if he didn't know or not," I snap, cutting her off before she can even finish the excuse. I'm in her face in an instant, my eyes blazing with a possessive rage that threatens to consume me. I know I'm coming off hot and intense, but I can't help it. The thought of another man's fangs sinking into her flesh, of his lips on her skin... it's enough to make my blood boil.

She stares up at me with defiance, her chin lifting as she meets my gaze head-on. "As I was saying before, you so rudely interrupted me," she says with attitude. "It happened so fast I couldn't stop it. He was on me as soon as I landed in my apartment, almost draining me."

I see red.

The world around me fades away until all I can see is the image of Lucian's mouth on Dani's throat, his fangs tearing into her soft, tender flesh. I want to kill him, to wrap my hands around his scrawny little neck and squeeze until his eyes pop out of his fucking skull. I want to rip his balls off and shove them down his goddamn throat, to make him suffer for ever daring to lay a hand on what's mine.

I gently pull her hair back off her neck, my heart pounding as I search for the mark, the telltale—But I don't see a damn thing—which means...

Dani's voice cuts through the haze of rage before I can even move, her tone hesitant and almost apologetic. "He... he gave me his blood again."

And just like that, I lose it. I turn away from her, my hands fisting in my hair as I stalk down the wooden planks of the market, my boots thudding heavily against the weathered boards. I can hear Dani trailing behind me, her footsteps light and quick as she tries to keep up. But I can't face her, can't look at her, while I'm raging.

I stop at a secluded spot on the docks, my hands gripping the rope railing so tightly I can feel the fibers digging into my palms. I stare at the sea, the endless expanse of black water stretching to the horizon, and try to calm the storm inside me.

The stars twinkle brightly above, which would typically take my breath away. But tonight, their beauty is lost on me. All I can think about is wrapping my hands around my brother's throat and squeezing until the life drains from his smug fucking face.

The fury is like a living thing, coiled tight in my chest and ready to strike at the slightest provocation. The thought of Lucian's blood running through Dani's veins, of his essence mingling with hers... it's enough to make me want to tear the whole fucking world apart.

"Rhyland," Dani says softly, her voice barely more than a whisper as she comes up behind me. "Please, just listen to me. It's not what you think."

I take a deep breath, forcing myself to unclench my jaw and relax my grip on the ropes. I turn to face her, my eyes locking onto hers with an intensity that makes her shiver.

"Then tell me what it is, Dani," I growl, my voice low and rough with emotion. "Because from where I'm standing, it looks like my fucking brother is trying to stake a claim on my mate. And I won't stand for that shit, not now, not ever."

She steps towards me, her hand reaching to rest on my chest. I can feel the heat of her touch through the fabric of my shirt, the gentle pressure of her fingers against my skin. And despite everything, despite the rage and the fear and the fucking agony of knowing another man has put his lips on her—almost damn near killing her. I feel myself calming, the tension draining out of me at her touch.

"He doesn't remember, Rhyland," she says softly, her eyes searching mine with sympathy and determination. "He doesn't understand that I'm yours, that we're mated. And even if he did... it wouldn't change anything. I'm yours, body and soul, and nothing will ever change that."

I close my eyes, letting her words wash over me like a balm. I know she's right, and no matter what Lucian does or says or how much of his blood runs through her veins, she'll always be mine.

But that doesn't make it any easier to bear. Doesn't make the thought of his fangs on her skin any less agonizing, any less infuriating.

"I know," I say finally, my voice raw. "I know he doesn't remember. But that doesn't change the fact that he hurt you, that he took something from you that wasn't his to take. And I can't just let that go, Dani. I can't just sit back and watch while he tries to worm his way into your heart, into your blood."

She sighs, her fingers curling into the fabric of my shirt as she leans into me. "I know," she whispers, her breath warm against my skin. "And I'm not asking you to. But we have bigger problems to deal with right now, Rhyland. We have to find the Siren's Lyre; we must stop Calypso and find the stone—we can't do that if we're too busy fighting each other."

I take a deep breath, letting her scent fill my lungs and her body's warmth seep into my bones. She's right, as much as I hate to admit it. We have a job to do, a mission to complete. And as much as I want to tear Lucian apart for what he's done... I know that Dani's safety, that the fate of the whole fucking world, has to come first.

She reaches up and wraps her arms around my neck, her fingers tangling in my hair at the base of my skull. Her grip is tight, forceful, and it sends a jolt of electricity straight to my cock. But it's her eyes that do me in, those honey-gold orbs filled with fire and passion and something that fucking undoes me every damn time.

The soft glow of the oil lamps nearby casts a warm light on her face, revealing the raw desire in her eyes. "Kiss me, you sexy Viking asshole," she breathes, her voice demanding and sassy that sets my blood on fucking fire.

I don't even think—just act. I pounce on her lips, one hand fisting in her hair as I tilt her head back, the other sliding down her spine to grip her plump ass. I lift her off the ground, wrapping her body around mine as I claim her mouth with a ferocity that leaves no room for doubt. I slam her up against the side of the building that occupies the dock. She kisses me back with wild abandon, her hands fisting in my hair as she moans and gasps into my mouth, her body straining against mine with a need that matches my own.

"What have I told you about that filthy mouth? Huh, Angel?" She only smiles, like the damn vixen she is, as I retake her mouth.

My hands are everywhere, desperate to touch, to feel every inch of her soft, smooth skin. I rip her dress at the slit, the delicate fabric tearing like paper under my fingers. She gasps, her body arching back as I expose her to the cool night air. I reach down between us, my fingers sliding through her wet petals with possessive intent. "I need this," I growl, my voice rough and demanding. "I need you right here and right fucking now."

I set her back on her feet, the heat of her body searing my palms as I tear the remains of her dress off her plump tits, baring her to the night. She's fucking gorgeous, her skin flushed and her eyes half-lidded with desire. I take one of her tight nipples into my mouth, my lips closing around the taut peak with a suction that makes her cry out. The cool air and the heat of my mouth work their magic, making her nipples tighten even further as they pebble against my tongue.

She grips the back of my neck, her fingers curling into my hair as she urges me. "Rhyland," she gasps, her voice breathless and pleading. "Please..."

And that's all the encouragement I need.

I whisk us inside the empty building in a flash, moving faster than the human eye can follow. The only illumination is a hearth flickering in the far corner, casting a warm, intimate glow across the room.

It's a secluded boat repair shed, just private enough for our needs. There's a sturdy workbench against one wall that'll do nicely and enough rope and tools lying around to make things interesting if we're feeling adventurous. The place reeks of wood and salt, but right now, all I can focus on is the scent of Dani and the need burning in my veins.

I'm going to mark her, cover her in my scent, my cum, my blood. I will brand her as mine and leave an indelible claim on her body and soul. The thought sends a jolt of possessive satisfaction, a savage joy that burns hot in my veins.

DANICA

33

I feel Rhyland's anger and frustration pulsing through our bond like a live wire. He's pissed off, upset, and probably fantasizing about ripping Lucian's head off and using it as a soccer ball for what he's doing.

I get it. I really do.

That undeniable, possessive tug in our bond, the primal urge to keep each other close and untouched by anyone else—it's like a cosmic "no trespassing" sign that's been hardwired into our very souls. It's the same possessive feeling that had me ready to go all "jealous girlfriend" on that bitch barmaid who was eye-fucking Rhyland like he was the last piece of man-candy on earth.

But at the same time, I can't really fault Lucian for his behavior. He's running on pure vampire instinct right now, his centuries of self-control and understanding of his own nature wiped clean like a hard drive after a system reset. He's like a newborn vamp, all impulse and no restraint.

Maybe this whole situation, as screwed up as it is, is precisely what Rhyland needs to feel secure in our relationship. To know, deep down in his bones, that I'm not going anywhere, that I'm his, and he's mine, no matter what. Hell, it's what I need, too—a reminder that our bond is unbreakable, that nothing and no one can come between us.

It's like we're two pieces of a puzzle that fit together perfectly, and this experience, as bizarre and uncomfortable as it may be, is just another way of reinforcing that connection. A twisted, vampire-induced way of saying "I love you" and "I'm yours forever."

As much as I want to smack Lucian upside the head for his antics, I know I need to cut him a little slack. He's not himself right now, and it's up to me to be the level-headed one (for once).

I whimper as Rhyland's mouth leaves my skin, my body craving more of his touch, more of him. His eyes rake over me, drinking in every inch of my exposed flesh with a hunger that matches my own.

"Goddamn, you're so beautiful," his voice rough with desire. "So sexy."

His words thrill me, igniting sparks of pleasure in every nerve ending. I can feel my arousal pooling between my legs, hot and slick, begging for his attention. He cups my breasts, his thumbs teasing my hardened nipples as he watches the play of emotions on my face.

I reach down, needing to touch and feel him like he's feeling me. My hand finds his thick, hard cock, and he hisses at the contact, his hips jerking forward. "Fuck, Dani," he groans, his voice strained. "You have no idea what you do to me, baby."

I lean in close, my lips grazing his open chest, "I'm happy to find out." I whisper, with promise.

Without hesitation, I sink to my knees, my hands tugging at his pants. I can feel his gaze scorching my skin as I free his impressive length. I stroke him slowly, relishing the feel of his thick, veiny cock in my hand and the way his breath catches.

Then, I take him into my mouth without warning, swirling my tongue around the sensitive head as I suck him deep. His taste floods my senses, salty and musky, sending a shudder of desire through me. I hollow my cheeks, taking him deeper, my hand trying to wrap around the base of his shaft as I start bobbing my head in a steady rhythm.

"Shit, baby," he hisses, his fingers tangling in my hair. "Just like that. Fuck. Take it all."

I take him deeper, my tongue teasing and swirling as I work him. When he moans, urging me on, I push further, letting his cock slide down my throat until he's hitting the back of it. Ignoring my gag reflex. Spit leaks from the corners of my mouth as I swallow around him, taking him even deeper until my lips meet the sexy hairs on his pelvis.

The gentle rhythm of the ocean and the crackling fire provide a sultry soundtrack to Rhyland's pleasure, with waves softly caressing the docks like a teasing lover's touch.

"Fuuuck," he grunts, his hips thrusting against my face. "That's it. Take every inch of this cock. Let me see how hungry you are."

I moan around his thick length. His filthy words ignite the fire in my core, sending molten heat straight to my clit. Knowing I'm pleasing him, bringing him to the brink, turns me on like nothing else. I want him to lose control, to come undone because of me.

"Ah, fuck... An...gel," Rhyland whimpers, his voice strained and desperate, like he's teetering on the edge of oblivion. The sound of his raw, unfiltered desire nearly sends me over the edge. It's like a siren's call, urging me to give in to the throbbing ache between my legs and chase my release.

Hearing Rhyland like this, so vulnerable and consumed by his desire for me, is the most erotic thing I've ever experienced. It's a heady rush, knowing I have the power to reduce this strong, fearless Viking to a quivering mess.

So I swallow around him again, my throat working his length in a way I know will drive him wild. I moan and whimper around him, my hands gripping his thighs as I take him deeper still. And when I feel him tensing, his body coiled tight, I hollow my cheeks and swallow him to the root.

He comes with a roar, his fingers tightening in my hair as he thrusts once, twice, spilling himself down my throat. I swallow every drop, milking his orgasm until he's spent and shaking, his breath coming in harsh pants.

I release him slowly, letting his cock slide from my lips with a lewd pop. His eyes darken with renewed lust as he takes in the sight of me on my knees, my lips swollen from his cock.

"Goddamn, baby," he rasps, his voice wrecked. "I'm nowhere near done with you."

Oh, I know. This man is insatiable, ready to go round after round.

He hauls me to my feet, his mouth crashing down on mine as he devours me with a kiss. I can still taste him on my tongue, salty and musky and oh-so-fucking-good. He tears at my clothes again, his hands desperate as he strips away the last remnants of my dress until I'm bare to the night.

"*Mine*," he snarls against my lips, his hands gripping my ass, grinding our bodies together. "All fucking mine."

And I can't help but agree. In this moment, in every moment, I am his, and he is mine.

He lifts me effortlessly, my legs wrapping around him as he blurs us to a dark corner of the room. The cold wood of a rum barrel meets my bare ass as he sets me down, making me squeal.

I glance around, eyes wide, realizing that anyone could walk in, catch us, and see what we're doing. It's thrilling and nerve-wracking all at once. My heart races and my breath comes in short gasps as I anticipate what's coming.

I think I want to get caught.

Before I blink, Rhyland has his hands on the underside of my thighs, spreading me wide as he leans in. "I'm fucking parched, baby," he rumbles, his voice a sexy command that makes me shiver. "Drown me in this sweet cunt."

His hot mouth descends on my clit, his tongue swirling over the sensitive nub with expert precision. I moan and squirm against him, already so close to the edge after sucking his glorious cock. My juices coat my thighs as I grind against his face, desperate for more friction.

And he gives it to me. He laps at my arousal, growling in approval as he devours me. His tongue works me mercilessly, driving me higher and higher until I'm a quivering, mewling mess, my hands fisting in his hair.

As I'm sprawled across the barrel, my legs fall open, splayed wide like a feast. My neck hangs off the back as Rhyland controls the lower half of my body. The rough wood contrasts deliciously with the heat of Rhyland's mouth on my core. He's hunched over me, his hands gripping my thighs, holding me open as he feasts on me.

"Fuck..." I gasp, my head falling back as pleasure crashes over me. "Yes, Rhyland." I whimper. "Make me come..."

He growls, the vibrations against my sensitive flesh making me cry out. Then he plunges two thick fingers into me, pumping them in and out as he sucks hard on my clit. It only takes a few thrusts of his skilled fingers before I shatter, my body bowing off the barrel as a scream tears from my throat.

Rhyland's hand clamps over my mouth, muffling my cries of ecstasy. But he doesn't relent, his fingers pumping into me as I clench and gush around them. "Goddamn, Angel," he breathes, his voice rough with desire. "You're so fucking sexy when you come for me."

I'm panting, my chest heaving as I try to catch my breath. But Rhyland doesn't give me a chance to recover. His mouth is back on me, licking and sucking, drinking down my release like it's the finest wine. "Mmm...delicious," he murmurs against me. "I could feast on this pussy forever."

He quickly yanks me up and flips me, bending me over the barrel, my hands splayed against the rough wood. I gasp as I feel his hard cock nudging at my entrance, my body buzzing with anticipation. I'm so ready for him, my clit throbbing and my pussy aching to be filled.

I wiggle my ass against him, biting my lip at the feel of his thick tip pressing against me. "Fuck me," I demand, my voice hoarse and needy. "Don't make me wait another goddamn second, Rhyland."

"So fucking needy for my cock," he growls, rubbing his stiff length through my dripping wetness, coating himself. "When did you become so demanding, huh?"

I whimper, my ass bucking against him as he continues to tease me, dragging his thick, veiny shaft along my slit with agonizing slowness. "Rhyland, please," I beg, my voice breathless and desperate. "Stop teasing me and just fuck me already."

A low chuckle rumbles from his chest, his dark timbre against my skin, prickling the air between us. His fingers tighten, possessive and commanding, while his breath skims my cheek. "Look at you," he murmurs, lips grazing the shell of my ear. "So desperate. You'd do anything, wouldn't you, my sweet little whore?"

Jesus, his filthy mouth is driving me wild, my core tightening as I gush in anticipation, just waiting for him to impale me on his monster cock. He calls me a whore, but to me, it's music. I'll happily be his whore any fucking day.

I moan wantonly, my head falling back against his chest as my body trembles with the sheer force of my arousal. "Fuck yes," I gasp, my tone sassy and defiant, even in my desperation. "I want you to wreck me, Rhyland."

Rhyland grabs a fistful of my hair, yanking my head back as he lets out a low growl, the vibration reverberating through my entire body. His other hand is clamped onto my hip, fingers digging into my flesh hard enough to leave bruises.

"Careful what you wish for, baby," he warns his voice a low, threatening rumble that makes my toes curl. "You keep talking like that, and I might just lose control and fuck you into oblivion."

And with that, he slams into me, his cock plunging deep into my wet heat with one brutal thrust that has me crying out and my fingers digging into the wood of the barrel. "Fuck!" I gasp, my head falling back as the pleasure-pain of his possession rips through me. "*God*, yes, more..."

"Yeah?" He pants, his breath hot against my neck. "You want more of my cock? I'll give you more than you can handle, baby." His deep voice has my core clenching around him in anticipation. "You better keep quiet, though—as much as I love hearing you scream for me, we can't get caught."

I get wetter at the thought.

His thumb brushes over my lips, and I nod eagerly, my body thrumming with need. I'm so ready to come again, the tension coiling tighter and tighter inside me.

He doesn't wait for my response. His large hand covers my mouth, silencing me as he pounds into me. "That's it, baby, scream into my hand," he grunts, his hips snapping forward, burying himself to the hilt inside me.

I bite down on his hand, and he hisses, his grip on my hair tightening to the point of pain. I rake my nails down his arm, marking him as he marks me. Then his teeth are in my neck, biting down hard as he slams into me. I scream into his palm, the sound of our flesh meeting obscenely loud in the quiet building. But I don't care, I am lost in the feeling of him.

His venom floods my system, making my walls flutter and clench around his throbbing cock. I can feel him twitching inside me, his thrusts becoming erratic as my blood mixes with his venom, pushing us both closer to the edge. He pulls back from my neck, licking a hot stripe up my throat, sucking hard on the marks he's left as my blood trickles down my chest.

Then he pushes my face down into the barrel, his hand tangling in my hair to hold me in place. "Don't you fucking move," he commands, his voice a rough growl. "I'm going to fuck you until you can't walk straight."

I couldn't move if I wanted to. My hair curtains my face, my breasts crushed against the barrel, the wood biting into my sensitive nipples. My entire body quakes with the force of his thrusts, each one hitting that perfect spot inside me that makes me see stars.

He has me completely at his mercy, his body caging me in—his hand grips my hip as he controls every aspect of my pleasure. It's intoxicating, being so thoroughly possessed by him, and I can't help but arch my back, tilting my hips to take him even deeper.

He kicks my legs further apart, changing the angle and making me gasp. I feel every thick inch of him buried inside me, and I can't hold back my cries.

"That's it, baby," he grunts, his voice heavy with lust. "There's my desperate little slut. Take every fucking inch. Scream my name."

I can't even form words—all that's coming out of my mouth are moans and groans, my throat already raw from the noises he's wringing out of me. But damn, I can't help but smirk and giggle at the thought that here I am, literally getting fucked over a rum barrel on a pirate island. It's like something straight out of a dirty adventure novel.

"Something amusing, Angel?" Rhyland growls, his voice laced with authority. He thinks I'm giggling because he's not fucking me hard enough to make me lose my damn mind.

As if.

His thrusts become downright brutal, pounding into me, and I forget all about my playful detour and giggles, gasping as he takes me to the edge.

"I don't hear you giggling now." he pants behind me as he ruts into me.

The wet slap of our bodies, the thumping of the barrel against the wall, is obscene. His heavy balls smack against my clit with every thrust, the pain blending deliciously with the pleasure. He leans down, biting my shoulder before sucking hard, making me sob. His hips stutter as I clench around him.

"Bathe me, baby," he growls, his voice rough with need. "I know it's there. I can feel it building."

He's right; my orgasm is coiled tight inside me, a spring waiting to be released. He's hitting that spot, that sweet spot deep within me that has my walls clenching and my juices flowing like a damn fountain. That familiar feeling of needing to pee washes over me, and Rhyland senses it, the clever bastard. He knows me, my body, and when I'm about to combust.

Rhyland slaps my ass hard, the sound reverberating through the small room and making me cry out. He spanks me a second time. The sharp sting is fucking incredible. "Give it to me, Angel," he demands, his voice desperate and harsh.

And I do. I shatter with a muffled scream, my body shaking violently as my release crashes over me. My cum gushes around his cock, my walls clamping down on him like a vice as he fucks me through it. I can barely breathe, barely think, as wave after wave of ecstasy washes over me. I'm lost in the pleasure, feeling of him, of us.

"*Fuck yes,* that's it," Rhyland growls, his voice strained and guttural. "Good girl. That's what I want."

His thrusts become erratic, his hips jerking as he chases his own release. I can feel his cock pulsing inside me, growing impossibly harder just before he comes with a primal roar that sends goosebumps across my skin. He fills me with his hot seed, coating my walls with his essence as he rides out the waves of his orgasm.

Rhyland collapses against me, his breathing coming in erratic huffs. His heart is pounding against my back like he just ran a damn marathon. My mouth feels drier than the Sahara, and I try to swallow, but it's like trying to gulp down sandpaper.

As Rhyland slips out of me, I can feel the evidence of his release trickling down my thighs, a deliciously naughty reminder of our passionate encounter. The sensation of his warm seed painting my skin sends a shiver down my spine, a tangible mark of his claim on my body and soul.

Rhyland falls to his knees behind me and spreads me wide open, "Goddamn, look at that, baby," he murmurs before diving face-first into my cum coated depths, tasting himself and me all at once. It's so fucking filthy and erotic that I can't help but moan into the rough wood beneath me.

I can feel his tongue swirling and plunging into my pussy, lapping, sucking, slurping up our combined juices like he's starving for it. His moans vibrate through me as he savors every drop, clearly getting off on the taste of us together. It's so fucking hot that it nearly sends me careening over the edge again.

He yanks me up, fisting his hand in my hair and claiming my lips in a bruising kiss. His tongue plunges into my mouth, ensuring I thoroughly taste our combined flavors. I moan into the kiss, meeting his tongue stroke for stroke, lost in the raw passion that only this man can ignite in me.

He breaks away, "God damn, we taste fucking incredible together."

Rhyland is like a force of nature—raw, primal, and unapologetically alpha. He's a damn animal, and he's all mine.

The sound of slow, sarcastic applause reaches my ears, and Rhyland and I tear our lips away from each other, whirling around to face the source of the interruption.

"Bravo! Encore! That was a performance worthy of a standing ovation," Lucian drawls, with sarcasm. He's lounging in a chair like he's the damn king of the world, acting as if he didn't just get a front-row seat to our X-rated show.

Rhyland quickly tugs up his pants and whips off his shirt, draping it over me in a polite gesture that would be sweet if we weren't both still panting and flushed from our very public romp.

"I mean, the passion, the intensity, the raw animalistic energy...I'm getting all tingly just thinking about it," Lucian continues, fanning himself dramatically. "So, tell me, sweet cheeks. You like it rough, huh? Because from where I'm sitting, it looks like you're quite the little firecracker in the sack." he winks. "Just the thing I'm into."

Rhyland's growl is so low and menacing that it's a wonder Lucian doesn't piss himself on the spot. "You've just signed your fucking death warrant, you son of a bitch," he snarls, and I can feel his rage and possessiveness flooding through our bond like a tidal wave.

My heart is pounding like a jackhammer, and my worry is reaching stratospheric levels. This whole situation is a powder keg waiting to explode, and I'm not sure if I have the strength to be the voice of reason anymore.

"Rhyland...." I warn.

God, please don't kill him.

Please don't kill him.

Lucian, you fucking idiot!

"Oh, come on, Honey Pot! You're breaking my heart here. I thought we had a real connection, you know? A bond forged in the heat of the moment, sealed with a little love bite on that delectable neck of yours..." He clutches his chest dramatically. "The way you let me taste your sweet, sweet nectar—was like a religious experience. I saw the face of God, and she was wearing your skin."

Lucian throws his head back, lost in the memory. "Oh, and let's not forget about the passion of that kiss we shared." he closes his eyes as if remembering it. "Ah, the memories. They'll keep me warm on those cold, lonely nights. But don't worry, sweet cheeks. I won't tell Tall, Dark, and Growly over there about our little tryst. It'll be our secret." he winks.

Oh...fuck.

I conveniently forgot to mention the whole lip-locking extravaganza, and now the secret's out like a cat with a jetpack. Lucian might as well start planning his funeral because he's about to become vampire confetti.

Rhyland lunges across the room in a blur of motion, his muscles coiled and ready to strike. Before Lucian can even blink, Rhyland slams into him with the force of a freight train, sending them both crashing onto a nearby table. The sound of splintering wood and shattering glass fills the air as the table disintegrates beneath their combined weight.

I cringe, my heart leaping into my throat as I scramble to my feet. Darting to the other side of the room, I desperately attempt to distance myself from the chaos.

The situation is spiraling out of control, and I can feel Rhyland's rage coursing through our bond like molten lava, searing and all-consuming. It's a warpath, pure and simple, and in this moment, I don't think he gives a damn about the fact that Lucian is his brother or the memories they share. All that matters is the red haze of fury that's taken over his mind.

"Rhyland, stop! Both of you, knock it the fuck off!" I scream, my voice raw and desperate, but it's like trying to reason with a hurricane. They're too far gone, lost in the primal dance of violence and rage.

They clash like titans, trading blows with a speed and ferocity that's almost inhuman. Ever the agile, Lucian weaves and dodges around Rhyland's massive fists, his movements a blur of motion. It's a twisted déjà vu, a sickening reminder of their sparring session at WhisperVale, only this time, there's no holding back, no restraint.

The fight drags on, seconds stretching into eternities as they lay waste to everything around them. Furniture is reduced to kindling, shards of glass and debris littering the floor like the aftermath of a war zone. The building itself seems to groan and shudder under the onslaught, walls cracking and supports straining.

And then, it happens. A sickening snap echoes through the room like a shattered bone, and my blood runs cold.

DANICA

34

I watch in horror as Rhyland crumples to the floor, his body twisted unnaturally. My heart stops, my blood turning to ice as Lucian's gaze locks onto me, a feral hunger burning in his eyes. Blood drips from his lips, a testament to the vicious blows Rhyland managed to land, but it's the sheer, unadulterated bloodlust in his expression that sends shivers down my spine.

How he managed to one-up Rhyland in their little tussle is beyond me. Must've been a lucky shot or some cosmic fluke.

"Oh, you can see it, can't you, Honey Pot?" his voice a twisted mix of snark and primal need. "The hunger, the craving, the all-consuming desire for that sweet, crimson Kool-Aid pumping through your veins."

Rhyland's unscheduled nap on the floor has me up shit creek, staring into Lucian's eyes right now, with that feral grin spreading across his face; I've got one thought loud and clear:

I'm totally fucked.

He stalks towards me. His movements are fluid and predatory, his eyes never leaving the blood that still glistens on my neck. "I've been fighting it, trying to keep the beast caged, but your blood... and this little thing between us," he points his finger at me then himself, "I felt your desires, your sweet, sweet need for release..."

His tongue darts out, licking the blood from his lips in a slow, sensual motion. "Watching him drink from you, the scent of your essence thick in the air... it's like mainlining pure, undiluted ecstasy. A hit that goes straight to the primal core of my being like a fucking junkie."

I back away slowly, my heart pounding so hard I swear it's going to burst out of my chest. Fear and adrenaline course through my veins, a sickening cocktail that makes my head spin faster than a merry-go-round.

"Lucian, don't..." I whisper, my voice trembling with fear and desperate hope. "I will kick your ass if I have to." I throw on my best bravado.

He takes another step closer, his eyes burning with a raw and all-consuming hunger. "It's taking every ounce of willpower I have not to pin you against the wall and drink my fill of you. Consequences can suck my undead dick. To lose myself in the taste of you again—until I can't even remember my own fucking name, let alone how to spell it."

My hands ignite in flames, fear being their usual spark like a damn flamethrower. I don't trust Lucian as far as I can throw him right now; the man is lost in some bloodthirsty haze, and I'm the all-you-can-eat buffet.

"Lucian..." I warn, "I don't want to hurt you."

Please, God—or whoever's listening up there—don't let this turn into a shit show. I send a silent prayer into the universe, hoping someone's got my back.

He smirks, eyeing the flames dancing in my palms like they are nothing more than cute little birthday candles. "Those are adorable," he drawls, "but they won't stop me, Honey Pot."

I don't even register him moving before he's on me in a heartbeat, his teeth sinking into my neck, feeding deeply. I open my mouth to scream, but Lucian slaps a hand over it, silencing me. I press my burning hands against his chest and push with everything I've got, my fingers scorching his shirt. He barely flinches, intent on draining me dry.

As dumb as it sounds, I don't want to hurt the fucking idiot.

His venom courses through my veins, mixing with the remnants of Rhyland's toxic cocktail, and I can feel my body going limp, my strength seeping away like water through a sieve.

Lucian cradles me against him, his growls and moans of pleasure vibrating against my skin as he continues to pull at my blood viciously. The edges of my vision blur, the world fading away like a bad dream.

No, no...not again.

This can't happen again—I don't think Lucian will stop.

My knees buckle, and I start to sink to the floor, my body no longer able to support its weight. I reach for my power, trying to summon the flames, the light, anything to fight back, but it's like trying to start a fire in a rainstorm. The venom and the blood loss have me weak, helpless, and unable to defend myself.

Please, someone...something...

Help.

I pray to whoever in the universe can hear me.

A blinding flash of light sears my retinas and Lucian's weight is suddenly torn away from me. There's a sickening thud as he's hurled across the room like a rag doll. I crumple to the floor, my legs about as helpful as overcooked spaghetti, my ears ringing from the deafening sound that follows, like a sonic boom mixed with an EMP blast.

Blinking away the spots dancing in my vision, I slowly lift my head. And holy shit, if it isn't the last person I expected to see this side of Judgment Day.

"Dani, are you alright?" Seraphina's at my side in an instant, her hands gripping my shoulders like she's afraid I might float away. Those honey-colored eyes of hers are swimming with worry.

Ears still ringing, "Seraphina?" I croak, my voice sounding like I've been gargling gravel. "How—? Why are you here?" I'm half convinced I'm hallucinating from blood loss.

"I heard your call," she says, all angelic concern. "I knew I had to help. That *thing* almost killed you." The way she says 'thing,' you'd think Lucian was something she scraped off her celestial shoe.

"Yeah..." I mumble, rubbing at the still bleeding wound on my neck. "He's not exactly firing on all cylinders right now. Memory wipe—lost his marbles—the whole shebang." I struggle to my feet, feeling like a newborn foal, and peer over at Lucian's crumpled form in the corner. "Is he dead? Please tell me you didn't just nuke his ass into oblivion."

Seraphina shrugs, her expression unapologetic. "I can't say I'd feel too bad if I did. What he was about to do to you, Dani... it's unforgivable."

A groan from across the room catches my attention. Rhyland's stirring, clutching his neck like he's just gone ten rounds with a heavyweight champ.

I stumble over to him, my legs still wobbly. "Hey," I manage because, apparently, near-death experiences have robbed me of my usual wit. Rhyland's on his feet in an instant, his eyes darting around the room, searching for Lucian.

Rhyland's eyes land on Lucian's unmoving form on the floor before snapping back to me. Then, as if he can't believe what he's seeing, he spots Seraphina standing there in all her angelic glory. His eyes go wide, and then he's moving, coming up to my side and wrapping his arms around me like he's afraid I might disappear. "What the hell happened?"

I lean into his embrace, taking a moment to breathe him in before I answer. "Rhyland, meet Seraphina. She kind of just saved my ass from becoming Lucian's personal juice box."

I feel Rhyland's embarrassment pulsing through our bond. He feels like he failed me again by being unable to protect me. I squeeze his hand and give him a wave of reassurance, trying to let him know that I don't blame him and that it wasn't his fault.

He gives me this look that screams, *'Don't try to sugarcoat my fuck up, babe.'* Then, turning back to Seraphina, he says with genuine gratitude, "Thank you."

Seraphina shrugs, her white wings rustling softly with the movement. I can't help but notice that they've changed color since the last time I saw her, from a shimmering gold to a pure, pearlescent white. "It was a choice I had to make: either interfere and deal with the consequences or let you die. I chose the former."

I look at her, confusion written all over my face. "Hold up, what are you saying? What consequences?" I step closer to her, my worry skyrocketing.

The last time she interfered, when I almost became a shish kabob in the Whispering Woods, she mentioned that she wasn't allowed to step in but did it anyway. She said there would be hell to pay if my father found out—if the Gods got wind of it.

She stares at me, her honey-gold eyes, so similar to mine, filled with determination and resignation. Her long, golden-blonde hair frames her flawless face, and her plump lips are pressed into a thin line. "Seraphina, spill. What consequences are we talking about here?"

She lets out a long, heavy sigh as the world's weight rests on her perfect shoulders. "Your father told me not to go or answer your call. He said that if I did, I would be banished from Atheria, cast out of the realm of light."

I'm pretty sure my jaw just hit the floor. I must look like a fucking idiot, standing here gaping at her. "I'm sorry, *what?*" I manage to choke out, my voice rising in pitch with each word. "Banished? For saving my life? What kind of fucked up logic is that?"

"We—Angelic beings are not allowed to interfere with mortal decisions—outcomes—"

"Seraphina, I know all that. But what the hell is my father's problem? He'd rather banish you for saving his daughter—his supposed *savior*? That's some serious bullshit right there." I cut her off, my sass meter hitting an all-time high.

I'm frustrated, pissed off, and confused as all hell. My own father would instead let me die than offer help, and Seraphina, being the absolute angel that she is (pun totally intended), would instead take the punishment to save my sorry ass.

"Your father doesn't approve of you being tethered to these..." she pauses and looks at Rhyland, "*beings.*"

And there it is again. My choice of soulmate has *Daddy Dearest* seeing fifty shades of pissed off. He's so butthurt over his rebellious daughter's life choices that he'd rather throw in the celestial towel and let the Apocalypse happen. Talk about a cosmic temper tantrum. I mean, way to prioritize, Dad. Your ego or the fate of the world? Tough call, apparently.

"And he was quite displeased that we interfered before by giving you the Atherite stone too early," Seraphina adds, her voice as sweet and innocent as a cherub's lullaby.

Well, hot damn, looks like I just snagged the "Most Dysfunctional Family" trophy. Go me!

"Prematurely?" I can't resist asking, my eyebrow arched in a perfect "excuse me?" pose.

"Oh, yes," Seraphina explains, with angelic sincerity. "The plan was to give it to you later. But Jophiel told your father how much you needed it. And, well, that's why I've been banished for meddling again."

I reach out and pull her into a hug, holding her close and inhaling the sweet scent of jasmine and something uniquely her. "Thank you, seriously. I'm so sorry that he's done this to you. What exactly does banishment mean for you, though?"

I'm curious now. Where does that leave her if she can't return home to Atheria?

She pulls back, taking my hands in hers. "It just means that I can't go back—I'll have to find somewhere else to stay, to lay low for a while. The good news is that I get to keep my powers. The bad news is that I was stripped of my title in Atheria and lost my golden wings."

She's explaining this to me like I'm supposed to have a PhD in Celestial Studies, but I'm lost as hell. I had no clue that angelic beings came with different wing colors, like some heavenly mood ring. And her title? For all I know, it could've been "Chief Feather Duster" up there.

Mental note: *add "Angelic 101" to my ever-growing list of shit to figure out.*

"Seraphina, honey, you're staying with us. Or better yet, crash at my place with Emily and Sable. They'll keep you safe, and you all can have epic girls' nights complete with face masks, trashy reality TV, and enough wine to make even an angel forget her halo."

She looks at me like I've just offered her the keys to heaven—ironic, considering. "Dani, I couldn't possibly impose like that. I don't want to endanger anyone because of my choices."

I roll my eyes so hard I'm sure I see my brain. "Oh, please. You're family now, sister. We take care of our own. Plus, I'm pretty sure Emily and Sable would kill for another girlfriend to swap gossip and beauty tips with."

Rhyland, standing there like a deliciously brooding work of art, finally decides to join the conversation. "Dani's got a point," he rumbles, his voice all rough and sexy, like a mix of whiskey and dark chocolate. "You're more than welcome to stick with us for as long as you need. It's the least we can do after your sacrifice."

Seraphina looks between us, her eyes shimmering with unshed tears. "I... I don't know what to say. Thank you—both of you. Your kindness means more than you could ever know."

I grin, pulling Seraphina in for another hug. "That's what family's for, babe. We're like a dysfunctional celestial sitcom now. All we need is a laugh track and—"

A groan from the floor cuts me off, and we all whirl around. Lucian's standing up, his back to us, stretching like he just woke up from the world's most intense power nap.

"Uhhh..." he drawls, "What in the nuclear reactor *fuck* was that? Did someone slip me some angel dust, or did I just get bitch-slapped by a supernova?"

Lucian slowly turns around—his eyes lock onto us like a heat-seeking missile. Suddenly, Lucian's whole demeanor shifts—his eyes glaze over, and I swear I can see the exact moment his brain short-circuits.

Lucian clutches his chest and collapses to the floor.

LUCIAN

35

I can't breathe.

My heart's beating faster than a squirrel on speed—like it's trying to punch its way out of my chest Alien-style. And it's all because of the drop-dead gorgeous blonde bombshell angel standing in front of me, looking like a goddamn snack.

My mate.

My mate?—Holy fuck! My very own slice of heaven.

I felt it the second I laid eyes on her, like a fucking epiphany from the love gods above—my heart kicking on and beating loudly in my chest.

After she walloped me with her light grenade, all the memories flooded back like a tidal wave of holy shit-I-remember-now. Dani, Rhyland, the prophecy, my part in this whole fucked up play—saving Dani's perky little ass not once—but twice. My broody, stick-in-the-mud brother Rhyland, who I live to annoy just for shits and giggles. Erik, my stoic, honorable bro who's got a stick so far up his ass you could hang a flag on it. Azrael, Adrian, Luminara—the whole dysfunctional family. It all came back in a rush, like a high-def movie montage on steroids.

And now, here she is, my mate, standing before me in all her ethereal, heart-stopping glory. I always prayed I would get my own angel one day, and damn, the universe did not disappoint. I can feel it in my gut, a thread pulling me towards her like a magnet, an all-consuming need to claim her, make her mine in every sense of the word.

She has to be Dani's guardian angel, the one and only—Seraphina. I mean, who else would swoop in like a divine fucking intervention to save Dani from my dumb-ass, memory-challenged self? It's not like we've got a rolodex of angels on speed dial.

I remember how Rhyland described what he felt when he first saw Dani—that aching feeling in his chest, that soul-deep need to claim, couldn't think straight—She's real, and she's the one who can keep me from falling into darkness, and despair, the light to my eternal fucking night.

And the physical effects? Holy shit, it's like I've been hit by a truck loaded with emotions and sensations. My heart hasn't beat in centuries and is now pounding like a drum solo at a metal concert. Emotions I thought were long dead and buried are rising like zombies on a mission. And the world around me? It's like someone cranked up the resolution to ultra-fucking-HD. Colors are brighter, scents are more potent, and every inch of my body hums with newfound energy.

Speaking of scents—Oh, sweet chimichanga-scented heaven! I'm getting a nose full of her like a bloodhound on steroids. Dani's scent is like a watered-down version of this angelic confection standing in front of me. It's taking every ounce of willpower I have not to start drooling like a goddamn Pavlovian dog—the urge to taste her is so fucking intense that I can practically feel my taste buds doing a happy dance in anticipation.

This angel's fragrance is like a vanilla-spice smoothie with a shot of her own secret sauce. It's making my brain do the cha-cha slide, and my fangs practically scream, "Feed me, Seymour!" I want to faceplant into that neck like it's an all-you-can-eat taco buffet and just huff until my lungs file for divorce.

And her face? Sweet mother of all that's holy and unholy! It's like someone cranked the resolution to "You can see into the future" mode. I can spot every freckle, every microscopic hair. Hell, I could probably read her thoughts if I squint hard enough! She's the Mona Lisa in a world of crayon drawings, people!

Picture this: long, golden blonde hair that glows like a halo, framing a face so perfect it could make grown men weep. Smooth, sunkissed skin that begs to be touched, eyes like golden pools of caramel with lashes longer than the list of people who want to kick my ass (and trust me, that's one loooong list). And those lips? Plump, kissable pillows that could make you forget your own damn name. But that's not even the best part...

Those breasts? They're playing peek-a-boo with that dress, and let me tell you, I've never wanted to play a children's game so badly in my life. They're like two perfect scoops of ice cream trying to escape their cone, and I'm all about that jailbreak.

And she's fun-sized! I'm talking, 'gotta stand on her tippy-toes to reach my chin' kinda small. Plus, it means I can scoop her up easily. Manhandling made easy—now that's what I call ergonomic!

Those hips? Sweet, merciful mayhem! They've got more curves than a racetrack, and I'm ready to take them for a spin. I could get lost exploring those curves for days. Hell, send out a search party 'cause I'm going on an expedition, and I might never return.

In short, she's the kind of woman that makes you believe in intelligent design. Because only a higher power with a wicked sense of humor could create something this perfect and then let me anywhere near it.

I can feel the beast inside me rattling its cage, howling for me to take what's mine, to claim her in every way possible.

But I know I can't just pounce on her like a rabid animal. I've got to play this cool. Take it slow. Woo her with my charm and wit, make her fall for me as hard as I've fallen for her.

It's a fucking test of my self-control, but I'll be damned if I let my baser instincts turn me into a drooling moron in front of my mate.

She's my salvation and future—all wrapped up in one mind-blowingly perfect package.

Shit is about to get real, folks. Lucian's found his mate, and the world better buckle up 'cause this love story's gonna be one for the ages.

"Lucian?" Dani's voice snaps me out of my thoughts. "Are you okay?"

I don't know how long I've been standing here gawking like an idiot at my mate, so I flash Dani my signature panty-dropping grin. "Never better, Princess. Miss me?" I glance over at Rhyland, who looks like he's about two seconds away from strangling me again. "Hey, Rhy-Rhy—No need to get your panties in a twist. I'm all good, bro."

Dani, being the brains of this operation, lets out a sigh of relief. "Oh, thank God. His memories are back." She hunches over, hands on her knees, catching her breath.

I stride up to the angelic bombshell, a grin spreading. "Well, hello there, gorgeous. Seraphina, right? The name's Lucian—your one and only mate, at your service." I say it like I'm commenting on the weather, like finding my soulmate is just another day in the life of yours truly.

Great job breaking the ice, dumbass.

I take her hand in mine, my skin buzzing at the contact. Bringing her hand to my lips, I place a gentlemanly kiss on her soft, delicate skin, my eyes never leaving hers. It's like staring into twin pools of molten gold, and I can feel myself getting lost in their depths.

Seraphina gasps a little at the contact.

"I must say, the universe certainly has a sense of humor, pairing a devilishly handsome rogue like myself with an angel straight from the pages of a Victoria's Secret catalog. But who am I to question fate?" I flash her my most charming grin, the one that's been known to make ladies weak in the knees and men question their sexuality.

Beside me, Dani makes a noise that sounds like a cross between a cough and a cat hacking up a hairball. Seraphina yanks her hand away from me like I've got the plague, her eyes wide. "Excuse me?"

"Yeah, what she said," Dani chimes in, her voice hitting a pitch that could shatter glass. " Lucian, did you hit your head harder than we thought when you went airborne?"

I smirk, my eyes never leaving Seraphina's. "Hit my head? Oh, please, Princess. If anything, that cosmic bitch slap knocked my noggin back into place. Now, I'm seeing clearer than a hawk on Adderall."

Seraphina looks at me like I've grown a second head, but I wink at her, undeterred. "Now, now, my angelic cupcake, no need to play coy. I know it's a lot to take in, being mated to a specimen like myself, but I promise you, it will be one hell of a ride."

Dani groans, facepalming so hard I swear I hear her brain rattle. "Lucian, I don't think—"

But I wave her off, my focus solely on Seraphina. "Trust me, baby girl, you and me? We're going to be the stuff of legends. Lucian and Seraphina, a love story for the ages."

Seraphina stares at me, blinking like a deer in headlights before she turns to Dani with a look that screams, *"Help me, I'm trapped in a romance novel with a lunatic."*

Dani, ever the voice of reason, chimes in. "Luci, can I talk to you for a sec?"

But do I listen? Of course not. I'm too busy eye-fucking my angelic soulmate.

"Lucian!" Ah, there's Rhyland, right on cue to cock-block me like the brooding asshole he is.

I roll my eyes, "One min—" is all I manage to get out before Rhyland grabs me by the neck like a misbehaving puppy and pulls me away.

Next thing I know, I'm being dragged to the corner of the ramshackle hut we so graciously demolished, tripping over debris and shit along the way. I finally pry

Rhyland's meaty paws off me and straighten myself out. Can't have Viking Fuckface making me look like a toddler in front of my lady love.

Dani, looking like she just went ten rounds with a sex hurricane and only barely came out on top, fixes me with a stare. "Lucian, are you sure you're okay? You're saying some weird things—"

"Oh, come on, guys. Don't tell me you can't see it. The connection, the chemistry, the undeniable pull between me and Seraphina. It's like the universe just handed me my slice of heaven on a silver platter." I sigh, my patience wearing thinner than Rhyland's excuse for a personality.

Rhyland, ever the eloquent wordsmith, growls out, "No... What the fuck are you talk—" He pauses, looking at Seraphina, then back to me like trying to piece together a fucked up puzzle. "You can't be serious?"

Dani, still confused, "What? What the hell am I missing?"

I throw my hands up in exasperation. "Oh, for fuck's sake. Do I have to spell it out for you two? Seraphina. Is. My. Mate. My other half, my better half, the yin to my yang, the hot sauce to my burrito. She's the one I've been waiting for, the light to my darkness, the angel to my demon. Capiche?"

Dani and Rhyland exchange a look that's equal parts shock and concern like they're mentally debating whether to call a priest or a psychiatrist. But I grin, my eyes drifting back to Seraphina.

Dani raises her hands, waving them around like she's trying to swat away an invisible fly. "Whoa, whoa, whoa. Hold the hell up." She turns to Rhyland, her eyebrows practically hitting her hairline. "Is he for real?"

I let out a scoff that could win an Oscar for Best Dramatic Performance. "Oh, come on. Is it so hard to believe that I, Lucian, the epitome of charm and sex appeal, could have a destined mate? I'm wounded, truly." I place a hand over my heart, feigning hurt.

"Look, just ask tall, dark, and brooding over here what he felt when he first laid eyes on you, sweet cheeks. Then maybe you'll stop looking at me like I just grew an extra dick."

Rhyland, ever the conversationalist, crosses his arms over his chest like a disapproving father. But the look he shares—one of those sickening, soulful gazes that say they're having a whole fucking conversation without words.

Ugh.

They know exactly what I'm talking about—that undeniable pull, the primal need to protect, claim, own, mate. It's written all over their disgustingly lovestruck faces.

I grab Dani's hand, placing it over my now beating heart. "Feel that?" Dani's eyes widen in shock. "Told you."

Dani stares at me, her eyes shimmering with unshed tears. For a moment, I think she's going to go all Hallmark movie on me and start sobbing about the beauty of love or some shit.

"Oh my god, Lucian..." She cups her hands over her mouth, her voice quivering. "I... I can't believe it. You finally have new spank bank material. I'm so proud."

Rhyland, the smug bastard, throws his head back and laughs like he just heard the joke of the century. I, on the other hand, am not amused.

I roll my eyes. "Ha ha, very funny. Now, if you two lovebirds will excuse me, I have a soulmate to woo."

And with that, I stroll back towards my Halo Hottie, a swagger in my step and a gleam in my eye. I'm ready to sweep her off her feet and into my arms, where she belongs. Seraphina, my love, my mate, prepare to be wooed like you've never been wooed before.

The Lucian Express is coming, and it's a one-way ticket to Paradise.

DANICA

36

Well, isn't this a delightful plot twist straight out of a daytime soap opera? Never in a million years did I expect Seraphina, the heavenly hall monitor, to be mated to Lucian, the walking, talking personification of a vampire frat boy. Mr. Charm-Your-Pants-Off himself would be the lucky fiend to snag my guardian angel.

As Lucian was busy drooling over Seraphina like a lovesick puppy, Rhyland and I had a little telepathic pow-wow to sort out this cosmic curveball. Lo and behold, my brooding Viking confirmed that Lucian's not just spewing a load of nonsense—he really has found his eternal match in my celestial guardian.

Rhyland reminded me of the "undead heart beating again, buried feelings resurfacing, centuries-old ice caps melting" shebang he experienced when he first locked eyes on me. A little trip down memory lane to that fateful moment when he busted down my bathroom door like a horny Neanderthal on a mission, professing his undying love and how I'd melted his icy heart faster than a popsicle in hell.

Back then, I was clueless, completely oblivious to the whole "soul-deep bond" and "primal mating instincts" thing that had Rhyland's fangs in a tizzy.

All I knew was that I felt this weird, inexplicable tug toward Rhyland, like an invisible leash was pulling me in his direction. It was like my body was a compass, and he was my true north. Then, the separation anxiety—being away from him for too long felt like I was going through withdrawal from the world's most addictive drug.

But now, as I watch Lucian stare at Seraphina with that same intense, all-consuming gaze that Rhyland gets whenever he looks at me, the pieces finally click into place.

It's not just a case of wanting to take a little nibble from the celestial buffet—oh no, this is the real deal. Lucian's eyes are brimming with a depth of emotion and longing that can only come from finding your other half, your soul's counterpart.

The kind of look says, "I would burn down the entire universe just to keep you safe and by my side."

Who would have thought that beneath all that cocky bravado and shameless flirting beat the heart of a true romantic, yearning for his destiny to be fulfilled finally? Lucian, the eternal bachelor and self-proclaimed love 'em and leave 'em playboy, has finally met his match in the most unlikely of mates.

This is going to be one hell of a love story to witness, that's for sure.

I stroll back over to Lucian and Seraphina, trying not to laugh at the poor girl's expression. She's listening to whatever verbal diarrhea Lucian is spewing with a look that screams "SOS" louder than a siren on a bender. Time to stage a little angelic intervention before Lucian talks her ear off—literally.

"Hey, Seraphina," I chime in, with false cheer. "Why don't we get you some new clothes and maybe, uh..." I eye her stunning feathered wings, wondering how the hell we're going to disguise those bad boys without causing a scene. "A really, *really* big coat?"

Seraphina catches my drift, her eyes sparkling with joy. "Oh, my wings? No worries, I've got this." And just like that, with a mere flick of her thoughts, her wings vanish in a puff of glittery magic, leaving her standing in her gorgeous dress, as wingless as a plucked chicken.

"Well, damn. That's handy," I mutter, my jaw practically hitting the floor. "Wish I could make my problems disappear that easily."

Lucian—never one to miss an opportunity for a dirty joke. "Mmm..that is a nifty trick. Think you could work that magic on my pants later? I've got a not-so-little problem that could use your divine intervention if you catch my drift." He waggles his eyebrows suggestively, his grin widening as Seraphina's cheeks flush a delicate shade of pink.

Her eyes widen, shock and morbid curiosity flickering across her face before she quickly schools her features into a mask of angelic indifference. "I will do no such thing," she stammers, her voice slightly higher. "I will stick to using my powers for... celestial purposes only."

I can tell she's equally scandalized and intrigued by Lucian's bold proposition, but she's trying her damnedest not to show it. Her eyes dart to Lucian's crotch for the briefest of moments, as if she's trying to gauge the severity of his "problem," before she quickly averts her gaze, a blush creeping up her neck.

Lucian, of course, is undeterred. "Celestial purposes, huh? Well, I can think of a few heavenly activities we could get up to that would definitely make you see stars, if you know what I mean." He shoots her a wink, his grin turning positively devilish.

I groan, stepping between them before Lucian can further corrupt the poor girl. "Okay, that's enough, you walking Viagra ad. Let's focus on the task at hand, shall we? We need to get Seraphina some new clothes and figure out our next move."

Seraphina nods vigorously, latching onto the change of subject like a lifeline. "Yes, clothes. That sounds like a wonderful idea, Dani. Please, lead the way."

As we make our way out of the shack, I can't help but notice Seraphina sneaking glances at Lucian, her brow furrowed in a mix of confusion and fascination. It's like she's trying to reconcile the idea of a vampire with the concept of a soulmate and failing miserably.

I hope she's prepared for the emotional whiplash that comes with being the object of Lucian's affection. Because if there's one thing I know about Lucian, it's that he doesn't do anything half-ass—especially when it comes to pursuing his mate.

But for now, I'll focus on playing chaperone and making sure Lucian doesn't scar Seraphina for life with his relentless innuendos. The last thing we need is an angelic smiting because Lucian couldn't keep his dirty thoughts to himself.

The obnoxious chatter of merchants below rudely awakens me. Seriously, don't these people have anything better to do than ruin a girl's beauty sleep?

I'm tucked in beside Rhyland, his heat enveloping me like a deliciously warm, sexy blanket. By the window, Seraphina sleeps soundly, blissfully unaware of the auditory assault outside.

After yesterday's bullshit, we quickly found decent accommodations and crashed harder than a narcoleptic at a mattress convention. As soon as my head hit the pillow, I was out like a light, dead to the world and dreaming of a place where pirates knew the meaning of indoor voices.

Lucian and Erik are shacked up next door, probably snoring loud enough to wake the dead and scare them back to sleep. We're supposed to meet Gideon later to figure out our next moves, but right now, I want to burrow deeper into Rhyland's arms and pretend the outside world doesn't exist.

Stretching like a cat in a sunbeam, I start to sit up, but Rhyland grabs my hip and yanks me closer. I'm still only wearing his shirt, which swims on me like a sexy long nightgown. "And where the hell do you think you're going, Angel?" he growls, his voice sleepy, smoky, and sexy as sin.

I grin at him, batting my eyelashes innocently as I swing my leg over his torso, straddling him. He grips my bare thigh, his hand running up to cup the edge of my ass, and I can't help but purr at the contact. I swear, this man could make a nun think twice about her vows with just a single touch.

"Just wanted to see what time it is, you possessive brute," I tease, my voice breathy and coy. "Sucks not having a watch around here. Gotta do everything the old-fashioned way and look at the sun like I'm some explorer or something."

Rhyland chuckles, the sound low and rumbling in his chest. "Fuck the sun, Angel. I'll tell you what time it is. It's time for you to get your sweet little ass back in this bed, and let me show you how a real man starts his day."

His hand slides higher, squeezing my ass with just the right amount of pressure to make me squirm. "Oh, is that so?" I purr, my lips curving into a wicked grin. "And what exactly does a real man's morning routine involve, pray tell?"

Rhyland's eyes flash with hunger and mischief, his grip on me tightening. "I think you fucking know, you little tease. But if you need a reminder, I'm more than happy to oblige."

I shiver at the promise in his words, my body already responding to the heat in his gaze.

Rhyland smirks, his hands tightening on my hips as he pulls me down against him, letting me feel every inch of his desire. "How about I show you instead of telling you, Angel? Actions speak louder than words, after all."

And with that, he flips us over, pinning me beneath him as he captures my lips in a searing kiss that steals the breath from my lungs, and the smart-ass retorts from my tongue.

Rhyland pulls back from my thoroughly kissed lips, a smug grin on his face. "First things first, baby. I need my goddamn breakfast."

Before I can even process what he means, he's ducking under the sheet and settling between my legs. I quickly glance over at Seraphina, who's still sleeping like the dead, and pray to God to keep my big mouth shut and my moans to a minimum.

But then Rhyland's tongue is lashing out against my clit, and I'm arching off the bed like I've been electrocuted. He grabs my thighs in his big, rough hands and pushes my legs apart, spreading me wide open for his hungry mouth. I see him get up on his knees, and then he's devouring me like a man starved, his entire warm, wet, delicious mouth covering my pussy as he sucks and savors me like I'm the best damn thing he's ever tasted.

My eyes roll back in my head as I reach under the sheet and tangle my fingers in his hair, holding him right where I want him. He moans quietly against my wet sex, letting me know just how much he's enjoying his little morning feast. "Fuck, baby, you taste even better marinated," he growls, his voice muffled by my flesh.

I know he's talking about his cum and mine from last night, and the thought of him lapping up our combined juices like it's his favorite fucking breakfast has me clenching around nothing. He pulls away suddenly, and my clit instantly goes cold from the loss of his mouth. But before I can even whine in protest, he's biting into my inner thigh, marking me as his.

I have to grab the pillow and muffle my moan, biting down on the fabric to keep from screaming as he drinks from my inner thigh, his fingers fucking into me slowly, agonizingly. It's torture, sweet, delicious, and maddening all at once, and I know I won't last long under his relentless onslaught.

"Rhyland...." I whisper. "I'm going to come..."

Rhyland releases my thigh. His mouth back on my sensitive clit—warm and delicious. "Good, 'cause I'm starving," he mumbles.

As if on cue, my orgasm crashes over me before I can even register what's happening. My face flushes with heat as I struggle to stifle my cries. My pussy clenches around his fingers, pulsing and fluttering as he coaxes every last shred of pleasure from my body. I feel the wetness trickling down my ass and onto the sheets as Rhyland drinks in my release, his mouth sealed against my core, moaning and gulping.

Fuck that's hot.

"Mmm...baby," he rasps, his breath scorching against my sensitive flesh as he pushes my thighs up and back, spreading me wider and opening me to him completely. "I would die a happy man drowning in you."

He's referring to my squirting—a phenomenon I'd never experienced before meeting him. Whatever he does to me, it triggers something primal, a release so intense it feels like I'm coming undone at the seams.

Rhyland's tongue gives me the complete VIP treatment, going places no passport has ever been issued for. He's everywhere—inside me, outside me. But when that clever little muscle flicks against my ass, I have to bite my tongue to keep from screaming. It's like a good spanking—painful and pleasurable all at once, leaving me wondering if I should thank him or slap him.

With a satisfied growl that says, *'Mmmm, that hit the spot,'* he pulls back from my lady bits like he's surfacing after a deep-sea dive. And let's be honest, he basically did. This man has tongue skills that would make the mythical creatures of the deep blush.

He sits back, looking all sorts of pleased with himself, and licks his lips like he's just sampled the most delectable dessert on the damn planet. If seduction had a face, it would be Rhyland's after a taste test south of my border.

"Damn, Angel," he murmurs, his voice low and thick with desire. "I could wake up to—"

"Good morning!" Seraphina chimes from the corner of the room, her voice as chipper and bright as a songbird at sunrise.

I quickly shove Rhyland off of me, sending him tumbling off the side of the bed with a grunt and a thud. "H-Hi..." I clear my throat, acting like I wasn't just getting my pussy eaten by my irresistible Viking. "Good morning. How did you sleep?"

Rhyland pops his head up from the side of the bed, his lips a shiny sheen from my arousal and looking like a disgruntled puppy who just got booted off the couch. "What the hell, Angel?" he grumbles, rubbing his head where it connected with the floor.

I shoot him a look that says, *'Shut up and play nice,'* before turning back to Seraphina with a bright, totally-not-fake smile. "I hope we didn't wake you with all the... uh... commotion."

Seraphina blinks, her head tilting to the side like a curious bird. "Commotion? I didn't hear anything. I was admiring the view from the window. The sunrise over the sea is quite beautiful."

I breathe a sigh of relief, thanking whatever gods are listening that angels have the observational skills of a distracted toddler. "Oh, yes. It's really stunning, isn't it, Rhyland?" I say, with false enthusiasm as I try to act like I wasn't just caught with my hand in the proverbial cookie jar.

Rhyland, who's still sprawled on the floor like a petulant child whose favorite toy was just snatched away, shoots Seraphina a look that's half annoyed, half incredulous.

"Oh yeah, it's *really* something," he drawls, his voice thick with sarcasm. "Almost as stunning as the view I had a few seconds ago before someone decided to interrupt."

I shoot him a warning glare. "Right," I say, clapping my hands together desperately trying to change the subject. "We should get moving. We have a lot to do before we meet with Gideon, and by that, I mean clothes—lots and lots of clothes."

Seraphina tilts her head, looking adorably confused. "Clothes? But I thought we would discuss our next steps and plans for finding the key and stopping Moretemis."

I nod, my smile turning sly and mischievous. "Oh, we are, sweetie. But first, we need to make sure we look the part. I mean, we can't very well go traipsing around the high seas looking like a bunch of landlubbers, now can we? No, if we're going to be taken seriously as badass pirates, we need to dress the part."

Rhyland snorts, finally hauling himself off the floor and dusting off his pants. "Since when do you care about looking the part, Angel? Last I checked, you were more interested in getting me out of my clothes than putting me in new ones."

I shoot him a wink, my grin turning positively wicked. "Oh, trust me, big boy, I'm always interested in getting you out of your clothes. But even I know there's a time and a place for everything—but right now? It's time to go shopping."

Seraphina still looks a little lost, but there's a spark of excitement in her eyes now, a hint of curiosity and anticipation. "Shopping? For pirate clothes? I... I've never done anything like that before. It sounds... fun."

I laugh, "Oh, honey, you have no idea. Stick with me, and I'll show you the ropes. By the time we're done, you'll be the most stylish swashbuckler on the seven seas."

DANICA

37

After a whirlwind shopping spree at the local merchants, where we scored some seriously badass outfits that would make even the most grizzled pirate do a double-take, Seraphina and I look like the ultimate swashbuckling bombshells.

Of course, that's after Rhyland decided to play a little game of "surprise sex" in the changing room. Mr. Insatiable snuck in while I was trying on a particularly sexy little number and bent me over, claiming he wasn't done with his 'morning routine.' I had to bite my tongue to keep from screaming as he pounded into me against the wall, praying that no one would hear the telltale slap of skin on skin or the muffled moans I couldn't quite contain.

What's a bit of public indecency between soul mates, right? It's just another day in the life of being bonded to a possessive, alpha-as-fuck vampire Viking. I swear, the man's libido is as endless as his stamina. Not that I'm complaining, mind you. There are certainly worse ways to start the day than with a mind-blowing orgasm courtesy of my own personal sex god.

I'm rocking a fitted black leather vest that cinches at the waist, showing off my curves in all the right places. It's paired with a flowy white blouse that's just sheer enough to be tantalizing without venturing into full-on scandalous territory. The sleeves are billowy, giving me that perfect 'I'm ready for adventure' vibe, and the neckline is low enough to keep things interesting without risking a wardrobe malfunction at the first gust of wind.

My legs are encased in tight, high-waisted black pants that hug my hips and thighs. They're tucked into knee-high leather boots with just enough heels to give me a little extra swagger in my step. A wide, buckled belt slung low on my hips completes the look.

Seraphina has gone for a slightly more refined take on the pirate aesthetic. She's wearing a deep burgundy corset top that laces up the front, accentuating her slender waist and giving her an air of regal elegance. The rich color complements her golden hair and sunkissed skin perfectly, making her look like a goddamn Renaissance painting come to life.

Her skirt is a flowing, tiered affair in a soft ivory hue, with delicate gold embroidery along the hem that catches the light with every step. It falls just above her ankles, revealing a pair of dainty, heeled boots in warm brown leather. A thin, gold chain belt rests on her hips, and a matching gold choker adorns her slender neck, adding sparkle and shine to her ensemble.

We spent the entire day roaming around the local shops, ogling all the shiny wares and trinkets like a bunch of magpies on a treasure hunt. Seraphina was like a kid hopped up on sugar at Disneyland—she'd never experienced anything like this before, and it showed in how her eyes sparkled with wonder and delight at every turn.

I asked Lucian and Erik to sit this little shopping trip out, much to Lucian's vocal displeasure. He whined and grumbled like a toddler. But, eventually relented. I mean, don't get me wrong, I love the guy, but I need some quality one-on-one time with my guardian angel to ease her into this whole crazy adventure without Lucian and his perpetually horny ass scaring the poor girl off.

We navigated through the crowded stalls like a bunch of seasoned bargain hunters on Black Friday, dodging elbows and haggling with merchants. By the end of the day, Seraphina had turned into a regular wheeling and dealing pro, batting her eyelashes and flashing her angelic smile like some secret weapon. Even the surliest vendors were putty in her hands, practically tripping over themselves to give her the best deals and the prettiest baubles.

But as the sun starts to dip below the horizon, painting the sky in shades of orange and pink, we know it's time to call it a day. We have a meeting with Gideon at the bar, and as much as I would love to keep playing dress-up with Seraphina, duty calls.

We make our way through the winding streets, the sound of laughter and music spilling out from the various taverns and inns we pass. The air is thick with the scent of roasting meats and spiced rum.

As we step into the bustling tavern, we're the main attraction at the world's thirstiest circus. Heads snap in our direction so fast that I'm pretty sure a few of these pirates will need neck braces. Jaws are dropping left and right, and I'm half expecting a cartoon wolf to pop out from behind a barrel and start panting, tongue lolling out and eyes bugging from his head.

Rhyland—the possessive ass, looks like he's about to go full caveman and toss me over his shoulder for another round of "hide the Viking sword" in some dark corner. Seriously, the man loses his shit faster than a seagull spotting a french fry whenever someone so much glances my way or comments on my outfit. *"Do you always have to look sexy in everything you put on?"*

Well, excuse the fuck out of me for not dressing like a nun. What am I supposed to say to that? "Sorry, babe, I'll try to look more like a potato sack next time"? Not that I'm complaining, mind you. It's nice to have a man who thinks you're sex on legs even when you look like you've been dragged through a hedge backwards. Bed head? He's all over it. Morning breath? Bring it on. It's like living with a horny complement machine, and honestly? I'm not mad about it.

Lucian is practically drooling at the sight of Seraphina, his eyes glazing over with a mix of awe and desire. I can practically read his mind right now—it's a one-way ticket to X-ratedville.

The tavern is a cacophony of sounds and smells, the air thick with the pungent aroma of stale beer, sweat, and the faint tang of salt from the sea. The clamor of clinking mugs, raucous laughter, and the occasional burst of off-key singing create a lively backdrop as we make our way through the crowd.

We spot Gideon at a table in the back, his feet propped up on a chair and a lazy grin on his face as he surveys the room. As we approach, he raises a hand in greeting, his eyes twinkling with mischief and maybe just a hint of something else as they land on Seraphina.

"Well, well, well," he drawls, his voice low and smooth as honey. "Look what the tide dragged in. I was startin' to think ye lot had gotten lost in the market, distracted by all the shiny things and pretty faces."

I roll my eyes, plopping down in the seat across from him and reaching for the pitcher of ale in the center of the table. "Please, like we'd ever be that easily swayed. We're professionals, Gideon. We know how to keep our eyes on the prize."

Seraphina slides into the seat next to me, her ethereal beauty starkly contrasting the dingy surroundings. Rhyland takes his place on my other side. Ever the opportunist, Lucian tries to wedge himself between Seraphina and me, his eyes gleaming with mischief. But I'm having none of it. I shove him away, fixing him with a stern glare. "Sit your ass down on the other side, Casanova," I growl, pointing to the empty seat across from us.

Trying to ease Seraphina into this wild ride, especially with Lucian's antics, is like teaching a cat to fetch—hilarious but not exactly easy.

Lucian pouts, but I'm having none of it. With a firm shove and a pointed glare, I send him stumbling to the opposite side of the table, his protests falling on deaf ears. With a dramatic sigh, he flops down into the seat opposite us, his eyes never leaving Seraphina's face.

I introduce Seraphina to Erik and Gideon, and I swear, Gideon looks like he just got smacked upside the head with a hefty dose of love dust. "Aye... lass... nice to meet ye," he stutters, his usually smooth pirate swagger nowhere to be found. "So, you're a friend of our dear Dani here?"

I hear Lucian growl low in his throat, and I've got to do a double-take. Wow. I don't think I've ever heard Lucian get all territorial before, but it's pretty damn evident that Gideon is attracted to Seraphina, and Lucian is picking up on it like a bloodhound on a fresh scent.

"Hey, Captain Horndog!" Lucian calls out with irritation. "I know my girl here is a total smoke show, but how about you keep your eyes above sea level, if you know what I mean? Wouldn't want you to strain something trying to undress her with your mind."

Erik coughs, choking and sputtering like a drowning man smacked in the face with a tidal wave of Lucian's sudden jealousy streak. The man is usually as calm and composed as a cucumber in an ice bath, but even he can't keep his stoic facade intact in the face of Lucian's territorial bullshit.

Gideon blinks, taken aback by Lucian's sudden display of possessiveness. "Apologies, mate. Meant no disrespect to ye or the lady. Just tryin' to be friendly-like is all."

"Lucian," Erik admonishes, his voice strained but still somehow managing to sound like he's scolding a misbehaving child. "Perhaps it would be wise to show a bit more decorum in front of our new acquaintance."

Lucian rolls his eyes, his grin turning sharp and dangerous. "Decorum? Is that what we're calling it now? Nah, I think I'll stick with good old-fashioned honesty, thanks. And honestly? Captain Charmless over there needs to keep his eyes and thoughts to himself before I show him exactly what happens when you try to poach another man's mate."

"Seraphina, it is a pleasure to make your acquaintance," Erik says, his tone polite and composed, even as he's still trying to catch his breath from his little choking fit.

Seraphina smiles serenely, seemingly oblivious to the testosterone-fueled drama unfolding around her. "It's lovely to meet you all."

Gideon salutes his mug and winks, "Cheers, lass."

Lucian looks like he's about two seconds away from leaping across the table and throttling Gideon with his bare hands.

His gaze darts back to Seraphina, and he shoots her a wink, his eyes sparkling with mischief and possessiveness. Seraphina blushes, caught off guard by the sudden attention from both men, her cheeks turning a delightful shade of pink.

Everyone launches into a heated discussion about ship repairs and our next move. I chime in, reminding them of our need to head to Serraphatic Cove to find the key I'm supposed to locate.

How the hell am I going to accomplish that feat is anyone's guess, but I've learned to roll with the punches when it comes to this whole "Chosen One" gig.

I lean in close, my voice low and laced with concern. "I know this all may seem really strange to you. I'm so sorry, Seraphina, that you're in this position." The words feel hollow, inadequate in the face of her sacrifice. She lost her home, her very purpose, because of me, because of my father's actions.

But Seraphina, ever the picture of grace, shakes her head, and her smile is gentle and understanding. "Don't blame yourself, Dani. It was my decision, my consequence. I'm okay with it."

She sniffs and then stares into her mug as if the universe's secrets might be hidden in its murky depths.

Sensing her unease, I nudge her gently. "It's ale; it has a kick to it. Try it." I encourage her, hoping to distract her from her heavy thoughts.

She raises the mug to her lips, taking a tentative sip. Almost immediately, she starts coughing, her eyes watering as the alcohol burns its way down her throat. "It burns," she gasps, rubbing at her neck. But to my surprise, she goes back for more, her eyes widening with each gulp. "But it's good," she admits, slamming the empty mug on the table.

The table falls silent, everyone's jaws practically hitting the floor as we watch this angelic creature throw back her drink like a seasoned sailor. Oblivious to our stunned reactions, Seraphina wipes her mouth with the back of her hand. "More?"

Lucian, who looks like he's about to combust, leaps to his feet, his chair clattering to the ground in his haste. He stumbles over to Seraphina, his usual cocky swagger replaced by a nervous energy that's both endearing and hilarious. "Yeah, I-I got it... just wait, right there," he stammers, his voice cracking like a pubescent boy's.

I can't help but laugh at the sight of Lucian, the smooth-talking, unflappable vampire, reduced to a bumbling mess in the presence of his celestial mate. For her part, Seraphina seems blissfully unaware of the effect she's having on him. She smiles that sweet, innocent smile. "Thank you," as if he's just offered to pass the salt.

"Erik says Seraphina's scent is... distracting," Rhyland's deep, commanding voice echoes through my mind, his tone laced with a hint of primal possessiveness.

I glance over at Erik, noting how his muscles are coiled tight, his jaw clenched as if fighting an internal battle. Shit. If Erik, the master of self-control, struggles to keep his cravings in check around my scent, I can only imagine the effect Seraphina's pure Atherian essence has on him.

"Is he going to be okay?" My concern bleeds through our mental connection.

"He'll manage," Rhyland assures me. *"But it's not easy. She's potent, her scent a siren's call to our baser instincts. Even I'm finding it... challenging to ignore."*

I can feel the tension rolling off Rhyland in waves, his every muscle flexed as he fights to maintain control. It's a side of him I rarely see, the raw, animalistic power that lurks beneath his calm exterior. The knowledge that Seraphina's mere presence can bring such powerful vampires to the brink of their control is both thrilling and terrifying.

"What can we do to help?" I ask, my mind racing with possibilities.

"For now, we endure. We are not slaves to our impulses. We are warriors and leaders. We will master this, as we have mastered every challenge before."

His words show a steely determination. At this moment, Rhyland is every inch the alpha male, the unquestioned leader of his kind. His strength, his unwavering control, is a force to be reckoned with.

Erik and Rhyland struggle against their instincts. Our very essence calls to them a temptation that would bring lesser beings to their knees.

But my vampires are no ordinary men. They are warriors, leaders, and kings among their kind. And they will not be brought low by base desires, no matter how potent the lure.

"Lucian, on the other hand..." Rhyland's voice trails off, a hint of concern lacing his words.

"What about him?"

"It's different with him. She's his mate. Every instinct in his body screams at him to protect and cherish her. He'd sooner starve himself into madness than ever lay a finger on her in harm." Rhyland's tone is solemn, his words hanging heavy between us.

I gaze at Lucian, watching as he stares at Seraphina with a longing so intense it's almost palpable. The depth of emotion in his eyes is staggering, a testament to the unbreakable bond between a vampire and his mate. At this moment, I know with absolute certainty that Lucian would move mountains and walk through the fires of hell before he allowed any harm to come to Seraphina.

"How long can he hold out if Seraphina doesn't accept the bond?" The question tumbles out of me before I can stop it, a nagging worry plaguing me since Rhyland offered me his own bond.

What would have happened if I had made him wait? If I had refused?

Rhyland is silent for a moment, his brow furrowed in thought. *"It's difficult to say,"* he admits at last. *"It varies from vampire to vampire, depending on their strength of will. Some of our stories speak of those who waited years, decades, or even centuries for their mate to accept the bond. Others..."* He hesitates, a shadow passing over his features. *"Others fell to their darker nature when faced with rejection from their fated partner."*

I swallow hard, my mouth suddenly as dry as the desert sands. The thought of what could have happened to Rhyland, of the pain and madness he might have endured had I not accepted our bond, sends a shiver spider down my spine. And now, watching Lucian, seeing the raw need etched into every line of his face, I can't help but fear for him.

Lucian is strong, his mind is as sharp as a steel trap, and his will is unbreakable. But everyone has a breaking point, a limit to what they can endure. And the bond between a vampire and his mate, the all-consuming need to claim and be claimed in return... it's a force that can bring even the mightiest to their knees.

"We'll just have to hope it doesn't come to that," I murmur, my heart aching for the struggle I know Lucian must be facing. *"Seraphina may be an angel, but she's not heartless. Surely, she won't let him suffer needlessly."*

Rhyland nods, his jaw tight with unspoken emotion. *"We can only pray that she sees the truth of their bond and accepts the gift that fate has bestowed upon them. Because if she doesn't..."*

He doesn't need to finish the thought. We both know the stakes, the terrible price Lucian may be forced to pay if Seraphina rejects him.

As I watch the interplay of emotions across Lucian's face, the way his eyes never leave Seraphina's form, I can't help but feel a flicker of hope. Because, in the end, love always finds a way. And if anyone deserves a happily ever after, it's Lucian—the vampire with a heart of gold beneath his smartass exterior.

"I'm just so fucking happy he's finally back to his old self and has stopped drooling over your delectable ass," Rhyland's relief flows through me. *"Now he can focus on his own goddamn mate and keep his fucking hands and fangs to himself. I won't have to rip him apart limb from limb for sniffing around what's mine."*

I can't help but snort at that. *"Aww, were you feeling a little threatened there, Fjord Fluff? Afraid Lucian might sweep me off my feet with his charming wit and dashing good looks?"*

Rhyland hasn't breathed a word about *the kiss*—Lucian and his loose lips just had to spill the beans. I'm counting my lucky stars that Rhyland's keeping mum. Maybe he's just as eager as the rest of us to put this whole clusterfuck behind us.

"Watch it, Angel. You know damn well that you're mine and mine alone. I won't hesitate to remind you of that fact, even if it means bending you over this table right here and now and showing everyone in this fucking tavern who you belong to."

I feel a rush of heat flood my body at his words, my thighs clenching involuntarily at the thought of Rhyland claiming me so publicly, so possessively. But I'll be damned if I let him know just how much his little display of dominance affects me.

"Whoa there, Berserker Beau," I tease, *"Let's keep the public mating rituals to a minimum, shall we? We wouldn't want to give Seraphina a crash course in Vampire Kama Sutra 101. I'm pretty sure her angelic sensibilities aren't quite ready for the sight of your bare ass in all its glory."*

Rhyland's answering chuckle is dark and filled with wicked promise. *"Oh, I think she'd survive, baby. But you're right. We shouldn't subject the poor girl to our passion's raw, untamed force. She's got enough on her plate dealing with Lucian's piss-poor attempts at wooing."*

I can't help but snicker at that, my eyes darting to where Lucian sits, his gaze still glued to Seraphina like a lovesick puppy drooling over a juicy bone.

"By the way, I felt that, Angel."

I play dumb, batting my eyelashes with exaggerated innocence. *"Felt what, exactly?"*

Rhyland leans over, his breath hot and heavy against my ear, his hand gripping my thigh with possessive intent. "You got fucking excited when I mentioned taking you right here on this table, in front of everyone," he whispers, his words a sinful caress against my skin. "I think my Naughty Little Angel has a kink for public sex, for being watched, worshipped, dominated. You've proven that twice now. Or should I say, Little Devil?"

I close my eyes and try to steady my breathing, but it's a losing battle. Rhyland's words, his touch, the very thought of him claiming me so openly, so possessively, in front of a room full of strangers—it sends a spark of molten desire straight to my clit, my body betraying me in the most delicious way possible.

Fuck, I am one dirty, shameless bitch.

Rhyland throws his head back and laughs, the sound equally intoxicating and infuriating. "See? I knew it, baby. You can't hide from me, not even in the depths of your own mind."

I shoot him a mental middle finger. *"Yeah, yeah, laugh it up, you smug bastard. Just remember, two can play at this game. Keep teasing me like this, and I might give the good people of this tavern a show they'll never forget."*

Rhyland's eyes flash with hunger and challenge, his grin turning feral. "Don't make promises you can't keep, baby. You know I'll take you up on that offer in a fucking heartbeat."

I lean in close, my lips brushing against his ear in a whisper-soft caress. "Who says I can't keep them? Maybe I want to be *bad,* to let everyone see how thoroughly you own me, body and soul."

Rhyland's answering growl is a rumble of pure lust, his hand tightening on my thigh in a grip that's sure to leave bruises. "You're playing with fire, Angel. Keep this up, and I won't be held responsible for my actions."

I grin, "Well then, hot stuff, it looks like you've got your work cut out for you. Better find a way to douse these flames, 'cause right now? I'm a regular ol' fire hazard."

It's a dance of dominance and submission, a push and pull of passion and provocation that never fails to leave me breathless and aching for more.

And fuck, if I don't love every single second of it.

RHYLAND

38

The more I learn about Dani and all her filthy little fantasies, the more it blows my fucking mind and sets me on fire. Every time she reveals a new kink, my cock gets so hard it could cut diamonds. I want to give her everything she craves and then some, even if it means going against every possessive, alpha instinct that's hardwired into my DNA.

Twice now, this kinky little scenario has reared its head—first in her dream, and then when I caught her getting wet watching Faderyn get railed and decided to make her come so hard, she saw stars. Fuck me, that night is seared into my brain like a brand.

And just last night, when Lucian watched us, did I feel even a hint of shame or embarrassment through our bond? Hell no. What I felt was pure, raw, fucking arousal pouring off her in waves. I can't help but smirk, realizing I've struck gold with this filthy, wild, insatiable little vixen I get to call mine. What I wouldn't give to pry open that dirty mind of hers and see every depraved, naughty fantasy she's hiding in there. It'd be like the kinky fucking cherry on top of the dirtiest sundae imaginable.

But I'm a patient man. I know these things have a way of unfolding, and with me pushing all her naughtiest buttons, this game will be the highlight of my entire existence.

After knocking back enough drinks to drown a damn elephant, hashing out our next moves, and heading back to our Inn, Dani pulls her usual stunt. She bats those golden eyes at me, begging me to bunk with my brothers for the night, so she and Seraphina can have some goddamn "girl time." She's determined to make sure Seraphina feels all cozy and comfortable. In the end, I cave like a fucking house of cards, helpless against those swirling golden eyes and the way she kisses me like she's trying to devour me whole. She leaves me with a raging hard-on and an ache in my balls that I know won't quit until I'm buried inside her again.

So here I am, stuck in a room beside the girls with my brothers. Lucian won't shut up about Seraphina. "Bro, can you fucking believe this? Did you see her? She's so fucking beautiful, it hurts to look at her."

Erik stares at him, his face as blank as a freshly wiped ass. "Yes, Lucian. You've mentioned it once or twice... or a dozen times."

I take a look around our temporary room. It's not the fucking Ritz, but it'll do for a few days. The room is spacious, with a window that looks out over the sea. It's got an authentic Caribbean vibe, with walls painted in soothing shades of teal and furniture made of white-washed wood. The salty tang of the ocean breeze mingles with the faint scent of rum and the sweet, fruity aroma of the flowers blooming in the lush foliage that spills from a small table in the center of the room. Two queen-sized beds take up opposite sides of the space, with a couch that's seen better days shoved up against one wall. There's a bathroom that's barely bigger than a fucking broom closet and some dressers that have probably been around since the dawn of time.

I flop on the couch and kick my feet up on the table, fixing Lucian with a look. "So, what's the plan, Romeo? How are you going to convince your Juliet to accept the mating bond? Because right now, it seems like she'd rather chew off her own arm than let you put a mark on her."

Lucian gets this shit-eating grin on his face like he's about to drop the most pro-found fucking wisdom of the century. "Oh, I've got a plan, my brother. A foolproof, panty-dropping, angel-seducing plan that'll have her begging to be my mate faster than you can say 'holy matrimony.'"

Erik and I exchange a look, and I can practically hear him rolling his eyes. This should be good.

I think back to when I first laid eyes on Dani. I was a stubborn bastard, fighting tooth and nail against the idea that she could be my mate. But eventually, even I couldn't deny the truth anymore. I embraced my alpha instincts and took a chance, claiming her as mine. Dani, being the perfect little submissive, melted under my dominance and control, accepting me as her mate. But Lucian? He's a different breed altogether. He's not known for his alpha tendencies or his ability to dominate. No, he's more of a smooth-talker, a charmer who can talk his way out of any situation. It might work on Seraphina, but it will be one hell of a show to watch.

"I'm gonna take my sweet time with her, you know, test the waters..." Lucian trails off, running his fingers through his hair with a smirk that screams 'I'm a cocky bastard.' "But before all that, I gotta say my mea culpas for the whole 'almost turning your girl into a juice box' fiasco. Let's just say I wasn't exactly playing with a full deck, if you know what I mean."

I nod, my jaw clenching tight. "I know that, and I accept your apology. But first things first, you son of a bitch." I stand up and stalk over to Lucian, who stands his ground like the cocky bastard he is, ready for whatever I'm about to do. I wrap my arms around him in a fierce hug, squeezing him so hard I swear I hear his ribs creak. "Welcome back, brother."

Lucian tenses up at first as if expecting a knife in the back. But then he's hugging me back, his arms tight around me. "Aww, I missed you too, you big softie. No homo, though."

I pull back, looking him dead in the eye with a smile that's all teeth and no warmth. He grins back at me, and then I twist his neck with a sickening crack, watching as he crumples to the floor like a marionette with its strings cut. "That's payback, asshole."

I step over his lifeless body and sit back down on the couch, propping my feet up on the table like I'm the fucking king of the castle. Erik's deep, rumbling laugh fills the room, and I can't help but flash him a grin.

"Was that really necessary?" Erik asks from his spot by the window—his arms crossed. He looks out over the sea with a smirk on his face.

Before I can answer, he shakes his head. "Never mind. Knowing Lucian and his bullshit, I'm gonna go with a 'hell yes' on that one."

DANICA

39

"Seraphina, I know this is hard to wrap your pretty little head around, but it's the real deal, honey," I slur, the alcohol making my tongue looser than usual. "I don't have all the answers, but I know that Lucian is your mate. Don't you feel... I don't know... something? Anything? A tingle? A spark? A sudden urge to rip his clothes off and have your wicked way with him?"

We're in our cozy little room next to the guys. The soft glow of the oil lamp casts warm shadows on the walls. The open window lets in a gentle sea breeze, carrying with it the scent of salt and the distant sound of waves crashing against the docks.

"It's unheard of," Seraphina spats, her voice tinged with disbelief and disgust. "It goes against everything we've been taught, everything we've been protecting ourselves against—the darkness. Their kind—their species drain us, kill us..."

Seraphina pauses for a moment, her brow furrowed in deep thought.

I plop onto the sofa cushions, bouncing under my weight. "But...?" I prod, my eyebrows waggling with drunken curiosity.

Seraphina meets my gaze, her golden eyes swirling with a kaleidoscope of emotions. "But... I do feel something. Something I can't quite put my finger on, something that both terrifies and thrills me in equal measure. It's like... like a spark—" She shakes her head, her hair cascading around her face in a curtain of gold silk. "No, this isn't right. It can't be right."

I let out a long-suffering sigh, my head spinning slightly from the alcohol. "Ok, listen up. I know what you're used to and what Atheria has drilled into your pretty little head, but times have changed. Some vampires have evolved. No offense, but you guys just sit up in the sky with your halos and harps, not really keeping up with the Joneses down here."

Seraphina huffs, her feathers ruffled by my less-than-flattering assessment of her kind. "We are not allowed to spy or watch all the time, it goes—"

"Against the rules, I know, I know," I interject, waving my hand dismissively. "But let's be real here, Sera. Look at me and Rhyland. We're mated, and it's freaking magical."

I lean forward, my eyes locked on Seraphina's, trying to make her see the truth in my words. "If I've got this right, fate is calling the shots here, not us. We don't get to pick and choose who we fall for, who our souls are bound to for all eternity."

Seraphina sits on the sofa beside the window, the breeze ruffling her hair. "Yes. And I'm happy for you. But they're tied to darkness, Dani. We've had this discussion already when I warned you about mate-bonding with Rhyland."

"Ah, yes, you did," I acknowledge, a sly grin on my face. "But you also said that Rhyland is not lost to the darkness and still has light in his soul. Did you not?"

Seraphina shifts uncomfortably, her gaze darting away from mine. "I... I may have said something to that effect, yes."

"Ha!" I crow triumphantly, pointing at her with a slightly wobbly finger. "So, if Rhyland can have light in his soul, why can't Lucian? Why can't any vampire, for that matter? Maybe it's time for Atheria to update their playbook, hmm? You can't just paint them all with the same broody, bloodsucking brush, Seraphina. That's like saying all angels are stuck-up, rule-following prudes with sticks up their asses."

Seraphina gasps, her hand flying to her chest in offense. "Dani!"

I wave her off, my inhibitions lowered by the alcohol coursing through my veins. "Oh, don't get your halo in a twist. I'm just saying maybe it's time to open your mind a little. Trust what you feel, not what you are told."

Seraphina blushes, her eyes darting away from mine. "I don't know, Dani. It's all so... confusing. I've never felt *this*—whatever this is—before."

I lean forward, my hand resting on her knee in a gesture of drunken camaraderie. "That's because you've never met your mate before, silly. Trust me, I know exactly how you feel. When I first met Rhyland, I was all kinds of confused and conflicted. But then I realized that sometimes, the heart wants what it wants. And mine? It's screaming for that broody, possessive, Viking alpha vampire like he's the last slice of pizza at 3 AM."

Seraphina giggles, her hand covering her mouth in a vain attempt to stifle the sound. "Dani, you're terrible."

"No, I'm honest," I correct her, my words slurring slightly. "And honestly? I think you and Lucian would be perfect together. He needs someone to keep him in line, and you need someone to loosen you up a bit. It's a match made in... well, maybe not heaven, but definitely in some cosmic, fate-driven universe."

Seraphina falls silent, her gaze drifting out the window to the endless expanse of the sea.

"Seraphina, I need you to listen to me," my voice low and intense. "Love is love, no matter what form it takes or who it's between. And if fate has decided that your soulmate is a vampire, then who the hell is Atheria to say otherwise?"

I sit back, my arms crossed over my chest, my expression defiant and un-apologetic. "So maybe it's time for Atheria to get with the program, to stop judging an entire species based on some outdated, narrow-minded bullshit. Because I gotta tell you, Sera, if they can't see the beauty and the magic in a love like mine and Rhyland's? Then maybe they're the ones who need to do some soul-searching, not us."

My head lolls against the back of the sofa; I can't help but smile at the thought of Seraphina and Lucian together. They may be an unlikely pair, but something tells me they're exactly what each other needs.

"I always assumed that my mate—my Soul-Tie, would be someone from Atheria. Never in a million years would I have imagined this," Seraphina says, her voice tinged with wonder and disbelief.

I quickly sit up straight, my alcohol-addled brain latching onto the mention of the *Soul-Tie*. "Seraphina, that reminds me, how exactly does this whole Soul-Tie thing work for you guys up there?"

Seraphina ponders my question for a moment, furrowing her brow in thought. "Honestly, I haven't a clue. With your father and mother, they were supposed to find someone to help with their Soul-Tie, but you know what happened with that," a hint of sadness creeps into her voice. "Since I can remember, our kind haven't needed to tie ourselves to one another, as we've stayed safe and secluded in Atheria, far away from everything."

I chew on my bottom lip, my mind whirring with possibilities. If a vampire's mate bond is, in fact, a Soul-Tie, then that would explain why Calypso only mentioned Erik and Lucian's souls being untethered while Rhyland's was con-spicuously absent from her little roll call of unbound vamps.

According to Erik and Rhyland, vampires haven't had a true mate since dinosaurs roamed the Earth, with Rhyland and I being the freaky outliers. Oh, and now Lucian and Seraphina are joining our exclusive club. If that's the case, Rhyland and I are already Soul-Tied. It's like the universe is screaming at us, "Hey, dumbasses, you're Soul-Tied! Congrats, now go forth and make sweet, sweet love!"

I turn to Seraphina, my expression serious. "Sera, I hate to be the bearer of bad news, but I truly believe that a mate bond with vampires is, in fact, a Soul-Tie. And if that's the case, then you need to understand that if you don't accept Lucian's bond or tie yourself to him in the way that fate seems to be pushing you towards, bad things can happen to him. Like, really bad things. And as much as he drives me crazy sometimes, I kind of love the big idiot, and I don't want to see him suffer."

Seraphina's eyes widen, her face paling at the implications of my words. "Wh at... what kind of bad things?" her voice barely above a whisper.

I sigh, running a hand through my hair. "I'm not entirely sure, to be honest. But from what Rhyland has told me, a vampire who is rejected by their mate, who is denied the bond that their very soul craves... it can drive them mad. It can twist, warp, and turn them into a shell of their former selves. And I don't want that for Lucian. I don't want that for you, either."

This gets me thinking—What if all these vampires who have gone off the deep end, diving headfirst into the bloodlust and evil pool, did so because they lost their mate? Or worse, get rejected by them? Or, even more tragically, couldn't hold out long enough to find their one true love?

What if that's the case with Azrael? That dude's got more issues than a newsstand. And all these vamps who have fallen off the wagon and embraced their inner darkness are just a bunch of lovelorn, mate-deprived saps.

Seraphina is silent for a long moment, her gaze distant and thoughtful. "I... I had no idea," she murmurs, her voice thick with emotion. "Are you absolutely certain that the mate bond and the Soul-Tie are the same?"

I reach out and take her hand, my grip firm and reassuring, my eyes locking onto hers with an intensity that cuts through the haze of alcohol. "I'm a thousand percent sure, Seraphina. And with both you and Lucian untethered, you're vulnerable, exposed. You're like two bright, shining beacons in the darkness, just waiting for something to come along and snuff you out." I pause, letting the weight of my words sink in, watching as understanding dawns on Seraphina's face. "Calypso is packing the last piece of the Soul Stone..."

Seraphina takes a deep, shuddering breath, her eyes shimmering with unshed tears. "I... I don't know," she admits, her voice small and uncertain. "I need... I need time to think and to process all of this. It's just... it's so much, Dani. It's so overwhelming."

I nod, my heart aching for my conflicted guardian angel. "I get it, Sera. Believe me, I do. When Rhyland first told me about the mate bond, about the intensity of the connection between us, I was scared shitless. I didn't know if I was ready for that commitment—that all-consuming love."

I squeeze her hand, my voice gentle but firm. "But you know what? I took a chance. I took a leap of faith. And it was the best damn decision I ever made. Because being with Rhyland and tied to him in every way possible, it's like coming home, like finding a piece of myself I never knew was missing."

Seraphina's smile is small, a flicker of hope amidst the uncertainty. "You make it sound so beautiful, Dani. So... so right."

I grin, my eyes sparkling with mischief. "Oh, it is, girl. It really is. And you know what else? The sex is mind-blowing. Like, toe-curling, earth-shattering, 'oh my god, I think I just saw the face of God' kind of good."

Seraphina blushes, her cheeks turning a delightful shade of pink. "Dani!" she admonishes, her voice scandalized but slightly intrigued.

I laugh, the sound bright and joyful in the cozy little room. "What? If you take a chance on love, you might as well go all in. And trust me, with a vampire? You'll be going all in—all night long."

The way she's blushing and squirming at my scandalous talk has me wondering if Seraphina's love life is as pure as freshly fallen snow. Not that it's any of my business, but I'm starting to think her halo might double as a chastity belt.

Seraphina shakes her head, a reluctant grin tugging at the corners of her mouth. "You're incorrigible, you know that?"

I shrug, my grin turning sly and wicked. "Hey, if you've got it, flaunt it. And from what I've seen of Lucian? He's definitely got it. And he wants nothing more than to give it to you in every way possible."

Seraphina's blush deepens, but there's a spark of something in her eyes, a hint of curiosity, longing, and desire. "I... I'll think about it," she murmurs, her voice soft but filled with a new kind of determination. "I'll think about everything you've said, Dani. And I will... talk to Lucian. I will try to understand this—"

I let out a whoop of joy, throwing my arms around her in a fierce, drunken hug. "That's my girl! Oh, Sera, you won't regret this. I promise you, whatever happens, it will be one hell of a ride." I gasp, my hands flying to cover my mouth, "Oh my god, we would be sisters-in-law."

We start giggling and hugging like a couple of lovesick fools, all giddy and goofy with the sheer absurdity of the situation.

Suddenly, Seraphina's expression turns serious. Her eyes widen, and she becomes curious, "Will he have to bite me?"

I pause for a moment, weighing my words carefully. "I'm not going to lie to you, Sera," my voice gentle but firm. "Yes, he will have to bite you. It's part of the whole 'vampire mating' thing, a way for him to mark you as his, to claim you in the most primal, intimate way possible."

Seraphina's eyes widen even further, a hint of fear flickering behind the curiosity. "And... and what does it feel like?" her voice barely above a whisper. "Does it... does it hurt?"

I can't help but smile at that, a wicked, knowing grin spreading across my face. "Oh, honey," I purr, with mischief. "Trust me when I say this—once he bites you for the first time, you'll be begging for more. It's not just about the pain, about the sharp sting of his fangs sinking into your flesh. It's about the pleasure, the rush of endorphins and adrenaline and pure ecstasy that comes with it."

Seraphina's cheeks flush a deep, rosy pink, her eyes glazing over slightly as she tries to imagine it. "Really?" she breathes, her voice trembling with a heady mix of nerves and anticipation. "It's that much of a... a—"

"Turn on?" I finish for her, my grin turning sly and knowing. "Yes. I mean, don't get me wrong, it's not just about the physical pleasure, although that's definitely a big part of it. It's about the connection, the bond that forms between you when he tastes your blood—when he takes a part of you into himself like that."

I lean forward, my expression serious, my eyes locked onto hers. "But Seraphina, I need you to understand something. This isn't just a one-time thing, a fun little kink to spice up your sex life. When a vampire bites their mate, it's a claiming, a marking. It's their way of saying, 'You're mine, now and forever.' It's a bond that can never be broken, not by time or distance or even death itself."

Seraphina swallows hard, her eyes searching mine for any hint of doubt or hesitation. But there is none to be found, only the steady, unwavering certainty from firsthand experience.

Seraphina's breath catches in her throat, her pupils dilating with a hunger that has nothing to do with food. "That... that sounds..."

"Incredible?" I supply, my grin turning wicked once more. "Oh, believe me, it is."

I sit back, my expression softening into something more tender, more understanding. "But hey, I know it's a lot to take in and wrap your head around. Lucian will understand and will wait for you as long as it takes. Because at the end of the day, Sera? He wants you, all of you, in whatever way you want to give yourself to him."

Seraphina nods slowly, her expression thoughtful as she mulls over my words. "I... I think I need some time," she admits, her voice soft but filled with a new resolve. "But... I also think I want to try."

I take her hand, giving it a gentle, reassuring squeeze. "And you will, Sera. In your own time, at your own pace. And when you do? It's going to be magical."

Seraphina smiles, "Thank you, Dani. For being such a good friend. I've always watched after you and watched you grow into the beautiful, confident woman you are today, and I couldn't be happier to have you as my friend."

My vision blurs as my tears well up, and I pull Seraphina into a fierce, heartfelt embrace. In this moment, I'm overwhelmed by the sheer depth of my gratitude and love for this incredible being who has been my guardian, my savior, and my unwavering support through every trial and tribulation.

"No, Sera, thank you," I choke out, my voice thick with tears. "I couldn't be more blessed to have you in my life, and I will spend every day trying to be worthy of the love and devotion you have shown me."

Seraphina's eyes are shining with tears of her own, and she pulls me back into another hug, squeezing me tight. "I love you too, Dani," she whispers, soft and fierce. "More than you could ever know."

And as we sit here, clinging to each other like a couple of emotional koalas, I can't help but feel like the luckiest bitch in all the realms.

LUCIAN

40

I'm hanging over the ship's railing like a limp noodle, my face practically kissing the waves as I hurl my guts out for the third goddamn time since we set sail. It's like my stomach has declared mutiny and is trying to secede from the rest of my body. Sweat is pouring down my face like I'm in a fucking sauna, and the sickening churning in my gut just won't quit.

Apparently, I missed the memo about needing sea legs for this little adventure. It was one thing when we landed here in the middle of a freaking Michael Bay movie, explosions and all, but it's a whole different ballgame when the constant rocking of the ship is making me feel like I'm on a never-ending roller coaster from hell.

"Aye, mate. You'll get your sea legs soon enough," the Captain shouts from his perch on the helm, his laughter grating on my nerves. He seems to be getting a real kick out of watching me suffer.

I try to muster up a witty retort, something along the lines of 'Yeah, well, fuck you too, you salty son of a bitch,' but another wave of nausea hits me like a tsunami, and I'm back to painting the side of the ship with a lovely shade of blood red. It's like my insides are staging a coup, and my esophagus is the unfortunate battlefield.

I'm clinging to the railing like it's my last lifeline, my knuckles turning white from the death grip. The wood feels like it's made of sandpaper and broken dreams, with splinters stabbing into my hands like tiny, vindictive toothpicks. The ocean is spitting salty mist into my face like a pissed-off llama, and it's mixing with the sweat and tears pouring down my cheeks like a tragic cocktail of bodily fluids.

I must look like a hot mess, but I couldn't give a flying fuck at this point.

It's fucking humiliating, but I can't seem to stop the revolt happening in my stomach. I'm starting to wonder if this is some cosmic punishment for all the shit

I've pulled over the years—like the universe is finally saying, 'Hey, asshole, time to pay your dues. Hope you like the taste of your blood because you'll see a lot of it.'

I'm trying to think of anything but the swirling, churning, 'fuck-my-life' feeling in my gut.

Seraphina.

My mind wanders back to that juicy conversation I overheard at the Inn between Seraphina and Dani the other day. You know, right after Rhyland snapped my neck like a damn toothpick. I came to just in time to hear Seraphina's angelic voice while I was shamelessly eavesdropping like the nosy bastard I am.

And guess what? My celestial snickerdoodle is willing to give this crazy ride a shot! Cue the happy dance. Seriously, kudos to Dani and her wondrous girl talk. She's the wingwoman I never knew I needed but am eternally grateful for, like finding a surprise chimichanga in the fridge when you're starving.

Speaking of my cosmic cupcake, I smell her before I see her. My senses are tuned into her frequency, picking up on her angelic presence like radar. She comes up to the side of the boat where I'm perched, clinging to the railing like it's my last hope of salvation. I don't want her to see me like this, all pathetic and green around the gills. It's not exactly the image of Suave, debonair Lucian, which I'm trying to project here.

"Hi, are you going to be okay?" Her sweet, angelic voice has me swooning like a Victorian lady in a corset. It's like auditory ambrosia, soothing my battered soul and settling my stomach, if only for a moment.

I gather myself, putting on my best 'I'm totally fine' face. Can't look like a pussy in front of my love, now can I? "Yeah, I'll be good. Don't worry about me, beautiful. I'm just communing with the ocean, you know...getting in touch with my inner sailor." I flash her a grin, hoping it comes across as charming and not like I'm two seconds away from hurling again. "How are you doing?"

She giggles and blushes, and holy shit, it's the cutest fucking thing I've ever seen. I want to wrap her up in my arms and never let go. Motion sickness be damned. "I'm great," she says with a smile that could light up the ocean. "This is amazing, isn't it? Just so beautiful." She looks out at the open seas, her eyes sparkling with wonder.

The bright blue waters stretch out for miles as we head towards Serraphatic Cove on a mission to find this key Calypso has demanded of Dani. It is beautiful, I'll give it that. But I can't take my eyes off her. She's the real view here, the most stunning thing in this whole goddamn realm. "Not as beautiful as you," I say with my patented panty-dropping smirk.

Smooth, Lucian. Real smooth.

Seraphina looks over her shoulder at me, a blush creeping up her neck like a delicate rose. And fuck me, that neck. I want to lick it, suck it, kiss it, worship it like the divine temple it is. She's so perfect, it's almost unreal. I can't believe she's mine. But she is, and I will have her, claim her, and make her fall head over heels for yours truly.

I'll be the Casanova to her Aphrodite, the Gomez to her Morticia. I'll make her swoon, weak in the knees, and make her forget every other man she's ever been with because that's what she deserves. The best of the best, the crème de la fucking crème.

I lean against the railing, trying to look suave even though my complexion probably rivals the Hulk on a bad day. I flash Seraphina my most charming grin. "So, cupcake, I know we got off on the wrong foot, what with me almost killing your bestie and all. But in my defense, I was having a really bad day—a bad week, actually. Woke up on the wrong side of the coffin, you know?"

Seraphina and I have been doing this awkward dance of small talk for the past few days while we're stuck on this floating flea island they call Driftwood Market. She's been keeping her distance like I'm carrying some kind of vampire cooties— which, okay, fair point. But hey, I've been on my best behavior, taking whatever crumbs of attention she'll toss my way like a starving pigeon in Central Park.

Meanwhile, Dani's been playing helicopter mom, hovering around Seraphina like she's Secret Service protecting the president. She has this "don't breathe wrong in her direction" vibe. Like, seriously? Me? Upset my angel cake? That's like accusing a unicorn of tax fraud—it just doesn't compute.

I tried negotiating visitation rights with Dani (and by negotiating, I mean whining like a teenager who got their Xbox taken away). Still, she shut that down faster than a speeding ticket. So, instead of getting quality time with my celestial cupcake, I got stuck bunking with my brothers. Talk about cruel and unusual punishment.

And don't even get me started on Rhyland, Mr. Brooding-Is-My-Middle-Name. Three days of listening to him whine about being separated from Dani like some lovesick teenager at summer camp. Welcome to the club, bro! Now you know how it feels to be cockblocked by circumstances beyond your control. Karma's a bitch, and her name is Dani Pierce.

Seraphina raises an eyebrow, a hint of a smile playing at the corners of her lips. "Is that your idea of an apology?"

"An apology? Nah, I don't do apologies. Too mainstream. I'm more of a 'grand gestures and witty one-liners' kind of guy. But for you, I might make an exception." I give her my best puppy-dog eyes, which probably look more like a deranged raccoon, but hey, it's the thought that counts.

She can't help but laugh, and *Christ,* it's the most beautiful sound I've ever heard, like a symphony of tinkling bells and pure joy. I feel my pants tighten and make a mental note to thank the universe for baggy pirate trousers.

"Has anyone ever told you that you have the most beautiful laugh in the history of the universe? Because damn, it's like someone took a bunch of wind chimes, mixed them with puppies giggling, and sprinkled some fairy dust on top. It's officially my new favorite sound in the universe, right up there with the sweet melody of my enemies crying." The words are projectile vomiting out of my mouth faster than I can catch them, but fuck it, I'm on a roll. I'd recite the entire phone book backward while doing the Macarena if it meant hearing that heavenly sound again.

Seraphina blushes, ducking her head shyly. "You're just saying that because I'm—" she stops herself from saying 'mate.' "It's like some supernatural flattery reflex."

"Trust me, beautiful, I may be many things—devastatingly handsome, incredibly witty, a god in the sack —but a liar isn't one of them. When I say your laugh is the most beautiful thing I've ever heard—I mean it. Scout's honor." I hold up my hand in a mock salute.

"What is a scout? And why do I feel you never were one of these... *scouts?*"

I can't help but chuckle at her naivety and the way she's already calling me out on my bullshit. It's like she's got a built-in Lucian lie detector. "A scout is someone who is supposed to be all about honor, integrity, and helping little old ladies cross the street. You know, all that goody-two-shoes crap."

Seraphina leans against the railing, her body angled towards me, and sweet baby Jesus, she looks like a fucking wet dream come to life. Her burgundy corset is hoisting her perfect tits up like they're an offering to the gods, and the way her waist nips in and her hips flare out is making my pants feel tighter than a nun's asshole. A tantalizing glimpse of leg peeking out from her skirt. My dick is harder than a fucking diamond right now.

"Hmm..." she hums, my balls tighten at the sound. "So, you're saying you're a man of integrity?"

I step closer, caging her in with my arms on either side of the railing. She sucks in a breath, but to my surprise and delight, she doesn't try to escape. I lean in, my lips brushing the shell of her ear. "Baby girl, when it comes to you, I'm a fucking Boy Scout. Loyal, trustworthy, and always prepared." I punctuate the last word with a subtle roll of my hips, letting her feel just how 'prepared' I am.

Seraphina's cheeks flush a delicious shade of pink, and I can practically feel the heat radiating off her. She's so innocent, it's like corrupting a fucking angel. Which, I guess, is exactly what I'm doing. "I-I talked to Dani about...you know, figuring this thing out between us. But you must understand, Lucian, this is all new to me." Her voice trembles slightly, and I can tell she's nervous as hell.

"I know, beautiful. And I'm not trying to push you into anything you're not ready for. But Jesus, take the wheel; you drive me crazy. I've never wanted anyone the way I want you." I pull back just enough to look into her eyes, letting her see the sincerity behind my words. "We can take this as slow as you need. I'll be a perfect gentleman. Well, as much of a gentleman as I can be with a permanent hard-on for you."

She giggles at that, and my dick twitches. She's gonna have to stop laughing, or I'm going to embarrass myself. "A gentleman, huh? I'll believe that when I see it."

"Oh, you'll see it, sweetheart. And feel it. And taste it." I waggle my eyebrows suggestively. "But only when you're ready. Until then, I'll just be over here, taking a lot of cold showers and thinking about baseball."

Seraphina laughs again, shaking her head. "You're ridiculous, you know that?"

"Ridiculously charming? Ridiculously handsome? Ridiculously skilled in the art of seduction?" I grin, pressing a hand to my chest. "Stop me when I'm getting warm."

She rolls her eyes, but I can see the smile she's trying to fight. "How about ridiculously full of yourself?"

"Ooh, you wound me, Cupcake." I clutch my heart dramatically. "But you know what they say. It ain't bragging if it's true."

She shakes her head again, but this time, she leans into me a little, her body soft and warm against mine. "You're lucky you're cute, Lucian. Otherwise, I might have to smite you for your impertinence."

"Smite me? *Fuck*, that's hot. You can punish me anytime, baby girl. I've been a very, *very* naughty boy." I let my voice drop to a low, seductive growl—her heartbeat speeds up.

"I-I'll keep that in mind," she stammers, her blush deepening. "But for now, how about we focus on getting to know each other? Without all the innuendo and flirting?"

I sigh dramatically, but I'm grinning like a fucking idiot. "If you insist, sweetheart. But just so you know, flirting is like breathing for me. It's not something I can just turn off."

"Well, you better learn to hold your breath, then. Because I want to know the real Lucian, not just the smooth-talking charmer." She looks up at me, her swirling-gold eyes serious but warm.

"The real Lucian, huh? Well, I hope you're ready for a wild ride, beautiful. Because behind all the wit and charm, I'm a fucking mess. But for you, I'll try to be the man you deserve." I brush a strand of hair behind her ear, letting my fingers linger on her soft skin.

"That's all I'm asking for, Lucian. Just be yourself, and let's see where this takes us." She smiles, and it's like the sun coming out from behind the clouds.

"You got it. One genuine, unfiltered Lucian is coming right up. Brace yourself because it's gonna be a bumpy fucking ride." I grin, and she laughs, the sound wrapping around me like a warm hug.

With the nausea finally subsiding and my stomach no longer trying to secede from the rest of my body, I feel like a fucking million bucks. "Wow, Cupcake, you must have some kind of mystical healing voodoo in that voice of yours. I think it's your laugh—gotta be the laugh—cause I'm cured!" I reach out and run my fingers through her silky golden locks, marveling at how they feel like strands of pure sunshine.

Seraphina flashes me a smile brighter than a supernova, and I nearly bust a nut. "It seems all you needed was a little distraction from the waves and the motion of the ocean."

Her voice is like a fucking eargasm, wrapping around me tighter than spandex on a superhero's ass.

I could *totally* run with that and milk the humor for all it's worth, but she's asked me to dial it back, so I clamp my mouth shut and just drink her in with my eyes.

Being this close to her, soaking in her angelic presence? Yeah, that's enough for me right now. Hell, it's more than I deserve.

As we stand here, the sea breeze whipping around us and the sun setting on the horizon, I can't help but thank the fucking universe for this woman—I've finally found something worth holding onto. Something genuine and fucking beautiful.

Even if it means being vulnerable and honest and all that terrifying shit. Because for Seraphina, I'd face down an army of demons with nothing but a spork and a smile.

She's worth it. And damn it all to hell, so am I.

DANICA

41

After two days of playing pirate on the high seas, we finally made it to Serraphatic Cove. We drop anchor about a mile off the coast. The view from the ship is like something straight out of a travel brochure. Mountains that could give the Rockies a run for their money, waterfalls that would make Niagara look like a leaky faucet, and water so blue that it looks like someone melted down sapphires and poured them into the ocean.

Gideon's ship is looking pretty damn spiffy. It's like it just rolled out of the pirate shipyard, all shiny and new after the crew put in some serious elbow grease. You'd never guess it was the same vessel that nearly got turned into driftwood not too long ago.

Speaking of driftwood, I ran into Izabelle on our little nautical adventure, the backstabbing sea harlot herself. When she saw me, she scurried behind Gideon like a cockroach. It would've been funny if I wasn't so pissed off.

Rhyland gave me the lowdown on her little betrayal, how she threw me to the sharks (literally) and left me to deal with Bloodbane's crazy ass all on my own. And while I may not be able to give her the ass-kicking she so richly deserves right now, you better believe her time is coming.

Karma's a bitch, and so am I.

My eye snags on a distant island off in the distance, cornering Serraphatic Cove, and before I know it, I'm playing twenty questions with Gideon.

"Aye, that be Selkie Shores," Gideon informs me, sounding like he's about to launch into a pirate's version of a nature documentary. "The Selkies keep to themselves, and you rarely see 'em at all."

Selkies? Sounds like a brand of designer dog food. "Selkies?" I repeat, hoping for more info. I vaguely remember reading about them in the Book of Aquaria, but apparently, my brain decided to file that information under "Useless Trivia" instead of "Important Magical Creatures."

"Half man, half seal, from what we've gathered," Gideon explains, describing some bizarre genetic experiment gone wrong. "They like to stir up trouble, and we call 'em the dogs of the sea."

Now, I'm even more confused. "Why?" I ask, wondering both about the dog comparison and their reclusive nature.

"They're playful, like dogs," Gideon says with a shrug as if that explains everything. "And the Queen has forced 'em to stay on their island, or else they'll be hunted for sport and killed on sight."

Well, that escalated quickly. I mean, talk about an overreaction. What did these seal people do, pee in Cordelia's royal swimming pool?

I squint at the distant island, trying to catch a glimpse of these mythical creatures. But unless they're waving giant "Hello, we're Selkies!" signs, I'm not seeing squat.

This whole situation is fishier than a tuna cannery. Why are they exiled? What could these adorable seal people possibly do that's so terrible? In our world, seals are water puppies. Here, they're treated like the plague with flippers.

Since I was the designated blood donor for this trip—Seraphina wasn't quite ready to share her angelic juice yet, which is understandable. Lucian, who typically jumps at the chance for his dose, whined like a toddler and insisted he should only drink from his mate now. Rhyland, ever the supportive brother, agreed, but I had to step in and tell him to quit bitching. We are on a tight schedule and need to get a move on. After some grumbling and eye-rolling, Lucian finally caved and took his dose.

Of course, because nothing can ever be easy, I had to do it the old-fashioned way, with a knife, some glasses, and Rhyland playing nurse. It was like a fucked-up version of a tea party, only with more blood and less crumpets.

Erik, my favorite silver fox, managed to snag my daggers from the tavern on that fateful night of my impromptu pirate adventure. He's been keeping them safe like some weapon-hoarding dragon.

He hands them over with a hint of a smile. "I am of the opinion that these are rightfully yours, Little Huntress."

I can't help but throw my arms around him in a bear hug. Erik might act all stoic and broody, but deep down, he's just a big softie. Moments like these remind me why he's the badass big brother I never knew I needed. Who else would think to rescue my weapons while I'm off getting kidnapped by pirates? That's some next-level thoughtfulness right there.

Erik, Seraphina, and Lucian have decided to stay on the ship and wait for us to return—no need to bring everyone on this treasure hunt.

Rhyland and I pile into the dinghy, the small boat creaking ominously under our combined weight.

As we row towards shore, the island seems to come alive. Birds I'd never seen before swoop overhead, their calls a strange mix of melodic and haunting. The air grows thick with the scent of exotic flowers and salt spray, making my head spin.

When my feet touch the sand, a jolt goes through me, like I've stepped on a live wire. The beach is unlike anything I've ever seen—sand so white it is almost blinding, dotted with seashells in colors I didn't even know existed in nature. Palm trees sway in a breeze I can't feel, their leaves whispering secrets in a language I can't understand but somehow feel I should know.

I turn to share my awe, only to find Rhyland frozen in place, his expression a mix of wonder and wariness. My unflappable Viking vampire looks like he's seen a ghost—or maybe something even more unsettling.

That's when I hear it—a beautiful song that makes my heart ache, carried on a wind that shouldn't exist. As one, we turn towards the source of the sound, and I feel my breath catch in my throat.

The most breathtaking creature I've ever seen is perched on a rock in the pool at the bottom of the mountains. A mermaid, with skin that shimmers like mother-of-pearl and hair so red and vibrant, bounces like living seaweed. When her eyes meet mine, they are the same impossible blue as the water around us.

I can tell she's a mermaid just by looking at her. For one—she doesn't have those telltale shark fins running down her back like some aquatic mohawk. And her voice, while easy on the ears, doesn't have that creepy, mind-controlling vibe that sirens are known for. You know, the kind that makes you want to jump off a cliff or allow some sexy siren with abs for days to clamp a tracker around your neck?

She dives into the water, vanishing beneath the surface, and we start walking towards the massive oceanic pool that dominates the island's center. Suddenly, she's there again, popping up like a curious little mermaid, her expression a mix of intrigue and wariness.

"Hello," I say, plastering on my most charming, *I'm not here to cause trouble'* grin. "I'm Dani." I introduce myself, channeling my inner Disney princess and trying not to break into song. "You must be Ariel?" I can't help but snicker as Rhyland chuckles beside me, clearly on the same wavelength.

Seriously, this chick is like a walking, swimming advertisement for the Little Mermaid. She's got the whole package—fiery red hair, porcelain skin that's probably never seen a blemish, and even a damn bra made of pearls.

Her tail? It's like someone took a handful of glitter and a bucket of turquoise paint and just went to town. The scales shimmer in the water like a disco ball, catching the light and throwing it back in a dazzling display of aquatic fabulousness.

Her torso and arms are covered in sporadic patches of glittery scales—like she rolled around in a vat of glue and then took a swan dive into a pool of sequins.

"No, I am Mirella," she states flatly, her tone about as warm as a polar bear's ass. "Why are you here?" She looks pissed like we just crashed her private beach party and ate all the shrimp cocktails.

I play nice, putting on my most charming, disarming smile. "I'm sorry to bother you, but I'm here to find something—a key. Maybe you might know where I can start?"

Now that I think about it, Calypso gave me fuck-all regarding directions. Gideon mentioned something about an underwater cave, but that's about as helpful as a fart in a windstorm.

Mirella bobs in the water, flicking her tail in what I can only assume is mermaid for 'I'm getting real tired of your shit.' But then, her expression softens a bit, like maybe she's decided we're not complete assholes after all. "No one is allowed on this Island? Did the Queen send you?"

Shit.

I know she's talking about Cordelia, but what should I say? *'No, actually, the sea witch sent me, and I'm under a Coral Pact, so lead the way, fish girl?'*

Yeah, I don't think that's going to fly. But she didn't specify *which* queen, and Calypso seems to have crowned herself the new Queen Bitch of the Seven Seas, so I figure a little white lie can't hurt. "Yup, she sure did," I say, crossing my fingers behind my back like a kid trying to get out of trouble.

I know the merfolk are under Cordeila's rule just as the Sirens are under Calypso's rule—the war of the fishes.

Rhyland shoots a wave of unease down our bond, clearly not thrilled with my lying to this poor, unsuspecting mermaid. I quickly send him an 'I got this' vibe, hoping he'll trust me to handle this without blowing our cover.

I wait for Mirella to respond, my heart flip-flopping in my chest. Come on, little mermaid, take the bait. Mama's got a key to find and a realm to save, chop-chop!

"What is that on your head? A tiara? It's beautiful. I want to hold it," Mirella states, reaching out with a gleam in her eye that sets off all kinds of alarm bells in my head.

I quickly back up, holding my hands up in a 'whoa there' gesture. "Uh, sorry. It doesn't come off." I mentally kick myself for not thinking to hide the damn thing before we set foot on this island.

Way to go, Dani. Might as well have painted a big old target on my forehead.

Mirella's expression shifts from mildly annoyed to intensely curious.' "It's stunning, and I would like to hold it. That is the price to pay for my help," she states, her tone leaving no room for argument.

Damnit. How the hell am I supposed to get out of this one? "Look, as much as I would love to let you hold it, it doesn't come off." I demonstrate by giving the headpiece a good yank, showing her it's not budging.

But Mirella is not to be deterred. "Then I would like to touch it and get a closer look," she insists, her eyes never leaving the glittering tiara.

I sigh, weighing my options. What's the harm in letting her get a closer look? Maybe if I indulge her curiosity, she'll be more inclined to help us. So, against my better judgment, I lean closer to the water, giving her a clear shot at the tiara.

Mirella reaches out, her fingers grazing the jewels, and then the little thief tries to yank it off my head! "Ouch!" I screech, swatting her hands away. But of course, the tiara doesn't budge, and I lean back, giving her a look that could curdle milk. "Were you really going to try and steal it?"

Mirella looks completely unrepentant. "I like trinkets and beautiful things," she says with a shrug as if that explains everything.

I pinch the bridge of my nose, feeling a headache coming on. "Look, I get it. It's pretty and eye-catching, but this," I point to the tiara, "is my thingy-ma-bob and belongs to me as the Savior of the Seven Realms. It can't be taken. You can look at it all you like and touch it, but that's how it goes. Now, will you help us or not?"

Mirella pouts, her tail flicking in the water like an irritated cat. For a moment, I think she's going to tell us to fuck off and find our own damn way. But then, she seems to have a light bulb moment, her expression smoothing into something more surprised. "The *savior,* you said?"

I clear my throat, "Yeah, it's just a figure of speech." Not wanting to get into the whole 'I'm the Savior Spiel.'

Then, like some underwater flash mob, more merfolk pop out of the water, all gawking at us like we're the latest aquatic attraction. I gape at them as they keep their distance, probably afraid I'll contaminate their precious ocean with my human cooties.

"Mirella, what is the meaning of this?" A merman with long blue hair asks, looking like he's got a fish bone stuck sideways.

"Nothing for you to worry about, Kaelan." Mirella snaps, rolling her eyes.

"You know the rules, Mirella. This place is forbidden to outsiders. The Queen—"

"The Queen sent them, Kaelan." Mirella counters, her voice dripping with 'duh.'

Kaelan scrunches his face like he's trying to solve a complicated math problem. "No, Mirella. She would not send anyone here. *Ever.*"

Well, shit. Now we're screwed. This Kaelan is about to blow my cover.

"So, how'd you get your hands on that sparkly little number?" Mirella asks, her eyes glued to my tiara like it's the most fascinating thing since the invention of the clamshell bra.

I stand there, gaping at her and the other merfolk. "Oh, you know, it was sort of gifted to me," I shrug, trying to play it cool. "Like a mystical hand-me-down from the universe."

That's the best I can pull out of my ass without resorting to blatant lies or diving headfirst into the whole spiel. I mean, how do you break it to a mermaid whose biggest concerns are probably swimming and seaweed macramé that you're the Savior destined to rescue the world from certain doom? It's not exactly small talk material.

She glances over her shoulder at the other merfolk, bobbing in the water like a bunch of curious buoys.

"Very well," she says, her voice smooth. "Only because the *Queen* commands it—follow me," she says with a wink.

"Mirella, this is suicide! You cannot go against the Queen." Kaelan snaps, his voice tighter than a clam with lockjaw.

"Mirella, you are making a mistake." A female mermaid with long purple hair chimes in, probably the underwater equivalent of a Karen.

"What's your problem? They said they were sent by the Queen herself. Do you all really want to take the chance of exiling them when it was her command in the first place?" Mirella counters, sounding about as convincing as a shark trying to sell life insurance to a school of fish. "You want to test that theory and possibly lose your fins?"

Oh, shit on a seashell. Cordelia sounds just delightful—in a morbid, 'might-just-ruin-your-day' kind of way. Looks like the underwater kingdom's got its very own Aquatic Attila. And here I thought mermaids were all about singing with crabs and collecting dinglehoppers.

"It's your funeral." Kalean snaps, then dives under.

Purple-haired Karen shakes her head and follows Kaelan.

With that, Mirella dives back beneath the surface, leaving us to scramble after her like a bunch of landlubbers trying to keep up with a seasoned sailor. I exchange a look with Rhyland, a silent 'here goes nothing' passing between us.

Damnit, I just got my leathers cleaned, too.

Suddenly, my bracelet starts vibrating and glowing like it's auditioning for a rave. I raise an eyebrow at it, wondering what in the magical hell it's doing now.

Rhyland sees it and asks, "What's it doing?"

I shake my head, "Haven't got a clue. Maybe it's trying to communicate with its home planet." I motion toward the water, "Shall we follow the yellow brick road?"

As we wade into the water, I can't help but feel like we're walking into the lion's den—or, in this case, the mermaid's lagoon. But hey, at least the water's nice and warm. And who knows, maybe Mirella will be the helpful, friendly type who wants to braid our hair and swap sea shanties.

...Yeah, and maybe pigs will fly out of my ass and start singing show tunes.

I take a deep breath, fill my lungs with as much air as they can hold, and dive down after Mirella. The moment I open my eyes beneath the surface, I'm blown away by the crystal-clear water. It's like someone turned up the resolution on reality, every detail sharp and vivid in a way that almost hurts to look at.

The saltwater stings my eyes for a second, but the sensation quickly fades, leaving me free to take in the underwater wonderland around me—and holy shit, what a wonderland it is.

I spot Mirella's shimmering tail ahead, cutting through the water like a turquoise blade. She's swimming towards what looks like an underwater cave, a hidden oasis of coral and rock formations that takes my breath away (or it would, if I had any breath to spare).

As I swim closer, I can see the intricate patterns and colors of the coral, a kaleidoscope of pinks, purples, and oranges that seem to glow with an inner light. Schools of tropical fish dart in and out of the nooks and crannies, their scales flashing like jewels in the filtered sunlight.

It's like something out of a dream—a beautiful hidden world beneath the waves. I feel a sense of peace wash over me, a tranquility that seems to seep into my bones and quiet the constant chatter of my mind.

As we swim deeper into the cave, I feel the burn in my lungs, a growing ache that tells me I'm running out of air. Mirella seems oblivious, her tail flicking ahead of us as she leads the way, but Rhyland is at my side, his strong arms pulling me up toward the surface.

We burst through the water, gulping down lungfuls of sweet, sweet oxygen. "She must forget we need air to breathe," I gasp, clinging to Rhyland as I catch my breath.

He holds me close, his chest heaving with exertion. "It's easy to forget when you're used to living beneath the waves," he says, his voice a low rumble that I feel as much as I hear.

Mirella's head pops up a few feet away, her expression contrite. "I'm so sorry. I keep forgetting—here. Stay close. It's not far." She dives back under, swimming towards us with a few assertive flicks of her tail.

I take another deep breath, filling my lungs, and grab Mirella's hand. She gives me a reassuring squeeze, and then we're off, cutting through the water like a pair of torpedoes.

Rhyland swims at my side, his hand clasped firmly in mine.

We swim deeper into the coral caverns and enter a new world, an underwater oasis of twisting tunnels and hidden chambers. The colors are even more vibrant here, and the coral formations take on strange and wondrous shapes that defy the laws of physics.

I'm so caught up in the beauty of it all that I almost don't notice when Mirella starts pushing me towards the surface. But then my head breaks through the water, and I gulp air like it's the elixir of life, my lungs expanding with relief.

We've emerged into a hidden cave, the rocky walls dripping with moisture but sparkling like glitter and the air heavy with the scent of salt and sea life. It's like something out of a pirate movie, a secret hideaway where treasure and danger lurk equally.

As I look around, taking in the eerie beauty of the place, I can't help but feel a sense of excitement thrumming through my veins. I can feel we're getting closer to the key, to the answers we seek.

Rhyland bursts through the surface, sending ripples cascading across the tranquil water. In an instant, he is at my side, his eyes scanning me for any signs of distress. He grips the rocky ledge, his muscles flexing as he hoists himself up and out of the water with an effortless grace that never fails to take my breath away.

Then, he reaches for me, his large hands wrapping around my waist and lifting me as if I weigh no more than a feather. I cling to him, my body molding against his as he sets me gently on the cave floor.

The heat in the cave is oppressive, the air thick and muggy, but with our clothes soaked through and our skin slick with moisture, it's almost a relief.

Mirella bobs in the water below us, her tail flicking back and forth as she stares at me with those eerie, luminous eyes. "Through there," she says, pointing to a nook in the corner of the cave, "are the Pools of Reflection; you must look into them to gain access to the next area. This is as far as I go. No one has ever escaped this trial—I wish you luck! But I have a feeling you won't need it." She winks.

And then, without another word, she dives back beneath the surface, her shimmering tail disappearing into the depths with a flick and a splash. I'm left staring after her, my mouth hanging open, trying to process her words.

I swivel to face Rhyland, my eyebrows trying to climb off my forehead. "Well, that was reassuring," I quip, trying to lighten the mood. "Looks like it's just you, me, Rhy-Pie, and whatever fun-house mirrors from hell await us. Shall we?"

LUCIAN

42

"So, Cupcake, whaddya wanna know?"

We're chilling on the quarterdeck, snuggled up on a blanket with some pillows propped against a couple of barrels. It's like our little love nest, minus the rose petals and scented candles. Though, I could probably rustle some up if I really tried. Never underestimate the power of a determined vampire with a romantic streak.

Seraphina is tucked up next to me, fitting perfectly against my side like a sexy angelic puzzle piece. The vast expanse of the ocean stretches out before us, the waves lapping gently against the ship as we wait for Dani and Rhyland to return from their little adventure. Honestly, I couldn't give two shits what they're up to.

Don't get me wrong; I'm all for the "saving the world" thing. It's noble and heroic and blah blah blah. But when you've got a literal angel in your arms, the rest of the world can take a backseat. Priorities, people. And right now, my priority is making sure Seraphina is safe, sound, and thoroughly seduced by my irresistible charm and wit.

Not that I'm trying to get in her pants or anything.

Okay, that's a lie.

I'm definitely trying to get in her pants. But can you blame me? Have you seen this woman? She's like a walking, talking fantasy come to life. And the fact that she's my mate, my other half, my missing puzzle piece? Well, that just makes it all the sweeter.

So, yeah. Dani and Rhyland can take their time doing whatever they're doing. Slaying monsters, finding ancient artifacts, braiding each other's hair... I don't care. The rest of the world can wait as long as I've got Seraphina.

Suck it, Shakespeare. This is what true romance looks like.

Seraphina takes a swig from her mug of rum, courtesy of our gracious captain. She downs it like a seasoned pro.

Impressive.

"Hmm..." she muses, pondering her next question. "How about you tell me how you became a vampire? What was your life like before?"

Oh, great. The million-dollar question. Not exactly my favorite topic, but if it keeps my celestial chimichanga engaged, I'll bite. Figuratively speaking, of course.

"Buckle up, buttercup, 'cause this story's a doozy," I warn her, taking a deep breath. "Picture it: England, 1822. I was a strapping young lad of twenty-two, living the simple life in a quaint little village. I had a family, a job, and a future so bright, I needed shades."

Seraphina leans in, her honey-gold eyes fixed on me, and I can't help but feel a twinge of something in my chest. It's probably just indigestion from all the rum.

"Enter Lilith, the fire-red-haired temptress who sashayed into town. She was a vision, all pale skin and emerald-green eyes. Every man in the village was tripping over themselves to get a piece of that, myself included. Little did we know, she was more interested in our jugulars than our hearts."

I pause, the memories rushing back like a tidal wave of shit I've tried to bury for centuries. "Long story short, Lilith took a liking to yours truly. And I got a one-way ticket to Bloodsuckersville, population: me."

Seraphina's eyes widen, her hand coming to rest on my arm. The touch is electric, sending shockwaves through my undead body.

"Turns out, Lilith is a very old vampire and had a thing for turning pretty young things into her eternal playthings. I was just another notch in her bed-post, another pawn in her sick little game. She made me do things, Cupcake. Things that still haunt me, even after all these years."

I clench my jaw, the anger and betrayal as fresh as the day it happened. "I was her puppet, her little blood-sucking protégé. She reveled in the kill, in the power she held over me. And I hated every fucking second of it."

Serphina's gaze is still locked on mine. "How did you escape her?"

"It took decades, but I finally grew a pair and broke free—made her release me. I struck out on my own, vowing never to be anyone's bitch again. Until I met my brothers, we all share the same maker. I use my wit and charm to mask the pain. It's a lot easier to crack jokes than to face the darkness, you know?"

Seraphina nods, her thumb tracing soothing circles on my skin. "I know we're still getting to know each other, but I want you to know that you don't have to hide with me. I'm here for you, Lucian, no matter what."

I swallow hard, my throat suddenly tight. "Careful, Cupcake. Keep talking like that, and I might fall for you harder than I already have."

She smiles, and it's like the sun breaking through the clouds. "I think I can handle that." I want to kiss her badly. "May I ask how you made her release you? What does that mean?"

I let out a breath and take a swig of rum, letting the burn distract me from the memories. "In Vampire 101, when a Maker turns you, they basically slap a 'Property of' sticker on your forehead. It's like being stuck in a never-ending game of 'Simon Says' where Simon's a sadistic asshat."

I clear my throat, trying to dislodge the lump of centuries-old pain. "Eventually, I got fed up with being her blood-sucking puppet and pulled the ultimate 'uno reverse' card. Told her to cut me loose, or I'd punch my own ticket to the great beyond. Of course, she folded faster than a cheap lawn chair at the thought."

Seraphina gasps, her eyes wide with horror. "Oh, no, Lucian. You wouldn't have... you know...?"

"Kill myself?" I finish for her, watching her gulp and nod. "Back then? I was ready to swan dive into the great unknown. It was a horror show, sweetheart, and I wanted out of that toxic circus more than I wanted my next meal."

Her eyes, those gorgeous pools of honey, fill with worry and something that looks suspiciously like... care? For me? It's enough to make my heart do a little jig.

"So, she released you? What does that mean for you, now?"

I let out a laugh about as laughable as a funeral dirge. "She cut the puppet strings. Now I'm a real boy, Pinocchio style, minus the growing nose and the whole 'wanting to be human' schtick."

I take another swig of rum, letting it burn away the bitter aftertaste of memories. "It means I'm free to be the charming pain in the ass you see before you without any vampire mind-control shenanigans. No more 'Simon Says' from the bloodsucking bitch who turned me."

I shrug, trying to play it cool, but there's a hint of relief in my voice that I can't quite hide. "As for Erik and Rhyland, well, misery loves company, right? We're like the world's most dysfunctional boy band, brought together by the same psycho manager. I'd bet my left fang their stories are about as pretty as a dumpster fire in a glitter factory."

I catch that giggle, but I'm not fooled. Her swirling gold eyes are like a mood ring; right now, they're screaming, "sad puppy." If she only knew the half of it... Hell, if she knew even a quarter of the shit I was forced to do, she'd probably sprout her wings and fly far, far away from this mess of a vampire.

But I'll be damned if I'm gonna taint my celestial snack cake with that level of fucked-up right now. No way am I unleashing that Pandora's box of horrors on her angelic ears. She doesn't need that kind of nightmare fuel.

So instead, I plaster on my best 'everything's peachy' grin. It's about as convincing as a dollar store toupee, but hey, I'm trying here.

"Oh, man. Talking about Lilith dredges up all kinds of fucked-up memories. Azrael and Paige...? Those sadistic bastards tried to pull the same shit on me. They wanted to mold me into their perfect little killing machine, just like Lilith."

It's like déjà vu all over again. I knew it was all kinds of wrong—hated every second of it, especially when they made me kill that poor girl.

I may not have had my memories, but I sure as hell had my conscience, and that shit didn't sit right with me.

Seraphina stiffens beside me, her grip on my arm tightening, "Azrael tried to...?

I nod, my jaw clenching at the thought. "Yeah. Fucker thought he could mold me into his own personal murder machine—joke's on him, though. Turns out, even with a case of supernatural amnesia, I'm still the same stubborn, rebellious bastard I've always been. But you know what? Fuck 'em. Fuck Lilith, fuck Azrael, and fuck anyone who tries to control me. I'm done being someone's plaything. I may be a vampire, but I'm nobody's bitch. Not anymore. I've spent centuries learning to be my own man, even if that man is a sarcastic, emotionally stunted work in progress. But hey, at least I'm a work in progress with a great ass and a killer sense of humor."

I figured this is how I scored my vampire mind control powers. It actually makes a weird kind of sense—my brain's like Fort Knox when it comes to letting others take the driver's seat. So, naturally, my superpower came from that ironclad will of mine.

But here's the thing—I'm not some power-hungry douchebag who abuses this gift like a kid with a magnifying glass and an anthill. Nah, I'm more of a "use my powers for good" kind of guy. Well, mostly good. And if it happens to benefit me in the process, hey, that's just a bonus! I'm like a mind-controlling Robin Hood, except instead of stealing from the rich and giving to the poor, I'm ensuring everyone's on Team Lucian. It's a win-win situation, really.

Seraphina's eyes shimmer in the fading light as she gazes deeply into mine, her expression a mix of empathy and admiration. "Lucian..." she whispers my name, her voice as soft as the breeze. "You've been through so much, endured so much pain. But look at you now. You came out on top and refused to bend. That speaks volumes about your strength, your character."

I feel a lump form in my throat, my chest tightening with emotions I've kept buried for so long. How she looks at me like I'm something precious and worthy is almost too much to bear.

Swallowing hard, I reach out and tuck a stray strand of her golden hair behind her ear, my fingers lingering on the soft skin of her cheek. "That's my tragic backstory, Cupcake. Told you it was a doozy."

I try to keep my tone light, but my voice is rough, betraying the depth of my feelings.

"But you know what they say," I continue, smiling. "What doesn't kill you makes you stronger. Or, in my case, what doesn't kill you makes you a wise-cracking, undead pain in the ass with a heart of gold buried somewhere beneath all the snark and innuendo."

Seraphina laughs softly, the sound mingling with the gentle crash of waves against the ship's hull. "And what a beautiful heart it is," she murmurs, her hand coming up to rest over my now beating heart—because of her—*my mate.* "Buried or not, I see it. I see you, Lucian. And I think you're pretty damn amazing."

I cover her hand, marveling at how her smaller fingers fit perfectly against mine. "Careful there, angel face. Keep saying things like that, and I might start believing them."

She smiles, her eyes sparkling with mischief and affection. "Well, then. I guess I'll have to keep saying them until you do."

We sit here, lost in each other's gaze, as the ship rocks gently beneath us. The salty tang of the sea air mixes with her skin's sweet, intoxicating scent, creating a heady perfume that makes my head spin and my heart ache with longing.

"You know," I murmur, "if this were a movie, this would be the part where the dashing hero sweeps the beautiful maiden off her feet and kisses her senseless beneath the setting sun."

Seraphina's lips curve into a playful smirk. "Oh? And are you the dashing hero in this scenario?"

I grin, leaning in closer until our noses are almost touching. "Sweetheart, I'm the dashiest hero there ever was. And you, my Goddess of Giggles, are the most beautiful maiden ever to grace the Seven Realms."

She laughs, her breath mingling with mine. "Laying it on a bit thick there, aren't you?"

"*Thick* is my specialty," I quip. "But in all seriousness, Phina, baby... I may not be a hero but for you? I'd slay dragons, battle armies, and even sit through a Nicholas Sparks movie marathon."

Seraphina's laughter rings out, a melodic sound that seems to dance on the ocean breeze. It's a laugh that could make demons fall to their knees. And holy fuck; it's doing things to my body that would make a succubus blush.

I rein myself in, reminding my overexcited anatomy that all good things come to those who wait. And oh, the things I have in store for my halo honey. The things I want to do to her, with her... they'd make the devil himself clutch his pearls and fan his face.

I watch her laugh, the sound wrapping around me like a warm embrace. Her mouth is open, her head thrown back in abandon, and the world has slowed to a crawl. Every detail is magnified, from how her hair catches the fading sunlight to the delicate curve of her neck. She's a vision, a goddamn masterpiece, and I'm just a lowly admirer basking in her radiance.

"But enough about my sordid past," my voice low and intimate. "Let's focus on the present, shall we? Specifically, the present company. Because I gotta say, beautiful, you're a sight for these jaded, world-weary eyes."

I let my gaze travel over her, taking in every curve and dip of her body. From the swell of her breasts to the flare of her hips, she's a work of art—a masterpiece crafted by the gods themselves.

"And I'm not just saying that because I'm trying to get in your pants," I continue, my lips curving into a wicked grin. "Though let's be real, that's definitely a factor."

Seraphina's eyes widen, her cheeks flushing a delightful shade of pink. "Lucian!" she admonishes, swatting at my chest. "You can't just say things like that!"

"Why not?" Catching her hand and bringing it to my lips. I press a kiss to her knuckles, my eyes never leaving hers. "It's the truth. I want you, Seraphina. In every way possible. And I'm not ashamed to admit it."

She swallows hard, her pupils dilating as she stares up at me. "I... I... we need to take things slow. I'm not... I've never..."

"I know, sweetheart," I murmur, cupping her cheek with my free hand. "And I would never push you into something you're not ready for. But that doesn't mean I can't tell you how I feel. How much I desire you."

I lean in, my lips brushing the shell of her ear. "How much I *ache* for you," I whisper in a low, seductive rumble. "How much I want to worship every inch of your body until you're crying out my name in ecstasy."

Seraphina shivers, a soft gasp escaping her lips. "Lucian..."

"Shh," I soothe, kissing gently to her temple. "We've got nothing but time, Cupcake. I'm not going anywhere. And when you're ready to ride on the Lucian Express, I'll be here. Waiting. Wanting. Panting after you like a dog in heat. Forever yours and all that sappy shit."

She giggles, her eyes glistening with emotion like she's about to cry tears of joy at my romantic prowess. "Okay... thank you," she breathes, her voice all breathy and sexy, like she's already imagining me rocking her world.

But then, my brain short-circuits like a faulty toaster, and I backtrack faster than a politician caught in a lie. "Wait, hold up. Rewind. You've never *what* now?" I ask, my eyebrows shooting up so high they practically wave hello to my hairline.

I mean, I know she's innocent. Hell, she's a literal angel, all pure. But surely, she doesn't mean...

"I-I've never, you know..." she stammers, looking away shyly like a schoolgirl confessing her crush.

Holy mother of *FUCK*. No way. No fucking way.

A virgin?

My mate, my other half, my goddamn soulmate, has never experienced the mind-blowing, toe-curling, life-altering magic of sex? Of orgasms? Of being worshipped by a man who knows his way around a woman's body like a kid in a candy store?

I think my dick just wept a single tear of joy.

This is too good to be true. It's like winning the lottery, but instead of money, I've hit the jackpot of sexual inexperience. I feel like I should be doing a fucking victory dance, spiking an imaginary football and screaming "Touchdown!" at the top of my lungs.

But I rein myself in, trying to play it cool—wouldn't want to scare off my blushing virgin bride with my overwhelming enthusiasm for popping her cherry.

"Cupcake, are you telling me..." I begin, my voice low and seductive, "that no man has ever had the pleasure of exploring your heavenly body? Of tasting your sweet nectar? Never experienced the earth-shattering, mind-blowing, oh-sweet-baby-Jesus orgasms that leave you a trembling, boneless heap?"

Seraphina flushes a delightful shade of pink, like a strawberry dipped in whipped cream.

Mmm, now there's an idea for later.

"N-no," she whispers, biting her lip in a way that makes me want to do it for her with my teeth. "I've never been with anyone. I've never... done anything."

Fuck me sideways and call me a virgin whisperer.

I mean, seriously, what are the odds? It's like I've stumbled into a unicorn sanctuary while wearing horseshoe underwear and carrying a four-leaf clover.

Forget about striking oil or finding a vein of pure diamonds. I've just discovered the Holy Grail of inexperience, the Ark of the Covenant of innocence, the freakin' Excalibur of untouched territory!

I'm watching her like a hawk, taking in every little detail. The way her breathing quickens, the flush spreads across her skin like wildfire. And that scent, that intoxicating aroma of arousal? It's hitting me like a freight train, making me want to drool like a starving man at a feast.

She's knocked back a few mugs of rum, and I can see the inhibitions melting away, the walls crumbling down. Her caramel eyes are swirling with desire, the golden flecks in her eyes shimmering like precious treasures. And fuck, I could drown in those depths and die a happy man.

"Lucian..." she breathes, her voice barely above a whisper. "I've never....been kissed."

Those words, that confession? It's like a punch to the gut and a shot of adrenaline simultaneously. We're so close now, our breath mingling, our lips a hair's breadth apart. I reach up, cupping her cheek with a tenderness I didn't know I possessed.

My fingers tangle in the silken strands at the nape of her neck, a gentle anchor in the storm of our desire.

"Well then," I murmur, my voice rough with want. "Don't let me keep you waiting. May I kiss you, beautiful?"

She stares deep into my eyes, and I swear I can see straight into her soul. Her chest is heaving, those perfect breasts straining against the confines of her corset, begging to be freed. And fuck, I want to bury my face in that heavenly valley and never come up for air.

"Y-yes..." she whispers, and it's like the heavens themselves have parted.

I close the distance, pressing my lips to hers with a reverence I've never known. And sweet baby Jesus, they're softer than I ever could have imagined. Plump, yielding, begging to be devoured. I push harder, coaxing her mouth open with my own, and she follows my lead like a dream.

And then, I slide my tongue inside, tasting her, claiming her. She mimics my actions, her tongue tentatively brushing against mine, and the sensation is enough to make my knees weak. She moans into my mouth, the sound vibrating through me like a fucking tuning fork, and I swear to God, I nearly come in my pants like a teenager.

It's electric, cosmic, and everything I never knew I needed. As we lose ourselves in the kiss, the world around us fades away; I can't help but think that this...right here—is what heaven must feel like.

I pull back, needing to ensure she's okay with this and that I'm not pushing her too fast. Her eyes fly open, and she grips my shirt like it's a fucking lifeline. "More. Please don't stop. Do that again," she breathes, and holy shit, if that isn't the sexiest thing I've ever heard.

I almost laugh at her eagerness, but who am I to deny my mate what she wants? I dive back in, taking the lead. I deepen the kiss, my grip on her hair tightening as I tug her flush against me. The moan that escapes her lips vibrates through, shaking me to my very core.

It's taking every last shred of my self-control not to let loose and paint the town white. But I'm a classy guy, a real Prince Charming type, and I'll be damned if I let her think I'm some minute man who's all bark and no bite.

No, sir, I'm in this for the long haul, ready to take her on a pleasure cruise that'll last longer than the Titanic (minus the whole "sinking" part, of course). I'm talking about a marathon of passion, an endurance test of ecstasy.

So I pour all my focus into the kiss, into making her feel good. I guide her through the motions, showing her how to move her lips and how to tangle her tongue with mine. And goddamn, she's a quick study. It's like she was made for this, made for me.

The way she molds herself against me, the little noises she makes, the taste of her on my tongue... it's enough to drive me insane. And I'm pretty sure I've already booked a one-way ticket to crazy town because I can't get enough of her.

Breaking away from her lips, I trail a path of searing wet kisses down the column of her throat. She arches into me, gasping as I explore the smooth expanse of her skin. Fuck. What I would give to sink my teeth into her silky flesh—but I'll wait. Wait until she's begging for my bite.

I lick a hot stripe up her neck, feeling her pulse jump beneath my tongue. I find that sweet spot just below her ear and latch, sucking and nibbling until she's squirming against me.

Her hands fly up to my hair, fingers curling into the strands and tugging me closer. "Lucian..." she whimpers, and fuck me runnin', the way she says my name makes me want to do all sorts of dirty, depraved things to her.

I work my way back up, peppering her skin with open-mouthed kisses until I reach her lips again. I capture them, my tongue delving into the sweet recesses of her mouth. She meets me stroke for stroke, her tongue tangling with mine in a sensual dance.

The heat between us is so intense that I'm surprised we haven't spontaneously combusted. The sounds she's making, the little sighs and moans, are like a symphony to my ears. A filthy, X-rated symphony that's making my dick harder than a diamond in an ice storm.

It's a fucking rush, knowing that I'm the one making her feel this way. I'm introducing her to the world of pleasure and passion. And I swear on all that's holy, I will make it my mission to rock her world in every way possible.

And together, we're going to set this fucking world on fire.

RHYLAND

43

The air is thick with the scent of salt and ancient secrets as Dani, and I approach the alcove beyond the pool we just entered. The winding tunnels amplify every sound, from the echoing slap of our footsteps against the slick rock to the steady *drip, drip, drip* of water that seems to come from everywhere and nowhere all at once. I keep Dani's hand clasped tightly in mine as we navigate the twisting passageways, my senses on high alert for any sign of danger.

Every now and then, the tunnels open up, offering tantalizing glimpses of the cavern far below. The water is a brilliant, impossible blue, so clear and bright it almost hurts to look at. Beneath the surface, I can see a kaleidoscope of rocks and coral in every color imaginable, like a fucking underwater rainbow.

When we finally reach the spot Mirella pointed out to us, we find ourselves standing at the edge of a massive pool that takes up most of the cavern. The water churns and swirls like a whirlpool, making me feel dizzy just looking at it. "So, what the hell are we supposed to do now?" I ask, my voice echoing off the cave walls.

Dani shrugs, her lips pursed in thought. "Beats me. Calypso just said to go through the Pools of Reflection, something about a pure soul or whatever."

I snort, my confidence taking a nosedive faster than a lead balloon. Pure souls? Yeah, I'm pretty fucking sure that counts me out. Dani must feel my doubts through our bond because she reaches up and cups my cheek, her honey-gold eyes locking onto mine.

"Hey," her voice soft but firm. "None of that broody bullshit, mister. We're in this together, no matter what. So quit your moping, and let's figure this out, okay?"

I can't help but smile at her sass, even as my heart clenches with a love so fierce it takes my breath away. "Okay, baby. Together."

Dani leans forward, peering into the swirling depths of the pool. The current is so strong that it whips her hair around her face like a tornado, the chestnut strands dancing in the eerie blue light that seems to emanate from the water itself.

Suddenly, a voice booms out from around us, so loud and deep that it makes my bones vibrate. *"What is your reflection?"* it asks the words echoing off the cave walls until it sounds like a chorus.

I whip my head around, trying to locate the source of the voice, but there's nothing there. Just the empty cave and the endless expanse of water. "What the fuck?" I mutter under my breath, my hand instinctively reaching for the weapon at my side.

The whirlpools have disappeared, leaving behind a surface as smooth and still as glass. The water is so clear and perfectly calm that it looks more like a mirror than a pool. I can see every detail of the cave reflected in its surface, from the jagged rocks that line the edges to the faint glow of the bioluminescent algae that cling to the walls.

What lies beneath that glassy surface? What secrets does this ancient place hold? I have no fucking clue.

Dani, being the sassy little minx that she is, just cocks her head to the side and grins. "A talking pool? Well, that's a new one. What's next, a singing toilet? Should I start reciting 'mirror, mirror on the wall' and hope for the best?"

I can't help but laugh at her quick wit, even as I shake my head in disbelief. "I don't think that's gonna cut it this time, Angel. Wrong fairytale."

Dani nods, her lips twitching with amusement. "Right. Okay, let's try this again." She leans forward, staring into the still pool like she's trying to see straight through to the other side. "Hello? Anybody home? We come in peace, I swear."

I step up beside her, my shoulder brushing against hers as I peer into the water. Our reflections stare back at us, calm and still. But there's something else there, too, something just beneath the surface that I can't quite make out. It's like trying to see through a veil of mist, all shadowy shapes and half-formed images that slip away before I can grasp them.

"What do you see?"

Dani squints, leaning in even closer, "I'm not sure. It's like... like something is moving down there, but I can't quite make it out."

As she speaks, the voice rings out again, louder this time. *"What is your reflection?"* it demands, the force of it making the water tremble and dance.

I take a deep breath, steeling myself for whatever the fuck is about to happen next. "Guess we're about to find out," I mutter, reaching for Dani's hand and lacing my fingers through hers.

I stare into the pool, my own reflection staring back at me. But then, suddenly, the image shifts, rippling and changing like a movie reel. I see Dani and me in a home I don't recognize, looking happy as hell. Dani's laughing, her head thrown back in pure joy, and the sight of it makes my heart clench.

The scene shifts again, and now Dani is in a room, sitting in a rocking chair with her back to me. I move closer, my footsteps echoing in the stillness until I'm standing right behind her. She's holding something close to her chest, singing a lullaby in a sweet voice that makes my eyes sting. When she looks up at me, the love in her eyes is so fucking intense it steals the breath from my lungs. She pulls the blanket down, revealing the most perfect, beautiful baby I've ever seen. "Say hello to your daddy, Rhylica," she whispers, her voice so soft it's like a caress.

The baby opens her eyes, and I'm lost. They're just like Dani's, a swirling gold with flecks of silver that seem to see straight into my fucking soul. *"Rhylica?"* I breathe, the name feeling like a prayer on my lips.

Just as quickly as it appeared, the scene vanishes, leaving me staring at my stunned reflection again.

I feel Dani shaking me, her voice urgent in my ear. "Rhyland. What did you see?"

I turn to look at her, my eyes misting over with the weight of the incredible vision I just witnessed. I open my mouth to speak, but before I can get a word out, the voice booms out once more. *"Your reflections are worthy; you may enter, Saviors."*

Saviors? As in more than one? Either I need to get my ears checked, or I'm losing my fucking marbles.

"Rhylica? Who the hell is Rhylica? I heard the name in your thoughts." Dani looks at me, her brow furrowed in confusion. "Aww, babe..." She reaches up, her thumb brushing gently over my cheek, wiping away a tear I didn't even realize had fallen.

I never fucking cry. I'm the big bad alpha and supposed to be strong and unshakable no matter what. But that vision... it hit me like a goddamn freight train. My heart is lodged so far up my throat I can barely breathe, and I don't know what to make of what I saw.

Was it real?

A glimpse of the future?

Or just my own fucked-up brain conjuring up fantasies of a life with Dani that I know can never be?

I take a shuddering breath, trying to get my shit together. "I saw you, and me, and..." I pause, swallowing hard against the knot in my throat. "A baby," I whisper, the word feeling like a prayer and a curse all at once.

Dani's eyes go wide, her mouth falling open in shock. "A baby? Like, *our* baby?" She shakes her head like she can't quite wrap her mind around the concept. "But that's...impossible. Vampires can't have kids. Right?"

I shrug, feeling just as lost and confused as she looks. "As far as I know—it's unheard of our kind. But that's what I saw. You were holding her, singing to her. And she was perfect. So fucking perfect." My voice cracks on the last word, and I have to look away, blinking hard against the sudden burn of tears in my eyes.

This has to be some sick, twisted joke. A fucked-up mind game that this goddamn pool is playing to mess with my head. Our kind can't have kids. It's just not possible. It's never fucking happened in the history of ever. So to see that vision, to see Dani—the woman I love more than my own goddamn life—my mate—giving me the one thing I want most in this world? It's like a sucker punch straight to my fucking balls, a knife twisting in my heart.

I feel like I can't breathe, as if the walls of this cave are closing in on me. My chest is so tight it feels like it might crack open from the pressure, spilling out all the desperate, aching hope that I've kept locked away for so fucking long.

Because that's what it is, isn't it? Hope. The kind of hope that's so fragile, so dangerous, that I've never let myself even consider it before.

But now, with that vision seared into my brain like a brand, I can't shake it—can't stop thinking about what it would be like to hold my child in my arms—our child—to watch Dani's belly swell with new life, to build a family and a future together. It's everything I've ever wanted and never thought I could have.

And the worst part? The part that makes me want to roar with fury and fall to my knees all at once? It's not fucking real. It can't be. It's just a cruel illusion, a taunt from the universe to remind me of everything I'll never have. All the dreams that will never come true, no matter how much I might wish for them.

It's a bitter pill, a reality check I never asked for. But as much as it hurts and makes me want to rage against the unfairness of it all, I know I can't let it break me. I have to be strong for Dani if nothing else. She needs me to keep my shit together, to be the rock she can lean on when things get tough.

Dani's hand finds mine, her fingers twining with my own. "Hey," she says softly, waiting until I meet her gaze. "Whatever it was, whatever it meant... we'll figure it out together. Just like we always do."

Dani steps closer, her arms winding around my neck like a lifeline. She pulls me down into a kiss, her lips soft and warm against my own. I cling to her like a drowning man, pouring all the pain and hurt and desperate longing I'm feeling into this kiss. Even if I could never have that vision and that perfect little girl would never be more than a beautiful dream, I still have this. I still have Dani, this incredible, amazing woman who loves me with every fiber of her being, just as I love her.

When she pulls back, her eyes find mine, holding my gaze with an intensity that steals the breath from my lungs. "For whatever that was, Rhylica is a beautiful name," she says softly, her lips curving into a tender smile.

I can't help but smile back, even through the ache in my chest, because she's right. It is a beautiful name. A perfect name for the perfect little girl, with Dani's eyes, my smile, and a bright future that hurts to imagine. Even if she'll never be more than a figment of my imagination, a bittersweet glimpse of what might have been, I know I'll carry the memory of her face with me for the rest of my days.

Dani's hand finds mine again, her fingers lacing through my own like a promise. "Come on, babe," she murmurs, tugging me gently toward the pool's edge. "Let's see what other surprises this magical puddle has in store for us."

So I take a deep breath, shoving all that pain and longing deep where it can't touch me. I square my shoulders, set my jaw, and turn to face whatever fresh hell this fucking pool has in store for us next. Because that's what I do. That's who I am. And no matter what kind of mind games the universe wants to play, that will never change.

"What about you? What did you see?" I can't help but ask, still reeling from the mind-fuck of my reflection, or vision, or whatever the hell that was.

Dani glances back at the pool and then meets my gaze with a smirk. "I saw the future of the realms," she says like it's no big fucking deal. "And let me tell you, babe, it looks pretty goddamn epic."

I raise an eyebrow, impressed and a little scared by her nonchalance. Before I can ask her to elaborate, she's swinging her legs over the side of the pool, her boots dipping into the glassy surface. "I think it wants us to take the plunge. You coming, or what?" She holds out her hand, her eyes sparkling with challenge.

I scoff, shaking my head—as if I would ever let her dive into the unknown without me by her side—or wouldn't follow this woman into the depths of hell itself if she asked me to.

So I swing my legs over the ledge, my hand finding hers like a magnet. Our fingers lace together, a perfect fit, as we exchange a loaded glance. Whatever waits for us beneath the surface, we'll face it together. No question.

I take a deep breath, filling my lungs with the damp, earthy air of the cave. Dani does the same, her chest rising and falling in sync with mine. And then, with a silent count of three, we push off from the ledge and dive in, plunging into the cool, clear water.

The moment we break the surface, the world falls away. The water envelops us, cradling us in its embrace as we sink deeper and deeper into the depths. It's peaceful down here, quiet in a way that seems to reach into my very soul. I can feel Dani's hand in mine, anchoring me to reality even as the rest of the world fades away.

We kick our legs, propelling ourselves forward through the crystal-clear water. Schools of luminescent fish dart past us, their scales glinting like jewels in the ethereal blue light that seems to emanate from everywhere and nowhere all at once.

And then, just as I'm starting to wonder if we'll ever reach the bottom, I see a shimmering portal hovering in the water like a mirage. It pulses with energy, a kaleidoscope of colors that shift and change every second.

I glance at Dani, seeing the same awe and anticipation reflected in her eyes. She squeezes my hand. *"I've seen these before—it's okay."* She pushes into my mind to reassure me.

And with that, we kick forward, propelling ourselves straight into the heart of the portal and the unknown adventure that awaits us on the other side.

DANICA

44

Rhyland and I pop out of the portal like a couple of spitballs, emerging into calm waters that feel like a damn spa compared to the toilet-flush ride we just took. I have no idea where the hell we are or what Water Gate we just stumbled through, but at this point, I'm just happy to be alive and not drowning in some interdimensional plumbing.

For a moment, I'm unsure which way is up, my head spinning like I just got off a particularly wild carnival ride. My lungs are screaming at me, burning like I just inhaled a pack of cigarettes and chased it with a shot of battery acid.

Rhyland, bless his heart. He seems to have a better sense of direction than I do. He grabs my hand, his grip solid and reassuring, and drags me upwards. I kick behind him, trying to help, but let's be real—he's doing most of the work. The man's built like a fucking tank, and his powerful strokes cut through the water like a hot knife.

The surface seems impossibly far away, a distant glimmer of light that taunts me with its promise of sweet, sweet air. My lungs are on fire, screaming at me to just take a breath already, but I know that's a one-way ticket to Drowning City. So I grit my teeth and keep kicking, trusting Rhyland to get us there before I pass out from lack of oxygen.

Finally, we break the surface. I gulp in a massive lungful of air, coughing and sputtering like a drowned rat. Rhyland pulls me close, his strong arms wrapping around me as he leads us toward the edge of whatever body of water we've found ourselves in.

I have no damn clue where we are. For all I know, we could be in Narnia. All that matters is that we're alive and one step closer to figuring out this "Siren's Lyre" business.

As we get closer to the edge, I take in our surroundings. We're in some underground cavern, the walls slick with moisture and glowing with an eerie blue light. It's like something out of a sci-fi movie, all alien and otherworldly.

"Where the hell are we?" I ask, my voice echoing off the walls.

Rhyland shakes his head. His brow furrows in concentration as he scans the area for signs of danger. "I don't know," he admits."But whatever this freaky-ass place is, we need to keep our eyes peeled and guard up. No telling what nasty surprises it might have in store for us."

I nod, my senses on high alert. We may have survived that Water Gate, but something tells me we're not out of the woods yet. Or the water, as the case may be.

Rhyland boosts me onto solid ground as we reach the edge with an almost insulting ease. I mean, I know I'm not exactly a heavyweight, but damn. The man makes it look like he's lifting a feather instead of a full-grown woman.

I flop onto my back, my chest heaving as I try to catch my breath. Rhyland hauls himself up beside me, water streaming off his muscular form in rivulets. He looks like some fucking sea god, all glistening skin and rippling muscles. It's enough to make a girl forget all about her near-death experience.

"Well, that was fun," My voice raspy. "Let's never do that again, yeah?"

Rhyland just grunts, his eyes scanning our surroundings with a wary intensity. I can practically see the wheels turning in his head, trying to figure out where the hell we are and what kind of trouble we've landed ourselves in this time.

But for now, I'm content to lie here and breathe, letting the solid ground beneath me anchor me back to reality. Because let's face it—after the mind-fuck of those reflection pools and the wild ride through the Water Gate, I could use a bit of boring old reality.

Of course, knowing our luck, that's probably too much to ask for.

Rhyland reaches out his hand to me. "We need to find this fucking key and get the hell out of Dodge, Angel. This place gives me the creeps, and I don't want to stick around long enough to find out why."

I nod, taking his hand, and he pulls me to my feet. "Agreed, and not in a fun, haunted house way."

We make our way deeper into the cavern, the walls narrowing until it feels like they're closing in on us. Our footsteps bounce off the stone, echoing in the eerie silence.

I glance around, my eyes widening as I take in the scene. Dead skeletal remains are scattered everywhere, littering the ground like some kind of screwed-up Halloween decoration. I grip Rhyland's arm, trying to get his attention without losing my shit completely. "Look," I hiss, my voice barely above a whisper.

I watch Rhyland's gaze sweep the area, his jaw clenching tighter every second. "This can't be fucking good." I can practically feel the tension radiating off him in waves, his every muscle coiled and ready to act at the first sign of trouble.

"Oh, you think?" I shoot back. "What gave it away, the piles of bones or the fact that we're trapped in a murder tunnel with no way out?"

Rhyland looks at me, "Now is not the time for your sass, woman."

I can tell he's on edge, every inch of him primed and ready for a fight. And honestly, I can't blame him. This place is giving me the heebie-jeebies like nobody's business.

We see a narrow fissure in the rock filled with a dark, swirling mist that sets my nerves on edge. "Well, that looks inviting," I mutter, eyeing the ominous gap with a healthy dose of skepticism.

As we step closer, the mist seems to come alive, whispering and hissing like a nest of snakes. Then, out of nowhere, a voice rings out, clear as a bell.

"Only one may answer—three riddles you must solve to pass through this gate. Each answer will stop a blade, but beware, for if you're late, the blades will swing again, and more will drop down, trapping you within this deadly town."

Oh, isn't this just adorable? A rhyming mist? What's next, a singing fog machine?

Then, the universe decides to flip me the bird and the mist parts like the Red Sea, revealing a set of blades that begin to swing like a deadly pendulum. They look like they were ripped straight out of a horror movie. "Oh, you have got to be fucking kidding me," I groan. "A deadly pop quiz. Just what I always wanted."

Rhyland's jaw clenches so hard I'm surprised his teeth don't shatter, his eyes narrowing as he studies the fissure like it insulted his mother. "Stay calm," he murmurs, his hand tightening around mine until I'm sure my fingers are turning blue from lack of circulation.

I shoot him an incredulous look, my eyebrows climbing so high they're practically merging with my hairline. "Stay calm? Are you kidding me right now?" I screech. "We're trapped in a fucking murder tunnel with no way out, and you want me to stay calm?"

Rhyland gives me a look, saying, "I'm the alpha male here, and I know what I'm doing." Which is complete and utter bullshit. But hey, if it makes him feel better to pretend like he's got this under control, who am I to burst his bubble?

"We can't afford to lose our shit right now," his voice low and steady, like he's trying to talk me down from the ledge of a full-blown freak-out. "Panicking will only make this whole fucked-up situation worse."

I let out a bark of laughter that sounds more than a little unhinged, even to my ears. "Worse? How could things possibly get any worse than this?" I gesture wildly at the swinging blades, the piles of bones—the whole fucked-up situation we've found ourselves in.

Rhyland shakes his head, a small smile tugging at the corner of his mouth. "You'd be surprised," his tone dry. "Trust me, baby. We've got this."

The blades swing back and forth like they're trying out for the world's deadliest pendulum competition, each pass getting closer to turning us into human sashimi. I whip my head around, desperately searching for another way out, but it's like we're trapped in a goddamn Saw movie. The walls are closing in, the tunnel narrowing until it feels like we're stuck in a freaking straw, and the only way out is through the murder hole.

The voice echoes through the cavern again, the first riddle hanging in the air like a noose.

"I flow without a form; my light ignites the storm. What am I?"

I scowl at the riddle, my brain doing its best impression of a hamster on a wheel as it tries to make sense of the clue. "Flow without a form... light ignites the storm... Hell, I don't know. Electricity?" I throw out, hoping that maybe, just maybe, I'll get lucky and the universe will decide to cut me a break for once.

But, of course, the blades keep swinging, their deadly arcs getting closer and closer. The panic claws its way up my throat, my heart pounding like it's trying to break out of my chest and make a run for it.

"Wrong answer," the voice intones, and I swear I can hear the sadistic glee from every word. *"Try again."*

I take a deep breath, trying to force myself to focus past the mind-numbing terror coursing through my veins.

What the hell flows without form?

I dig deep into the recesses of my mind, dusting off that analytical part of my brain that I love so much but always seems to short-circuit at the worst possible moments.

Light, storm... Shit. Come on, Dani, think! And then, like a jolt, it hits me. "Okay, okay. Flow without a form... light ignites the storm... Wait, could it be... water?"

The moment the word leaves my lips, one of the blades shudders to a stop, frozen in place. I let out a whoop of triumph, my pulse racing with adrenaline.

"One down, two to go," Rhyland murmurs, his voice tense. "Keep going, baby. You've got this."

The voice rings again, the second riddle hanging like the Sword of Damocles, just waiting to drop and slice us in half.

"In darkest depths, I softly glow, A beacon for the lost below. What am I, in ocean's keep, That guides the weary from the deep?"

Oh, for fuck's sake.

This one is harder than trying to solve a Rubik's cube blindfolded, and I can practically hear the gears in my brain grinding to a halt. I have to focus, or we're going to end up dead.

I chew on my lip like a piece of gum, my mind racing. "Darkest depths, softly glow... beacon for the lost... Shit, I don't know. A lighthouse?" I blurt out, immediately regretting the words as soon as they leave my mouth.

"Wrong again," the voice taunts, *"One more chance, or face the consequences."*

The blade that had stopped now kicks back to life, and I let out a groan of defeat that sounds like a dying whale. The blades' deadly dance gets faster until they're nothing but a blur of glinting metal. And then, because the universe can fuck right off, another set of blades drops down behind us with a sickening clank, cutting us off and trapping us in.

Shit! Oh my god. I'm pretty sure my heart is about to explode out of my chest like a xenomorph, and Rhyland's grip on my hand is so tight I'm pretty sure he's rearranging my bone structure. He tries to Jedi mind-trick those blades into stopping, but it's about as effective as using a squirt gun on a forest fire.

Rhyland's jaw is clenched tight, and he's sweating more than a sinner in church as he gives it another go. The blades sound like a pissed-off blender, slowing down for a hot second before Rhyland drops his hands, looking like he just went ten rounds with a hurricane.

Shit.

I guess we can't count on vampire superpowers to save our asses this time. Time for Plan B... if only I had one.

"Darkest depths, softly glow... beacon for the lost..."

"Try bioluminescence, baby," Rhyland's voice echoes in my mind, clear and insistent. He knows damn well that only one of us can answer these stupid fucking riddles.

That's good—genius.

"Wait, could it be... bioluminescence? Like that glowing shit we saw earlier?" I ask as I pray to every god I can think of that I'm right.

Because if we're not...

Two blades shudder to a stop, frozen in place. I let out a shaky breath—my knees weak with relief.

"Two down, one to go," Rhyland murmurs, his voice strained with the effort of keeping calm. "You've got this, baby. Just one more."

The final riddle echoes through the cavern, the voice heavy with malice.

"In water's grasp, I flicker bright, A dance of shadow and of light. What am I, in liquid's flow, That makes the depths above me glow?"

For the love of all that's *holy* and unholy!

The panic now is a living, breathing thing inside me, clawing at my throat and squeezing my lungs until I can barely breathe. It's like a thousand tiny spiders crawling under my skin, a million ants marching through my veins, and I swear to god, if I don't get out of this fucking tunnel soon, I'm going to lose my shit.

The blades behind us are getting closer with every second, the sound of their swinging filling my ears until it's all I can hear.

We're forced to shimmy closer to the one blade swinging in front of us, the metal glinting in the eerie light like the teeth of some monstrous beast. I can feel the heat of Rhyland's body pressed against mine, the tension in his muscles, the way his breath comes in short, sharp bursts. He's just as scared as I am, and that terrifies me more than anything else.

"Water's grasp, flickering bright... shadow and light... Ugh, I don't know. A flashlight?"

All three blades drop back down with a sickening clang, swinging faster now, the air whistling as they slice through it—I have to fight back a scream as they get closer and closer until I can practically feel the metal brushing against my clothes.

"Wrong again," the voice taunts, making my blood cold. *"Time's up, little saviors. Prepare to meet your doom."*

The blades are so close now that I can feel the air they displace, the way they make my hair flutter and dance like I'm in the middle of a tornado.

"Babe, I don't know what to do," I whisper, my voice small and broken. Rhyland doesn't respond, but I can feel the way his body tenses, the way his grip around my torso tightens until it's almost painful.

The tears are flowing freely now, hot and salty, against my skin, and I can taste the despair on my tongue, bitter and cloying. My mind is a whirlwind of half-formed thoughts and fragmented memories, snippets of my life flashing before my eyes like some jacked-up highlight reel.

I squeeze my eyes shut—a scream of pure desperation tears from my throat as I dive deep within myself, clawing desperately for that elusive time-bending power. It's like trying to grab a fistful of smoke in a hurricane, but I keep pushing, straining, until I finally brush against that familiar spark.

Something shifts.

The world around me shudders, then slows. With a final shuddering scream, everything just... stops. The silence that follows is so absolute, so all-encompassing, that for a moment, I wonder if I've gone deaf. Or maybe just died.

I crack open an eye, half-expecting to see those psycho blades still doing their best Cuisinart impression on my sorry ass. But no...instead, those circular death dealers are just hanging there, frozen mid-slice. It's like the universe decided to buffer right in the middle of my execution.

I'm half-tempted to wave my hand in front of my face to make sure I haven't accidentally stumbled into a glitchy video game cutscene. But knowing my luck, that'd probably trigger some boss battle I'm in no shape to handle right now.

"What the hell?" Rhyland's voice is a hoarse whisper in my ear, his breath hot against my skin. "How...? Did you do that?"

I spin around to face him, my eyes wide with shock. Holy shit, I did. But usually, my power only lets me slow time down, not stop it completely. And it's always been a solo gig, but now Rhyland is stuck in this weird-ass time bubble with me.

"I-I think so," I stammer, my voice shaking with adrenaline and disbelief.

Rhyland, being the practical bastard he is, doesn't waste time analyzing this bizarre turn of events. He grabs my hand, and we slip through the fissure like thieves in the night, the frozen blades looming over us.

I cling to that sensation like a lifeline—the one keeping us suspended in this bizarre time bubble. Every fiber of my being is focused on maintaining this fragile state as we shimmy through the deadly obstacle course. We duck under the frozen blade, its edge gleaming wickedly mere inches from our heads.

Rhyland moves with me, his grip on my hand never faltering. The fact that he's here, frozen in this moment with me, is a mind-fuck all its own. I mean, unless my vampire boyfriend suddenly developed time manipulation powers when I wasn't looking, the only explanation is that my mojo decided to go plus-one tonight due to our physical contact when I tapped into this power, pulling him into my little time-out corner of reality.

As we weave our way through this deadly sculpture garden, I can't help but wonder if this is what it feels like to be a cat with nine lives. Or maybe we're just starring in our own action movie, complete with slow-mo escape scenes. Either way, I'm not complaining. I'll take "miraculously not dead" over "sliced and diced" any day of the week.

We make it to the other side, and then I let it go—the world snaps back into motion, the blades whirring to life with a vengeance, like they're pissed off that we dared to cheat death.

I think back to the riddle, turning the words over like a Rubik's cube, "Water's grasp, flickering bright... shadow and light..." And then it hits me.

It's so simple, so damn obvious, that I almost want to laugh. The way light dances on the water's surface, casting shadows and illuminating the depths, is a simple concept that holds so much meaning and power.

"The answer to the riddle is Reflection!" I shout, my voice bouncing off the tunnel's walls like a pinball.

And just like that, the blades grind to a halt, the mist dissipating like a fart in the wind. We're left standing there, panting and shaking, our hearts pounding in our chests like jackhammers.

"Holy shit," Rhyland breathes, his eyes wide with awe and disbelief. "That was too fucking close."

I nod, my legs trembling beneath me as the adrenaline wears off. "You're telling me. I thought we were goners for sure."

"How the fuck did you pull that off?" Rhyland pants, his hands braced on his knees like he just sprinted a mile. "That whole freezing time shit? That's a new one, even for you."

I shrug, my breath coming in ragged gasps. "Beats me, but I'm sure as hell not complaining." I pause, my brow furrowing as I consider the implications. "Maybe my powers are leveling up or something? Like, I just unlocked a new skill in the world's most screwed-up video game."

Rhyland snorts, shaking his head. "Only you would compare a near-death experience to a damn video game."

I grin, the adrenaline still buzzing through my veins like a live wire. "Hey, if the shoe fits..."

Rhyland rolls his eyes, but I can see the relief in his gaze, the way his shoulders sag as the tension bleeds out of him. "Well, whatever it was, I'm just glad it worked."

I nod, my relief so sharp it's almost painful. "You and me both, babe. I guess the universe decided it wasn't done with us yet."

Rhyland's lips twitch, a hint of his usual smirk returning. "Or maybe it just didn't want to deal with your sassy ass in the afterlife."

I gasp, "Excuse you, my ass is a fucking delight. The afterlife would be lucky to have me."

Rhyland chuckles, the sound warm and rich in the damp chill of the tunnel. "Whatever you say, baby. But let's try to avoid testing that theory anytime soon, yeah?"

I nod, my smile fading as the reality of our situation settles back in. "Agreed. We've got shit to do, and I'd rather not end up dead before we finish it."

Even as I say it, I know it's a lie. Because as much as I hate to admit it, as much as it scares the ever-loving hell out of me... I live for this shit. The danger, the adrenaline, the rush of knowing that we're alive and beaten the odds once again.

Rhyland grabs my hand and pulls me through the tunnels, "Come on, Angel. We ain't done yet."

LUCIAN

45

Okay, so it's been a whole goddamn day, and we still haven't heard a peep from Dani and Rhyland. Who the fuck knows what kind of trouble they've gotten themselves into this time? Probably off battling some ancient evil or trying to solve some cryptic-ass riddle to find this stupid key. I swear, it's like they're on a never-ending episode of *"Scooby-Doo,"* but with more sexual tension and less talking dogs.

If something terrible happened to them, I'd know. I felt Dani's fear earlier, like a kick in the nuts from the universe itself. But it went away quickly, so I'm guessing they're okay now. Whatever fresh hell they stumbled into, they probably punched it in the face and walked away like the badasses they are.

Thanks to this blood-sharing deal, I'm a mood ring for Dani. I can feel every little thing she feels, which is about as fun as a root canal when I'm trying to focus on my little piece of heaven right here. Don't get me wrong, I love Dani like a sister. I'd take a bullet for her, jump in front of a train, the whole shebang. But when her fear hits me, it's like this primal urge to go full-on superhero mode.

And then there's Seraphina, my precious little worry-wart. She's like a broken record, constantly asking me if Dani is okay or out of danger. Her concern is so strong it's like being crushed by a giant teddy bear. I get it, though. She loves Dani, too. Guardian angel duties and all that jazz. But we both know Dani's a tough cookie. She stared death in the face and flipped the bird. She's like a damn cockroach, impossible to kill. So, Seraphina and I keep reminding each other of that, trying to keep our minds out of the gutter of worst-case scenarios.

After Seraphina had her mind thoroughly blown by our little makeout session on the quarter deck, she surprised me by being the one to put the brakes on. Don't get me wrong, the girl was clearly into it. Her skin was flushed and hot, and the scent of her arousal was so thick I could've cut it with a knife and spread it on toast.

But even though every fiber of my being was screaming at me to keep going, to give in to the primal need that was consuming us both, Seraphina had the presence of mind to slow things down. She asked me, all sweet and polite, to step back. And as much as it pained me to do so, I had to respect her wishes.

I mean, I may be a lot of things—devastatingly handsome, charming as hell, and hung like a horse—but I'm also a man of my word. I promised her I'd be a gentleman, take things slow, and let her set the pace. And damn it all to hell, that's precisely what I'm going to do.

Even if it kills me, which, let's be real, it just might.

Just as I was about to suggest we take a cold dip in the ocean to cool off, Seraphina's stomach let out a growl that could've woken the dead. And that's when I realized, in my haste to devour her delectable lips, I'd forgotten that my poor girl hadn't eaten in who knows how long.

So, being the attentive and doting mate I am, I took it upon myself to rectify the situation immediately. What kind of gentleman would I be if I let my lady love starve?

I took her hand in mine, marveling at how perfectly it fit, and led her back below deck to the galley. As we walked, I couldn't help but think about all the other firsts I wanted to experience with her.

We're now chilling below deck in the mess area with our little ragtag group of misfits: Gideon, Erik, and some other crew members who probably don't deserve to be in the same room as my celestial goddess. But hey, who am I to judge?

Seraphina is going to town for this fish dinner as if it's the last meal she'll ever eat. Watching her devour everything in sight is like watching a fucking masterpiece unfold. Who knew watching someone stuff their face could be such a turn-on?

Barnaby, the ship's resident Gordon Ramsay wannabe, whipped up this spread of fish, potatoes, greens, and these rolls that are so damn good, they'll make you want to smack your grandma. And Seraphina? She's making noises that should be illegal in all seven realms.

"I've never tasted anything so delicious," she moans, her mouth full of food, and it's so fucking cute. I want to feed her, like some cheesy romance novel hero. But you know what? I'm totally down for that role.

I can only imagine the kind of boring-ass food they serve up in Atheria. Probably some magical kale smoothie that tastes like a unicorn's ass. But down here? We've got the trifecta of deliciousness: fat, salt, and carbs, baby. And my girl is experiencing it all for the first time, like a virgin on her wedding night.

"Aye, thank ye, lass," Barnaby says, looking all proud of himself. "I do enjoy me some good fish."

Barnaby, who looks like the unholy lovechild of Chunk from *The Goonies* and a pirate who hasn't seen a bar of soap in a decade, is shoveling food into his face like it's his day job. He's eyeing my angelic goddess like she's the main course, and I'm about two seconds away from stabbing him with my fork.

Meanwhile, Gideon and Erik huddle in the corner, talking strategy and chugging rum like it's the elixir of life. They're probably discussing some super serious, world-saving shit. Still, all I can focus on is the way Seraphina's hair catches the candlelight, making her look like a fucking renaissance painting come to life.

"It's wonderful," Seraphina gushes, swallowing her food like a champ. "May I have some more?"

Before Chef Boyar-ugly can even think about getting up, I'm already out of my seat, ready to cater to my girl's every whim. "Allow me, Cupcake," I purr, laying on the charm thick. "You can have all you want and more. And I do mean more."

I give her a wink that's so loaded with innuendo it could make a porn star blush. I pile her plate high with seconds, thirds, and fuck it, fourths. My baby girl wants to eat, then I am sure as hell going to make sure she's satisfied.

As I set the plate down in front of her, I lean in real close, my lips practically grazing her ear. "Eat up, gorgeous," I whisper, with promises of things to come. "You're going to need your energy for what I have planned later."

The way she shivers and blushes tells me she's picking up what I'm putting down. And hot damn, I can't wait to follow through on all the filthy things running through my mind.

How her breath hitches, and cheeks flush tells me she knows exactly what I'm implying. And fuck, I can't wait to make good on that promise.

But for now, I'm content to sit back and watch her enjoy her meal, marveling at how she savors every bite like a religious experience. And who knows? Maybe it is.

And the best part? I'm the lucky son of a bitch who gets to be here for all her firsts. Her first taste of real food, her first kiss, her first... well, let's say I've got a whole list of firsts I can't wait to introduce her to.

After a while of watching her and discussing boring-ass ship repairs with Gideon and Erik, Seraphina leans back in her chair, patting her stomach like a satisfied lion after a big kill. "I'm full," she declares, and I can't help but grin at the contented look on her face.

After watching her put away enough food to feed a small army, the rest of us can't help but laugh. "I'm sure you are, baby girl," I chuckle, standing up and offering her my hand. "Come on, let's go walk off that food coma."

We make our way back up to the main deck. The sun's just starting to set, painting the sky in a whole fucking rainbow of colors. It's like Bob Ross got drunk and went apeshit on the horizon. Seraphina leans against the ship's side, taking a deep breath of that salty sea air.

"So, tell me again about your life before you were, you know..." she trails off, looking at me with those big, golden, curious eyes.

"Turned?" I finish for her, raising an eyebrow. "Before I became the devastatingly handsome creature of the night, you see before you?"

She rolls her eyes, but I can see the smile tugging at the corners of her mouth. "Yes, that. What did you do? What were you like?"

I lean against the railing beside her, staring at the ocean as the memories flood in. "I lived in this quaint little village in England, where everyone knew everyone else's business."

I pause, letting the nostalgia wash over me. "I was a blacksmith's apprentice if you can believe it. I spent my days pounding at metal, making horseshoes, tools, and whatever the village needed. It was hard work, but I loved it. There was something satisfying about taking a raw piece of metal and shaping it into something useful."

Seraphina listens intently, her gold eyes never leaving my face. "What about your family? Your friends?"

I shrug, a wistful smile playing on my lips. "I had a family, sure. A mother and father, and a couple of siblings. We weren't rich by any means, but we had each other.

As for friends, well... let's just say I was a bit of a troublemaker back then. Always getting into scrapes, pulling pranks, chasing after pretty girls."

I give her a wink, and she blushes, shaking her head. "Some things never change, I guess."

"You got that right, angel face," I grin, bumping my shoulder against hers. "But you know, even though I was a bit of a handful, I was always there for the people I cared about. If someone needed help, I was the first one to volunteer. If there was a problem that needed solving, I was the one who came up with the plan."

I sigh heavily, looking down at my hands like they hold the secrets to the universe. "I guess you could say I was a bit of a hero, even back then. Always trying to save the day, always putting others before myself. It's what got me into trouble with Lilith in the first place."

Seraphina's brow furrows, her lips pursing in confusion. "What do you mean?"

I run a hand through my hair, really not wanting to take this trip down memory lane. But I know she deserves the truth, even if it's not pretty.

"So, remember how I told you Lilith came to my village? All of us young guys were practically tripping over ourselves to get her attention. She was gorgeous and mysterious, making you feel like you were the only man in the world when she looked at you."

I shake my head, a rueful smile on my lips. "She worked as a seamstress for a while, but none of us knew what she *really* was. A vampire, a seductress, a manipulative bitch who played us all like fiddles."

Seraphina listens intently, her hand resting on mine, anchoring me to the present.

"Anyway, there was this one night when a bunch of us were at the local tavern, drinking and carrying on like the young idiots we were. Lilith was there, too, flirting and teasing, making us all think we had a shot with her."

I take a deep breath, steeling myself for the next part of the story.

"I noticed she was paying extra attention to my friend, Thomas. He was a good guy, kind of naive and easily swayed. I saw something in her eyes that night—something unnatural. I could see Lilith was reeling him in, and I didn't like it. Call it intuition, but something about her just didn't sit right with me."

I pause, the memories playing out like a twisted nightmare.

"I tried to warn Thomas and get him to see that Lilith was bad news. But he was too far gone, too caught up in her spell. He brushed me off, told me I was just jealous that she wanted him and not me."

I let out a humorless laugh, shaking my head. "If only he knew how wrong he was. I couldn't have cared less about Lilith's affections. I just wanted to keep my friend safe."

Seraphina squeezes my hand, her eyes full of sympathy and understanding.

"Later that night, I saw Thomas leave the tavern with Lilith. I had a bad feeling, so I followed them. They headed into the woods, and I kept my distance, not wanting to intrude. But then I heard Thomas scream."

I close my eyes, the sound still echoing in my mind after all these years.

"I ran towards the noise, my heart pounding in my chest. And that's when I saw her, Lilith, with her fangs buried in Thomas's neck. She was draining him dry, and he was lying there, helpless and afraid."

Seraphina gasps, her free hand coming up to cover her mouth.

"I don't know what came over me, but I charged at her, tackling her to the ground. We struggled, and she was so strong, so fast. But I managed to get in a few good hits, enough to make her let go of Thomas."

I take a shaky breath, the weight of the memory pressing down on me like a physical force.

"I told Thomas to run, to get help. But it was too late—he was dead. Lilith, she was pissed. She came at me with a fury I'd never seen before, her eyes glowing red and her fangs bared."

I unconsciously rub at my neck, remembering her bite.

"She overpowered me easily, pinning me to the ground like I was nothing more than a rag doll. And then she bit me, her fangs sinking into my flesh like hot knives. I screamed, I fought, but it was no use. She was too strong, and I was just a human."

Seraphina's eyes are wide, her face pale as she listens to my tale.

"The last thing I remember before blacking out was her voice whispering in my ear. *Such fire in you—you're mine now, Lucian. Forever.* And then everything went dark."

I let out a long, slow breath, the weight of the memory finally lifting from my shoulders.

"When I woke up, I was different. Changed. Lilith had turned me, made me into a monster like her. And that's how I became a vampire, by trying to save my friend..." I breathe deep, "who in the end died anyway."

I stare into Seraphina's eyes, scanning her face like a paranoid TSA agent, half-expecting to find even a trace of fear or disgust. But instead, I'm greeted by an endless ocean of understanding and empathy, and it's like a swift kick to the emotional nuts. I'm laid bare, my soul exposed like a naked hitchhiker on a busy highway, but somehow, in her presence, I feel completely safe and accepted. It's a mindfuck of the highest order.

"You see, angel face? Even back then, I was willing to throw myself under the proverbial bus for the people I gave a damn about."

Seraphina's eyes are filled with a cocktail of sadness and curiosity, "Just like when you sacrificed yourself for Dani," she says, her voice as soft as a kitten's purr. It's not a question but a statement of fact.

I lock eyes with her, my mind buzzing with unasked questions like a swarm of caffeine-addicted bees. "So, you've heard about that little incident, huh?"

Seraphina nods, her golden curls bouncing with the motion. "Yes, Dani told me what happened before she made it to Aquaria. She shared how you willingly put yourself in harm's way...for her," she says, her voice barely above a whisper. "She's alive because of your bravery."

I swallow hard, the memories of Azrael pinning me down and that witch making scrambled eggs out of my brain all so Dani could get to safety. "It's just who I am, for better or worse. Mostly worse." I wink.

Seraphina's smile is like a ray of sunshine piercing through the clouds of my fucked-up existence. Her hand reaches to cup my cheek, and I lean into her touch like a touch-starved puppy. "For better, Lucian. Definitely for better. You are not like them—the ones lost. Or like Lilith. You are better than all of them."

I gaze into her eyes—my own darting back and forth like a metronome on crack, trying to detect even a glimmer of doubt or hesitation. But there's none to be found. I'm stripped down to my core. My heart laid out on a silver platter for her to do with as she pleases. It's a level of vulnerability that would normally have me running for the hills but with Seraphina? I've never felt so safe, accepted, or completely at home. It's like she's the missing puzzle piece I never knew I needed.

It's a lot to process, even for a smooth operator like myself. I clear my throat, trying to dislodge the boulder-sized lump of emotions suddenly taking up residence there. "So, let me ask you something, my precious angel cake. I know I've got a metric fuck-ton of feelings for you, but can you tell me how you feel? You know, about this whole 'destined to bump uglies for all eternity' thing?"

Seraphina's smile is like a ray of sunshine piercing through the clouds of my fucked-up existence."At first, it scared me," she admits, her voice soft and contemplative. "We've always been taught that your kind is tied to darkness, that you'd snuff us out given the chance. Our blood calls to you, which should be a bad thing."

She pauses, and I feel my heart doing somersaults in my chest. But then she continues, her words wrapping around me like a warm, fuzzy blanket of hope.

"But after talking with Dani—understanding her experience with it and getting to know you? I've started to form my own opinions and feelings."

"Like what?" I prompt her, my voice barely above a whisper. I need to know what's going on in her beautiful head and hear her say the words that will either make or break me.

"It's like... I feel this *spark* between us, this pull towards you. It's deep inside, like a part of me I never knew existed until now. And it's not just physical, though; trust me, that's definitely a factor."

"Oh, do tell, my naughty little seraph," I purr, waggling my eyebrows at her. "I'm all ears, and other parts, too."

She blushes, and I feel a surge of pride, knowing that I'm the one who put that rosy hue on her cheeks.

"I—I've never felt anything..." she stammers, trying so hard to explain, and it's fucking adorable, "physical. Or attracted to anyone. It's emotional, too. Like my heart recognizes yours, like a puzzle that just clicked into place."

I nod, my throat tight with emotion. "I feel the same way, Cupcake. But for me, it's more primal, more instinctual. I need you in every way possible. And I need you to know I would never, *ever* hurt you—unless you ask me to, of course. Then I'm totally down for a little consensual rough play."

Seraphina laughs, the sound like a choir of angels singing a dirty limerick.

I take her hand in mine, placing it over my chest where my heart beats a steady, strong, and sure rhythm. "Do you feel that? That's because of you, Seraphina. You make me feel alive in a way I never thought possible." She nods, her eyes glistening with unshed tears. "And also, like, super horny. But that's beside the point."

She giggles, "Oh, Lucian, you have such a way with words."

"What can I say, baby girl? I'm a cunning linguist," I quip, giving her a suggestive wink. "All I want to do is protect you, love you, worship you like the goddamn goddess you are. I want to be your knight in shining armor, your personal love slave, your—"

Before I finish my impassioned speech, Seraphina silences me with a kiss that would make the angels weep with envy. Her lips are soft and sweet, like sugar dipped in cinnamon, and I can't help but melt into her embrace.

I wrap my arms around her, pulling her close and devouring her mouth like a starving man. A rare moment of clarity strikes me, and I break away, gasping for air. "Whoa there, my eager Heavenly S'more! At least buy me a drink first before you go all in. I'm a gentleman, and gentlemen—"

But once again, Seraphina cuts me off, smashing her lips against mine with an enthusiasm that could start a forest fire. She wraps her arms around my neck, pulling me closer, and I can feel every delicious curve of her body pressed against mine.

She pulls back just enough to whisper against my lips, her voice breathy and sexy. "Shut up and just kiss me, Lucian."

Well, fuck me sideways and call me a bitch. My sweet and spicy chimichanga just turned up the heat, and I am so here for it. I mean, who am I to deny my mate what she wants? Especially when what she wants is me.

Oh, she's going to be begging me to fulfill her every desire, to make her scream my name until she's hoarse and seeing stars. And I am more than happy to oblige with gusto and enthusiasm.

Because that's just the kind of mate I am. Attentive, devoted, and always ready to please.

Pleasing Seraphina will be my new favorite hobby. Sorry, knitting; you've been replaced.

RHYLAND

46

The tunnels seem to stretch on forever, winding and twisting like the guts of some giant, fucked-up sea monster. The air is thick with the stench of salt and decay, clinging to the back of my throat like a bad taste I can't shake. It's dark as shit in here, the only light coming from the eerie glow of the bioluminescent algae clinging to the damp walls.

As we slog through the endless twists and turns, I can't help but notice the water level rising with every step. It starts as a trickle, a minor annoyance that has us splashing through puddles. But before long, we're wading through the murky depths, the water sloshing around our thighs and soaking us to the bone.

"Well, this is just wonderful," Dani grumbles, her voice echoing off the narrow walls. "Maybe we should've brought a goddamn raft."

I can hear her nervousness and how she falls back on her signature sass when feeling out of her depth. But I know my girl, and she's tougher than she gives herself credit for. "Nowhere to go but forward, baby," I say, keeping my voice low and steady. "This tunnel's gotta lead somewhere. Just keep moving."

Dani doesn't respond, but I can practically feel the eye roll she's shooting my way. We trudge through the water, the level rising each step until we're neck-deep in the brackish liquid.

Suddenly, Dani lets out a blood-curdling screech that makes my heart slam against my ribs. "Oh my fucking god, something just touched my leg!"

I'm at her side instantly, my eyes scanning the dark water for any sign of a threat. But there's nothing—no ripple, shadow, or hint of movement beneath the surface.

"There's nothing, Angel," I reassure her, trying to keep my voice steady. "Come on, we gotta keep moving."

The water keeps rising, forcing us to bob and weave through the narrow passage like a couple of fucking corks. The stench of death is getting stronger now, so thick I can almost taste it on my tongue.

Up ahead, the cave ceiling drops low, leaving us no choice but to dive under and swim through the submerged section. Dani stops short, treading water as she stares at the dark opening with wide, wary eyes.

"Looks like we're going for a dip," her voice tight with apprehension.

I reach out, cupping the back of her neck and pulling her in for a hard, desperate kiss. "I'll be right behind you, baby. I promise," my forehead pressed against hers. "Always."

Dani conjures up an orb of her light and nods, taking a deep breath before diving beneath the surface. I follow close behind, the icy water closing over my head like a suffocating shroud. I can feel the current tugging at my limbs, trying to pull me off course, but I keep my eyes locked on the pale glow of Dani's light up ahead, using her as my guide through the darkness.

We swim for what feels like an eternity, our lungs burning and our muscles screaming with the effort. Just when I think I can't hold my breath a second longer, we burst through the surface into a massive, underground, flooded chamber that steals what little air I have left.

The chamber is vast and cavernous, with soaring arched ceilings that disappear into the gloom above us. The walls are ancient, crumbling stones, their surfaces pitted and worn by centuries of water and decay. They seem to loom over us, pressing in from every side like they're trying to swallow us whole.

But what's in the center of the room really steals the breath from my lungs. There, rising out of the murky water like a ghost from the past is a massive pirate ship. It's old as fuck, the wood rotted and blackened with age, the sails hanging in tattered shreds from the masts. It looks like something straight out of a nightmare, a relic of a bygone era with no business in this forgotten tomb.

"Holy hell," Dani pants beside me, her breath coming in ragged gasps as she treads water. "We need to get to higher ground before something decides to make us its next meal."

I nod, my eyes scanning the chamber for anything we can use to our advantage. The ship looms over us like a goddamn mountain, its decks so high they might as well be in the fucking clouds. No way we're climbing that beast without some serious gear.

The walls of the cavern are slick as shit, with no handholds or ledges to grab onto. We're bobbing in this death pool like a couple of corks, surrounded by nothing but water and debris.

"Fuck," I growl, frustration clawing at my insides. We're sitting ducks here, exposed and vulnerable in this watery hellhole. I scan the room again, desperation fueling my search. There's got to be something, some way out of this clusterfuck.

My eyes lock onto a glimmer of hope in the far corner. A wooden ladder, half-rotted and barely clinging to the wall, leads up to a narrow ledge that might be our ticket out of this watery hell. It's a long shot; the wood looks like it's one splinter away from crumbling to dust, but it's the only option we've got.

"Over there," I grunt, jerking my chin towards the ladder. "If we can get to that ledge, we might be able to find a way out of this shithole."

Together, we strike out towards the ladder, our arms and legs churning through the water as we dodge the floating debris. It's slow going, the weight of our clothes and the exhaustion of the last few hours dragging at our limbs like lead weights. But we keep pushing forward, our eyes locked on that narrow strip of wood like it's the only thing in the world that matters.

Dani eyes the ladder skeptically, her brow furrowing with doubt. "No way. That thing looks like it's one splinter away from crumbling into sawdust. It'll never hold my weight."

But we don't have time to debate the finer points of structural integrity. We need to get out of this water, and we need to do it now. Without a word, I duck beneath the surface, resurfacing a moment later with Dani perched on my shoulders.

She lets out a squeal of surprise, her thighs clamping around my neck as she struggles to keep her balance. "Jesus, Rhyland! A little warning next time?"

"Just grab the fucking ladder, baby," I grunt, my muscles straining as I try to keep us both steady in the murky water. It's like trying to balance on a surfboard, but I'll be damned if I let us both drown in this watery grave.

Dani reaches for the ladder, her fingers scrabbling against the slimy wood as she tries to find a grip. I can feel her boots digging into my shoulders, her weight shifting as she tries to haul herself onto the bottom rung.

"Sorry, sorry," she mutters, her voice strained with effort as she shimmies up the ladder. Her daggers scrap the rocks. I can feel her boot pressing down on the top of my head, the pressure making my skull throb like a son of a bitch. But I grit my teeth and bear it, using every ounce of strength to keep us both steady as she climbs.

Finally, Dani reaches the top of the ladder, hauling herself onto the ledge with a triumphant grunt. She turns back to look down at me, her face flushed with exertion and relief.

"Holy shit," she pants, a giddy laugh bubbling up from her throat. "I can't believe that worked."

I grin up at her, my heart pounding with the adrenaline rush. "Never underestimate the power of a good boost, baby. Now, how about you find something to help haul my ass up there before I start growing gills?"

Dani nods, scanning the ledge for anything she can use as a makeshift rope. "On it, babe. Just hang tight and try not to drown on me, okay?"

"No promises," I mutter, but there's no real heat behind the words. We've made it this far, and I'll be damned if a little thing like a flooded chamber is going to take me out now.

I tread water and watch as Dani searches the ledge, my mind already racing ahead to whatever fresh hell this place has in store for us next.

Suddenly, I feel something scrape against my leg, sending a jolt of adrenaline surging through my veins. I whip my head down, eyes scanning the murky water, but nothing is there. Just the swirling darkness and the faint glimmer of debris floating by.

Probably just a piece of driftwood, I think to myself, trying to shake off the unease prickling at the back of my neck. "Today, Angel," I shout at Dani, my voice echoing off the damp stone walls.

"Hold your damn horses, I'm looking," Dani sasses back. "There's nothing up here but twigs and shit."

I let out a frustrated breath. The longer I tread here, the more the water starts to leech the warmth from my body. I feel something bump against my leg again, the force of it sending me reeling backward through the water.

"What the fuck?" I hiss, my heart slamming against my ribs as I spin around, trying to get a glimpse of whatever the hell just touched me. But there's nothing there, just the endless expanse of dark, churning water.

I scramble towards the broken ladder, my heart slamming against my ribs as I try like hell to hurry up the slick wall. But it's no use—the damn thing is too high, too far out of reach, and I can't get a grip on the slimy stone no matter how hard I try.

"Danica, hurry the fuck up!" I bellow, my voice raw with rising panic as I feel something brush against my leg again, the touch sending a jolt of pure, primal terror surging through my veins. "There's something in the water, and—"

Before I finish my sentence, something wraps around my ankle, yanking me beneath the surface with a force that steals the air from my lungs. I thrash and kick, my eyes flying open as I'm dragged down into the murky depths, but all I can see is a swirling mass of bubbles and the faint, distorted glow of the chamber above.

I look down at my leg, my heart seizing in my chest as I catch a glimpse of the slimy, pulsating tentacle wrapped around my ankle. It's thick as a tree trunk, the flesh mottled and slick with some viscous fluid that makes my skin crawl.

I yank and pull at the tentacle, my lungs burning with the need for air as I fight to free myself from its grasp. But it's no use. The thing is too strong, too massive, and I can feel myself being dragged deeper and deeper into the abyss, the light fading away above me like a dying star.

Fuck, fuck, fuck.

My vision starts to blur around the edges as my oxygen-starved brain screams for relief. I can feel the pressure building in my chest, the agonizing burn of my lungs as they strain for air that isn't there.

I focus all my energy, rage, fear, and desperation into a single, concentrated blast of telekinetic power. I feel it—building in my mind, a pressure that grows and grows until it feels like my skull might split open from the force of it. And then, with a silent scream of fury, I unleash it on the creature, pouring every ounce of strength into the attack.

For a brief, shining moment, it works. The tentacle around my ankle loosens its grip, the slimy flesh recoiling as if burned by the force of my power. I don't hesitate; don't stop to think. I kick towards the surface with everything I have, my lungs screaming for air as I claw through the murky water.

I break through the surface with a gasp, my head spinning as I gulp down a lungful of damp, stale air. I feel that sickening tug on my ankle again, and I'm being yanked back into the depths.

I hear Danica above me, her screams piercing through the murky depths like a knife to the gut. Even muffled by the water—her raw, unbridled panic, the sheer terror that shoots down our bond like a lightning bolt.

That fear, that desperate, clawing need to return to her, gives me the strength to keep fighting. I thrash and kick against the tentacle's grip, my lungs burning with the need for air as I claw at the slimy flesh with my fingers. I can feel Dani's fear mixing with my own, a feedback loop of pure, primal terror threatening to swallow me whole.

I'm going to die down here, I realize with a sickening lurch of my stomach. I'm going to drown in this godforsaken chamber, pulled down into the depths by some eldritch horror that's been waiting for centuries to make me its next meal.

DANICA

47

I'm losing my damn mind as Rhyland is yanked beneath the surface by whatever hellspawn is lurking in the depths.

"Rhyland!"

Oh god, what do I do? Jump in after him like some discount action hero?

Yup, that's precisely what I'm going to do. But I need...

My eyes dart around the chamber, desperate for something—anything—to haul Rhyland's ass out of that nightmare. I'm about to start ripping my hair out when Rhyland resurfaces, gasping for air. Before I can even breathe a sigh of relief, he's dragged back under, the water churning and frothing like a blender set to "fuck you up."

I'm on the verge of a full-blown panic attack when I spot a battered old barrel tucked away in the far corner of my little island of safety. I scramble over to it, my heart pounding so hard I'm pretty sure it's about to burst out of my chest. I try to pry the damn thing open, but it doesn't budge like it's welded shut with the tears of a thousand frustrated sailors.

I'm about to start kicking and screaming like a toddler in a tantrum when my hands fire up, the glow building. Without even thinking, I blast the barrel with everything I've got. The thing disintegrates like a piñata, and I'm left blinking away spots as the debris rains down around me.

Then, like a gift from the gods of shitty situations, I spot a length of rope among the wreckage. "Rhyland, hang on...please don't fucking die," I whisper, my voice cracking with desperation.

I snatch up the rope and race back to the ledge, my heart in my throat as I watch the water churn and boil like a witches' cauldron. I can see the fight raging just below the surface, a blur of thrashing limbs and frothing bubbles, and I know I have to act fast, or Rhyland will end up as fish food.

I don't waste a second. I tie one end of the rope around my waist and secure the other to the pillar behind me with a knot.

Then, I jump...

The icy liquid hits me like a slap in the face, stealing the breath from my lungs and making my eyes sting. I force my eyes open, trying to make sense of the blurry mess of limbs and what looks like a creature straight out of a Lovecraftian nightmare. But I don't have time to dwell on the fact that we're in a real-life horror movie. Rhyland needs me, and I'll be damned if I let some overgrown sushi roll take him out.

I don't waste a second; I blast my light. The water around me explodes a burst of pure energy so bright it's like an atomic bomb going off. The creature lets out a shriek that vibrates through the water like a physical thing, and then it's gone, scurrying away into the depths like the cowardly piece of shit it is.

Rhyland is there, breaking the surface with a gasp and a sputter, his face pale and his eyes wild. He looks like he just went ten rounds with a great white shark, but he's alive, and that's all that matters.

"Rhyland!" I yell, my voice cracking with relief as I grab him like a lifeline. He's weak and battered, his skin paler than a ghost, and his eyes glazed over with pain. But he reaches for me like I'm the last solid thing in the world, his fingers scrabbling at my arms. "We gotta climb, babe. Now."

Rhyland doesn't waste a second. He grips the rope, his muscles straining as he hauls us towards the wall. "Climb on, baby," he grits out, his voice rough with exhaustion and pain.

I don't argue. I clamber onto his back like a koala, wrapping my arms and legs around him as he starts to climb. His muscles strain with the effort, the veins in his arms standing out like cords as he hauls us up inch by painful inch.

Finally, we reach the ledge. I scramble over Rhyland's shoulder, my limbs shaking with adrenaline and exhaustion as I claw my way onto solid ground.

Rhyland is right behind me, his fingers scrabbling at the edge of the landing as he tries to haul himself up—his arms are trembling, and his grip is slipping. He's running on fumes and will fall if I don't do something fast.

I lunge forward, grabbing onto his arms and yanking with everything I've got. I can feel the veins in my neck popping, the muscles in my back screaming with the strain. But I don't let go. I can't let go.

"Come on, you stubborn bastard," I grunt, my teeth gritted with the effort. "Don't you dare quit on me now."

For a moment, I'm sure we're both going to go tumbling back into the water, but then Rhyland gets his feet under him and uses the momentum to propel himself up and over the ledge. He lands on top of me in a tangle of limbs and gasping breaths, his weight crushing the air from my lungs.

But I don't care. I don't care about anything except the fact that he's here, alive and safe. I wrap my arms around him and hold on like he's the only thing keeping me tethered to this world. My face is buried in the crook of his neck as I breathe in his scent, the solid, reassuring warmth of his body.

We lay there, gasping for air and trying to get our bearings.

Against all odds, against every fucking thing this hellhole has thrown at us, we're alive.

He takes a shuddering breath, his hand finding mine and gripping it tight. "I'm okay," he rasps, his voice thin and thready. "I'm okay, Angel."

I let out a sob of relief, "Don't you ever fucking do that again," I choke out, my words muffled by his skin. "Don't scare me—I can't lose you, Rhyland. I can't."

I know deep down it wasn't his fault, but holy hell. What else am I supposed to say right now? I was scared out of my ever-loving mind, so sue me for having a momentary freak-out.

Your brain doesn't fire on all cylinders when your man is inches from becoming some watery hellspawn's dinner. It's not like I had time to consult my "How to Gracefully Handle Near-Death Experiences" handbook.

I'm running on adrenaline, fear, and whatever's left of my sanity at this point.

He holds me tighter, his breath warm against my ear. "You won't," he promises, his voice fierce and strong. "I'm not going anywhere, baby. Not without you."

And I believe him. Because if there's one thing I know about Rhyland, it's that he's a stubborn son of a bitch who never breaks a promise. Not to me, not to anyone.

Rhyland looks down at me, his dark hair a wet, sopping mess dripping over my face. "Thank you," his voice rough with emotion. "I probably would've been that fucking thing's dinner if it wasn't for you."

Before I can even open my mouth to respond, he's crushing his lips against mine, kissing me with a desperate, hungry intensity. I can taste the fear and the relief on his tongue, feel the way his body trembles against mine with the aftershocks of adrenaline.

Of course, I'd save him—what, did he think I would let him become fish food? I didn't even think; I just acted. It's not like I had time to weigh the pros and cons of diving into monster-infested waters. "Save hot vampire boyfriend" was pretty much at the top of my to-do list.

He breaks away, his eyes so blue and intense they could melt icebergs. "But if you ever do something so fucking reckless again," he growls, his voice low and dangerous, "I will bend you over my knee and spank that sexy ass of yours until you can't sit for a week. You hear me, Angel?"

I can't help but roll my eyes, even as a shiver runs down my spine. "Oh please, like you could stop me. Someone's got to keep your stubborn ass alive, and it might as well be me. Besides," I add with a smirk, "is that supposed to be a threat or a promise?"

Rhyland's eyes darken, a wicked grin spreading across his face. "Oh, it's a fucking promise, baby. And you know I always keep my promises."

I arch an eyebrow, ignoring the heat pooling in my belly. "Big talk for a guy who just got his ass handed to him by the Loch Ness Monster's ugly cousin. Maybe you should focus on staying alive instead of making empty promises."

He growls, the sound sending tingles to my clit. "Empty promises? I'll show you empty promises, little angel." He leans in closer, his body radiating heat. "How about I bend you over right here and now, show you exactly what happens to naughty girls who don't listen?"

I swallow hard, my heart racing. But I'm not about to back down. "As tempting as that sounds, Sailor Stud, we've got bigger issues. Like, you know, saving the world and all that crap. But rain check?"

Rhyland chuckles, the sound low and dangerous. "Oh, don't you worry, baby—I'm going to cash in that rain check. And when I do, you will be begging for mercy."

I grin despite the heat in my cheeks. "Promises, promises. Now, how about we focus on getting out of this watery hellhole before you start writing checks your ass can't cash?"

Rhyland smirks, crushing his lips to mine again and kissing me with so much want and need that I'm pretty sure my toes are curling inside my soggy boots. When he finally pulls away, I'm left more breathless than if I'd just run a marathon underwater.

As much as I want to lose myself in the moment—and boy, do I want to—I know we don't have time for a steamy makeout session in the middle of this aquatic nightmare. I break away from the kiss, my chest heaving as I try to catch my breath and remember how to form coherent thoughts.

"Easy there, Sir Seduces-a-lot," I quip. "I know I'm irresistible, but we have a job to do. You can thank me properly later, preferably somewhere with a bed and a distinct lack of murderous sea monsters."

Rhyland's eyes flash with a heat that could probably boil the water around us. "Don't tempt me, woman," he rumbles, his voice low and dangerous enough to make my insides do a little happy dance. "I'll throw you over my fucking shoulder and find a bed right now if you keep looking at me like that."

I can't help but laugh, the sound echoing off the walls like a gunshot. "As much as I appreciate the caveman act, I think we both know that's a terrible idea," I say, my tone dry as the Sahara. "Besides, I'm not into exhibitionism. At least, not when there's a risk of tentacle monsters joining in."

He shakes his head, that infuriating smirk still playing at the corner of his mouth. "You sure about that, baby? 'Cause I seem to recall you getting all hot and bothered at the thought of me bending you over that table in the bar and showing everyone who you belong to."

I punch his chest, my face flushing hotter than a sunburned tomato. "That is so not true," I protest, but even I can hear the lie in my voice.

Because the truth is, the idea of Rhyland taking me like that, claiming me in front of everyone like the possessive alpha he is? It has me tingling in all the right places, a rush of heat pooling low in my belly.

Rhyland's eyes darken, his gaze raking over me like a physical caress. "Don't try to deny it, Angel. I can smell how much you want it, how much you *need* me to fucking own you."

I bite my lip, my thighs clenching together as I try to ignore the ache building between them. "You're delusional," I manage to get out, but my voice is breathy and weak, even to my ears.

Rhyland chuckles, the sound dark and wicked. "Keep telling yourself that, baby. But we both know the truth."

He leans in close, his breath hot against my ear. "One of these days, I'm going to bend you over in front of everyone and show them all who you belong to. I will make you scream my name so loud they'll never forget it."

I shudder, my eyes fluttering closed as his words wash over me. I can picture it so clearly—Rhyland's hands on my hips, his body pressed against mine as he takes me hard and fast, not caring who sees or hears.

It's wrong. It's dirty. It's so fucking hot I can barely stand it.

I flush even harder, my mind spinning with all the filthy, delicious possibilities. But I can't let myself get distracted—can't let him see how much he affects me, how easily he can turn me into a needy, desperate slut with just a few words. Not now, not when we're so close to getting out of this hellhole.

"As much as I'd love to lay here and listen to you talk dirty to me all day, we've got shit to do. So why don't you put your money where your mouth is and help me find this damn key?"

Rhyland's grin widens, his eyes glinting with a challenge. "Oh, I'll put my mouth wherever you want me to, Angel. Just say the word."

I roll my eyes but can't help but smile. "You're impossible."

"Yeah, but you love me anyway," he shoots back, his voice softening with affection.

I shake my head, my heart so full it feels like it might burst. "God help me, I do," I whisper, the words a confession and a prayer all at once.

Before I lose my nerve, I lean in and press a quick, hard kiss to his lips. "Now come on, big guy," I murmur against his mouth. "Let's find this key and get out of here. We've got a world to save and a future to plan, and I don't want to waste another second."

Rhyland grins, standing up and taking me with him. "Lead the way, baby. I'm right behind you."

LUCIAN

48

I decide it's time for a little change of scenery. I mean, don't get me wrong, kissing my beautiful girl on the upper deck with the sun setting and a bunch of smelly pirates is a kink I never knew I had, but I want my sweet little cinnamon roll all to myself. So, I blur us below deck hoping to find a quiet spot where we can really let loose.

Seraphina gasps as we suddenly stop, breaking away from our kiss like she's just surfaced from a deep dive. Her hair is mussed, her cheeks flushed, and her lips swollen from my attention.

In other words, she looks like a goddamn snack, and I'm ready to feast.

"That was... exhilarating," she breathes, her eyes sparkling with excitement and lust. And then, before I can even come up with a witty response, she launches herself at me like a sexy missile, her lips crashing into mine with a fervor that makes my knees weak.

Now, I pride myself on being a graceful motherfucker, but even I have my limits. Caught off guard by Seraphina's sudden attack, I stumble backward, my foot catching on a stray rope or a coil of netting or some other pirate-y bullshit that's littering the floor. And down we go, tumbling ass over teakettle into a pile of sails and rigging and whatever the fuck else they keep in these cargo holds.

"Oomph!" I grunt as the air is knocked out of my lungs, but Seraphina doesn't seem to notice. She's too busy trying to devour my face like it's the last supper, and she's starving.

But I'm not about to let a little thing like falling on my ass ruin the moment. I wrap my arms around her, holding her close. The floor beneath me is hard and unforgiving, but I barely feel it. All I can focus on is the way Seraphina's tongue is dancing with mine, the way her hands are roaming over my chest like she's trying to memorize every inch of me.

She's like a woman possessed, her lips never leaving mine as she grinds against me like a cat in heat. The feeling of her soft curves pressed against my rock-hard body is enough to make even a seasoned pervert like me blush.

Little Lucian is standing at attention, ready and willing to storm her castle. The way she's moving against me, all passion and need, is enough to drive me to the brink of insanity. I want nothing more than to flip her over and show her exactly what this vampire can do, to make her scream my name until the whole fucking ship knows who she belongs to.

"I think..." Seraphina starts, her breath coming in short, sharp gasps, "I'm addicted to kissing you. I could—" She slams her lips back onto mine, her tongue thrusting into my mouth with a skill that belies her innocence. "Kiss you all day."

Oh, sweet merciful *fuck*. If this is what she's like just from kissing, I can only imagine what a goddamn nymphomaniac she'll turn into once I really show her the ropes. The thought alone is enough to make my dick throb with anticipation.

"Show me more... please." Her words are like a fucking siren song, and I'm helpless to resist. Show her more? Oh, baby, I'll show her everything. I'll worship every inch of her perfect body until she's screaming my name like a prayer.

Seraphina straddles my waist, and I sit up—her nestled in my lap as my lips trail kisses and licks along the creamy expanse of her exposed breasts, peeking out tantalizingly from the top of her corset. She moans, the sound shooting straight to my dick as I work my way up her neck, nibbling and sucking at the delicate skin of her throat. My fangs ache—needing to taste her—I won't bite her, not yet. Not until she begs me for it. And from the way she's writhing against me, I have a feeling that won't be long.

She's grinding on my cock like she's trying to start a fucking fire, and it's taking every ounce of my self-control not to come right here and now, like some overexcited teenager. But I won't. I can't. Not until I've given her the pleasure she deserves.

My hands slide up under the hem of her skirt, caressing the smooth, supple skin of her thighs before cupping the most perfect tight ass in my existence. She squirms on top of me, her hips rocking in a rhythm that's as old as time itself, as I continue my assault on her neck, sucking and licking until she's panting and moaning like a bitch in heat.

She grabs my face, her fingers tangling in my hair as she pounces on my lips again, kissing me with a ferocity that steals my breath and my sanity in equal measure.

Fuuuuck, she's so needy and demanding, and I love every fucking second of it.

I lose myself in her, my tongue dancing with hers in a primal tango of lust and desire. Her taste, her scent, her fucking everything is driving me to the brink of madness, and I never want it to stop.

"Lucian... more." Her plea is like a command from the heavens, and I am but a humble servant eager to obey. With an agility born of centuries of practice, I untie her corset, the damn thing falling away, exposing the most perfect breasts I've ever seen.

Holy handfuls of heaven! These luscious mounds are like two perfectly ripe cantaloupes begging to be squeezed and savored. And perched atop each glorious globe? The most delectable, rosy little nubs that are practically screaming, "Suck me, lick me, worship me!"

I've seen my fair share of nip-tastic sights in my day, but these? These are the crème de la crème, the top shelf of titillation, the gold standard of glandular greatness.

"Holy unfiltered f-bombs," I mutter, with more awe than a geek at a comic con. "I think I just found my new religion."

I latch onto one, sucking and tugging gently as my hands come up to cup and squeeze, feeling the weight of her in my palms. She throws her head back, her eyes fluttering closed as she lets out a moan that could wake the dead.

"Yes..." she whispers. Her fingers grip my hair, guiding my mouth to feed on her perfect tits. "that feels so good, Lucian."

"Fuck, Phina-baby," I growl against her skin, my voice rough with need. "You're so goddamn perfect. I could feast on you for days and never get enough."

She whimpers, her fingers tightening in my hair as she arches into my touch, silently begging for more. And who am I to deny her?

I switch to her other breast, lavishing it with the same attention as the first, my tongue swirling and flicking over the hardened peak until she's trembling and gasping above me. My free hand slides down, skimming over the curve of her waist and the flare of her hips before dipping between her thighs to cup the heat of her through her underwear.

She's *soaked*, the thin fabric no match for the flood of her arousal, and the knowledge that I did that, that I made this perfect, angelic creature so wet and wanting, is almost enough to make me come on the spot.

"Please," she begs, her hips grinding down against my hand, seeking friction, seeking release. "Touch me—please, Lucian. I need... I need..."

"I know, baby girl," I murmur, my fingers stroking her through the damp fabric, teasing her with the promise of what's to come. "I know what you need. And I'm going to give it to you. I'm going to make you feel so fucking good; you'll forget how to breathe."

She whines, high and needy, and I know I can't tease her much longer. Not if I want to keep my sanity intact.

With a growl that's half pleasure, half pain, I tear her underwear away, the flimsy fabric shredding like tissue paper under my strength. And then, before she can even gasp at the sudden exposure, I'm sliding a finger deep inside her, curling it just so until I find that spot that makes her see stars.

"Oh, God!" she cries out, her head thrown back, her body bowing. "Lucian, yes. Right there, don't stop, please don't stop."

And I don't. I pump my finger in and out of her, my thumb finding her clit and rubbing in tight, hard circles until she's clenching around me, her walls fluttering and pulsing as she hurtles toward the edge of oblivion.

I grip her neck with my free hand, needing her to look at me; her eyes fly open, swirling pools of gold with flecks of silver, blown wide with lust, "That's it, sweetheart," I encourage her, my voice a low, filthy rasp. "Come for me. Let me feel you come. Let go for me; I want to drown in you."

I focus back on her perfect tits, sucking and licking like a man possessed, while my fingers are doing some awe-inspiring acrobatics inside her tight little pussy. And let me tell you, when I say tight, I mean fucking tight. My dick is weeping with joy in my pants, begging me to let it come out and play.

But as much as I want to bury myself inside her and never come out, I know I need to take this slow—to make sure she's good and ready before we get to the main event. And right now, I need to taste her more than anything. To taste the sweet nectar of her arousal on my tongue and feel her come apart under my mouth.

So, with a move that would make a ninja proud, I flip her over and yank up her skirt. She's panting and gasping, her perfect breasts heaving with each ragged breath, and I know she's close. So fucking close. It's not gonna take more than a few well-placed licks and sucks before she's coming all over my face like a fucking geyser.

"What... what are you doing?" she asks, her voice barely a whisper, confusion and anticipation warring in her tone. And fuck me sideways if that isn't the most adorable thing I've ever heard.

"I'm gonna take you to heaven, angel face," I purr, spreading her legs wide and getting my first real look at her pretty pink pussy. And holy mother of all that is good and pure in this world, she is perfect. Slick, shaved, and wet—glistening like a fucking diamond in the rough. I'm practically drooling at the sight of her, my mouth watering with the need to taste her.

"Ohh gods above..." I moan at the sight.

I dive right in. I lap at her engorged clit like a man dying of thirst, and she nearly bucks me off with the force of her reaction. Her hips jerk and twist, her body writhing under my touch, and I have to grip her thighs to keep her still.

"Oh! Oh, god... Yes. More. Do that again," she demands, her voice high and breathy and so fucking sexy.

I smirk against her skin, my ego swelling with pride at her reaction. This time, I wrap my lips around her clit and suck, flicking my tongue over the sensitive bundle of nerves in a rapid-fire rhythm that has her arching off the floor, her back bowed like a damn rainbow.

"Hold still, baby girl," I murmur, my breath ghosting over her slick skin, making her shiver and moan. "Let me make you feel good."

Fucking Christ, she's so wet. Dripping.

And with that, I go to town. I suck and lick and flick and nibble, my tongue delving deep inside her before coming back up to circle her clit, over and over again. She tastes like a fucking dream, all cotton candy and strawberries and honey, with a hint of something uniquely her. It's like every sweet thing I've ever tasted rolled into one, and I can't get enough.

I moan into her pussy, the vibrations making her gasp and clutch at my hair, her fingers threading through the strands and tugging almost painfully. But I don't care. I'd let her rip my hair out by the roots if it meant I could keep tasting her, keep feeling her come undone under my mouth.

My dick is throbbing in my pants so hard it feels like it might explode. But I ignore it, focusing all my attention on the writhing, moaning angel beneath me. I slip my finger back inside her warmth, curling it just so, and she lets out a sound that's halfway between a sob and a scream.

"Lucian! Ohh..." she cries, her hips bucking wildly, grinding against my face like she's trying to merge us into one being. "Lucian, please...don't...stop."

And I don't. I keep going, my finger pumping and my tongue swirling, building her higher and higher until I can feel her start to clench around me, her walls fluttering and pulsing with her impending release.

"That's it, beautiful," I encourage her, my voice muffled by her slick flesh. "Come for me. Come all over my face like the good girl you are."

And with one final, desperate cry, she does. Her body goes rigid as she shatters into a million pieces, her pussy clenching and spasming around my finger as she rides out the waves of her orgasm, her release coating my hand.

I keep licking her through it, my tongue gentle now, soothing her through the aftershocks until she relaxes, boneless and spent.

"Holy...oh my god," she gasps, her chest heaving as she tries to catch her breath. "That was... that was..."

"Amazing?" I supply, grinning up at her from between her thighs. "Mind-blowing? The best orgasm of your entire existence?"

She laughs, the sound breathless and giddy, and reaches down to haul me up her body until we're face to face. "All of the above," she says, her eyes shining with awe and adoration. "I never knew it could feel like...*that.*"

"Sweetheart," I murmur against her lips, brushing a strand of hair from her face and cupping her cheek in my palm. "That was just the beginning. I will make you feel things you never even dreamed were possible. I'm going to worship every inch of your body until you're screaming my name and making you a mess for me to clean up."

She shivers at my words, her eyes darkening with renewed desire, my dick twitches in my pants like a fucking divining rod.

Before I can keep my promise, the sound of footsteps on the stairs makes us freeze. Then, a voice that's all too familiar rings out in the cramped space of the cargo hold.

"Hey, lovebirds! You two better not be fuckin' in me ship's supplies!"

Fuck. Me. Running.

It's Gideon, and from the sound of it, he's not alone. I can hear Erik's gruff voice and Barnaby's annoying cackle echoing behind him, and I know our little moment of paradise is about to be rudely interrupted.

But you know what? I don't give a shit. Because I just gave my mate the most mind-blowing orgasm of her life, and nothing, not even a bunch of cockblocking pirates, can take that away from me.

So, with a grin that's half smug, half apologetic, I help Seraphina to her feet and start straightening out her clothes, quickly tying her corset back, trying to make her look a little less like she just got thoroughly debauched on the floor of a pirate ship.

"To be continued," I whisper in her ear, giving her a wink full of promise and mischief. "And next time, I'm going to make you scream so loud, they'll hear you in all seven realms."

She blushes, but a glint in her eye tells me she's more than up for the challenge.

DANICA

49

Rhyland and I scour the landing like a couple of desperate treasure hunters, looking for anything that might help us get our asses over to that pirate ship. I've got a gut feeling that's where the key is hiding, and if there's one thing I've learned, it's to trust my gut, even when it's telling me to do something that will probably get us killed.

Not to mention, my bracelet has been glowing non-stop since we swam into this cavern.

As I scan the area, my eyes land on valves jutting out from the walls on the opposite side of the cavern. "Hey, check it out," I say, pointing to the valves. "What do you think those are for?"

Rhyland follows my gaze. "Could be used to control the water levels."

I grimace, my mind racing with all the ways that could go horribly wrong. Messing with those valves is like playing Russian roulette with a fully loaded gun. We have no idea which valve does what, and if we accidentally add more water to this hellhole, we're going to be fish food faster than you can say, "Oh shit."

I start walking along the ledge, my eyes scanning the walls for other options. And then I see it—a section of the wall separating us from the back of the cavern, crumbling and weak like one strong breeze away from collapsing.

I make my way over to it, running my hands over the cracked and crumbling stone. "Think you can use your superpowers to blast this thing?"

Rhyland's eyebrows shoot up, his expression skeptical. "You sure that's a good idea? What if the whole damn place comes crashing down on our heads?"

I roll my eyes, my patience wearing thinner than a threadbare thong. "Got any better ideas, tough guy? We need to get over there." I point to the back of the cavern, where I can see solid ground and a clear path to the ship.

Rhyland's jaw clenches, his eyes darting between the wall and the valves like he's trying to calculate the odds of survival. "Fuck it," he mutters, his hand clenching into a fist. "Stand back, baby. This might get messy."

I scramble back, my heart pounding as Rhyland approaches the wall. He closes his eyes in concentration as he reaches out with his power.

For a moment, nothing happens. Then, with a crack like a gunshot, the wall explodes outward, sending chunks of stone and debris flying through the air like shrapnel.

I yelp, ducking down and covering my head as bits of rock rain around us. When the dust settles, I peek out from behind my arms, my eyes widening at the sight of the gaping hole in the wall.

"Holy shit," I breathe, my voice shaking with awe and disbelief. "Nice work."

We peer through the hole like a couple of kids trying to sneak a peek at their Christmas presents, our eyes scanning the area for any sign of danger. But nothing but a vast, cavernous space stretches before us.

The sound of rushing water fills my ears, and I cock my head to the side, trying to pinpoint the source. "Do you hear that?" I ask Rhyland, my voice echoing off the walls like a ghostly whisper.

He nods, his eyes narrowing as he listens. "It sounds like a waterfall."

From how the sound bounces around the cavern, I'm guessing it's somewhere outside.

We go through the opening, picking our way over the rubble and debris like mountain goats. The cavern opens up even more as we go, revealing a world of glowing algae and scattered pirate shit that looks like it's been here since the dawn of time.

The smell of salt and decay clings to the back of my throat like a sour aftertaste. It's like someone left a fish to rot in a locker room, and the stench is enough to make my eyes water, and I have to fight the urge to gag. But I push through it, my eyes fixed on the prize ahead.

We wind our way around the cavern until we're on the backside of the pirate ship, the hulking mass of wood and metal looming over us like a giant. It's still a reasonable distance away, but we can see a way to get to it from this angle.

"I think if we can tie a rope up there," I say, pointing to a beam that looks like it's been grown into the walls like a tree, "maybe we can swing across like a couple of discount Tarzans."

Rhyland raises an eyebrow. "Discount Tarzans? Really?"

I shrug, a grin spreading across my face. "Hey, if the loincloth fits..."

He shakes his head, a chuckle rumbling in his chest. "You're ridiculous, you know that?"

I wink at him, my heart skipping at how his eyes darken with desire.

"There's a plank we can jump onto over there," Rhyland points to a rickety-looking board sticking out of the ship's side like a rotting tooth. "That seems like our best bet."

I follow his gaze. "You've got to be kidding me," my voice flat with disbelief. "That thing looks like it's one strong fart away from crumbling into sawdust."

Rhyland grins, the expression cocky and infuriating and sexy as hell. "What's the matter, baby? Afraid of a little adventure?"

I snort, "Adventure? More like a one-way ticket to a watery grave. That thing wouldn't hold a stuffed animal—let alone two grown-ass adults."

Rhyland's grin widens, his eyes glinting with a challenge. "Only one way to find out."

I shake my head, my stomach churning with fear and exasperation. "No way. No fucking way. I am not risking my life on a piece of driftwood that looks like it's been chewed up and spit out by Jaws himself."

Rhyland is done with my bullshit. He takes off like a bullet, leaping for the plank like he's got springs in his feet. He makes it in one jump, gripping the side and hauling himself up like it's nothing. His muscles strain against his shirt, and I can't help but stare in appreciation a little, even in the middle of this life-or-death situation.

He stands up, stomping on the plank to prove a point. "Looks pretty damn sturdy to me."

I roll my eyes, my heart pounding as I realize what he expects me to do. "Okay, smartass," I mutter under my breath.

"Your turn, baby," he calls out. "Just run and don't stop. I'll catch you." He says it like it's the easiest thing in the world as if he's asking me to toss him a beer from across the room.

Jesus Christ. I know I've got some serious Neo-level moves regarding combat, but long jumps? That's a hard pass. With my luck, I'd probably do a graceful swan dive straight into the water, only to become a snack for our friendly neighborhood sea monster. No thanks, I'll leave the Olympic-level leaps to the professionals and stick to kicking ass on solid ground.

But Rhyland, being the stubborn bastard he is, isn't taking no for an answer. "You got this, Angel," his voice softening slightly. "Come on."

I take a deep breath, my heart pounding like a jackhammer. I step back as far as I can, my eyes scanning the area for anything that might give me an advantage. And then I see it—a slight rise in the ground, just to my right. It's not much, but it might be enough to give me the boost I need.

I map out my jump like Sherlock Holmes, using the rise as a makeshift launching pad. I can practically see the equations floating in front of my eyes, the trajectory of my leap calculated down to the millimeter.

I'm gonna freaking die.

With a silent prayer, I dig my heels in and sprint like my life depends on it, which it does.

I wait until the exact second, my feet hitting the rise in the ground like I'm stepping on a trampoline. And then I launch myself into the air, my arms outstretched.

For a moment, I'm sure I will miss my mark. Rhyland and the plank seem to be moving away from me, the distance growing larger every second. But then, I feel this pull—like a magnet, my fingers close around Rhyland's wrist, his grip firm and sure on my arms.

I'm hanging on for dear life, my legs and lungs burning with the effort. But Rhyland, being the show-off he is, lifts me like I weigh nothing, crushing me against his chest as he blurs us off the narrow plank onto the ship's deck.

I collapse against him, my heart pounding. "Jesus," I gasp, my voice shaking with adrenaline and relief. "That was..."

Rhyland grins, his arms tightening around me like he'll never let go. "Told you I'd catch you, baby."

It had to be his telekinesis. That's the only explanation for how I felt like I was suddenly auditioning for Cirque du Soleil mid-air, defying gravity and managing to stick that landing like an Olympic gymnast.

One second, I think, "Well, this is how I die," and the next, I float through the air like Mary Poppins on a sugar high.

"Okay, Obi-Wan. Did you use your Jedi mojo to turn me into a human projectile? Because I'm pretty sure I didn't grow wings in the last five minutes."

Rhyland, the smug bastard, grins. "What can I say, baby? I couldn't let you go for another swim with our resident sea monster. Besides, you've got to admit, it was pretty impressive."

I roll my eyes. I hate to admit it, but I know he's right. Rhyland will always be there to catch me, no matter how far I fall.

We waste no time scouring the ship, looking for anything resembling a key. The boards creak and groan beneath our feet, but they hold steady, which is a minor miracle, considering this vessel looks like it's been around for centuries.

We find a set of stairs leading below deck, and as we descend into the ship's bowels, my jaw nearly hits the floor. We're greeted by a treasure trove that would make even the most seasoned pirate weep joyfully.

"Well, slap my ass and call me a landlubber," I breathe, my eyes wide with wonder. "This is quite the haul."

Everywhere I look, treasure chests overflow with glittering jewels, shiny coins, and enough gold to make Midas himself green with envy. The entire floor is blanketed in a sea of riches, the sheer luxury almost blinding.

Rhyland, being the cocky bastard he is, apparently takes my snarky commentary as an open invitation. He delivers a sharp smack to my leather-clad ass, the crack of it echoing through the chamber like a gunshot.

"Damn straight, it's a haul."

I squeal and whip around, my eyes narrowing to slits as I level him with my most withering glare. "Excuse you, Captain Grabby Hands," I snap, "I was speaking metaphorically, not issuing an invitation."

Rhyland smirks, "Don't pretend you don't love it, baby. That sweet little ass of yours was made for my hands."

I snort, "Oh, I'll show you sweet, Bitey Boy," I mutter, my tone dark with promise. "Keep it up, and you'll sleep with that tentacle creature tonight."

Rhyland grins, utterly unfazed by my threat. "Bring it on, Angel. You know I can take anything you dish out and beg for more."

I laugh, "Oh, I'll make you beg all right," I mutter darkly, my eyes glinting with mischief. "Beg for mercy when I'm through with you, Rhy-Pie."

Rhyland's brows furrow like he's just now catching onto my creative name game. "What's with all the damn nicknames?" He growls, and I can tell I'm getting under his skin in the most delicious way possible.

I smirk, batting my eyelashes innocently. "Aw, what's wrong? Not feeling the love, Fjord Fluff?"

"Not entirely," he grumbles, his nose wrinkling adorably. "Especially *Rhy-Pie*. Sounds like something you'd call a fucking cupcake."

I laugh, "Well, get used to it, babe. I've got a whole arsenal of pet names locked and loaded, ready to make you blush like a schoolgirl."

Rhyland grins, his teeth flashing white in the dim light. "Fuck, I love it when you get all feisty," he growls, his voice a low rumble that sends shivers down my spine and makes my nipples tingle. "Gets me rock hard for you."

He stalks closer, his movements predatory and full of intent. "Keep sassing me like that, and I might just have to put that smart mouth of yours to better use."

I tilt my chin up defiantly, meeting his heated gaze with a challenge of my own. "Bring it on," I taunt, my tongue darting out to wet my lips. "I can handle anything you dish out."

Rhyland chuckles darkly, his hands coming to rest on my hips as he pulls me flush against him. I can feel the hard length of him pressing insistently against my stomach, and it takes every ounce of my self-control not to grind against him like a cat in heat.

"Tread carefully, baby," he murmurs, his breath hot against my ear. "You know what I'm capable of."

I huff out a breath, torn between the desire to knee him in the balls and the urge to climb him like a tree. "Keep it in your pants, Neanderthal," I grumble, poking him in the chest with one finger. "We've got a job to do, remember?"

Rhyland catches my hand in his, his grip firm and unyielding. "Oh, I remember," he murmurs, his eyes burning into mine with an intensity that steals my breath. "But don't think for a second that I will forget this little moment. Once we're done here, I will remind you who's in charge."

"You're impossible," I mumble, trying and failing to hide my smile. "Can we please focus on the task at hand? You know, the whole 'saving the world' thing we came here for?"

Rhyland chuckles, the sound rich and dark. Then, he changes the subject. "How do we know what we're looking for? I know it's a key, but did Calypso give you any indication of what it might look like?"

I shake my head, my lips pursed in a frown. "No, she was frustratingly vague on the details. We'll have to dig through this mess and hope for the best. It's got to be here somewhere, right?"

Rhyland nods, his jaw set with determination. "Right. Let's get to work."

I spot a desk in the corner as we navigate through the hoard. Its surface is littered with ancient maps and nautical charts. It's like stepping into a time capsule, a glimpse into the life of a long-dead pirate captain.

We split up, each tackling a different section of the treasure hoard. I start with the desk, rifling through the maps and charts. But as the minutes tick by and the key remains elusive, I can feel my frustration mounting.

"This is like looking for a needle in a goddamn haystack," I grumble, tossing aside a particularly ornate compass. "We could be here for days and still come up empty-handed."

Rhyland looks up from the chest he's been rummaging through, his eyes glinting with amusement. "What, you're not enjoying our little treasure hunt? And here I thought you were the adventurous type."

I shoot him a withering glare, my hands on my hips. "Oh, I'm plenty adventurous, big guy. But even I have my limits. If I have to sort through one more pile of cursed doubloons, I might lose my mind."

Rhyland chuckles, the sound rich and warm in the musty air of the ship's hold. "Well, we can't have that, can we? Tell you what, why don't we make this a little more interesting?"

I raise an eyebrow, intrigued despite myself. "I'm listening."

He grins, the expression equal parts wicked and charming. "The first one to find the key gets to choose where we go on our first real date when we return to our realm. Loser has to pay up in sexual favors."

I consider this momentarily, my mind racing with possibilities. "Deal," my voice firm with resolve. "But just so you know, I have a very vivid imagination. You'd better hope you can handle what I dream up."

Rhyland's eyes darken, and his gaze rakes over me in a way that makes my skin tingle. "Oh, trust me, baby," he purrs. "I have no intention of losing this bet. I hope you're ready to pay up when I win."

I flush, my cheeks heating with desire. What sexual favors could he possibly have in mind this time? Knowing him, it'll be wild and daring, like our last little adventure at Playful Pint.

The thought makes my clit ache, my body reacting to the memory of that night. The way he took control and pushed me to my limits and beyond... It was equally thrilling and terrifying, and I'd be lying if I said I didn't want to do it again.

But I'm not about to let him know that. Not yet, anyway. First, I have to win this bet and show him just how creative I can be when it comes to pleasure and pain.

"Bring it on, big boy," I taunt, my lips curving in a smirk. "I hope you're ready to worship at the altar of my body because when I win, you're going to be my personal sex slave for the night."

Rhyland growls, the sound low and primal in his throat. "Fuck, baby," he rasps, his eyes blazing with hunger. "You keep talking like that, and I might just let you win on purpose."

I laugh, the sound bright and teasing in the musty air of the ship. "Where's the fun in that?" I quip. "I want to earn my prize fair and square. And trust me, when I do, you'll be begging me for mercy."

Rhyland's grin widens, "We'll see about that, Little Angel. You seem to forget who the fuck begs in this relationship."

After hours and hours of digging through this endless sea of shiny shit, we're still coming up empty-handed on the key front. I'm starting to wonder if this whole treasure hunt is just one big cosmic joke or if we somehow managed to take a wrong turn and end up in Davy Jones' fucking junk drawer.

I come across another crumbling map that looks like it's been through hell and back. *Tempest Isle* is scrawled across the top in fancy lettering, with a detailed image of a key in the corner and what looks like a harp marked on a specific location.

This is the location Calypso told me about.

I show Rhyland, my eyebrows raised in a silent question. "That's the island Gideon mentioned," he grunts, his eyes narrowing as he studies the map.

"Calypso, too. And I'm guessing this fancy-ass harp is the Siren's Lyre," I quip, my tone dry. I look closer at the key, my nose wrinkling at the sight of the creepy-ass skeleton on the tip, complete with jagged teeth and a blue jewel set into the eye sockets. "Bingo," I smile. "This is what we need to find if we want to get the hell out of this underwater hellhole."

Suddenly, a voice hisses in my mind, making me jump. *"Free me, and I will give you the key,"* it rasps, scaring the ever-loving shit out of me.

I whip around, nearly face-planting in the process. Rhyland is immediately at my side, his arms wrapping around me. "What the hell, baby?" he growls, his eyes wide with concern. "What's wrong?"

"Did you not hear that creepy-ass voice just now?" my voice shaking.

Rhyland frowns, his grip on me tightening. "No, I didn't hear shit," his tone laced with worry. But then his eyes lock onto my crown, widening with realization. "The stone," he breathes, his voice barely above a whisper. "It's glowing. The Faerite..."

My head begins to buzz like a swarm of angry bees, and that's when it hits me. That slimy, tentacled fucker from the depths is trying to chat me up like we're old pals.

"It's that thing in the water."

"Sorry, sushi boy," I respond, *"I don't deal with creatures with more arms than a Hindu goddess. You can take your offer and shove it up your fishy ass."*

Rhyland's eyes go wide, his jaw clenching with tension. "Really? What the hell is it saying?"

I nod, my stomach churning with fear and disgust. "It wants me to set it free in exchange for the key. Because that's totally a legit offer and not at all a trap."

The Faerite stone is like a damn cosmic telephone, letting me chat it up with every creature under the sun—or in this case, under the sea. But let me tell you, having some tentacled freak of nature whispering in your head is about as pleasant as a root canal without anesthesia.

I can feel the thing's hunger, desperation, and all-consuming need to break free from this underwater prison it's trapped in. It's like a leech, latching onto my mind and trying to suck me dry of any sympathy or goodwill.

Suddenly, the ship lurches beneath our feet, the creature's rage manifesting in a physical tantrum that nearly sends us sprawling. I cling to Rhyland, my heart pounding in my throat.

"Okay, okay," I gasp. "Maybe we could—I don't know—figure out how to spring Cthulhu from his watery cage."

Rhyland's grip on me tightens as he tries to make sense of my sudden change of heart. "How the fuck—?" But then his eyes widen, a glimmer of understanding dawning on his ruggedly handsome face. "Tell that thing we'll help it out, but only if it coughs up the key first. No key, no freedom, got it?"

I grin, "One order of blackmail. Coming right up."

I close my eyes, focusing on the slimy, slithering presence in my mind. *"Listen up, sushi breath,"* my voice firm and unyielding. *"We'll help you out of your little predicament, but only if you hand over the key first. No negotiations, no exceptions. You want your freedom? Then you better pony up the goods."*

Rhyland and I cling to each other, our hearts pounding in sync as we wait for the creature's next move. The silence stretches on, broken only by the creaking of the ancient ship and the distant sound of water lapping against the hull.

Suddenly, a splash echoes outside, followed by a loud thunk rattling the deck above our heads. We exchange a look of, "Oh shit," before scrambling up the stairs like our asses are on fire.

A brown leather box sits on the deck like a gift from the gods of bad decisions. I lunge for it, fumbling with the latch to open it.

And there it is—the skeleton key, its blue gem eyes glinting up at me like a beacon of hope in this underwater hellscape.

"I've given you what you desire; now give me mine," the creature demands, its voice slithering through my mind like an eel through seaweed.

I turn to Rhyland, my eyes wide with triumph and terror. "It wants us to hold up our end of the bargain," my voice trembling slightly. "But how the hell are we supposed to free it? And more importantly, how the hell do we get out of here?"

"The valves," his voice low and urgent. "That has to be the way."

Rhyland marches over to the ship's side like a man on a mission, his jaw clenched tight. I watch, half-impressed and half-terrified, as he zeroes in on those valves as if they've personally offended him.

He raises his hands, and then, holy shit, those valves start moving. They're creaking and groaning like arthritic joints, spinning as if possessed by some demented poltergeist.

The whole scene is equal parts impressive and utterly terrifying. Because let's face it, when your vampire boyfriend starts playing ghostly puppeteer with ancient underwater plumbing, you know things are about to get really interesting. And by "interesting," I mean potentially catastrophic.

For a moment, the world seems to hold its breath, the silence broken only by the creaking of the ancient ship and the thundering of my heart in my ears. But then, with a groan and a squeal that sounds like the gates of hell opening, all chaos breaks loose.

Water geysers out of the walls like fire hoses, the pipes bursting and spraying like a ruptured artery. The room fills with water so fast, the level rising higher and higher until the ship starts to bob like a cork on the ocean.

"Rhyland!" I shriek, my voice hitting octaves only dogs should hear as I stare up at the rocky ceiling looming over us like the world's worst game of 'Will It Crush Us?'

"Care to share which part of your brilliant master plan covered us becoming the world's most fucked-up submarine sandwich?"

Rhyland grins, that infuriating, cocky smirk that makes me want to kiss him and smack him at the same time. He swoops me up, and I squeal as he carries me below deck.

He sits me on a desk, his hands firm and reassuring on my hips. "Those walls are going to crumble like a sandcastle at high tide," he explains, his voice rough with adrenaline. "The pressure's too much—they don't stand a fucking chance."

I stare at him like he's lost his mind, my eyes wide with disbelief. I quickly peek out the portside window, and sure enough, the walls are starting to crack and crumble like they're made of paper mache.

The ship lurches forward, and I go flying, my heart leaping into my throat as I brace myself for impact.

Rhyland is there, his arms wrapping around me like a safety net, his body solid and reassuring against mine. "Hold on tight, Angel," he murmurs, his breath hot against my ear. "It's gonna be one hell of a ride."

My eyes widen as the realization hits me. "Wait," I gasp, my voice barely audible over the roar of the rushing water. "Are you saying what I think you're saying? Are we about to go over a fucking waterfall?"

Rhyland grins, his eyes glinting with excitement and something darker—a look that makes me want to smack the shit out of him. "Bingo, baby. God, you're so fucking smart."

Before I can process anything, his lips crash against mine in a searing kiss as the ship pitches forward. That gut-wrenching, weightless sensation hits me, and I can't help it—I scream.

"I HATE WATERFALLS!"

RHYLAND

50

I wrap my arms around Dani, holding her close against my chest as we brace ourselves for the inevitable impact. The ship plummets through the air, the force making my stomach lurch and my heart hammer against my ribs. The weightlessness is disorienting, a sickening sensation of freefall that seems to stretch forever.

And then, with a bone-jarring jolt, the ship suddenly stops mid-fall, the momentum sending us flying forward. I twist my body at the last second, taking the brunt of the impact as we slam into the wall with a sickening crunch. Pain explodes through my shoulder and back, a white-hot agony that steals the breath from my lungs.

The ship is tilted at a precarious angle, the nose pointing straight down into the churning water below. I can feel it swaying and creaking beneath us, the ancient timbers groaning under its weight. We must've snagged on a rocky outcropping or a hidden reef, but I know it's only a matter of time before the ship tears itself free and plunges into the depths.

I try to push myself up, my muscles screaming in protest as I struggle to find purchase on the tilted deck. Before I can get to my knees, the ship drops again, the sudden jolt slamming me back against the wall with a force that makes my vision blur and my ears ring. Dani screams, a piercing, terrified sound that echoes through the cramped space like a banshee's wail.

The ship swings wildly against the current, the waterfall's relentless pounding making the whole structure shudder and groan like a wounded beast. The deck beneath us is slick with spray and algae, making it almost impossible to find a grip. Every time I try to stand, the ship pitches and rolls, sending me stumbling back to my knees.

Dani clings to me like a lifeline, her face buried against my chest as she trembles. I can feel her fear pulsing through our bond, a sickening, all-consuming terror that threatens to drown us both. But I can't let it take hold or let it paralyze me. Not now, not when our lives depend on my clear head.

"Hold on to me, baby," I rasp, my voice barely audible over the roar of the water and the ship's creaking. "I'm going to try to get us out of here."

Dani nods, her arms nearly choking me as she wraps herself around my front. I take a deep breath, steeling myself against the pain, the fear, and the overwhelming sense of helplessness that threatens to crush me. With a grunt of effort, I lunge forward, half-crawling, half-dragging us toward the gaping hole in the ship's side.

It's a nightmare of jagged edges and splintered wood, a yawning abyss that seems to swallow the light. But it's our only way out, our only chance of escape before the ship finally gives way.

The spray from the waterfall is blinding, stinging my eyes and making it almost impossible to see. But I keep pushing, my muscles burning as I haul us both towards the edge.

I lunge forward, my fingers scrabbling for purchase on the ship's ripped siding. The jagged edges of the torn wood bite into my palms, but I barely feel the pain. All I can focus on is the death grip Dani has on me, her arms wrapped around me so tightly I can barely breathe.

"I need you to grab the rocks," I shout over the waterfall's roar, my voice raw and desperate. "Can you do that, Angel? I won't let you fall, I promise."

Dani nods, her face pale and streaked with tears, but I can see the determination in her eyes. She reaches out with shaking hands, her fingers clawing at the wet-slicked side panels of the ship as she starts to crawl toward the gaping hole in the hull.

The water pours down around us in a relentless torrent, making the wood slick and treacherous beneath our feet. I can feel it pounding against my back, the force of it threatening to rip me away from my precarious perch at any second.

But I grit my teeth and hold on, my muscles screaming with effort as I brace myself against the ship's crumbling frame. My foot finds a hold on something solid, a jutting piece of timber or a rusted nail, and I use it to push myself upwards, shoving Dani through the jagged opening with a grunt of effort.

The darkness beyond is absolute. I have no idea how high up we are or what horrors might be waiting for us on the other side. But I don't let myself think about it or let the fear take hold. All that matters is getting Dani to safety, no matter the cost.

"I got it!" Dani's voice rings out over the din of the waterfall and the ship's dying groans. I glance out the side of the hull and see her standing on a small ledge on the cliffside, her fingers digging into the slick, moss-covered rocks like claws.

A wave of relief washes over me, so strong it weakens my knees. But I don't have time to savor it, don't have time to do anything but move. I haul myself up, and through the opening, my hands scrabbling for purchase on the cliff face as I try to wedge myself into the narrow space beside Dani.

She scoots over as much as she can, her body pressed flat against the rocks to give me room. I feel the heat of her through my soaked clothes, the rapid rise and fall of her chest as she pants for breath.

I get a grip on the cliff, my fingers digging into the crevices and fissures of the stone. I take a deep breath, my heart hammering against my ribs as I prepare to jump, to launch myself towards the safety of the ledge above.

Before I can even tense my muscles and move, the ship beneath me gives a final, shuddering groan, and the world drops out from under my feet.

I hear Dani scream, a high, piercing sound that cuts through the waterfall's roar like a knife. My stomach lurches, and my heart stops as the ship plummets away beneath me. The hull spins and cracks as it hurtles toward the churning water below.

"Rhyland!"

Fucking hell.

For a single, terrifying second, I'm hanging in midair, my fingers scrabbling uselessly against the slick rock as I start to fall. By some miracle of fate or sheer dumb luck, my hand finds a hold, a tiny outcropping of stone that bites into my palm.

I hang there, my arms straining and my fingers bleeding, as the ship crashes into the base of the falls with a sickening crunch of wood and metal. The sound echoes through the chasm like a death knell, a final, haunting reminder of how close we came to joining the wreckage below.

What the fuck was I thinking, letting us go over in the ship like that?

I find a foothold and pull myself up, "It's okay, I'm okay, baby," I pant, my voice ragged with exhaustion as I try to ease the panic I can feel thrumming through our bond. Dani lets out a shuddering breath, her fingers digging into my arm like she's afraid I'll disappear if she lets go.

Even as I try to reassure her and cling to her like a lifeline, I can't ignore the cold, creeping dread that's taking hold in my stomach. Because now that the immediate danger has passed, now that we're no longer hanging off the edge of a fucking cliff, I'm starting to realize just how fucked we are.

I look around, my eyes straining to pierce the gloom, but all I can see is a yawning abyss of black water, the waterfall pounding down around us in a deafening roar. It's like being trapped in the heart of a fucking hurricane, the wind and the spray and the sheer, overwhelming power of it making it almost impossible to think straight.

"What do we do?" Dani shouts, her voice barely audible over the crashing water.

I grit my teeth, my mind racing as I devise a plan. I catch something that makes my heart skip a beat out of the corner of my eye. The cliff face to our right, which had seemed like a dead end just moments before, is starting to curve inward, the stone worn smooth by centuries of pounding water.

I tug on Dani's hand, jerking my head towards the narrow ledge, starting to take shape in the shadows. She nods, her eyes wide with understanding, and together, we begin to inch our way along the wall, our backs pressed flat against the slick stone as we baby-step through the spray.

It's slow going, each step a heart-stopping gamble as we test the rock beneath our feet, praying that it won't crumble away and send us plummeting into the abyss. We keep moving and pushing forward, our hands clasped so tightly.

Finally, after an eternity of gut-churning terror, I see it. A flat stretch of ground just behind the waterfall, a tiny oasis of safety amid the chaos.

I guide Dani towards it, my hand never leaving hers as we stumble and slip across the final few feet of treacherous stone. And then, at last, we're there, collapsing onto the blessedly solid ground in a tangle of shaking limbs and heaving lungs.

I pull Dani into my arms, burying my face in her damp hair as I hold her close. My heart is pounding with a clusterfuck of emotions—relief, gratitude, and a whole damn lot of others I can't even begin to put a name to.

Dani sits up and punches me in the chest. Hard. "What the actual fuck, Rhyland?" She shouts over the pounding water, her voice sharp with anger and disbelief.

I lay there, taking her fury like a man. I know I fucked up, and I'm kicking myself in the ass for my dumbass decision. She could have fucking died falling through that waterfall. "I'm sorry," I pant out, still trying to catch my breath. "I'm so fucking sorry, baby. I wasn't thinking."

"No shit, Captain Clueless!" Dani spats above me, swatting as I cover my head in a feeble attempt to defend myself. "That was really stupid, Rhyland. Like, epic levels of dumbassery."

I grab her hands and pull her down to my chest, meeting her fierce, molten gold eyes. They're filled with anger, frustration, and, beneath it all, an unwavering love that humbles me. I grip her hair, holding her gaze steady. "I know, baby. It was stupid and careless as fuck. I swear to god, it won't happen again."

"It better not," she grumbles, still glaring at me. "Or I'll kick your ass myself, you reckless bastard."

I miscalculated, plain and simple. I thought we weren't that far up, but those fucking caves and tunnels played tricks on my senses.

Not an excuse, just a cold hard fact.

Dani softens, collapsing onto my chest with a heavy sigh. I can feel her heart pounding against my own, the adrenaline still coursing through her veins. "I'm just glad we made it," she murmurs, her voice muffled against my skin. "But seriously, Rhyland, if you ever pull a stunt like that again, I will personally ensure that your dick falls off from lack of use. We clear?"

I wince at the threat, knowing full well she means every word. "Crystal fucking clear, Angel," I assure her, my hand rubbing soothing circles on her back. "I promise, no more dumbass stunts. From now on, it's safety first, all the way."

She nods, satisfied with my answer, and I let out a breath I didn't realize I was holding. Crisis averted, for now at least. But fuck, if this little misadventure hasn't hammered home just how much I need to get my shit together. Dani deserves better than a mate who risks her life with careless decisions.

"Please tell me you didn't lose the key," I rasp, my voice muffled against her skin.

Dani pulls back, her eyes blazing with a fierce, unshakeable determination that catches my breath. "Got it," a triumphant grin spreads across her face as she pulls the box from her pocket.

I let out a breathless laugh, my head falling against the stone as the tension drains from my body. Thank fuck. I don't even want to think about what we would've had to do if that key had ended up at the bottom of the falls.

Before I begin to savor the victory—even open my mouth to tell Dani how fucking amazing she is, the ground beneath us lets out an ominous groan, and the world starts to tilt sideways.

What the fuck now?

I scramble to find purchase on the slick stone, my fingers clawing uselessly at the rock as I feel myself starting to slide. Dani is struggling beside me, her eyes wide with terror as she tries to brace herself against the crumbling ledge.

But it's no use. The ground is too wet, too unstable—we're falling, plummeting down the side of the cliff like a couple of ragdolls.

I hit the ground hard, the impact driving the air from my lungs and sending a bolt of agony shooting through my battered body. I can hear Dani somewhere nearby, her breath coming in ragged gasps as she tries to push herself onto her hands and knees.

I crawl towards her, my vision blurring and my head spinning as I try to focus through the pain. I reach her and pull her close. The ground shifts again, and we're falling, tumbling head over heels into the darkness below.

I hear Dani scream, the sound cutting through the roar of the water and the pounding of my own heart. I feel the rush of the wind, the sting of the spray, the sickening lurch of my stomach as we plummet into the unknown.

And then, with a bone-jarring thud that feels like getting hit by a fucking semi-truck, we hit the ground again, Dani on top of me, and the world goes black and silent and still like the goddamn grave.

I come to with the taste of Dani's sweet blood on my tongue, her voice cutting through the fog in my head like the sweetest beacon. "Rhyland, sweetie. Come on." I blink, my vision swimming as I try to focus on her face. She's got her wrist slit, the crimson liquid dripping down her arm as she presses it to my lips.

I don't hesitate, my instincts taking over as I latch onto her wrist and gulp down the life-giving elixir like a man dying of thirst. The power of it surges through me, knitting my bones and mending my wounds with every swallow.

I sit up, my head clearing as the last of the fog dissipates. And that's when I see it—the pain etched into every line of Dani's face, the way she's holding her side like it's about to fucking fall off. And she's worried about *me*? After taking a fall that could've fucking killed her?

Not on my watch.

"Come here," I growl, my voice rough with concern as I feel her pain pulsing through our bond like a damn siren.

She winces, her face twisting in agony as she tries to move away from me. "I think I broke a couple of ribs and maybe my ankle."

Fuck that noise. I don't waste a goddamn second, tearing into my wrist with my fangs and shoving it towards her mouth. "Drink," I command, my tone leaving no room for argument or any of her sassy bullshit.

My blood seeps out, dripping down her chin as she latches on and drinks deep. I can feel the power of it flowing into her, mending her broken bones and knitting her wounds back together.

"That's it, baby. Fuck. I'm so sorry." As I watch her drink, the words are a rough whisper, a plea for forgiveness. Her caramel-gold eyes snap open, locking onto mine with a heat that makes my blood fucking sing. I can see the pain receding, replaced by a heady mix of lust and love and want that makes me want to fuck her right here on this fucking cave floor.

I pull my wrist away when I'm sure she's had enough, gathering her into my arms and holding her close as I listen to the snap and pop of her bones knitting back together. I know she's got that fancy-ass rock to heal her, but I'm not about to sit on my ass and wait for it to do its job when I can get it done faster and better.

I take a moment to survey our surroundings, my eyes adjusting to the dim light of the underground cavern. I spot a calm, blue pool surrounded by glittering, electric-blue rocks that cast an eerie glow over everything. It's beautiful, in a creepy sort of way.

The same ethereal, blue glow emanates from the rocks beneath the water's surface, casting a mesmerizing light that dances and shimmers through the crystal-clear depths. It's like something out of a dream, a hidden oasis of beauty and calm amid all this chaos.

"Looks inviting," Dani purrs, her lips brushing against the sensitive skin of my neck. She stands slowly, testing out her newly healed ankle with a cautious step. "Damn, that blood of yours is amazing stuff."

I rise with her, a smirk tugging at the corner of my mouth as I meet her gaze. "Not as good as yours, baby." I throw in a wink for good measure.

Dani's eyes darken the heat in them enough to set me on fucking fire. But instead of launching herself at me as I half-expect her to, she turns her back, strolling over to the edge of the pool with an extra sway in her hips that makes my mouth go dry.

Without a word, she starts to undress, her fingers deftly unzipping her top and shrugging it off her shoulders like a goddamn tease. I stand there, transfixed, as she reveals inch after tantalizing inch of smooth, golden skin; the curve of her spine and the dimples at the base of her back are enough to make me weak in the knees.

But it's when she hooks her thumbs into the waistband of her pants and shimmies them down over the luscious swell of her ass that I nearly lose my goddamn mind. I'm half-convinced that I will spontaneously combust from the sheer, overwhelming need coursing through my veins.

She toes off her boots, kicking them aside with a careless flick of her foot, and then she steps into the water, a sigh of pure bliss falling from her lips as the cool liquid envelops her like a lover's embrace.

And fuck me, the sight of her like that—naked and glistening in the ethereal blue glow, her hair fanning out around her like a halo—is enough to bring me to my knees. I can feel the blood rushing south, my cock swelling in my pants until it's almost painful, every nerve ending in my body screaming at me to take her, to claim her, and who the hell am I to deny what my mate is so obviously asking for?

RHYLAND

51

I dive into the water, the warmth embracing me, but it does little to quench the fire burning within me for the beautiful woman who awaits.

Dani is a vision of perfection beneath the pool's ethereal blue glow, her skin radiant and her eyes smoldering with raw, unrestrained need. Our bodies crash together, sending ripples across the surface as our mouths collide in a hungry, desperate kiss that tastes of longing, relief, and the primal passion that always simmers between us.

Her hand wraps around my throbbing cock, her touch electric. "I need *this* inside me now, Rhyland," she begs, her lips brushing mine with every word. "Don't make me wait another second. I need to feel you stretching me, filling me."

Fuck, when Dani talks dirty like that, it's like a switch flips in my brain. My cock hardens to an almost painful degree, ready and eager to fulfill her every filthy request. She knows exactly what to say to drive me wild with lust, and she wields that power like a weapon, keeping me perpetually on edge and craving more.

"You know just how to push my buttons, don't you, you insatiable minx?" I growl, nipping at her plump lower lip, swollen from our fevered kisses.

Dani's fingers tangle in my hair, tugging me closer until there's no space between us. "We almost lost each other," she breathes, her voice thick with emotion. "I need to feel you inside me, to erase the memory of it all, to prove to myself that we're alive and together."

She starts to stroke my cock, and my eyes damn near roll back in the sockets, "Fuck, you're needy tonight," I growl, but there's a smirk tugging at my lips. "Begging so prettily for my cock. How can I resist when you ask so nicely?"

How can I refuse her anything when my own need for her consumes me? A white-hot ache pulsing through my veins.

"And what about our little wager?" I ask as my hands roam her curves, gripping her firm, perfect ass. "Weren't you going to make me beg?"

A wicked smile curves her lips, a challenge gleaming in her eyes as she arches into me, offering herself up like a goddess to be worshipped. "That's on hold until I claim my prize. And just to be clear, I won."

"I beg to differ, baby," I retort. "I think it was a team effort, finding that key. We both played our parts."

Dani licks a hot, wet trail up my neck, her teeth grazing my earlobe in a way that makes me groan with need. "Just fuck me, Rhyland," she whispers, her breath hot against my skin. "We can argue about who won later."

"Noted," I rumble, with hunger. Without another word, I lift her, pressing her against the slick, wet rocks with a possessiveness that verges on primal.

I grab her wrists, pinning them above her head. "You want it, baby?" I growl, my lips brushing her ear. "You want me to stretch this tight little pussy, fill you up until you can't think straight?"

Dani's nipples tighten, "Yes."

We haven't had a moment to ourselves since we got here, no chance to just lose ourselves in each other without an audience or my annoying, cock-blocking brother getting in the way. Right now, all I want is to make my angel scream my name, to feel her coming apart around me in the most delicious way possible.

No distractions, no interruptions. Just me and my girl, the way it's meant to be.

Dani moans wantonly at my promise, echoing off the cavern walls. I tease her slick entrance, drinking in the sight of her before me, her breasts glistening with moisture, her eyes bright and golden with need.

I hoist her up, her legs wrapping around my waist as I line myself up with her entrance. And then, with one hard thrust, I'm buried to the hilt inside her, swallowing her cry of pleasure with a bruising kiss.

I grind into her with deep, driving thrusts that rock her body and send pleasure spiking through us both. "Fuck...yes...Rhyland, God, you feel so good." she keens, clinging to me desperately. "More."

"There's my needy girl. So fucking perfect," I groan against the soft skin of her neck, lost to the blissful sensation of her silken walls gripping me tight.

I will always crave Dani—with a junkie's desperation. I take her with almost brutal force, slamming into her over and over, and she takes it all, meeting me thrust for thrust, always eager for more.

The way she takes my cock, the way I crave giving it to her, will always be my ultimate weakness. I'm not gentle, and she fucking knows it—craves it just as much as I do. And that knowledge, that primal understanding between us, gets me rock fucking hard and panting with need every single goddamn time.

Dani squeezes me tight with her legs as I grip her ass, holding her right where I want her. I find the sweet spot at the juncture of her neck and shoulder, sinking my teeth into her delicate skin. She moans as I apply pressure, drinking her blood and infusing her with my venom, the bond between us intensifying with every exchange of our essences.

And let's not forget, my blood coursing through her veins is like fucking rocket fuel for her desire. It's like I've lit a goddamn fire inside her, every drop of my essence stoking the flames of her need until she's burning up from the inside out, desperate for me to quench the inferno with my cock. She's never more greedy, more ravenous for my touch than when she's high on the taste of me, and fuck if that doesn't make me harder than steel. Knowing that I'm the one who can satisfy her, the only one who can give her what she craves... it's the ultimate aphrodisiac.

My cock swells to an almost painful degree inside her, and Dani becomes wetter and slicker, her inner walls clenching around me like a velvet vise. I grit my teeth and force myself to slow down, to hold back the flood that threatens to wash over me. It gets better and better with her, every damn time taking me to the brink and leaving me wanting more.

"Rhyland...."

Her voice is like a fucking siren song, calling to me, beckoning me to my ruin.

"Yeah, baby?" I grit out, my hips snapping forward, driving my cock deep inside her. Fuck, she feels incredible. Her heat surrounds me, tight and wet and perfect.

She flips me with effortless grace, her confident smile daring me to challenge her. My back hits the rocks, and she settles above me, eyes shimmering with desire. "I think it's time I take the lead, Viking." Her voice is throaty, filled with seductive promise.

I raise an eyebrow, my desire for her burning in my eyes. "You sure about that, little angel? Think you can handle it?"

"I'm sure," she teases, her hands trailing down my chest, sending shivers down my spine. She leans down, her eyes daring me to resist. "Unless you're afraid I'll wear you out, big guy."

A low chuckle escapes me as I grip her hips. "Afraid? Of you? Baby, you have no idea what power you hold over me." I hold her gaze, my expression intense. "But I'll indulge your desire for control. This time."

The only other time I let Dani take control was in her car after her parents died. Her need to feel in charge, to have some fucking control over something in her life, was so raw and desperate that I surrendered to it. Watching her take what she needed—riding me with such fierce determination... fuck, it was the hottest thing I'd ever experienced. The memory of her wild abandon that night still makes my cock throb.

Dani grips my shoulders as she lowers herself onto my aching cock. I hiss through my teeth at the sensation, the feel of her tight heat swallowing me whole.

"God. Rhyland..." she pants, her hips rolling in a sensual rhythm that has me seeing stars. "You're so thick, so big, so damn good."

My fingers dig into her hips, guiding her as she rocks against me. "Jesus. Fuck, baby," I growl, my gaze locked on those golden eyes burning with need. "You have no idea what that filthy mouth does to me."

Her hips roll with confident grace, her golden eyes flashing with pleasure and dominance as she moves above me. "Yeah? You like it when I get naughty for you?" she teases, her voice breathy but full of challenge.

I can't help but let out a guttural moan as Dani shifts her position, taking me deeper. Her movements are swift and purposeful. She rocks herself down onto me, hard, impaling herself on my thick length. "Fuuuck, baby," I groan, my hand reaching up to grip her hair at the base of her neck, needing to feel her, to anchor myself to her. "Ride that fucking cock..."

Dani's tits are magnificent, bouncing and jiggling with every roll of her hips, the soft flesh glistening. I can't resist reaching up to cup those perfect globes, kneading and massaging them roughly as I pinch and tug at her nipples. The way she moans, her head falling back in ecstasy, the sound so fucking wanton and needy... it has my cock twitching inside her like it's got a mind of its own. I swear, this woman is going to be undoing—the way her pussy clenches around me, so tight and wet and perfect... I know I won't last long, not with her taking me so deep, so fucking good.

My lips seek hers in a desperate, needy kiss. My hips move on their own accord, thrusting up to meet her as she rides me with wild abandon. The sound of our bodies coming together echoes through the cavern, a primal symphony of passion and desire.

"Rhyland... I love you," Dani moans, her words punctuated by gasps of pleasure as she loses herself in the sensations, in the feeling of our bodies joined as one. "I love you so much, I need this...I need you."

And at this moment, with the woman of my dreams riding me like the damn deity she is, I'm in heaven. She's everything I never knew I needed, a gift from the heavens themselves, and I'm overcome with a wave of emotion so intense it nearly takes my breath away.

My mind drifts back to the vision I saw in the reflection pool, the image of our daughter, and I feel my eyes sting with unshed tears. I grip Dani's hip with one hand to slow her movements, and I cup her face in the other, my gaze locking with hers, trying to convey the depth of my feelings with a single look. "I love you so fucking much—I want that with you *so bad*, baby," I whisper, my voice raw with emotion. "A beautiful future."

Dani slows her movements, her hips still undulating gently as she searches my face. Her expression is one of tenderness and love. "I know..." she whispers, her fingers threading through my rough beard, then up through my scalp.

I don't even need to say it for her to understand what I'm conveying.

I kiss her then, pouring every ounce of my love and devotion into the press of my lips against hers. When I pull back, my forehead resting against hers, I speak the words burning in my heart since I saw our possible future. "A family with you, a child of our own. It's... all I want. It's all I have ever wanted."

Tears spill down Dani's cheeks, glistening in the ethereal blue light of the cavern. "I want that, too," she breathes, her voice thick with emotion. "So fucking much. I... I just don't think I can give that to you and..." she wipes a tear, " wasn't sure if that's something you wanted after..."

She trails off, and I know exactly what she's referencing—the family I lost, my children. She's worried I would never want that again, that the pain of that loss would keep me from ever wanting to be a father again. But fuck, she couldn't be more wrong.

"Angel, listen to me," my voice low and intense as I grip her hair at the base of her neck, forcing her to meet my gaze. "What happened in the past, the family I lost... that doesn't change a goddamn thing about how I feel about you, about us. You're my fucking world, baby. My everything."

I brush my thumbs over her cheeks, wiping away her tears with a tenderness that belies the fierceness of my words. "I want it all with you, Dani. I want the house, the kids, the fucking white picket fence if that's what you want. I want to build a life with you, a family. I want to watch your belly grow round with my child, to hold our baby in my arms and know that we created that perfect little miracle together."

My voice cracks with emotion, but I push on, needing her to understand the depth of my feelings, the sheer magnitude of my love for her. "You're not a replacement for what I lost, Angel. You're my mate—my soul—my goddamn future. And I'll be damned if I let the ghosts of my past keep me from embracing that future with both fucking hands."

I press my forehead against hers, my breath mingling with her own as I stare into her eyes, willing her to see the truth of my words. "I love you, Danica. I love you with every fucking fiber of my being. And I want nothing more than to spend the rest of my life loving you, building a family with you, creating a future that's all our own. Do you understand me?"

She nods, a watery smile breaking through her tears as she runs her hands through my hair, holding me close. "I understand," she whispers, her voice filled with wonder and joy.

She presses her lips against mine and rocks slowly against me, my cock still buried deep within her warmth. "Can you imagine?" she whispers, "A little girl with your eyes and my sass running around and causing trouble?"

I can't help but chuckle at the thought, my heart swelling with love and anticipation. "She'd be a handful, that's for sure. But with your brains and my charm, she'd have us wrapped around her little finger in no time."

Dani laughs—the sound music to my ears. "God help us if she inherited your stubbornness, too. We'll be in for a wild ride."

I grin, nuzzling my nose against hers. "Hey, my stubbornness is what got me you, right? I'd say it's a valuable trait to pass on."

She rolls her eyes, but I can see the love and amusement shining in their depths. "Yeah, along with your talent for getting into trouble and your knack for driving me crazy."

"Crazy in love with me, you mean," I counter.

I brush my thumbs over her cheeks, wiping away more of her tears. "You changed everything for me, Angel. You gave me a reason to fight, hope, and believe in something bigger than myself. And I promise I will spend every day forever making sure you know how loved and cherished you are."

Dani smiles, her eyes shining with love and happiness. "Forever, huh? You sure you can handle me for that long?"

I grin, my hands sliding down to grip her hips as I thrust up into her, making her gasp. "Oh, I think I can manage. After all, we have a lot of practicing to do if we want to make that baby, don't we?"

Dani's giggles turn into a moan as she starts to move on me again, her hips moving in a sensual rhythm that sends shockwaves of pleasure rippling through my body. But as much as I love having her on top, taking control and riding me like a fucking dream, I can't resist the primal urge to take over, to pound into her with all the love and passion I have.

In a blur of movement, I have her bent over the rocks. Her arms outstretched in front of her, hands braced against the smooth surface. I lean over her, my chest pressing against her back as I nip at her earlobe. "Now get on those tippy-toes and hang on, baby," I demand.

I grip a handful of her hair at the base of her neck, tugging her head back gently but firmly, exposing the elegant column of her throat. "I need to fuck my woman the way she likes it," I murmur against her skin, my lips trailing a path of fire along her neck and shoulder.

I grip Dani's hip, my fingers digging into her soft flesh as she rises on her toes and arches her back beautifully. I inch my way inside her tight, wet heat, groaning at the way her pussy clenches around me, choking my cock in the best possible way.

"Holy shit," Dani pants, her voice strained with pleasure. "Goddamn, Rhyland, your cock is...fucking huge."

I smirk, leaning down to nip at her earlobe. "Yeah? Love feeling every thick, hard inch of me stretching you open, filling you up?"

She lets out a breathy laugh that turns into a moan as I slam into her, my hips snapping forward with a force that makes her cry out in ecstasy. "Y-yes. *God,* yes. I love it," she gasps, her hands scrabbling for purchase on the slick rocks.

Fucking her like this, with her bent over and me slamming into her from behind? Yeah, she's feeling every goddamn inch of me, taking me so deep I'm practically in her throat. This is why this position is my absolute fucking favorite—I can go harder, faster, deeper than any other way. She's entirely at my mercy, just the way I like it, and the way she moans and cries out with every brutal thrust tells me she's loving every second of it, too. There's nothing quite like watching her come undone on my cock, knowing I'm the one who gets to wreck her, to claim her, to make her scream my name like a fucking prayer.

It's the ultimate power trip, and damn if it doesn't get me off like nothing else.

Dani pushes back against me, meeting me thrust for thrust, her ass bouncing deliciously against my pelvis. The sound of our bodies coming together, skin slapping against skin, echoes through the cavern, mingling with our moans and gasps of pleasure.

"Fuck...Rhyland. Oh. My. God."

I can feel her tightening around me, her inner walls fluttering and clenching, and I know she's close. I reach around, my fingers finding her clit and rubbing in firm, insistent circles, determined to push her over the edge.

"Give me what I want, Angel," I command, my voice strained with the effort of holding back my release. "I want to feel you come apart around me, want to hear you scream my fucking name."

"Rhy...!" Dani manages to choke out, her voice strangled with pleasure. Her walls clench around me, squeezing me, and I know she's teetering on the brink of ecstasy. "Oh, FUCK!"

"Fucking flood me, Angel," I growl against her throat, my teeth grazing the tender flesh before biting down hard. Her walls clench around my cock as she screams, her sweet essence gushing over me in waves. The force of her release nearly pushes me out, but I slam back in with a savage thrust, refusing to leave her heat for even a second.

"That's my good girl," I snarl, my hips pistoning faster as her body trembles beneath me. "Losing control, soaking me with this sweet pussy. Fuck, you're drowning my cock, baby." Her whimpers of pleasure drive me wild, urging me closer to my own release as I claim what's mine.

"Yes, yes...ohh...fuuuuck." she growls. "Rhyland, I'm coming...I'm coming." the sound bounces off the walls, a symphony of pure, unbridled ecstasy. Her body convulses beneath me, the force of her orgasm making her tremble and quake. I don't let up for a second, slamming into her with a punishing rhythm that has her screaming, her voice echoing off the cavern walls. My cock is drenched in her essence as she squirts again and again, coating me in her sweet nectar.

"Fuck, Angel, look at you," I growl, my eyes drinking in the sight of her lost in ecstasy. "Coming apart on my cock, squirting like a fucking fountain. So goddamn beautiful, so fucking dirty."

I've never seen anything like it—never felt anything so primal and raw. It's the sexiest thing I've ever witnessed, and I can't help but marvel at the goddess beneath me.

"You're so goddamn perfect, baby. My beautiful, dirty little angel."

This is what I live for, what I crave like a junkie craves his next fix—the feel of her silken heat gripping me like a fist, the taste of her essence on my tongue, the sound of her cries of pleasure filling the air. It's an addiction, a drug that I can never get enough of, and I never want the high to end.

I can feel my orgasm building, the pressure coiling in my balls and at the base of my spine, and I know I won't last much longer. Not with Dani clenching around me, milking me for all I'm worth, her body begging for my cum.

With brutal thrusts, I bury myself to the hilt inside her, my cock pulsing and twitching as I empty myself in her. "Jesus. Fuck!"

I roar my release, the sound primal and animalistic, and Dani answers with a keening cry of her own, her body shaking and trembling as she rides out the aftershocks of her pleasure.

I collapse on top of her, my sweaty limbs tangling with hers, our heaving breaths mingling in the air between us. Our bodies are still joined, our hearts hammering in perfect fucking sync like they're bound together with an invisible cord.

"Don't move," I command. I slowly pull out of her, every inch a sweet torture. My cock is still rock hard, straining toward her like a goddamn heat-seeking missile.

I bend down behind her, spreading her legs wide to give me a perfect view of her glistening pussy. Our cum leaks out of her, dripping down her thighs, and I can't help the primal growl that rips from my throat. This woman... she's mine, marked by my touch, filled with my release.

I swipe my fingers through the wetness, mixing our essences, and push them back inside her. Dani moans, her hips rocking back and forth as she fucks my fingers, her walls clenching around them like a goddamn vise. "You like that, baby? You like being filled with my cum?"

"Yes," she pants. "It's so hot, so dirty..."

I don't know when the hell I developed a breeding kink, but holy shit, it's going strong now—the thought of having her carry my child is now a constant fucking temptation. And right now, seeing her pussy filled to the brim with my cum, watching it drip out of her like liquid fucking gold...I'm ready for round two—to fill her up even more.

I dive in, licking and sucking at her swollen lips, tasting the mingled essence of us. Her juices are so fucking sweet, and the taste of my cum on her pussy sends a jolt straight to my cock. I groan as I feast on her, claiming her like the fucking animal I am.

DANICA

52

Not wanting to head back to Gideon and the crew, Rhyland and I decide to lie here and breathe while unpacking everything.

Ever the curious cat, Rhyland starts grilling me about the vision I saw in the reflection pools. I hesitate, not wanting to burst his bubble of post-coital bliss with talk of doom and gloom.

"Well, it was a bit like a choose-your-own-adventure novel," I quip, trying to keep things light. "In one version, all the realms were happy and thriving. Everything was sunshine and rainbows and singing woodland creatures."

I conveniently leave out the part about the other, darker path I saw. The one where everything goes to hell in a handbasket and Rhyland gets sucked into the darkness. That little nugget of nightmare fuel is staying locked up tight in the vault of my brain. Thank you very much.

Rhyland raises an eyebrow, clearly sensing there's more to the story. "And the other version?" he prompts.

I shrug, trying to play it off like it's no big deal. "Who knows? The future is fickle. For all we know, those Reflection Pools could've just been showing me some trippy alternate realities. Like, maybe in one of them, we're all just characters in a romance novel written by some bored housewife up in Washington State."

Rhyland snorts, shaking his head in amusement. "Cute, baby. Real cute."

I grin, batting my eyelashes at him in mock innocence. "Yeah, but you love it, right?"

Rhyland growls, his arms tightening around me as he buries his face in the crook of my neck, his beard tickling my skin, making me giddy inside. "More than anything in this world or any other," he murmurs. "I know there's something else you saw, something you're not telling me. And that's okay—for now. But don't think for a second that I won't find a way to coax it out of you, one way or another."

I melt into his embrace, my heart doing a little tap dance in my chest as I breathe in his scent, a heady mix of sandalwood, the Nordic seas, and pure, alpha male. Damn him for knowing me so well, for being able to read me like a book even when I'm trying my best to keep the pages closed.

But the truth is, I'm not ready to dive into the darker aspects of my vision or reflection just yet. Not when we're still basking in the glow of our victory, of the love and connection we share. And then there's Rhyland's vision to consider—is it just some weird, wishful thinking brought on by the magic of the Reflection Pool?

Or could it be a glimpse of a future that's possible despite everything we thought we knew about vampire biology?

Seeing Rhyland break down like that, so raw and vulnerable over his vision—it was like a sucker punch straight to the heart. I had no fucking clue that Mr. Broody Viking had a secret desire to join the diaper-changing club? It's not like we can populate a nursery with little fang-babies, right? Vampires and procreation go together, as well as peanut butter and motor oil.

But if we could? If, by some miracle of supernatural science or cosmic joke, we could actually make a mini-me-and-him?

Sign me the fuck up for that roller coaster of sleepless nights and spit-up stains. To see Rhyland grinning like an idiot over a squalling, pooping bundle of joy? Our squalling, pooping bundle of joy?

To give him the family he never thought he could have?

I'd move heaven and earth, even if it meant my uterus staging a revolt in the process.

Talk about a plot twist. Here I am, trying to save the world, and suddenly, I'm daydreaming about babies and tiny vampire onesies.

What the actual fuck has my life become?

I need to change the subject ASAP before I start yelling out baby names or asking if vampires can get sperm donors. Because let's face it, "Rhylica" is already stuck in my head like the world's most adorable earworm, and if I don't redirect this conversation, I will turn into a blubbering mess. And nobody needs to see that, least of all my Daddy Vike.

"You're not the only one with secrets, you know," I murmur, my lips curving into a playful smirk as I tilt my head back to look up at him. "Your lightning trick and background ring any bells?" Rhyland sighs in defeat, "But I suppose I can let you try to pry them out of me if you think you're up for the challenge."

Rhyland grins. "Oh, I'm up for it, baby," he rumbles, his hand sliding down to give my ass a possessive squeeze. "And I feel you'll enjoy every second of my interrogation techniques."

I laugh, the sound echoing off the cavern walls. "Uh-huh," I tease as I gaze up at Rhyland. "So, your lightning trick," I say, my fingers dancing along his chest, tracing the lines of his tattoos. "Care to explain how that's even possible, oh mighty God of Thunder?"

Rhyland's eyes darken, a storm brewing in their depths as he pulls back, his brow furrowed. "Honestly, baby, I have no fucking clue," he admits. "I never knew my father."

I stiffen against him, my heart clenching at the pain that flashes across his face. Well, shit. Looks like we've got more in common than just our need for one another. "Hey," I murmur, my hand cupping his cheek, my thumb brushing over his thick beard that I can never get enough of. "You're not alone in that boat, babe. My dad was a mystery, too, remember?"

Rhyland leans into my touch, his eyes closing as he takes a deep breath. "I know, Angel," his voice low and raw. "It's just... it's not something I talk about much, you know?"

I nod, my heart aching for the little boy he once was, yearning for a father he never knew. "I get it, Rhy. Believe me, I do. But hey, you've got me now, right? And I'm not going anywhere."

A small smile tugs at the corner of his mouth, his eyes opening to meet mine. "Thank fuck for that," he murmurs, his hand coming up to tangle in my hair, his fingers twisting in the strands. "I don't know what I'd do without you, baby."

I grin, my nose wrinkling as I kiss his jaw. "Probably brood a lot and punch things," I tease. "What about your mother?" I ask softly, my fingers threading through the silky strands of his hair.

Rhyland's jaw clenches, his eyes taking on a faraway look as he delves into the painful memories of his past. "My mother's name was Freya," his voice barely above a whisper. "She said she was named after the Norse Goddess Freyja. She was all I knew, and she filled my head with stories of the gods descending from the heavens and gifting her with me...or some shit like that."

I smirk. "So, you're telling me you're the result of some divine booty call?" I ask, my fingers trailing down his chest, my nails scraping lightly over his skin. "That's one hell of an origin story, babe."

Rhyland snorts, shaking his head as he rolls his eyes. "Yeah, well, as much as I wanted to believe I was some kind of divine gift, I grew up and realized that I was more than likely the result of some deadbeat knocking my mother up and leaving her high and dry."

I wince at the bitterness in his tone, my heart breaking for the man in my arms. "I'm sorry, babe," I whisper, kissing his chiseled chest softly. "That's a tough pill to swallow, no matter how old you are."

Rhyland shrugs, his expression hardening into a mask of indifference. "It is what it is, Angel," his voice gruff with emotion. "Can't change the past, no matter how much we might want to."

I nod, my mind already whirring with possibilities. "True," I concede. "But maybe we can uncover some answers about your father and, in turn, shed some light on that lightning mojo of yours."

Rhyland's eyes narrow. "What are you getting at, baby?"

"I'm saying," I muse, my fingers tracing that sexy dark hair trail leading straight to the promised land. "What if there's more to the story than we know? I mean, think about it. You've got these insane powers that no other vampire has. That's got to mean something, right?"

Rhyland frowns, "I don't know, Angel," he admits, hesitating. "I've never really given it much thought. I just assumed it was some fluke, a glitch in the vampire matrix, or some shit."

I shake my head, my grin widening. "Nuh-uh, Viking," I counter. "I don't believe in coincidences, especially regarding you. There's got to be a reason for your lightning powers, and I'll be damned if we don't get to the bottom of it."

Rhyland chuckles, his arms tightening around me as he pulls me closer. "You're not going to let this go, are you?" he asks, his voice a low rumble in his chest.

"Not a chance, babe," I confirm, my fingers walking up his chest to tap him on the nose. "You should know by now that once I sink my teeth into something, I don't let go until I've gotten to the bottom of it."

Rhyland groans, his head falling back against the stone floor with a thunk. "Fuck me," he mutters in amusement. "I've created a monster."

I giggle, my lips kissing the underside of his jaw. "You love it," I whisper, my breath ghosting over his skin. "Admit it, you're just as curious as I am about your lightning trick and where it comes from."

Rhyland sighs, his hand coming up to cup the back of my head, his fingers tangling in my hair. "Yeah, I am," he admits. "But honestly, baby, I'm not sure I want to know the truth. What if it's something I can't handle? What if it changes everything?"

I pull back, my eyes searching his swirling baby blues. "Hey," my voice is soft and reassuring. "No matter what we find out, it doesn't change who you are, Rhyland. You're still the same stubborn, brooding, sexy-as-hell vampire Viking I fell in love with. And nothing, not even some divine deadbeat dad, can change that."

Rhyland's eyes soften, a small smile tugging at the corner of his mouth. "I love you, Angel. I don't know what I did to deserve you, but I'm sure as hell not going to question it."

I grin, my heart swelling with love for this beautiful, broken man. "I love you too," I whisper, my lips brushing against his in a soft, sweet kiss. "And you deserve everything, babe. Don't ever forget that."

Rhyland groans, his tongue delving into my mouth, claiming me with a hunger that sets my blood on fire.

Our little cuddle session is rudely interrupted by the sound of splashing because, apparently, the universe just can't let us have one fucking moment of peace.

We scramble to our feet, frantically pulling on clothes and grabbing weapons, ready to face whatever fresh hell has decided to crash our party.

I've got my daggers in hand, poised to strike, half-expecting that creepy-ass sea creature to come slithering out of the water, ready to claim us as its mid-afternoon delight. Instead, Mirella emerges from the depths like a mermaid on a mission, her expression all business and no play.

I sigh in relief, sheathing my daggers and trying to calm my racing heart. "Mirella? What the hell are you doing here? I hope it's not to critique our technique—we're rather fond of our methods, you see."

Mirella, clearly not one for small talk or innuendo, cuts straight to the chase. "The Queen has summoned you, and you cannot refuse," she informs us, suggesting that 'no' is not an option.

Rhyland and I share a look of mutual bewilderment. "And pray tell, what happens if we do refuse?" I inquire, my eyebrow arched in question. "Not to be difficult, but we're on a tight schedule."

Mirella's expression tightens, her eyes flashing with a hint of warning. "If you refuse, there will be consequences," she states. "I don't wish to be unpleasant, but please, Dani. The Queen desires an audience with you both, as you have survived the trial."

Crap.

Can't exactly tell Miss Protocol here that we're running a con to snag a key for a seriously impatient sea goddess. The whole "meeting the Queen" thing definitely wasn't in the brochure—my bad for not reading the fine print. Calypso isn't exactly known for her warm and fuzzy patience, and something tells me, "Sorry, your sea goddess-ness, we got held up at a royal meet-and-greet" won't fly.

"Look," I say, channeling my inner diva, "I know we're basically the hottest thing since sliced bread around here, but I don't have time to deal with my adoring fans right now." I quip, trying to sound more annoyed than panicked. "Can't you tell your queen we'll take a raincheck? Maybe pencil her in for next week after we've—" I catch myself before I spill the beans, "after we gather ourselves? We're kinda exhausted."

Mirella stares at me, her fire-red hair glowing in the pool's blue lights. Her expression turns almost...scared..? "I'm afraid that's not possible," her voice firm. "The Queen's summons is not a request but a command. You would be wise to heed it."

I groan, my head falling back in frustration. "Fiiiine," I grumble. "But just for the record, I'm doing this under duress. And if your queen tries to make me curtsy or some shit, I'm out."

Mirella's face relaxes like I've just offered her a lifeline, but something's still off. My empathy meter is going haywire, blaring like a five-alarm fire in my head. It's like she's radiating worry in waves, and I'm the unwitting surfboard catching every single one.

I've got a sinking feeling that we're about to dive headfirst into a whole new ocean of trouble.

Rhyland picks up on my unease through our bond—the guilt gnawing at me for dragging this poor, dutiful mermaid into our mess of lies and schemes—wraps a steadying arm around my waist. She's just doing her job, following orders from what sounds like the aquatic version of Miranda Priestly, and here we are, about to royally screw her over.

"Let's see what the Queen wants," Rhyland offers, probably saving this poor mermaid from getting her fins handed to her by her boss.

Great, looks like we're about to add 'awkward royal audience' to our growing list of shit-hitting-the-fan moments.

I nod, my jaw clenched tight. "Yeah," I mutter, trying to swallow down the guilt lodged in my throat. "Let's just hope this doesn't last all night." I force my best 'bored socialite' impression like this is just another tedious obligation rather than a potentially catastrophic wrench in our plans.

Time to play the bored-but-compliant guest and pray we don't end up in some underwater dungeon for attempted magical theft.

Mirella nods, the pearls in her hair glistening at the movement, her face impassive. "Understood," her tone clipped and professional. "Now, if you'll follow me, the Queen is waiting."

"By the way, how the hell did you find us? Not that I know where we are exactly..." I can't help but ask.

"You're in Crystal Falls," she says as if it's clearly evident. "And how I found you was one of only a few options. Now, may we go?"

I have no idea where Crystal Falls is without looking at a map, so I leave it at that.

"Uhh, just one small detail," I interject. "We fragile humans have this pesky little requirement called oxygen. You know, that thing we need to survive? I'd hate for you to forget that minor detail *again* and have us drowning before we even reach Her Majesty."

Mirella's blue eyes catch the light as she expresses apology and exasperation. "Yes, I do apologize for that oversight," her tone is sincere. "Please, enter the water, and I will bestow the gift of breath upon you. It should allow you to breathe underwater until we reach the palace."

I pause, my mind processing her words. "Hold up, are you saying I can breathe underwater? Like, *actually* breathe, not just hold my breath and hope for the best?"

"Yes, the magic of the *Merfolk* grants us the ability to give breath to humans, allowing them to travel underwater with ease," Mirella explains, her tone matter-of-fact. "Unlike the others..."

She says this with a clear indication that Sirens, for all their sexy singing and enchanting good looks, are lacking in the underwater breathing department.

Well, well, well, isn't that an interesting little factoid?

"Well, color me impressed," I muse, my eyebrows raised in surprise. "I suppose there's more to you, Merfolk, than just pretty faces and shiny tails, huh?"

Mirella smiles, a hint of pride glimmering in her blue eyes. "Indeed, our magic runs deep and serves many purposes. Now, shall we proceed? The Queen is not known for her patience."

She looks edgy as hell, so let's just rip off the damn Band-Aid and get this over with.

I nod, taking a deep breath and steeling myself for whatever lies ahead. "Lead the way, my finned friend. Let's see what your illustrious leader wants with little old us."

I need to invest in a wetsuit at this point. My leathers are so salt-crusted and stuck to my skin that they might as well be a second layer of epidermis. Daggers sheathed, I dive down into the crystal-clear waters, the blue crystals illuminating the area like some underwater version of the Northern Lights. It's so clear and beautiful down here that I half expect to see Poseidon's tour guide pop up with a "Welcome to Atlantis" sign.

Mirella reaches me, her movements as fluid as...well, water. She places her lips over mine, and for a moment, I'm tempted to quip about buying me dinner first. But then she breathes air into my lungs, and suddenly, it's like my need for oxygen vanishes.

I take a tentative breath, half-expecting to choke on a mouthful of seawater. But to my surprise, nothing happens. The water fills my lungs as easily as air, and I feel no discomfort. It's like my body has suddenly decided that H2O is an acceptable substitute for oxygen.

The sensation is so strange and yet so natural that I can't help but marvel at it. I take another breath, then another, each one as effortless as the last. This is not what I experienced with the Siren when being dragged down to Calypso; clearly, this is the magic only mermaids wield.

She repeats the same steps with Rhyland, and I feel a twinge of irrational jealousy. I know it's just magic mermaid CPR, but those lips are mine. Thank you very much. I make a mental note to chat with Rhyland later about accepting kisses from other women, even if they are life-saving, underwater-breathing kisses.

I glance at Rhyland, wondering if he's experiencing the same surreal feeling. His expression is of wonder and amusement. *"Well, this is new,"* he says, using our mental communication pathway.

Mirella grabs my hand and tugs us down, Rhyland holding mine as we swim into the unknown.

LUCIAN

53

R hyland and Dani fucked off to find that damn key. And yeah, I know they're fine. I mean, I've got this whole blood bond thing with Dani, which is excellent for keeping tabs on her emotional state. But let me tell you, when I felt her arousal, I noped the fuck out of that connection faster than a virgin on prom night.

I do not need to be privy to whatever freaky shit they're getting up to, thank you very much.

But you know what *really* tickles my funny bone? Pissing off my dear, sweet, stick-up-the-ass brother, Rhyland. I mean, the guy's got a perpetual case of resting bitch face, and it just brings me so much joy to ruffle his feathers.

Especially when it comes to Dani, I swear, the mere mention of her name from my lips makes him go all twitchy and broody. So, naturally, I make it my mission to piss him off at every opportunity I can to watch him squirm—and this one will definitely get a rise out of the fuckface.

I'm sure they'll come strutting back any moment now, regaling us with tales of their daring exploits and narrow escapes. But in the meantime, my little cupcake, Seraphina, has been keeping herself busy all day by soaking up knowledge like a fucking sponge. She's already got Erik, Mr. Stoic McBroodyson himself, eating out of her hand. He's been teaching her how to wield a sword and hot damn; she's a natural.

It must be an angelic or Atherian thing, having the skills of a goddamn ninja assassin. She knocked me on my ass during a sparring session, and all I could do was laugh and try not to jizz in my pants at the same time. It was a delicate balance, let me tell you.

But Erik, the stoic, serious type, takes pride in training my little hostess cake. He even crafted her a custom Bo staff when she said the sword felt too heavy and awkward. And holy fuck, watching her twirl that thing around like a deadly ballerina is enough to make a grown man weep. She had the entire crew on their asses in a matter of seconds, each one eager to test their skills against the angelic warrior princess.

From what I've learned about my little celestial snack pack, Seraphina is missing a few key ingredients from the standard angel recipe.

No angel fire? Check.

No fancy-schmancy time warp tricks? Double check.

But light grenades? Oh, hell yeah. And those things pack a serious punch—just remembering when she smacked me upside the head with one has me grinning like an idiot.

According to my angelic amuse-bouche, the angel fire thing is reserved for the warrior bloodline in Atheria. Seraphina fits into "guardian angel" territory. Meanwhile, Dani goes all Human Torch at the slightest provocation.

What Seraphina lacks in pyrotechnics, she more than makes up for in ass-kicking abilities. She could probably take on a whole Martial Arts league with one hand tied behind her back. It's like watching a ballet of violence, and it's fucking beautiful.

It's been a real treat watching her come into her own and discover new strengths. She may be a sweet, innocent angel, but she's got the soul of a fighter. And I gotta say, it's pretty fucking hot.

There's just something about watching your mate kick ass and take names that gets the engine revving.

"That was a blast!" Seraphina practically skips over to me, her Bo staff casually propped against her shoulder like a goddamn action hero. Erik, however, is sprawled out on the deck, staring up at the sky like he's contemplating his entire existence. "I saw his leg sweep coming from a mile away, but I countered and took him down," Seraphina explains, grinning.

"I know, baby girl, I saw the whole thing," unable to keep the pride out of my voice. "You were fucking magnificent."

"Could you kindly reiterate the reasons that compelled me to undertake this endeavor?" Erik groans from his prone position, seriously regretting his life choices.

Seraphina giggles, taking a swig of water from her canteen. "Because you agreed to help me hone my combat skills, which is needed and—"

"Necessary for you to learn, yeah, yeah, I know," Erik finishes for her, waving his hand in defeat. He sighs, sitting up with a grunt, "It has been a pleasure in sparring with you; it brings to mind the time I instructed our Little Huntress in the art of combat."

Fuck, that feels like a lifetime ago when Erik was teaching Dani the fine art of ass-kicking in Luminara. Seriously, so much has gone down in the blink of an eye. It's insane to think about how tight-knit we've all become after wading through the hot mess that is our collective lives.

"Hey, there's no shame in learning from the best," I quip, giving Seraphina a wink. "And right now, the best just happens to be a gorgeous, ass-kicking celestial snack cake with a heart of gold."

Seraphina blushes at the compliment, ducking her head shyly. But I can see the glint of pride in her eyes, how she stands slightly taller and holds her head slightly higher. It's a beautiful thing to witness, watching her come into her own and realize just how fucking incredible she truly is.

"Well, I couldn't have done it without your guidance," turning to Erik with a grateful smile. "You're an amazing teacher, and I'm lucky to have you as a mentor."

To his credit, Erik looks genuinely touched by her words. "It's been my pleasure, Seraphina," looking at her like she just hung the fucking moon. "You're a natural, and it's an honor to help you cultivate your skills."

I mean, seriously, the guy's practically swooning. If he had a tail, it'd be wagging so hard it'd create a goddamn breeze. But hey, I can't blame him. My girl's got that effect on people. She's like a walking, talking ray of sunshine, and even a stoic hardass like Erik can't resist her charms.

I can't help but feel a swell of affection for my brother at this moment. I mean, sure, we give each other shit all the time, but at the end of the day, we've got each other's backs. And seeing him take Seraphina under his wing, helping her become the best version of herself? It's enough to make even my heart grow three sizes.

"Alright, alright, enough with the sappy shit," I interject, clapping my hands together. "What do you say we take a break and grab some grub? All this ass-kicking has me working up an appetite."

Seraphina laughs, eyes sparkling. "You're always hungry, Lucian."

"What can I say, baby girl? I'm a growing boy," waggling my eyebrows suggestively. "I'm always hungry for a certain cosmic cupcake."

She rolls her eyes, but I can see the fondness in her expression. "Let's go raid the galley before you start gnawing on the mast or, worse, me."

And with that, we make our way below deck, Erik trailing behind us with a bemused shake of his head. It's moments like these, the simple, everyday moments of camaraderie and laughter, that make all the bullshit we've been through worth it.

It all happened so fucking fast. One minute, we're walking down to the galley, laughing and joking, Seraphina's hand warm in mine. The next, I am waking up on the floor in the dank, dark bowels of the ship, my neck screaming in agony. I slowly get to my feet, rubbing the tender flesh where my spine meets my skull—the sensation of my neck being snapped is always a dead giveaway. The pain and disorientation of waking up from that particular brand of death is something I'll never get used to.

Some fucker snapped my neck like a twig from behind, and now I am all kinds of confused.

I look around frantically, my heart pounding against my ribs like a caged animal. "Seraphina!?" my voice raw and desperate, echoing off the damp, wooden walls.

I race up to the main deck, my heart pounding in my chest, only to find Gideon and the entire fucking crew bleeding out and barely clinging to life. Erik is sprawled on the deck, his face ashen and shirt soaked with crimson.

What the actual fuck happened here?

I grab Gideon by the lapels of his coat, hauling him to eye level, my hands shaking with fear and rage. "Where's Seraphina?" I demand, my voice barely recognizable, even to my own ears.

He coughs a spray of blood splattering across my face, then looks at me with a grim expression, his teeth stained red. "They took her, lad."

They? Who the fuck is they? Someone took my girl, my fucking mate?

I see red, my vision tunneling, the icy rage that threatens to consume me. "Who? *Who* the fuck took her?"

Gideon shoves my hands away, collapsing back onto the deck as Izabelle frantically tries to stem the flow of blood from his wounds. "Bloodbane, the scurvy dog. He ambushed us when we least expected it, mate. Boarded the ship quiet as a church mouse an' took us out 'fore we even knew what hit us. The bastard lookin' for Dani, he was."

I feel like I've been sucker-punched, the air rushing out of my lungs in a painful whoosh.

Who the fuck is this Bloodbane asshole? And more importantly, why take Seraphina? What could he possibly want with her?

Oh my fucking god.

I grip my hair, my fingers tangling in the strands, tugging so hard I swear I will rip it out by the roots. The sheer panic that's coursing through my veins right now is enough to make me want to scream, to rage, to tear the whole fucking world apart. I just found her, and now she's taken!

I haven't sealed the bond with her.

I can't find her, can't mentally connect with her.

I'm flying blind, and it's the most terrifying thing I've ever experienced. I'm going to lose my fucking mind.

I can only imagine she didn't go easy. My girl's a fighter through and through. She would have kicked, screamed, and fought with every ounce of strength. But what if...oh god...what if they hurt her? What if they...

I collapse on the deck, my knees slamming into the blood-soaked wood as I hurl, the coppery taste of blood filling my mouth. The sickening thought of them laying a hand on her, of causing her harm, is enough to make me want to tear my own heart out and use it as a fucking piñata.

I can feel the rage building inside me, a white-hot fury threatening to consume me entirely. If they've hurt her, if they've so much as touched a single hair on her head...there will be no force in heaven or hell that can save them from the ass-kicking of a lifetime.

I get up, my legs still a little shaky from the whole "puking my guts out" thing, and stumble over to Erik. "We need to go after them, like, yesterday, dude. Time's a-wastin'!"

Erik nods, his face as stoic as ever, but then he points to the sails. "While I share your urgency, Lucian, repairs come first on the sails, lest we find ourselves stranded here indefinitely."

I look up and see the tattered shreds of the sails, our only fucking way off this floating deathtrap, and with the crew doing their best impression of corpses on the deck, it looks like it's up to me and Erik to play seamstress.

It's like the pirate version of a dick move. Slash the sails and leave 'em high and dry while you sail into the sunset with their precious cargo. I gotta hand it to this Bloodbane guy, he may be a raging asshole, but he knows how to fuck with a ship.

"You good, bro?" I ask as he stands next to me, trying to gauge just how much of a beating he took.

"I endeavored to defend the ship and crew to the best of my abilities," Erik says, his voice all formal and shit, even though he looks like he's about to keel over. "But alas, their numbers were great, and they employed wooden swords, exploiting our inherent weakness."

Well, fuck me sideways with a wooden stake. So now they know what we are and how to take us down. This is so not good. Like, on a scale of one to "we're totally fucked," this is a solid eleven.

I wish Dani and Rhyland would've given me a heads-up about this Bloodbane douche canoe. Hell, even Gideon or Erik could've dropped a hint or two. But fuck no, everyone's gotta be all mysterious and shit, keeping secrets like it's going out of style.

I let out a frustrated growl, running my hands through my hair. "Okay, so we're dealing with a bunch of vampire-savvy pirates who have a hard-on for kidnapping my mate. Fan-fucking-tastic. Any other good news you want to share with the class, Erik?"

Sometimes I wish my stick-up-the-ass brother would just unleash his inner beast and go all Mortal Kombat on douchebags. You know, rip out a spine here, tear off a head there—really embrace that whole "vampire" thing we've got going on.

But nooooo. Erik's gotta be all noble and shit. He is like the Batman of vampires, if Batman had a perpetual case of constipation and a hard-on for honor. I swear, the guy probably irons his cape and alphabetizes his bat-gadgets.

It's like he missed the memo that being a vampire means you get to be a badass. Instead, he's over here trying to win the "Most Honorable Bloodsucker" award.

News flash, bro: that's not a thing!

Erik gives me one of his patented stoic looks that makes you feel like he's staring into your soul and finding it lacking. "I believe our time would be better spent focusing on the task at hand, Lucian. The sails will not mend themselves, and every moment we tarry is a moment Seraphina remains in peril."

I sigh, knowing he's right. As much as I want to charge off half-cocked and rain down unholy vengeance on these fuckers, we need to be smart about this. We need a plan.

And step one of that plan is getting this fucking ship seaworthy again.

DANICA

54

Holy mother of pearl, we've just stumbled into what I can only describe as the long-lost city of Atlantis. I'm talking about an underwater wonderland that would make even King Triton jealous.

We just went through one of those underwater portals—Water Gate—that feels like you're being flushed through interdimensional plumbing, complete with swirling water and the distinct feeling that you'll hurl your guts out.

Mirella swam us up through the palace to this opening, and suddenly, we're all standing again and breathing air like a bunch of land-dwellers at a mermaid convention.

As I take in the breathtaking surroundings, my eyes can't help but wander over to Mirella. Gone is the shimmering tail that made her look like a mermaid princess, replaced by a pair of legs that seem to go on for days.

It's not just the legs that catch my attention. No, the sporadic mermaid scales barely cover the goodie areas—much like Calypso's—leaving just enough to the imagination. The scales are a beautiful, shimmering turquoise, the same mesmerizing hue as her tail when she had it. It's like she's taken a piece of the ocean with her, even in human form.

But holy shit, this place is unreal. The walls are made of this shimmering mother-of-pearl that seems to change color with every light shift, going from a deep, mesmerizing blue to a dazzling, golden hue. And the ceilings? They're so high that you could fit a whole pod of whales here without grazing a fin.

Everywhere I look, there are these incredible statues of merfolk and sea creatures, each so lifelike that I half expect them to start swimming around and asking for directions to the nearest coral reef. Some are made of this gleaming, polished stone that looks like it was carved straight from the ocean floor, while others are inlaid with precious gems and metals that glitter like a treasure hoard.

The floors are an intricate mosaic of blues and gold, with patterns that swirl and twist like ocean currents.

But the real showstopper is the massive, ornate fountain in the center of the room. It's made of shimmering, iridescent crystal that seems to glow from within, casting a soft, ethereal light over everything, making it feel magical.

I glance at Rhyland, wondering if he's as blown away as I am. From the look on his face, I'd say he's pretty damn close to picking his jaw up off the floor. And honestly, I can't blame him.

Mirella guides us to the dining area; my eyes widen at the sight before me. The table is a veritable feast fit for Poseidon himself, overflowing with an array of seafood delicacies that make my mouth water and my stomach growl.

Succulent crab legs, their vibrant red shells, are piled high on silver platters. Whole fish, their scales gleaming in the light, are artfully arranged alongside mountains of plump, juicy mussels and clams. There are dishes I can't even begin to identify, but they all look plucked straight from the pages of a gourmet underwater cookbook.

My stomach lets out a rumble that could rival a whale's mating call, reminding me that I haven't had a decent meal in the last twenty-four hours. I've been substituting on a diet of stress, adrenaline, and the occasional swig of seawater, and my body is staging a mutiny.

"You must be hungry. Please, help yourselves," Mirella offers, gesturing to the bountiful spread. "We will meet with the queen shortly."

I don't need to be told twice. I dive for the table, piling my plate high.

Table manners? Never heard of her.

Rhyland watches me with that sexy smirk of his, probably wondering if he should call an exorcist or just enjoy the show.

This seafood is so fresh that I half expect it to slap me and swim away. Aquaria's pristine waters must be the secret ingredient because this stuff is divine. Sorry, Red Lobster, but you've just been dethroned.

Mirella returns moments later after I've fully stuffed my face, leading us toward a set of massive double doors carved from solid gold.

My palms are getting sweaty as I fidget. No clue what kind of shit show we're walking into here—could be anything from an awkward tea party to an underwater execution.

Guess there's only one way to find out.

The doors swing open, revealing the throne room in all its glory. I let out a low whistle. The room is surrounded by floor-to-ceiling windows that offer a breathtaking view of the vast open sea—just like Calypso's lair.

And there, sitting on a throne that looks like it was carved straight out of a giant pearl, is Her Royal Highness herself.

Holy mother of mermaids, this Queen serves some serious underwater realness. Her hair's a blonde-and-blue masterpiece that puts my best hair day to absolute shame, adorned with more ocean bling than a sunken pirate ship.

Her scales are navy blue and shimmering. And that dress? It's like someone liquefied the Northern Lights and poured them into fabric form.

Perched on her royal noggin is a crown that would make the Hope Diamond weep with jealousy. But the glowing staff in her hand is catching my eye—and apparently, my spidey senses, too. A familiar tug in my gut screams, "Important magical item alert!"

My crown starts to buzz and hum like it's trying to tell me something. And with a sudden, startling clarity, I realize precisely what it is.

"Rhyland..." I whisper into his mind. He tightens his grip on my hand, signaling that he hears me. *"Her staff—she has the Aquanite stone."*

Rhyland's eyes dart to her staff, and he gives my hand another assuring squeeze.

"I extend my gratitude for accepting my invitation. I am Cordelia, sovereign of this realm. I sincerely hope Mirella provided you with a pleasant escort during your journey."

I take a deep breath, knowing I gotta play my cards right to get my hands on that stone. "Oh, absolutely, Your Majesty. Mirella was a real peach, though I gotta say, the whole 'breathing underwater' thing? Not exactly a skill I was planning on adding to my resume."

The Queen's gaze remains steady, her expression unreadable. "I believe you know the reason for this summons, my dear. By freeing my pet, you have undoubtedly acquired the key it guarded."

I can't help but do a double-take. That monstrosity was her *pet?*

Is she off her royal rocker? Last I checked, pets were supposed to be cuddly and obedient, not man-eating sea beasts.

"I'm sorry, did you say 'pet'? Don't get me wrong, I'm all for exotic animals, but that thing? It was less 'Fluffy the Sea Monster' and more 'Nightmare Fuel on Crack.'"

Cordelia remains unfazed by my sass, her voice as smooth as silk. "I understand your confusion, but I assure you, the creature served a vital purpose in guarding the key. Its unique nature was necessary for the task at hand."

"Riiight, because nothing says 'top-notch security' like a giant, man-eating sea beast with a serious case of the munchies. Got it." I quip back.

Cordelia's lips quirk into a smile that doesn't quite reach her eyes. She extends her hand, palm up, and snaps her fingers at me like I'm some trained seal. "The key, if you please. I require it in my possession forthwith."

I'm about to give Her Royal Hign-*ASS* a piece of my mind when Rhyland steps in front of me, all six-foot-something of pure, protective alpha male. "Hold up, *Your Highness*," he growls, practically spitting out the title like it leaves a bad taste in his mouth. "You don't get to just demand shit from us without some fucking answers. Why do you want the key so badly, and why the hell couldn't you get it yourself? We're not handing over a damn thing until you start talking."

I smirk a little at Rhyland's no-nonsense attitude. He may be rough around the edges, but he has a point.

Cordelia sighs heavily like she is explaining something painfully obvious to a particularly slow child. "The key you hold is the gateway to Pandora's box, a treasure trove of untold power and danger. As the ruler of this realm, it is my solemn duty to ensure that it remains sealed and hidden from those who would misuse its contents."

I know damn well that this key opens—the Siren's Lyre. But what's got Little Miss Fancy Fins over here quaking in her seashells is the real question.

Unless she's hiding something.

She halts, fixing Mirella with an icy glare. "It appears this impudent mermaid has granted you access without so much as a whisper of my approval. Thus, I demand to know your intentions and the means by which you secured such an unwarranted privilege."

I glance at Mirella; she looks terrified, scared out of her wits. I shift my gaze back to Cordelia and realize she hasn't the foggiest clue what I am or why I'm here.

Ignorance is bliss, I suppose.

I raise an eyebrow, not buying her cryptic bullshit for a second, and done with her shit. "Calypso herself sent us to retrieve this key. You know, the goddess of the sea? And call me crazy, but I'm more inclined to trust her judgment than someone who keeps a giant, man-eating sea monster as a pet." I hold up my wrist showing her the bracelet. "Not to mention, I am under a Coral Pact—thingy."

Mirella gasps behind me, and Cordelia's features shift from calm and collected to royally pissed in the blink of an eye. She stands up, her shimmering gown flowing around her like a waterfall of rage. "Calypso, you say?" She starts pacing, her voice rising with each step. "Let's get one thing straight. Calypso is *not* the sea goddess of this realm; I AM!" She practically roars the last word, her eyes blazing with a crazy kind of anger.

Water erupts outside, and the sea suddenly becomes furious, mirroring her outburst. It's like her emotions are directly tied to the ocean itself.

Holy shit—looks like I hit a nerve.

I glance over at Rhyland, who looks as shocked as I feel. "Well, that escalated quickly," I mutter under my breath.

"You entered into a Coral Pact with her!?" Cordelia seethes, her eyes flashing with anger and disbelief. "You foolish, reckless child!"

I bristle at her condescending tone, my temper flaring. "Look, lady, I didn't have many options, okay? In case you haven't noticed, Calypso's not exactly the type of mermaid you say no to."

Cordelia sighs, shaking her head in a way that makes me feel like a toddler who just finger-painted on her favorite dress. "You have no idea what you've done, do you? The repercussions of your actions, the gravity of the situation you've placed yourself in?"

She's right. I don't have a fucking clue. I'm flying by the seat of my ass here, relying on instinct and a healthy dose of snark to get me through, but admitting that to Her Royal Mermaidness? Not a chance.

"Enlighten me, then," I shoot back, crossing my arms over my chest. "Since you seem to have *all* the answers, why don't you fill me in on exactly what I've gotten myself into?"

Cordelia's gaze hardens, her lips pressing into a thin line. "A Coral Pact is not something to be entered into lightly, you insolent *girl*. It is a binding agreement that cannot be broken without severe consequences. By agreeing to Calypso's terms, you've placed yourself under her control, her power and influence. She will use you as she sees fit, and there is little you can do to stop her."

A shiver runs through me like someone just walked over my watery grave. Cordelia's words echo in my mind, and I can't help but think back to my little heart-to-heart with Calypso.

The Sea Witch had clarified that breaking our pact was a big no-no. She'd sworn up and down that she wouldn't go back on her word, but let's be honest—when it comes to ancient, powerful Sea Witches, pinky promises don't hold much weight.

I try to shake off the feeling of impending doom, but it clings to me like a barnacle on a ship's hull. Calypso may have promised not to break our agreement, but that doesn't mean she won't find a way to twist it to her advantage.

I sneak a quick peek at Mirella, who's been doing her best impression of a mute statue this whole time. Her face is about as expressive as a poker player's, but something in her eyes sets off my internal alarm bells.

I force myself to keep my expression neutral, not wanting to give Cordelia the satisfaction of seeing me squirm. "Okay, so I made a deal with the devil. It wouldn't be the first time. But if it means saving the people I care about, I'd do it again in a heartbeat."

Cordelia's eyes flash with something I can't quite read. Anger? Frustration? Maybe even a hint of grudging respect?

"You are either incredibly brave or incredibly foolish," her voice softening. "But I fear that your actions may have consequences far beyond just you and those you seek to protect."

"Watch your goddamn mouth when you speak to my mate." Rhyland growls, a severe warning to the Mer Queen.

I swallow hard, trying to ignore the sinking feeling in my gut. I know I've stepped in it this time, but what other choice did I have?

"So, what do we do now?" I ask, my voice sounding a lot more confident than I feel. "How do we fix this mess?"

Cordelia sighs again, and for a moment, I see a flicker of something that looks almost like pity in her eyes.

"I need that key. Calypso cannot get her hands on it by any means necessary. One thing is certain—we must act quickly before Calypso's plans come to fruition. And we must be prepared for the storm that will follow."

Do I hand it over like it's a spare house key and not some mystical artifact that could potentially unleash who-knows-what kind of aquatic apocalypse? I mean, sure, Cordelia's got that whole regal "I'm the queen, do as I say" vibe going on, but her idea of security involves a man-eating sea beast with anger management issues. Not exactly inspiring confidence here.

On the other hand, maybe she's got a point. What if this Siren's Lyre is the underwater equivalent of a nuclear warhead, and Calypso's just itching to push the big red "destroy everything" button?

It's like being stuck between a rock and a hard place, except the rock is a potentially world-ending magical artifact, and the hard place is a mermaid queen who thinks "extreme petting zoo" is a valid security measure.

How the hell am I supposed to make this call? My "save the world" resume is pretty thin, and I'm pretty sure "gave the magical key to sketchy sea queen" isn't going to look great on it either way.

Maybe she'll trade me for the stone? All I have to do is recite my role in this prophecy for the umpteenth time and pray to every deity in the sea that she buys it.

I feel like a broken record at this point, constantly hitting replay on the "I'm the Chosen One" mixtape. If I had a dollar for every time I've explained this cosmic destiny BS, I'd be swimming in cash instead of potentially trading this world ending key for a magical rock.

As much as I want to poke the bear (or, in this case, the pissed-off mermaid), we must tread carefully. If we want to get our hands on that stone and figure out what's really going on here, we can't afford to make an enemy out of the Queen of Aquaria.

So, I take a deep breath and put on my most diplomatic smile. "Look, Your Highness, we may have gotten off on the wrong foot here. Why don't we all take a deep breath, maybe count to ten—or, you know, however high mermaids can count—and start over?"

I can feel Rhyland's gaze boring into my head like he's silently telling me to shut the hell up before I make things worse.

"Let's talk, Your Majesty. No more games, no more cryptic bullshit. Just the truth. What's *really* going on here, and why is everyone so hot and bothered about this key? What does it do?"

I can't lay all my cards on the table just yet. I've got to get this mermaid to spill the tea first.

Cordelia straightens her posture, her voice regaining its regal composure. "As I said, I require that key to maintain the status quo. It has immense powers, ones that can tip the scales. I cannot allow you to work for that... *witch* and undo everything I've strived to accomplish to keep—"

"Your Highness..." A merman with massive muscles, and a damn eight-pack with beautiful long blonde hair, I hadn't noticed pipes up from across the room, effectively putting a cork in her royal monologue.

Cordelia clears her throat, looking about as comfortable as a fish out of water. It's obvious she's mentally kicking herself for almost spilling the proverbial beans about what the hell is going on in this underwater circus.

I arch an eyebrow, my suspicions going into overdrive. "Look, I don't know what you were about to spill, but—"

"Angel, we've got a fucking problem," Rhyland's gruff voice cuts through my thoughts. *"Lucian just reached out. That bastard Bloodbane's has Seraphina."*

Oh my god.

Of course, the universe decides to toss another monkey wrench into the works as if on cue. I nearly choke on my spit.

I whirl around to face Rhyland, my mind racing. *"What the actual hell?"* I fire back into his mind. *"How did this happen?"*

Rhyland's eyes cloud over with a deep sadness, and I can feel his worry pulsing through our bond. Or is that my anxiety I'm feeling? It's hard to tell where his emotions end and mine begin.

Damnit.

This whole situation is spiraling fast.

What the hell am I supposed to do now? The stone's right there, practically gift-wrapped and ready for the taking. Cordelia is about to help me out of this Coral Pact, but Seraphina needs me. I can't just leave her high and dry. She'd never abandon me, and that's not who I am—family and friends always come first, even if it means dealing with psycho pirates and temperamental sea queens.

"Are you two quite all right?" Cordelia asks, eyeing us with a mix of suspicion and concern.

I quickly shoot a mental message to Rhyland. *"We're bailing. Back to the ship, pronto. We'll deal with this hot mess express after we rescue Seraphina."*

Out loud, I plaster my best 'everything's fine' smile. "Oh, we're just peachy, Your Majesty. Quick question, though—you wouldn't happen to have a little mermaid's room around here, would you? Nature calls, and all that." I do a little improvised pee-pee dance for good measure.

Cordelia stares at me momentarily, wondering if all humans are this weird before her lips curve into a polite smile. "Yes, of course. Mirella, please escort..." she pauses, clearly fishing for my name.

"Dani," I supply helpfully.

"Ah, yes. Mirella, please escort Dani to the restroom."

Mirella inclines her head, "Of course, Your Majesty."

Mirella turns to me, giving me a look harder to decipher than ancient hieroglyphics. Is it a warning? A plea for help?

Hell, if I know.

As we make our grand exit stage left, I can't help but think that this whole situation is fishy as fuck. And something tells me Mirella's cryptic look is just the tip of the iceberg lettuce in this underwater salad of secrets.

As we follow Mirella, I send another mental message to Rhyland. *"The second we're out of this bougie throne room, I'm conjuring a portal. We're bouncing out of here.'"*

Rhyland's mental reply is terse. *"Got it. Let's move."*

"Oh, and Dani..." Cordelia's voice stops me dead in my tracks.

I whirl around to face her, plastering on my best "who, me?" expression.

"I expect you to hurry and get back so we can discuss this further with the *key,*" her eyes narrowing into icy slits of suspicion. "And don't even think about leaving. I have Merguards surrounding this entire palace. There is only one way in and one way out."

Well, damn. That's about as subtle as a brick to the head.

Message received, Your Royal Bitchness.

"Please," gesturing back to Mirella with a smile. "Do hurry."

Pfft..if she only knew what I can do.

I find myself dropping into a curtsey in a moment of pure, absolute idiocy. Yeah, you heard that right. A fucking curtsey—like I'm some debutante at an underwater ball instead of a snarky human trying to outmaneuver a mermaid queen.

So much for my earlier declaration to Mirella about not bowing and scraping.

I pair this graceful, awkward-as-hell gesture with a smile that is so fake that it could probably be used as shark repellent. "Of course, Your Majesty. Wouldn't dream of it," I chirp, lying through my teeth.

Then, like the brave hero I am, I turn tail and scurry after Mirella. Nothing says, "I'm definitely not planning to escape," like running away at Mach 3.

This has to be the weirdest exit strategy I've ever participated in. But when you're dealing with kidnapped angels, a mermaid queen who's one scale short of a tail, and now we're trying to pull off the underwater equivalent of a dine-and-dash, and the urgent need to pee (fake or otherwise), you work with what you've got.

Here's hoping we can make our great escape before things get any crazier. But knowing our luck? I'm not holding my breath.

Well, figuratively speaking, anyway.

DANICA

55

Twenty turns, four hallways, and fifty-four doors later, we finally reach the restroom. Jesus, this place is massive!

"Wait outside; I'll call you in once I get it open," I inform Rhyland through our mental pathway.

Rhyland leans against the wall, arms folded across his massive chest, the picture of nonchalance. "I'll just wait out here," he says out loud, ensuring Mirella hears him. I can feel his tension thrumming through our bond.

I step into the most stunning bathroom I've ever seen. It's like walking into a work of art, with white and blue hues splashed across the walls like an abstract painting. The gold fixtures gleam like treasure, and for a moment, I'm dazzled by the sheer luxury of it all.

I can't afford to lose focus, not now. I'm ready to conjure up a portal and get the hell out of Dodge when Mirella follows me in. "Uhh... I think I can manage this solo, thanks," I quip, raising an eyebrow. "Unless you're planning on holding my hand while I do my business?"

Mirella's expression is far from amused, and I can tell she's not here for a bathroom break. She grasps my hands, her eyes wide and pleading. "Don't do what I think you're going to do," she begs, her voice trembling.

I decide to play dumb because hey, it's worked for me so far. "Don't do what exactly? Pee? Because I gotta tell you, that's non-negotiable at this point."

Mirella shakes her head—frustration evident on her face. "I know who you are, Dani, and why you're here. If you leave, Cordelia will—" She stops abruptly, her head falling forward like she's fighting against some invisible gag order.

"Just don't leave yet," she continues, her words coming out in fits and starts. "There will be consequences if you leave now... just..."

I pull my hands away, my frustration bubbling over. "Okay, hold up. What the hell is going on, Mirella? You're telling me you know who I am, and you've just been, what? Playing along? Spill it, sister."

Mirella takes a deep breath, her hands shaking like she's about to have a full-blown panic attack. "Yes, I know who you are—the savior and why you're here. But..." She stops again, her tongue seemingly tied in knots.

"I can't say more," she finally manages, her voice strained. "Just know that I want to help you. You have to hide the key. You cannot give her the key, Dani."

I stare at her, my mind racing. Hide the key? Fucking where—In my ass? And why? I've got more questions than a Jeopardy contestant, but something tells me Mirella's not exactly in a position to give me a straight answer.

"Alright, I'll bite," crossing my arms. "Let's say I do hide the key. Then what?"

God, this is frustrating—I need to get to Seraphina before something terrible happens to her, or worse, I'm too late. Not to mention, Lucian is probably going ape-shit crazy right now, and I'm surprised he's not rattling around in my head, screaming at me to get back to the ship. I can almost hear him now: "Dani, what the actual fuck are you doing? Playing hide-and-seek with mermaids while Seraphina's in danger? Get your ass back here!"

Mirella grabs my arm tight, her fingers digging into my skin like she's trying to anchor herself to reality. "You cannot give Cordelia that key, no matter what. And you can't leave...She will.... Hide the key, tell her you lost it, whatever you must do. Please... trust me on this."

Trust her? Is she fucking serious right now? This is the same mermaid who tried to swipe my crown like it was a shiny seashell at a beachside gift shop. I narrow my eyes, ready to tell her exactly where she can stick her trust, when I notice the tears welling up in her eyes.

Seeing her so desperate and afraid is like a punch to the gut. Something isn't adding up here, and it's making my bullshit detector go off like a foghorn in a lighthouse.

I take a deep breath, trying to make sense of this whole clusterfuck of a situation. On one hand, I've got a mermaid I barely know telling me to lie to the Queen and hide a key that apparently everyone and their mother is after. On the other hand, I've got my guardian angel in danger and a vampire brother probably tearing his hair out with worry.

I hate to admit it, but Mirella's fear seems genuine. And if there's one thing I've learned in my crazy, fucked-up life, it's that sometimes you have to trust your gut, even when your head is screaming at you to run the other way.

"Okay, fine," I cave, my voice low and urgent. "I'll hide the key and...wait. But you better have a damn good explanation for all of this, Mirella. Because right now, I'm flying blind, and I don't like it one bit."

Mirella nods, relief flooding her features. "I know, and I'm sorry. I wish I could tell you more, but... it's...complicated. Just know that I'm on your side, okay? I want to help you, but we have to be careful."

I roll my eyes because, of course, it's complicated. When is it ever *not* complicated in my life?

I don't know what to make of this, but I don't have time to dwell on it now. I've got a key to hide and a bitchy royal mermaid to lie to.

As I formulate a plan to hide the key and deal with Cordelia—

"What's going on?" Rhyland's voice booms in my head, his tone laced with worry and impatience.

"Change of plans," I quickly inform him of Mirella's cryptic warning, trying to prevent my doubts from seeping into my words.

Rhyland isn't having any of this shit.

He's through the door like a heat-seeking missile and in front of me in a blur. Mirella yelps and backs away, leaving me with Rhyland's heat, "Nope. Fuck that," he growls, his alpha male instincts kicking into high gear. "Lucian and the crew need us right now, Dani. And let's not forget about your guardian angel, who's currently at the mercy of a fucking psychotic pirate—Lucian's mate, no less."

I close my eyes, feeling the sting of tears threatening to spill over. The weight of the situation crashes down on me, threatening to pull me under. "I know, Rhyland. I know. But something is off about this whole thing, with Cordelia and—"

"I don't give a flying fuck, kära," His tone is sharp, laced with an alpha male authority that demands compliance. And there's that name he uses again when I'm pissing him off and going against him. It's like a verbal slap, a reminder that he's unhappy with my choices.

"But Mirella said something terrible would happen if we leave now," I counter, my frustration bubbling over like a pot of boiling water. "She said we can't leave. We have to—"

"No," Rhyland's tone is final, leaving no room for debate. His Nordic blue eyes blaze with a fierce intensity, his irises darkening like a stormy sea. "Conjure the portal, Dani. I'm done talking about this."

I can feel his tension through the bond, a tightly coiled spring ready to snap. His fear for his brother, Lucian's desperate need to get to Seraphina, pulses through our connection like an electric current.

I let out a huff of exasperation, feeling caught between a rock and a hard place. I know Rhyland's right. Seraphina and Lucian need us; every second we waste here is another second they're in danger. The thought of Seraphina, my guardian angel, at the mercy of that psychotic asshole, makes my blood run cold.

But I can't shake the feeling that Mirella's warning is more than just a bluff. There's a desperation in her eyes that I can't ignore, a pleading that tugs at my heartstrings and makes me question everything.

Why?

Why am I falling for this?

I can't shake the feeling that there's more to this situation than meets the eye.

You know what? Screw this; screw Cordelia and her weird temper tantrum and Mirella's vague warning. "Fine, but Mirella comes with us."

She's scared of Cordelia, so what's the harm in taking her along for the ride?

Mirella's eyes widen in shock, and fear creeps into her expression. "No... I can't—"

"Why the hell not?" my patience wearing thin. "I don't have time to play these underwater games of clue. Either come with us or stay, but make a choice, and make it now, Mirella."

She hesitates for a moment. Then, slowly, she nods. "Yes, I will come with you, but please...hurry."

Rhyland starts pacing like a caged tiger, his agitation rolling off him in waves. "Dani, we don't need to bring her along and get caught up in whatever underwater bullshit is going on here. Stick to the fucking plan, and let's go."

I briefly ponder if there's some underwater penal code that covers mermaid-napping. Is there a particular prison for those who abduct merfolk? A magical version of Alcatraz hidden beneath the waves?

I quickly shake off those thoughts, realizing now is not the time to contemplate oceanic law's finer points. We've got bigger fish to fry, and by fish, I mean a certain pirate captain who's about to learn the hard way that you don't fuck with my friends.

I stand my ground, folding my arms over my chest and giving him my best "don't mess with me" look. "No. She's coming with us, Rhyland. End of story."

He growls low in his chest, a warning that I'm pushing his buttons. His alpha nature clashes with my stubborn streak, and I know he hates it when I go against him. It's a dance we've done before and always ends with "punishment," which I am all too happy to take.

Focus, Dani.

I turn to Mirella, my eyes narrowing. "If this ever comes back to bite me in the ass, or if you even think about betraying us, I'll make sure there's not an ocean deep enough for you to hide in. Got it?"

Mirella swallows hard, nodding frantically. "Got it. But please, Dani... trust me. I'm risking everything to help you."

I don't have time to dwell on her words—Seraphina and Lucian are in danger. I focus on Lucian, Gideon's ship, and escaping this underwater nightmare.

With a flick of my wrist, a swirling vortex appears, the portal shimmering like a mirage. It's never as clear when I focus on a person rather than on a specific location, but I know it will get us where we need to go.

I grab Mirella's hand, yanking her through the portal with me. Rhyland is right on our heels, his presence a solid wall of muscle and fury.

As we step through the portal, I can feel the crackle of energy surrounding us, the rush of wind, and the sensation of falling.

And then, just as quickly as it began, it's over. We're standing on the ship's deck, the portal closing behind us with a snap.

I take a deep breath, trying to calm my racing heart. We made it. We're back on the ship, and Mirella is with us.

Now, all we have to do is find Seraphina, kick some pirate ass, and figure out what the hell is going on with Cordelia and her underwater kingdom of secrets.

RHYLAND

56

I leave Dani and Mirella in my wake as I hunt down my brothers, my strides purposeful and determined. I make a beeline for the captain's deck, my boots hitting the wooden planks, echoing like a war drum. The ship's already slicing through the waves at a breakneck pace, and I find Gideon at the helm, looking way too fucking chipper for a man who was supposedly knocking on death's door.

"Gideon," I bark, my voice sharp as a whip.

"Ahoy, mate!" there's an edge to his enthusiasm, a tightness around his eyes that belies his upbeat tone. "We be settin' sail for Blood Reef, where that scurvy dog Bloodbane is no doubt headin' with the lass!"

Before I can get a word in edgewise, Lucian materializes at my back like a pissed-off poltergeist. "Well, look who finally decided to show up!" he snarls. "What the actual fuck, Rhyland? While you were off playing hide-the-salami with Dani, I was stuck here playing nursemaid and seamstress to this floating deathtrap!"

I don't need to be a mind reader to know that by "nursemaid," he means he's been playing vampire medic, force-feeding the crew his blood to bring them back from the brink. Gotta give credit where it's due—it was a smart move, even from Lucian.

"Stow it, Lucian," I growl. "I don't need to hear your bitching. What's the situation? And don't spare the gory details."

Lucian's eyes flash, his fists clenching at his sides. "The situation? The situation is that some dick-cheese pirate with delusions of grandeur has my fucking mate, and I'm stuck here with my thumb up my ass instead of ripping his spine out through his nostrils!"

Erik approaches, his steps measured and his posture rigid despite looking like death warmed over. It's clear he hasn't fed in way too fucking long, but the stubborn bastard's discipline and fortitude are still rock solid.

"Brother, your return is most welcome in this dire hour," his voice formal and controlled.

"Jesus *Christ*, Erik. You look like hammered shit. When was the last time you sank your fangs into something that wasn't your damn pride?"

Erik shrugs, his posture stiff as a board. "You know I do not partake in the act of feeding unless it is freely offered, brother."

I let out a frustrated growl, my patience about as thin as a cheap condom. Erik needs some serious sustenance, and a willing donor would be fucking ideal right about now. Dani's blood might keep him from keeling over, but it's not enough to get him back to fighting form, and there's no way in hell I'm letting her become a goddamn feeding tube for anyone, even my own brother.

Gideon clears his throat, his expression grim. "Aye, I be willin' to offer me own neck to the lad, if it be what he needs."

We all turn to gauge Erik's reaction, but before he can utter a word, Izabelle steps forward, her turquoise eyes blazing with determination. "No, Captain. 'Tis I who shall provide the sustenance he requires." She runs her hands up and down Erik's chest, and the poor bastard looks like he'd rather walk the plank than take her up on her offer.

Erik shoots me a pleading look, silently begging for an out, but I give him a firm nod. He needs to feed, and he needs to do it now if he's going to be any use to us in the shitstorm that's brewing on the horizon.

With a resigned sigh, Erik turns and follows Izabelle below deck, looking like a man walking to his own execution. I almost feel sorry for the guy, but desperate times call for desperate measures, and right now, we need every able-bodied vampire we've got if we're going to take down Bloodbane and get Seraphina back.

"That scurvy bilge rat Bloodbane caught us with our breeches down. Stormed the ship like a bleedin' hurricane and made off with the lass. We're hot on his trail, but there be no tellin' what foul deeds he's got planned for the poor girl."

I feel my rage simmering beneath the surface, a volcano ready to erupt. I know all too well the fear and desperation Lucian's feeling—I've been there, and it's not a place I ever want to revisit. But we can't afford to lose our heads, not when Seraphina's life hangs in the balance.

"Oh, when I get my hands on this cock-juggling pirate cunt, I'm gonna go so medieval on his ass; it'll make the Spanish Inquisition look like a tea party," Lucian snarls. "This shit-ticket's about to star in his own snuff film, and spoiler alert: it's gonna be more gruesome than a Tarantino-Cronenberg collab. I'm gonna rearrange his organs so creatively; med students will need a fucking treasure map to pass their exams."

Well, holy fucking shit. I don't think I've ever seen Lucian this goddamn pissed off before, and it's starting to make me sweat a little. The bastard looks like he's about to go nuclear, his eyes blazing with a rage that could melt fucking steel.

It's not just anger—something more profound, more primal—the kind of fury that makes even a hardass like me take a step back and reassess the situation.

Dani and Mirella come rushing towards us, and I can't help but double-take at the sight of Mirella. It's like someone went to town on her with a can of turquoise glitter spray paint, covering all her naughty bits while leaving the rest of her bare as a baby's ass. I never clocked her look until now.

Gideon nearly chokes on his tongue beside me, his eyes bugging out of his head. "Well, shit. Is that a real-life mermaid on my ship?"

Dani rolls her eyes, her sass level cranked up to eleven. "Gideon, Mirella. Mirella, Gideon. There, introductions made. Now, can we skip the pleasantries and get to the part where we figure out how far we are from Bloodbane's ship?"

"Yeah, can we focus on the task instead of ogling the fish chick? My mate's out there with some psycho pirate, and I'm about two seconds away from going full-on berserker mode."

I shoot him a look, my eyes narrowing. "Cool your jets, Lucian. We're all on the same page here. Gideon, how long until we catch up to Bloodbane?"

Gideon tears his gaze away from Mirella, his expression sobering. "Aye, we be gainin' on 'em, but it'll still be a few hours 'fore we be within spittin' distance. The Seraph is a fast ship, but The Crimson Fury is still faster."

"Oh, hell no. Not on my fucking watch," Dani snarls, her eyes flashing with fierce determination. She closes her eyes, her brow furrowing in concentration as she focuses inward. "Never tried this before, but screw it, it's worth a shot."

I turn to face the vast expanse of the sea, my heart pounding in my chest as I watch a ripple in reality begin to form before my very eyes. It's like watching the fabric of the universe tear itself apart, and I realize with a start that Dani is actually opening a goddamn portal to Bloodbane's ship.

"Holy shit, baby. That's it." my voice thick with pride and awe. "Think of his ship—the red sails, the galleon..."

As Dani concentrates harder, the portal grows wider, and suddenly, there he is—Bloodbane himself, standing on the deck of his ship, sailing fast, like a king surveying his kingdom. It's the most surreal thing I've ever seen— like two different realities have collided and merged into one.

Beads of sweat begin to form on Dani's brow as she focuses even harder, her eyes pinched shut with the effort. I can feel the raw power emanating from her, and it's enough to make the hair on the back of my neck stand on end.

"Holy mother fucking fuck of multiverses!" Lucian hollers over the waves crashing.

I watch her in awe, marveling at her strength and determination. This woman—my mate—never ceases to amaze me. Even in the face of impossible odds, she's pushing herself to the limit, drawing on reserves of power I didn't even know she had.

"That's it, Angel," I murmur, my voice rough with pride and concern. "You've got this."

"Whooo, sweet cheeks! Tear that interdimensional asshole wider!" Lucian yells.

And then, before I can even blink, we're ripping through the portal like a bat out of hell, hot on Bloodbane's tail. The portal snaps shut behind us with a loud crack, and Dani exhales, her body sagging against mine.

"Damn, baby, you did good," holding her close and pressing a fierce kiss to her temple. "I'm so fucking proud of you."

Holy shit, I can't believe what I just witnessed. Dani, my beautiful, brilliant, badass mate, did the impossible. She created a portal and pushed an entire fucking ship through it like it was nothing.

I can see the bastard himself, standing on the deck with a look of utter shock and disbelief. He *clearly* wasn't expecting us to show up out of fucking nowhere like this, and I can't help but feel a surge of vicious satisfaction.

His eyes narrow into slits, and I can practically see the gears turning in his head as he tries to figure out how the fuck we managed to get the drop on him like this.

Well, tough shit, asshole. You're fucked.

"All hands on deck, ye scurvy bilge rats!" Gideon roars, his voice booming across the ship like a thunderclap. "Drop the sails and prepare the cannons! We've got a score to settle with that black-hearted bastard Bloodbane, and by the gods, we'll send him to the depths of Davy Jones' locker before the sun sets on this day!"

LUCIAN

57

Damn, Dani and her mind-blowing, reality-bending, ass-kicking portal powers. One second, we're trailing behind Bloodbitch's ship, and the next, we're right on top of them, close enough to see the whites of their beady little eyes. My heart's pounding like a jackhammer, and my blood's singing with the need to spill some pirate guts.

"Hold your fire, you trigger-happy fucknuggets!" I bellow, my voice echoing across the deck. "Nobody shoots until I've got my hands on Seraphina, you hear me? Anybody jumps the gun, and I'll personally shove a cannon up your ass and use you as a meat puppet!"

I mentally connect with Dani, I know I'm probably going to hear it from my asshole brother, but I don't give a shit, *"Dani, baby, I need you to work your portal mojo and get me on that floating shitheap. Like, yesterday."*

She's at my side in a flash, panting like she just ran a marathon through a minefield. "Lucian, you magnificent dumbass, you can't just charge in there solo!"

I give her a look that could melt steel; my jaw clenched. "Watch me, Princess. Now, open up a portal and send me over there before I start getting creative with my transportation methods. And trust me, you don't want to see what I can do with a catapult and a jar of lube."

Dani plants her hands on her hips, her eyes narrowing dangerously. "Oh, for fuck's sake, Lucian. I'm not letting you go alone, you colossal dipshit. If you think I'm letting you waltz onto that ship without backup, you've got another thing coming. I'm coming with you, end of story."

I start to protest, but she shuts me up with a glare that could melt my balls off. "Zip it, Lucian. Seraphina's important to me too, and I'll be damned if I'm going to sit back and twiddle my thumbs while you go off half-cocked. Besides, some-one's gotta be there to save your sorry ass when shit inevitably hits the fan."

A shit-eating grin spreads across my face, pride and affection for this feisty little firecracker swelling in my chest. "Alright, alright, you win, you stubborn sibling. But don't come crying to me when your brooding boy-toy throws a hissy fit and takes it out on your sweet ass."

"Leave Rhyland to me to worry about."

The ship lurches violently as an explosion rips through the air, Bloodbane's cannons finding their mark. The deck pitches beneath our feet, threatening to send us all overboard.

Fuck!

I lunge for Dani, my hand shooting out to snag her arm before she can hit the deck. In the same breath, my other hand latches onto the nearest rope, my fingers clenching so tight I feel the fibers digging into my palm.

The acrid smell of gunpowder fills the air, mixing with the salty sea spray. My eyes dart around, assessing the damage and looking for the next threat. Every muscle in my body is coiled tight, ready to react.

This isn't a game anymore. This is war, and that bastard Bloodbane just fired the first shot. As another blast rocks the ship, I grit my teeth, a snarl escaping my lips. Playtime's over, fuckers. It's time to show these pirates what happens when you piss off a vampire with a grudge.

With a flick of her wrist, a shimmering portal springs to life, the gateway to chaos and ass-kicking beckoning us forward like a siren's call. Rhyland's spidey senses start tingling as if on cue, and he whips around, his eyes wide with alarm.

"Danica! Don't you fucking dare—"

I crack my knuckles, a feral grin splitting my face ear to ear. "Ladies first, Princess. Let's introduce these bastards to a whole new world of pain. And by pain, I mean the kind that involves lots of screaming, crying, and begging for mercy."

Danica and I don't hesitate for a single fucking second. We dive through that portal like a couple of kids cannonballing into a pool, and the next thing we know, we're in the dank, dark bowels of the ship. The sound of pirates yelling, cannon fire, and water pounding against the hull, the creaks and groans of the timbers fill our ears, and the stench of mold and rat shit assaults our nostrils.

"Seraphina?" I call out, my voice echoing through the gloom. But there's no response, just the distant shouts and curses of the crew above us.

I'd assumed Dani would've portaled us straight to Seraphina's location, but as I look around, there's no sign of my angel anywhere. Just a bunch of fucking barrels and coils of rope and other pirate bullshit.

We start tearing the place apart, searching every nook and cranny, but it's like looking for a needle in a goddamn haystack. The shouting from up top is getting louder, and I know it's only a matter of time before they realize we're down here and come looking for us.

Out of the corner of my eye, I glimpse something blonde. My heart stops, and I whirl around, my eyes straining to see through the darkness. And there she is, lying on the floor in a crumpled heap, her golden hair spilling out around her like a halo.

"Fuck!" The word tears from my throat as I reach Seraphina's side instantly, Dani right on my heels. The sight of her chained to the wall like a goddamn animal makes my blood boil, and I have to clench my jaw so hard I think I might crack a tooth to keep from losing my shit entirely.

Dani doesn't hesitate for a second. Her hands start glowing, her otherworldly light burning bright as she focuses on the chains. The metal melts almost immediately, the cuffs and links falling away and hitting the pissed-soaked floor with dull clangs.

I scoop Seraphina up in my arms, cradling her against my chest like she's the most precious thing in the universe. Because she fucking is. Her body feels too light, too fragile, and it only fuels the rage burning in my gut.

I press my ear to her chest, holding my breath as I listen for the steady thump of her heartbeat. And when I feel the gentle rise and fall of her chest, the whisper of her breath against my skin, I nearly collapse with relief.

She's alive. My cupcake, my everything, she's alive.

But she's out cold, and who knows what those fuckers did to her before we got here. I want to storm up those stairs and rip every last one of those bastards limb from fucking limb.

But I can't. Not yet. Not until I know Seraphina is safe.

"Let's get her the fuck out of here. Now, Dani."

My eyes dart around the room, looking for any sign of an immediate threat. Every muscle in my body is coiled tight, ready to unleash hell on anyone who tries to stop us.

The need to protect Seraphina and get her to safety is overwhelming, as is everything else.

We need to move, and we need to move now.

Dani nods, her face grim and determined. "I'll open another portal. Get ready to move."

I hold Seraphina in my arms, clutching her close as Dani works her magic. The portal shimmers to life in front of us, a glowing doorway back to the safety of our ship.

But just as we're about to step through, the door at the top of the stairs bursts open, and a horde of pirates comes pouring down, their swords drawn and their eyes glinting with malice.

"Fuck!" I snarl, my grip tightening on Seraphina's limp form. "Dani, we need to move!"

But Dani's already in motion, her daggers drawn whirling through the air as she charges towards the pirates, a battle cry tearing from her throat. "Go!" she shouts over her shoulder. "Get her to safety! I'll hold them off!"

I hesitate for a split second, torn between my need to protect Seraphina and my desire to fight alongside Dani. But I know what I have to do.

With a roar of frustration and rage, I leap through the portal, Seraphina clutched tight against my chest. The last thing I see before the shimmering gateway snaps shut behind me is Dani, a whirling dervish of deadly grace, her daggers singing through the air as she takes on the entire fucking horde single-handedly.

DANICA

58

These filthy assholes stink to high heavens as I fight them off, their body odor a pungent mix of sweat, grime, and what I can only assume is the lingering scent of their last victim's blood. I can practically see the stink lines wafting off their unwashed bodies. It's enough to make me gag, but I don't have time for that luxury.

I'm a whirlwind of motion, my daggers flashing in the dim light as I fend off their attacks. I trip one particularly foul-smelling bastard, and he goes down hard, his ass hitting the deck with a satisfying thud—no time to celebrate, not when I've got another one trying to sneak up behind me.

I spin in time, my daggers clashing against his sword with a bone-jarring clang. The vibrations shoot up my arms. I grit my teeth and push back with everything I've got. I'm not letting some two-bit pirate get the best of me.

My peripheral vision catches a weathered barrel to my right. In a heartbeat, I feint left, the pirate's blade whistling past my ear. I pivot, my boots finding purchase on the barrel's curved surface. The wood groans under my weight as I coil, then explode upwards.

For a split second, I'm airborne, the dank air of the ship's hold rushing past my face. Time seems to slow as I twist, my legs pistoning forward. My feet slam into the pirate's chest with a sickening thud, the impact jolting up my legs. His eyes bulge, breath exploding from his lungs in a wheezing gasp.

The force of my kick sends him reeling backward. He pinwheels through the air, crashing into a stack of crates with a thunderous cacophony of splintering wood and clanging metal. Debris rains down around his crumpled form as he lies motionless amidst the wreckage, the acrid smell of gunpowder mingling with the metallic tang of blood.

The others are on me instantly, their blades flashing in the flickering light. I let my instincts take over, my body moving on pure adrenaline and muscle memory.

Gripping my daggers tighter, I slice through the neck of another pirate, his blood spurting everywhere like a macabre geyser. He grips his throat, a sickening gurgle escaping his lips as he drowns in his blood—no time to revel in the kill, not when another one comes at me from the left.

I tap into my time-warp power, the world around me slowing to a crawl as I see his next move before he can take his next breath. I tuck and roll, coming up behind him in a flash. With a savage twist, I sheath both daggers into his carotid arteries, his blood coating my hands in a slick, sticky mess. Using my foot, I kick off his back, dislodging my daggers to face the next filthy pirate charging me.

He swings his sword with a roar, and I meet his blade with both daggers, the weight of his swing sending shockwaves up my arms. The bastard releases one hand from his sword, and before I can react, his fist connects with my face in a sucker punch that snaps my head back. Stars explode behind my eyes, and for a second, I swear I can see through time.

But I'm not about to let this walking petri dish of bad hygiene get the best of me. I drop to the ground, sliding beneath the pirate's legs. With a vicious thrust that would make a proctologist wince, I shove my daggers up into his groin. His scream of agony is music to my ears, a beautiful symphony of karma and instant regret. "Didn't your mother ever teach you it's not polite to hit a lady, asshole?" I quip. "Or did she drop you on your head one too many times as a baby? Actually, don't answer that. I think we both know the answer."

"Goddamn it, Dani," Rhyland's voice echoes in my head, his worry palpable through our bond. *"I'm coming. Just hold on."*

I quickly roll to my feet, another pirate slamming me up against the wall, a barrel digging into my back. White-hot pain shoots through my lower spine, but I refuse to let it show. "You're out of your league, little lass," he sneers, his rancid breath washing over me in a putrid stench.

Spittle flies from his black, rotting teeth, and it takes every ounce of willpower I have not to vomit. I channel my inner Rhyland, remembering his *Viking Fighting 101* lessons. With a quick jerk, I slam my forehead against the pirate's nose with a sickening crunch.

He staggers back, blood gushing from his shattered nose. His hand comes up to cup his face, his eyes wide with shock and pain. I don't give him a chance to recover. With a fierce cry, I slam my foot into his gut, putting every ounce of strength I have behind the blow. He goes down like a sack of bricks, his body crumpling to the ground in a heap of filthy rags and unwashed flesh.

I finally get some breathing room, the remaining pirates circling me like sharks. One of them, a particularly ugly bastard with a face like a bulldog chewing on a wasp, leers at me with a predatory grin.

"You're going to pay for this, bitch," he snarls. "And when I get my hands on you, I'm going to take my dick and fuck you until you scream, until you wish you were dead. Then I'm going to fuck your corpse."

I feel my stomach churn at his words, a wave of revulsion washing over me. But I don't let it show, my face a mask of sassy defiance. "Sorry, ugly," I fire back. "I don't do necrophilia. And even if I did, I'd rather fuck a cactus than let your tiny, shriveled excuse for a dick anywhere near me."

His face contorts with rage, his eyes bulging as he lets out a roar of fury. It's like looking into the face of a rabid dog, all frothing madness and primal fury.

He charges at me, his sword raised high above his head, ready to cleave me in two. But I'm not about to let that happen. I've been through too much, fought too hard, to let some scurvy-ridden bastard take me out now.

I can feel the familiar heat building in my hands—that inner fire—always simmering beneath the surface. It's a part of me, as much as my snark and attitude. And right now, I'm tired, pissed off, and in desperate need of a bathroom break.

With a flick of my wrists, my daggers burst into flames, the blades erupting with a brilliant, white-hot glow that illuminates the dank, shadowy bowels of the ship. It's like I'm holding two miniature suns in my hands, the heat so intense I can feel it on my face.

Holy shit. Okay, that's new.

I stare at my flaming daggers in shock, my mind struggling to process what I see. I've always known that my angelic heritage gave me specific abilities. But this? This is something else entirely.

The bastard's ugly face hardens. "Witch!" He lets out another roar, tinged with a hint of desperation, and lunges at me with all his might. But I'm ready for him.

Our blades collide in a cacophony of metal and magic, my flaming daggers hissing and spitting against the cold steel of his sword. The clash sends sparks flying, each a miniature star born and dying instantly. The heat is oppressive, warping the air around us into shimmering waves, but I remain laser-focused, my senses heightened by the rush of battle.

We weave a deadly dance, our weapons flashing in the dim light like lethal lightning. The pirate moves with a fluid grace that speaks of years of combat, but against the inferno raging through my veins, his skill is a candle before a wildfire.

With a primal roar that tears from my throat, I channel every ounce of my angelic fury into one devastating strike. My blazing daggers cleave through his sword as if it were nothing more than parchment, the metal liquefying and then shattering in a shower of molten droplets and glittering shards.

The pirate staggers backward, his face a mask of terror and disbelief. The acrid stench of fear mingles with the heavy smoke and sweat. His eyes, wide with horror, reflect the dancing flames of my daggers as realization dawns—he's staring death in the face.

I lunge forward, my body moving with inhuman speed. My daggers trace twin arcs of searing light through the air, leaving fire trails in their wake. They find their mark with brutal precision, sinking deep into flesh and bone.

The pirate's scream of agony is cut brutally short, replaced by the sickening sizzle of burning flesh. His body crumples to the ground, smoke rising from the charred ruin of his chest. The smell of cooked meat and scorched hair fills the air, a grim testament to the devastating power of angelic fire.

The other pirates watch in horror as their comrade falls. I stand amidst the carnage; my daggers still wreathed in flames. "Who's next?" I taunt, my voice ragged as I pant, chest heaving. "Come on, boys. Let's dance."

The pirates hesitate, their eyes darting between me and their fallen friend, his body still smoking on the floor. I can see the fear etched into their faces, the dawning realization that they've stepped into a world of shit they never could have imagined. They know they're outmatched and facing something far beyond their meager comprehension.

Before they can move, a familiar voice cuts through the tension, "You're all fucked."

The pirates whirl around, their faces draining of color as they face the massive Viking vampire. He stands there like an avenging angel, his azure eyes blazing with fury, his fangs bared in a snarl that promises nothing but pain and death.

I grin, feeling relief like a cool breeze on a hot day. "Looks like the cavalry is here, boys," I quip. "And trust me, he's not nearly as nice as I am."

The pirates try to scatter like rats fleeing a sinking ship, their courage failing in the face of Rhyland's wrath. But there's nowhere for them to run, nowhere to hide. Rhyland is on them in a blur of motion, his body moving with a speed and grace that defies belief.

I watch in morbid fascination as he tears through them. His fangs sink into flesh, tearing out throats with a savage efficiency that borders on artistry. Blood splatters the walls and floor, painting the ship's bowels in a macabre canvas of crimson and gore. The screams of the dying fill the air, a symphony of agony and despair that echoes through the confined space like a twisted lullaby.

I know I should be recoiling in horror, averting my eyes from the brutal spectacle unfolding before me. But I'm transfixed, my gaze locked on Rhyland as he tears through our enemies like a hurricane of flesh and fang. There's a savage beauty to his movements, a deadly grace that's as mesmerizing as terrifying.

Rhyland is a force of nature unleashed, a Viking god. His eyes blaze with an unholy fire, his muscles rippling beneath blood-spattered skin as he deals out death with terrifying efficiency. It's violence in its purest form, unadulterated and unrestrained.

Goddamn, I'm utterly captivated.

Watching Rhyland like this and seeing the full extent of his capabilities doesn't scare me. It thrills me to my very core.

I'm witnessing the unleashing of a primal force, a glimpse into the heart of the predator that lurks beneath Rhyland's civilized exterior. And God help me, but I've never been more turned on in my life.

In a matter of moments, it's over. The pirates lie crumpled at Rhyland's feet, their bodies broken and lifeless. Blood drips from his mouth, staining his beard and running down his chin. He looks like a god of war, a primal deity of blood and death.

I stare at him, my breathing still in ragged gasps, my heart pounding. Rhyland stares back at me, his eyes filled with a swirling maelstrom of emotions. There's fury there, a white-hot rage that could consume the world. But there's also love, a fierce, protective devotion that takes my breath away.

I know I've pissed him off, that he's furious with me for putting myself in danger. But looking at him now, seeing how he's torn through our enemies like they were nothing more than paper dolls, I can't bring myself to care.

"What the fuck were you thinking, Dani?" Rhyland growls. "You could have been killed."

I shrug, "But I wasn't," my tone sassy and unapologetic. "And besides, I had it under control."

Rhyland snorts. "Under control? Is that what you call nearly getting your throat slit by a bunch of filthy pirates?"

I grin, twirling my still-flaming daggers in my hands. "Hey, it's not my fault they underestimated the power of a pissed-off angel with a set of magic daggers."

Rhyland stalks towards me. His movements are predatory and deliberate, like a wolf closing in on its prey. His chest rises and falls with each breath, his emotions bleeding into me through our bond like a tidal wave crashing against the shore.

Oh yeah, he's *fucking* pissed.

The kind of anger that simmers beneath the surface, waiting to explode. But there's more than just rage coursing through him. I can feel the adrenaline pumping through his veins, the relief that I'm still standing, still breathing. But above all else, there's the fury, the searing wrath of an alpha male whose mate has defied him not once but *twice*.

I drop my flaming daggers to the floor. A surrender?

He reaches out, his hand wrapping around my throat like a vise, his fingers digging gently into my skin with slight pressure. I moan at the contact.

"Dani," he growls, his voice low and dangerous, sending heat straight to my core. "I will punish you for this. You've gone against me twice today in a matter of an hour."

I look at the blood on his mouth, the crimson stains painting his lips like a deadly work of art. My eyes trace back up to his, those swirling storms of blue that seem to pierce straight through to my soul. "What are you going do, babe?" I taunt, my breath ghosting across his skin, my lips so close to his that I can almost taste the coppery tang of blood.

The tension between us is electric, a palpable force that crackles and sizzles like a live wire. I can feel the heat of his body pressed against mine, the hard planes of his muscles molding to the soft curves of my own. His cock is rock-hard against my stomach. It's intoxicating, the way he makes me feel and sets my blood on fire with just a touch, just a look.

Rhyland's grip on my throat tightens, his fingers flexing against my skin in a silent warning. "You're playing with fire, Little Angel," he rumbles, his voice a low, feral growl that makes my toes curl. "You know what happens when you push me too far."

Oh, I do.

And right now, I'm so goddamn turned on it's not even funny. When your man's out there looking like a Viking god of war and destruction, morals tend to take a backseat to pure, unadulterated lust.

I arch an eyebrow. "Maybe I like playing with fire," I purr. "Maybe I want to see how far I can push you before you snap."

Rhyland's eyes flash with an almost feral hunger, a primal need threatening to consume us both. "Be careful what you wish for, baby," he warns. "You might just get it."

I lean in closer, my breath hot and heavy against his skin. "Promise?" I whisper a mix of sass and seduction, a challenge and an invitation all rolled into one.

I know I'm pushing him, pressing all his buttons like a kid in an elevator, but damn, I can't help myself. There's just something about how Rhyland's punishments make me feel, the way they set every nerve ending in my body on fire and leave me craving more. Call me twisted. I'm addicted to the rush, the thrill of knowing that I can drive him to the brink of madness just the same.

I know he'll never hurt me, not really. Oh, he might leave a few delicious bruises, might make me scream and beg and plead for mercy, but it's all part of the game we play. Because beneath all that alpha male dominance, the growls, snarls, and fierce possessiveness, there's a love that's so deep, so pure, it makes my heart ache.

Rhyland would rather cut off his arm than cause me any actual harm, and that knowledge is like a safety net, a cocoon of warmth and security that allows me to push him to the limit, to dance on the edge of the knife without fear of falling.

Maybe I am a sick bitch, a glutton for punishment who gets off on riling up her man until he's ready to explode. But you know what? I wouldn't have it any other way. Because in the end, when the pain fades and the pleasure takes over, when Rhyland holds me in his arms and whispers words of love and devotion against my skin, I know that every moment, every challenge, every push, and pull of our twisted little dance, is worth it.

And if that makes me a twisted bitch, well, so be it. I'll wear that label like a badge of fucking honor.

Rhyland growls, his grip just shy of cutting off my air supply. "You have no idea what you're in for, baby," he promises—a dark, sensual purr that weakens my knees. "But you're about to find out."

RHYLAND

59

The desire to punish my angel is a raging inferno inside me, but I've got bigger issues to deal with right now—namely, that cocksucker Bloodbane. I storm up to the upper deck, Dani hot on my heels, and it's like stepping into a goddamn war zone. Gideon's crew and Bloodbane's are going at it like rabid dogs, the clash of steel and the screams of the wounded filling the air like a fucked-up symphony.

We'd swung over and boarded Bloodbane's ship as soon as we got within spitting distance, and now it's all hands on deck—literally. I catch a glimpse of Erik in the middle of the shitstorm, his sword flashing in the sunlight as he cuts down pirates left and right like they're nothing more than fucking weeds. The stubborn bastard's back to his old self now that he's got some fresh blood pumping through his veins, and he's unleashing holy hell on these poor, unsuspecting fucks.

And then, like a bolt from the blue, I spot Bloodbane. The fucker's right there, in the thick of it all, and I don't waste a single goddamn second. I blur to him faster than a blink of an eye; my fangs bared in a snarl as I sink them deep into his neck with a sickening crunch. The bastard squirms and fights like a man possessed, his strength almost a match for my own, but I'm running on pure, unadulterated rage now, and no force in heaven or hell can stop me.

The metallic taste of blood floods my mouth as I rip and tear, my jaw locking like a fucking pit bull. With a vicious jerk of my head, I tear his throat out, unleashing a geyser of crimson that paints the deck in gruesome splatter.

Bloodbane's scream turns into a wet, gurgling rasp, the sound of a man drowning in his blood. I flip him onto his back, the impact echoing like a thunderclap across the ship. His eyes, wide with terror and disbelief, lock onto mine as I call upon my power.

The air around us crackles with energy as I focus my telekinesis, forcing his blood to choke him from the inside out. I can feel every pulse, every desperate attempt to breathe as I squeeze tighter and tighter. Bloodbane's body convulses, his hands clawing at his throat as if he could somehow stop the inevitable.

I lean in close, my face inches from his. His blood drips from my lips, splattering onto his cheeks like some fucked up war paint. "This is for fucking with what's mine, you piece of shit," I snarl, my voice a guttural growl that barely sounds human.

With one final, savage pulse of power, I let it all go. The result is instantaneous and horrifying. Bloodbane's body explodes in a shower of gore, chunks of flesh and bone raining down around me like some twisted, gruesome confetti. The air is thick with the coppery scent of blood, the deck slick with viscera.

I stand there, chest heaving, covered in the remains of my enemy. The rage slowly ebbs, replaced by a cold, savage satisfaction. Let this be a fucking lesson to anyone who dares to threaten what's mine.

My eyes sweep the deck, searching for Dani amidst the chaos and carnage. And then I see her, locked in a deadly dance with two of Bloodbane's goons, her blades wreathed in the searing white flames of her angel fire. She's a vision of lethal grace, her movements fluid and precise as she dodges and thrusts, but I'll be damned if I let her face these bastards alone.

I blur to her side in a heartbeat, my hands finding the throats of the two savages who dared to threaten my mate. I squeeze with all my might, feeling their windpipes collapse beneath my fingers like fucking paper, and then I wrench their necks to the side with a sickening crack, the sound of their spines snapping like music to my ears.

Dani's eyes lock with mine as I let the bodies drop to the deck, and the heat in her gaze is enough to set my blood on fire. I can feel her arousal thrumming through our bond like a live wire—smell it and taste it on my tongue—the primal part of her responding to the sight of me unleashing my darker side. It's a heady fucking feeling, knowing that she accepts every part of me, even the parts that most people would run screaming from.

Focus.

We throw ourselves back into the fray, our blades and bodies moving in perfect sync as we cut a bloody swath through Bloodbane's crew. It's a fucking massacre, the deck of The Crimson Fury running red with the blood of the fallen, but we don't stop, can't stop, not until every last one of these bastards is dead or dying at our feet.

Just as suddenly as it began, it's over. The last of Bloodbane's men fall with a gurgling scream, and an eerie silence descends over the ship, broken only by the ragged sound of our own breathing and the gentle lapping of the waves against the hull.

Despite all this death and destruction, I can't take my eyes off Dani. She's a damn vision—a goddess of war, her hair wild and her eyes blazing with a golden feral light that sets my soul on fire. And I know, with a bone-deep certainty, that there's nothing in this world or any other that I wouldn't do to keep her safe and by my side for all eternity, even when she goes against me.

With The Crimson Fury nothing more than a smoldering wreck on the horizon, Dani and I finally have a moment to breathe. We'd washed up and changed out of our blood-soaked clothes, and now we're standing on the upper deck of The Seraph, watching the last remnants of Bloodbane's ship burn like a fucking funeral pyre.

Lucian's holed up below with Seraphina, practically snarling at anyone who dares to come within ten feet of her until she wakes up. The poor bastard's been through hell and back, so we all decided to give him some space, even Dani, though I could tell it was killing her to leave her friend's side.

Gideon's got us pointed towards Tempest Isle and says we should be there within a day or two if the winds hold steady. It's a welcome respite after the shitstorm we just weathered, but there's still one little matter that needs attending to—namely, Dani's punishment for scaring the ever-loving fuck out of me with that portal stunt.

I spin her around and cage her in with my arms, my hands gripping the railing on either side of her as I lean in close. "Now, back to what we were discussing, woman," my voice low and dangerous. "Your punishment."

Dani tilts her head back, her caramel gold eyes flickering with apprehension and false bravado as she meets my gaze. "Oh, is that so, big guy?" she challenges, her tone aiming for sass but falling short. "And just what did you have in mind? Because let me tell you, I can handle anything you dish out...I think."

Fuck, this woman drives me crazy. She's trying to put on a brave face—bait me. But I can see the uncertainty lurking beneath the surface. She knows damn well I'd never lay a finger on her in anger, but the anticipation of the unknown is getting to her. I could edge her for hours, driving her to the brink of insanity with pleasure until she is begging me for release. Or I could spank that perfect ass of hers until it's red and raw, then heal her with my tongue and start all over again. Hell, I could even tie her up and leave her spread open and aching for me until we reach the island, teasing her mercilessly the whole damn way.

Or, if I'm feeling particularly sadistic, I could do all fucking three.

The possibilities are endless, and I feel my cock twitching in anticipation as I lean in close, my lips brushing against the shell of her ear. "Oh, I've got plenty of ideas, baby. And trust me, by the time I'm done with you, you'll be lucky if you can walk straight."

Dani meets my gaze. "Oh really, Mr. Big Bad? And here I thought the fierce Viking was going soft on me. Why don't you prove me wrong... if you dare?"

"Don't push me, woman." I warn.

"All I'm hearing is talk," she taunts back, pressing closer. "No action. Maybe you're not the alpha male, everyone thinks—"

My control snaps. In one swift motion, I throw Dani over my shoulder, her startled squeal of protest only spurring me on as I stride purposefully toward our cabin. "You want action, baby? I'll give you fucking action," I promise darkly.

By the time I'm done with her, she'll be so thoroughly fucked and satisfied that she won't even remember what she did to deserve this punishment in the first place.

That's just the way I like it. And from the way Dani's squirming against me, her arousal permeating the air, I'd say she likes it, too.

LUCIAN

60

I'm sitting in our quiet cabin on the ship, hunched over the bed like a gargoyle, clutching a damp washcloth. I'm gently dabbing at Seraphina's face, wiping away the grime and blood, my heart racing with each ragged breath she takes. She sprawls out on the bed like a fallen angel. Her golden hair fanned across the pillow, her skin radiant and beautiful.

I'm trying to hold it together, to be the stoic hero she needs, but inside? I'm a complete mess. My mind races, conjuring all sorts of horrible scenarios about what those sick bastards could've done to her. I can't take the peanut gallery's pitying looks and hushed whispers anymore.

I snap. "Everybody out!" I snarl, eyes wild and desperate. "I need some quality time with my mate, so kindly fuck off and let me brood in peace!"

They scatter, leaving me alone with my comatose angel and the oppressive silence. I stagger to my feet, legs shaking, and approach the liquor cabinet. I grab the nearest bottle of rum, not bothering to check the label and take a long, burning swig.

The alcohol scorches my throat, but it's a welcome distraction from the icy fear clawing at my insides. I slump against the wall, the bottle dangling from my trembling fingers, allowing my gaze to drift back to Seraphina.

She looks so fragile, so breakable, lying there like a shattered porcelain doll. It tears me apart to see her like this. I want to scoop her up in my arms and protect her from all the darkness in this fucked-up universe.

I'm torn; part of me wants to rip open my wrist and force-feed her my blood like the world's most fucked-up smoothie, thinking it will heal her and bring her back to me.

But then my conscience decides to pop up like an unwanted parasite, waving a red flag the size of Texas: "Hey, numbnuts, remember what happened with Dani?" No, I want my cupcake to sip from my veins because she wants to—because she craves that intimate connection with me. I'm not about that non-consensual blood-sucking life, no matter how much my body is begging me to just go for it.

So here I am, stuck between wanting to be a savior and not being a complete asshole. It's like being in a terrible choose-your-own-adventure book where all the endings suck.

Instead, I'm left doing the one thing I fucking hate—waiting. I'm drowning my sorrows in booze that tastes like it was filtered through a hobo's sock, praying to every god, demigod, and comic book hero I can think of.

I'm praying those golden eyes will open and light up my world again—losing her now, after just finding her? That's a twist I'm not ready for, a punchline I can't handle.

So I sit here, marinating in my helplessness, hoping that somewhere in the cosmos, someone's listening to the desperate pleas of a lovesick vampire. Come on, universe. Don't screw me on this.

And then, like a Hallmark movie, "Lucian?"

The bottle slips from my fingers, shattering on the floor in an explosion of glass and wasted alcohol. I couldn't care less about the mess. I'm at her side in a flash, my hands hovering over her, afraid to touch, scared I might break her even more.

"Hey, baby girl," I whisper, my voice thick with emotion. "Welcome back to the land of the living. You had me worried there for a second. How ya feeling? Like you got trampled by a herd of elephants or just a really enthusiastic marching band?"

She lets out a weak chuckle. "More like a marching band of elephants," she croaks, her eyes fluttering open to meet mine. "You came for me? Saved me?"

The way she asks the question, like it's a surprise, makes my heart clench. I cup her face, my thumbs brushing over her cheekbones. "Of course, I came for you, Cupcake," I say fiercely, my eyes locked onto hers. "I would've moved heaven and earth to get to you. Hell, I would've taken on the whole fucking universe if that's what it took. You think I'd just leave you hanging like a forgotten ornament? Not a chance in hell, sweetheart."

I shake my head, my jaw tightening at the memory of those agonizing hours spent not knowing if she was alive or dead. "It was a nightmare not being able to get to you sooner," I admit. "I've never felt so helpless in my life. And trust me, I've been in some pretty fucked-up situations, but this? This was a whole new level of suck."

Seraphina sighs, her sunlit gold eyes watching me. Her voice is soft and exhausted, like a whisper in the wind. "They gave me something—put it over my face—it smelled horrible. I couldn't breathe—I couldn't fight them—they were so strong and—"

She's trying so hard to explain, and each word is a struggle. It tears me up inside, like watching a wounded bird trying to fly.

"Shhhh, easy there, angel face," gently combing my fingers through her golden locks. It feels like touching spun sunshine, if sunshine could get traumatized. "You're okay now. You're safe now."

My mind races, piecing together this fucked-up puzzle. Sounds like those assholes hit her with some knockout gas, probably chloroform or something equally nasty.

Her eyes, those golden pools I'd happily drown in, shimmer with unshed tears. Her voice barely above a whisper, "I saw what they did to you, Lucian. It hurt so much—I thought they killed you. I screamed and—"

The thought of her witnessing that hits me like a freight train. I close my eyes for a moment, trying to keep my composure, but I can feel the rage and pain bubbling beneath the surface.

"Phina-baby," my voice low and intense, fighting to keep it steady. "I'm okay... see? I'm right here, baby girl. Not going anywhere."

I want to make a joke, to lighten the mood, but I can't find the words. All I can think about is how terrified she must have been, how much it hurt her to see me like that. It makes my chest ache in a way that has nothing to do with physical pain.

Before I can even blink, she launches herself at me, her arms wrapping around my neck tightly. Her embrace knocks me off balance, and we tumble back onto the bed in a tangle of limbs.

"I'm so glad you're okay...thank you," she whispers into my ear, her breath hot against my skin. "Thank you for saving me."

I bury my face in her neck, breathing in her sweet, intoxicating scent. She smells like cinnamon, sugar, and everything good in this world, and I never want to let her go. I wrap my arms around her waist, holding her close, feeling the steady thump of her heartbeat against my chest.

"I'll always save you, Cupcake," I murmur, my lips brushing against her pulse point. "No matter what it takes or what I have to do, I'll always come for you. You're my everything, baby girl. My whole fucking world. Without you, I'm just a sad, lonely sack of shit with a healing factor and a smart mouth."

She laughs, the sound sending shockwaves through my body like an earthquake. Little Lucian stands at attention, ready to salute the skies, and I'm pretty sure Seraphina can feel the effect she's having on me.

"You're not lonely, Lucian. Not anymore. You are so brave... caring," she pauses, "And..."

She stands up, her movements fluid and graceful, positioning herself directly before me. I sit up on the edge of the bed, my eyes glued to her every move as her fingers thread through my hair, tugging gently as she nudges her way between my legs. The sensation is so intense, so overwhelming, that my eyes roll back, and I have to fight back a moan.

I reach up, my hands finding her luscious hips, anchoring myself to her like she's the only thing keeping me from floating away.

She bends down, her lips hovering just a hair's breadth from mine, her breath hot and sweet against my skin. "And so, so handsome." She licks her lips and straddles me. "Lucian," she whispers, "make love to me. Now."

Well, fuck. My eyes snap open, and I stare at her like a deer caught in the headlights of a semi-truck. "Are you, umm... sure that's wise right now?" I stammer, my brain short-circuiting at the thought of what she's asking. "I mean, with everything that's happened, and you just waking up, and—"

She cuts off my rambling with her lips, kissing me with a passion and intensity that steals the breath from my lungs. Her tongue dances with mine, teasing and exploring, and I can taste the need, desperation, and raw, unbridled desire on her lips.

"I can heal, Lucian—I'm feeling better than ever and seeing things clearly. I see you. Please," she breathes, her words hot and heavy against my mouth, "just shut up and make love to me—show me how it's done. Teach me, Lucian. I need to feel closer to you, and I want all of you inside me."

Holy fucking mother of all things divine and sacred. She's begging me, pleading for me to take her, to claim her, to make her mine in every possible way. And I can't be happier, can't be more fucking honored and humbled—and terrified—all at once.

I lean back just enough to lock eyes with her, and what I see there would knock me flat on my ass if I wasn't already sitting. There's love, trust, and a need so intense it could melt vibranium. It's like staring into the sun—if the sun were made of pure desire.

Her body is pressed up against me—Little Lucian is standing at full attention, saluting like his life depends on it. It's taking every ounce of self-control not to dive in like it's the world's sexiest swimming pool.

"Are you sure about this, sweetheart?" my voice rougher than sandpaper. "Because this ain't no test drive, Cupcake. Once we cross this line, no U-turns are allowed. I'm talking full-on, no-takebacks, til-death-do-us-part kinda deal here. You'll be mine in every way possible, body and soul, for all eternity. We're talking longer than a Marvel movie marathon, including all the post-credit scenes."

I'm trying to be responsible and offer her an out if she wants it. But every fiber of my being is screaming to shut the fuck up and claim her already.

She smiles, her hand coming up to cup my cheek, her thumb brushing over my lower lip as if she's trying to memorize every curve and contour. "Lucian, I've never been more certain about anything in my entire existence," her voice soft but filled with a fierce determination that makes my heart skip a beat.

"I want what Dani and Rhyland have, that beautiful, all-consuming love that defies the very laws of nature. And you, my darling demon, make me laugh, smile, and feel things I never even knew were possible." She pauses, her fingers threading through my hair like she's trying to weave herself into my very being.

"I want to be yours, Lucian, in every sense of the word. I want to belong to you—body, soul, and everything in between. So please, make me yours."

With those magical words, any last shred of doubt or hesitation vanishes like a fart in the wind. I surge forward, capturing her lips in a kiss that's pure teeth, tongue, and primal, desperate need. My hands roam all over her like an over-caffeinated octopus, mapping out every curve and hollow, committing every glorious inch of her to memory.

I rip open her corset like a kid on Christmas morning, but instead of presents, I'm unwrapping the most delectable pair of breasts I've ever laid eyes on. The flimsy fabric doesn't stand a chance against my raging desire for this angel in my arms. Her breasts bounce free, perky, and perfect, like two scoops of heavenly ice cream begging to be devoured.

She grinds against my hips, her hands tangling in my hair as I flip her onto the bed, her body open and willing for all sorts of deliciously sinful things.

"I want you so damn bad, beautiful," I growl against her skin, my lips blazing a trail down her neck, across her collarbone, and over the swell of her perfect, bouncy breasts. "I'm gonna make love to you like you've never been loved. I'm talking full-on worship of every single inch of you until you're screaming my name, seeing stars, and forgetting everything else except my hands on this amazing body."

This isn't what I had envisioned for her first time. I had this unconventional yet undeniably romantic scenario cooked up in my head. A moonlit picnic in a secluded spot, complete with chimichangas, tequila, and a serenade from yours truly. Maybe a little skinny dipping to set the mood, followed by a sensual massage with whipped cream and chocolate sauce. You know, classy shit like that. I wanted her first dip in the Lucian Love Pond to be an unforgettable, wild ride.

My innocent little angel deserves the most mind-blowingly unique and tender introduction to the art of making love, not some hasty, desperate romp on a creaky bed in a fucking pirate ship cabin.

But hey, when life gives you lemons, you say, "fuck the lemons," and bail. Or, in this case, when life puts you on a pirate ship with your girl begging you to pop her cherry, you grab life by the balls and go for it.

Adapt, improvise, overcome.

Sure, it might not be the most conventional setting for deflowering my sweet, innocent angel, but damn if it isn't going to be the most mind-blowing, earth-shattering, soul-bonding experience of my entire existence. The way she's looking at me, the way she feels, the way she's begging me like a prayer... that's the kind of shit that stays with a man.

Ultimately, all that matters is connecting on the deepest level possible, giving each other everything we have. And that, my friends, is the real fucking romance right there.

She arches into my touch, fingers raking down my back, breath coming in short, sharp gasps like music to my ears. "Yes," she whimpers. "Please, Lucian. I need you. I want to feel... this. Show me everything."

I can't resist her, not when she's begging so sweetly and looking at me like I'm the last chimichanga in a world full of salads. I latch onto one of her nipples, sucking, nibbling, and teasing it until it's as hard as my moral dilemmas. She writhes beneath me, her hips bucking in search of friction. With a quick shimmy, I get her out of that skirt, the fabric falling away to reveal miles of smooth, sun-kissed skin just begging to be licked, bitten, and marked as mine.

Then, in a blur of motion that would make the Flash look like a geriatric turtle, I'm out of my clothes, standing in all my naked glory. Little Lucian is ready for action, standing tall and proud, leaking a bead of precum glistening at the tip like a fucking crown jewel.

Seraphina's eyes lock onto my cock like it's the Holy Grail, her breath catching in her throat, her tongue darting out to wet her lips in a way that makes me want to shove it down her throat and face-fuck her until she's gasping for air.

Later, Lucian.

"Is that... going to *fit?*" Her voice is laced with awe and trepidation—like she's not quite sure whether to be scared or excited by the prospect of taking my massive length inside her.

I can't help but laugh at her adorable innocence, even as my cock twitches and throbs at the thought of sinking into her tight, virgin heat. "Oh, it's gonna fit, Cupcake," I assure her, my voice low and rough with desire. "I'll go nice and slow—you'll love every second of it. I'm going to stretch you open and fill you up and make you come so hard you'll forget what two plus two is."

Seraphina's eyes are dark with desire, her pupils blown wide like she's high on the world's most potent aphrodisiac. The taste of her arousal on my tongue? It's headier than a triple shot of whiskey, sweeter than ambrosia, and more addictive than any drug on the market.

She reacts to my words like they're a direct line to her libido, and I'm filing that little tidbit away for future reference. Dirty talk is like catnip for my celestial sweetheart—good to know.

I lay over her on the bed, her legs falling open like a fucking invitation, her pussy glistening and ready for me. "But first," I murmur, my eyes darkening with hunger as I feast my gaze on the wet, pink perfection of her pussy, "I've gotta get you nice and wet, sweetheart. I want to make sure you're ready for me, that you can take every inch of my cock without breaking."

I spread her legs wider, my fingers digging into the soft flesh of her thighs as I lower my head between her legs, my breath hot against her skin. Her eyes light up, and she bites her lip, a soft, desperate moan escaping her throat. "Yes, please," she whimpers, her hips bucking up towards my face in a silent plea. "Do that... thing again with your tongue..."

I smirk. I don't need to be told twice. I dive in like a man possessed, my mouth latching onto her clit and sucking hard, my tongue flicking and swirling until she's thrashing beneath me, her hands fisted in my hair as she tries to grind herself against my face. I lap at her like a man dying of thirst, my tongue delving deep into her tight, dripping hole, my nose nudging against her clit with every thrust.

"God... Lucian... yes."

Either I'm the pussy-eating champion of all the seven realms, or Seraphina's just one of those girls who can come faster than a speeding bullet. Maybe it's a virgin thing, like a hair trigger on a loaded gun.

She comes apart like a fucking supernova, her back arching off the bed as she screams my name like it's the only word she knows. Her pussy's clenching and fluttering around my tongue like it's trying to keep me there forever, and I sure as hell ain't complaining. I keep going, licking and sucking her through the aftershocks until she's a boneless, whimpering mess beneath me. When I finally come up for air, my face shines like a glazed donut, and I lick my lips with a satisfied smirk, savoring every last drop of her sweet nectar.

"Damn, sweetheart," I pant. "You taste like the sweetest fucking candy in the world. I could feast on this delectable little pussy of yours all goddamn day and never get tired of it."

But my insatiable Nimbus Nugget is not having it, not when she's so desperate for more, for every inch of my throbbing dick. She reaches for me with trembling hands, her eyes glazed over with a heady cocktail of lust and need that's making me harder than Chinese algebra. "Yes, I would love that. Your mouth, the things you do with your tongue... it's... it's indescribable," she whimpers, her voice cracking with pure, unbridled desire. "But...I need..."

"I know what you need, baby girl."

I crawl up her body, my cock leaving a trail of precum on her skin as I go until I'm hovering over her, the tip of my dick nudging against her entrance. "This might hurt a little," I warn her, my voice strained with the effort of holding back, of not just slamming into her and fucking her into oblivion. "But I promise, it'll be worth it. I'm gonna make you feel so fucking good; you'll never want anyone else inside you."

She nods, her eyes locked on mine with anticipation and trepidation. Her breath quickens as she braces herself for the pleasure to come. I gently nudge the head of my cock at her entrance, teasing both of us with the promise of what's to come. A wave of raw, electric ecstasy shoots through me as I begin to penetrate her inch by glorious inch.

Seraphina moans, a soft whimper escaping her lips as she feels the stretch. "Just relax and breathe, sweetheart," I murmur, my voice hoarse with desire. "I'll take it slow and gentle, savoring every moment with you."

I capture her lips in a deep, passionate kiss, my tongue tangling with hers as I slowly inch my way inside her. She squirms beneath me, her body adjusting to the invasion, her walls clutching at me like a silky velvet vise. I swallow her moans, our tongues dueling in a rhythm as old as time.

With every gentle thrust, I delve deeper into her core, our bodies locking together like two pieces of a puzzle finally fitting into place. Seraphina squirms beneath me, her body demanding more, needing to feel me buried to the hilt. She wraps her legs around my waist, pulling me closer, a silent plea to drive home and claim her fully.

With one swift, sure thrust, I bury myself inside her, my balls slapping against her ass as I bottom out. I feel the light snap against my cock—her innocence—and I groan with need.

She cries out, her nails digging into my shoulders, her pussy clenching around me, and for a moment, I'm afraid I've hurt her, that I've ruined this perfect fucking moment.

But then she starts moving beneath me, her hips rocking up to meet mine, her legs squeezing around my waist tighter than a sexy koala, pulling me deeper into her scorching heat. That's when I know she's more than okay—she wants this just as badly as I do, if not more.

"Holy fuck, Phina-baby," I groan, my forehead pressed against hers as I start to move, my hips snapping forward in a rhythm that's as steady and relentless. "You feel so fucking incredible. So tight, so perfect, like you were custom-made just for me, like a bespoke suit but a million times better."

She giggles, whimpers, and moans, her head thrown back on the pillow as I rock into her, my cock stretching her open and filling her up in a way she's never been filled before. "I feel...so full," she pants, her voice high, breathy, and desperate. "you're so big—don't stop, please don't stop. I need more, harder, faster, please."

I comply with a growl, my hips pistoning forward as I fuck her with abandon, the bed creaking and groaning beneath us as we move together, our bodies slick with sweat and her juices. I can feel her getting close, her pussy fluttering around my cock, her breathing coming in short, sharp gasps, and I know that I'm not far behind, that I'm going to fill her up with my cum and make her mine in every way possible.

My eyes can't help but wander down to the space between our bodies, and holy shit; it's like a fucking work of art. There, glistening on my cock, is the unmistakable evidence of her innocence. It's the most delicate shade of pink, a beautiful contrast against my skin, and it's all because of her blood. Her virgin blood.

And fuck me sideways, but I want to dive in face-first and taste it. I want to savor every last drop of that precious innocence, to let her blood dance on my tongue like some kind of forbidden elixir. I can practically feel my fangs tingling with anticipation, begging me to just go for it.

I know, I know. You're probably thinking, "Lucian, you sick bastard! That's some twisted shit right there." But hey, I'm a vampire, remember? We're not exactly known for our conventional tastes. The sight and scent of blood is like a goddamn aphrodisiac to us, and when it's the blood of our soulmate? Of an angel, no less? Well, let's just say it's like mainlining pure ecstasy straight into our veins.

Fuck, she feels fantastic. Better than anything I've ever experienced in my entire messed-up existence. Her pussy squeezes me tight, making me see stars and shit. I kiss her deeply, my tongue tangling with hers as I pound my cock into her snug little hole. She's moaning and squirming and begging for more, like a damn nympho, and I am *living* for it.

She breaks away, breathless and panting, "Lucian..." she wines, and her eyes drift closed as she arches her back, riding the waves of pleasure beneath me.

"Yeah, baby girl? Tell me what you're feeling. Do I need to dial it down a notch, or can you handle more of the Lucian Special?" I smirk, sucking her tight nipple.

"Oh, god..." She bites her lip, her eyes fluttering open to meet mine. "I feel like I'm about to—"

"Explode like the motherfuckin' Fourth of July?" I finish for her with a grin, "explode for me, sweetheart," I command, my voice rough and strained with the effort of holding back my release. "Come on my cock like a good girl; let me feel you, beautiful."

And she does, her back arching off the bed as she screams my name, her pussy clamping down on me like a fucking vise as she comes apart beneath me. "Oh, *GOD*, Lucian!"

I stare down at her in awe, and I follow her over the edge with a roar, "Ungh, fff-fuuuck!" my hips slamming into hers one final time, my cock pulsing and twitching as I paint her insides with thick ropes of cum.

I tumble onto her, both of us gasping for air like we just ran a marathon. I find her mouth and kiss those sweet, angelic lips like they keep me alive. She kisses me back with a hunger that sets my soul on fire.

"That was... oh my goodness. The most incredible thing I've ever felt," she murmurs against my lips, her voice soft and filled with wonder.

And she's right. It was earth-shattering. Seraphina, my beautiful angel, my soulmate—the best sex of my entire existence, and I know it will only get better from here. "I know, Cupcake. You were un-fucking-believable. A goddamn natural."

She kisses me again like she's starving for my touch—like she can't get enough. Then she pulls back, her golden eyes glowing with a renewed hunger that makes my spent cock grow and twitch with interest. "Can we... can we do that again? Please?" her voice sweet and innocent yet filled with unquenchable desire.

I can't help it—I burst out laughing, the sound filled with pure, unadulterated joy. My girl, my greedy, perfect girl, is going to be the death of me, and I couldn't be happier about it.

I laugh, kissing her forehead. "We can do that as many times as you want. By the time I'm done with you, the only coherent thought in that pretty little head of yours will be my name, echoing like a broken record. Prepare to be thoroughly and utterly Lucian-ized, baby girl."

Her answering smile is blinding in its brightness, and she pulls me down for another kiss, her eager body already moving against mine. Round two, here we come.

Pun fucking intended.

DANICA

61

"Come on, baby, I know you've got one more in you," Rhyland growls, his voice a sinful caress that sends sparks shooting through my veins. "Give it to me. Give me what's mine."

I'm a quivering, boneless mess. My body wrung out from the relentless onslaught of pleasure he's inflicted upon me for the past...'I don't even know any more hours,' I feel like I've been fucked into oblivion and back again, every nerve ending raw and exposed.

So much for punishment, this is pure bliss wrapped up in a sadistic, sexy-as-hell package.

Sure, he spanked me all right. Each stinging slap sent jolts of electricity straight to my core, leaving me panting and writhing, craving more of that delicious pain. And when he sank his fangs into my tender flesh, his venom set my blood on fire, transforming my already dripping pussy into a veritable waterfall of need.

Now, he's got me straddling his lap as he sits on a wooden chair, my hands bound behind my back with a leather belt. The supple leather rubs against my skin, the sensation only fueling the inferno raging inside me as he impales me on his monster cock. "So perfect," he growls. "This pussy is a fucking paradise, baby. Wrap those legs tighter around me. Ride me hard, and take every inch of me."

Holy shit, his filthy words short-circuit my brain, reducing me to a mindless creature of pure lust. His fingers dig into my hips hard enough to bruise as he controls my movements, slamming me down onto his thick length until I see stars.

He edged me for hours until I was a writhing, whimpering mess, begging for release like it was oxygen and I was drowning. I screamed, pleaded, and I cursed him. I even threatened to portal his sexy ass to the seventh circle of hell if he didn't let me come. But he just smirked that infuriatingly sexy smirk of his and kept right on tormenting me—all just music to his sadistic little ears.

By the time he finally decided to show some mercy, my voice was so hoarse from all the begging that I sounded like a pack-a-day smoker with a severe case of laryngitis.

Now, he's making me come every five minutes—which I didn't even know was possible, and now I'm begging for a whole new reason. My body is so oversensitive that each orgasm feels like I'm being struck by lightning, pleasure so intense it borders on pain.

Rhyland's voice is pure sin, "Fuck, you're so goddamn beautiful—taking my cock like a greedy whore." he rocks up into me, his tip bumping my cervix—that elusive spot that makes my eyes roll back. "Just like that, baby. Take it all."

And then, because he's determined to kill me with pure sexual pleasure, he leans forward and captures my nipple between his teeth. The sharp sting of his bite sends lightning bolts straight to my core, which, at this point, is a raging inferno of need.

I'm pretty sure I make a noise that's half moan, half whimper as he lavishes attention on my sensitive peak. It's like there's a direct line from my nipple to my clit, and every flick of his tongue, every scrape of his teeth, and the delicious scrape of his beard just winds me tighter and tighter.

The ship begins to rock violently, the motion adding a whole new intensity to our already explosive connection.

It's like the ocean itself is conspiring to drive me crazy, the rhythm of the waves synchronizing with the roll of my hips. I'm riding him hard now, rising and falling on his thick length like my life depends on it.

The wooden chair creaks beneath us, a counterpoint to our ragged breathing and the slap of skin on skin. I'm vaguely aware of the sound of waves crashing outside, but it's drowned out by the pounding of my heart and the rush of blood in my ears.

Rhyland's grip on my hips is tight, "Fucking *Christ*, woman," He groans as he guides me up and down his thick length. "You feel that? The way my cock fills you up so perfectly?"

"Please, Rhyland," I gasp, my voice hoarse from hours of screaming and moaning. "I can't... I don't think I can..."

But even as I protest, I feel that familiar tightening in my core, that building pressure that signals another impending explosion. God help me, but it looks like my body's determined to give him exactly what he wants—one more earth-shattering orgasm.

He chuckles darkly. "Oh, you can, and you will, filthy girl. You'll come for me as many times as I demand. Because this pussy? This body? It's *mine.* And I'll take what's mine, over and over again, until you can't function."

And then I fall. My body crashes over the edge like a wave breaking, and I come with the force of a thousand suns. My body becomes a conduit for pure pleasure, and I come—hard. I clench and spasm around him, my nectar flowing over his cock and marking him as mine.

Rhyland growls, a sound of equal pride and sheer male satisfaction. "That's it. Good girl..." he praises. "Make a mess of me, baby. Let me feel how much I make you shake."

Holy hell, this man is my kryptonite! The way he gets off by making me lose control. With every release, I drench him, and the heat between us intensifies with every drop. He's the flame to my wildfire, the spark to my explosion, and I love every scorching moment.

Suddenly, Rhyland and I are flying across the small room as the ship starts its best impression of a bucking bronco. Outside, we hear men yelling, the wind howling, and waves battering the ship's sides.

Rhyland, ever the gentleman, quickly unties me and helps me get dressed. Now we're at the helm with Gideon, trying to keep our footing as the waves rise and fall around us like a demented roller coaster.

I swear to God, I'm going to grow fucking gills at this point. I'm half-tempted to portal back to the mortal realm and buy myself a damn wetsuit so that I can have a fighting chance of staying dry for more than five minutes at a stretch.

"What the hell is going on?" I shout over the crash of the waves, my voice barely audible over the roar of the wind and the pounding of the rain.

Bless his salty sea dog heart, Gideon grips the wheel tighter and grits his teeth. "Aye, it's the damn Sea Witch and her Dark Tides, lass," he yells back, his voice rough and strained with the effort of keeping the ship on course. "Best get back to shelter if you know what's good for you!"

Dark Tides? What the ever-loving hell? Calypso promised she wouldn't hinder my little quest for her, but apparently, the bitch lied. Is it because we killed Bloodbane, or does she know I went and had a little chat with Cordelia behind her back?

Before I can even begin to process this new development, Mirella is at my side, her eyes wide and urgent. "Dani, the Dark Tides, you must get below deck," she urges, her voice barely audible over the howling wind.

I nod, my hair plastered to my face in a wet, tangled mess. "Mirella, go," I shout, my voice nearly lost in the crash of the waves. "I'll be right behind you."

The clouds above us are an angry, roiling mass of black, the rain pounding down on us like a hailstorm. My clothes are soaked through, clinging to my skin like a second layer of flesh, and my hair is a soggy mess.

Rhyland, ever the protector, takes my hand and blurs us below deck in a flash of superhuman speed, his grip on me tight and reassuring.

As Rhyland and I stumble into the galley, trying to keep our footing on the wildly pitching deck, I'm greeted by a comforting and slightly disturbing sight. Erik, Lucian, Seraphina, and a handful of the crew are all gathered around the table, looking like they're trying to ride out the storm by sheer force of will.

But when I see Seraphina, alive and well and not looking any worse for wear after her little misadventure with Bloodbane, I feel a wave of relief crash over me. "Seraphina." I cry out over the chaos. "Thank god you're alright!"

I try to rush to her, but the ship chooses that exact moment to rock, sending me reeling into the table like a drunkard. I manage to right myself, and some-how, I make it to Seraphina's side and pull her into a bone-crushing hug.

"Are you okay?" I ask, my voice muffled against her shoulder as I cling to her.

Seraphina squeezes me back, her arms strong and reassuring. "Yes, I'm fine, Dani," her voice soft and soothing despite the chaos around us. "Thanks to you."

I feel a tug on my arm, and I reluctantly let go of Seraphina, only to see Lucian reaching for her. Seraphina slides back into his lap, cradling his head against her chest like a mother soothing a fussy baby.

Lucian, for his part, looks like he's about to audition for a role in *"The Exorcist."* His face is a sickly shade of green that makes me wonder if he will start spewing pea soup any second now. But Seraphina holds him close, murmuring soft words of comfort in his ear as she strokes his hair.

Seeing the usually unflappable Lucian reduced to a queasy mess is strange, but I can't blame him. The storm outside is raging like a pissed-off kraken, and even with my sea legs, I'm feeling a little green around the gills myself.

I'm clinging to a pole in the middle of the galley, trying to keep my balance as the ship tosses and turns. Rhyland comes up, caging me against his body, anchoring me to him like he's afraid I might go flying off into the great beyond.

Mirella stumbles down the stairs, her usually graceful movements reduced to a series of flailing limbs and near misses as she tries to find something—anything—to hold onto.

"Well, this is just freakin' great," I rant as I grip Rhyland's arms hard enough to leave bruises. "Calypso obviously can't even keep a goddamn Coral Pact promise without trying to drown us all in the process."

I let out a huff of frustration as the ship takes a nosedive, sending us all stumbling. Mirella shakes her head, her red hair flying around her face like a mermaid in a wind tunnel. "Not Calypso," she gasps before the ship pitches again, sending her flying.

Erik is there before she can crash into the wall, snatching her out of midair. He plops her down on his lap and wraps his arms around her, holding her steady like a human seatbelt.

"I've got you, Little Fish," he says, his voice low and soothing, like he's trying to calm a spooked horse.

Mirella's eyes go wide momentarily as if unsure what to make of this sudden display of chivalry. But then she relaxes against him, letting out a little sigh of relief. "Thank you."

The ship rights itself again, and I take the opportunity to catch my breath. "What do you mean, not Calypso?"

Mirella shakes her head, her face scrunching up like she's trying to solve a complicated math problem. "I can't..." she starts before letting out a growl of frustration. "Uugh!"

It's like watching someone try to talk through a mouthful of marbles, all sputtering and half-formed words and nonsensical gibberish. And suddenly, it hits me—Mirella's under some gag order, like a magical version of a non-disclosure agreement.

She's trying to tell me something, but she can't—the words are stuck in her throat and refusing to come out. It's the same kind of cryptic bullshit that Calypso pulled, all vague hints and half-truths and infuriating evasiveness.

I groan in frustration. I'm pissed off, in desperate need of a nap, and sick of this rocking ship; I bang my head against the pole like a particularly dense woodpecker. "My god," I mutter, my voice muffled against the wood. "Can't anything be easy?"

"Paper and quill," Mirella says urgently as if she's trying to impart the universe's secrets in three little words.

I stare at her momentarily, my mind racing to try to make sense of her words. It's like she's speaking in code—like there's some hidden message in her words that I'm supposed to decipher.

And suddenly, it clicks—she's trying to find a way around the gag order, a loophole in the magical red tape keeping her from talking.

Finally, the storm has fucked off to whatever watery hell it came from, and we can breathe without feeling like we're trying to inhale the entire ocean. We pick ourselves up off the floor and start cleaning up the galley, righting chairs, and chasing down all the shit that went flying during Calypso's little temper tantrum.

Most importantly, I managed to scrounge up a quill and some paper for Mirella because that's the key to unlocking whatever secrets she's been keeping.

We all gather around the table like it's storytime at the local library, and Mirella starts to spill her guts. "I learned to write after I found books," her voice all wistful and dreamy, like she remembers a long-lost love. "So many books, I love to read. That's how I found your tome, Dani—the book of the savior."

I do a double-take so hard I nearly give myself whiplash. Hold the damn phone—there are more books out there? About the prophecy?

And the fact that Mirella taught herself to read and write? That tells me this girl's probably got a stack of books taller than I am hidden away somewhere.

"Makes sense," Lucian chimes in from his side of the table, looking significantly less green now that the rocking has stopped and Seraphina is comfortably perched in his lap.

He gives a casual shrug, his trademark smart-ass smirk firmly in place. "I mean, every realm's got to have its own little stash of lore and prophecy, right? It's like a collector's edition with exclusive content."

"I found them in the Atlantean Ruins a while ago," she continues, all casual like she's talking about finding a particularly interesting seashell on the beach. "Cordelia doesn't know, of course."

Of course, she doesn't, because why would anything in this goddamn realm ever be simple? I look at Mirella, waiting for her to drop the next bombshell.

"Anyway, I read about you, coming with a crown and powers. Once I saw the crown—"

"The one you tried to steal," I remind her, with enough attitude to drown a small village.

Mirella has the decency to look embarrassed, her cheeks flushing a delicate shade of pink. "Yes, I am sorry," she says, all contrite. "I wanted to see if it was truly what the book spoke about, and I got a little grabby—once you mentioned you're the Savior and saw you complete the trial and retrieve the key, I knew you were the one foretold."

I sigh because what else is there to say? "Forgiven. Go on," I urge her.

That's when Mirella grabs the quill, dips it into the squid ink, and scribbles...

Cordelia stole my voice

I look up at her, my brow furrowed in confusion. "Wait, she did what?" I ask. "She stole your voice? As in, she literally took away your ability to speak about certain things?"

Mirella nods, her eyes wide and filled with relief and urgency. "Yes, that's precisely it," she confirms, her voice carrying a note of excitement at finally being able to communicate this crucial information.

I sit back in my chair, my mind racing to process the implications of this revelation. Stealing someone's voice is a level of magical control I've never encountered before, a gag order taken to the extreme.

What the hell is this queen hiding?

And with that, Mirella starts scribbling away again...

She has ~~tour~~ cursed and stolen all mer-
maid's voices to ~~speke~~ speak the truth

Mirella is writing at lightning speed, struggling to spell her words. Or maybe, since self-taught, she still has a bit to learn.

"What truth, Mirella?" I ask, my voice softening. I can see the weight of this secret in her eyes, and it tugs at my heart.

Mirella gives me a small, grateful smile, appreciating my patience. She dips her quill again, the gesture deliberate and careful. I lean in, my eyes fixed on the paper, eager to unravel this mystery burdening her.

What truth could be so crucial that Cordelia would go to such lengths to keep it hidden? And, more importantly, how will it affect our journey?

There's a tension in the air, thick with anticipation. Whatever Mirella's about to reveal, it's clear it's not just some trivial tidbit. It's something big, something that could change everything.

I take a deep breath, trying to calm my racing thoughts.

Cordelia controls the Dark Tides

DANICA

62

"**H**old up, Cordelia's pulling the strings with the Dark Tides?" I ask, my eyebrows shooting up so high they practically hit my hairline. "I thought Calypso was supposed to be the resident sea witch with a monopoly on all things aquatic."

Mirella shakes her head as she dips her pen back into the ink. With a few quick strokes, she scribbles out a response.

The stone Cordelia ~~potes~~ possesses control
the waters.

"The Aquanite stone." I muse, my mind racing to connect the dots. "So that's the secret behind the Dark Tides? But why? And more importantly, why let Calypso take the fall? And what curse?"

Mirella takes a deep breath, frustrated. "It is easier to show you than try to tell you."

"Okay, how do you show me?"

"The Atlantean Ruins has the answers. There's a book down there written by a mermaid scribe—a seer named Nixie."

Nixie?

That name hits me like a ton of bricks. "Nixie? As in the Gypsy on Captain's Haven?"

Mirella's eyes light up like she just won the underwater lottery. "You know Nixie?"

"I met her once," I confirm, my brow furrowing as I try to piece together this mind-bending puzzle. "She read my cards to me..." I squint my eyes shut, shaking my head. "Are you sure we're talking about the same person here? Because I'm pretty sure the Nixie I met had legs, not fins."

Mirella nods her head so frantically I'm half-worried it might fall off. "Yes, that's her... It's..." She struggles again, her words getting caught in her throat like a fish in a net. I point to the paper, silently urging her to write it down before she pops a blood vessel.

I can't blame her—if I couldn't speak my mind freely, I'd be pretty pissed off, too. She quickly scribbles again, her quill flying across the parchment...

> *Nixie ~~scibed~~ scribed her ~~vicion~~ vision. She*
> *was a mermaid before she traded her fins*
> *for legs to ~~permenetly permane escp~~ escape*
> *the sea and the curse*

Holy shit. If someone had told me that Nixie, of all people, would be tangled up in this underwater shit show, I would've laughed in their face. But here we are, and apparently, the Gypsy who read my fortune is a former mermaid with a direct line to the secrets of Atlantis.

Go figure.

And this curse she's talking about? I'm willing to bet my left tit that it's got everything to do with Mirella's magical gag order and Cordelia.

I turn to Mirella, my mind already racing ahead. "Okay, so the next order of business is for us to get our hands on that book and see what it says. I want to know everything."

Because let's face it, knowledge is power. And in a world where Mirella can't even voice what the hell is going on without choking on her own words, this book might just be our golden ticket to the truth.

Mirella nods her head in agreement, a determined glint in her eye. "I can go retrieve it; I know exactly where they are," she says, and I don't doubt her for a second.

"What about the Siren's Lyre?" Erik asks, "We need to get that first, don't you think?"

Erik has a valid point; I shouldn't be deterred from questing to the Atlantean Ruins right now. Maybe Cordelia will throw another tantrum, trying to drown us.

"Okay, let's divide and conquer," I offer. "Mirella, you grab the scrolls, book, or whatever, and we will stay the course and head to Tempest Isle."

"Whoa, whoa, hold your seahorses there, Princess," Lucian cuts in, his smartassery dialed up to eleven. "You're seriously thinking about sending little mermaid here, who's got strings pulled by some sea queen with a throne lodged up her ass, on a solo mission to Indiana Jones her way through ancient ruins and bring back some magical paperwork unscathed? Really? Are we in the same movie here?"

Lucian makes a fair point, and I can't help but smirk. "Alright, smart-ass, what's your grand plan, then?"

"We'll go with Mirella," Seraphina declares, cutting Lucian off at the pass. "I would love to see the Ruins."

I can't help but snort at the look on Lucian's face. It's like someone just told him his favorite leather pants are out of style.

"No way, Cupcake. I'll go with Mirella, and you, with your sweet, angelic ass, will stay right here where it's safe. No arguments." Lucian fires back.

Gideon saunters in like he just battled Poseidon, taking a seat at our table. He pours himself a pint of ale and downs it in one go. "Got the ship righted, and we be on course to Tempest Isle."

"Great. How far is that from the Atlantean Ruins?" I fire back, my mind already racing ahead.

Gideon's brow furrows like a confused seagull. "Not far at all, love," scratching his beard. "It be on the way to that cursed Isle. Why do ye ask?"

"Perfect!" I exclaim, a grin spreading across my face. "We'll be making a little pit stop. Mirella, Lucian, and Seraphina will snag the scrolls, book, or whatever the hell it is while we continue to Tempest Isle. Gideon, you'll drop us off and follow up to wait for our little mermaid squad."

Rhyland, quiet as a predator on the hunt, finally breaks his silence. "Damn, baby," he drawls, a flirty smirk playing on his lips. "When the hell did you become such a badass military strategist?"

Erik clears his throat. "I do believe the Little Huntress has learned from the best; by that, I mean myself." He punctuates his words with a wink, and I can't help but let out a snort of laughter.

"Oh great," Lucian cuts in, throwing up his hands. "Erik's getting an ego boost now? Just what we need. Nope, sorry. That's my gig. You can take your newfound swagger and fuck right off with it, pal. There's only room for one charming asshole in this group, and that spot's already taken. I mean, really, what's next? Rhyland learning to smile? Dani making a bad decision? The apocalypse is clearly upon us, folks! Batten down the hatches and prepare for the end times because Erik just tried to be funny. May the gods have mercy on our souls."

I can't help but laugh, shaking my head in amusement.

Erik arches an eyebrow. "Lucian, your insecurity is showing. Perhaps if you spent less time trying to assert your supposed charm and more time honing your wit, you wouldn't feel so threatened by a mere quip. As for your role in this group, I believe 'court jester' would be more fitting than 'charming asshole.' But fear not. Your position is secure. After all, someone needs to provide comic relief, even if it's unintentional. Now, if you'll excuse me, I have more pressing matters than engaging in a battle of wits with an unarmed opponent."

Erik quickly gets up from the table and stomps off, and I damn near choke on my tongue at his retort. Knowing him, he's probably off to sharpen his sword for the millionth time until it can split a hair lengthwise.

Lucian's jaw drops, his eyes wide as saucers. For a moment, he sputters incoherently, clearly caught off guard by Erik's unexpected verbal jab.

"I... you... what... did you just... holy shit-balls on a stick! Did Erik just... sass me? Am I having a stroke? Is this real life? Someone pinch me. I must be dreaming. Or maybe I've died and gone to some bizarro alternate universe where Erik has a personality. Quick, someone check if pigs are flying outside!"

He dramatically clutches his chest, faking a heart attack. "Oh, the pain! The agony! I've been wounded by words sharper than Erik's usual glare. How will I ever recover from such a devastating blow to my ego?"

Still perched on his lap like the world's most angelic armrest, Seraphina giggles. Her laughter is clear and musical, like a chorus of tiny bells. It starkly contrasts Lucian's theatrics, and I can't help but smile myself.

"Alright, Count Dracula," I drawl, fighting back a smirk. "Maybe save the theatrics for the sirens? You can distract them with your Oscar-worthy performance while the rest of us snag the lyre."

He drops the act, that familiar mischievous grin spreading across his face. "Why, Princess, you wound me. And here I thought my skills deserved at least a Golden Globe nomination."

"In what century?" I scoff, arching an eyebrow. "The 1500s? Your acting's about as fresh as a decomposing corpse."

Poor Mirella sits there, eyes wide like saucers, watching the exchange unfold. She looks utterly bewildered at our sassy and smart-ass barbing.

Meanwhile, the captain is in stitches; deep belly laughs rocking his broad frame as he slams another pint of ale.

Seraphina's giggles die to soft chuckles, but amusement still dances in her eyes. I can't help but marvel at the scene before me—here we are, on the brink of a potentially world-ending clusterfuck, and we're cracking jokes like it's just another Tuesday night.

But you know what? Maybe that's precisely what we need. A moment of levity before we dive headfirst into the cosmic shitstorm that awaits. Because if we can laugh in the face of danger, maybe—just maybe—we've got a shot at coming out the other side with our sanity intact.

RHYLAND

63

The cave entrance looms before us like the gaping maw of some ancient, eldritch horror, a yawning void that seems to swallow the very light itself. The cave mouth is framed by twisting vines and what looks like two female statues.

The dense forest surrounding us is a claustrophobic tangle of gnarled trees and twisted vines, their leaves rustling in the faint breeze like the whispers of long-dead spirits. The only sound is the distant roar of a waterfall, its thunderous echo reverberating through the stillness like the heartbeat of some slumbering titan.

It's taken us the better part of the day to trek to this godforsaken spot, with Erik Dani and myself loaded down like pack mules with enough gear to supply a small army. Water, food, and enough vials of Dani's blood to keep us going if shit hits the fan. We took one dose on the ship before we hit ground.

She offered some of her blood to Lucian, too, but the stubborn bastard turned her down—something about Seraphina giving him all the sustenance he needed. I just hope to fuck he's right.

It warms the cockles of my heart to see those two lovebirds getting closer by the day. It's only a matter of time before Lucian grows a pair and seals the bond, and then he'll never have to worry about losing himself to the bloodlust or any of the other hellish shit our kind goes through without a mate. Which brings me to Erik, the stoic son of a bitch.

Don't get me wrong, the man's a goddamn force of nature, with a patience and endurance that would put a monk to shame. But even he has his limits, and I can only pray to whatever fucked-up gods are listening that he finds his mate soon, before the loneliness and the hunger drive him to the brink of madness.

Gideon dropped anchor a mile off the shore, and Dani portaled us onto this godforsaken rock they call Tempest Isle, not wanting to take our chances with the

Sirens and Jesus; this place is creepy as fuck. The massive island is a sprawling expanse of jagged cliffs and dense jungle stretching forever. As we made our way inland, we passed the crumbling remains of ancient civilizations, their stone statues and ruined temples a silent testament to the passage of time and the fragility of life.

And now, here we stand, at the threshold of the unknown, our path lit only by the faint glow of Dani's light. The cave yawns before us like the mouth of some primordial beast.

"Shall we proceed?" Erik inquires from behind me. "Is this indeed the path that leads to the lyre?"

It's a damn good question and one I don't have a fucking answer to. Dani spent more time with Mirella after our little storytime session, poring over her notes and trying to make sense of this whole lyre situation while Erik and I scrounged up gear for this little excursion.

"Yeah, can't you hear the whispers?" Dani asks, her voice serious and sass. Erik and I exchange a look of pure fucking confusion. We don't hear jack shit.

"According to Mirella's notes, the path to the lyre starts with a cave opening marked by whispers and two siren statues that weep saltwater," Dani explains, scanning the entrance with keen intensity.

Intrigued, I start walking toward the statues, my boots crunching on the dense underbrush with each step. As I draw closer, I'll be damned if those creepy-ass statues aren't actually crying, silent tears streaming down their stone faces like some fucked-up fountain.

"Looks like we're on the right track after all," I mutter, turning back to face them. We exchange a brief nod before heading into the cave mouth, our weapons at the ready.

I take the lead, hacking through the thick vines with my sword like a machete. Erik does the same on the other side, his blade flashing in the dim light as he clears a path. I move the sliced vines out of Dani's way, holding them back so she can duck underneath without getting tangled up in the mess.

As we pass the siren statues, I can't help but notice their eerie expressions. One is the picture of sorrow, her features contorted in a mask of eternal grief, while the other wears a smile that's just a little too wide, a little too gleeful for comfort. It's creepy as hell, and I can feel the hairs on the back of my neck standing on end as we venture deeper into the cave.

The air grows colder and damper with each step, the sound of our footsteps echoing off the stone walls like the beating of some giant, invisible heart. The darkness seems to press in on us from all sides, broken only by the faint glow of Dani's ball of light as she leads the way.

"So, what other nuggets of wisdom did Mirella impart upon you, baby? I'd like to know we're not just wandering around this dank-ass cave for shits and giggles," I ask, my voice echoing off the stone walls as I bring up the rear.

"Well, according to her, we should watch for a flooded chamber, a coral bridge, a harmonious pool..." Dani trails off, her brow furrowing as she tries to recall all the details Mirella shared with her. "Oh, and a melody chamber, followed by an altar that glows with light."

"And we're supposed to find these things in that exact order?" I can't help but ask, my tone skeptical. It all sounds a little too convenient, a little too much like a fucking video game quest for my liking.

"Yup!" Dani quips back, her voice brimming with confidence. "I've got it all memorized, locked, and loaded in my big, beautiful brain. Mirella and I went over it multiple times, just to be sure."

And the thing is, I believe her. If there's one thing I know about my girl, she's smart as a whip and twice as deadly. Her scientific mind is like a fucking steel trap, latching onto every little detail and refusing to let go until she's got it all figured out.

The sound of rushing water reaches my ears, growing louder with each step, and I know we must be getting close to the first of Mirella's landmarks—the flooded chamber.

I tighten my grip on my sword, my senses on high alert as we round a corner and find ourselves standing at the edge of a vast, underground lake.

"Well, would you look at that," I mutter, my eyes scanning the chamber for any signs of danger, "Mirella knew her shit after all."

I realize this isn't just some ordinary flooded chamber as we approach the water's edge. No, this is something else entirely. The water is crystal-clear, almost unnaturally so, and glowing algae illuminate it from within, casting an ethereal, greenish-blue light throughout the cavern.

But that's not even the creepiest part. I hear whispers as we stand here, taking in the surreal beauty. They are faint at first but grow louder with each passing second.

"She's here."

The Savior..."

"It's her..."

"What the actual fuck?" I mutter, my grip tightening on my sword as I scan the chamber for signs of danger. But there's nothing there—just the glowing water, the whispering echoes, and a strange, circular stone platform rising from the flooded chamber's center.

I can see that the platform is covered in intricate engravings, a complex web of symbols and patterns that seem to hint at some greater meaning. And in the center of it all, carved into the very heart of the stone, are a series of instruments. Lyres, harps, flutes...it's like a fucking miniature orchestra.

Damn, this place just keeps getting weirder and weirder. We dive into the glowing water without a second thought, swimming towards the raised platform. I help Dani first, my hands gripping her waist as I hoist her onto the stone. Erik and I follow close behind, our eyes scanning the intricate engravings covering every inch of the platform.

"So, do you have any ideas what these fancy squiggles mean?" Dani asks as she crouches down to examine them closer.

I lean in, my brow furrowed in concentration as I study the symbols. There are otherwordly looking designs, but if I had to guess—musical notes etched beneath each instrument—drums, flute, harp, and of course, the fucking lyre. But here's the thing...I can't read music for shit.

"Don't look at me, baby," I mutter, shaking my head. "I'm about as musically literate as a tone-deaf goat."

"This oval-shaped note with a stem represents a half note, lasting two beats," Erik explains, his voice calm and measured as he points to each symbol. "The open oval is a whole note, four beats. The filled oval with a stem is a quarter note, one beat. And this filled oval with a stem and a flag is an eighth note, lasting half a beat."

I stare at him, my jaw practically hitting the fucking floor. "Since when did you become a goddamn music prodigy?"

Erik shrugs, silver eyes glinting. "I used to play the piano, brother. A very long time ago."

Dani, meanwhile, is off in her own little world, her head cocked to the side like she's listening to something only she can hear. "They're telling us to play the musical notes," she murmurs, her voice distant and dreamy.

I glance around the chamber. "Play them with what, exactly? I don't see any fucking instruments lying around."

"We hum," Erik replies like it's the most obvious thing in the world. He turns to Dani, his expression serious. "Hum this beat, Dani." He demonstrates a note, and Dani mimics it perfectly. Then he does the same for me, and soon enough, we're all humming in harmony like some otherworldly choir.

And that's when the magic happens. As our voices blend, words materialize on the stone above the musical notes, glowing with an eerie, pulsing light.

"Holy hell," I breathe, my eyes widening in awe. "Is that...a song?"

Erik nods, his long silver hair falling into his eyes, his gaze intense as he reads the words aloud.

"In the calm, the light shall glow,

with a whisper where secrets flow.

Melodies of joy we weave,

to unlock the path, we believe."

We fall silent, waiting with bated breath for something—anything—to happen. But the chamber remains still and quiet. The only sound is the gentle lapping of the water against the platform.

"Okay, so...now what?" I ask, my voice echoing off the stone walls.

Erik frowns. "Perhaps we need to sing the melody," he suggests, his tone thoughtful. "Like this..."

And then, to my utter fucking amazement, he begins to sing. His voice is soft and haunting, the notes rising and falling like the ebb and flow of the tide. Dani and I exchange a glance, our eyes wide with wonder, before joining in, our voices blending in a harmony that sends shivers down my spine.

As we sing, the chamber begins to change. The water starts to glow even brighter, pulsing in time with the rhythm of our song. The engravings on the platform shimmer and shift, revealing hidden pathways and secret doors that were invisible before.

And then, with a final, resounding note, the chamber falls silent again. But everything has changed. The path forward is clear now, illuminated by the soft, pulsing glow of the water.

"Damn, that was some seriously impressive shit," I mutter. "Didn't see that coming."

Dani grins, her eyes sparkling as she turns to Erik. "No kidding, Mr. Stoic," she quips. "Who knew you had such a set of pipes on you?"

Erik smirks slightly, his expression as unreadable as ever."I am a man of many talents, Little Huntress. But perhaps we should focus on the task at hand."

"Right, right," Dani says, waving a hand dismissively. "Guess we'd better see where this yellow brick road leads, huh?"

I nod. "Damn straight, baby. Let's get this over with."

I can't help but think if Erik wasn't here to unfuck this music situation, where the hell would that leave us? Up shit creek without a goddamn paddle, that's where.

Shaking my head, we head through the now visible door, our weapons at the ready and our hearts pounding with anticipation. Erik takes the lead, his movements precise and calculated as he scans the path ahead for any signs of danger.

The passage is narrow and winding, the walls slick with moisture and glowing with that same eerie, pulsing light. But we press on, our footsteps echoing off the stone as we venture deeper and deeper into the heart of the cave.

And then, just when I'm starting to wonder if this fucking tunnel is ever going to end, we emerge into a vast, open chamber that takes my breath away. The walls are lined with shimmering crystals, each pulsing with a different color—blue, green, red, and purple. And in the center of the room, rising from a raised dais, is a sight that makes my heart skip a beat.

It's the coral bridge. The second landmark on Mirella's list. And it's even more breathtaking than I could have imagined.

The bridge is a masterpiece of natural beauty. It is a delicate arch of living coral that spans a chasm so deep and dark that it seems to have no bottom. The colors are vibrant and alive, shades of pink, orange, and red that seem to glow from within.

"Holy *shit*," I breathe, my eyes wide with wonder. "Would you look at that?"

Dani nods, her long chocolate brown hair laying like wet silk down her back, her expression of pure awe. "It's incredible. I've never seen anything like it."

Even Erik seems impressed, his stoic facade cracking just the tiniest bit as he takes in the sight before us. "It is a marvel," he agrees, with genuine appreciation.

I step forward, my boots crunching on the rocky ground as I approach the chasm's edge. The bridge looks sturdy enough, but I know better than to take anything for granted in this fucked-up place.

"Alright, listen up," my voice low and serious. "We cross this thing one at a time, nice and slow. No sudden movements, no fucking around. Got it?"

Dani and Erik both nod, their expressions grim but determined. They know what's at stake here and are not about to let anything stand in our way.

So, with a deep breath and a muttered prayer, I step out onto the bridge, my heart pounding as I begin to make my way across the chasm. The coral is surprisingly sturdy beneath my feet, but I can feel it shifting and swaying with each step, a reminder of just how fragile this whole fucking setup is.

The howling winds roar up from the dark chasm beneath my feet, their force nearly knocking me on my ass.

But I keep going, my gaze fixed straight ahead as I put one foot in front of the other. And then, when I think I might make it to the other side without incident, I hear a sound that makes my blood run cold.

A crack. A fucking crack in the coral echoes through the chamber like a gunshot.

Before I can react, the bridge crumbles beneath my feet, the once-solid surface giving way to a gaping void of nothingness. I lunge forward, my hands scrabbling for purchase on the rocky ledge, but it's too late. I'm falling; Dani's scream is all I hear as I plummet into the darkness below.

"RHYLAND!"

LUCIAN

64

"I swear on my impressive collection of limited edition comic books, Cupcake, I would never even dream of hurting you," I declare solemnly as we cuddle up in our cabin, waiting for the signal to dive into the Atlantean ruins.

Seraphina, being the irresistible minx that she is, straddles my lap as I sit in a chair, her arms snaking around my neck like a sexy boa constrictor. Her skirt pools around us, and I can feel the scorching heat of her body pressed against me. It's like a goddamn inferno, and I'm ready to play firefighter.

"I know, Sparky McSnark. I trust you with all my heart," she breathes against my neck, her angelic voice sending shivers straight to my already needy erection. We may have just had a wild romp between the sheets a couple of days ago, but I'm already itching for rounds four, five, and—hell, let's throw in a round six for good measure.

Seraphina started calling me "Sparky" because of our electric connection and, well... my snarky mouth. She says I ignite a fire in her, and who am I to argue with a gorgeous angel who thinks I'm the hottest thing since ghost peppers? I've been called many things in my life—most of them not fit for polite company—but *"Sparky"*? It's growing on me like a fungus but in a good way. A sexy, tingly fungus that makes me want to do unspeakable things to this celestial beauty in my arms.

"I promise I'll be as gentle as a fluffy bunny at a tea party. It should feel like a little slice of heaven, or at least a really good hickey," I reassure her, trying to keep my cool as Seraphina grinds against me. She's wiggling like a sexy worm on a hook, and it's taking every ounce of my gentlemanly resolve not to dive in and feast.

I'm trying to take things slow, not wanting to rush my heavenly desire or push her too fast. But damn, she's making it hard (in more ways than one) with her enthusiasm and willingness to let me sample her sweet nectar.

When I turned down Dani's blood offer before they departed for Tempest Isle, Seraphina stepped up like an absolute goddess and offered me her crimson ambrosia. Holy hell, I am drooling at the thought of tasting her essence—it's like being handed a golden ticket to the chocolate factory, except instead of candy, it will be the most delectable blood I have ever had the pleasure of sinking my fangs into.

Dani is only half angel, and her blood is like crack to all of us—so I can only imagine what Seraphina will taste like.

I'm determined to be a gentleman about it, even if it means enduring the sweet torture of her body pressed against mine, teasing me with the promise of ecstasy. I'll take my time, savoring every moment and making sure Seraphina's first blood-sharing experience is nothing short of magical. After all, a lady like her deserves nothing less than the utmost care and devotion from her dashing, albeit slightly deranged, vampire lover.

I run my tongue along the silky smooth skin of her neck, tracing a tantalizing path from her collarbone to her earlobe. She shivers beneath my touch, her skin erupting in a constellation of goosebumps. I grin against her flesh, knowing I'm the one making her body sing like the finest instrument. She tightens her grip around my neck, her fingers digging into my skin, silently urging me. I take my time, savoring the moment, peppering her pulse point with kisses and gentle nips. Her skin is like silk beneath my lips, and I can't resist sucking on that tender spot, marking her as mine.

"Lucian...please...." Seraphina whispers. "Bite me. Take me into you."

I groan, and with deliberate slowness, I sink my fangs into her delicate flesh, piercing through like a hot knife through warm butter. She lets out a gasp that's half "oh, fuck yes" and half "holy shit, that hurts," and it's like music to my ears.

She's clinging to me so tightly that you'd need a map and a compass to find where one ends and the other begins.

I start drawing her blood into my mouth, holy mother of all things sweet and sinful. I nearly lose control—she tastes like heaven on earth! It's like a goddamn flavor explosion in my mouth: vanilla ice cream, cinnamon, and a hint of something zesty that I can't quite identify. My eyes roll back in my head as I let out a guttural moan against her neck, my senses overwhelmed by the sheer ecstasy of her essence.

Seraphina arches her back, tilting her head to give me better access to her throat. It's a test of willpower not to gulp her down like a ravenous beast, but I force myself to take it slow, savoring every drop like a connoisseur. She's grinding against me, her hips moving in a way that's making me see stars. The venom I'm pumping into her veins is clearly doing its job, and I can't help but feel a surge of pride at the potency of my supernatural love juice.

I grab a fistful of her silky hair, holding her head in place. She's putty in my hands, a whimpering, writhing mess of desire. "Lucian...oh my god..." she whimpers. "please," she breathes, her voice needy.

I know what she wants. I can fucking smell it, and that's all the invitation I need.

Without missing a beat, I fumble with my pants like a fucking noob, finally freeing myself. I hook my fingers in her panties, lightly touching her soaked clit, and shove them aside, groaning into her neck as I feel the scorching heat of her soaking wet core. She's so ready for me, so desperate, and I hope she's not still sore from our earlier sexapades, but her body is practically begging for an encore. I release her neck, licking a wet stripe up her neck.

Our eyes lock, molten gold meeting blazing brown, and I can see the raw, unbridled lust swirling in her gaze.

Slowly, torturously, I guide the head of my cock to her waiting heat, watching in awe as her face contorts with pure pleasure as I penetrate her inch by glorious inch.

"Gods...you're *so*...big." She whispers against my lips.

I smirk at that. "It's all yours, sweetheart."

She pushes down on me, taking me deeper with each thrust, riding me like a goddess on a mission. I latch onto her neck once more, drinking deeply from the well of her desire as she rocks in my lap, her tight walls gripping me.

"Don't stop, Lucian," she moans, with need. "I need to feel you... all of you. Your bite, your body... consume me."

Holy hell, her words are like an aphrodisiac mainlined straight to my core. The way she's so open, so wanton in her desire, it's blowing my mind in the best possible way. Knowing that she craves my bite, that she gets off on me drinking from her? It's like pouring gasoline on the raging inferno of my lust. This woman is going to be the death of me, and I couldn't imagine a sweeter way to go.

It's a feedback loop of pleasure; each pull of her blood and each clench of her core pushes us both closer to the edge of oblivion. She's a goddess in my arms, and I'm her willing worshipper, ready to follow her to the ends of the earth and back.

When I release her neck, it feels like someone just plugged me into a live wire. The connection is so strong—like a force of nature—and I know I need to make her mine—permanently—forever and ever, amen.

I fumble for the knife in my pants, nearly stabbing myself in the process, and then I'm slicing into my own throat like a madman. "I want you to taste me, Cupcake. Take me into you," I rasp, my voice rough with need.

Seraphina's eyes go wide, and I swear I can see fear and arousal battling it out in those caramel-gold depths. I could get lost in those eyes, drown in them, and never come up for air. "Is this..." she gasps, grinding down on me so hard I think she's trying to break me in half. All I can do is pray not to blow my load. "The bond? I need to drink from you, too?"

I grab her hips, trying to slow her down before she turns me into a one-pump chump, but it's like trying to stop a runaway train with a feather. "Yeah... ahhh... shit..shit...*shiiiit.* Fuck, you feel so good..." I pant, my breath coming in ragged gasps as she rocks against me. "Yes—it's the bond, baby girl. Be mine, sweetheart—forever."

She gives me a smile that's pure sex and sin, like she knows exactly what she's doing to me, and she's loving every second of it. She's reveling in watching me come undone, reducing me to a babbling, incoherent mess.

Please, beautiful. Accept this. Accept me.

Then she's kissing me, her tongue plunging into my mouth like she's trying to taste my soul. I meet her stroke for stroke, our tongues tangling together. She pulls back, "Yes," she breathes against my lips, then licks my neck, her tongue lapping at the wound like a kitten with a bowl of cream. "I want to be yours, Lucian. Make me yours."

Oh, sweet baby Jesus, I nearly black out from the sensation. Every nerve ending in my body is on fire, consumed from the inside out. I grip her so hard I'm pretty sure I'm leaving bruises, but I can't help it. I'm thrusting up into her like a man possessed, her mouth on my neck and her walls wrapped around my cock. It's fucking euphoric.

She keeps drinking from me, pulling my essence into her like she's dying of thirst, and I'm the only oasis in the desert. The sensation is indescribable, like nothing I've ever felt before. It's pure ecstasy—like every pleasure center in my brain is firing off at once.

Is this what it's like to bond with your mate? Because if so, sign me the fuck up for a lifetime subscription.

The words are etched into my very being, a primal instinct taking over and pouring out in a torrent of emotion. The mating vows spill from my lips, a sacred pledge that binds us together, heart, body, and soul. It's a promise of forever, of love that knows no bounds, and as I speak the ancient words, I can feel the weight of their significance settling over us.

As she drinks, something shifts inside me, like the fabric of my being is being rewoven. Every molecule in my body reaches out to her, twining together until I can't tell where I end and she begins. Time slows, the world fading away until there's nothing left but the two of us, our hearts beating in perfect sync.

I can feel her physically and on a level beyond the flesh. It's like I'm inside her head, heart, and soul. I can feel her emotions, thoughts, and desires swirling together in a kaleidoscope of color and sensation. It's overwhelming, almost too much to bear, but at the same time, it's the most incredible thing I've ever experienced.

We're two pieces of a puzzle, finally clicking into place after a lifetime of searching. We fit perfectly, our jagged edges smoothing out until we're one seamless whole. I can feel her pure, unconditional love for me wrapping around me like a warm blanket on a cold night. And I know, with a bone-deep certainty, that I will love her for the rest of my days and move heaven and earth to keep her safe and happy.

As the bond solidifies, I feel our essences merging, our life forces becoming one. It's like a supernova exploding inside me, a burst of light and energy threatening to consume me whole. I'm drowning in her, lost in the depths of our connection, and I never want to come up for air.

Seraphina releases my neck and throws her head back in bliss. She's grinding against me like her life depends on it, her moans echoing off the cabin walls. I tangle my fingers in her hair, tilting her face towards mine. "Eyes on me, gorgeous."

When her gaze meets mine, it's like looking into the heart of a star—radiant, intense, and filled with a love that takes my breath away.

"I feel... so much." She moans, "So much... I feel you...everywhere."

I crash my lips against hers in an intense kiss that could power a small country for a week. I'm pouring every last drop of my love, devotion, and undying (pun intended) affection into this searing lip lock, trying to convey just how much she means to me.

The effects of my blood are no joke. It's like I've just injected her with a concentrated dose of pure, unfiltered horniness. She's practically vibrating with arousal, her body humming like a tuning fork of desire.

But that's not all, folks! She's also feeling the full force of our bond, the unbreakable tie that binds us together for all eternity. It's like a cosmic superglue, fusing our souls into one perfect, dysfunctional, beautiful mess.

"You're mine now, beautiful," I murmur against her skin, my voice low and possessive. "From this moment on, you belong to me, and I belong to you. We're in this together, forever and always, no matter what kind of crazy shit the universe throws our way."

"Lucian... ohh GOD!" Seraphina's voice cracks like a whip, her eyes rolling back, and she screams my name like a prayer. Her tight walls clamp down on me—the pleasure is so intense I'm pretty sure my eyeballs just jumped out of their sockets.

"Fuuuck...such a good girl—take what you need from me. Ride my cock, angel face."

She's so wet—her cum is drenching my dick and dripping down my balls.

My venom and blood are like a one-two punch of pure, unadulterated pleasure, sending Seraphina on a one-way trip to O-Town—population her.

I can't help myself. I rip open her corset, my hands greedy for the treasures within. I grab a handful of her delectable tit, the soft flesh filling my palm like nature's finest pillow.

Her nipple pops into my mouth like a cherry on top of a sundae, and I suck and nibble at it until it's as hard as my resolve not to blow my load. She's screaming my name, her body convulsing with aftershocks as waves of pleasure wash over her. It's like riding a rollercoaster, and I'm unsure how much more I can take before I pop.

I reach down, hooking my arms under her knees for leverage. I blur her to the wall, and then I'm pounding into her, slamming home again and again, my hips snapping forward, ensuring she feels every inch of my cock.

Seraphina's moaning incoherently, a symphony of pleasure and need that sends shivers down my spine and makes my heart sing. Then, with one final, soul-shattering thrust, I come harder than a comet crashing into the sun.

"Sweet... fucking... fuuuuck!" I bellow, my voice bouncing off the cabin walls like a pinball as I erupt inside her with the force of a thousand nuclear warheads. It's like Hiroshima and Nagasaki had a love child in my balls, and now it's detonating inside her like the Fourth of July, Christmas, and New Year's Eve all rolled into one explosive package.

I run my tongue across my lips, savoring her taste before diving in for another kiss. She clings to me, and I can't help but chuckle. "Sweet sassafras, Cupcake, you're gonna suck the life right out of me—literally!" I gasp, my lips still tingling from our fiery lip lock. "Death by dick drainage... what a way to go!"

Seraphina's giggle sends shockwaves through my body, her inner walls doing a cha-cha on my cock that has me panting like a dog. "Gah! Fuck... Easy there, giggle monster." I yelp, my oversensitive cock twitching inside her like it's been zapped with a cattle prod.

I'm pretty sure my eyes are crossing, and I'm making noises that would make a wounded walrus sound dignified by comparison. "Woman, are you trying to kill me? Because if so, mission accomplished! I'm dead, deceased, shuffled off this mortal coil. Send my regards to the big guy upstairs, and make sure they bury me with my limited edition comics, okay?"

Seraphina gazes up at me, her eyes sparkling. "Oh, my goodness. That was... wow. I feel like I took a trip down a rollercoaster made of stardust and rainbows. Is this what being cosmically bonded feels like?"

I can't help but grin, my heart dancing in my chest. "Baby girl, if this is a trip, strap me in and call me a frequent flyer. We're talking first-class tickets to Cloud Nine, complete with mind-blowing orgasms and a side of eternal love."

Seraphina giggles, and the sound is like tinkling bells mixed with sass. "Well, in that case, I hope you packed your bags because you're stuck with me for eternity. No refunds, exchanges, or even if you find a shinier model."

"Pfft, as if there could be a better model," I scoff, pulling her close. "You're like the limited edition, gold-plated, diamond-encrusted version of perfection. I'd be a certified idiot to even think about trading you in."

"Aww, you sweet-talker, you," Seraphina coos, booping my nose with her finger. "Keep that up, and I might just have to keep you around for a millennia or two."

"Only a millennia or two? Challenge accepted, Cupcake. I'll have you begging for an extension before you can say 'holy matrimony.'"

Seraphina's laughter fills the air, a sound so pure and joyful it could probably cure cancer. "Oh, Lucian," she sighs, her eyes twinkling with adoration. "What am I going to do with you?"

"Well, I've got a few ideas," I reply with a wink, blurring us to the bed. "And they all involve making you laugh, scream my name, and question your life choices—not necessarily in that order."

"Holy shit, Phina baby, get a load of this!" I shout, my voice echoing through the vast, cavernous hall.

The Atlantean Ruins are straight-up bonkers, like something out of a fever dream. Picture this: a massive underwater palace with walls glistening with coral and gems and water cascading down like an ethereal indoor waterfall.

Thanks to Mirella's magical underwater breathing kiss, we can dive deep into the heart of the Atlantean Ruins without needing scuba gear. Honestly, I never thought I'd be doing my best Merman impression while exploring a mythical palace that's supposedly Poseidon's bachelor pad.

Getting into this place was like a real-life game of Tomb Raider, minus the tight shorts and... well, you know the rest. We had to channel our inner Lara Croft, navigating through some seriously claustrophobic underwater passages and squeezing our way through tight crevices. I'm pretty sure I left a piece of my dignity behind in one of those cracks, but that's the price you pay for adventure, right?

After playing underwater limbo and contortionist, we finally emerged into this cavern, and bam! We're breathing air again, walking around in what feels like a submerged graveyard filled with ancient relics, crumbling architecture, and that distinct smell of 'old and damp.'

We followed Mirella through the labyrinthine halls, and she led us to a hidden chamber fit for water gods, like the Library of Alexandria. Shelves upon shelves of ancient tomes and scrolls are just waiting for some curious soul to crack them open and unleash untold knowledge (or maybe a curse or two; who knows?).

I'm flipping through one of these dusty old books, handling it like a newborn baby made of glass, when Seraphina's voice cuts through the silence. "What have you got there, handsome?" she asks. The scent of vanilla, sugar, and spice that follows her everywhere is like a damn aphrodisiac.

"Not sure," I reply, carefully turning the crumbling pages. "I can't make heads or tails of this language, though. It's like trying to read a doctor's handwriting after they've downed a bottle of tequila."

Seraphina laughs as I hand her the book. She takes it with the reverence of a scholar handling a priceless artifact. Settling down on a nearby rock, the picture of grace and intelligence, "Let me take a look."

And just like that, I'm putty in her hands. Watching her work that brilliant mind of hers is like witnessing a master artist at work. I lean back against a coral-encrusted pillar, content to bask in the glow of my girl's genius. "Take your time, Cupcake," I say with a grin. "I've got all the time in the world when it comes to you."

Mirella strolls back into the room, her fishy bits replaced with legs that would make a supermodel weep. "Ta-da! I've got Nixie's journal," she announces, waving the book like it's a golden ticket to Willy Wonka's chocolate factory.

"Hell yes! One more item crossed off our 'Save the World' scavenger hunt list. Now let's see if we can find some juicy tidbits about Dani and this prophecy nonsense."

I turn to Seraphina and holy hell. She's flipping through that book like it has a "self-destruct in 10 seconds" timer. Her eyes bounce across the pages faster than a caffeinated squirrel on a sugar rush.

"This is the Book of Shadows and the Dead," she announces, casual as ever, like she's just telling me what we're having for dinner.

My jaw drops. "What the actual fuck? How did you...? Are you shitting me right now?"

Seraphina nods, a smile playing on her lips. "I'm very serious, Sparky."

Jesus, this is the book Erik and I couldn't find at the Obsidian Enclave, even if our lives depended on it. And here's my angelic girlfriend, reading it like it's the back of a cereal box.

"Hold the phone. Are you telling me you just read that entire thing in the time it takes me to scratch my ass? And you *actually* understood it?" my voice squeaking like a prepubescent boy.

Seraphina saunters to me, hips swaying. She hands me the book and kisses my lips, making my dick twitch. "Yep, it's old Greek—speed reading is just one of my many talents. Didn't I mention that?"

I shake my head, feeling like a clue-by-four has hit me. "So, let me get this straight. You can read anything just by giving it the ol' once-over? Like, literally anything?"

"Mmhmm," she hums, looking as innocent as an angel in a lingerie store.

I spot another dusty old tome nearby and snatch it up, handing it to her. "Alright, Ms. Speed Reader Extraordinaire, what's this bad boy about?"

She opens the book with the grace of a ballerina, flips through it faster than I can say, "Holy shit," and hands it back to me. "This one's all about Asgard and the Norse gods. Thor's abs get a whole chapter, by the way."

Holy shitballs on a stick, folks! Not only did this walking wet dream of an angel decide to hitch her wagon to my crazy train, but she's also constantly blowing my fucking mind.

It's like someone took my brain, dunked it in a vat of LSD, and then plugged it directly into the Matrix. I can feel every single one of her emotions and desires buzzing through me like I just licked a 9-volt battery of pure ecstasy. We're talking next-level connection here, people—the kind that would make even the sappiest rom-com writer say, "Whoa, dial it back a notch, buddy."

I mean, seriously, how did I get this lucky? Did I save a bus full of nuns and puppies in a past life? Because being eternally bonded to this heavenly hottie who's equal parts sexy librarian and badass warrior feels like I've won the cosmic lottery, cashed in all my karma points, and got a 'Get Out of Hell Free' card all rolled into one mind-blowing package.

Dani is going to shit a brick when she hears of this.

DANICA

65

My heart nearly leaps out of my damn chest as I watch Rhyland plummet into the gaping maw of the cavern. The bridge collapses beneath his feet and for a gut-wrenching moment, I'm convinced I'm about to watch my mate become a pancake on the jagged rocks below.

But thank the gods for Rhyland's lightning-fast reflexes. Somehow, he managed to grab onto the rocky ledge, his fingers scrabbling for purchase against the slick stone. Now, he's just hanging there, dangling like a worm on a hook over that gaping maw of darkness that seems all too eager to swallow him whole.

Erik's at the edge in a flash, his eyes scanning the area with a laser-like focus. I can practically see the gears turning in his head as he tries to figure out how to get Rhyland back to safety. We brought all kinds of shit in our trusty backpacks—rope included— but what the hell good is that going to do with Rhyland stranded on the other side of the cavern, separated from us by a chasm that looks like it could be the gateway to the underworld itself?

I watch, my heart in my throat, as Rhyland grips the ledge and starts to haul himself up. His muscles strain against the fabric of his shirt, veins popping on his arms and hands as he inches his way upward. It's like watching a real-life game of cliffhanger, except the stakes are so much higher than some stupid plastic mountain.

Rhyland finally reaches the top and pulls himself over the edge. I let out a breath I didn't even realize I was holding, my lungs burning with the sudden influx of air.

He takes a moment to catch his breath, his chest heaving as he stands and assesses the situation. "Get the rope and toss it over to me," he calls out to Erik, his voice echoing off the cavern walls.

Erik's already on it, dropping his bag and grabbing the rope we brought. We tie the ends together, creating a makeshift lifeline that we pray will be long enough to span the distance between us and Rhyland.

It takes a few tries, but finally, Rhyland manages to catch the rope's end. He ties it off securely to the former bridge's column, anchoring it with a knot that could probably hold the weight of a small elephant.

Erik does the same on our end.

"Now what?" I ask, my voice breathy and shaky as I've just run a marathon through a quicksand field.

Rhyland's answer is so matter-of-fact it's almost infuriating. "You'll have to shimmy across," he says like it's the most natural thing in the world.

I blink, convinced I must have misheard him. "What?" I ask again, my brain struggling to process the sheer insanity of what he's suggesting.

He can't possibly expect me to tightrope walk across that chasm like some circus acrobat, can he?

"Little Huntress," Erik chimes in, his tone infuriatingly calm. "You will be fine. Go first, and I will be right behind you."

Oh. My. God. They're actually serious about this. They want me to fucking shimmy across, with nothing but a flimsy rope and a prayer standing between me and a one-way ticket to splat city.

I swallow hard, my mouth suddenly dry. My palms are sweating, and my heart is racing so fast I'm half-convinced it's trying to beat its way out of my chest.

I look at the rope, then back at Rhyland and Erik. They're both watching me expectantly, waiting for me to sprout wings and fly across the gap.

"You've got to be shitting me," I mutter, my voice trembling despite my best efforts to sound tough. "I'm not a fucking tightrope walker, guys. I'm a scientist, not a Cirque du Soleil performer."

But even as the words leave my mouth, I know I don't have a choice. It's either shimmy across the rope or turn back, and there's no way in hell I'm letting a little thing like certain death stop me from getting to that lyre.

With shaking hands, I grab onto the rope, my knuckles turning white from the force of my grip. I can feel the rough fibers digging into my palms, and for a moment, I'm convinced I will lose my nerve and turn back.

But then I think of Mirella, trapped in her silent prison. I think of Aquaria, cursed to live under the tyrannical rule of a power-hungry queen. And I think of Rhyland, my mate, love, and everything.

I can't let them down. I won't.

So, with a deep breath, I dangle, and with trembling hands, I wrap my ankles securely around the rope, the rough fibers biting into my skin through the fabric of my pants. My fingers grip the rope so tightly that I feel the circulation starting to cut off, but I don't dare loosen my hold.

Here goes nothing.

"You've got this, baby," Rhyland's voice is like a soothing balm, wrapping around me like a warm, reassuring embrace. "I'm right here; just keep coming to me, Angel."

I take a deep, shaky breath, steeling myself for what I am about to do.

And then, I start to move. Inch by agonizing inch, I pull myself across the chasm, my heart lodged so firmly in my throat that I'm half-convinced it's trying to make a break for it and flee the scene entirely.

My hair cascades toward the yawning abyss like a chestnut waterfall as I shimmy across the rope upside down, feeling like the world's most terrified sloth.

"This is fine," I mutter through gritted teeth, trying not to think about the fact that I'm dangling over certain doom like the world's most reluctant bat. "Totally normal. Just your average Tuesday, hanging out... literally."

I inch forward, my arms and core muscles screaming in protest. Who needs a gym when you've got life-or-death situations to keep you fit?

"If I make it out of this alive," I grunt, my face probably as red as a tomato from all the blood rushing to my head, "I'm never complaining about planks again."

The rope sways and bounces with each movement, sending fresh jolts of terror racing down my spine like icy fingers trailing along my vertebrae. It's like being on the world's most horrifying amusement park ride, except there's no safety harness, no emergency stop button, and the only thing waiting for me at the bottom is a one-way ticket to oblivion.

But I keep going, refusing to let the fear consume me. Hand over hand, I shimmy my way across the chasm, my eyes locked on Rhyland's reassuring presence on the other side.

The darkness below seems to call out to me, its whispers growing louder and more insistent with each passing second. It promises relief and an end to the terror and the struggle. All I have to do is let go, give in to the pull of gravity, and allow myself to be swallowed whole by the abyss.

But I won't do it. I can't. Not when Rhyland is waiting for me, his arms outstretched, ready to catch and pull me back from the brink.

So I keep shimmying and pushing forward, even as my muscles scream in protest and my lungs burn with the effort of dragging in each ragged breath. The rope bites into my palms, leaving angry red welts in its wake, but I barely feel the pain. All that matters is reaching the other side, closing the distance between myself and Rhyland until I'm safely in his arms again.

Rhyland's hands close around my waist, his grip firm and sure as he pulls me from the rope and the yawning chasm. I collapse against him, my arms wrapping around his neck in a desperate, clinging embrace.

I'm shaking like a leaf, my heart racing so fast. I bury my face in the crook of Rhyland's neck, breathing in his familiar scent, letting it ground me and chase away the lingering tendrils of fear.

"It's okay, baby," he murmurs, his arms tightening around me, holding me close. "I've got you. You did it."

And I did. I really did. I faced my fears, stared death in the face, and somehow, miraculously, came out the other side unscathed.

But even as relief washes over me in dizzying waves, I can't shake the memory of Rhyland dangling over that chasm, his life hanging by a thread. The thought of losing him, of watching him be swallowed alive by the darkness, is enough to make my blood run cold and my stomach twist with nausea.

I know he can heal with his vampire abilities, but how the hell do I know what is down there in that bottomless pit?

I cling to him even tighter, as though I can somehow anchor him to me, keep him safe through sheer force of will alone. Because the truth is, I don't know what I would do without him. He's my rock, my guiding light, the one constant in a world that seems hell-bent on throwing us curveball after curveball.

Behind us, I hear Erik making his way across the chasm, his movements sure and steady despite the perilous drop beneath him. A moment later, he's standing beside us, his face etched with relief and grim determination.

"We should keep moving," he says, his voice low and urgent. "There's no telling what other dangers might lurk in these caves."

He's right, of course. We can't afford to linger here, not when the fate of the realms hangs in the balance. But for a moment longer, I allow myself to savor the feeling of Rhyland's arms around me, the solid warmth of his body pressed against mine.

Because in a world where danger lurks around every corner and death is always just a heartbeat away, these moments of connection, love, and comfort are more precious than all the treasures in the realms combined.

As we venture deeper into the cave, the air grows thick with anticipation, like we're on the cusp of something big. And then, when I'm starting to wonder if we've taken a wrong turn somewhere, I hear it.

Beautiful notes like instruments. We stumble upon a sight that takes my breath away.

It's a pool, but not just any pool. No, this kind of pool belongs in a fairy tale or a high-end spa resort. The water is crystal clear, shimmering with an otherworldly light that seems to dance and play across its surface. And the sound... oh, the sound.

This is the next landmark Mirella spoke about—this must be the harmony pool.

It's like nothing I've ever heard, a symphony of musical tones that seems to rise from the pool's depths. Droplets of water fall from the stalactites above, each creating a unique note that blends seamlessly with the others, weaving a hauntingly beautiful and strangely soothing melody.

"Wow." I breathe. "This is incredible."

I can feel the pull of the pool, the way it seems to call out to me on some deep, primal level. It's like the water is alive, imbued with a power that I can't quite name but can feel thrumming through every fiber of my being.

"We should take a closer look," Erik suggests, his voice cutting through my reverie. "There may be clues here—something that can help us."

He's right, of course. We didn't come all this way to admire the scenery, no matter how breathtaking it might be. So, with a nod of agreement, we start to make our way around the pool's edge, following a stone path that looks like ancient hands carved it.

As we walk, I can't help but marvel at the path's intricacy. The stones fit together like pieces of a puzzle, each bearing a unique pattern that seems to tell a story all its own. It's like we're walking through history, the very heart of the ancient world that gave rise to this place and all its secrets.

And then, just when I'm starting to think that maybe we've hit a dead end, that the pool is nothing more than a pretty distraction—I see it. A pedestal stands at the water's very edge, its surface worn smooth by time and the elements.

But what really catches my eye is what's on top of the pedestal. It's a riddle etched into the stone in a language I've never seen before. The symbols seem to dance and shift before my eyes, teasing me with their hidden meaning.

"Well, shit," I mutter, my brow furrowing as I try to make sense of the cryptic words. "Looks like the ancients were big fans of brain teasers."

Rhyland steps beside me, his dark hair and chiseled jaw sexy in this lighting. His baby blue eyes narrow as he studies the riddle. "It must be a clue."

I look around, trying to make sense of this crazy musical pool situation we've stumbled into. But all I see is the glowing water shimmering like a disco ball, and I hear the sounds of harmony echoing off the cave walls like we've landed smack dab in the middle of a mystical orchestra pit.

I glance back at the writing on the pedestal, my eyes narrowing as I notice something I hadn't picked up on before. "Hey, Erik," I call out, my voice bouncing off the damp stone. "Are those musical notes above each word, or am I just seeing things?"

Erik leans in closer, his silver brow furrowed in concentration. "Yes," he confirms, his tone matter-of-fact as always. "The first is C." He continues, rattling off the notes like he's reading from a music sheet. "E. G., and A."

"Well, that's just great," I mutter, throwing my hands up in exasperation. "We've got the notes, but how the hell are we supposed to turn that into some kind of secret message? It's not like we've got a piano handy."

Something catches my eye as I scan the cave for clues we might have missed. There, etched above us on the stalagmites, are letters. Freaking letters, like we've stumbled into some kind of twisted spelling bee.

"Look!" pointing up at the ceiling. "I think that's the answer."

We follow the drip of the water, watching as it falls in perfect time with the letters above. I make my way over to the 'C,' standing beneath it like I'm waiting for a goddamn baptism. And then, after what feels like forever, the water finally falls, hitting the pool with a musical note that sends goosebumps across my flesh.

But that's not all. As I peer into the shimmering water, I see a silvery phrase floating there, like a message in a bottle from the great beyond. "In harmony, we seek the light," I read aloud, my voice hushed with awe.

"Whoa!" I exclaim, repeating the message before disappearing like a mirage in the desert.

Erik and Rhyland look at each other with pure wonder, like they can't quite believe what they see. "Go to the next note, Little Huntress," Erik instructs, his voice tinged with excitement. "E."

I don't need to be told twice. I scramble around the pool's edge, eyes scanning the ceiling for the elusive 'E.' And there it is, etched into the stone like a beacon of hope. I wait with bated breath, my heart pounding in my chest as the water drips down, down, down.

Then, with a musical chord that echoes through the cavern like a heavenly choir, another phrase appears in the pool. "With courage found, we take our flight." I read, my voice trembling with anticipation.

I repeat the phrase like a mantra, determined not to let it slip away. And then I'm off again, searching for the following letter in this crazy, musical scavenger hunt. 'G,' where the hell are you?

I finally spot it at the front of the pool, sprinting over, my feet slipping on the damp stone. I wait for the drip, my breath caught in my throat. When it falls, the words that appear in the water nearly bring tears to my eyes.

"A leap of faith shall guide our way."

"One more, baby," Rhyland encourages, his voice low and steady.

But the final letter, that damn 'A,' is nowhere to be seen. I circle the pool like a shark on the hunt; my head cranes back as I search every nook and cranny. And then, finally, I spot it, tucked away in the back corner like a shy child at a party.

I scramble over the stones, my heart racing as I wait for the final drip...

"To the treasures that softly sway."

And then, we wait. We wait for something, anything, to happen. A hidden door to open, a magical staircase to appear, a freaking genie to pop out of a bottle and grant us three wishes.

But nothing happens. Nada. Zip. Zilch.

I sigh in frustration, my shoulders slumping as I repeat each message like I'm trying to decipher some ancient riddle.

"In harmony, we seek the light; With courage found, we take our flight. A leap of faith shall guide our way to the treasures that softly sway."

Just when I'm about to throw in the towel and call it a day, the cave starts to rumble. It's like the very earth beneath our feet is shifting, groaning like an old man getting out of bed in the morning.

I watch in amazement as the floor beneath the pool separates, the water dumping through like a pair of majestic waterfalls. It's like the cave itself is transforming before our very eyes, revealing secrets that have been hidden for centuries.

"Oh my gosh," I breathe, my eyes wide with wonder. "This is it."

I stand there, my jaw practically hitting the floor, as the water drains into the depths below, revealing a gaping hole that seems to go on forever. The cave has opened its secrets to us, inviting us to dive headfirst into the unknown.

Without hesitation, I step into the now-empty pool, my feet slipping on the slick stone.

I peer over the hole's edge, my stomach doing a little flip-flop as I take in the sheer drop. Down below, I can see that all the water has settled into a larger chamber, forming a pool that could swallow a small army.

I glance down at my wrist, where my bracelet glows brighter than a supernova. Clearly, it's flashing "This Way, Genius!"

I look at Rhyland, our eyes locking in a silent exchange that speaks volumes. We both know what's next and what the final piece of the puzzle must be. We all say in unison, our voices echoing through the cavern like a chorus of destiny.

"A leap of faith shall guide our way."

RHYLAND

66

I grip Dani's hand like a fucking lifeline, my fingers intertwined with hers so tightly I can feel her pulse racing against my skin. "On the count of three," I murmur, my voice low and intense as I meet her gaze.

Dani nods, her honey-gold eyes locked on mine with a trust that takes my breath away. She knows, beyond a shadow of a doubt, that I won't let her go, that I'll move heaven and earth to keep her safe as we make this insane leap of faith.

And it is insane.

The drop is at least fifty feet, a yawning chasm of darkness stretching forever. But we don't have a choice. The only way out is down, and the only way down is together.

"One," I count, my heart pounding like a war drum. "Two..."

Dani takes a deep, shuddering breath, her nerves cycling through our bond like a fucking feedback loop. I can feel her fear, her uncertainty, but I push it back with a wave of confidence and calm, wrapping her in a cocoon of reassurance and love.

"Three."

We launch ourselves off the edge, our bodies arcing through the air. I wrap myself around Dani like a second skin, holding her so close I can feel her heart pounding against my chest. The wind rushes past us, a deafening roar that drowns out everything else—my stomach in my throat—then we hit the water, hard and fast, the impact knocking the breath from my lungs in a rush of bubbles and foam. The cold shocks my system, a thousand icy needles piercing my skin as we sink beneath the surface.

I don't let go of Dani. Not for a fucking second. I kick hard, propelling us back towards the light.

We break the surface with a gasp, Dani coughing and sputtering as she struggles to catch her breath. I pull her close, crushing her against my chest as I tread water, my heart still racing with the adrenaline of the jump.

"I've got you, baby," I murmur, my lips brushing against her ear. "I've always got you."

Dani nods, her face buried in the crook of my neck as she clings to me, her body trembling with a mixture of cold and relief. And then, just as I'm starting to wonder if Erik chickened out on us, he splashes down beside us, his silver hair plastered to his forehead as he surfaces with a gasp.

"Damn, that was intense," he says, his voice rough with adrenaline. "You two okay?"

I nod, my arms still wrapped around Dani like I'm afraid she might disappear if I let go. "We're good, brother. A little wet, but we'll live."

Dani lets out a shaky laugh, her fingers digging into my shoulders as she clings to me. "Speak for yourself, babe," she quips. "I think I left my stomach back up on that ledge."

I grin, and it feels like it might split my face in two. "Nah, baby, you've got bigger balls than that," I tease, pressing a quick, hard kiss to her temple. "You're a fucking warrior, remember?"

Dani rolls her eyes, but I can see the smile tugging at the corners of her mouth, the way her body relaxes just the tiniest bit in my arms. "Yeah, yeah, whatever you say, Captain Save-a-Hoe," she mutters, with sass as she gives me a playful shove. "Guess I should be thanking my lucky stars. I've got such a big, strong man to protect little old me, huh?"

I smile as my lips brush against her ear. "Damn straight, baby. You know I'd do anything to keep you safe. Even if it means jumping off a fucking cliff like some kind of discount Batman."

Dani snorts. "Please," she scoffs. "You're way hotter than Batman. And you don't need some fancy-ass gadgets to get the job done."

I can't help but puff up a little at that, my ego swelling like a fucking balloon. "Damn right, I don't," I agree. "I've got something much better than gadgets."

"Oh yeah?" Dani asks, her eyebrows raised in a playful challenge. "And what might that be, tough guy?"

I lean in even closer, my breath hot against her skin as I whisper the words like a promise. "You, baby. I've got you."

And it's the truth. Because with Dani by my side, I feel like I can take on the whole fucking world. She's my strength—my courage, the fire that burns in my veins and keeps me going even when the odds seem impossible.

Dani blushes, and Erik clears his throat, getting our attention back on track.

I turn to Erik, my expression sobering as I take in our surroundings. The chamber we've landed in is even more massive than the one above, the walls stretching up and up until they disappear into the darkness. The water is deep and clear, the bottom lost in shadow, and I can feel the ancient magic thrumming through it like a heartbeat.

Dani's bracelet casts a brilliant light, illuminating the water around us in a vivid glow. It seems to do its light-up dance whenever we're near the artifacts, almost as if it's guiding us.

"Alright, let's get moving," as I swim toward the chamber's far end. "We've got a lyre to find and a realm to save, and we're not going to do it by treading water all day."

Erik nods, his expression grim, as he falls into place beside me. His powerful strokes cut through the water like a blade. Dani follows close behind; her more petite frame is no match for our speed, but her determination is more than making up for it.

As we reach the water's edge, I hoist myself onto the rocky ledge with a grunt, my muscles flexing with the effort. I turn back to Dani, my hand outstretched, and pull her up to me with a single, powerful tug. She collides with my chest, her body molding to mine like it was fucking made for me.

I take a moment to drink her in, my eyes roaming over her figure with unabashed hunger. Her leathers are drenched, clinging to her curves. The wet fabric hugs her tits, highlighting their perfect shape and the way her nipples strain against the material, begging for my touch. And fuck me, her zipper is sitting low, teasing me with a tantalizing glimpse of her cleavage.

I reach out, my fingers grazing the exposed skin of her chest as I slowly, deliberately zip her up. The action is possessive, a silent claiming, and how her breath hitches tells me she feels it, too.

"Careful, baby," I rumble. "Keep flashing me like that, and I might just have to take you right here, audience be damned."

I punctuate my words with a wink, my lips curving into a wicked smirk. Dani shivers, her gold eyes darkening with desire, and I know she's picturing it—me bending her over the nearest rock and fucking her until she screams.

But as much as I'd love to make that fantasy a reality, we've got shit to do. Erik is already moving ahead, his keen eyes scanning the cavern for any signs of trouble. I reluctantly step back from Dani, my hand settling on the small of her back as I guide her forward.

"Come on, Angel," I murmur, my breath hot against her ear. "Let's go find this lyre so I can get you back to the ship and finish what we started."

She nods, her body trembling with anticipation, and together, we set off deeper into the cave. With every step, the heat between us grows, the promise of what's to come hanging heavy in the air. And I know, without a shadow of a doubt, that when I finally get her alone, I'm going to finish what I started on that ship—her punishment—the way I make her come so hard she sees fucking stars.

I take a moment to survey our surroundings, my eyes widening as I take in the sheer scale of this underground cave. It's fucking massive, like something out of a goddamn fantasy novel. The walls are covered in glowing coral, casting an eerie, pulsing light that dances across the damp stone. The sound of trickling water echoes through the chamber, a constant reminder of the power and mystery surrounding us.

I spot a trail leading deeper into the cave and grab Dani's hand, my fingers intertwining with hers as I start leading the way. We walk for what feels like forever, our footsteps echoing off the walls like a heartbeat. And then, just when I'm starting to wonder if we're going in circles, we reach another opening and stop dead in our tracks.

"The altar," Erik says, his voice low as he points toward the chamber's far end. "It's there."

I follow his gaze, and sure enough, there it is—a stone altar glowing with an otherworldly light that seems to pulse in time with the beating of my heart. And there, resting on top of it like a fucking crown jewel, is the Siren's Lyre.

"There it is," Dani breathes, her voice filled with relief and awe. "We finally found it."

As we draw closer, I start to notice something strange. The lyre is surrounded by a shimmering water barrier, like a curtain of liquid light that ripples and dances with a life of its own. And there, at the altar's base, is an old-looking keyhole, its surface covered in intricate carvings and symbols.

"Baby, the key," I murmur, my eyes locked on Dani's.

She's already reaching into her pocket, her fingers closing around the skull-shaped key with the glowing blue gems. The key seems to pulse with an energy of its own, like it's been waiting for this moment all along.

"I've got it," her voice trembling with excitement and nerves. "Let's see if this works."

With that, she steps forward, clutching the key tightly as she approaches the altar. I hold my breath, my muscles tense and ready to act at the first sign of trouble. But as Dani inserts the key into the lock, there's a soft click, and the barrier shimmers and disappears like a mirage.

Dani reaches out, her fingers trembling as she lifts the lyre from its resting place. It's a thing of beauty, all gleaming gold and intricate carvings, and as she cradles it in her hands, I swear I can feel the power emanating from it like a physical force.

"We did it," she whispers, her voice filled with joy and disbelief. "We actually fucking did it."

I wrap my arms around her, pulling her close and burying my face in her hair. I can't help but feel a sense of triumph and wonder. We've come so far and faced so many challenges and obstacles, yet here we are, standing at the end of our quest with the prize we sought held tightly in our grasp.

It's a moment I know I'll never forget, a memory I'll cherish for the rest of my days.

"Alright, we've got what we came for. Let's get the hell out of here before this place decides to throw any more curveballs our way."

Dani grins, her eyes sparkling as she cradles the lyre close to her chest. "What's the matter, big guy?" she teases. "Afraid of a little adventure?"

I snort, shaking my head in amusement. "Baby, I think we've had enough adventure to last us a lifetime," I reply, my lips twitching with a smile. "But if you're not ready to call it quits just yet, I'm sure we can find some trouble to get into on the way back to the ship."

Dani laughs, the sound echoing off the cavern walls. "Tempting. But I think I'll save the trouble-making for another day. Right now, I just want to get back to the others and figure out our next move."

I nod, my expression serious as I think about the task ahead of us. "Let's go."

Dani nods, her eyes closed, already focusing on opening a portal. "Way ahead of you, Mr. Tall, Dark, and Brooding," she quips. "One express trip back to the S.S. Gideon, coming right up."

DANICA

67

So, after our little underwater cave adventure, we return to the Seraph, soaked and smelling like a bunch of drowned rats. As I descend below deck, I'm greeted by the sight of Mirella, Lucian, Seraphina, Finn, and Gideon, all huddled together like they're plotting world domination.

Seraphina practically tackles me in a hug, squeezing me so tight my ribs creak. "Dani!" she shouts, her voice muffled against my shoulder. "Thank the gods, you're back and in one piece!"

I hug her back, inhaling the familiar scent of my angel bestie and feeling some of the tension I've been carrying around melt away. Don't get me wrong. I knew Lucian would never let anything happen to her on their little side quest to the Atlantean Ruins. But still, a girl can worry.

"Aye, good to see ye back, lass," Gideon chimes in, his pirate accent thicker than the stew he's been slinging in the galley.

I flash him a grin and a nod, "Thanks for not abandoning us."

"Well, well, if it isn't my favorite damsel in distress," Finn drawls, sauntering forward with that ridiculous red bandana perched atop his messy mop of brown hair. "Nice to see yer not doing yer best impression of a drownin' rat this time. It's a good look on ya, lass."

I roll my eyes but can't help the grin tugging at my lips. "And here I thought you missed playing the dashing hero, Finn. Don't worry, I'm sure there are plenty of other helpless maidens just dying to be rescued by your scurvy-ridden self."

Finn laughs. "Aw, come now, lassy. You know you're the only waterlogged princess for me."

"Charming as ever, I see," I retort, giving him a playful shove. "So, tell me, oh great savior of the seas, have you managed to keep the hold clear of unexpected floods? Or should I be worried about taking an impromptu swimming lesson every time I step below deck?"

Finn's smirk widens. "Aye, lass, the hold's as dry as a nuns... well, you know. But don't let that stop ye from calling for me if you ever feel the urge to practice your drowning technique again."

"I'll keep that in mind, Finn."

After a quick bath (and by "bath," I mean splashing some water on my face and hoping for the best), Rhyland and I change into dry clothes for once and head back down to the galley.

And bless his heart, Erik's got a bowl of steaming seafood stew waiting for me like he knew my stomach would stage a mutiny if I didn't get some grub in me pronto. I don't waste a second, diving in like a starving wolf and slurping down every last drop.

Erik sits there, watching me with this little smile like he's the world's most over-grown mother hen. Always looking out for me, that one. It's enough to make a girl feel all warm and fuzzy inside.

"Thank you," I mumble around a mouthful of stew, my manners temporarily taking a backseat to my ravenous hunger. Once I've licked the bowl clean (literally, no shame), I fish out the Siren's Lyre and plop it down on the table like a trophy.

Not to be outdone, Mirella produces Nixie's journal with a flourish, sliding it over to me like she's passing me the keys to the kingdom—time to get to the bottom of this curse nonsense and figure out what the hell Cordelia's been up to.

I reach for the journal, ready to crack it open and spill its secrets. Before I can even flip to the first page, Rhyland's got me in his lap, his arms wrapped around me, tight.

"Seriously, babe?" I grumble, trying (and failing) to wriggle free. "I'm trying to solve a cosmic mystery here, not play *'The Princess Bride.'*"

Rhyland chuckles, his breath warm against my ear. "Relax, Angel," his voice all low and rumbly. "You've been through a lot today. Let me hold you for a minute, yeah?"

And damn it all to hell, I can't argue with that. Because as much as I hate to admit it, being in Rhyland's arms feels like coming home, like the safest place in the world. And after our day, I could use a little safety and comfort.

With that, I start to read. I'm staring at this journal like it's written in freaking hieroglyphics, my brain doing somersaults trying to make sense of the cryptic scribbles. But then, like a ray of sunshine cutting through the fog, Seraphina pipes up.

"Here, allow me," her voice all sweet and knowing, like she's about to drop some profound wisdom on us.

I look at her, my eyebrows shooting up. "Wait, what? You can read this ancient mumbo-jumbo?"

"Trust me, Princess. Wait till you see this shit. It's like watching a librarian on speed-reading steroids." Lucian snarks.

I hand over the journal, still skeptical but figuring it can't hurt to let my guardian angel take a crack at it. And holy hot damn, Seraphina starts flipping through those pages like she's skimming a trashy romance novel. I swear, her eyes are moving so fast, they're practically leaving scorch marks on the paper.

Within a minute (a freaking minute!), she hands the journal back to me, a serene smile on her face. "Okay, here's the deal," her voice all calm and collected, like she didn't just perform a miracle of speed-reading.

And then she starts to spill the tea, and let me tell you, it's a doozy. I'm talking drama, intrigue, and plot twists that would make even the most seasoned soap opera writer clutch their pearls in shock.

I lean back in my chair, my mind reeling from the bombshell Seraphina just dropped on us. "Okay, let me get this straight. Cordelia and Calypso are sisters? And their dad, Aeces, pulled a classic case of 'trade in the old model for a newer one' when he ditched Undinite for Rillia?"

Seraphina nods, her expression of sadness and understanding. "Yes, Dani. It was a terrible situation for all involved. Rillia, Calypso's mother, was to crown her queen next in succession."

I snort, shaking my head in disbelief. "Yeah, no kidding. And then Undinite went all *'fatal attraction'* and murdered Aeces and Rillia? Talk about a family drama."

Seraphina sighs, her voice soft and melodic as she continues. "Undinite then crowned Cordelia as queen and then took her own life. It's tragic, Dani. In her grief, Cordelia lashed out at Calypso. She cursed her with a once-a-month mermaid tail."

"Because nothing says 'I love you, sis' like turning her into a magical fish out of water, right? Cordelia must have missed the memo on healthy sibling relationships."

I take a moment to reflect on our encounter with Calypso. She was lounging in a pool, her mermaid tail on full display, and then, after dinner, she was suddenly over our presence, ready to kick us out.

But then it hits me. What if that was her swim day? Her one chance to rock that tail before being cursed with land legs for the rest of the month?

If you only had one day a month to embrace your inner mermaid, wouldn't you want to make the most of it?

So maybe Calypso's abrupt dismissal wasn't about being rude but about cherishing her limited time as a mermaid. And honestly, I can't blame her for that.

Seraphina, all sweet and knowing, "And if that wasn't enough, Cordelia cursed all the Merfolk, stealing their voices and banishing Calypso from the palace."

"A most despicable act, indeed." Erik finally supplies.

Lucian chuckles. "Whoa, that's some serious *Game of Thrones* action right there! I bet George R.R. Martin is taking notes."

I nod. "And let's not forget the cherry on top of this dysfunctional sundae. Cordelia gives Calypso the Soul Stone, a cursed family heirloom that amplifies emotions and drives the wearer to murder. Because nothing says 'sisterly love' like a homicidal accessory."

Rhyland's brow furrows. "But why the fuck would Cordelia make Calypso wear the Soul Stone? What's her endgame here? And how?"

I tap my chin thoughtfully, my mind racing with possibilities. "Maybe she's trying to paint Calypso as some soul-sucking monster? You know, make herself look like the good guy while her sister takes the fall?

"And maybe it's part of the curse—to force her to wear the damn thing."

Lucian nods, "Well, no fucking shit. Remember how Calypso was acting all kinds of cray-cray when we met her? It was like watching a schizophrenic squirrel on a cocaine bender."

He leans back, crossing his arms over his chest as he continues his analysis. "She was more conflicted than a vegan at a barbecue—like she was constantly wrestling with her inner demons. One minute she's all sweetness and light; the next, she was trying to tear my heart out of my fucking chest."

Seraphina gasps in horror, rushing back over to Lucian.

I shudder, remembering the way Calypso's eyes had flickered between desperation and malice. "Yeah, it was creepy as hell. Like she was two different people trapped in one body."

Erik, so stoic, sheds some light. "Perhaps the Soul Stone is corrupting her, turning her into a twisted version of herself."

I nod, my heart sinking at the thought. "Or maybe she's just desperate and needs our help, even if she's going about it in the worst possible way."

Mirella finally speaks up, her voice soft and hesitant: "That stone is pure evil—I read about it—whatever it's doing to her can't be good."

"Oh, I know damn well what this stone is capable of and how it works—what baffles me is how Calypso can seem so clear-headed and still in control," shaking my head, confused.

"It's one of the deadliest stones in existence, and she's only got a fraction of it," I continue, raising an eyebrow for emphasis.

Mirella's eyes widen, filled with innocent concern. "Wait, so there's more of it out there?"

I nod. "Yep. We have the other pieces. The plan is to get Calypso's, fuse them all together, and then lock it up tighter than Fort Knox until I figure out what the hell we're dealing with."

I glance around at the others, "Because, you know, babysitting ancient evil artifacts is kind of my thing now. Who knew I'd have such a knack for it?"

I lean against Rhyland's chest, my mind reeling with the implications. "So, we've got a cursed species, a vengeful sister, and a smear campaign involving the Soul Stone that is turning Calypso into a homicidal maniac? And I thought my family was fucked up."

Lucian is practically vibrating with glee. "See? What did I tell you? My girl's got mad skills, yo. She could probably recite Shakespeare's works backward while doing a handstand and juggling chainsaws."

Seraphina giggles, returning to Lucian's lap and kissing him as she sits down.

I roll my eyes but can't help but grin. "Alright, alright. But can we focus on the task at hand? Like, I don't know, the fact that Cordelia's apparently a psychotic mermaid with a vengeance."

Lucian, in all his smart-ass glory, "Jesus, with a family like that, who needs enemies? I'd rather get a fruitcake for Christmas than a one-way ticket to Murder Town."

Either way, it's a fucked-up situation all around. And it's starting to look like I'm the only one who can untangle this mess and bring some balance back to this underwater shit show.

Danica Pierce, professional curse-breaker and part-time mermaid therapist—at your service.

"Damn, this is a lot to unpack," I mutter, shaking my head in disbelief.

Mirella nods so vigorously that I'm half-afraid her head might fall off.

I pause momentarily, trying to wrap my head around this convoluted mess of a family drama. "But why isn't anyone standing up to Cordelia? If everyone knows she's not the rightful ruler, why not stage a coup or something?"

Mirella's already scribbling away, her quill flying across the page like it's got a mind of its own.

No one will go against her in ~~feer~~ fear of
the stone or losing our fins Everyone can ~~life~~
live happy if no one ~~speeks~~ speaks of it

"Ah, so that's her trump card," I muse, the pieces finally falling into place. "She's got the magical equivalent of a nuclear deterrent and is not afraid to use it. Plus, with that gag order in place, no one can speak out against her without risking her wrath.

Mirella scratches out another message and hands it to me.

The curse sits within the Sirens Lyre.

I stare at the words, my mind racing with the possibilities. "The Siren's Lyre? That's the key to all of this. The one thing that can turn the tides and undo the curse?"

Mirella nods, her expression fierce and unwavering. And suddenly, it all makes sense—why Calypso sent me on this wild goose chase, why Cordelia was so desperate to get her hands on that damn key.

I glance behind me at Rhyland and can practically see the gears turning in his head as he tries to process this bombshell. He looks about as shocked as I feel like someone just smacked him upside the head with a wet fish.

Erik takes a sip of his ale and clears his throat. "What of the Sirens?" he asks, his voice all business and no-nonsense.

"What do you mean, big guy?" I ask, because apparently, I need things spelled out for me like a kindergartener.

Erik straightens up like he's about to give a lecture on underwater politics. "Are the Sirens also affected by this evil enchantment, or do they remain unscathed?"

I have to hand it to him; the man has a point—the Sirens seem to be under Calypso's command, which begs the question of where they fit into this whole curse conspiracy.

I turn to Mirella, my eyebrows raised in expectation. She shakes her head no.

And just like that, a new can of worms has been opened. We all sit here in silence, our minds whirring as we try to piece together this latest puzzle.

If the Sirens are immune to Cordelia's curse, what does that mean for the bigger picture? Are they allies in this twisted game of underwater politics, or are they just caught in the crossfire?

"You know, it's quite clever when you think about it," Seraphina reflects. "Why would Cordelia even consider cursing the Sirens? It's clear they're immune. I doubt anyone in their right mind would choose to listen to a Siren's song, knowing it could lead to a heap of trouble."

She pauses, thinking. "It's logical that the curse is intended to impact only the non-Siren species. Cordelia isn't foolish enough to squander her time and magic on beings everyone is already steering clear of. That would be such a waste, wouldn't you agree?"

Lucian, the little shit, lets out a groan that sounds suspiciously like a poorly disguised orgasm. "Fuuuuck, I love it when you get all intellectual on me. It's like dirty talk for nerds, and I am *here* for it, baby girl."

Seraphina giggles.

Lucian, with his golden hair spiked every which way, leans back in his chair, a lazy grin spreading across his face. "But you're absolutely right, Cupcake. Cordelia's not gonna waste her time finding a curse for a bunch of fish-tailed femme fatales that everyone's already running scared from. She's got bigger fish to fry, like keeping her scaly ass on that underwater throne."

I can't help but snort at Lucian's unique brand of eloquence, "Well, there you have it, folks," I quip. "The Sirens are safe from Cordelia's magical meddling, all thanks to their reputations as the underwater world's biggest heartbreakers."

Then, like a lightbulb moment, something clicks in my brain. Calypso informed me that the Siren's Lyre was actually whipped up as a weapon for the Sirens. What if the lucky duck wielding this bad boy can curse any species they want? My mind starts to do cartwheels, but I rein it in. I'll get to the bottom of this fishy business soon enough, mark my words.

Seraphina and Lucian start kissing while she's perched on his lap like a contented kitten, and he's got this dopey grin on his face that screams "smitten." They are all over each other, all cute and couple-ly, lost in their little world. It's adorable as hell seeing them like this. Seraphina's practically glowing with happiness, and Lucian? He's like a lovesick puppy, all wagging tail and heart eyes.

Rhyland rolls his eyes. "For fuck's sake, you two, get a goddamn room already. Some of us are trying to keep our lunch down over here without watching you suck face."

Lucian pulls back from Seraphina, his face split in a grin. "Well, well, well, look who's talking. Mr. 'I Can't Keep My Hands Off Dani For Five Fucking Seconds' is giving me a lecture about PDA? That's richer than your trust fund, Rhy-Rhy."

I have to admit, he's got a point. I'm currently perched on Rhyland's lap like it's my throne, as his hands grip my inner thighs like he's afraid I might float away if he lets go.

Rhyland narrows his eyes. "Watch it, asshat. Don't make me come over there and rearrange your pretty boy face."

Lucian clutches his chest, gasping dramatically like he's auditioning for a telenovela. "Oh no, please, anything but that! I need this face for, like, everything." He pauses, then winks, "Aww, what's the matter, Rhy-Rhy—afraid of a little competition in the PDA department? Worried that Phina and I might steal your crown as the resident horndog couple? That's adorable."

Rhyland snorts, his hands running up and down my thighs in a way that makes me quiver. "You're a real fucking comedian, you know that? Keep it up, and I'll ensure the only action you get is from your right hand and a bottle of lotion."

Lucian grins, blowing Rhyland a kiss that's equally mocking and affectionate. "Aww, I love you too, big bro. Now, if you'll excuse me, I have some unfinished business to attend to with my lady. These lips don't kiss themselves, you know."

Rhyland scoffs. "TMI, dude. Just keep it in your pants until we're done here. God knows you can't stay focused on the task at hand for more than five fucking seconds. Then you can go nuts, for all I care."

Lucian grins, giving Rhyland a mock salute that's more middle finger than respect. "That's a hell no, Captain Cockblock. Your wish is *not* my command. In fact, it's not even in the same zip code as my to-do list."

Erik rolls his eyes. "The incessant bickering between these two never fails to astonish me."

I can't help but laugh, caught in the crossfire of their ridiculous banter. Moments like these remind me why I love these idiots so much, even when they're driving me absolutely insane.

DANICA

68

I'm perched on the side of the ship's deck with Seraphina, taking in the endless expanse of the sea as we make our way back to Driftwood Market. We desperately need supplies and a shower that doesn't involve salt water and fish pee.

With the Siren's Lyre being our golden ticket to breaking this underwater curse, we're obviously heading back to Calypso's place. Where exactly that is? Well, your guess is as good as mine. I haven't yet figured out how to send a magical underwater telegram to our favorite part-time mermaid.

I turn to Seraphina. "So, you and Lucian, huh?" I waggle my eyebrows suggestively.

Seraphina's eyes light up like a kid on Christmas morning at the mere mention of Lucian's name. "Yes," her voice as sweet as honey. "I can't quite explain it... it all happened so fast."

I laugh at her sudden bashfulness. "Don't be shy, Sera. You can't resist the pull of your mate; trust me, I know. I was very stubborn with Rhyland." I chuckle at the memory of my stubborn ass fighting tooth and nail against the inevitable.

Seraphina sighs dreamily, her eyes glazing over with that lovesick look. "It's just... everything," she gushes. "I never knew true love—finding your soulmate—would feel like this. And if I'm being honest, I couldn't be more thrilled to have been kicked out of Atheria to experience it."

I grin, patting her on the shoulder. "Can't say I blame you, sister. You've done your angelic duty, Sera. Now it's time to live a little and experience all the naughty, fun stuff you've missed out on."

Seraphina blushes, but her smile is radiant. "You're right, Dani. I'm ready for this new chapter in my life. But I will never stop protecting you."

"That's my girl," I say with a wink. "Just remember, if Lucian ever gives you trouble, I've got your back. I know where he sleeps."

Seraphina turns her gaze to the vast expanse of the sea. Her voice tinged with uncertainty and a hint of guilt. "Do you think we... went too fast?"

I shake my head. "No, absolutely not," I reassure her, my tone firm but gentle. "What you guys have? It's not some run-of-the-mill, swipe-right-on-Tinder kind of deal. We're talking true love here, honey—the soul-deep, write-epic-poems-about-it kind of love."

I reach out and squeeze her hand. "Your soul recognizes him, and he recognizes you. It's like...your spirits do this cosmic happy dance whenever you're together. There's no expiration date on that kind of connection—no 'best if used by' stamp."

Leaning in, I catch her eye, ensuring she listens. "Look, Sera, when it comes to matters of the heart, there's no such thing as a rulebook or a timeline. You go with what feels right, and trust me, following your heart? That's never wrong. It's like...an emotional GPS. It might sometimes take you on some weird detours, but it always gets you where you need to be."

I grin, nudging her playfully. "Besides, have you seen the way Lucian looks at you? That man is so obsessed; I'm surprised he hasn't started leaving little heart-shaped clouds everywhere he goes. So stop worrying and enjoy the ride, sweetie. True love doesn't come knocking every day, you know."

"I know," Seraphina sighs, her eyes still fixed on the horizon. "I feel him on such a level that I never even thought was possible—the blood thing..."

I look over at her, knowing exactly where she's going with this. Her cheeks are flushed, and she's fidgeting like she's about to confess to stealing cookies from the cosmic cookie jar.

"It's so... dirty and... and..." she stammers, struggling to find the right words.

"Erotic?" I finish for her, unable to keep the smirk off my face.

Seraphina's blush deepens to a shade that would make a tomato jealous. "Yes," she admits, her voice barely above a whisper. Then, as if a dam has broken, she bursts out, "And it's crazy. I love it!"

I can't help but laugh at her enthusiastic confession. "Oh honey, I know," giving her a conspiratorial wink. "It's more addictive than chocolate-covered crack, isn't it?"

She nods eagerly, her eyes sparkling. "It just feels right and freeing and so much more."

"Oh, it is freeing," I agree, my mind drifting to my own experiences. "Allowing your man to take himself into you, to take away all your pain, your fear, your anxiety with his bite... it's like the world's most intense therapy session, only with way more orgasms."

I nudge her playfully. "It truly is something else, girl. Just wait until you really get into it. You'll be walking around with a permanent goofy grin and bite marks in places you didn't even know could be bitten."

Seraphina giggles, her earlier guilt seemingly forgotten. "Is it always like this?" she asks, her voice filled with wonder.

"Oh, sweetie," I reply with a grin. "Trust me when I say you haven't seen anything yet. This is just the appetizer. The main course? It'll blow your celestial mind."

We sit there momentarily, grinning like lovestruck idiots as we watch the waves crash against the ship. It's a rare moment of peace amid all this chaos, and I can't help but feel a surge of gratitude for the fantastic people I've got by my side.

"So..." Seraphina starts, her voice uncertain. "Are all vampires... you know, big?"

I catch sight of a pod of dolphins frolicking in front of us, their sleek bodies flipping and splashing in the water. I can't help but smile at their playful antics.

My mind wanders to my vampire guys—Rhyland, Erik, Lucian—all towering over me with their impressive heights and muscular builds. "Yeah, I mean, Rhyland is 6'4", Erik is the same height, and Lucian is only a smidge shorter."

I think about Azrael and Adrian, too, both of them built like brick houses. "Maybe it's a vampire thing," I shrug, assuming she's talking about their overall size.

Seraphina blushes, dipping her head and clearing her throat awkwardly. "No, I meant... in the nether regions department."

OH. *OH!*

Little Miss Guardian Angel has got a naughty side!

I cackle, realizing I totally missed her not-so-subtle reference. "Umm, I wouldn't know if *all* of them are packing heat down there," I manage to say between giggles. "But personally? Let's say Rhyland's... equipment... matches his impressive height."

Seraphina's eyes widen to the size of dinner plates, and I swear I can see steam coming out of her ears.

"So, Lucian's working with a broadsword too, huh?" I wink at her, enjoying her embarrassment, maybe a little too much. "Why am I not surprised? Must be a vampire thing. Maybe it's all the blood flow."

She giggles, covering her face with her hands. "I can't help it! It's just... wow."

"Welcome to the big leagues, honey," I say, patting her back. "Just remember, it's not the size of the boat. It's the motion of the ocean. Although, in our case, I'd say we hit the jackpot in both departments."

We dissolve into laughter echoing across the waves. Who knew angels could be so delightfully naughty?

I may be half-angel—my halo's got a bit of a tilt to it. And the best part? I'm still learning, still uncovering new depths to my desires and fantasies. It's like I'm on this wild, sensual journey of self-discovery, and Rhyland is my oh-so-willing tour guide.

So yeah, I may have angel blood running through my veins, but trust me, there's plenty of devil in me, too. And I'm not afraid to let that freak flag fly.

"What're you two giggling about over here?" Rhyland's deep voice rumbles in my ear as he comes up behind me and wraps his arms around my waist, pulling me flush against his rock-hard chest.

I flash Seraphina a conspiratorial wink. "Oh, you know, just some good old-fashioned girl talk."

Seraphina winks back, a sly grin on her face. "Speaking of which, I think I will go find Lucian. You two lovebirds, have fun!" She turns on her heel, leaving Rhyland and me alone in our little bubble of sexual tension.

Rhyland nuzzles my neck, his breath hot against my skin. "So, what were you two really talking about, Angel? With all those giggles, it sounded like you were spilling some juicy secrets."

I shiver as he places an open-mouthed kiss on my neck, his teeth grazing my sensitive flesh. "A lady never kisses and tells," I lie, my voice a little breathier than I'd like to admit.

Rhyland chuckles, the sound low and sinful. "Is that so? Because from where I'm standing, it seems like you and Seraphina were having quite an intimate conversation."

I tilt my head back, giving him better access to my neck. "Maybe we were, maybe we weren't. What's it to you, Bothersome Berserker?"

He growls, nipping at my earlobe. "It's everything to me, baby. I want to know every dirty little thought that runs through that pretty head of yours."

I can't help but laugh, even as desire coils hot and heavy in my belly. "Wow, possessive much? I didn't realize my *girl talk* was subject to your approval, Mr. Alpha Male."

Rhyland spins me around, pinning me with his Nordic blue gaze. "Regarding you, Angel, everything is subject to my approval. I want to know every inch of you, inside and out."

I roll my eyes, even as my heart races at his words. "Easy there, caveman. I'm not some damsel in distress waiting for you to club me over the head and drag me back to your man cave."

He grins, the expression equal parts wicked and sexy. "Nah, you're too much of a pain in the ass to be a damsel in distress. But that doesn't mean I don't want to know every part of you and those delicious thoughts and claim them."

I arch an eyebrow, my lips curving into a smirk. "Is that a promise or a threat, Rhy-Pie?"

God, he's a work of art. All hulking muscle, tan, and irresistibly handsome. His white shirt is slightly open at the neck, giving a tantalizing glimpse of his tattoo. His dark hair is cut high and tight, emphasizing his chiseled, bearded jaw. And those eyes—those stunning, ocean-blue eyes that could make my knees buckle with just one look.

He leans in close, his lips brushing against mine. "It's a fucking guarantee, baby. Now, why don't you stop being such a tease and tell me what you and Seraphina were talking about?"

I laugh, pushing him away playfully. "Not a chance, Bitey Boy. A girl's got to have some secrets, after all. Keeps things interesting."

Rhyland shakes his head, a rueful smile on his face. "You drive me crazy, woman."

I grin, pressing a quick kiss to his lips. "Ditto."

And with that, I stroll away, leaving him standing there with a look of pure hunger in his eyes.

Oh yeah, this is going to be fun.

I'm suddenly knocked off balance, my ass meeting the deck in a less-than-graceful display of coordination. Meanwhile, Rhyland's playing a game of "pin the tail on the barrel."

Oh, for the love of Poseidon's soggy balls! One minute, I'm getting cozy with my Norse beefcake, and the next, this ship's pitching and rolling like crazy.

The crew's in full panic mode, rushing around like headless chickens as they peer overboard to see what's rocking the ship. I see a tentacle thicker than a redwood slithering up the vessel's side like a perverted python.

"Kraken!" some genius pirate screams behind me. No shit, Sherlock. What gave it away? The giant, ship-molesting appendage?

Pirates are scattering like roaches, and the Kraken's tentacles are slithering all over the ship like a handsy date you can't get rid of.

Holy shit—Is this the same sushi-craving son of a squid that tried to make Rhyland its personal chew toy? Because I swear, it wasn't this ginormous last time. What, did it hit some underwater gym and bulk up on protein shakes made of unfortunate sailors?

Well, not today. This overgrown calamari platter isn't going to have us for dinner—not if I have anything to say about it—time to channel my inner Carrie and go full-on Firestarter on this aquatic asshole.

Summoning all my strength and focus, I call upon my powers, feeling the familiar surge of energy coursing through me. With determination, I unleash a powerful blast combining searing light and intense flame, aiming straight for the creature.

As my attack races toward the massive beast, the air crackles with heat and energy. I hope this will drive it away or make it think twice about messing with us again. My heart pounds in my chest, and fear and adrenaline fuel my resolve to protect us from this terrifying threat.

The Kraken screeches like a banshee, its tentacles recoiling from the ship. But the damage is done. The ship's rocking like a cradle in a hurricane, and I'm starting to think we might take an unplanned swim. I'm on my ass, clinging to anything within reach to keep from sliding into the ocean's not-so-gentle embrace.

Rhyland is at my side in an instant. "What the fuck?" he exclaims, his eyes wide with disbelief.

"Looks like our friendly neighborhood sea monster is stopping by for round two of your delicious ass," I quip.

Suddenly, a tentacle slams down next to us, and Rhyland has none of it. He unleashes a telekinetic blast that sends the slimy appendage flying back. But the tentacle's not going down without a fight. It tears through the ship's side like tissue paper, leaving a hole big enough to drive a truck through.

Shit. As if we didn't have enough problems.

Erik and Lucian burst onto the deck, ready to throw down with our unwelcome sea monster party crasher. Erik, the overachiever he is, immediately starts going full

Ginsu on the tentacles, slicing and dicing them like he's auditioning for Iron Chef: Kraken Edition.

"Friend of yours?" Lucian quips, his trademark smirk firmly in place.

I shoot him a withering glare. "Oh, totally. We were just about to sit down for a nice chat over some tea and biscuits. You know, catch up on old times, swap recipes, the usual."

"Ah, my mistake. I didn't realize you two were so close. Should I give you a moment alone, or...?"

"Just get your snarky ass up to the helm and help the Captain," I snap over the deafening roar of the Kraken and the splintering of wood. "And try not to get eaten. I'd hate to explain to Seraphina why her boyfriend is now calamari."

Lucian gives me a mock salute. "Aye, aye, Captain Sassy Pants. I'll ensure our fearless leader doesn't steer us straight into Davy Jones' locker."

With that, he bounds up to the top deck, ready to play first mate to the Captain. I can only imagine the bullshit pearls of wisdom he's dropping.

I'm about to fire off another round of angel-fueled whoop-ass when I hear a scream that turns my blood to ice. I whip around just in time to see Finn, the Captain's first mate, being dragged overboard by a tentacle wrapped around his leg. The kid's face is a mask of pure terror as he claws at the deck, desperate to hold on.

"FINN!" I scream, scrambling to my feet. But it's too late. The tentacle yanks him over the side with a sickening crack, and he disappears into the churning waters below.

For a moment, I'm frozen, my heart shattering into a million pieces. Finn was just a kid, barely old enough to shave. He'd saved my life when I nearly drowned, and now...now he is gone, just like that.

Tears blur my vision as a wave of grief and rage crashes over me. This fucking Kraken is going to pay. I will make sure of it.

I focus my energy on the Faerite stone, channeling my thoughts through its ancient power. *"Why are you doing this?"* I demand, with fury. *"I freed you from your prison, you ungrateful bastard. Attacking us is how you repay me?"*

The Kraken's presence slithers into my mind like a cold, oily serpent, its thoughts dark and twisted. *"I seek retribution for the wrongs done to me,"* it hisses, its voice echoing in the depths of my consciousness.

"Stop this madness!" I plead, my heart pounding in my chest. *"No one here has harmed you. It was Cordelia who imprisoned you, not us."*

A massive tentacle lashes out with terrifying speed as if in response to her name. Time seems to slow to a crawl as I watch in horror, the appendage slamming into Lucian with the force of a battering ram. His body goes limp as he's catapulted off the ship, disappearing into the churning waters below.

The breath is ripped from my lungs as I feel Lucian's pain and confusion through our bond, the sensation so intense it brings me to my knees.

This can't be happening.

Not again. Not another friend lost to this nightmare.

My blood roars in my ears, drowning out all other sounds until a scream pierces the chaos, a sound that will haunt me for the rest of my days.

"LUCIAN!!" Seraphina's voice is raw with anguish as she clings to the ship's railing, her eyes wide with desperation. Before I can draw a breath to call out to her, she leaps over the side, plunging into the sea after her fallen mate.

"Seraphina, no!" I scream, my voice cracking with emotion. I stumble to the railing, my hands gripping the weathered wood so tightly that my knuckles turn white. The waves below are a frenzied maelstrom, the Kraken's tentacles churning the water into a deadly whirlpool.

I search for any sign of Lucian or Seraphina, my heart in my throat.

I can't lose them—not like this.

LUCIAN

69

Holy tentacle porn, Batman! This is not how I pictured my day going. There I was, just minding my own goddamn business when suddenly, I'm being dragged into the frigid depths of Davy Jones' locker by a Cthulhu-looking mother-fucker that probably crawled out of the deepest, darkest crevice of Satan's asshole.

The salty water stings my eyes as I struggle to see through the inky blackness, bubbles obscuring my vision like I'm in a fucking jacuzzi from hell. I can feel the air being squeezed out of my lungs by the crushing pressure, my chest burning like I've swallowed a gallon of battery acid.

I try to fight against the slimy, pulsating tentacle wrapped around my body, but it's like trying to wrestle a greased-up sumo wrestler. The more I struggle, the tighter it seems to squeeze until I'm pretty sure my ribs are about to snap like fucking twigs.

As I'm being dragged deeper and deeper into the abyss, my mind starts to wander to Seraphina, my beautiful angel cake. I can picture her face, those sparkling golden eyes, and that smile that could light up the whole damn world. The thought of leaving her behind, of her being mateless and alone, is more painful than any physical torture this octopus bastard could inflict.

Will she feel the same unbearable pain ripping through her soul that I would if I lost her? Will the loss drive her to the brink of madness, turning her into a fallen angel consumed by darkness and despair? The very idea makes me want to tear this fucker limb from slimy limb.

I summon every last ounce of strength I have left, thrashing and kicking like a wild animal caught in a trap. But it's no use. My lungs are screaming for air, and my vision blurs around the edges as the icy water seeps into my bones.

I feel my consciousness slipping away. My thoughts drift back to Seraphina. I hope she knows how much I love her and how I would move heaven and earth just to see her smile—to hear her laugh. In our brief time together, I hope to show her the true depths of my devotion and make her feel cherished and adored in every possible way.

Most of all, I hope I was able to give her a taste of the mind-blowing pleasure she deserves, to worship every inch of her body until she was a quivering, moaning mess of ecstasy. If I'm going to die, at least I'll go out knowing I rocked her world like a fucking hurricane.

Bright lights dance across my vision, growing more colorful and intense with each passing second. My body goes limp—weightless—no longer being squeezed to death—succumbing to the sea's cold embrace. I drift towards the light, and a vision of Seraphina's face appears before me, radiant and perfect and so fucking beautiful it makes my heart ache.

If this is what death looks like, then maybe it's not so bad. Because in the end, there's no sight I'd rather see than the face of the woman I love, the angel who stole my heart and made me believe in something greater than myself.

"Lucian..." Seraphina's voice echoes through my mind like a siren's song, sweet and haunting and so fucking perfect it makes my heart clench.

"I'm sorry, sweetheart," I whisper, the words bubbling from my mind in a stream of silent regret. I know she can't hear me, but I need to say it anyway: to put my feelings into the universe like a message in a bottle. *"I hope you know I love you, baby girl. More than anything in this fucked-up world."*

Suddenly, I feel the softest, most delicate hands cradling my face, followed by the feather-light brush of lips against mine. It's like being kissed by my sweet, sweet angel, and I swear, I can almost hear the hallelujah chorus singing in the background.

And then, like a fucking miracle, air rushes into my lungs, sweet and pure and so damn good I could cry. The burning in my chest eases, replaced by a warmth that spreads through my entire body like liquid sunshine.

I force my eyes open, blinking against the sting of the saltwater, and find myself staring into the most breathtaking pair of golden eyes—Seraphina—that sparkle with love, relief, and fierceness that takes my breath away all over again.

I feel a tug on my body, and suddenly, we're moving upwards, cutting through the water. My limbs are useless, but I can feel Seraphina's strong, slender arms wrapped around me, holding me close as she propels us toward the surface.

And then I see them—her wings, those magnificent, iridescent wings, unfurling behind her like the most beautiful fucking thing I've ever seen. They're glowing with an ethereal light, each powerful stroke sending us rocketing through the water like a pair of feathered torpedoes.

It's like something out of a goddamn fairy tale, watching my angel soar through the depths, her wings shimmering like stardust in the filtered sunlight. I can feel the raw power emanating from her, the sheer determination and love driving her to save the man she loves.

As we break through the surface, gasping for air and clinging to each other, I can't help but stare at Seraphina in awe. She's a fucking vision, her golden blonde hair plastered to her face, her cheeks flushed with exertion, and her eyes blazing with a fire that could put the sun to shame.

"You came for me," I croak. The saltwater has done a number on my throat, but it's the overwhelming surge of emotions that has me feeling like I'm about to choke up like a little bitch at a Nicholas Sparks movie. "You saved my life, baby girl. You're like my own personal superhero, minus the spandex and the tragic backstory."

Seraphina smiles as she presses her forehead against mine. Her hands cradle my face like I'm the most precious thing in the world—I can feel the warmth of her love seeping into my skin like a balm for my battered soul.

"I will always come for you, Lucian," she murmurs, her voice trembling with a fierce intensity that makes my heart skip a beat. "I would move heaven and earth to get to you. You think I would just leave you hanging like a forgotten ornament?" She gives me a knowing smile. "I will always find you in this life and the next."

I can't help but grin like a fucking idiot, my heart swelling with so much love and gratitude it feels like it might just burst out of my chest like the world's most awkward baby alien. She's throwing my own words back at me, the same cheesy-ass line I used when I rescued her from that douchecanoe pirate, Captain Bloodbitch, or whatever the fuck his name was.

But coming from her lips, those words take on a whole new meaning, a promise of forever that makes me want to shout from the rooftops and do a little victory dance.

Seraphina smiles, "And...I love you, too," she whispers, her words sweet with more sugar than a diabetic's nightmare.

My brain short-circuits faster than a toaster in a bathtub. Wait just a motherfucking minute. She heard my entire internal monologue? The private radio station broadcasting straight from my twisted mind while I was in Squidward's ass? Holy shit. Call me a psychic because this can only mean one thing—our bond is leveling up like a Pokemon on steroids. We're going full Professor X here, complete with the mental walkie-talkie action.

I can't resist the urge any longer. I grab Seraphina and plant a big, fat, sloppy kiss right on her perfect lips, pouring every ounce of love and gratitude and sheer fucking relief into it like I'm trying to win a gold medal in tonsil hockey. And bless her angelic heart, she kisses me right back, her lips moving against mine in a dance that's both familiar and electrifying, like coming home and discovering a new world all at once.

Our little makeout session is rudely interrupted by the sound of cannon fire blasting through the air like a fucking Fourth of July parade. The Kraken bastard is still trying to drag the ship to the briny depths like a kid with a bathtub toy.

Seraphina doesn't hesitate. With a powerful beat of her wings, she launches us out of the water like a fucking surface-to-air missile, holding me close as we soar toward the deck of the ship.

We land on the deck with a bone-jarring thud, and I'm pretty sure I'm going to be feeling that shit in my tailbone for weeks. No time to dwell on my aching ass because Dani and Rhyland are going full Super Saiyan on the giant tentacles, blasting them with energy beams and magic missiles like they're in a fucking anime battle sequence.

The ship rocks and sways, and I'm starting to regret that third bowl of fish soup I had for lunch. Dani catches sight of me, her eyes wide and puffy and still glistening with tears like she's been crying her fucking eyes out over my sorry ass.

"Lucian, holy shit, you're okay!" she yells, her voice barely audible over the sound of splintering wood and eldritch screeching. "I thought you were calamari for sure!"

I open my mouth to reply with some witty one-liner, but before I can get a word out, another tentacle slams down on the side of the ship like a fucking wrecking ball, tearing a hole the size of a Buick in the hull.

"You two stay out of the way!" Dani shouts, her voice strained with the effort to keep the ship from being dragged under. And as much as it fucking kills me to admit it, she's right. I may be a badass vampire with a potty mouth for every occasion, but I don't have the kind of superpowers that my stick-in-the-ass brother and his pint-sized powerhouse of a mate are packing.

So I do the only thing I can do. I grab Seraphina like she's my life raft, pulling her close and ducking down behind a pile of crates and barrels to keep her safe from the chaos erupting around us. The deck is slick with seawater, and god knows what else. The air is thick with the stench of brine, burnt wood, and coppery tang of blood.

But through it all, Seraphina remains a beacon of calm, her presence soothing the frayed edges of my nerves like a balm on a raw wound. She clings to me just as tightly, her wings wrapping around us both like a protective cocoon, shielding us from the worst of the debris and the flying tentacles and the fucking insanity of it all.

DANICA

70

I'm so freaking relieved that Lucian and Seraphina are okay. Seraphina just dove in like a boss to save her man, and I'm feeling all sorts of proud, relieved, and pissed off at the same time.

I mean, what in the actual *hell* was she thinking? Then again, I can't really talk, considering I pulled the same stunt for Rhyland. When your mate's in trouble, it's like this primal instinct kicks in, and suddenly, the concept of self-preservation goes right out the window.

I focus my energy on the overgrown sushi roll, giving it one last chance to back off.

"Listen up, asshole," I growl. *"You've got one chance to untangle yourself from this ship, or I swear to every god in the sea, I will turn you into a floating pile of ash."*

I don't even know why I'm bothering to negotiate with this asshat. It's not like reasoning with a Kraken is high on my bucket list, but hey, I'm feeling generous.

The slimy bastard slithers back into my mind, its presence as welcome as an oil spill in a pristine ocean. *"I will never surrender again,"* it hisses, its voice like nails on a chalkboard in my brain.

Fine, then. Have it your way, you colossal piece of shit.

I let out a primal scream, unleashing every last ounce of power within me. Light and fire explode from my hands, eyes—my very being, engulfing the Kraken in a blaze of holy retribution. It's like I'm channeling the sun, a supernova of righteous fury that engulfs the Kraken in a blaze of holy hellfire.

By some miracle (or maybe just my incredible aim), my power targets the Kraken like a heat-seeking missile, leaving the ship unscathed.

The monster shrieks in agony, its tentacles flailing as it tries to escape the inferno. But there's no escape from my wrath. I pour everything I have into the attack: every shred of pain, every ounce of grief for Finn, for the brave souls lost to this monster's rampage.

And then, as suddenly as it began, it's over. The Kraken sinks beneath the waves, its charred and smoking remains disappearing like a bad dream. The ship is battered and broken, but somehow, it's still afloat. We're alive, but the cost...the cost is too damn high.

I hear a faint whisper as the adrenaline fades: *"Thank you."* —a final message that makes my blood run cold.

Thank you? What the ever-loving fuck?

Did this overgrown calamari want to die? Was it so far gone, so broken from centuries of imprisonment, that death was its only release?

I sink to my knees, my body trembling with exhaustion and a sickening sense of understanding. No creature, no matter how monstrous, should suffer like that. And in the end, I gave it the only mercy it could comprehend.

But the bitter taste of victory turns to ashes in my mouth as I survey the destruction around me. The deck is slick with blood and seawater, the bodies of fallen crewmen scattered like broken dolls. And Finn...brave, sweet Finn...he's gone. Lost to the depths, never to see another sunrise.

I feel Rhyland's arms around me; his strength keeps me from shattering into a million pieces. I bury my face in his chest, my tears soaking his shirt as the weight of it all comes crashing down on me.

This is the price of being a savior—the burden I must bear. But in moments like this, when the cost is measured in lives cut short and dreams unfulfilled, I can't help but wonder...

Is it worth it?

After our much-needed detour to Driftwood Market, we're squeaky clean, freshly clothed, and loaded with enough supplies to survive the end of the world—or at least another Kraken attack. Our ship's been patched up (which looked like it had gone ten rounds with a cheese grater); we're all set to play "Where in the World is Carmen San-Calypso?"

Of course, I'm mentally kicking myself for torching that tracking device. Way to go, Dani. You just had to play the rebellious heroine, didn't you? That little gadget probably would've led us straight to Calypso's underwater hideout, complete with turn-by-turn directions and a "You have arrived at your destination" announcement.

But no, we're doing this the old-fashioned way: sailing aimlessly and hoping we stumble upon Calypso. It's like trying to find a specific fish in the ocean—Oh, wait.

We've been lounging around for two weeks, letting our batteries recharge and our sea legs recover. Now, we're all suited up and ready to set sail on this wild goose chase... or should I say, wild fish chase?

At this rate, I might need to invest in a waterproof GPS. Do they make those for mythical underwater kingdoms? Asking for a friend.

As I'm strutting towards the ship, feeling like a brand new woman, a familiar figure catches my eye. Tucked away inside a small, unassuming building, I spot none other than Nixie herself, shuffling her tarot cards with an air of mysterious knowing.

I practically sprint inside, my curiosity burning. "Hello, Dani," Nixie greets me, her voice as smooth as sea glass. "It's good to see you thriving and on the right path."

I plop down in the seat across from her, the words tumbling out of my mouth. "Why didn't you just tell me everything from the start?" I blurt out, my frustration as clear as the crystal waters of Aquaria. "It would've saved me a lot of trouble and confusion."

Nixie continues to shuffle her cards, the rhythmic motion seeming to soothe her. "If I had revealed to you from the beginning that Calypso was innocent and laid bare all of Cordelia's misdeeds, would you have truly believed me?" she asks, her eyes piercing into my soul.

I open my mouth to protest, to insist that I would have believed her, but then I pause.

Would I have?

When we first met, I was skeptical of her fortune-telling and cryptic messages, but everything she said had been spot-on. "Yes," I finally say, my voice quieter now. "I would have believed you."

Nixie sighs, a sound as ancient as the sea itself. "It's not that simple, Dani," she explains, her voice tinged with regret. "You see, I was once a part of Cordelia's court, a trusted advisor and confidante. But as her heart grew darker and her actions more twisted, I knew I could no longer stand by her side."

She sets down her cards, her eyes distant with memory. "I made a choice, a sacrifice. To escape the curse and retain my voice, I traded my fins for legs, my home in the sea, for a life on land. But in doing so, I also bound myself to a sacred oath, a promise not to interfere directly in the realm's affairs."

I lean forward, my brow furrowed in confusion. "But why? Why make that kind of promise?"

Nixie smiles sadly. "Because I knew the truth would have to be discovered, not handed out like a gift. The savior, destined to break the curse and restore balance, would need to walk their path, learn and grow, and make their own choices."

She reaches out, her weathered hand grasping mine. "I couldn't tell you the full story, Dani—because your journey and discoveries are all part of a greater tapestry. *You* needed to learn and see things with your own eyes to make decisions based on the truth you uncovered."

I sit back, my mind reeling with this new revelation. "So, the journal...Mirella ...?"

Nixie nods. "They were my way of guiding you. I knew Mirella would find and read it—the book I wrote of you and your journey as the savior."

She fixes me with a stare that seems to pierce through to my very core. "Your task, Dani, is to restore balance to all the realms. To mend what has been broken, to unite what has been divided. And to do that, you needed to see the world, experience its wonders and horrors, and understand the forces at play and the stakes at hand."

I take a deep breath, letting her words sink in. It's a lot to take in, a lot to shoulder. But somehow, deep down, I know she's right. Every twist and turn, every revelation and heartache... it's all been leading me to this point, preparing me for what's to come.

"I understand," my voice steady with newfound resolve. "I may not like it, but I wish you could've just given me a roadmap from the start... but I get it. I had to walk this path on my own."

Nixie smiles, pride shining in her ancient eyes. "And walk it you have, child. You have grown so much and learned so much. You are ready to face the final challenge and bring peace to Aquaria once more."

She releases my hand, sitting back in her chair. "Now go, Dani. Speak with Calypso, break the curse, and set things right. The fate of Aquaria, of all the realms, rests in your hands."

I stand, my heart pounding with fear and excitement. "I won't let you down," I vow, my voice ringing with conviction. "I won't let any of you down."

And with that, I turn and stride out of the building, my steps sure and my head held high.

"Oh, and Dani," Nixie's voice stops me in my tracks just as I'm about to make my dramatic exit. I turn, my eyebrows raised in question. "Calypso is hiding in the Atlantean Ruins, in case you didn't know." She throws me a wink like she's just handed me the keys to the underwater kingdom before returning to her card shuffling.

I blink, my mind racing. The Atlantean Ruins? Are you kidding me? Has Mirella been holding out on us this whole time? No, there's no way. She would've spilled the beans by now, probably with a side of underwater interpretive dance.

Then again, I've never actually been to these ruins myself. For all I know, they could be the size of a small country with enough nooks and crannies to hide an entire army of mermaids.

I nod at Nixie. "Thanks for the tip," I say with a wink.

As I make my way back to the ship, I can't help but feel a surge of determination and just a hint of nervous excitement. This is it, the final stretch—the endgame. And I'll be damned if I let Cordelia win.

So watch out, Cordelia. The savior is coming for you, and she's bringing a tidal wave of sass, wit, and pure, unadulterated badassery.

Your days of cursing innocent mermaids and stealing voices are numbered.

The tides are turning, and I'm ready to ride the wave to victory.

DANICA

71

We stand before Calypso. The weight of the Siren's Lyre in my hand feels like the key to unlocking a long-buried truth. The Atlantean Ruins stretch out around us, a vast underwater city frozen in time, and Calypso sits on her throne, a small island of power amidst the ancient grandeur.

It's the same place she took me captive—the same dark and eerie lair. Naturally, I asked Mirella if she knew Calypso was hiding down here, and she shook her head, swearing she had no idea. Given the sheer size of these ruins, it's no wonder Calypso's domain only occupies a small portion of the entire structure.

"You have returned, my dear," Calypso greets me, a smile playing at the corners of her lips. Her gaze sweeps over my crew—Lucian, Erik, Seraphina, Mirella, and Rhyland—a silent assessment of the strength I've brought with me. "And I see you've got your entire army."

I meet her eyes, my voice steady with the weight of the knowledge I now carry. "Yes, and I know everything."

Calypso's eyes widen, a flicker of vulnerability breaking through her regal composure. She rises from her chair, her movements fluid and graceful, even as I see the pain etched into every line of her face. "You know the truth?" she whispers, her voice trembling.

I nod, my throat tight with the weight of her suffering. "I'm so sorry about your mother, your father," I manage to say, the words feeling inadequate in the face of such tragedy.

Calypso closes her eyes, a single tear tracing down her cheek. When she opens them again, I see a depth of grief that takes my breath away. "It was tragic, yes," she says softly, her voice barely above a whisper. "It was unwarranted and something that I can never unsee."

The realization hits me like a tidal wave, stealing the air from my lungs. She witnessed her parents' deaths and watched as her world was shattered in a moment of senseless violence. The weight of that trauma, the scars it must have left on her soul, is almost too much to comprehend.

The Faerite stone vibrates through me, channeling her pain, and it nearly knocks me on my ass.

I take a step forward, my heart aching with the need to offer comfort, to let her know that she's not alone anymore. But I know that words cannot heal the wounds she carries.

Instead, I reach into my bag, my fingers closing around the cool, smooth surface of the Siren's Lyre. Calypso inhales sharply, her hands trembling at her sides.

"I have come to help you," my voice ringing with conviction, "and to break this curse."

I hold out the Lyre, a tangible symbol of the hope and freedom I want to offer her. Calypso's eyes are fixed on the instrument, a mix of longing and fear playing across her face.

At this moment, I feel the full weight of my role as a savior, the responsibility I carry to set things right. But more than that, I feel connected to Calypso, a shared understanding of the pain and loss that can shape a life.

"You're not alone anymore," I say softly. "We're here to stand with you, fight for you, and help you reclaim what was taken from you."

Calypso's chocolate brown eyes meet mine, and at this moment, I see a flicker of hope, a glimmer of the strength and resilience that has carried her through all these years of suffering.

"Thank you," she whispers, her voice raw with emotion. "Thank you for believing in me, for seeing the truth."

I turn to Mirella, a smile of gratitude on my face. "She helped me," I explain, gesturing to the mermaid who has become more than just an ally but a true friend. "She was able to find the journals from Nixie, the key to unlocking the truth."

Calypso's eyes widen at the mention of Nixie's name, a flicker of recognition sparking in their depths. "Nixie?" she asks, her voice soft with memory, "I remember a Nixie at court before everything changed. She always had a way of seeing beyond the surface, of speaking the truth even when it was difficult to hear."

I nod, understanding the weight of Calypso's words. "She's a seer," I explain, my voice filled with a newfound respect for the enigmatic fortune-teller. "She saw all of this unfolding, and she made sure to record it, to leave a trail for us to follow."

Calypso looks stunned momentarily, her eyes distant as if she's seeing the past play out before her. Then, slowly, she nods. "I see. Well, thank the God Poseidon for that—for your foresight and bravery in such darkness."

She turns to Mirella, her black scales glistening in the dim light, her long dreadlocks swaying as she moves. "Thank you for your honesty and seeking the truth," her voice fills with gratitude.

Mirella dips her head in a show of respect.

Calypso steps forward, her expression contrite. "I am sorry for my...methods," she begins, hesitating. "I just knew that you could obtain the Lyre, and I was so desperate to—"

"Say no more," I cut her off, holding up a hand. "I get it, trust me. You've been dealing with some serious shit, and desperate times call for desperate measures. Consider it water under the bridge."

Lucian scoffs, rolling his eyes. "Speak for yourself, Little Miss Forgiveness! You're not the one who almost had your heart ripped out by a crazed mermaid on a power trip."

I level a glare at him that could make hell feel like a ski resort. "Lucian, I swear—"

Seraphina jabs Lucian in the ribs with her elbow. He yelps, rubbing his side, pouting.

"Ow! What was that for, you celestial menace?" he whines.

"For being an insensitive..." Seraphina stops, her mind searching...

"Jackass." Erik supplies happily.

"Yes, that! Can't you see that Calypso is trying to apologize?" Seraphina scowls.

Lucian grumbles under his breath, but he wisely keeps his mouth shut. I have to bite back a smile—it's not often that someone can put Lucian in his place, but Seraphina seems to have a real knack for it.

The bracelet on my wrist vibrates, startling me as it slips from my skin and clatters to the floor. At that exact moment, I notice Calypso's bracelet mirroring the action, falling in perfect synchronicity with mine.

"Our pact is complete, "Calypso breathes. The weight of the moment hangs heavy in the air between us. "I do hope it guided your path."

Looking back, I realize it did. It lit up whenever I was on the right track to the relics. I nod and smile.

I feel a question burning in my mind, a need to understand the depth of Calypso's suffering. "May I ask," I begin, my voice hesitant, almost afraid to give voice to the words, "When all of this happened? How long? The curse?"

"One thousand, fifty-six years, eight months, and five days." Calypso's answer is immediate, the words falling from her lips with the weight of centuries.

I feel Rhyland stiffen at my side, and a subtle shift in his posture sets off alarm bells in my mind. But I'm too stunned by Calypso's words to focus on anything else. Over a thousand years. A millennium of suffering, of isolation, of bearing the weight of a curse that was never hers to carry.

The realization hits me, stealing the air from my lungs. Mermaids can live that long? I had no idea, no concept of the sheer scope of their existence. And yet, here stands Calypso, a living testament to the enduring power of the sea, to the strength of a spirit that refuses to be broken.

I swallow hard, my heart aching with the weight of her pain. "I'm so sorry," I whisper. "I can't even begin to imagine what you've been through, the toll this has taken on you."

Calypso's smile is tinged with sorrow, her dark eyes flickering with the weight of centuries-old grief. "It's been a long and lonely road," she confesses, her voice a fragile whisper, threatening to break under the burden of her pain. "But even in my darkest moments, I clung to the hope that you would someday come. That you would uncover the truth and help lift the..."

Her voice trails off, the word "curse" trapped in her throat, stolen by the enchantment that has haunted her for so long.

With a gentle touch, Calypso reaches out, her hand resting on mine. Between us, the Siren's Lyre pulses with a soft, ethereal glow, a tangible connection to the power of truth and the promise of freedom.

"When I was just a small child," she begins, her eyes distant with memory, "my mother would tell me stories of a great savior, a hero crowned with a wreath of precious gems. She spoke of how this savior would come to the realms, a beacon of light against the encroaching darkness, and deliver us from an ancient evil that seeks to consume our very existence."

Calypso's gaze drops to the seashell necklace resting against her chest, the Soul Stone glimmering with an ominous beauty. "I never imagined that my own fate would be so intricately entwined with this prophecy," she admits, her voice heavy with the weight of her unwanted role in this cosmic dance.

She looks up, her eyes meeting mine, and in their depths, I see a flicker of hope, a glimmer of the unbreakable spirit that has carried her through the long centuries of isolation and pain. "And now, thanks to you, that long-awaited day has finally arrived."

"What have we here?" Cordelia's voice slices through the air like a well-sharpened blade, shattering the moment into a million bitter pieces.

We all whirl around, heart in my throat. Cordelia stands in all her evil glory, her dark blue gown shimmering like the ocean's depths. The Aquanite stone perched atop her staff pulses with an eerie, azure light, casting an otherworldly glow across her cold, beautiful features.

The tension in the air is so thick you could cut it with a knife and serve it on a silver platter. A thousand years of sisterly betrayal and bitterness hang between Calypso and Cordelia, as tangible as the salt in the sea. Calypso's hand tightens on mine, her fingers trembling with a silent plea for strength, for the courage to face the darkness that's haunted her for centuries.

I hold up the Lyre like a talisman. "Game over, Cordelia. Your reign of terror is about to come to a screeching halt. The truth is out, and your dirty little secrets are exposed."

Cordelia laughs, with condescension. "Oh, you naive little girl. Do you have any idea what I'm capable of? The power I wield?" She raises her staff, and suddenly, water comes rushing up through the small pools scattered throughout the room, like geysers.

The space quickly becomes a whirlpool of chaos. The raging currents sweep us off our feet. I'm pretty sure I swallow half the ocean before Cordelia throws her arms down, and the water retreats.

We all slowly get to our feet, dripping and drenched with seawater.

"Hand over that Lyre," she demands, "and I might just let you walk out of here with your limbs intact."

I can't help but laugh, the sound echoing through the room like a battle cry. "Seriously, Cordelia? Do you even know who you're fucking with?" I toss the Lyre to Rhyland and whip out my daggers, the blades bursting into flames with my angel fire. "The way I see it, you've got two choices: stand down or get ready for a serious ass-kicking."

"Sister, please..." Calypso begs. "It doesn't have to come to this—not anymore."

"Oh snap! My money's on the sassy angel!" Lucian grins, waggling his eyebrows at Cordelia. "Sorry, Aqua-Ho, but I've seen Dani go full 'Carrie' at prom, and trust me, it ain't pretty. You might want to rethink your life choices, like, now."

Cordelia waves her staff, trapping Lucian, Mirella, Seraphina, and Erik inside a water bubble. They struggle as they float suspended, their lungs burning for air. Acting quickly, Mirella uses her magic to give them the breath of life, ensuring they survive in the aquatic prison.

"Sister, stop!" Calypso's voice rings out, bouncing off the cavern walls like a bullet.

Cordelia's eyes narrow as she begins to pace the floor, her movements as fluid and menacing as a shark circling its prey. "What? What could you possibly have to say to me, Calypso?" she sneers, with venom.

The air crackles with tension, the weight of centuries of pain and betrayal hanging between the two sisters like a suffocating fog. As I stand here, daggers blazing and heart pounding, I know this is it.

The final showdown.

The moment of truth.

Calypso sighs, the sound heavy. "I don't want to fight with you anymore, Cordelia. I know you blame me for what our father did to your mother, but that's not on me. You can't hold me responsible for his choices, for finding his *true mate*."

Calypso's words seem to hit Cordelia like a slap in the face, and she loses her shit. "His true mate was my MOTHER!!" she screams, her whole body shaking with a rage that's been simmering for centuries. "Your mother put a spell on him—cursed him—tricked him into thinking she was the one. Then she turned around and murdered OUR father, then killed herself!"

Oh, how wrong she is on that tidbit. Her mother twisted the story before she offed herself.

I can't help but roll my eyes at the dramatics. Seriously, this is like watching a supernatural soap opera, and I'm stuck in the middle of it. I half expect Cordelia to start throwing vases and slapping people.

Calypso shakes her head, a sad smile playing at the corners of her mouth. "No, sister, that's not how it was. I remember how my parents looked at each other, the pure love and devotion in their eyes. It was real, Cordelia. Did you ever see that with your mother? Did she ever gaze at our father like he hung the moon and stars? My mother did not..."

Calypso pauses, taking a deep breath to calm the storm inside her. "I'm sorry your mother couldn't accept the truth and bear the pain of losing him."

Cordelia's mask slips momentarily, the broken little girl beneath the icy exterior. "I... I don't know," she admits, her voice small and uncertain. "She was always so angry with Father, always furious with me." But just as quickly, the vulnerability is replaced by a snarling rage. "And it's all because your mother was a WHORE! Stealing men, stealing MY father! My mother's pain was too much to bear—to take her own life because of what your bitch of a mother did to our family!"

Calypso's shoulders slump like she's carrying the world's weight, and she practically collapses onto her throne. "No, Cordelia, it wasn't my mother's fault. You've been fed a lie. It was the Soul Stone," she says, her voice heavy with the truth. "It changed your mother, twisted everything good inside her into something dark and ugly."

She looks up at Cordelia, and I swear I can see the pain etched into every line of her face. "It's doing the same thing to me, sister," she whispers. "Every day, it eats away at my resolve, whispering in my ear, pushing me to do terrible things, to give in to hate and cruelty."

I stare at Calypso, my jaw practically hitting the floor. Holy shit—how has this woman managed to resist the evil call of the Stone for so damn long? I've seen firsthand what that thing can do, how it can warp souls into something monstrous.

My mind flashes back to Azrael and Amara, how they succumbed to the Stone's influence like it was nothing, their desire to cause harm as natural as breathing. And yet, here's Calypso, fighting tooth and nail against its pull, clinging to her humanity with everything she's got.

"How?" Cordelia asks, her voice barely above a whisper, as if afraid of the answer. "I made sure to lock that stone to you, never to take it off. How are you able to ignore its cause?"

Calypso smiles, and it's a sad, broken thing that makes my heart ache. "Because I never lost hope that one day, you and I would find a way to mend what's been broken between us. My love for you, sister, is buried deep inside me. And I've refused to let this cursed stone take that away from me, no matter how hard it tries. You were lied to, Cordelia. And I don't fault you for that."

I am witnessing something intimate, raw, painful, and beautiful. It's like watching a flower bloom in the middle of a war zone, a testament to the resilience of the human spirit.

"Why would you force your sister to wear that cursed thing?" I ask, my voice a mix of disbelief and horror. "You saw what it did to your mother, how it twisted her into something unrecognizable. How could you inflict that same fate on Calypso—your own sister?"

Cordelia turns to me, her expression a mask of bitterness and resentment. "Because I wanted the person," she spits, shooting a nasty glare in Calypso's direction, "who tore my family apart to experience the same pain and hatred that my mother endured. I wanted Calypso to suffer, to know the agony of being consumed by darkness and despair."

I stare at her, my mouth hanging open in shock. "Let me get this straight," I say slowly, trying to wrap my head around her twisted logic. "You blame Calypso, your *sister*, for simply being born? For existing? Cordelia, do you hear how absolutely batshit crazy that sounds?"

Calypso's voice is whispery, her eyes shimmering with unshed tears. "Sister, we were so close once, the best of friends and confidants. It shattered my heart when you did this to me, to us. How could you let your anger and jealousy poison the bond we once shared?"

I nod, my heart aching for the pain and betrayal etched into Calypso's face. "She's right, Cordelia. Your father made his choices, and they were his alone. Blaming Calypso for his actions, for the fact that he fell in love with Rillia—her mother, is like blaming the sun for rising in the east. It's a fundamental truth of the universe, not some personal slight against you."

Cordelia's face twists. "You don't understand!" she hisses, her fingers curling at her sides. "You didn't see the way our family crumbled, the way my mother withered away under the weight of her grief and rage. Someone had to pay for that. Someone had to suffer as she suffered!"

I take a step forward. "And you thought that someone should be Calypso? Your own flesh and blood? Cordelia, that's not justice, that's cruelty. You let your pain and anger blind you to the truth, to the love and compassion that should have guided your actions. It was *your* mother, Cordelia, that murdered them, not Rillia."

Cordelia flashes her eyes at me as if I slapped her.

Calypso reaches out. "Please, sister," she begs, her voice cracking with emotion. "It's not too late to make this right, to heal the rift between us. I forgive you, Cordelia. I forgive you for everything because I know the true you, the sister I love and cherish, is still in there somewhere. You didn't know the truth. Now you do."

Cordelia's expression wavers momentarily, a flicker of vulnerability and longing passing over her face. But then her features harden, her lips twisting into a sneer. "Forgiveness?" she scoffs. "I don't need your forgiveness, sister. I did what I had to do, what my mother's memory demanded of me. My mother is not a murderer!"

I sigh, shaking my head sadly. "And look where that got you, Cordelia. Alone, bitter, and consumed by a hatred that will never truly satisfy you. Is that really the legacy you want to leave behind?"

Cordelia opens her mouth to retort, but no words come out. She stands there, her chest heaving, her eyes darting between Calypso and me like a cornered animal.

I can't help but feel a surge of admiration for Calypso. I mean, here's a woman who's been through hell and back, who's had every reason to give in to the darkness, to let it consume her whole.

But she hasn't. She's fought, endured, and held onto that tiny spark of hope like it's the only thing keeping her alive. And in a way, maybe it is.

Because hope? It's a powerful thing. It's the light in the darkness, the beacon that guides us home when we're lost at sea. And Calypso? She's been holding onto that light for centuries, refusing to let it go out, no matter how hard the winds of fate try to snuff it out.

It's humbling to be in the presence of that kind of strength and love. I watch Cordelia's face, see the flicker of understanding in her eyes, and feel the tiniest crack in her icy facade. I can't help but feel a glimmer of hope myself.

Cordelia's face then twists into a snarl. "I don't believe a word of this bullshit," she spits. "How could you say my mother did all this? How could you possibly love me after everything I've done to you? I don't want your love, and I sure as hell don't need it!"

And with that, all hell breaks loose.

Cordelia slams her staff against the ground. The cavern walls shudder like they're about to crash around us. Water comes rushing in from every direction, a tidal wave of chaos and destruction threatening to sweep us away.

Rhyland's there, scooping me into his arms like I weigh nothing. He blurs us to higher ground, moving so fast that the world around us becomes a blur of color and sound.

As the water swells and rages beneath us, I realize with a sinking feeling that Rhyland and I are the only ones left standing. Lucian, Erik, Seraphina, and Mirella have all been swept away by the churning waters, their fate unknown.

And Calypso? She's caught in the middle of the maelstrom—no mermaid tail—can't swim—her body tossed and turned like a ragdoll in the grip of her sister's fury.

"Damnit," I mutter under my breath, my heart pounding.

This is bad, like, really bad.

"**I**'m gonna deal with this bitch once and for all," I growl to Dani, my eyes never leaving Cordelia's furious face. "You stay put, Angel. I got this."

Dani scoffs, her hands on her hips as she glares at me. "Excuse me? What do you mean, 'deal with her'? Rhyland, I swear to god, if you kill her, I will personally kick your ass from here to the surface."

I sigh at her stubborn defiance. My woman can never just let me handle shit. "Relax, baby. I'm not gonna kill her. Yet."

And with that, I move, blurring across the cavern to where Cordelia stands, her staff raised in a defensive posture. I lunge for the weapon, my hands closing around the slick metal, and with a sharp twist, I wrench it from her grasp.

"Heads up, baby!" hurling the staff towards my mate. She snatches it out of the air with ease, her reflexes honed to perfection.

The instant the staff leaves Cordelia's hands, the churning waters die down, the roaring torrent fading to a gentle trickle. Calypso lies on the cold, wet stone, her chest heaving as she gulps in the stale air.

Cordelia whirls on me, her eyes flashing with rage and disgust. "How dare you interfere!"

I bare my fangs, my eyes glinting with a dangerous light. "Enough of this bullshit, lady," I snarl. "Your little reign of terror is over. You either kiss and makeup with your sister, or I'll find a permanent solution to this family feud. We clear?"

I hand the Lyre to Calypso, gently helping her to her feet. She clutches the instrument to her chest, her eyes wide and grateful as she stares at me.

Cordelia sneers, her hand outstretched as she summons her staff back to her grasp. It flies into her palm, and she grins at me, a twisted, ugly thing. "You've just made a grave mistake," she cackles. I wait for the waters to engulf us, holding on to Calypso as I prepare to blur. But nothing happens.

Cordelia looks around, confused.

"Performance issues?" Dani quips from across the cavern. "Don't worry, I hear it happens to everyone. Well, everyone except Rhyland, of course. That man is a fucking machine."

I shoot her a heated look, my cock twitching at the blatant praise. And then I see it—the Aquanite stone in her crown glowing and pulsing an aqua blue.

I watch with pride and amusement as Dani hops down from her perch, sauntering over to Cordelia with a swagger.

Cordelia glares at Dani, her face twisted with rage and disbelief. "How?" she demands, her voice shaking with impotent fury. "How did you get the stone?"

Dani smirks. "Oh, that's simple," she drawls. "So, funny story. Apparently, there's this whole 'Dark Prophecy' thing that's been floating around the Seven Realms like a bad rumor. You know, the one about a savior who's supposed to swoop in and save the day when everything goes to hell in a handbasket? Well, guess what? Turns out, that savior? Is yours truly."

She stops in front of Cordelia, her hands on her hips, and I can't help but admire the way her leather pants hug her curves, the way her breasts strain against the tight fabric of her soaked top. Fuck, my woman is a goddamn work of art.

Dani continues, her voice sharp and unyielding. "And I need these stones to fulfill it. So, I will be taking what is *divinely* mine, and I'll be damned if I let anyone, especially a bitter mermaid with a serious case of sibling rivalry, stand in my way."

Calypso walks over to her throne and sits, "Sister, please. I told you the stories were true..."

"Make amends and end this tyrant bullshit," Dani continues. "Or, as my man said, we will find a permanent solution to end this fuckery—which involves a not-so-nice ending for you."

I chuckle darkly, my fangs glinting in the dim light of the cavern.

Cordelia's eyes dart between us, her face a mask of fear and desperation. I can practically smell the stench of her terror, the bitter tang of her defeat. She knows she's lost, knows that she's no match for us.

"You can't do this," she whispers, trembling with impotent rage. "I am the queen of this realm. I am the rightful ruler!"

"No, Cordelia. Calypso was crowned the rightful ruler, chosen by the people, and blessed by the gods. Your mother couldn't accept that, couldn't bear the thought of her daughter being second best. So she poisoned you, twisted your mind with her bitterness and jealousy until you could no longer see the truth."

Dani steps closer, her golden eyes blazing. "And then, in the ultimate act of selfishness and cruelty, she murdered your father and Calypso's mother. She took two innocent lives and destroyed a family, all because she couldn't let go of her pride and ego. The Soul Stone was an acting catalyst to your mother's already lost mind, Cordelia."

Cordelia flinches as if Dani struck her, her eyes wide and haunted. "No," she whispers, shaking her head in denial. "No, that's not true. My mother loved my father...She wouldn't have..."

The cavern fills with a beautiful, harmonious melody as Calypso begins to play the Lyre. Everyone falls silent, transfixed by the enchanting notes that echo around us. Glittering water swirls around Calypso and the instrument, a shimmering vortex of magic and music. Suddenly, she takes a deep, shuddering breath and collapses to the floor, her mermaid tail again in place.

A shockwave rips out from the center of the room, the sheer force of it nearly knocking me on my ass. Dani's hair whips wildly around her face, and Cordelia is left standing there, utterly speechless.

Calypso looks up at Dani, her eyes shining with unshed tears. "Thank you."

Dani and I rush to Calypso's side, carefully helping her into one of the nearby pools. She flicks her tail, sending droplets of water splashing around her. I retrieve the Lyre and place it gently beside her, my gaze never leaving Cordelia as she begins to weep.

"I'm..." she hiccups, her voice barely audible. "Sorry," she whispers between sobs.

I narrow my eyes, uncertain whether her apology is based on genuine remorse or the bitter realization of her defeat.

Dani, ever the compassionate one, approaches Cordelia just before she crumples to the stone floor. "Hey, it's okay," she soothes, her voice gentle and understanding. "It's a lot to let go of and swallow—I get it."

Calypso gestures for my assistance, and I help her out of the pool, setting her down on the floor. Her shimmering tail fades away, revealing her long, slender, chocolate-brown legs once again, her modesty preserved by a smattering of glittering scales. "Sister..." she calls out, tentatively approaching Cordelia.

Cordelia raises her head, her face streaked with tears, her blue-blonde hair sticking to her face. "I—I am so... sorry," she chokes out, her words heavy with regret. "I...didn't know..."

Calypso closes the distance between them, pulling her sister into a tight embrace. She holds Cordelia close, shushing her quietly as she sobs into her shoulder, her body shaking with the weight of her emotions.

Calypso's words hang in the air, heavy with emotion and the weight of years of separation. "It's all true. I am sorry for your mother and her actions. I forgive you, sister. I have missed you."

As I listen to her heartfelt declaration, realization dawns on me like a fucking freight train. This isn't just about a power struggle or a petty grudge. No, this is about a shattered bond, a childhood connection torn apart by a mother's jealousy and a cursed stone's influence.

It's clear to me now that Cordelia and Calypso once shared a deep, sisterly love, the kind that's forged through shared experiences and inside jokes through late-night giggles and whispered secrets. But somewhere along the way, that bond was poisoned, twisted by Cordelia's mother's actions and the insidious power of the Soul Stone.

I can't even imagine the pain and betrayal Calypso must have felt, watching her sister turn against her, consumed by jealousy and hatred that wasn't entirely her own. And yet, despite everything, she never gave up hope. She never stopped loving her sister, never stopped believing that somewhere beneath the anger and the bitterness, the real Cordelia still existed.

And now, as I watch the two sisters embrace, their tears mingling as they cling to each other like lifelines, I know that Calypso was right. Their bond never truly died, no matter how much the Soul Stone tried to destroy it.

It's a testament to their love's strength and the unbreakable ties of family and sisterhood. It reminds us that even in the darkest times, even when all seems lost, there's always a chance for redemption, forgiveness, and healing.

I glance at Dani, my heart swelling with love and pride as I take in her soft, understanding smile. She gets it, too. She knows the power of second chances, choosing love over hate, forgiveness over revenge.

Adrian's the prime example. After his ultimate betrayal—stabbing both her and me in the back, betraying all of us—she went ahead and forgave him. Me? I couldn't see past that shit as I tried and failed.

It's one of the many reasons why I love her so fucking much. Why I would follow her to the ends of the earth and beyond and lay down my life for her without a second thought.

Because in a world that's so often filled with darkness and pain, she is my light. My hope. My everything.

As I watch Cordelia and Calypso slowly begin to rebuild what was broken, their laughter mixing with their tears as they cling to each other like the sisters they were always meant to be, I can't help but feel a sense of hope for the future.

In a future where love triumphs over hate, forgiveness is always possible, and the bonds of family and friendship are strong enough to weather any storm.

A future that Dani and I will build together, side by side, come hell or high water.

And I wouldn't have it any other fucking way.

Dani returns to my side, and I instinctively pull her close, my arm wrapping possessively around her waist. Lucian, Mirella, Erik, and Seraphina emerge from the other side of the cavern, looking like a pack of drowned rats.

"Well, that was quite the adventure," Lucian quips, his trademark smirk firmly in place despite his unkempt appearance. "Remind me to pack a snorkel next time we decide to play underwater heroes."

I watch Mirella clasp her hands together, her knuckles turning white as she bites down on them, her eyes shining with tears, hope, and disbelief. "Finally!" she breathes, the word escaping her lips like a prayer, like a fucking benediction.

I can see the world's weight lifting off her shoulders, the burden of years of silence and secrecy finally easing as she watches Calypso and Cordelia reconcile.

Calypso turns to Dani, her eyes shining with gratitude and something else, something that looks a hell of a lot like hope. "Dani, this belongs to you," her voice trembling as she grips the necklace holding the Soul Stone.

"Please take it." She pleads.

Dani reaches out and tugs the necklace from Calypso—I feel the crackle of energy between them, the weight of destiny and fate. "Do what you're born to do, sweet child," Calypso murmurs, her words a benediction, a fucking prophecy. "Do not listen to it's whispers. I know you are strong, Dani. Whatever you do, do not let this take your light."

I know those whispers all too fucking well—those insidious voices that slither into your mind like venomous snakes, sinking their fangs deep into your psyche. They worm their way into your thoughts, twisting and corrupting everything they touch until you can't tell what's real and what's a lie. They promise you power, but it's a false gift, a poisoned chalice that'll drive you to the brink of madness and beyond. Those whispers are the stuff of nightmares, and they'll tear you apart from the inside out if you let them.

Dani, my brave, beautiful Dani, clutches that stone like a lifeline, the final piece of this cursed Soul Stone. I feel her love, her relief, her fucking joy through our bond, and it's so intense, so overwhelming, that I can barely breathe.

The Faerite stone pulses with energy, feeding off the emotions of the women—amplifying Dani's already bleeding heart until I feel it in my chest, a physical ache that steals my breath and makes my eyes sting with unshed tears.

And then Calypso is hugging Dani, both crying, their tears mingling as they cling to each other. It's a moment of pure, unadulterated emotion, and I can't help but be swept up in it, my heart swelling with pride and love.

Being the observant little shit that he is, Lucian picks up on it immediately.

"Well, well, well, look who's getting all misty-eyed!" he crows, with gleeful mockery. "Is that a tear I see, oh mighty Rhyland? Don't tell me the big bad Viking is going soft on us!"

I glare at him, but it only seems to fuel his amusement.

Fucking prick.

I quickly make my way to the other side of the room, closer to my brothers, shoving Lucian none-too-gently as I pass. He stumbles back a step, laughing like the asshole he is.

"Aww, did I strike a nerve?" he taunts. "Poor widdle Whyland, getting all emotional over a little family reunion. Shall I fetch you a tissue, my liege?"

"Careful, dick," I growl, my fists itching to beat into his smug fucking face. "Keep talking shit, asshole, and I'll show you just how *soft* I am."

"Ooh, kinky!" he quips, waggling his eyebrows suggestively. "Didn't know you were into that sort of thing, Rhy-Rhy. Does Dani know about your secret BDSM fetish?"

I step forward, ready to wipe that smirk off his face...

"Boys, boys," Dani scolds. "Can we not do this right now? We just saved a fucking realm, in case you forgot."

I shoot Lucian one last glare before facing my mate, my expression softening instantly. "Sorry, baby," I murmur, my voice low and apologetic. "You know how Lucian gets under my skin."

Dani rolls her eyes. "Oh, I know," she sighs, shaking her head. "You two are like a couple of overgrown children, I swear."

Lucian gasps, clutching his chest in mock offense. "Moi? A child? I'll have you know, my dear sweet sister-in-law, that I am a paragon of maturity and sophistication. It's not my fault Rhyland here has the emotional range of a teaspoon."

Seraphina giggles. Clearly in love with Lucian's shit.

I snort, crossing my arms over my chest. "I'll show you emotional, you little—"

"Perhaps we could save the bickering for later," Erik suggests, his tone dry as fucking bone. "Such as getting back to our realm."

I sigh, running a hand through my dark hair. "Yeah, yeah, you're right," I concede, my gaze drifting back to Dani. "We should probably head back. I'm sure there's a fuck-ton of shit to unfuck back home."

Dani nods, her expression turning serious. "Agreed," her fingers closing around the seashell in her hand, "We need to see what shitshow Azrael has come up with."

Lucian, never one to let a moment of solemnity last too long, claps his hands together gleefully. "Rightio!" he chirps, bouncing on the balls of his feet. "Let's go save the universe and all that jazz. Hey, do you think they'll erect statues in our honor? I've always wanted a statue. Preferably one with a massive co—"

"Lucian!" Dani and I snap in unison, cutting him off before he can finish that thought.

He holds up his hands, a shit-eating grin on his face. "Alright, alright, keep your pants on. Or don't, in Rhyland's case. I know how much he loves to let it all hang out."

I sigh, shaking my head. Done with Lucian's shit. "Alright, let's head back to Gideon, grab whatever shit we came here with, and get the fuck out of this underwater nightmare."

Lucian, being the relentless little fucker that he is, just won't let it go. "Ooh, ooh, or maybe a movie!" he exclaims, practically vibrating. "I call dibs on Ryan Reynolds playing me."

"You're a fucking idiot, you know that?" I grumble.

As much as Lucian drives me up the fucking wall, I can't deny that his ridiculous antics are a welcome distraction from the heavy shit we've been dealing with.

Lucian takes my insult as an invitation to keep pushing. He grins, slinging an arm around my shoulders. "Aww, don't be jealous, Rhy-Rhy," he coos, batting his eyelashes at me. "I'm sure they can find someone to play you too. Maybe that guy who played the Hulk? You've got the whole 'angry and brooding' thing down pat."

I shove him off, but I can't help the small smile that tugs at my lips. Fucking Lucian.

You know what? I take that shit back. Maybe there are some things that I can't forgive after all. Like this asshat and all the bullshit he puts me through on a daily fucking basis.

Even as I think about it, I can't help but laugh at myself. Because honestly? I love the guy, no matter what kind of fuckery he pulls. He's my brother, my family, and that means something.

So maybe, love really does conquer all in the end—even when it comes to dealing with a pain in the ass like Lucian.

DANICA

73

Cordelia and Calypso finally decided to put on their big girl panties and rule together like the badass sister duo they were always meant to be. Hallelujah, praise the sea gods! It only took them a thousand years and a metric fuck-ton of drama to get there.

Man, I'd love to stick around and see what these magical mermaids have up their sleeves for this realm. But after chatting with the sisters, it's pretty clear that things are about to get a major facelift around here. We're talking truth-telling, creature-uniting, realm-transforming stuff. It's gonna be a wild ride, and I'm bummed I'll miss it!

But I'm sure this isn't the last I will see of Aquaria.

The Soul Stone's hanging out in my pocket until I can get it home and under severe lock and key. It's whispering sweet nothings, but joke's on it—I've mastered the art of selective hearing—thanks to Lucian.

This damn stone—talk about a demanding piece of jewelry! This thing had Calypso playing supernatural UberEats driver, forcing her to collect souls of the recently deceased like they were takeout orders. Untethered souls hang around like awkward party guests who don't know when to leave, and Calypso, against her will, has to vacuum them up into that creepy rock. Not exactly the kind of job you'd want to brag about.

The Sirens were in fact Immune to the curse, just like Seraphina thought. But here's the real plot twist—these gorgeous, mythical beings have been painted as the story's villains for centuries when, in reality, they're about as evil as a basket of kittens.

Sure, they've got the whole "Siren's call" thing going on, the ability to bend minds to their will with just a few haunting notes. But the whole "luring sailors and pirates to their watery graves" shtick? Total bullshit, a complete fabrication cooked up by none other than Cordelia herself.

Not to mention it kept treasure hunters and pirates away from the Lyre—clever but bullshit.

The Sirens knew the real story: Calypso was the rightful ruler. They saw Cordelia's jealousy and bitterness for what it was— a poison that threatened to destroy her soul and the fabric of their society.

People bought it. For centuries, the Sirens have been vilified and feared, their true nature obscured by a veil of lies and propaganda. They've been hunted and persecuted, driven into hiding by those who would rather believe a convenient lie than face the uncomfortable truth—the same for the Selkies.

The Aquanite stone is home in my crown, nestled like a cozy aquatic Airbnb. The moment I snatched that sucker from Cordelia's staff, it practically leaped into place, snuggling up to the other stones like they were long-lost besties.

The feeling was like diving into a cool, refreshing pool on a hot summer day. A wave of calm washed over me, and for a moment, I forgot all about the crazy Cordelia and her temper tantrum.

I'm unsure what to do with this new addition to my magical girl arsenal. But if Cordelia's little display of aquatic acrobatics is anything to go by, this stone is all about emotions and using water as a cosmic conduit.

I will have to be extra careful around any body of water larger than a puddle. The last thing I need is to accidentally summon a tidal wave because I got too excited about a buy-one-get-one-free sale at my favorite shoe store.

Or, turning a romantic beach getaway into a scene from *"The Perfect Storm"* because Rhyland forgot our anniversary. Yeah, not exactly the kind of "savior" moves I want to be known for.

"I will miss you, Gideon." I give him a big ol' bear hug, and damn, the man smells like he bathed in a tub of rum and sea salt. There's something else in there, too, but I'm not about to sniff a pirate to figure it out.

"Aye, lass. It was an absolute pleasure helping ye. Ye did what ye came to do, and ye did it." Gideon grins, his eyes twinkling with pride.

"You will be written about in history books, I'm sure of it. Gideon Sterling, Pirate sidekick to the Savior." I smile, already picturing the epic tales that will be told about our adventures.

"Aye, love. That would be great to see." Gideon's cheeks turn red, and I can't resist planting a big smooch on one of them.

I mean, come on, the man deserves some love after putting up with our ragtag crew of supernatural misfits.

I turn to Mirella, and my heart aches as I see the tears streaming down her gorgeous face. It's like watching a mermaid version of a Hallmark movie, and I'm not ashamed to admit that it's getting to me.

"Aww, Mirella, don't cry," I say, trying to keep my own waterworks in check. "I promise this isn't the last time you'll see my fabulous self. We're like besties now, and besties don't just disappear on each other."

But even as I say it, I can feel the familiar ache in my chest—her emotions swimming through me due to the Faerite stone.

I'm beginning to have a love-hate relationship with this damn thing.

This whole making friends and then leaving them behind thing? It sucks ass. I mean, first Axilya, Faderyn, Meadow, and now Mirella and Gideon? The universe is determined to make me the savior of the realms and the queen of goodbyes.

Mirella pulls me into a hug, and damn, the girl smells like the perfect beach day—ocean, sea salt, and a freshness that makes me want to bottle it up and sell it as a perfume.

"Thank you for helping me, Dani," she sniffs, wiping her nose adorably. "You will never be forgotten."

And that's it. The floodgates open, and I'm crying with her, our tears mingling like the sea and the rain. I want to blame it on the Faerite stone, with its annoying ability to turn me into an emotional sponge, but let's be honest—I've grown fond of Mirella. She's like the cool mermaid sister I never had, and the thought of saying goodbye is hitting me harder than I expected.

"I couldn't have done it without you; don't forget that," I choke out.

With her knowledge and her unwavering support, I don't know if we would have made it this far. She's been the unsung hero of this whole underwater adventure, and I'll be damned if I let her forget it.

I pull back, "Say goodbye to Nixie for me?"

Mirella nods her head, "Of course."

As much as it hurts, I know this isn't the end. We're connected now, bound by the threads of friendship and the shared experience of saving an entire realm. And if there's one thing I've learned on this crazy journey, it's that the bonds we forge along the way are more substantial than any curse or evil mastermind.

So yeah, saying goodbye sucks major ass. But you know what? It's not really goodbye. It's more like "See you later, alligator," or in this case, "Catch you on the flip side, mermaid."

Izabelle decides to sashay her skanky ass over, draping herself over Gideon like a cheap, pirate-themed curtain. "Aye, the land-lubber finally leavin'?" she sneers.

I turn to face her, my eyes narrowing as I remember all the crap she put me through. The backstabbing, the scheming, the whole "let's throw Dani to the sharks" thing? Yeah, not cool, sister.

"That's right, Izabelle," my voice as sweet as poisoned honey. "I almost forgot my parting gift."

She detaches herself from Gideon and saunters towards me, a smirk on her face that I'd love nothing more than to wipe off with a well-placed fist. "Oh? And what's that?" she snarks, like a cat about to get a face full of karma.

Without a second thought, I rear back and let my fist fly, connecting with Izabelle's face in a symphony of cartilage and regret. There's a satisfying crunch as she goes down, hitting the deck with all the grace of a drunken elephant. Blood gushes from her nose, probably ruining her "I'm a conniving pirate whore" aesthetic.

"That's for being a grade-A, certified bitch," shaking out my hand. "Hope you enjoy your new look. I hear broken noses are all the rage this season."

Behind me, Lucian's cackling like a hyena that just discovered laughing gas. He strolls to Izabelle's crumpled form, grinning like an idiot.

"Holy *ship*, JIZZabelle!" he exclaims. "That looks like it hurts more than that one time when I tried to high-five a jellyfish. Here, let me help. How many fingers am I holding up?"

He waves his hand in front of her face, alternating between flipping her off and making other crude gestures.

Izabelle's pride is more bruised than her face, and she swats at his hand like an angry cat. Lucian dances back, still chuckling. "Whoa there, tiger! I was just trying to help. Maybe we should get you an ice pack... and a personality transplant while we're at it."

Rhyland's got a smirk that could cut glass, and Erik? He's giving me a look of pride that warms my heart.

It feels good. Damn good. Because sometimes, just sometimes, a bitch needs to get punched in the face. It's like the universe restoring balance, one broken nose at a time.

Here we are, another realm saved, another stone acquired, and another step closer to fulfilling this "savior" gig.

It's been one hell of a ride so far, and I wouldn't trade it for anything.

DANICA

74

I step into my apartment, ready to collapse on the couch, binge-watch some trashy reality TV, and stop dead in my tracks.

"What the hell?" I whisper, my eyes widening as I examine the scene before me. It looks like a tornado, a hurricane, and a pack of wild animals had a rave in my living room.

Rhyland stiffens beside me, his nostrils flaring. "Smells like fucking dog."

Lucian and Erik both give a quick nod, their faces set in grim lines. It's like watching a synchronized brooding routine.

Shit is everywhere, from overturned furniture to shattered glass, and I'm pretty sure that stain on the carpet is going to require some industrial-strength bleach.

I run, searching around my apartment for Emily and Sable.

"Emily?" I shout, my voice echoing in the eerie silence. "Sable?" I know she said they had this place locked down tight with more magical wards than Hogwarts, but from the looks of it, that didn't do jack shit.

We portaled back and walked into this shitshow. Was it Azrael? Did that asshole finally make his move?

"She's not here," I tell everyone, my voice shaking. "I—I don't know what to do..." Panic is rising in my throat like bile, threatening to choke me.

Rhyland is at my side in a heartbeat, his strong arms wrapping around me. "Calm down, baby," his voice low and reassuring. "Don't go jumping to conclusions. We'll figure this out."

But I can't calm down. The thought of something happening to Emily is like a knife to my gut, twisting and tearing me apart. She's my rock, my best friend, and if anything happened to her, I'd never forgive myself.

"Hey, check this out." Lucian's voice cuts through the fog of my panic, and I whip around to see him holding up a familiar object—a cell phone, a shit-eating grin on his face. "Looks like our little Velma left us a clue."

I practically teleport to his side, snatching the phone out of his hand. A message from Emily on the lock screen—I unlock it with shaking fingers.

> We were attacked. Had to move. Call me when you get this.

Relief floods me, so strong it nearly brings me to my knees. "She's okay," I whisper, clutching the phone like a lifeline. "She's okay."

But how long ago did this happen? I quickly check the date on the message—two days ago. Shit. Panic starts to claw at me again. Emily, the clever bitch, left this knowing I'd find it when I got back.

I quickly call her, not wasting a second. She picks up on the second ring, and I practically shout into the phone. "Emily, thank god. What's going on?"

"Well, shit, look who finally decided to grace us with her presence," Emily drawls. "Took you long enough, bitch. I was starting to think you'd eloped with Aquaman and left me high and dry."

I can't help but laugh; the sound is borderline hysterical. "Please, you know I'd never leave you, Em. You're Bonnie to my Clyde." As I kick a broken plate across the floor.

"Damn straight," she quips, but I can hear the tension in her voice. "But seriously, we've got a major fucking problem. Those werewolf bastards attacked us—they were after the Soul Stone."

Goddamn werewolves, more than likely working for that shitstain, Azrael. I suck in a breath, my mind racing. God, please tell me they didn't get their mangy paws on it. I had that thing locked up tight in my safe.

No. No, no, no. This can't be happening.

I sprint to my bedroom, my heart pounding in my ears. I throw open the closet doors, and my worst fears are confirmed. The hidden panel is ripped from the wall, the safe torn from its hiding place like it was made of tissue paper.

"Goddamnit," I scream, slamming my fist against the wall. "Those bastards! They got the stone, Em. It's fucking gone."

I can hear Emily's sharp intake of breath, the weight of the situation hitting her like a ton of bricks. "Shit, Dani. I...I don't know what to say. We tried to stop them, but there were too many. We barely made it out alive."

Just then, water bursts from the pipes in my adjoining bathroom, reacting to my emotional outburst.

Shit—Just what I need right now.

Rhyland comes rushing in, quickly turning off the water.

I close my eyes, forcing myself to take a deep, calming breath. Losing my shit isn't going to help anyone right now. "Where are you, Em? Please tell me you're somewhere safe."

"We're at Sable's grandma's place in Olympia," Her voice strained. "Laying low until we can figure out our next move. God, Dani, I'm so fucking sorry. I should have done more, should have—"

"Stop," I cut her off, my voice firm. "This is not your fault, Emily. You did everything you could. I'm just glad you're okay. You are okay, right?"

There's a moment of silence and then a soft, humorless chuckle. "Yeah, I'm okay—a little banged up, but I'll live. Can't say the same for those furry fuckers, though. I may have set a few of them on fire with my mind."

Despite the gravity of the situation, I can't help but snort.

I sigh, running a hand through my hair, needing to calm down. "Couldn't you have scheduled the werewolf home invasion for next week? I had plans to binge-watch The Bachelor and eat my weight in ice cream."

Emily lets out a choked laugh, the sound somewhere between a sob and a snort. "Oh, well, excuse the fuck out of me, your highness. Next time, I'll be sure to clear my calendar of any pesky supernatural attacks before I pencil in your pity party. Wouldn't want to interrupt your crucial self-care routine."

"Damn right," I shoot back, forcing a grin even though she can't see it. "A girl's gotta have her priorities, you know. Saving the world is important and all, but so is maintaining my flawless complexion."

Emily groans, and I can literally hear her eyes rolling through the phone. "You're a real piece of work, you know that? I'm over here fighting off werewolves and trying not to piss myself from fear, and you're worried about your fucking skincare routine."

"Hey, if we're gonna go down in flames, I'm gonna do it looking fabulous," I quip, yanking clothes off my hangers. "Besides, someone's gotta keep up morale around here. Might as well be the resident hottie with the killer sense of humor."

Emily snorts. "You're impossible, you know that? But I love you anyway, you ridiculous bitch."

I feel a surge of warmth in my chest at her words, a reminder of our unbreakable bond. "Love you too, Em," my throat tight with emotion."Okay, you two stay put and keep your heads down. I will round up the cavalry and figure out our next move."

Emily laughs, the sound a little more genuine this time. "Got it. Just...be careful, okay? I have a feeling this is just the beginning. And Dani?"

"Yeah?"

"I know you've got your vampire beefcake and his merry band of misfits watching your back, but still. I can't lose you."

A sense of foreboding settles in my gut. "I know," my voice barely above a whisper. "But we'll get through this, Em. We always do."

"You all should get the hell out of there and lay low until we meet," Emily warns, her voice turning serious. "There's no telling what those fury pricks might do."

"Got it."

I hang up and grab my bag. Time to play a game of 'How much shit can I fit into one suitcase?' I start throwing things in haphazardly—clothes, shoes, my fun little rose vibrator Rhyland got me. You know, the essentials.

Lucian and Erik burst into the room like they are auditioning for an action movie. "We heard everything," they say in unison.

"I knew it was those werewolf fucks." Rhyland starts helping me pack, his muscles flexing in a way that's totally unnecessary but greatly appreciated.

Seraphina floats in, all angelic and concerned. "What can I do to help?"

Lucian turns to her, cupping her face in his hands like she's the most precious thing in the universe. "Nothing, baby girl," planting a kiss on her lips that's sweeter than a unicorn's fart. "Your presence is enough, beautiful."

Seraphina practically melts, a goofy smile spreading across her face.

I smirk at the two new lovebirds, "Hate to interrupt, but we've got a slight problem. Where the hell are we supposed to go?"

"I know where we can go," Lucian says, turning back to us with a smirk. "I've got a place that's so secret, even the CIA doesn't know about it."

I raise an eyebrow, skeptical as hell. "I don't think Karma will cut it this time, Luci. We need somewhere completely off the grid, somewhere that—"

"I know, I know," he cuts me off, waving his hand like he's swatting a fly. "Like I said, I've got a place. It's my super-secret, ultra-exclusive bachelor pad out on Mercer Island. It's got everything we need—a hot tub, a fully stocked bar, and a view that'll make you cream your panties."

Rhyland's head snaps up, his eyes narrowing. "Since when do you have a fucking house, dickwad?"

Lucian grins, all smug and self-satisfied. "Since I bought it years ago, dumbass. What, did you think I spent all my money on hookers and blow?"

I snort, shaking my head. Only Lucian could make a safe house sound like a fucking frat party.

"Alright, enough with the real estate chit-chat," I say, zipping up my suitcase with a flourish. "We need to get out of Dodge before the wolf pack returns for round two."

As Rhyland finishes packing up my belongings, I survey the wreckage of my apartment, my heart heavy with memories. Every shattered piece tells a story of the life I've built here, the love that has seeped into these walls.

But now, amidst the ruins, I realize that the warmth and comfort have been stripped away, replaced by a hollow emptiness. The werewolf attack, the theft of the Soul Stone, the violation of my sanctuary—it's tainted everything.

I run my fingers over the splintered remains of my favorite armchair, the one where Emily and I used to curl up with a bottle of wine and talk shit about our exes. I trace the jagged edges of a shattered picture frame, the smiling faces of my family now distorted and fragmented, like a twisted funhouse mirror.

The weight of what I'm leaving behind hits me like a punch to the gut. This place has been my anchor, my port in the storm of my crazy, fucked-up life. It's where I've laughed, cried, screamed, found love, and forged unbreakable bonds.

But I know, in the end, that home isn't a place. It's not four walls or a collection of possessions. Home is the people you love, the ones who stand by your side through thick and thin, who fight and bleed and die for you without a second thought.

Lucian rubs his hands together, his eyes gleaming with mischief. "I call shotgun!"

RHYLAND

75

As we pull up to the gated mansion in our Ubers, I can't help but let out a low whistle. This place is fucking massive, like something straight out of a goddamn movie.

The wrought-iron gates slowly swing open, revealing a long, winding driveway lined with perfectly manicured hedges and towering oak trees. The gravel crunches beneath the tires as we approach the house.

And then, there it is. The mansion itself, rising from the shores of Lake Washington like a fucking castle. It's all sleek lines and modern angles, with huge floor-to-ceiling windows reflecting the lake's shimmering waters. The exterior is a mix of dark wood and stone, giving it a rustic elegance that's both impressive and intimidating.

As we get closer, I can see the sprawling lawns surrounding the property, dotted with colorful flower beds and perfectly trimmed topiaries. There's a huge deck that wraps around the entire back of the house, complete with a built-in hot tub and an outdoor kitchen. The place reeks of luxury.

And then there's the view. Holy shit, the view. The mansion is perched right on the lake's edge, with a panoramic vista of the water and the mountains beyond. It's the kind of view that people would kill for, the kind that makes you feel like you're on top of the goddamn world.

I glance over at Dani, who's staring up at the mansion with wide eyes and an expression of awe. "Holy fuck," she breathes, her voice barely above a whisper. "Never would've thought Lucian to have a place like this."

The Uber stops at the base of the stairs, and I step out, my eyes still drinking in the grandeur. Lucian sidles up beside me, a shit-eating grin on his face.

"Not too shabby, eh?" he quips, elbowing me in the ribs. "I told you I had a secret hideout. Bet you're glad you didn't kill me all those times you threatened to, huh?"

I roll my eyes. "Don't tempt me, asshole," I growl, but there's no real heat behind my words. "I might just change my mind if you keep running your mouth."

Lucian laughs, slinging an arm around my shoulders as he leads us up the stairs. "Please," he scoffs. "You'd be lost without me, and you know it. Who else would keep you on your toes and make sure you don't take yourself too fucking seriously?"

I scoff but can't help but be a little impressed. I mean, don't get me wrong, Lucian's still a pain in my ass. But even I have to admit, the guy's got style.

As we make our way up the front steps, I feel the tension draining from my body. It's been a long fucking day, hell, a long fucking month, and the thought of crashing in a place like this is almost too good to be true.

As Lucian swings open the massive front doors, my jaw drops. "Holy fucking shit," I mutter, taking in the sight before us.

The interior is a goddamn work of art. Sleek, modern lines are everywhere, and the place has an open floor plan that makes it feel even bigger than it looked outside. The floors are polished concrete, gleaming under the soft light of designer fixtures hanging from the high ceilings. Floor-to-ceiling windows dominate one wall, offering a breathtaking view of Lake Washington and the twinkling lights of Seattle in the distance.

"Welcome to Casa de Lucian," our host announces with a flourish, grinning like an idiot. "Make yourselves at home, mi casa es su casa, and all that jazz."

Dani lets out a low whistle, her eyes wide as she takes in the surroundings. "Damn, Lucian. I didn't know being a pain in the ass paid so well. Maybe I should consider a career change."

I can't help but chuckle at that, even as I roll my eyes. "Don't even think about it, Angel," I growl playfully, pulling her close. "One Lucian in the family is more than enough."

Erik merely raises an eyebrow. "It's... adequate," his tone dry as the Sahara. But I can see the hint of approval in his eyes as he scans the room, no doubt already cataloging potential security risks and escape routes.

On the other hand, Seraphina looks like she's about to swoon. "Oh, Sparky," she breathes, her eyes glittering as she gazes at him adoringly. "It's absolutely perfect. Just like you."

I barely suppress my laugh at the nickname Seraphina has given Lucian.

Lucian is preening under her attention. "Only the best for you, Cupcake," he purrs, wrapping an arm around her waist and kissing her cheek.

"Alright, alright," I cut in before I have to witness any more of their lovey-dovey bullshit. "Can we get the grand tour already? I need a shower."

Lucian's grin widens if that's even possible. "Right this way, ladies and gentlemen," gesturing towards a sleek staircase that looks floating in midair. "Let me show you to your suites. And trust me, they're fucking spectacular."

We follow him up the stairs. The second floor is just as impressive as the first, with a long hallway lined with doors. The walls are adorned with modern art pieces that probably cost more than most people's cars, and the plush carpet feels like fucking clouds beneath our feet.

"Each suite has its own bathroom, walk-in closet, and balcony," Lucian explains as he leads us down the hall. "And don't worry, the walls are soundproof. So feel free to get as... enthusiastic as you want." He winks at Dani and me, and I resist the urge to punch him in his smug face.

Dani, of course, rolls her eyes. "Gee, thanks for the permission, Lucian," she drawls. "I was so worried about offending your delicate sensibilities with our wild, passionate lovemaking."

Seraphina giggles at that, her hand covering her mouth as she leans into Lucian's side. "Oh, I don't think Lucian has any delicate sensibilities left to offend," she says, her tone all innocence and light. "Not after—"

I groan, shaking my head. "TMI, Seraphina," I mutter, pinching the bridge of my nose. "Way too fucking much information."

Seraphina walks to a door and suddenly lets out a soft gasp. "Lucian," she breathes, her eyes wide as she stares at the door. "Is this... is this our room?"

I follow her gaze and nearly choke on my tongue. The door is a deep, rich red, with a gold nameplate that reads "The Love Nest" in swirling script.

Lucian grins, looking entirely too pleased with himself. "Of course, sweetheart," pulling her close. "Only the best for my cupcake."

I make a gagging noise, and Dani elbows me in the ribs. "Be nice," she hisses, but I can see the laughter in her eyes.

Erik, trailing behind us like a silent shadow, finally speaks up. "If you two are quite finished," he deadpans, "perhaps we could continue the tour? Some of us want to settle in."

"Spoilsport," Lucian mutters, but he leads us to the end of the hall anyway. "This one's for you, Erik," gesturing to a sleek black door. "I figured you'd appreciate the minimalist aesthetic."

Erik nods, a faint smile playing on his lips. "It will suffice," he says, and coming from him, that's practically a ringing endorsement.

Finally, we reach the end of the hall, where two massive double doors stand sentinel. "And this," Lucian announces, his voice grand and dramatic, "is the master suite. Also known as the fuck pad, the shag shack, the—"

"We get it," I cut him off. "It's where Dani and I will be staying."

Lucian grins, waggling his eyebrows suggestively. "Oh, I know," his tone evident with innuendo. "I made sure to stock the nightstand with plenty of lube. You know, just in case."

I am about to smack the fucker upside the head, but he throws open the door with a flourish, and even I have to admit, it's pretty damn impressive. The room is massive, with an Alaskan king-sized bed that could comfortably fit about six people. Floor-to-ceiling windows offer a breathtaking view of the lake, and an enormous fireplace on one wall begs to be lit.

But it's the bathroom that catches my eye. It's bigger than some apartments I've lived in, with a huge soaking tub, a separate glass-enclosed shower, and a fucking sauna. Yeah, you heard me right—a sauna.

"Holy shit," Dani breathes, her eyes wide as she takes it all in. "This is... wow."

Lucian grins, "I know, right?" his tone smug as hell. "And just wait until you see the closet. You could fit a small army in there."

I snort, shaking my head. "Only you would think that's a selling point, Lucian."

I wrap my arms around Dani from behind, nuzzling her neck. "Don't get too comfortable, Angel," my voice low and husky. "We're not out of the woods yet."

She leans back into me, a soft sigh escaping her lips. "I know," her tone of resignation and determination. "But for tonight, can we just pretend that everything's okay? That we're just a normal couple on a really, really nice vacation?"

I chuckle, pressing a kiss to her temple. "Whatever you want, baby," I tell her, meaning every word. "Tonight, we can be whoever the fuck you want us to be."

Lucian smirks, "You two lovebirds enjoy your little nest. The rest of us will be down the hall if you need anything. Like condoms. Or lube. Or—"

"Out," I growl, pointing to the door. "Before I throw you out."

Lucian laughs, takes Seraphina's hand, and leads her out of the room. I shut the door behind them more forcefully than necessary, turning to Dani.

"Alone at last," I murmur, pulling her into my arms. "Whatever shall we do with ourselves?"

Dani grins up at me, her eyes sparkling with mischief. "Oh, I'm sure we can think of something," she purrs, her hands sliding under my shirt. "After all, we wouldn't want to let this soundproofing go to waste, now would we?"

I growl low in my throat, my hands tightening on her hips. "Fuck, no," I rumble, capturing her lips in a searing kiss. "In fact, I think it's time we put it to the test. Thoroughly and repeatedly."

Dani laughs against my mouth, her body melting into mine. "But, first," she murmurs, her lips brushing against mine with every word, "I need a glorious shower in that beautiful bathroom. And you're coming with me."

I growl deep in my chest, my hands gripping her luscious ass as I hoist her up. She wraps her legs around my waist, and I can feel the heat of her through our clothes. It's enough to drive a man fucking insane.

I crash my lips against hers, devouring her mouth like a man starved as I carry her towards the bathroom. She tastes like sin and salvation, and I can't get enough.

The rest of the world fades away—the stolen Soul Stone, the werewolves—as we stumble into the bathroom, our hands tearing at each other's clothes. Buttons fly and fabric rips, but I couldn't give a single fuck. All that matters is getting her naked, getting my hands and mouth on every inch of her soft, perfect skin.

We finally enter the shower, the hot water cascading over us as I press her against the cool tile wall. She gasps as I trail my lips down her neck, my teeth grazing her pulse point. I can feel it thundering beneath my tongue, a reminder of how alive she is, how fucking precious.

"Rhyland," she moans, her nails digging into my shoulders as I explore her body with my hands and mouth. "Please..."

I know what she needs, what she's begging for. And I'm more than happy to oblige.

I hoist her up higher, her legs locking around my hips as I position myself at her entrance. With one swift thrust, I'm inside her, buried balls deep in her tight, wet heat.

"Fuck," I groan, my forehead falling against hers as I start to move. "You feel so goddamn good, Angel."

She whimpers, her hips rolling to meet mine with every thrust. "So do you," she gasps, her head falling against the wall. "God, Rhyland, don't stop."

As if I could. As if I would ever fucking want to.

76

Rhyland's cock is a masterpiece, a work of art crafted by the gods themselves. I swear, I could worship at the altar of his dick for eternity and never get enough. The way he fills me, stretching me to the brink, hitting that sweet spot deep inside with every thrust—it's pure ecstasy, sending me careening over the edge every damn time.

You know the old saying—size doesn't matter. Well, that's a fucking lie. Rhyland is the biggest I've ever had, and he's showing me what I've been missing my entire goddamn life.

He's got me pinned against the shower wall, my body trapped between the cool tiles and his hard, unyielding muscles. His hands grip my ass, his fingers digging into my flesh as he controls my movements, slamming me down onto his thick, pulsing length. His tattooed arms flex and ripple with each powerful thrust, a mesmerizing display of raw, primal strength.

I'm a writhing, moaning mess, clinging to him desperately as the hot water cascades over us, the steam rising in a heady fog. My nails rake down his back, leaving angry red lines in their wake, a physical manifestation of the pleasure tearing through my body.

"Fuck, woman," Rhyland growls against my neck, his breath hot and ragged. "You're driving me crazy." His hips piston into me with renewed vigor, his cock driving into me like a jackhammer, relentless and unforgiving.

"Give it to me, Angel," he commands, his voice a low, guttural rumble that vibrates through my very bones. "I can't last much longer with the way you're squeezing my cock, milking me for all I'm worth."

His filthy words are my undoing, pushing me over the precipice into mind-numbing ecstasy. I come with a keening cry, my inner walls clamping down around his throbbing length, pulsing and fluttering as wave after wave of pleasure crashes over me.

Rhyland's answering groan is animalistic and primal as he buries his face in the crook of my neck, his teeth grazing my sensitive skin. His hips stutter, losing their rhythm as he chases his own release, and then he's coming, his hot seed spurting deep inside me, coating my walls with his essence.

The sensation triggers another orgasm, my body shuddering and convulsing in his arms as the white-hot flames of rapture consume me. The wet, obscene sounds of our coupling echo off the shower walls, a lewd symphony of passion and desire.

We stay like that for a long moment, our bodies intertwined, our chests heaving as we struggle to catch our breath. The water continues to pour over us, washing away the evidence of our coupling, but the memory of it is seared into my mind, body, and soul.

After our steamy shower session, Rhyland and I dried off, got dressed, and I sent a quick text to Emily with Lucian's address. We made our way to the kitchen, and let me tell you, calling it a kitchen is like calling the Mona Lisa a doodle. This place is a gourmet wonderland, a culinary wet dream that would make The Food Network weep tears of joy.

It felt amazing to finally shower with actual products instead of a bar of kelp soap that smelled like low tide. Lucian's bathroom was stocked with every luxury, from high-end shampoos to fancy lotions that cost more than my entire wardrobe.

I'm perched at the kitchen island, rocking my favorite pair of cotton shorts and a cozy oversized sweater that hangs off one shoulder. It's the perfect blend of comfy and cute—like I'm ready for a lazy Sunday morning but still could kick ass if needed.

Rhyland, my caffeine hero, is brewing a pot of coffee that I've been craving like a junkie in need of a fix. I don't care if the sun is setting; I need my liquid energy, and I need it now.

As I perch on the kitchen island stool, still flushed from our steamy shower session, I can't help but ogle Rhyland as he moves around the kitchen. He's a walking temptation in nothing but low-hanging gray sweatpants, clearly borrowed from Lucian. His damp black hair is artfully tousled, cut tight on the sides with just enough on top to make me want to muss it up again.

That thick, well-groomed beard frames his chiseled jaw, still glistening with a few stray water droplets. My eyes trace the contours of his gloriously naked upper half, a masterpiece of golden tan skin and Nordic tattoos stretched over rippling muscles. From those washboard abs to the arms that easily manhandled me against the shower wall just minutes ago, every inch of him screams, 'Touch me.'

I'm mesmerized by the tantalizing trail of dark hair that starts below his navel and disappears into the waistband of those sweats, forming a 'V' that points like a neon sign to the impressive bulge I was intimately acquainted with earlier.

Seeing him and the lingering endorphins from our passionate encounter sends me a fresh wave of heat. My skin tingles, my heart races, and I'm pretty sure I'm grinning like an idiot. It's taking every ounce of willpower not to drag him back to bed, coffee be damned.

Rhyland must feel my eyes boring into his back. "Ready for another round, baby? Should I put this coffee on hold?"

I can't help but roll my eyes. Of course he knows exactly what I'm thinking—damn vampire senses. He can probably smell my arousal from across the room, the cocky bastard.

"Don't you dare stop that coffee," I warn, trying to sound stern but failing miserably. "I need caffeine if I'm going to keep up with your insatiable appetite, Mr. 'Let's-See-How-Many-Rounds-We-Can-Go.'"

He turns then, flashing me that devastatingly sexy smirk that never fails to make my heart skip a beat. "Can't blame a guy for trying, Angel," he purrs, his voice low and full of promise. "Besides, you weren't complaining about my appetite a few minutes ago."

I feel my cheeks flush even hotter if that's possible. "Coffee first," I insist, pointedly ignoring how my body screams for an encore. "Then we'll talk about satisfying other... cravings."

Rhyland's answering grin is positively wolfish. "I'll hold you to that, baby," turning back to the coffee maker. "Better drink up quick."

I quickly switch on the kitchen TV, needing a distraction from the Norse god in front of me—figuring I might as well catch up on the latest news while I wait for my life-giving elixir.

Let's see what chaos and mayhem the world has been up to while I've been playing mermaid in the underwater realm.

I find a news station and crank up the volume, the reporter's voice filling the room.

"Breaking news: Another werewolf massacre rocks Sammamish today as Wolf Pack leader and Sherriff of Area Twleve, Mason Brooks, claims the victims crossed territory lines, sparking the brutal attack. Stay tuned for more on this developing story at eleven. Back to you, Tom."

I stare at the TV, my jaw hanging open like a broken puppet. Rhyland, the caffeine-bearing godsend, sets a steaming mug of liquid gold before me. "Looks like we've got our work cut out for us, Angel," his hands land on my shoulders like a pair of heat-seeking missiles, kneading the knots out of my muscles like he's on a mission from the massage gods.

No shit. What the ever-loving fuck is Area Twelve?

"I can't believe this," I mutter, shaking my head in disbelief. "We've been so caught up in playing supernatural fix-it crew for the other realms that we've totally neglected our own backyard."

I sip my coffee, letting the bitter liquid scorch my tongue and jolt my brain into action. "Seriously, though, what the hell is going on? I know Emily mentioned that the wolves were claiming territories and shit, but what does this mean?"

"Werewolves have been trying to claim territories for eons, baby," Rhyland sighs, his fingers still working their magic on my tense muscles. "But I'm flying blind here. I need to do some digging and find out what the hell happened to the vampire council. I'll make some calls in the morning to see if I can get the lowdown on these packs and their little turf war."

I nod, taking another sip of my life-giving elixir. Suddenly, my phone buzzes like an angry hornet, demanding my attention. I snatch it up, hoping it's not another crisis to add to our ever-growing list of apocalyptic problems.

But when I see Emily's name on the screen, I can't help but grin like an idiot.

In route. We should be there in about an hour and a half.

Okay, drive safe. See you soon! And don't forget to bring the good snacks. You know, the ones that don't taste like cardboard and sadness.

I hit send, feeling a little lighter, a little more hopeful. Sure, the world might be going to hell in a handbasket, but at least I've got my crew. *My family.*

A wave of relief washes over me, the knots in my stomach loosening just a bit. Emily's on her way. My ride-or-die, my partner in crime, my platonic soulmate. With her by my side, I know we can take on anything.

Rhyland leans down, pressing a kiss to my cheek. "Emily's on her way?" he asks, his voice a low rumble that makes my nipples ache.

"Yeah," I nod, leaning into his touch. "Her and Sable. They should be here in an hour and a half, give or take a few bathroom breaks and snack stops."

Rhyland chuckles, his breath tickling my ear. "Good. We're going to need all hands on deck for this one. And if anyone can help us figure out this werewolf mess, it's Emily. That girl's got intel for this type of shit and a tongue sharp enough to cut through bullshit like butter."

I can't help but laugh, picturing Emily verbally eviscerating a bunch of posturing werewolves. "Damn straight. Those fleabags won't know what hit them. Between your brawn, Emily's witchy powers, and my dazzling wit and charm, we'll have this territory dispute sorted out in no time."

Rhyland snorts, "Dazzling wit and charm, huh? Is that what we're calling it now?"

I elbow him in the ribs, my grin widening. "Hey, don't knock it till you've tried it, buddy. I'll have you know my wit and charm are legendary. They're like the secret weapons in my savior arsenal."

"You sound like Lucian—he's rubbing off on you, Angel." Rhyland teases. "Just promise me you'll use your powers for good and not evil."

I bat my eyelashes at him, putting on my best innocent face. "Who, me? I'm practically a saint. A beacon of virtue and righteousness."

Rhyland laughs outright at that, the sound rich and warm. "Sure you are, baby. And I'm the Easter Bunny."

I laugh with Rhyland, the stress and anxiety of everything slowly dissipating like mist in the morning sun. It's like my brain is stuck in some cosmic whiplash, trying to reconcile the insanity of our inter-realm adventures with the mundane reality of our own world.

One minute, we're swimming through magical underwater kingdoms and battling ancient girl drama, and the next, we're back in the land of smartphones, luxury real estate, and gas-guzzling SUVs. It's like being yanked out of a high-fantasy novel and dropped into an episode of "Lifestyles of the Rich and Famous: Supernatural Edition."

I can't help but feel a little disoriented, my mind struggling to adjust to the jarring shift in reality. My brain is a rusty gear, grinding and rattling as it tries to switch between the different settings of the multiverse.

"Is it just me, or is this whole realm-hopping thing starting to feel like the world's most fucked-up case of jet lag?" I muse, my fingers tapping restlessly against the countertop. "I love a good adventure as much as the next girl, but sometimes I just want to sit down and watch some mindless reality TV without worrying about the fabric of the universe unraveling around me."

"I know what you mean, Angel. We don't get the luxury of a normal life."

I sigh, leaning my head back against his chest. "I know. And I wouldn't trade this life for anything. But sometimes, I wish we could take a break from the chaos, you know? Just be a regular couple and do regular couple things. Like arguing over what to watch on Netflix or fighting for the last piece of pizza."

Rhyland chuckles, spinning me in my chair and kissing my forehead. "Well, we might not be able to escape the chaos completely, but I think we can manage some normalcy now and then. How about this? After we deal with this werewolf situation and make sure the realms aren't going to implode, we take a day just for us. No magic, no monsters, no impending doom. Just you, me, and a lot of junk food and trashy TV."

I can't help but grin at the thought, my heart swelling with love for this man who always seems to know what I need. "That sounds perfect," I murmur, tilting my head to capture his lips in a soft, sweet kiss. "And you still owe me that date, mister," I remind him, my voice a playful purr.

"Ahh, yes, the date," Rhyland growls, his beautiful blue eyes darkening with desire and amusement.

He grips my waist with his large, calloused hands, effortlessly lifting me onto the kitchen island. Now at eye level, he steps between my parted thighs, his body a solid wall of muscle and heat.

I flashback to that first time in my apartment in this position when he sat me on my kitchen island and worked his magic fingers and tongue until I was a writhing, moaning mess. The memory sends a bolt of liquid heat straight to my core, and I squeeze my legs around his waist, pulling him closer.

My hands wander up his muscular chest, appreciating how his black tattoos beckon my fingers on his godlike physique—the gray sweatpants slung low on his hips. It should be a goddamn crime for him to look this good in loungewear.

And speaking of crimes, the way his monster cock is just swinging free beneath the thin fabric is practically a felony. I lick my lips, my mind flooding with all the filthy things I want to do to him. Again.

"You're doing it again," Rhyland smirks, his gaze roaming over my face, knowing I am practically drooling. "Have you decided yet on who won that bet, Angel?"

I smile at him, my fingers toying with the back of his hair. "Hmmm, I do recall winning that bet fair and square. And to the victor go the spoils, right?"

Rhyland's hands squeeze my hips, his fingers digging into my flesh in a way that makes me want to purr. "Mmm, I think it was a tie, baby—a team effort."

I arch a brow, my lips curving into a challenging grin. "Oh? Because last time I checked, that nasty creature was all up in my head, not yours. It reached out to me telepathically, which means I'm the one who had to deal with its creepy-ass voice invading my brain. Therefore, I am the victor, and you, my sexy Viking, owe me a date of my choosing and a whole lot of sexual favors."

Rhyland throws his head back and laughs, the sound so deep and rich that I swear I can feel it in my bones.

Damn, he should laugh more often. It's like auditory porn, sending shivers of desire racing down my spine and straight to my already aching core.

"Fuck, Angel, you drive a hard bargain," he rumbles, his eyes gleaming with amusement and hunger. "But I know when I'm beaten—I concede, baby. You won fair and square, and I'm man enough to admit it."

He crushes his lips to mine, his kiss fierce and demanding, stealing the breath from my lungs. After our shower, he trimmed his rustic beard, and now the slight tickle of his facial hair against my skin drives me wild. His hands rove over my body, caressing, squeezing, claiming every inch as if it's his own personal playground.

I moan into his mouth, my fingers tangling in his short, silky hair and tickling his beard as I give myself over to the sensation. Kissing Rhyland is like being consumed by a force of nature, wild and untamable and so fucking intense that it makes my toes curl, and my brain short-circuit.

I'm lost in the heat of Rhyland's kiss, my mind hazy with desire, when suddenly, a memory flashes through my brain like a lightning bolt. It's so jarring that I pull away from his lips, my brow furrowed in concentration. "Hey, remember when I asked Calypso how long she'd been cursed?"

Rhyland blinks at me, his expression of confusion and frustration. "Seriously, Angel?" he grumbles, his voice rough with arousal. "That's what you're thinking about while I'm trying to devour you? Fucking hell, woman, you're killing me here."

I can't help but grin sheepishly, feeling a flush creep up my cheeks. "Sorry, it just came to me out of nowhere. You know how my mind sometimes wanders, especially when I get stuck on a thought. Maybe it was the caffeine boost?"

Rhyland's expression softens, his eyes crinkling at the corners with fond affection. "Yeah, I remember," tucking a stray strand of hair behind my ear. "Why do you ask?"

I lean into his touch, savoring the warmth of his calloused fingers against my skin. "You stiffened up when she said how long," I murmur, my gaze searching his face. "I noticed it the second it happened, but everything was so crazy, I never got a chance to ask about it."

Rhyland's tattooed hand falls away as he drags it down his face, a heavy sigh escaping his lips. "Fuck, you don't miss a thing, do you?" he mutters, his eyes distant and pensive. "Yeah, her answer threw me for a loop. Because the length of her curse? It was exactly a hundred years after the year I was turned."

My eyebrows shoot up to my hairline, my mind racing with the implications. "Wait, you mean the year you were... turned? Like, when you became a vampire?"

Rhyland nods, his jaw tight with tension. "Yeah. It was 867 AD. And Calypso said she'd been cursed for nearly that long. That's the same time everything went to shit—when the Darkness retreated because your father closed off the realms."

My brain feels like it misfires, the gears grinding to a halt as Rhyland's words sink in. "Wait—what?" I blurt out, blinking rapidly as I try to process this bombshell he's just dropped. "You've never mentioned any of this to me before. How is it possible that your turning as a vampire was connected to the sealing of the realms and the retreat of the Darkness?"

He stares at me.

"And my father? How...how do you know all this?"

DANICA

77

"Do you remember the wall at the Valley of Ancients?" Rhyland asks, his voice low and intense, his eyes searching mine for understanding.

I nod, my mind flashing back to that moment we traveled to the Amazon rainforest, the awe and terror I felt as those paintings came to life before our eyes, telling a beautiful and horrifying story. "Yes, I remember," my fingers tightening on his shoulders. "It was like watching history unfold, like being transported back in time."

Rhyland's hands tighten on my waist, his fingers digging into my flesh as if trying to anchor himself to the present. "When I saw what Elysium did and what I felt that day when I knew I was going to die...I just put two and two together," his voice rough with emotion. "The same day I died was the same fucking day the realms were sealed off. I felt it, Angel. The Darkness was closing in, and then, all of a sudden, it just disappeared. Just like what we saw on that wall."

His voice is raw, almost tragic. "The Darkness retreated, and I felt this... this shift, like the world had been tilted on its axis. And now I know why. It was because your father had closed the realms and had sealed away the evil that threatened to consume us all."

I frown. My mind races as I process this revelation. "But what does it mean?" I whisper. "Why would dying and your turning be connected to the sealing of the realms? What purpose could it serve?"

Rhyland shrugs, a heavy sigh escaping his lips. "No fucking clue, baby. It could be a coincidence, or it could be something more. All I know is that day is burned into my fucked up brain like a brand. I remember every goddamn second, every sensation, every emotion. So when Calypso mentioned how long she'd been cursed, it just...threw me for a loop."

He pulls me closer, his hands trailing down to cup my ass, his touch a searing heat even through the thin fabric of my shorts. It's a desperate, needy gesture as if he's trying to lose himself in my body, in the comfort of our connection.

I can only imagine the horrors Rhyland must have faced on that fateful day, the pain and loss he endured as his world was ripped apart at the seams. My heart aches for him, for the centuries of torment and confusion he's had to carry on his broad shoulders.

Without thinking, I lean in and capture his lips in a soft, tender kiss, pouring every ounce of my love and devotion into the simple gesture. "I'm so sorry, Rhy," I murmur against his mouth, my fingers threading through his hair in a soothing caress. "I can't even begin to imagine what you went through, what you've been carrying with you all these years."

Rhyland leans into my touch, his eyes slipping closed as he takes a shuddering breath. "It's a mind-fuck, that's for sure," he admits. "But in a way, it's also a relief. Because now I know that it wasn't random, that my turning served a purpose, even if I don't fully understand it yet—It brought me to you."

The full extent of Rhyland's transformation into a vampire remains a mystery to me. The details of his maker and the ordeal he endured during his change are shrouded in darkness. But given the haunted look in his eyes whenever the subject arises, I can only imagine it was a hellish experience—certainly not something he'd celebrate or reminisce about fondly.

For the entirety of his undead existence, Rhyland has been a lone wolf, navigating the centuries without companionship or genuine connection. The thought of him wandering through the ages, isolated and burdened by his immortality, sends a pang of sorrow through my chest. It's a profound and enduring loneliness that makes my heart ache for him.

I press my forehead against his, our breaths mingling in the scant space between us. "I will always be here for you, Rhyland," I vow fiercely, my heart swelling with the force of my conviction. "Through the good times and the bad, through the light and the shadows, you're not alone anymore, and you never will be again. I promise you that."

Rhyland's answering growl is low and possessive, his lips claiming mine in a bruising kiss that steals the breath from my lungs. "Fuck, woman, the things you say and do to me," he rasps, his hands kneading my flesh with a desperate urgency. "I love you so goddamn much. It scares the shit out of me sometimes."

I can't help but smile against his lips, my heart soaring with the knowledge that this beautiful, broken, utterly incredible man is mine, now and forever. "I love you too," I whisper, my voice fierce with the depth of my devotion. "So, so much...it almost hurts how much—more than anything in this world or any other. And together, we're going to—"

"Ohh, for fuck's sake! Really? I give you two the honeymoon suite, and you're in here christening my kitchen island like a pair of horny teenagers," Lucian whines as he strolls in. "I mean, I'm all for a good kitchen kink, but at least put a sock on the door or something. A man needs warning before he walks in on a live porno."

Rhyland drops his head to my chest, a low groan of annoyance rumbling through him. "We're not fucking, you *ass*," he grumbles, pulling back and helping me hop off the counter. I settle back into my seat, sipping my coffee and trying to hide my grin behind the mug.

This is the first time I've ever seen Lucian without a shirt, and the view is not half bad. He stands in low-slung basketball shorts that ride dangerously low on his hips, making that V-shape point straight to his groin. His physique is something else—muscled and trim, a leaner but equally jaw-dropping contrast to Rhyland's hulk-like build.

He's sporting a few tattoos on his chest, with one that snakes around his torso. Lucian's golden hair is now cut shorter, and he's been growing some facial hair, giving him a slightly older, more rugged vibe. And those big, chocolate-brown puppy dog eyes of his? They're soft, relaxed, and unmistakably happy.

"Could've fooled me, big guy," Lucian quips as he rummages through the cupboards. "From where I stood, you two were about to reenact that scene from *Fifty Shades*. You know, the one with the ice cream?"

My cheeks flush at the mental image. "Jesus, Lucian, not everything is about sex, you know." I huff, trying to regain my composure.

Lucian gasps. "Lies and slander! In my world, everything is about sex. It's the glue that holds the universe together, the cosmic lube that keeps the gears of reality turning."

He rummages through the cupboards, his brow furrowed in concentration. "Speaking of lube, where's my stash of edible body paint? I could've sworn I left it next to the quinoa and kale chips."

I nearly choke on my coffee, my eyes watering as I struggle to contain my laughter. "My God, Lucian, how do you even function in polite society?"

He grins. "Bold of you to assume I do, sweet cheeks. Polite society is for chumps and people who don't know how to have a good time."

Rhyland rolls his eyes, crossing his arms over his chest. "Where's Seraphina?" clearly trying to steer the conversation away from Lucian's debauchery.

Lucian grins, a wicked gleam in his eyes. "Taking a well-deserved nap, my friend. I wore her out good and proper if you know what I mean. Gotta keep my baby satisfied, even if it means sacrificing my own beauty sleep."

I groan, burying my face in my hands. "TMI, dude. I do not need the details of your sex life. Especially when it concerns my guardian angel."

"Your loss, babe. I could write a best-selling memoir with all the kinky shit I've gotten up to over the centuries."

Eager to change the subject before Lucian can launch into a graphic play-by-play, I glance around the kitchen, taking in the gleaming surfaces and distinct lack of food. "We need to go grocery shopping," setting my mug down with a decisive clink. "You've got nothing to eat in this mausoleum you call a kitchen unless you count protein powder and ego as food groups."

Lucian waves a dismissive hand, biting into a pop tart that he seemingly pulled out of thin air—my mouth waters. "Already got it handled, sweet cheeks. My minions will be here bright and early tomorrow, armed with enough food to feed a small country. Or, you know, three hungry vampires and their insatiable mates."

I raise an eyebrow. "Minions? What, did you put out a classified ad for henchmen on Craigslist?"

Lucian snorts, crumbs flying everywhere as he gesticulates wildly. "Please, I'm not an amateur. These are highly trained professionals skilled in the art of grocery shopping and ass-kissing. They've been on vacation while we were off gallivanting in the other realms, but now that we're back, they're ready to cater to our every whim."

I can't help but laugh, shaking my head in disbelief. "Only you would have a team of professional ass-kissers on speed dial, Lucian."

He grins, popping the last of the pop tart into his mouth. "What can I say? It's a tough job, but somebody's got to do it. And trust me; these guys are the best in the biz. They'll have this place stocked and ready for action in no time."

Rhyland sighs, pinching the bridge of his nose. "I'm almost afraid to ask, but what kind of action are we talking about here?"

Lucian's smile turns positively devilish. "Oh, you know, the usual. Serving, cleaning, cooking, kissing ass. And maybe a little light bondage if we're feeling frisky."

I choke on my coffee again, my face turning an alarming shade of red. "Goddammit, Lucian, you can't just say shit like that!"

Clearly, he's talking about Staff for this mansion, not some Mad Max-style Seal team.

He cackles, clearly enjoying my discomfort. "Oh, but I can, my sweet summer child. In fact, I insist on it. Life's too short to be a prude, especially when you're immortal."

"Fuck off, Lucian," Rhyland barks.

I can't help but laugh, marveling at the easy camaraderie between these two ancient beings. It's like watching an odd couple sitcom, with Rhyland as the long-suffering straight man and Lucian as the wisecracking goofball.

"Well, as long as your 'minions' come bearing coffee and snacks, I suppose I can put up with your delusions of grandeur," I tease. "But if they forget my Pop-Tarts, there will be hell to pay. A girl's gotta have her processed sugar fix, ya know."

Lucian clutches his chest. "Perish the thought! I would never dream of depriving you of your artificial cherry goodness. I'm a lot of things, but suicidal isn't one of them."

Lucian saunters over to the cupboard, grabs a silver bag of Pop-Tarts, and tosses it my way with a wink. I catch it without missing a beat.

I grin, raising my mug in a salute. "Damn straight. I knew there was a reason I kept you around, Luci. Well, that and your sparkling wit and dashing good looks."

Lucian preens, running a hand through his artfully tousled golden hair. "Aww, stop, you're making me blush. But please, do go on. My ego could always use a little stroking."

Rhyland groans, burying his face in his hands. "I swear, you two are going to drive me into an early grave. Can we please talk about something else? *Anything* else?"

I laugh, reaching out to pat his arm in consolation. "Okay, okay, we'll behave—for now. But don't think you're off the hook, mister. I still fully intend to collect on that bet. And trust me, my imagination is running wild with all the delicious possibilities."

Rhyland's head snaps up, his eyes darkening with a heat that sends shivers to my toes. "Fuck, woman, you can't just say shit like that," he growls.

Lucian claps his hands, a shit-eating grin on his face. "Oooh, what's this about a bet? Do tell, my little lovebirds. Inquiring minds want to know."

I smirk, my eyes never leaving Rhyland's. "Let's just say that the spoils of war will be very, *very* sweet. And leave it at that."

"Aww, you're no fun." Lucian pouts. "But fine, keep your kinky secrets. I'll just have to use my imagination. And trust me, it's a wild and wondrous place."

Rhyland shudders, a look of mock horror on his face. "Please don't. I beg of you. There are some things even immortality can't cure, and the mental scars from your twisted fantasies are definitely on that list."

I can't help but laugh, the sound ringing through the kitchen like a bell. "Oh, I don't know. I think a peek inside Lucian's head could be entertaining. Like a cross between a porno and a Looney Tunes cartoon."

"You know it, baby. My mind is a wonderland of debauchery and chaos. And I wouldn't have it any other way."

As the three of us dissolve into laughter, I can't help but feel a sense of warmth and belonging wash over me. Because this, right here? This is what family feels like.

A bunch of snarky, inappropriate misfits who would walk through fire for each other.

And I wouldn't trade it for all the riches in the realms.

DANICA

78

"Holy shit, this place is fucking nuts," Emily says as she plops down at the kitchen island, her eyes wide with awe.

Ever the faithful friend, Sable sits beside her, looking just as impressed. Rhyland, in a rare display of domesticity, pours two cups of coffee for our guests and sets them down with a flourish.

"Well," Emily teases, sipping the steaming brew. "When did you turn into such a softie, big guy? I could get used to this whole 'attentive host' thing you've got going on."

I shoot Emily a warning glare, my eyes narrowing into slits. "Watch it, missy. That's my man you're talking about."

Emily laughs, utterly unfazed by my attempt at intimidation. "Whaaat?" she drawls. "It's a compliment, Dani. Clearly, you're rubbing off on the big lug, and I gotta say, it's a good fucking look on him."

Rhyland, never one to be left out of the snark-fest, lets out a low growl that rumbles through his chest like distant thunder. In one smooth motion, he scoops me up and plops me down on his lap, his strong arms wrapping around me like a cocoon of muscle and testosterone.

"Alright, enough with the chit-chat," he grumbles. "What's the fucking plan here? We've got a stolen Soul Stone, a pack of mangy werewolves, and a whole lot of shit to sort out."

Once Emily arrived, we escorted her and Sable to one of the countless rooms in Lucian's ridiculous mansion. Seriously, who needs this many bedrooms? Is he planning on starting a supernatural boarding school or something?

We're all gathered in the kitchen, ready to plot our next move. But before we dive into the nitty-gritty of our world-saving strategy, I need to know something.

"How's Damon?" I ask, trying to keep the worry out of my voice.

Emily gulps her coffee, her eyes meeting mine over the mug's rim. "He's good. But... I think you should call him. girl."

Instant panic mode: activated. "What? What's happened?" I demand.

Emily smiles calmly in the face of my freak-out. "Nothing. He's just starting to ask questions about you, is all. And since you plan on hanging around for a bit, I think it's best you connect."

I let out a sigh of relief so huge, it could probably power a small wind farm. Damon's safe. Thank fuck for that. But Emily's right—I need to call my little brother if only to reassure him that his darling sister hasn't been abducted by aliens or joined a cult or something.

"Okay, I will call him," I agree, already mentally preparing myself for the interrogation I know is coming. Damon's always been protective, and I feel he won't be thrilled about my little supernatural sabbatical or the lies I have been feeding him.

Lucian and Seraphina waltz in, looking like they just rolled out of bed (which, let's be real—they did).

Lucian, ever the charming bastard, "Oh fuck me runnin'. The Witchy Wonder Twins have arrived." He guides Seraphina to a seat at the kitchen island, treating her like a precious princess, before strolling over to the fridge.

"Gee, Lucian. Your hospitality is just overwhelming. I feel so welcomed; I might just puke rainbows and glitter, asshole." Emily fires back.

Sable waves. Her pink hair bounces as she does.

Unfazed by her snark, Lucian pulls out a bottle of Gatorade and fills a glass for Seraphina. "Oh, where are my manners?" he drawls, with fake sincerity. "Welcome to Chez Lucian, where the insults are as free as the booze, and the eye rolls are always on the house."

Emily doesn't skip a beat. "Aww...did someone piss in your blood bag this morning, Luci?" she says with a smirk. "Glad to see you've got your memories back, and you're not just some amnesic horny idiot anymore." Emily crosses her arms, her eyes gleaming with mischief. "You can drop the whole hospitable host act, golden boy. Not even your bougie-ass Gatorade can make the bullshit you're serving any easier to swallow. So, what's next on the agenda? You gonna wow us with your stash of stale-as-fuck snacks, too?"

Lucian grins and winks. "Looks like someone woke up with an extra-large serving of bitch flakes," he retorts. "Congrats on the upgrade from regular bitch to supreme bitch—really suits you.

"As for the snacks, I'll have you know my stash is top-fucking-notch. But I wouldn't want to overwhelm your delicate sensibilities with anything too bold or exciting. Wouldn't want you to choke on something other than your own bitchy remarks, now would we?"

"I'm confused," Seraphina murmurs. "Are they...always like this?"

She looks utterly lost by their exchange.

I can't help but laugh. "Oh, honey. This is just their twisted way of bonding. It's like watching a verbal sparring match—intense but oddly fascinating."

Emily snorts, taking a swig of her coffee. "Please, as if I'd ever bond with this overgrown man-child. I have standards."

Lucian clutches his chest theatrically. "Ouch, Em. You wound me deeply. And here I thought we had something special—a connection forged in the hallowed halls of sarcasm and bad puns. Guess I'll just have to drown my sorrows in more witty comebacks and ridiculous hijinks."

"In your dreams, DeadBoy," Emily retorts, rolling her eyes.

I notice Lucian stiffening, clearing his throat, and mimicking what Rhyland did to me. He swoops Seraphina up off her chair and sits her on his lap, lightly kissing her neck.

Emily looks confused, and I suddenly realize I haven't introduced Seraphina yet. Shit, I'm terrible at this. "Emily, this is Seraphina—my guardian angel—and Lucian's mate."

Emily nearly chokes on her coffee, wiping her chin as it dribbles down. "Hold up, rewind. Lucian's *what* now? *Mate?* As in, 'till death do us part, forever and ever, amen' kind of mate?"

Lucian grins, a smug look on his face. "That's right, Rainbow Brite. This angelic goddess has won the grand prize: Yours truly, in all my devilishly handsome glory. I know, I know—try to keep a lid on that envy. Green's not your color."

Seraphina smiles, and I swear the whole room gets a little brighter. "It's lovely to meet you, Emily. Dani has told me so much about you."

Still looking shell-shocked, Emily gestures to the seat next to her. "Oh, honey, I am so sorry. Come over here, and I'll protect you from this walking, talking bad decision."

Lucian scoffs, "Moi? A bad decision? I'm the best decision anyone could ever make. I'm like the personification of a good life choice."

Emily snorts. "Please. You're about as good a life choice as a tattoo on your face that says 'No Regrets.' Seraphina, sweetie, blink twice if you need me to stage a daring escape."

Seraphina giggles, snuggling deeper into Lucian's embrace. "That's very kind of you, Emily, but I assure you, I'm quite content where I am."

"Aww, what's the matter?" Lucian taunts. "Feeling a little left out? Hey, I'm sure if you keep stirring that cauldron of yours, you'll conjure up a halfway decent lay someday. Maybe a nice goblin or a particularly well-endowed toad."

"Hmmm... what was it you said a while back? It's right on the tip of my tongue," Emily muses, feigning ignorance before turning to Sable. "Help me out here, Sable. What was that delightful little nickname again?"

Sable chimes in with a grin, "Semen Demon, wasn't it?" before giggling.

"Alright, alright, put a cork in it, you two," Lucian interjects, his voice strained as he tries to regain some semblance of control over the situation. "As much as I'd love to continue this thrilling trip down memory lane, we've got bigger issues. You know, the whole 'fate of the world hanging in the balance, Thanos is coming, we're all gonna die' thing? Ring any bells?"

But Emily and Sable are having none of it, their laughter only growing louder and more raucous at Lucian's obvious discomfort. "What's the matter, *Semen Demon*?" Emily manages to choke out between laughs. "Afraid we'll spill your dirty little secrets in front of your angelic mate?"

Lucian shoots them a withering glare, his cheeks flushed with anger and mortification. "Oh, *ha ha*, very funny," he deadpans. "You two should take this show on the road. 'The Cackling Witches of Comedy,' coming to a theater near you. Tickets start at 'go fuck yourselves.'"

Bless her pure little heart, Seraphina looks utterly baffled by the whole exchange. "I don't understand," she murmurs, her brow furrowed in confusion. "What's a *Semen Demon?* Is that some supernatural creature I haven't heard of?"

Rhyland groans, his head thudding against my back in exasperation.

The question only sends Emily and Sable into another fit of hysterics, tears streaming down their faces as they cling to each other for support. Lucian, meanwhile, looks like he's about two seconds away from launching himself out the nearest window.

"No, baby girl," he grits out through clenched teeth, his voice strained with the effort to maintain his composure. "It's just a stupid joke that Emily and Sable think is hilarious because they have the sense of humor of a pair of twelve-year-old girls hopped up on pixie sticks and Mountain Dew."

I snicker at the absurdity of it all, my laughter bubbling in my throat despite my best efforts to hold it back. "Alright, alright," I manage to choke out, holding up my hands placatingly. "Let's all take a deep breath and try to focus, shall we?"

I will have to talk to Emily and get to the bottom of this mystery later.

After a couple of hours and three pots of coffee later, Emily has us all caught up. According to Emily, the werewolves have claimed four 'areas' and are now glorified guard dogs here in Washington State. Multiple packs throughout the US—California, Florida, the Midwest, Texas, New York, and Colorado.

Basically, all over the fucking place.

I hate these assholes—no good comes from them, and now they're everywhere, like a flea infestation.

Not to mention the same amount, if not more, in witch covens.

"Well, color me surprised," I drawl, rolling my eyes. "I already know who runs Area Twelve. What's their deal anyway?"

"Once Azrael took over vampire command..." I vividly remember Emily telling us this when we returned from Luminara: "he's given werewolves free rein to claim these territories, which also gives Azrael more power as the vampire council has been wiped out." Emily explains.

Rhyland's head snaps up, his eyes narrowing. "You're sure about this?"

"Yup. It was later discovered after you all got sucked into Narnia..."

"Aquaria." I correct her.

"Whatever—point is, after you took your little underwater sabbatical, it came out that Azrael murdered all the council members so he could seize control. Their bodies, or what was left of them, were found up in the mountains. Not exactly a pretty picture, if you catch my drift."

I cringe inwardly at the mental image of when Adrian died, the way his body froze up like a cold statue. A shiver runs through me at the memory, and Rhyland squeezes me, picking up on my unease.

Lucian leans back in his chair, his face a mask of disbelief. "Hold up, hold up. Are you telling me that the mortal law enforcement just sat back and twiddled their thumbs while this shit went down? What, did they all take a collective vacation to 'Not My Problem'-ville?"

"Not really." Emily starts, her voice laced with frustration. "I mean, yes, there are still laws and shit, but Azrael has too much power and influence for the mortal authorities to go against him. Everyone played nice and followed the rules when the vampire council was around to keep things in check, but now..."

"They're too chickenshit to stand up to him," I finish, my voice flat. "Azrael's got them all by the balls, and they're too afraid to even squeak in protest."

Lucian lets out a low whistle, shaking his head. "Well, isn't this just a regular shit show of epic proportions? Azrael's running around playing murder-happy dictator, the werewolves are marking their territory like a bunch of incontinent chihuahuas, and the humans are apparently on a permanent 'see no evil, hear no evil' sabbatical. Fucking wonderful."

Emily nods, her face grim. "It's a goddamn mess, that's for sure. But what I want to know is, what the hell are we gonna do about it? We can't just sit around with our thumbs up our asses while Azrael and his furry minions and witch bitches run roughshod over everything."

Azrael has the entire supernatural army at his beck and call. And now, he's got the damn Soul Stone to boot. So not only did we beef up his power stockpile while we were gallivanting in other realms, but we also went ahead and served his shadow power back to him on a silver platter.

Fuck. Me.

I sigh, rubbing my temples in a vain attempt to stave off the headache I feel brewing. "Honestly? I have no clue. But one thing's for sure—we can't let this continue. We have to find a way to stop Azrael and restore some semblance of order before everything goes to hell in a handbasket."

Rhyland nods, his jaw clenched. "Damn right. And the first step is getting that Soul Stone back. Once we have that, we can start working on a plan to take down Azrael and his little empire of bullshit."

"No," I state plainly, my voice cutting through the room like a knife.

Rhyland and everyone else freeze, their eyes snapping to me as if I've just grown a second head. "We need to fix this by connecting with leaders and putting together another vampire council—one that we can trust and powerful enough to make a difference. We need to meet with the covens and the packs, get their heads in the game, and ensure they're on the right side of this fight. We take away Azrael's power from the inside and watch him crumble like a house of cards. Then, and only then, do we go after the stone and put an end to that bastard once and for all."

The silence is deafening, stretching for an eternity as everyone digests my words.

"Your strategic understanding is impressive, Little Huntress. Your plan shows wisdom beyond your years. I take some credit for your skills, but your talent and determination are all your own."

All heads swivel in Erik's direction like a bunch of meerkats on high alert as he enters the kitchen. He's rocking a pair of gray sweatpants and a blue T-shirt, looking like he just stepped out of a goddamn athleisure catalog. His silver hair is brushed and groomed to perfection, not a single strand out of place.

His silver eyes scan the area, taking in the scene before him with an intensity that would make lesser men quake in their boots. But me? I smirk because I know beneath that stoic exterior lies a heart of gold and a wicked sense of humor.

"Well..." I drawl. "Look who decided to grace us with his presence. Nice of you to join us, Erik. I was starting to think you'd fallen into a coma."

Erik walks by me, his hand resting on my shoulder in a gesture of support and affection, a rare display of emotion from the usually reserved vampire. I can't help but smile—feeling a warmth bloom in my chest at his subtle but meaningful gesture.

As Erik heads toward the cabinet, he calls out to Lucian, his voice laced with dry amusement. "Lucian, this most certainly calls for a drink. Where do you keep the libations in this place? Surely, you have a stash that lives up to the grandeur of this momentous occasion."

Lucian throws his hands up in exasperation. "Oh, I'm sorry, I didn't realize we were celebrating something. What occasion is that, Erik? The fact that you're trying to take credit for Dani's brilliance, or the fact that she just came up with a plan so foolproof even you can't find a way to poke holes in it?"

Erik looks over his shoulder, a smirk playing at the corner of his mouth. "Both, of course. As her mentor, I think I'm entitled to some reflected glory, don't you?"

LUCIAN

79

I t's been a couple of weeks since our little kitchen kumbaya session, and let me tell you, I've been busier than a one-legged man in an ass-kicking contest. I've been burning up the phone lines, calling every vampire and their undead mother across this godforsaken globe. You know, just catching up with old pals and shooting the shit about the latest apocalyptic shitstorm courtesy of everyone's favorite winged douchebag, Azrael. Or, as I like to call him, Azhole.

These fanged friends of mine have all heard about the epic clusterfuck we've got going on here in the good ol' US of A, and they've agreed to fly their pale asses over here for a little pow-wow. Time to get the band back together and form some sort of council because, apparently, that's what you do when the world's about to go tits up.

Oh, and let's not forget about the whole Karma situation. I've had to take a step back from that particular shitshow while we sort out this colossal goat rodeo. My main man and partner-in-crime, Andrew, is holding down the fort for me. He's like the Alfred to my Batman, minus the British accent and the killer butler skills. He's keeping the booze flowing and the party going while I'm off playing hero.

Plus, let's be real: I'm not quite ready to introduce Seraphina to the debauchery and mayhem of Karma. I don't want to scare off my innocent little angel cake with the sight of drunken frat boys doing body shots off of each other. I mean, can you imagine her sweet, angelic face amidst all the debauchery and questionable life choices? It'd be like throwing a baby bunny into a pack of hungry wolves. Not gonna happen, my friends. Not on my watch.

No, I'll ease her into that world slowly, like a gentleman. A gentleman who owns a nightclub full of sin and questionable decisions, but a gentleman nonetheless.

Meanwhile, the Witchy Twins have set off on their own little adventure, probably to go braid each other's hair and talk about their feelings. Just kidding, they're actually off to rally the covens because now that Rainbow Brite has leveled up to become the most badass witch in history, she's ready to start her own little coven. Talk about a power move.

Erik, the brooding bastard, has fucked off to reconnect with an old furry friend. And no, I don't mean he's into that kinky shit. He will see if he can get some of the wolf packs on board with our little save-the-world shindig.

Once we all settled, I handed the goods to Dani and Rhyland—the tomes Seraphina and I heisted from the Atlantean Ruins. Man, you should've seen their faces: part shock, part glee, like kids who just found out their Halloween candy stash is twice as big as they thought.

Dani practically did a happy dance when she saw the Book of Shadows as she'd just hit the supernatural jackpot. But their curiosity was piqued even more when they saw the other book we grabbed—the Book of Asgard and the Norse Gods.

Rhyland gave it the side-eye, looking like he'd just found a turd in his cereal. "Why the hell was this book down in the Ruins?" he wondered out loud, clearly weirded out by its unexpected location. It's not every day you find ancient Norse mythology chilling in an underwater tomb, after all. But hey, who am I to question the crazy shit that pops up on our adventures?

As for the lovebirds, Dani and Rhyland? They've been playing mad scientist, trying to cook up some potion to mask Dani and Seraphina's scent. Because having a delicious-smelling mate is like wearing a fucking neon sign that says "Bite Me" to every fang-having motherfucker out there.

Dani's been going stir-crazy, cooped up in the house, and working non-stop on this little science project. But hallelujah, praise the lord and pass the ammunition because they finally cracked the code! The only downside? I can't smell my sweet little cinnamon roll when she drinks it, which is a real boner killer. It lasts about four hours for each dose—If we ever got separated, I'd be shit out of luck trying to sniff her out. Sure, we've got our little cosmic connection, but it's the principle of the thing. I need all systems go when it comes to my angel cake.

Speaking of my insatiable little angel, Seraphina. Holy fucking shit, this girl is curious with a capital "C," and it's got my pants tighter than a nun's asshole. She's always asking me these naughty little questions, wanting to try out all sorts of kinky shit. So, being the fucking genius that I am, I set her up with her very own computer and introduced her to the beautiful world of PornHub. You know, for educational purposes.

I just showed her how to type in the search bar and let her go to town. Watching her face as she discovers the joys of internet porn? Priceless. I'm talking wide eyes, flushed cheeks, and a jaw that's about to hit the floor. It's like watching a kid in a candy store if the candy store was full of dicks and pussy.

Class is in session, and I'm about to give my angel a crash course in carnal knowledge that'll make the Kama Sutra look like a fucking children's book.

I'm just chilling in our room, sipping on some bourbon and minding my own damn business, when Seraphina drops a bombshell that nearly makes me spit out my drink.

"What's pegging?" she asks, all wide-eyed and innocent.

It's like a record-scratch moment. I jump up faster than a cat on a hot tin roof to see what the hell she's looking at, and lo and behold, there it is: 'pegging' in all its glory, right at the top of most searched PornHub history.

I can't help but laugh my ass off. "Baby girl, my new safeword is Meatloaf—I would do anything for love, but I won't do that."

Seraphina tilts her head, her brow furrowing in that adorable way that makes me want to eat her up. "Safeword?" she asks, her voice all sweet and curious.

Man alive, how did I get so fucking lucky with this adorable, innocent little cinnamon roll?

"Yeah, Cupcake," I explain, trying not to grin like a fucking idiot. "It's a word you pick when you want to stop during sex or sexy times." I waggle my eyebrows suggestively.

She bites her lip, looking at me through those long, luscious lashes. "I would never want you to stop," she says sweetly, her voice all soft and full of promise.

Fuuuuck, this girl is going to be my death. I groan, feeling my dick spring to attention like a soldier at reveille. If only she knew the kind of depraved, twisted shit I'm into... But I'm trying to be a gentleman here, taking things slow for my precious little angel cake.

Don't get me wrong, I'd love nothing more than to corrupt her six ways to Sunday, but I've got to ease her into it, you know? Can't just dive into the deep end of the perv pool without some floaties and a safety lesson first.

But damn, the way she looks at me, all innocent and trusting... It's enough to make a man want to fall to his knees and worship at her feet. And trust me, I plan to do plenty of worshipping.

Before I can even process what's happening, Seraphina clicks play on the video, and holy shit, it's like watching a train wreck in slow motion. There's this chick with a dildo the size of a fucking baseball bat, just going to town on some dude's ass like she's trying to strike oil. And the guy? He's moaning and groaning like he's having the time of his goddamn life.

Seraphina's eyes are as wide as saucers, and her cheeks are flushed a delicious shade of pink. But that's not what hits me like a ton of bricks—it's her arousal, slamming into me like a fucking freight train. I can't take my eyes off her as she watches this chick absolutely destroy this guy's backdoor.

"Can we...Would you like to try that, Sparky?" she asks, her voice all breathy and full of wonder. "He looks like he enjoys it..."

Jesus, tap-dancing Christ, I think my brain just went offline.

Okay, so here's the thing: back in my wild and crazy vampire youth, I had my fair share of experimentation with the same sex. But I was always more of a pitcher than a catcher. Sure, I tried bottoming a few times, and let me tell you, that prostate orgasm is like a whole new level of fucking nirvana. But it's been centuries since I've even considered taking a trip down that particular memory lane.

But for Seraphina? Shit, I'd let her do just about anything to me, including turning my ass into her own personal playground.

"Really, Cupcake?" a shit-eating grin spreading across my face. "You want to rail my ass like a fucking champ?"

She nods eagerly, her eyes shining with curiosity and lust. "I want to make you feel good, Lucian," her voice all soft and sincere. "I want to give you that kind of pleasure."

Slap my ass and call me Cupid, I am so fucking in love, and I'm about to prove it by letting this sweet, innocent angel peg me like a fucking tent stake.

"Phina-baby. You already make me feel good. But..." I purr, pulling her close and nuzzling her neck. "If that's what you want to try, then who am I to deny you?"

Seraphina giggles into my neck, and I inhale her intoxicating scent like a man starved for air. No weird-ass potions masking her natural aroma today so that I can bask in every delectable note of her essence. She threads her fingers through my hair, all soft and sensual, and starts peppering my neck with kisses that feel like fucking heaven.

I can't help but groan at the feel of her mouth on my skin, my body responding like a goddamn Pavlovian dog. We've been going at it like horny teenagers the past couple of weeks, fucking like it's an Olympic sport, and we're gunning for the gold. And Seraphina? She's a fucking insatiable minx. It's like she can never get enough of my dick, and hell, if that isn't the best kind of mate a guy could ask for.

My cock is perpetually hard, ready to go at a moment's notice, and she's always more than willing to take it for a ride. Sometimes I wake up with my dick already buried deep inside her, like my body can't resist the magnetic pull of her sweet, tight heat. One slight move, and she's awake, ready to rock my world all over again.

"Tell you what..." I murmur, pulling back to gaze into her mesmerizing golden eyes. Before I can even finish my thought, she's crashing her lips against mine, her tongue delving into my mouth like she's trying to taste my very soul.

And just like that, all coherent thought flies right out the fucking window. I grab her perfect, round ass, squeezing those delectable cheeks as I pull her flush against me, kissing her back with a fervor that borders on feral.

She's wearing these sinfully sexy silk shorts that ride so high her ass is practically hanging out, begging for my attention—the spaghetti strap silk tank top, clinging to her curves like a second skin. I can see her hard nipples straining against the fabric, feel them pressing into my chest, and it's enough to make a man lose his goddamn mind.

It takes every ounce of willpower I possess to resist her intoxicating kisses, but I manage it somehow. "We will definitely try the pegging thing, pinky promise," I say with a wink, my mind already conjuring up all sorts of deliciously dirty scenarios. "But tonight, I have other plans for my beautiful girl."

Plans that I've been dreaming up since this ethereal goddess walked into my life and turned it upside down in the best possible way.

"Oh?" Seraphina asks, her voice all breathy and full of desire. She sucks on my bottom lip, and I swear to God, my eyes nearly roll back into my fucking skull from the sheer pleasure of it. "What plans do you have for me, Sparky?" she purrs.

Hot fucking damn, the way she says *Sparky* should be illegal in all fifty states and at least a dozen foreign countries. It's like audio porn, straight-up eargasmic seduction that has my cock straining against my pants like it's trying to stage a fucking jailbreak.

"Oh, Cupcake," I groan, my voice low and rough with lust. "You have no idea what you're in for. I'm going to make you feel things you never even knew were possible, take you to heights of pleasure that will ruin you for anyone else."

Seraphina shudders in my arms, a soft moan escaping her lips, and I know I have her right where I want her. "So what do you say, beautiful?" I murmur, nipping at her earlobe. "Ready to let me rock your world in ways you never dreamed of?"

Seraphina lets out a delighted squeal, her eyes wide with surprise and excitement.

I lean in and press a tender kiss to her cheek, fighting the overwhelming urge to say 'fuck it' to my carefully laid plans and just ravish her right here and now. But I resist because I'm a man on a mission, and I'll be damned if I let my dick derail the epic night of romance and seduction I've got in store for my girl.

She runs her fingers through my facial hair—the rugged beard I've been growing since we set foot in Aquaria. Seraphina seems to be digging the Lumberjack look. "I can't wait," she purrs, with anticipation. "But first, I want to try something." Her golden eyes twinkle with a mix of innocence and a hint of mischief, like a choir girl with a secret wild side. I can practically see the halo tilting off her head, making way for a pair of horns. Oh, this is gonna be good.

And just like that, my sweet-as-cherry-pie Seraphina is on her knees, and I'm pretty sure my heart stops for a solid three seconds at the sight. And holy Mother of fuck, my pants suddenly feel two sizes too small as she unleashes my rigid cock from its cotton prison. Her golden locks are flowing like a damn waterfall, and I just can't help myself. I gather that silky hair into a ponytail, giving it a gentle tug to tilt her head back. It's our little game, and she loves it.

It's game on, folks.

"You want a snack, Cupcake?" I ask, my voice cracking like a pubescent boy going through voice changes. Because, let's be real, Seraphina drives me insane.

"Mmm, hmm," she hums. "I want to know what you taste like, Sparky." And with that, she takes my entire length into her warm, wet mouth.

"Holy fuuuu..." my knees almost buckle at the sensation of her lips and tongue working their magic.

Sweet merciful crap on a cracker, her first time giving head, and she's blowing me away! Literally, my mind is fucking blown to smithereens, and I'm pretty sure I've forgotten how to blink. Her PornHub tutorials have leveled her up from novice to ninja, and I'm reveling in the sweet, sweet sensations she's bestowing upon my dangly bits.

I never pressured her into anything 'cause I'm all about that consent life and letting her explore her desires at her own damn pace. But when she's offering to take a stroll down Blow Job Boulevard, who the hell am I to say no?

Her mouth is like a pleasure portal, sending shockwaves of delight straight to my core. She's an angel sent from above to deliver me to cloud nine, and I love every delicious stroke. She's exploring like a damn Columbus of cocks, and I am here for this naughty voyage of oral delights! So bring on the throat massage, 'cause this girl is taking me to cock-sucking heaven, and I'm never coming back!

"Je-*zus*...." I groan. "You like that, Cupcake?"

Her beautiful gold eyes look up at me, my cock buried in her throat. She gulps around me, nodding.

She's got me wired tighter than a caffeine addict, and I'm teetering on the edge of orgasmic bliss in record time. Someone call the Guinness Book of World Records because this girl is rewriting the damn manual.

She's making these little choking sounds, so I grip her ponytail tighter, giving it a little yank, and holy shit, she takes me in even more, like she's trying to inhale my damn soul through my dick.

I feel myself sinking deeper into her throat, and I'm pretty sure I've died and gone to heaven. This girl's got skills that would make the devil blush.

No gag reflex? Check.

Suction that could rival a goddamn Dyson? Double check.

She's working me like a damn maestro, and I am loving every second of this wild ride.

She pulls off with a pop, and before I can catch my breath, she hits me with a request that makes my eyes roll back so far I can practically see my own cerebellum.

"Lucian, choke me," she whispers, her eyes watering slightly, and oh sweet mother of fuck, that's it. That's my kryptonite. I thrust my hips, and she takes the whole damn length of me, her spit dripping down my shaft, her eyes rolling back in pure pleasure.

"Fuck yes, baby girl," I grunt, feeling the tension coil tighter and tighter in my balls. "You want me to choke that gorgeous throat with my cock?"

She moans, and the sound vibrates through me like a thunderbolt, sending sparks of electricity straight to my groin. Her spit is gathering at the corners of her mouth, shining like a badge of honor—just the way I like it—nice and sloppy.

"Ungh...fuck, yes. Just like that, Cupcake." I thrust faster—harder. "Just fuck...ing...like...that." I'm gasping, unable to breathe.

Am I hyperventilating?

I can't hold back anymore. My cock pounds into her throat as she takes it like a damn champion.

I'm losing my shit at this point. My body's buzzing, and my knees are about as stable as Jell-O. I'm pretty sure galaxies are exploding in my head, stars colliding, and nebulae forming from the sheer force of my impending orgasm.

"Phina-baby, I'm gonna—holy shhh-it, I'm gonna—" I choke out, my voice ragged. "GOD, FUUCK—"

I'm coming down her throat like a volcano erupting, screaming her name like she's the cure to all my ailments. She swallows around me, milking me for every last drop, and I'm left a panting, sweaty, satisfied mess. My knees are weak, my heart's pounding like a jackhammer, and my vision's so blurry I can't even see straight.

Holy fucking Mother of Moses, this girl owns me, body and soul.

She's gazing at me that'd make the devil blush; her lips curved in a mischievous smile that's got my dick twitching in her hand. And then she goes and wipes her mouth seductively, muttering sensually, "Mmm, yummy."

Fuck yes, it was yummy. But you know what else is yummy? The taste of her lips, which is precisely what I claim as I crash my mouth against hers, sliding my tongue into her mouth to taste the sweet combination of her and me. It's like the world's most erotic cocktail, and I'm already drunk on it. My hands splay on her ass, pulling her close, and I can feel my body screaming to bend her over and have my way with her.

I reluctantly step back, putting some space between us before I forget all about self-control and go caveman on her delectable ass. Because self-control is my middle name. Well, okay, it's not. But a guy can pretend, right?

I have to save something for later, so I tease with a wink, and my signature Lucian smolder. "I don't wanna keep you waiting, Cupcake. If I recall correctly, you and the girls have appointments today."

And oh, for the love of fuck, the way she looks up at me with those doe eyes, all innocence and earnestness, "Was it okay, Sparky? Did I do it right?"

Oh, my-lanta—this girl!

Was it okay? DID SHE DO IT RIGHT?

I can barely stand! I'm pretty sure I've forgotten how to breathe. "Sweetheart," I rasp, my voice hoarse with desire. "That was the best damn thing I've ever experienced in my entire undead existence, second only to being mated to your glorious self."

She's blushing, biting her lip, and I just want to eat her up, lick by lick. This girl has me wrapped around her tiny finger, and she knows it. But who am I to complain? I'm just a helpless vampire in the clutches of her sinful mouth magic, and I'm loving every damn second of it. Hallelujah and pass the ointment, 'cause I'm pretty sure I've got whiplash from the pleasure express.

With a giggle and a swish of her hair, she's off to the closet, no doubt to change into something equally mouthwatering. But I'll be damned if I let my imagination run wild with those thoughts.

Got a plan for tonight, and I ain't gonna let my horniness derail that bad boy.

I just had the best mouth orgasm of my entire undead existence, and I can't wait for the next round.

Bring it on, Cupcake; this sparky's ready to set you on fire.

DANICA

80

I'm standing on the balcony, the stunning view of Lake Washington stretched out before me, but I can't even appreciate it. My nerves are wound tighter than a spring as I dial Damon's number, my heart doing a drum solo in my chest.

The phone rings, and then my baby bro's voice comes through, "Hello?"

I'm hit with a wave of emotion so strong that I'm afraid I might start ugly crying right here on this fancy-ass balcony. "Hey, little Demon," my voice wavering slightly as I use the nickname I've called him since we were kids. The familiarity of it feels like a balm on my frayed nerves.

"Holy shit. If it isn't my long-lost sister," Damon exclaims, his tone a perfect mix of surprise and sarcasm. "How did your little save-the-world trip to Ethiopia go?"

Wait, is that really where Emily said I was? Ugh, I will have to chat with that girl about her cover stories.

"It was good," I lie through my teeth, hoping he can't hear the guilt in my voice. "How are things going for you?"

"Can't complain. Just working at McKinley & Associates," he replies before his voice becomes somber. "You know I sold mom and dad's house, right? After—"

The lump in my throat feels like it's the size of a grapefruit. I close my eyes, the memories of their brutal murder still fresh and painful. "Yeah, I know. Emily told me—it's okay," I assure him, wanting him to know I understand.

"So, what's new with you? Are you back now, for good?" Damon asks, a hint of hopefulness creeping into his tone.

"Yeah, just a lot has happened. My apartment had a gas leak or something," I fib, hating myself for lying to him. But it's better than dragging him into this supernatural shit show. "So I had to evacuate—I'm staying with some friends now on Mercer Island."

"Mercer Island? Damn," Damon chuckles, impressed. "Ritzy-ass friends, you got there."

"Yeah, something like that," I deflect, eager to change the subject. "So, are you doing okay though? I know we didn't talk much after... you know—mom and dad."

Damon and I might indeed be adopted, but we both have a Ph.D. in burying our feelings and throwing ourselves into work to avoid the pain.

"Yeah..." he sighs, "I'm just keeping busy. All this supernatural stuff is hella weird, though; so much has changed here since you left. All these werewolves, witches, and now a new vampire leader or whatever." He pauses, "You know I hate all these freaks."

I wince at his words. Just like my parents, Damon despises anything supernatural.

"Yeah, tell me about it," I force a laugh, trying to lighten the mood. "Hey, if you're up for it, maybe you can spare some time and come for a visit? There's plenty of room here..." I trail off, hoping he'll say yes.

I'd just need to keep my fanged friends under wraps for a while, and Emily and Sable would have to dial back on their magical mischief. Piece of cake, right?

There's a pause, and for a moment, I'm afraid he will decline. But then, "Yeah, I would like that, actually. I have some things to tie up here for this week, but maybe I could come out next week or something?" His voice softens, a hint of vulnerability shining through. "I miss you, Dani-bear."

My heart swells at the nickname, a smile spreading across my face. "I miss you, too, Little Demon."

Damon laughs, the sound warm and familiar. "Alright, I will call you next week, and then you can send me the address."

"Got it. I will talk to you then. Stay safe, okay?" I say, trying to pour all my love and concern into those few words.

"I will. Talk to you soon. Love ya, sis."

"Love you, too," I whisper, my heart feeling lighter than it has in weeks.

As I hang up, I can't help but feel a mix of excitement and apprehension. It'll be so good to see Damon again, but I know I'll have to be careful about what I say and do around him. The last thing I want is to put him in danger.

But for now, I'm just going to bask in knowing that my little bro is safe and I'll see him soon.

And if I have to spin a few more tales to keep him in the dark?

Well, that's just what big sisters do.

After hanging up, I run back into our room to get dressed—I'm so freaking ecstatic that I can barely contain myself. We girls are about to hit the road for our much-anticipated spa day. I booked our appointments earlier this week; today is finally the day.

Seraphina and I can walk amongst the population with our secret potion. Sable helped Rhyland and I concoct it so we could use it without fear of being attacked by our scent alone. We can finally strut our stuff without worrying about some hungry vampire or supernatural freak trying to take a bit out of us.

A whole new world of possibilities has opened up, and I am here for it.

The shit tastes like *ass*, but It's a small price to pay for safety.

I've hidden my crown with just a thought—no need to flash the bling—and Lucian has the shard of the Soul Stone locked up tight in his massive vault beneath the mansion.

I can't help but chuckle at the thought of anyone trying to steal that shit. I immediately jump to that epic scene from *Fast and the Furious*, where Dom and Bryan jack the vault using those souped-up Dodge Chargers.

I can picture it now: a couple of dumbass supernatural thieves trying to recreate that stunt, only to find out the hard way that Lucian's mansion is a hell of a lot more secure than my measly apartment and cheap safe.

I shake my head, banishing the ridiculous thought—as if anyone would be stupid enough to try and pull a stunt like that.

Then again, in this crazy world of ours, anything's possible.

The guys have something planned for us tonight—not together, of course. Rhyland has our date night planned, and Lucian has something up his sleeve for Seraphina. I can only imagine what those two have cooked up. Knowing Rhyland, it's probably something equal parts romantic and badass. And Lucian? Let's say Seraphina better be prepared for a wild ride.

Bless her witchy heart. Emily has been progressing with a few covens. They plan to set up a meeting within a week to discuss joining hands. I've got to hand it to her; she's taking this witch role more seriously than I imagined. Then again, when you're basically a walking, talking clan of witches yourself, I guess you don't have much choice.

Sable, our resident supernatural Nancy Drew, has been a godsend. She's been keeping tabs on all the paranormal beings like she's got a crystal ball glued to her forehead. Azrael is still, indeed, trying to create his stupid fucking ritual to pull Moretemis over prematurely, but so far, no dice. I don't think he knows we've returned, which is good for us. Let him think we're still off gallivanting in some other realm while we get our ducks in a row.

Lucian's place is, in fact, off the radar, as he promised. We're talking state-of-the-art security, more cameras than a reality TV show, and enough magical protection to make Hogwarts look like a cardboard fort. Sable and Emily's unbreakable spells locked his place tighter than a military base. Seriously, I think even a cockroach would have trouble getting in here without the proper clearance.

Before he left, Erik helped Lucian put all the security measures in place, and we have guards everywhere on top of cameras. Erik, of course, made sure to do background checks on all security, and Lucian, being the general hustler, compelled them to do as they were told. At any other time, I would be against this mind control, but right now, with the stakes so high, we can't take any chances. We need everyone on the same page, even if that means using supernatural persuasion to get there.

I finally feel safe and can breathe for a second. I haven't been able to relax in what feels like years. It's like a weight has been lifted off my shoulders, and I can finally take a moment to just...be.

Lucian surprised me with the tombs he and Seraphina pulled from the Ruins. I was not expecting them to pull that out of their asses, but they did, and I couldn't be happier. We finally have the last book of the Seven Realms, and when it's time to delve into it, we have it. Not to mention the book of Norse Gods—I can't wait to sit down with Seraphina and dig into that knowledge.

Christmas came early, and Santa brought us the gift of ancient wisdom.

Aunt Flow reared her ugly head, and I have to be honest, I was sad. I cried and cried while Rhyland held me close, kissing me and reassuring me while my hormones were all over the place. He, too, was on the verge of tears—us both knowing what we knew in the back of our minds was impossible. I know Rhyland wants a family—a baby—as do I.

But vampires can't procreate.

It's unheard of.

Oh, and let's not forget the little IUD situation I've got going on down there! Yup, still rockin' that contraceptive bling. Funny thing is, I don't think Rhyland even knows about it. I mean, I probably should've mentioned it during our little "heat of the moment" chat, but somehow it just didn't come up. Maybe I'm a teensy bit worried he'll be pissed at me for not sharing that tidbit sooner.

I can just picture his reaction: "You've got a what in your where now?" Might be a tad miffed that I kept it on the DL, but hey, a girl's gotta have her secrets, right?

Ah well, one bombshell at a time, I always say!

Whatever that Reflection Pool meant doesn't change anything. I still love Rhyland with everything in my heart, body, and soul; nothing will ever change that, not even being able to have a family. I will gladly take him and him alone for the rest of my life. He is my everything, and I wouldn't trade him for all the babies in the world.

I mean, what was I thinking—that his magical vampire spunk would somehow Houdini its way past my trusty womb defender? Keeping this little plastic pal on security detail might not be such a bad idea right now—can you imagine trying to fight off an evil horde with a baby bump? Talk about a tactical disadvantage!

Once we've kicked ass, defied the odds, and saved the Seven Realms, I'll clue my Viking vamp in on my little secret. Then we can seriously start working on making that baby.

"Oh my god, this is the shit," Emily moans to my right as the nail tech works her magic on my feet. She sounds like she's one foot rub away from nirvana.

I grin. "Yeah, we haven't done this in forever. I'd almost forgotten what it feels like to be pampered instead of pummeled."

"What color should I get?" Seraphina asks from my other side, her voice sweet as honey. The massage chair is digging into my muscles like it's trying to find buried treasure.

"Hmm, what color do you like?" I ask, turning to her with a smile.

Seraphina purses her lips, deep in thought. "I'm not sure. I've never had the opportunity to experiment with nail polish before. What do you think would look good on me?"

I can't help but smile at her earnestness. It's easy to forget sometimes that Seraphina is still new to this whole "being human" thing. She's like a blank canvas, waiting to be painted with all the world's colors.

"I think a nice pastel blue would look lovely on you," I say, squeezing her hand. "It would bring out the color of your eyes and give you an ethereal vibe. Plus, it would match that cute little sundress you bought the other day."

"Ooh, getting all nostalgic on us, are you?" Emily chimes in. "Why don't you go for something a little more daring? Like, I don't know, blood red? Really embrace that whole 'angel dating a vampire' aesthetic."

Seraphina's face lights up like a Christmas tree, and she nods enthusiastically. "Blood red it is, then! Thank you, Emily. And I like your color a lot, Dani."

I shrug, trying to play it cool even as a warm feeling blooms in my chest. "What can I say? I'm a regular fashion guru. Just call me the supernatural version of Tim Gunn."

Emily snorts, rolling her eyes. "Please. The only thing you're a guru of is sarcasm and bad puns. But I guess even a broken clock is right twice a day."

"Hey, I resent that!" I say, giving her a playful smack. "My puns are top-notch, thank you very much. You're just jealous of my wit and charm."

"Yeah, that's definitely it," Emily deadpans. "I'm just green with envy over here. If only I could be as clever and witty as the great Dani Pierce."

Sable, who has been quietly enjoying her own pedicure, pipes up with a grin. "I don't know, Emily. I think Dani's onto something. Her puns are pretty *pun*-derful, if you ask me."

I let out a bark of laughter. "See? Sable gets it. She understands the art of the pun."

Emily shakes her head, a small smile tugging at the corners of her mouth. "You two are impossible. I don't know how I put up with you."

Watching our exchange with amused confusion, Seraphina chimes in with a knowing smile. "I think it's because, deep down, you love them. Even if they do drive you a little crazy sometimes."

Emily sputters, her cheeks turning a delightful shade of pink. "I... well... I mean... oh, shut up. You're one to talk, Miss 'I'm dating the walking, talking embodiment of sarcasm and bad jokes.'"

Seraphina shrugs, a serene smile on her face. "What can I say? I have a thing for charming rogues with hearts of gold."

I can't help but laugh at the look of outrage on Emily's face. "Face it, Em. We're all a bunch of lovable weirdos. And you wouldn't have it any other way."

Emily sighs, a reluctant smile spreading across her face. "Yeah, yeah. I guess you're right. But if any of you tell Lucian I said that, I'll deny it until my dying day."

We all laugh, the sound echoing through the spa like a symphony of joy and friendship. And in this moment, surrounded by the people I love most, I feel a sense of peace wash over me.

After a much-needed Brazilian wax (because who the hell has time for landscaping when you're trying to save the world?) and a massage that made me feel like I was floating on a cloud of pure bliss, we finally returned to the mansion. I feel like a million fucking bucks—and considering the price tag on some of these spa treatments, I probably should.

I park Lucian's ridiculously expensive, blacked-out Bentley Continental GT (which he so graciously let me borrow) and can't help but marvel at the sheer beauty of this beast. It felt good to get behind the wheel again, even if it was to chauffeur our little girl gang around town.

As we enter the mansion, I make a beeline for our room. Seraphina immediately starts searching for Lucian. Emily and Sable, on the other hand, make themselves at home in the living room, ready to binge-watch whatever trashy reality show they can find.

I grin as I watch them go their separate ways. It's funny how we still find time for the little things even amid all this supernatural chaos. Brazilian waxes, fancy cars, and trashy TV—it's the stuff that keeps us sane.

Well, as sane as a group of supernaturally-charged women can be, anyway.

I am mentally picking out which expensive ass outfit I will wear for my date night with Rhyland. Maybe that little black dress that hugs my curves in all the right places? Or the red one that makes me look like a goddamn femme fatale?

Decisions, decisions.

I fling open the door, and my jaw nearly hits the floor. There, sitting on the bed with a sexy-as-sin grin on his face, is Rhyland, looking like he just stepped out of a goddamn GQ photoshoot. Next to him is a huge black box with a pink ribbon, and I swear, if my ovaries could talk, they'd scream, "YES, PLEASE!"

He's rocking a dark blue tuxedo that fits him like a second skin, hugging every delicious curve of his muscular frame. His beard is trimmed to perfection, framing his chiseled jawline like a work of art. And don't even get me started on his hair—freshly cut and shaved on the sides, it's like he's channeling some sexy, brooding vampire James Bond.

Unable to resist the allure of this man any longer, I launch myself at him, tackling him onto the bed in a flurry of limbs and giggles. He laughs, the sound rich and warm as he brushes my freshly washed and blown-out hair out of my face. "Hi, Angel. Did you have a good time?"

I can't stop smiling, my cheeks hurting from the sheer force of my grin. "Yes, so needed. Girls' day, the spa... it was pure bliss."

"Good. I got you something," he says with a sexy smirk, motioning to the box.

I practically squeal with delight, kissing his lips before I can stop myself. I mean, can you blame me? The man is a walking, talking temptation, and I am but a weak, weak woman.

Finally, I tear myself away long enough to grab the box, my hands practically shaking with excitement. It's been so long since I got a present, and I almost forgot what it feels like to be spoiled like this.

I tear into that box like a kid on Christmas morning, my fingers practically trembling with anticipation. Rhyland props himself up on his elbow, watching me with amusement and anticipation that's sexy as hell.

As I lift the lid and peel the delicate tissue paper back, I swear my heart stops for a second. Nestled in a sea of tissue, is quite possibly the most breathtaking dress I've ever seen.

I let out a gasp that's somewhere between a squeal and a moan, slipping off the bed to pull it out in all its glory.

Holy. Fucking. Shit.

The dress is a masterpiece of silk and lace, a deep, rich burgundy that practically shimmers in the light.

It's a floor-length gown with a fitted bodice that looks like it was made to hug my every curve. The neckline is an open sweetheart cut, flaunting all the goods and leaving little to the imagination. I can't help but chuckle, wondering how Rhyland will keep his shit together, taking me out when I'm rocking this jaw-dropping dress. The back is all open and daringly low, skirting the edge of risqué with its provocative design.

But it's the details that make this dress unique. The bodice is adorned with intricate lace appliques, each hand-stitched with care and precision, which takes my breath away. The lace continues down the sides of the dress, drawing the eye to how the silk clings to my hips and thighs like a lover's caress.

And then there's the slit. *Oh, the slit.* It runs up the right side of the dress, starting at mid-thigh and ending just below the hip. It's the kind of slit that makes a statement, the kind that says, "I'm here to turn heads and break hearts, and I'm not sorry about it."

This isn't just a dress—it's a declaration of love, a promise of passion, and a celebration of everything that makes me feel beautiful and alive.

I turn to Rhyland, my eyes shining with unshed tears of joy and gratitude. "It's perfect," I whisper, my voice thick with emotion. "You're perfect."

Rhyland closes the distance between us, his strong arms snaking around my waist and pulling me flush against his hard, muscular body. His heat seeps through the fabric of my clothes, making me feel warm and tingly all over.

"Not as perfect as you, baby," he murmurs, his voice low and husky, sending heat coiling in my stomach. He leans in, capturing my lips in a gentle kiss—full of promise. His lips move against mine slowly, purposefully, like he's savoring every second of this moment.

Just as I'm about to melt into a puddle of desire right here on the spot, he pulls back and brings his hand down on my ass in a playful slap, the sharp sting of it making me yelp in surprise.

"Now go get dressed," he commands. "We have reservations, and I don't want to be late."

RHYLAND

81

D ani shuts the bathroom door, and I smirk as I make a beeline for the closet. I've got a few more surprises up my sleeve for tonight, and I'll be damned if I don't make the most of every fucking second.

I grab what I need and head back to the bathroom, knocking once before barging in. And holy fucking shit, the sight that greets me nearly brings me to my knees.

Dani's standing there like a goddamn goddess, wearing nothing but a scrap of black lace that barely qualifies as panties. Her perfect tits are out, golden and perky, begging for my hands and mouth. And fuck me; the highlights in her hair make her look even more irresistible if that's even possible. The golden streaks match those mesmerizing eyes of hers, adding a whole new level of sex appeal that has my cock straining against my zipper. It's taking every ounce of self-control I have not to throw her on the bed and ravage her right fucking now.

I swallow hard, my mouth suddenly dry as a desert. I adjust my painfully hard erection.

"I almost forgot your other gifts," my voice rough with desire as I set the Jimmy Choo box down on the counter.

Dani tries to play coy, covering her nipples with her hands like some blushing virgin. "Oh? And what's that, Norse god of Naughtiness?" she asks, her voice all breathy and innocent.

I just smirk at the name, stalking her like the predator I am. I circle behind her, leaning down to whisper in her ear. "Bend over, baby."

She shivers, her heart rate skyrocketing as she slowly places her hands on the counter. I grab her black lacy panties, moving them to the side as I run my fingers through her smooth, silky folds.

Fuck me, she's so goddamn perfect.

"Mmm, baby," I rumble, my cock painfully erect at the feel of her bare skin. "Did you do this for me?"

She looks over her shoulder, her gold eyes swirling with desire. "Maybe," she purrs, her hips pushing back against my hand. "Or maybe I just felt like being extra smooth today."

Knowing she's freshly waxed, smooth as fucking silk, has my blood pumping. I want to dive face-first into her sweet little pussy, lick and suck that pretty clit 'til she's wailing my name for all to hear. And don't even get me started on this tight, perfect ass. It's begging for my mouth, my teeth, my full fucking attention.

Later. I've got all of this night mapped out.

But hell, one little taste won't hurt, right?

I position myself behind her—kneeling, my voice a rough command. "Bend over further, baby. Let me see this gorgeous ass."

Like the good girl she is, she obeys. I spread her open, drinking in the sight. The arch of her back, the curve of her spine, the way her juicy ass jiggles, tempting me... Fuck. Not wasting another second, I bite on one cheek, reveling in her gasp.

Gripping her thighs, I spread her even wider. I flatten my tongue against her smooth cunt and drag it slowly upward until I reach that flawless little hole in her perfect ass.

Dani moans, dropping her head to the counter as I feast on her. Sucking, flicking, savoring every fucking inch. "Fuck, Rhyland... oh my god..." she whimpers, lost to the pleasure. "I love your mouth on me..."

"Yeah? You like being dirty for me, baby?" I growl, slapping her ass hard enough to leave a mark. "Like it when I eat this ass like a fucking animal?"

"Yes... god, *yes*," she pants, pushing back against my face as I devour her.

I'm relentless, burying my face between her cheeks, my cock leaking in my pants. I'm gonna get her soaked, desperate, aching for what I've planned.

My fingers find her clit, slick with her arousal. I rub soft, teasing circles as I continue to devour her ass, my tongue relentless. The combination has her gasping, her hips rocking desperately against my face.

"Rhyland, fuck... I'm so close..."

As much as I want to feel her come undone, to taste her release on my tongue, I know I have to hold back—I need her on the edge, desperate for more.

I've been gentle with my angel lately, treating her like spun glass as we navigated the dangers of Aquaria. But now, my naughty little vixen has a punishment coming, one that's *long* overdue. And by the time I'm done with her, she'll be a begging fucking mess for mercy, for release, for anything I'm willing to give her.

I pull away, my fingers trailing up to pinch her swollen clit between my thumb and forefinger. Her whole body tenses, every muscle coiled tight as I hold her right on the brink.

"No, no, no, no," she moans, her head falling back as she begs for release. "Rhyland... please, I need...let me come..."

I stand up and adjust my erection. I chuckle darkly, nipping at her earlobe. "Eyes forward, Angel."

She obeys, and I quickly wet the object in my mouth before slowly working it into her tight little pussy. She gasps and moans, her body trembling as I stretch her open.

"Fuck, *Rhyland*," she whimpers, her nails digging into the counter. "What...what is that?"

I ignore her question, pushing the toy in deeper. "Just relax."

When it's finally seated inside her, I pull her panties back into place, giving her ass a little slap for good measure. She yelps, spinning around to face me with fire in her eyes.

"Correct me if I'm wrong," she says, all haughty and demanding, "but I thought I was the one who won the bet. Therefore, you pay up in sexual favors."

I smirk, my eyes raking over her naked body. "You did, baby. But we never agreed on *when* I would pay on that bet."

Her eyes flash, her cheeks flushing with anger and arousal. "What? Dammit, Rhyland, you don't play fair! And what the *hell* did you put in me?"

"You'll see, baby. But first, I've got one more gift for you."

I hand her the Jimmy Choo box, watching her eyes widen with shock—suddenly forgetting our little argument. "No. No fucking way," she breathes, her hands shaking as she opens the lid.

Inside are the shoes I picked and bought for her—black high heels with asymmetric gold floral hardware, crystal embellishments, and a buckle ankle strap. They're sexy as hell, just like my girl.

"How? What?" she stammers, her eyes flying up to meet mine. "Do you know how expensive these are?!"

"Clearly, baby, I do."

"How the hell do you know my size?"

I laugh, pulling her into my arms. "Baby, I know more about you than you think," nipping at her bottom lip. "I've spent countless hours studying every inch of you, memorizing every curve and hollow. Your shoe size is just the tip of the fucking iceberg."

She narrows her eyes at me. "You sneaky bastard," she accuses, poking me in the chest. "Have you been snooping through my things?"

I shrug, completely unrepentant. "Guilty as charged, Angel. But can you blame me? I had to know everything about my sexy little mate, including what size heels she wears."

She scoffs, rolling her eyes. "You're impossible, you know that? Most guys ask a girl what she likes. They don't go rifling through her closet like a creeper."

I grin, my hands sliding down to grab her ass. "Ah, but I'm not most guys, now am I? And trust me, baby, by the time I'm done with you tonight, you'll be thanking your lucky stars that I'm so thorough."

Dani looks up at me, her hazel-gold eyes blazing with exasperation and heat. "You're lucky you're so damn hot, you know that? Otherwise, I might punish you for being such a creep."

"Punish me? *Fuck*, baby, that sounds like a challenge."

Her eyes narrow, that sassy little smirk playing on her lips. "Oh no, we are *not* going down that road, Rhyland. This is supposed to be my date night. A nice, normal date that I *won* fair and square."

"Mmhmm," I hum, not even trying to hide my amusement. Whether she realizes it or not, she's already thrown down the gauntlet.

"You know what? *Fine.* You want to play? We can play," she huffs, her chin tilting up defiantly. "But don't come crying to me when you can't handle what I dish out, you, Exasperating Eon-walker."

I lean in close, my voice a low growl. "Oh, I can handle anything you throw at me, Angel. The question is, can you?"

She pushes at my chest, but I can see the way her pupils dilate, the way her breath catches. "Now, if you'll excuse me, you brute, I need to put on this beautiful dress so you can take me out like a gentleman."

I let her shove me towards the door, not even trying to hide my shit-eating grin. "Whatever you say, Angel. Just remember you started this little game. Don't be surprised when I finish it." I grab her chin, forcing her to meet my gaze. "Do not take that out. Understand?"

She starts to roll her eyes, but I yank her attention back to me. "Don't," I growl, my tone leaving no room for argument. "And don't roll those gorgeous eyes at me."

She takes a shaky breath, her pupils dilating as she nods.

As I close the door behind me, I hear her mutter, "Fucking arrogant Viking." But there's no real bite to it, just a promise of the fun we're about to have.

Oh, this night just got a hell of a lot more interesting. My feisty little vixen thinks she can challenge me? Fuck, I'm gonna enjoy putting her in her place over and over again.

Let the games begin, Angel. You have no idea what you're in for.

DANICA

82

I slip into the front seat of the Bentley Continental GT, the luxurious leather cradling my body like a lover's embrace. Rhyland, looking like a goddamn snack in his tuxedo, saunters over to the driver's side and slides in, the picture of masculine grace.

As he fires up the car, the engine purring to life like a satisfied jungle cat, I shift in my seat, acutely aware of the foreign object nestled between my thighs. Oh, I know damn well what he's inserted inside me—another vibrator—silicone, egg-shaped, and currently pressing against all the right spots.

It's not uncomfortable, per se, but it's... different. A constant reminder of the delicious torture Rhyland has in store for me tonight.

As we pull away from the mansion, the city lights blurring past the windows, Rhyland glances over at me, his face barely illuminated by the soft glow of the dash lights. Even in the dim light, I can see the hunger in his eyes, the raw desire that simmers just beneath the surface.

"You look gorgeous, baby," his voice like velvet over gravel.

I preen under his praise, a flush of heat spreading across my skin. It's not just the words, but the way he says them—like I'm the most beautiful thing he's ever seen—like he can't quite believe I'm real.

And let's be honest, who can blame him? I'm a fucking vision in this dress, the fabric clinging to my curves like a lover's caress, the neckline plunging dangerously low, offering a tantalizing glimpse of the goods.

But it's more than just the dress. It's the way I feel in it—powerful, sexy, untouchable. I could walk into any room, own it, and bring kings to their knees with a smile.

"Thank you. You have good taste," I say with a smirk, trying to play it cool even as my heart races at the sight of him.

Rhyland nods, grabbing his phone from his pocket and pulling up an app, but then he gives me this look—you know, the one that promises all sorts of delicious trouble. It's the naughty look he gets when he's about to play, and sure as shit, that little toy inside me starts softly buzzing, making me jerk in my seat like I've been electrocuted.

"How's that feel?" he asks, his voice all low and growly, like a predator stalking its prey.

Holy shit.

I can't let him do this to me before our damn date! I'll be a wet fucking mess before we even sit down for dinner at this rate. "Rhyland... S-stop," I plead, even as the vibrator works its magic on my inner walls, sending sparks of pleasure shooting through my body.

But does he listen? Of course not. He just ignores me, his eyes glued to his phone like he's checking his fucking email or something. And then, because he's a sadistic bastard, the vibrations change. It starts slow and steady, an irresistible rhythm that has me biting my lip to keep from moaning. But just as I get used to it, the buzzing shifts into rapid-fire mode, quick and relentless, before easing back into that annoying, steady pulse.

I can't help it—I grab his arm, my nails digging into his skin as I let out an involuntary moan. It's too much, too good, and I'm already teetering on the edge of something dangerous and delicious.

"You're playing with fire, Norseman," I manage to gasp out, my voice breathy and strained. "Keep this up; I might just combust before we even reach the restaurant."

Rhyland chuckles, the sound dark and full of promise. "Nope. I won't let that happen. I know you, Dani—I know when you're at your fucking peak. This game has only started, baby."

And then, because he's a goddamn tease, he shuts off the vibrator, leaving me limp in my seat, frustration building until I'm ready to scream. I let out a growl, glaring at him with all the fury of a woman denied her orgasm. This edging shit is for the fucking birds—

"Are you kidding me with this edging bullshit, Rhyland?" I snap, my voice tight with pent-up need. "It's not cute, it's torture." Delicious, mind-blowing torture, but still. "You're going to kill me before this night is over, you sadistic ass."

Rhyland laughs, the sound rich and deep and infuriatingly sexy. "What have I told you about that bratty mouth, huh? Keep it up, and I might just have to put it to better use."

I clench my thighs together, my body throbbing with want at the promise in his words. Goddamnit, this man knows exactly how to push my buttons and wind me up until I'm ready to explode.

But two can play at this game.

Even if it kills me, I'm going to make this man work for every moan, every desperate plea that falls from my lips.

He wants to play? Fine. But he better be ready for the fight of his life.

After an hour of pure, unadulterated torture, we finally pull up to the restaurant. The entire ride, Rhyland's been flicking that fucking vibrator on and off like it's his toy, leaving me a writhing, cursing, moaning mess in the passenger seat.

So much for not making a sound—dammit!

I bitched, I begged, I threatened to cut his balls off if he didn't let me come, but did he listen? Hell no. He just sat there with that infuriating smirk on his face, looking sexy as hell—wanting to smack his face and kiss him at the same time.

This fucking vibrator is coming out, even if I have to perform a goddamn exorcism to get it done.

I should've taken it out before we even left the house, but no, I had to be a masochistic bitch and let him have his fun. Well, the joke's on me because now I'm stuck waddling around like a penguin with a sex toy shoved up my snatch.

Rhyland and his kinky shenanigans are going to be the death of me. Does he expect me to sit through an entire meal playing "How Many Ways Can I Make Dani Squirm?" Because let me tell you, at this rate, I'm about two appetizers away from bursting into flames right here in this swanky establishment.

I can just see the headlines now: *"Local Woman Spontaneously Combusts in Five-Star Restaurant —Authorities Suspect Vampire Foul Play."* Nope. Not happening. I refuse to become a cautionary tale about the dangers of supernatural foreplay in public places.

But even as I'm cursing his name, I can't help the thrill of excitement that runs through me. Because as much as I hate to admit it, I love it when he gets like this—All dominant and controlling, pushing me to the brink of insanity with his teasing touches and wicked words.

It's a dangerous game we play, but damn if it isn't the most fun I've ever had.

"I'll be right back," I tell Rhyland as we settle into our seats at the table, my voice too high-pitched to be casual.

He smiles at me, that sexy, panty-dropping smile of his, catching a glimpse of fang. The sight of it sends a jolt to my clit, and I have to fight the urge to climb into his lap and ride him right here in the middle of the restaurant.

I flag down a passing waiter and ask where the ladies' room is, trying to keep my voice steady even as my legs tremble with each step. As soon as I'm inside, I make a beeline for the nearest stall, locking the door behind me with shaking hands.

I yank up my dress, ready to perform an emergency eviction on this silicone squatter, but my lady parts have apparently formed their own security detail. They're locked down tighter than a Tupperware container at a potluck, and this vibrator just got VIP status.

It seems my vajayjay has grown quite attached to its new silicone BFF. I'm talking a level of clenching that would make even the most seasoned Kegel enthusiast weep with envy.

Fantastic. Just freaking great. I'm stuck in a fancy restaurant bathroom, playing tug-of-war with my own vagina. This is not how I pictured my evening going.

I try to channel my inner zen master. *"Breathe, Dani. Relax. It's just a sex toy, not the sword in the stone. You've got this."* My pep talk is about as effective as a chocolate teapot.

Of course, that's when Rhyland decides to invade my head like an unwanted telemarketer. *"Problems?"* I can hear the smirk in his mental voice.

"Nope," I fire back, shooing him out of my brain. His dark chuckle echoes in my mind before he vanishes, leaving me alone with my uncooperative clam-clenching cooch.

I let out a breath, close my eyes, and relax; I gently pull until the vibrator slides out of me with a wet pop. I can't help the little moan that escapes me at the sensation, my body clenching around the sudden emptiness.

I'm half tempted to throw myself a little one-woman party right here and now—a quick DIY orgasm and a big 'screw you' to Rhyland. But just as I embark on my solo adventure, the bathroom door swings open.

Great timing, random stranger. I roll my eyes and yank open the stall door, ready to make my grand exit.

I head for the sink, washing off the toy quickly and efficiently before tucking it away in my purse. I duck back into the stall to clean myself up as best I can, cursing under my breath at the wet mess Rhyland's left me in.

I adjust my dress, ensuring everything is in place before returning to face the music. Rhyland's waiting for me at the table, looking like sin incarnate in his tailored suit and devilish smile.

"Everything okay, baby?" his voice all innocent concern even as his eyes sparkle with mischief.

"Just peachy," I reply, my smile sharp enough to cut glass.

Rhyland chuckles, a dark, dangerous sound that makes me shiver. "For disobeying me and doing exactly what I told you *not* to do, there will be consequences, Angel."

I swallow hard, my mouth suddenly dry. He can't be serious, can he? What consequences could he possibly give me that he hasn't already at this point—

One look at Rhyland's face tells me he's not fucking around. His blue eyes are blazing with a fierce intensity, the kind that says he means business. And I know from experience that when it comes to these games, Rhyland takes this shit as seriously as a heart attack.

Because that's just who he is—a controlling, sadistic alpha-hole who gets off on pushing my buttons and driving me to the brink of insanity. And I'm the horny little bitch who can't seem to get enough of it.

I arch an eyebrow, trying to play it cool even as my heart races. "Oh really? You didn't specify how long I had to keep it in—don't tell me you're running out of tricks already."

His eyes flash, a predatory gleam that makes my insides quiver. "Trust me, Angel, I've got plenty of tricks up my sleeve."

I'm about to hit Rhyland with another sassy comeback when our waiter appears, his eyes instantly drawn to the generous display of cleavage my dress is offering up like a goddamn buffet.

I smile at the look on Rhyland's face—he's practically vibrating with rage, his jaw clenched so tight I'm surprised his teeth haven't shattered.

What the hell did he expect?

This will be fun.

"Good evening. My name is Jake. I will be your server tonight. May I start you with wine or a drink from the bar?" his gaze still firmly glued to my tits.

Jake's got that whole "aww, shucks" college boy charm going on—tousled blond hair like he just rolled out of bed after an all-nighter and eyes greener than a freshman's first attempt at tequila shots. He's tall and lean, like a beanpole with abs. But let's be honest; he's about as intimidating as a labradoodle puppy compared to my Viking stud muffin. Rhyland's got that "I'll ravish you senseless and then build you a longboat" vibe that Jake couldn't match if he tried.

I flash Jake my most dazzling smile, laying on the charm like it's going out of style. "Hi, Jake. Thank you... could you help me with the wine menu?" I scoot closer, batting my eyelashes up at him. "I forgot my reading glasses and can't see what this says."

It's a blatant lie, of course. I can read the menu just fine. But Jake doesn't need to know that.

"Sure thing," he says, leaning in closer, his eyes practically bugging out of his head as he gets an even better view of my assets. I can feel Rhyland's glare boring into me, but I studiously ignore him, focusing all my attention on the hapless waiter.

"What the fuck do you think you're doing, Dani?" Rhyland's voice rumbles in my head, the warning clear in his tone.

But I keep smiling, leaning closer to Jake until we're practically nose-to-nose. "Wonderful. I'll take the Riesling. Thank you, Jake," I purr, with sugary sweetness.

Jake turns bright red, stammering out a response before practically sprinting away from the table. I lean back in my chair, a self-satisfied smirk on my face as I finally meet Rhyland's gaze.

"What's the matter, babe? Can't handle a little competition?" I tease.

"You must enjoy pissing me off, woman," he growls. "That unlucky little shit is no competition—I don't expect you to flirt in front of me, Dani... purposely. Keep it up, and I'll bend you over this fucking table and show everyone in this restaurant who you belong to."

I shiver at the heat in his words, my body instantly responding to the dominance in his tone. My fantasy of him taking me in front of people—owning my body. But I'm not about to back down now.

Jake quickly returns, flustered. " I apologize, sir. May I get you a drink?" Jake left in such a hurry that he forgot Rhyland's drink order.

"Bourbon. Neat." Rhyland responds in a clipped tone.

Jake, a little shaken, nods and hurries away.

As I take in the stunning surroundings of the high-end Seattle restaurant Rhyland has chosen for our date, I can't help but be impressed by its sheer elegance and sophistication. The decor perfectly blends classic and modern, with plush velvet curtains, glittering chandeliers, and abstract art pieces adorning the walls. The tables are set with crisp white linens, gleaming silverware, and delicate china, each place setting arranged meticulously. But the breathtaking panoramic view of the Seattle skyline truly steals the show.

"So," I drawl, leaning forward on my elbows and giving Rhyland an eyeful of my ample cleavage. "What other delightful tortures do you have planned for me tonight, oh great and powerful Norse god?"

"That's for me to know and for you to find out, little minx."

Before I can devise a suitably sassy retort, Jake returns with our drinks and takes our orders. I can barely contain my excitement when my meal arrives—a mouthwatering filet mignon with truffle mashed potatoes and roasted asparagus. I'm pretty sure I'm drooling, and it's not just because of the sexy Viking sitting across from me.

As we dig in, Rhyland and I trade heated glances and easy banter, the sexual tension between us simmering just beneath the surface. But then he has to go and ruin the mood with a serious question.

"So, you spoke with your brother? How is he?" Rhyland asks between bites.

I shrug, spearing a piece of asparagus with my fork. "Oh, you know, living the dream. Working for some fancy-schmancy company, probably making more money than God. He's coming to visit next week."

Rhyland frowns. "Do you think that's wise, Dani?"

I roll my eyes, taking a sip of my wine. "Why wouldn't it be? He's my brother, Rhyland. I need to see him."

"Does he know yet? About...everything?"

I cringe, my stomach twisting with guilt. I hate lying to Damon and keeping such a massive part of my life a secret, but what choice do I have? The supernatural world is dangerous; the less he knows, the safer he'll be.

"No," I admit, my voice quiet. "He doesn't know."

Rhyland's gaze softens, his hand reaching across the table to cover mine. "Are you going to tell him?"

I sigh, suddenly feeling like the world's weight is on my shoulders. "I don't know yet. I just...I want to protect him, Rhyland. He's all the family I have left."

Rhyland nods, his thumb stroking soothing circles on the back of my hand. "I understand, Angel. But you know you can't keep this a secret forever. Eventually, he will find out, one way or another."

I know he's right, but that doesn't make it any easier. Rhyland knows Damon is not fond of the supernatural, and I fear that Damon will disown me.

How do you tell your baby brother that you're mated to a vampire—that you're some kind of supernatural chosen one destined to save the world?

It's a conversation I'm dreading but one I know I can't avoid forever.

But tonight? Tonight is about forgetting all of that, about losing myself in pleasure and passion and the man who sets my soul on fire.

So I push those heavy thoughts aside and focus on the delicious meal in front of me, on the way Rhyland's eyes darken with hunger every time they meet mine.

The rest of the world can wait. Tonight belongs to us.

Jake returns to our table with a smile that's just a little too eager. "Is there anything else I can get you? Dessert, perhaps?"

I lean forward, resting my elbows on the table and pushing my tits together until they're practically spilling out of my dress. Jake's eyes immediately zero in on the tempting display, his Adam's apple bobbing as he swallows hard.

I can feel Rhyland's glare again, but I ignore him, focusing all my attention on the flustered waiter. "Dessert sounds perfect, Jake," I purr. "What do you recommend? I'm in the mood for something...sweet and sinful."

Jake's face turns a delightful shade of crimson, his eyes darting between my cleavage and Rhyland's murderous expression. "Um, well, we have a delicious chocolate lava cake," he stammers, shifting uncomfortably from foot to foot. "It's served warm with vanilla ice cream and a raspberry coulis."

"Mmm, that sounds amazing," I moan, licking my lips slowly. "I do love something *hot* and *gooey* in my mouth."

Jake makes a strangled sound, his pants visibly tightening as his bulge grows more pronounced. He looks like he's about to pass out, his face flushed and his breathing shallow.

Rhyland clears his throat pointedly, his eyes flashing with fury. "We'll take two of those," his voice low and dangerous. "And the check, if you don't mind."

Jake nods frantically, practically tripping over himself in his haste to escape the table. I cross my legs, my core clenching, a self-satisfied smirk on my face as I meet Rhyland's gaze.

"What?" I ask innocently, batting my eyelashes. "I was just being friendly."

"You know *exactly* what you're doing," he warns, his eyes promising retribution—a dark promise. "Keep it up, and I'll show you just how *friendly* I can be."

I shiver at the heat in his words, my thighs clenching together under the table. God, he's so fucking hot when he's jealous, all possessive and dominant, and ready to stake his claim—It's like poking a bear with a stick, only instead of getting mauled, I get fucked within an inch of my life.

Jake returns with our desserts and the check, his face still flushed and his pants still straining against his obvious arousal. He sets everything down on the table with shaking hands, his eyes darting nervously between me and Rhyland.

"Thanks, Jake," I say sweetly, my finger tracing the rim of my water glass. "You've been *so* helpful tonight."

He swallows hard, his voice cracking as he replies, "It was my pleasure, m-ma'am. Have a wonderful evening." He looks at Rhyland, "Sir."

As he hurries away, I can't help but giggle, feeling a little drunk on the power of my seduction. But when I look at Rhyland, the heat in his eyes sobers me up quickly.

"You're in trouble now, Angel. I hope you're ready for what comes next."

Ruh-Roh.

LUCIAN

83

"Here, let me help you with that, sweetheart." I grab Seraphina's helmet and carefully place it on her head, making sure not to fuck up the gorgeous hair she spent hours perfecting or snag those sexy-as-hell dangly earrings.

"Oh my gosh, this is so exciting!" she gushes, her voice slightly muffled by the helmet. "What's this magnificent beast called?" she asks, gesturing to my pride and joy, my Ducati Panigale v4 bike.

"This, my darling angel cake, is a motherfucking speed demon on two wheels. And when I say fast, I mean 'hold onto your tits and pray to whatever god you believe in' fast." I wink.

"Ooh, I like the sound of that!" Seraphina giggles, her eyes sparkling with excitement. "I'll hold on tight, I promise."

I made damn sure my girl wore something that wouldn't chafe her delicate skin during the ride. And holy fucking shit, did she deliver. She's rocking this delicious as fuck black little tube top number, showing off her flat sexy stomach that makes her cleavage look like a goddamn snack. I just want to motorboat those perfect tits until I pass out from lack of oxygen.

She's got on these sinfully tight black yoga pants that hug her ass perfectly. You know the ones I'm talking about—the viral butt crack leggings that show off every mouthwatering curve and leave absolutely nothing to the imagination.

When she bent over to put on her boots, I nearly blew my load again. It was like staring into the face of God—if God had the most perfect, biteable ass in all of creation.

Especially after that mind-blowing blowjob—sweet merciful Christ! The way she took the initiative to make me see stars and holy hell, did she ever. I'm still reeling from it.

I pull the leather jacket on her and zip it up tight.

I slip on my helmet, snapping the visor down before I start the bike. Seraphina squeals as the engine roars to life, and I motion for her to hop on behind me.

"Saddle up, backpack." my voice barely audible over the purring engine.

I reach over and smack her visor down, because safety first, right? Then she swings her leg over the bike, scooting close behind me and wrapping her arms around my waist. I let out a low moan at the feeling of her pressed against me, her body heat seeping into my skin even through our clothes.

Holy shit, the way her thighs are squeezing my hips and her tits are pressed against my back... It's enough to make a man want to say, 'fuck the road trip,' and just spend the next week worshipping every inch of her body.

But I'm a man with a plan, and I'll be damned if I let a little thing like mind-blowing arousal derail my carefully crafted seduction scheme. So I take a deep breath, try to think about baseball stats and dead kittens to calm my raging hard-on, and rev the engine.

"Hold on tight, baby girl," I call over the bike's roar.

And with that, we peel out of the driveway like a bat out of hell, Seraphina's delighted laughter ringing in my ears as we speed off into the night.

The night air whips past us like a fucking symphony of speed and adrenaline. The real thrill? Those thighs of hers wrapped around me tight. She's squeezing me like she's trying to juice a lemon, and I'm the luckiest damn lemon in the world.

I've never let any other woman ride backpack on my baby before. So the fact that I'm popping Seraphina's motorcycle cherry has me grinning like a goddamn fool. I feel like the luckiest bastard on the planet, and I'm not ashamed to admit it.

I reach back with my gloved hand and give her thigh a possessive squeeze. She grinds even closer to me in response. My eyes practically roll back into my skull from the sheer pleasure of feeling her pressed so tightly against me—her heat searing into me even through the layers of leather and denim.

I squeeze her leg harder, my fingers digging into the supple flesh as I gun the throttle, urging the bike to go faster, harder, like I'm trying to outrun the concept of speed itself.

The engine roars beneath us, a primal scream of power and fury that sets my blood on fire. I can feel the adrenaline surging through my veins, a heady cocktail of excitement and raw, unbridled lust.

I missed you, baby. Talking about my bike.

From the sound of Seraphina's delighted squeals echoing through the helmet's built-in mic—I'd say she's feeling the rush as much as I am.

"Are you having fun, Cupcake?" I ask. My voice rumbling through the speakers.

Her laughter is like music to my ears. "Faster, Lucian!" she cries, her voice breathless with exhilaration. "I want to go faster!"

Hells to the yes! It's like she read my mind. I crank the throttle as far as it'll go, the front wheel nearly lifting off the ground as we rocket forward into the night.

The world blurs around us, a kaleidoscope of colors and sensations that bleed together until there's nothing left but the engine's roar, the rush of the wind, and the intoxicating feel of Seraphina's body pressed against mine.

About thirty minutes later, I bring the bike to a smooth stop on a bustling Seattle street, the engine purring like a contented kitten before I kill the ignition. I yank my helmet off in one smooth motion, my hair probably looking like I just stuck my finger in a light socket, but do I give a fuck? Not even a little bit.

Seraphina untangles herself from me, wiggling that perfect ass of hers as she dismounts the bike. Watching her swing her leg over and slide off the seat is like watching poetry in motion. Poetry that makes my dick harder than fucking calculus.

As soon as her feet touch the ground, I reach for her helmet, gently easing it off her head like I'm unveiling a masterpiece. When I finally get it off, I'm greeted by the most beautiful sight in the world: Seraphina's face lit up with a grin so bright it could power the entire city.

"Oh my god, Lucian, that was incredible!" she gushes. "I've never had so much fun in my entire life!"

I can't help but smile like a damn fool as I look down at her, my heart swelling with so much love and pride it feels like it might burst out of my chest. Despite the wind and the helmet, I smooth down her silky blonde hair, marveling at how perfect it still looks.

Most women I've known would be a fucking mess after a ride like that, all shaky legs and smeared makeup, bitching about their hair being ruined. But not my Cupcake, oh no. She's the opposite, practically vibrating with happiness and adrenaline, her eyes wide and her cheeks flushed with exhilaration.

It's like she was born to ride, born to experience the rush and the freedom that comes with tearing down the open road on two wheels.

"I'm so glad you enjoyed it, sweetheart," I murmur, cupping her face and brushing my thumb over her soft, pink lips. "Seeing you like this, so happy and alive? It's the most beautiful thing I've ever witnessed."

Seraphina leans into my touch, her eyes fluttering closed as she nuzzles her cheek against my palm. "Thank you for sharing this with me, Lucian," she whispers, her voice so full of love and gratitude it makes my throat tighten with emotion. "I never knew life could be this amazing, this exciting. You've opened up a whole new world for me."

I bend down and take her lips in a searing kiss, pouring every ounce of love and passion for her into this perfect moment. When I finally pull back, we're both breathing hard, our eyes locked in a gaze so intense it feels like the rest of the world falls away.

"Stick with me, Cupcake. I'll show you things you never even dreamed were possible. I'll give you the fucking stars."

Seraphina's giggle is like the fucking cherry on top of this sundae of awesomeness as I take her hand in mine, our fingers locking together like two horny teenagers at a drive-in movie. I lead her down the street, dodging pedestrians like I'm some ninja on a mission from God. And let's be real, I kind of am.

Our next stop on this wild and crazy night of romance and poor life choices? None other than Marination Mobile, aka the food truck that's going to make your taste buds shit rainbows and your arteries scream for mercy. They've got this insane Hawaiian-Korean fusion thing going on that'll make you want to slap your mama and call her a bad cook.

Now, I know what you're thinking. "But Lucian, you magnificent bastard, why the fuck are you taking your girl to a roach coach on date night? Where's the fancy-ass restaurant with the snooty waiters and the wine list that costs more than my rent?"

I'm about to drop some truth bombs on your ass. See, I'm not your average, run-of-the-mill romance novel fuckboy. I don't do that candlelit dinner, roses, and chocolate bullshit. That's for pussies who don't know how to keep it real.

I mean, I would totally do that if Seraphina asked me to, but that's beside the point.

I'm all about the authentic experience, baby. I want to show Seraphina the real Lucian—the one who'd sell his left nut for a good kimchi quesadilla and a side of

DGAF. I want her to see the world through my eyes, to taste the flavors that make my heart sing like a fucking gospel choir.

"Alright, Cupcake, get ready to have your panties blown clean off," I say, rubbing my hands together like a mad scientist about to unleash his greatest creation. "This place has the best goddamn spicy pork tacos in the entire fucking universe. And the kimchi quesadillas?" I kiss my fingers like I'm some fancy-ass French chef, my eyes practically rolling back in my skull at the mere thought of those crispy, cheesy triangles of pure ecstasy. "They're so good, they'll make you want to punch a nun in the face and steal her habit. Fucking perfection, I'm telling you."

Seraphina laughs so hard I can't help but smile. "Mmm...sounds amazing. I can't wait." she gushes, excitedly bouncing on her toes. "I can't wait to try everything!"

As we step up to the window to place our order, the heavenly aroma of sizzling meat and spicy kimchi wafting through the air like a siren song, I can't help but feel like the luckiest son of a bitch in the world.

Because of this right here? This is what happiness tastes like—sharing the things you love with the person you love, discovering new flavors and new adventures together, and creating memories that'll last longer than a vampire's morning wood.

"Well, well, well, look what the cat dragged in! Lucian, you sly dog, where the hell have you been hiding? And who's this gorgeous little thing you've got with you?"

"Jackson, my man! I've been out there living my best undead life; you know how it is. And this stunning creature right here? This is Seraphina, the light of my life and the fire in my loins. She's a total newbie to the orgasmic experience that is your food, so be gentle with her, will ya?"

Seraphina's cheeks turn the most adorable shade of pink as she smiles at Jackson, her eyes sparkling. "It's so nice to meet you, Jackson. Everything smells absolutely divine!"

"Ha! Divine? Oh, honey, you have no idea. Lucian's about to corrupt you in ways you never even dreamed of. And I'm not just talking about the food." Jackson winks.

I grin at Jackson's comment, my mind already racing with all the deliciously depraved ways I plan to corrupt my sweet little angel cake. But I've got to take it slow, ease her into the beautiful world of sin and iniquity one step at a time.

"Alright, Jackson, enough with the innuendos. Just hook us up with the usual, will ya? My girl's about to have her mind blown, and I want a front-row seat to the show."

"You got it, boss. Two orders of pure, unadulterated foodgasms coming right up!"

I take Seraphina to the most epic spot in all of Alki Beach Park, a little piece of heaven that'll make you want to burst into a fucking Disney song. The view is so mind-blowingly spectacular; it's like the Seattle skyline, and the beach had a baby and named it "Fuck Yes." The skyscrapers are lit like Christmas trees, and the sand is just begging for some naked moonlit shenanigans. The sound of the waves is like nature's ultimate wingman, setting the mood for some serious romance. It's the place that makes you want to rip off your clothes and run around like a wild animal, but I've got other plans for my girl.

Jackson drops off our order, "Here ya go, man. Enjoy."

"Thanks," I say as I hand Seraphina her tacos.

Seraphina takes her first bite of that spicy pork taco, her eyes rolling back in her head like she's having a religious experience. I can almost hear the hallelujah chorus singing in the background.

It's like watching art in motion, a masterpiece of culinary ecstasy unfolding before my very eyes.

And as she moans in delight, the sound sending shockwaves of desire straight to my dick, I know I made the right choice.

"Oh my *gosh*," Seraphina moans, her mouth full of pure taco goodness. "This is just..." She trails off, too lost in the orgasmic flavors to even form a coherent sentence.

A dribble of taco sauce escapes the corner of her mouth, making a break for freedom down her chin. And fuck, it's the most adorable thing I've ever seen. I reach out with a napkin to wipe it away, even though every instinct in my body is screaming at me to lick it off.

Stop, Lucian. You're in public.

"Amazing?" I finish for her, taking a big-ass bite of my kimchi quesadilla and letting out a moan of my own. The flavors explode on my tongue like a fucking supernova.

I've been dreaming about this goddamn quesadilla ever since I left for Aquaria with Dani, and let me tell you, it was worth every second of the wait.

"I told you, Cupcake," I say, waggling my eyebrows at her like the smug bastard I am. "This place is the real fucking deal. Once you go Marination, you never go back."

Seraphina nods, too busy shoving another bite of taco into her face to respond. And honestly? I can't blame her. If I had to choose between talking and eating this food, I'd choose the food every damn time.

We sit here in blissful silence, stuffing our faces like a couple of stoned teenagers at a 7-Eleven. And with every bite, I can feel the stress and bullshit of the past few weeks melting away, replaced by a sense of pure contentment.

This is what happiness tastes like. Good food, good company, and not a single fuck given about the rest of the world.

Take notes, kids—this is how you do date night right.

RHYLAND

84

I'm fucking livid as we storm back to the car, my grip on Dani's waist tight as steel. That little stunt with the waiter? Pushing her tits in his face, eye-fucking him, flirting with him, right in front of me? She's crossed a line.

She knows damn well what that shit does to me. It's one thing for some limp-dick asshole to drool over my woman. It's a whole other level of disrespect when she's the one doing the flirting. Well, congratu-fucking-lations, baby. You've got my full attention now, and you will regret every second of it.

We left the restaurant without dessert, my anger boiling as I dragged Dani out the door. She groaned in disappointment, but I was too pissed to care.

As we walk back to the car, my eyes devour every inch of Dani. She's a fucking vision in that sinful dress. The deep red fabric clings to her curves, hugging her hips and ass in a way that makes my mouth water. The neckline plunges dangerously low, offering that dumbass waiter and anyone else a glimpse of her cleavage, her tits threatening to spill out with every breath she takes.

What the fuck was I thinking?

Her silky brown hair, now streaked with golden highlights, cascades down her bare back like a waterfall. My fingers itch to trace the line of her spine, to feel the softness of her skin under my touch.

As she walks, the dress shifts, revealing a glimpse of her toned thigh through the daring slit. My cock strains against my zipper, but my rage overshadows my lust.

I take a deep breath, expecting to be hit by her intoxicating scent—that mix of honey and spice that drives me fucking wild. But there's nothing. That damn potion of hers has masked her scent completely. It's like a punch to the gut, unable to smell her. But even without her scent filling my nostrils, the sight of her alone is enough to make my blood boil with need.

I will teach my little Vixen a lesson she won't soon forget—she wants to act like a bratty tease? I'll treat her like one. And when I'm finished, she won't be able to sit pretty without remembering who the fuck she belongs to.

By the time this night is over, she's gonna wish she never pissed me off.

"Rhyland, let go," Dani huffs, trying to shrug off my grip, but I'm not having it.

We reach the car, and I push her back against it, caging her in with my body. Her breathing quickens, her golden eyes wide with fear and defiance.

Good, she should be scared.

I lean in close, my voice a menacing growl. "Did you have fun in there, Angel?"

Dani dares to look unfazed. "Yup, sure did. You?"

I resist the urge to bend her over the hood and spank that sassy ass raw. "Aren't you just precious? Think you've won, huh? Pissing me off, flirting with that piece of shit right in front of me, flaunting your tits like a bitch in heat? You wanna be treated like a whore, baby?"

Anger flashes in her eyes, but beneath it, I can smell her arousal. She's probably feeling my rage through our bond, knowing fully what her little stunt would do to me.

"I wasn't acting like a whore, Rhyland," she spits, her chest heaving with each labored breath.

My gaze drops to her breasts, barely contained by her dress. Dipping my head, I drag my tongue along the swell of her cleavage, working my way up her neck, feeling her throat bob as she swallows hard. "No? Could've fooled me, the way you were shoving these in that fucker's face."

"Fuck you," she hisses, even as her fingers tangle in my hair, pulling me closer. "I was just having a little fun. Not my fault you're a possessive asshole who can't take a joke."

I chuckle darkly, my fangs grazing her pulse point. "Oh, I can take a joke, Angel. But you and I both know that wasn't a fucking joke. That was you testing me, pushing my buttons like the bratty little temptress you are."

She's been on edge for hours, desperate for release, but I'm not about to give her that satisfaction. Not when she's earned herself a thorough punishment.

She gasps as I bite down, my fangs piercing her soft skin. I drink deeply, savoring the sweet and spicy honey taste of her blood on my tongue. "And now," I murmur against her throat, "you're gonna pay for it. I never got my dessert, after all. Guess I'll just have to settle for you instead."

Dani melts against me as I hold her up, drinking deeply from her throat. My venom courses through her veins, igniting every nerve ending with white-hot pleasure. She whimpers, rubbing her body against mine, my hard cock pressing into her soft belly.

I pull away, my fangs tearing into my wrist. Dani's eyes are half-lidded, glazed over with lust and need. "Drink," I command, pressing my bleeding wrist to her lips. "Drink it all down like a good little girl."

She's going to be so far fucking gone, so drunk on my blood and my venom, that she won't know which way is up. I want her completely under my spell, lost to everything but the pleasure and pain I give her and what I am about to do.

Dani's lips close around the wound, her tongue lapping at the crimson flow. Her pupils are blown wide, the golden irises nearly swallowed by inky black desire. The sight of her, the feel of her mouth on me, it's almost too much. My cock weeps in my pants, begging for release.

But I hold back, gritting my teeth against the onslaught of sensation. I won't give in, not yet. Not until she's completely lost in me—lost to what I have planned for her next.

"That's it, Angel," I growl, my voice a gravelly purr. My free hand tangles in her hair, guiding and possessing her. Take it all down." I feel her swallowing my essence and a shockwave of desire coursing through me. "That's a good girl."

My words soothe her, her golden eyes becoming heavy with desire and submission. Seeing her like this, trusting and needy, makes my inner beast purr with satisfaction.

I've never pushed her this far before, never given her this much of my blood and venom at once. But I need her pliant, entirely under my thrall, for what will happen. Only by surrendering to my power, my control, can she fully embrace the depths of her desire, the filthy fantasies she's kept locked away for so long.

It's a delicate balance, walking the line between pleasure and pain, dominance and submission. But I know my angel, know her limits and her needs. I'll push her to the brink, shatter her into a million pieces, only to put her back together again, stronger and more beautiful than ever.

She moans around my wrist, her body trembling as the blood and venom work their magic. I can feel her arousal through our bond, a tidal wave of need and desperation that threatens to consume us both.

But I ride it out, letting her drink her fill until she's teetering on the edge of oblivion. Only then do I pull away, licking the wound closed with a quick swipe of my tongue.

"Good girl," I murmur, my voice rough with hunger. "Now, let's see how long you can last before you're begging me to fuck you senseless."

We arrive at my next destination, Dani, in a daze beside me. "Where... where are we?" she murmurs, her voice thick with confusion and desire.

I ignore her question, step out of the car, and move to her side. I open the door, helping her to her feet. Her pretty pink toes are encased in those sexy black heels, and her long, sun-kissed legs swing out. She stands on unsteady feet, and I wrap an arm around her waist, pulling her flush against me.

Gripping her chin, I tilt her face up to meet my gaze. She's so far gone, drunk on my blood and venom, that I can feel her inhibitions melting away through our bond. Perfect.

Exactly where I want her.

Taking her hand, I lead her to the establishment's back entrance. The bouncer asks for my credentials, which I provide without hesitation.

As we step inside, it's like entering another world entirely. Low lights cast a seductive glow, sultry music pulsing through the air. People are everywhere, tucked away in hidden corners, lost in the throes of passion. Fucking, sucking, threesomes, and more—a decadent display of hedonism and desire. Vampires and other supernaturals mingle freely, indulging in every depraved act imaginable.

Thank fuck for Dani's potion, masking her scent from prying noses.

I discovered this exclusive exhibitionist club online last week, knowing it would cater perfectly to Dani's deepest fantasies of being taken, claimed, in public. I doubt even Lucian is aware of its existence. Gaining membership required a hefty fee and extensive vetting, but I didn't give a single fuck. I made the calls, paid the price, and now I get to play with my angel in the most delicious ways.

Dani sucks in a sharp breath as she takes in the scene before her, her eyes widening. "Rhyland..." she starts, a warning in her tone that comes out as more of a needy whimper.

Her grip on my bicep tightens as I lead her to the front desk. I give the attendant my name, and he nods in recognition, guiding us to our private table.

"Thank you, Mr. Erikkson. Please use the provided button when you're ready for the *other* room," he says, handing me a small device resembling a garage door opener. With a curt nod, he takes his leave.

I smirk, pocketing the buzzer. Oh, I have plans for that room—for my naughty angel. She has no idea what's in store for her tonight.

But first, I'm going to enjoy playing with her. Make her see what her teasing and bratty behavior has unleashed. And by the time I'm done with her, she'll be begging me to take her, to claim her in front of everyone.

Dani's eyes dart around the room, taking in the sights before her. The haze of desire still clouds her gaze, but a flicker of confusion breaks through. "Where the hell are we, Rhyland?" she asks, her voice breathy and strained.

I follow her line of sight, landing on a couple nearby. The man has a woman on her knees, his cock buried deep in her throat as she gags and sputters around his length. Dani's breath hitches, her thighs clenching together at the erotic display.

I know she likes to watch just as much as she wants me to claim her in front of everyone. Her desire spikes and I have to shift, adjusting my aching erection.

"Just a club," I lie smoothly, easing her closer to me on the plush leather bench. The soft material cradles our bodies as I grip the nape of her neck, tangling my fingers in her silky hair. With a firm tug, I force her to meet my gaze, her blown pupils ringed in molten gold. Her desire thrums through our bond, hot and heady.

Leaning in close, I brush my lips against the shell of her ear. "Ready to play, baby?" I purr.

She nods, a shiver running through her body at my words. Slowly, teasingly, I peel down the front of her dress, revealing one perfect, dusty pink nipple. The cool air of the club instantly pebbles her flesh, the rosy bud begging for my touch.

Unable to resist, I bend down, capturing her nipple between my lips. I suck lightly at first, then harder, flattening my tongue against her skin and laving her entire breast with worshipful attention. She tastes like heaven, sweet and intoxicating.

Dani moans, her head falling back against the seat as I work her sensitive flesh. I don't give a single fuck who sees this, who watches me worship my woman. Let them look. Let them see that no one else can touch her, that only I can give her what she needs. It's still a struggle for me, allowing others to feast their eyes on her naked beauty, but I'll endure it for *her*. For the kinky, filthy desires that make her blood sing.

Lost in her taste and feel, I almost miss the waitress approaching our table. "Drinks?" she asks, her voice cutting through the haze of lust that surrounds us.

I hastily order our drinks with the waitress, who seems utterly unfazed by the debauchery surrounding her. Clearly, she's seen it all. With a curt nod, she disappears, leaving me to return my full attention to Dani's delectable body.

Pulling down the other side of her delicate dress, I expose her neglected nipple to the cool air. It puckers instantly, begging for my touch. I oblige, licking and flicking the sensitive bud with the tip of my tongue. Dani's fingers tangle in my hair, tugging me closer, guiding my mouth exactly where she wants it.

"Rhyland... please... fuck, my body is on fire," she whimpers, her hips rolling against the leather seat, seeking friction. "I ache..."

I know exactly what she's feeling—my blood only intensifies her desires and needs.

I glance up, catching her gaze fixated on the couple nearby. The man has the woman's head bobbing up and down his shaft, her throat bulging obscenely with each thrust. Dani bites her bottom lip, a moan escaping her as she watches, her arousal spiking through our bond.

The waitress returns with our drinks, placing them on the table. I slip her a crisp hundred-dollar bill and dismiss her without a word. My focus is solely on Dani, on the need pulsing between us.

Reaching down, I unbutton my pants, freeing my aching cock from its confines. It springs out, hard as steel and throbbing with desire. Dani's eyes widen as she takes in my impressive length, her tongue darting out to wet her lips.

"On your knees, Angel," I command. "Time for your dessert since you wanted it so badly."

Dani looks up at me, her eyes wide and glazed with lust. "W-what?" she stammers, her tongue darting out to wet her lips.

I smirk, running my thumb along her bottom lip. "You heard me, baby. Didn't you tell that waiter how much you love something hot and gooey in your mouth? Well, I've got just the thing for you."

Her cheeks flush, realization dawning as she recalls her earlier words. "Rhyland, I was just—"

"Teasing?" I interrupt, my grip on her chin tightening. "Trying to get a rise out of me? Well, congratulations, sweetheart. It fucking worked. Now you're gonna get on your knees and eat your dessert like a good little whore. Right here in front of everyone."

Dani shivers. Slowly, she sinks to the ground, her movements graceful and deliberate. She looks up at me through her thick lashes, a coy smile on her lips.

"You want this, don't you?" I taunt, fisting my hand in her hair and guiding her mouth closer to my aching cock. "Want to wrap those pretty lips around my dick? Show everyone in this club what a good little cocksucker you are."

Dani moans, her eyes fluttering shut as she nuzzles against my shaft. "Yes," she breathes, her hot breath ghosting over my sensitive skin. "Want to taste you—feel you in my throat."

"Then do it," I command, tightening my grip on her hair. "Suck me, Angel. Make me come down your throat like the filthy girl you are."

With a needy whine, Dani parts her lips, taking the head of my cock into her wet, welcoming mouth. I groan, my head falling back as she begins to work me with her tongue, lapping at the pre-cum beading at the tip. The sight of her on her knees, her red lips stretched around my girth, is enough to make me want to fuck her face until she gags.

I hold back, determined to make this last as long as possible. Glancing around the room, I notice three men already fixated on Dani, their eyes glued to the sight of her lips wrapped around my cock. She takes me as deep as she can, her nose brushing against my pelvis, and I barely suppress a feral growl.

"Fuuck... that's it, baby. Eat my cock, swallow it down. Such a good girl," I praise, my voice strained with pleasure. Dani moans around my shaft, the vibrations sending shockwaves through my body. "See all these men watching you suck me off? You like that, Angel? Like being watched while I fuck your throat?"

Dani's arousal spikes higher, pulsing through our bond like a livewire. My cock thickens in response, stretching her lips obscenely. She splutters around my girth, drool and spit leaking from the corners of her mouth and down my balls. I growl at the sensation, at the feel of her silky throat constricting around me as I push her head down further. She can take it. My girl likes it rough, and she's had plenty of practice accommodating my nine-inch cock.

Suddenly, Dani pops off, gasping for breath. "Fuck," she pants, her chest heaving. "Rhy—"

I tighten my grip on her hair, tugging sharply at the roots. "Did I say you could stop?" I demand, my voice a low, dangerous rumble.

Dani's eyes, already watering from the gagging and pressure on her throat, widen at my tone. "N-no," she stammers, her breath coming in shaky gasps.

Without warning, I shove her head back down, forcing my cock to the back of her throat. She gags, the sound only fueling my desire. "Then get back on it and suck it like the cock-hungry whore you are, baby."

Dani squeezes her thighs together, a desperate groan muffled by my thick shaft. The vibrations make my balls tingle, tightening with impending release. I'm hitting deep now, controlling the bobbing of her head with my hand fisted in her hair. She's pliant, letting me fuck her throat with abandon.

"Eyes on me, baby," I command, positioning myself on the edge of the bench to get a better view of her face. "Let me look at those beautiful eyes while I fuck your throat."

Dani obeys, her tear-filled gaze locking with mine. The sight of her, mascara smudged, lips swollen and stretched around my cock, is enough to make me explode. But I hold back, determined to push her to the brink of ecstasy.

"Fuck, you look so good like this," I groan, my hips thrusting shallowly into her mouth. "My perfect little cocksucker, taking me so deep. You love this, don't you? Love being used, being watched, being my dirty girl."

Dani whimpers, her eyes fluttering shut as she surrenders to the sensation, to the filthy words falling from my lips. I can feel her getting more turned on by my words.

My orgasm comes quickly—the sight of her so beautiful, swallowing all of me, I can't take it anymore.

"That's it, Angel," I encourage, my thrusts growing more erratic as I near the edge. "Take it all, every fucking inch. Gonna come so hard down your throat, fill you up until you're choking on it."

With a final, brutal thrust, I bury myself in her sweet mouth, my balls on her chin, and my cock pulses as I shoot my load directly into her waiting throat. Dani swallows around me, milking every last drop as I ride out the waves of my orgasm.

I groan—loudly.

Finally, I pull out, a trail of saliva and cum connecting the tip of my cock to her swollen lips. She looks up at me, dazed and panting, with a satisfied smile.

"*Fuck,* baby," I praise, brushing a strand of hair from her forehead. My dick is still rock-hard and ready for more. "We're just getting started. The night is young, and I have so much more in store for you."

DANICA

85

I'm so freaking high on Rhyland's blood and venom right now I can barely keep my arousal at bay. My mind is a hazy, lust-filled blur, my body thrumming with need and desire.

So, here we are, in some fancy-ass exhibition club where public fucking is just par for the course. Our table is up on the upper level, which sounds great in theory, but in reality, it's like we're goddamn goldfish in a bowl, on full display for all the perverts below.

They're not even batting an eye at the live porn show Rhyland and I are putting on. It's just another day at the office for them, another couple of exhibitionists getting their rocks off in public.

But for me? It's a whole new level of fucked up and filthy, and I am here for it.

I lick my swollen lips, savoring the musky, sweet, and salty taste of Rhyland's arousal. It's a flavor I'll never tire of, a reminder of how he came down my throat, hot and hard and pulsing with pleasure. And the knowledge that we had an audience? That strangers were watching our little pornographic performance? Well, let's just say it adds a whole new level of 'hot damn' to the proceedings.

My eyes dart around the room, a shiver of excitement racing down my spine as I feel the weight of countless gazes upon me. It's like being caressed by invisible hands, each pair of eyes leaving a trail of heat on my skin. The air feels thick with desire, charged with an electric current of lust and anticipation.

But before I can fully bask in the intoxicating attention, Rhyland's strong hands are on me, pulling me up with an urgency that steals my breath. His lips crash against mine with a ferocity that makes my knees weak. It's not just a kiss—it's a claiming, a marking, a declaration to everyone watching that I am his and his alone.

He thrusts his tongue into my mouth, chasing the taste of himself, and I moan shamelessly, melting into his embrace. His hands are everywhere, gripping my hips, snaking up my ribcage until they find my aching, swollen breasts.

The taste of him—dark, rich, and sinfully delicious—floods my senses, drowning out everything else.

At this moment, with Rhyland's arms around me and the heat of strangers' gazes on my skin, I feel more alive than ever. It's dangerous, thrilling, and utterly intoxicating. As Rhyland's hands roam my body, leaving fire trails in their wake, I know this is just the beginning of a night that will push us both to our limits and beyond.

I groan as he kneads the sensitive flesh, my nipples hardening into tight, desperate peaks. I never thought Rhyland would be okay with this, with letting anyone else see me naked or pleasuring him. But I can feel it through our bond, the way he's pushing past his discomfort, his possessive instincts, all for me. For my fantasy.

And hell, if that doesn't make me love him even more.

I pour everything I'm feeling into our bond, letting him feel the depth of my desire, the intensity of my need. I show him how much this turns me on, how much I crave his touch, taste, and everything. And how, no matter who else might be watching, no one in this world or any other will ever compare to the man who holds my heart.

The man who gives me the most mind-blowing orgasms and is currently devouring my mouth like a starved animal.

When I teased the waiter earlier, I knew exactly what I was doing. I knew I was pushing Rhyland to the brink, testing the limits of his control. But even still, his reaction scared me as much as it aroused me.

To know I can still get under his skin and drive him to the edge of madness with an innocent flirt. It's a heady, intoxicating feeling. And the way he's so fiercely protective of me, so unapologetically possessive? It's like a drug, and I'm a hopeless fucking addict.

He's going to make me pay for my little stunt, and I'm going to love every damn second of it.

Because this man, this beautiful, infuriating, dominant Viking vampire? He's mine. And I'm his.

Rhyland wastes no time, lifting me onto the table like I weigh nothing. I'm at the perfect height now, my pussy lined up with his hungry gaze as he sits on the bench in front of me. He pushes my dress up slowly, teasingly, before spreading my legs wide and exposing me to the room.

My eyes dart around once more, my pulse racing. And sure enough, we've still got quite the captive audience. It's like we're the main attraction at some high-end, adults-only circus, and everyone's got front-row seats to the show.

One guy in particular catches my attention, and holy hell, talk about multitasking. He's got his cock buried so deep in some girl's throat. I'm half convinced she's going to need a breathing apparatus. But despite his, uh, current engagement, his eyes are locked on me with an intensity that could melt steel.

I feel a flush creeping up my neck, my skin prickling with heat under the weight of his stare.

"Eyes on me, baby."

I quickly look away and focus on Rhyland as he reaches for the glass beside me, plucking an ice cube from its depths with a wicked glint in his eye. I watch, my breath catching in my throat, as he slowly drags the frozen cube up my inner thigh, leaving a trail of icy fire in its wake.

I flinch at the sudden chill, a gasp escaping my lips as goosebumps erupt across my sensitive skin, my nipples pebbling painfully. Before I can even process the sensation, Rhyland's hot tongue is there, lapping at the moisture left behind, chasing away the cold with the searing heat of his mouth, his beard tickling my inner thigh in the most intoxicating way.

I moan, my head falling back as he works his way higher, his tongue tracing intricate patterns on my trembling flesh. He repeats the process on my other thigh, the contrast of hot and cold sending shockwaves of pleasure racing through my veins.

I feel his blood coursing through me, heating me from the inside out until I'm a writhing, panting mess of need and desire. The taste of his blood—spicy and sweet, cinnamon and chocolate, and I can see why their blood is so addicting—an aphrodisiac. My pussy aches, empty and clenching around nothing, desperate to be filled. My nipples are so hard, pebbled peaks begging for his touch, his mouth, his teeth.

And the need to come, to finally find release after hours of teasing and denial, is so strong that I can barely breathe. I'm on the edge of something huge, something earth-shattering, my body wound tighter than a bowstring.

Rhyland pulls away, his mouth leaving my skin with a final, teasing lick.

I whimper, my hips bucking up off the table in a desperate search for friction, for anything to ease the ache between my thighs. Rhyland chuckles, his Nordic-blue eyes dark with the promise. He places the ice cube back into the glass.

Rhyland pulls my lacy underwear to the side, baring my aching, needy pussy to his gaze, and everything else fades away.

Yes, fucking finally!

"Look at me, baby," he commands, his voice low and rough with desire. My eyes snap to his, getting lost in the swirling depths of blue, the love and arousal I see there stealing the breath from my lungs. "Watch me while I devour what's *mine.*"

God yes!

And then his head is between my thighs, his tongue flicking out to taste me, and holy fuck, I nearly come on the spot. I'm so sensitive from all the edging, so desperate for release, that even the slightest touch is almost too much to bear.

Rhyland doesn't stop, doesn't slow down. He pushes me back onto the table, the white tablecloth cool against my overheated skin as I lean back on my elbows, giving him better access to my dripping core.

He spreads me wide, his fingers digging into my thighs as he holds me open for his hungry mouth. His tongue is everywhere, licking and sucking and flicking over my clit in a relentless assault of pleasure that has me seeing stars.

I tangle my fingers in his hair, holding him in place as I grind against his face, chasing the release that's been denied to me for so fucking long. I'm so close, *so goddamn close*, my nipples pebble and aching, my pussy clenching around nothing as I teeter on the brink.

I risk another peek behind me, my heart skipping a beat as I realize that we're still being watched, that all those hungry eyes are devouring the sight of Rhyland eating me out like I'm his favorite meal.

"Fuck, Rhyland," I pant, my voice high and breathy with need. "I'm gonna come, baby. Don't stop."

Of course, because he's a sadistic bastard who lives to torment me, that's precisely what he does. He pulls back, leaving me empty and aching, as I let out a frustrated whine.

"Hold that thought, Angel," he says with a wicked grin, his lips and beard glistening with my juices. "We're just getting started."

I want to scream, to punch him, to tackle him to the ground and ride his cock until I finally get the release I so desperately need. But I know that's exactly what he wants, what he's been waiting for all night.

"You're an asshole, Rhyland," I snarl, with equal parts fury and desire. "But if you think I'm going to beg for you, you've got another thing coming. I am done with your games tonight."

Rhyland's grin is pure sin, his eyes glittering with a dark promise as he leans in close, his breath hot against my ear. "Oh, I don't think, baby," he purrs, his fingers skating up my thighs, making me shake with need. "I know. By the time I'm done with you tonight, you'll be begging me for mercy, screaming my name so loud they'll hear you in *Valhalla*."

I shiver at the promise in his words, my body already aching for his touch, for the sweet torture I know he has in store.

Rhyland pulls my dress back down, covering my exposed flesh from the hungry gazes of the room.

I catch a flash of anger in his eyes, a possessive fury that sends a thrill down my spine before he slips his mask of cool indifference back into place. He's trying to play it off like he's unfazed, but I know better. The thought of all these people seeing me, wanting me, is driving him crazy.

And I'd be lying if I said I didn't love every second of it.

Before I can dwell on that thought for too long, the gentleman from earlier appears at our table, a knowing smirk on his face. "Right this way, sir," he says, gesturing for us to follow him.

I frown in confusion as Rhyland helps me to my feet, his hand possessive on the small of my back.

Where the hell are we going now?

As we approach the back of the building, down a long hallway lined with glass panels, I start to get an idea. People are crowded around each panel, their faces pressed against the glass as they gawk at whatever's inside.

And when I finally see for myself, my jaw nearly hits the floor.

In one room, two men are going at it like animals, one slamming his cock into the other's ass while he begs for more, harder, faster. In the next, a woman is tied up with intricate rope work. Her body is contorted into a beautiful, erotic sculpture as her partner fucks her from behind.

And in the last room, a woman straddles a blindfolded man, riding his cock with wild abandon as the onlookers press their faces against the glass, their breath fogging up the surface with each panting gasp.

It's like something out of a goddamn porno, a live sex show put on for the viewing pleasure of anyone with a pulse and a pervy streak. And as much as the rational part of my brain is screaming at me to run, to get the hell out of this den of sex and sin, I can't deny the thrill of excitement that runs through me at the thought of being watched, of putting on a show of my own.

Rhyland must sense my thoughts through our bond because he leans close, his lips brushing against my ear as he speaks from behind me as I stare at the woman grinding on the man's cock. "Still think you won't beg, Angel?" he murmurs, his voice low and rough with promise. "We'll see about that."

With that, he takes my hand and leads me to an empty room at the end of the hall. The glass walls offer an unobstructed view of the plush, king-sized bed—a kinky wonderland of cuffs, whips, chains, and Fifty Shades of "Oh My!"

Oh, fuck. What have I gotten myself into?

DANICA

86

I can feel Rhyland's discomfort through our bond like a giant neon sign flashing, "I'd rather eat glass than do this." He's already given me quite the show on that table.

I know he's doing this for me, and I love him so much for it—I snap out of it.

I stop short, grabbing his arm like it's a life preserver in this sea of sexual tension. "Rhyland," I whisper, looking up into those baby blues that could make a girl forget her own name. "I... I don't want this."

Rhyland's eyes soften. "Are you sure?" he asks, probably wondering if I've been body-snatched.

"Yes," I nod, tugging him like a stubborn puppy on a leash. "Take me home, you big Viking lug."

We zoom through the city, the lights blurring like a neon fever dream, my mind racing faster than Rhyland's driving. Sure, that room probably would've been hotter than Satan's sauna, but I can't push Rhyland into something he's not comfortable with. Even if the thought of it makes my lady bits sing the cha-cha.

I know he's still itching to punish me for my little flirting stunt earlier. The way he's gripping my thigh, you'd think it was the steering wheel. His eyes are glued to the road like he's afraid it'll disappear if he looks away, and he's giving me the silent treatment.

Oh boy, I feel I'm in for one hell of a "talking to" when we get home.

Should I even consider pushing my luck with what I've got up my sleeve?

Rhyland parks the car and opens my door like the chivalrous Viking he is. As we enter the mansion, he takes my hand, clearly ready to drag me upstairs for what I'm sure will be a very... thorough discussion about proper restaurant etiquette.

"Hold your horses, Romeo," I say, my heart pounding. "I'll meet you up there. Gotta grab something first."

Rhyland gives me a look that's part suspicion, part 'what are you up to now?' It's like he can smell the mischief brewing. He drops my hand. "Okay, baby. Be quick," he says, rounding the corner and heading upstairs.

The moment he's out of sight, I bolt for the kitchen like my ass is on fire. I grab what I need—a little surprise Sable and I have been cooking up. Part of me is excited to try this on Rhyland, but another part is wondering if I should start writing my will now.

I stand there, biting my lip hard enough to leave marks, pouring two glasses of bourbon. My hands shake like I'm diffusing a bomb instead of making drinks.

Fuck it.

I'll deal with the fallout later. Now, it's time to flip the script and cash in on that bet. I won fair and square, so I'm collecting my winnings.

As I head upstairs, drinks in hand and secret weapon cleverly disguised as innocent bourbon, I can't help but grin like the cat who got the cream. Oh, Rhyland has no idea what's coming. Let's see how Mr. Alpha Viking handles being caught with his horns down for once.

I open the door carefully, trying not to spill his spiked drink. And there he is, my Nordic Adonis, staring out on the balcony like he's contemplating world domination or maybe just how he's going to punish me. His back to me, all muscle and man in that tailored suit that should be illegal in at least forty-nine states.

He looks over his shoulder, and holy hell, those baby blues are blazing hotter than a supernova. There's heat, there's hunger, and there's *definitely* a promise of retribution for my little stunt tonight. His dark hair and neatly trimmed beard frame those chiseled features like Michelangelo himself carved them.

Holy hell. This man could make me come with just a look, and I'm already more wound up than a jack-in-the-box after hours of denied orgasms.

Alright, Dani, keep it together. You've got a plan, remember? Time to turn the tables on our resident Viking vamp. Let's see how he likes being the one left breathless and begging for once.

"Brought us a drink," I chirp, sauntering towards him like I'm not about to unleash chaos in a glass.

Rhyland smirks, taking his glass like it's not laced with vampire kryptonite. "Hmm... need to take the edge off, baby? Worried?"

I swallow the knot in my throat. Worried? Ha! I'm about as worried as a mouse in a room full of cats. But Sable and I tested this on Erik—our willing guinea pig—and it worked like a charm. Who knew vampires were so susceptible to magical roofies?

I smile, trying to look innocent. "Yeah, you know, all that edging. I need a stiff drink."

Rhyland's smirk turns predatory. "Oh, I'll give you something stiff, alright, baby, right after I turn that pretty ass of yours red for your little stunt tonight. And don't think I've forgotten about your heroic bullshit in Aquaria."

I groan, rolling my eyes. "Seriously? You're still pissy about that? It's not like I could just stand by and watch The Moron—aka Lucian—go in half-cocked to get Seraphina."

"You went in blindly, and it was not safe Dani," he growls, his alpha male showing. "We're supposed to do things together, remember? When will you get it through your pretty head that my job is to protect you from harm? You went against me."

I roll my eyes again, this time with extra sass. "Yes, oh mighty *Thor*," I drawl. "When will you realize I don't always do as I'm told? Shocking, I know."

Rhyland moves closer, his heat wrapping around me like a blanket made of pure sex. "Oh, I'm well aware you don't do anything you're told. Not even when it means staying safe—for that, you'll learn, Angel."

I swallow hard, feeling like I just poked a sleeping dragon with a very short stick.

He leans down, his breath hot against my ear, "Roll those pretty eyes at me one more time, sweetheart, and I'll give you something to roll them about."

I take a shaky breath, raising my glass like I'm about to toast the end of my sanity. "Cheers."

Little does he know, school is about to be in session—and I'm the headmistress tonight. Bottoms up, big boy!

Rhyland steps back, smirking like he's got this shit in the bag. "Cheers." He raises the glass to his lips and gulps it down like it's the elixir of life.

I hold my breath, waiting for the fireworks to start.

Rhyland's face morphs from smug to utterly bewildered as he starts swaying like he's on the deck of Gideon's ship during a hurricane. He stumbles to the chair, looking up at me with those blazing blues now clouded with confusion. "What the fuck?"

"Sorry, babe. All's fair in love and war, right?"

I quickly approach him, helping his stumbling ass to the bed before he becomes a Viking-shaped puddle on the floor. "Up ya go, big guy," I grunt, maneuvering him onto the mattress.

"Dani... what... did... you...?" He falls back on the bed, his eyes drooping fast.

Sable and I worked our asses off on this little witch's brew. Turns out, Sable's grandma—a witch so powerful she could probably turn you into a toad just by thinking about it—knows of an herb that can knock a vampire on their supernatural ass—Shadows Grasp (because, apparently, witches aren't big on creative naming), and it's been a secret weapon for centuries.

Sable and I turned it into a magic potion that can be slipped into a drink with no muss, fuss, or telltale smell or taste. I figured this was easier than trying to stab my vampire with a needle. Plus, way less chance of me accidentally stabbing myself in the process.

I couldn't believe my eyes when we tested this little cocktail on Erik. It worked like a charm, turning our resident stoic vampire into a pile of undead goo. It's our ace in the hole now, and tonight, it's my secret weapon to turn my Viking into putty in my hands. For the next few hours, he'll be about as threatening as a kitten on catnip.

I maneuver him into position on the bed, feeling like a naughty kid rearranging the furniture while the parents are out. Only in this case, the furniture is a 6'4" vampire who usually calls all the shots.

As Rhyland slips deeper into his forced siesta, I can't help but grin. Oh, how the mighty have fallen—time to see how Mr. Alpha handles being the submissive for once. Let the games begin, and may the odds be ever in *my* favor.

I leap off the bed like a ninja and dash to grab my secret weapon, numero dos—rope.

Time to undress the sleeping beauty. And holy hell, who knew an unconscious vampire could weigh more than an elephant?

"Come on, big guy," I grunt, wrestling with his jacket like it's trying to eat me. "Work with me here!"

Rhyland flops back onto the bed, out cold. I attack his clothes with the determination of a woman on a mission. Shirt? Gone. Pants and boxers? Sayonara. Shoes? See ya!

And there he is, in all his glory. All yummy tatted chest, skin golden from his newfound ability to sunbathe without bursting into flames. His colossal cock, lying at half-mast on his stomach. Those chiseled abs rise and fall slowly as he snoozes away in la-la land. Christmas came early, and I got the world's sexiest present.

Time for some creative gift wrapping. I tie Rhyland up by his hands to the headboard, feeling like a naughty girl scout earning her bondage badge. Then I work my way down to his feet, securing them to the bedposts. He's spread out like a Viking buffet, open to my every whim. Bon appétit!

For the finishing touch, I cup my hands over each rope, channeling my power. My hands glow as I seal the bonds. Unless I say so, he's not getting free. There's no telling what he'll do when he gets his strength back, but that's a problem for future Dani. Right now, I've got a Viking to ravish.

This ride's about to get wild, and I'm holding the reins. Who's giving orders now, huh? Spoiler alert: it's not the guy currently drooling on the pillow.

Sorry, babe, but class is in session, and Professor Dani is about to teach you a lesson in humility.

RHYLAND

87

I come to, my head pounding like a fucking jackhammer.

What the hell happened?

I haven't felt this shitty since I was drugged fucking ages ago. That's a memory I'd rather forget.

Shadows Grasp.

I force my eyes open, taking in my surroundings, and instantly notice I'm tied up. I yank on the ropes, but it's useless. I'm weak as fuck. Even my telekinesis is out of my grasp. My mouth is drier than a bone.

That's the power with this shit—it takes away all your strength, your supernatural abilities, your energy and leaves you weak as any mortal.

I growl low in my throat, frustration and anger bubbling up inside me. This fucking bullshit hasn't reared its ugly head in goddamn eons. I'd hoped it was lost to the world, buried deep where no supernatural fucker could ever find it again. But apparently, the universe loves to shit all over me.

"Dani?" I croak out, my voice rough and strained.

How the fuck did she get her hands on this shit, and why the hell would she drug me? I'm pissed off and ready to rain down holy hell on her bratty ass. If this is her idea of getting even, she's in for a world of hurt.

I try to sit up against the headboard, but I'm as immobile as a fucking statue. Fuming, I gather what strength I have. "Danica!" I roar, my voice bouncing off the walls like a sonic boom.

The bathroom door creaks open, and I hear Dani's footsteps approaching. "No need to shout, babe. I can hear you just fine," she purrs, with fake innocence.

I can't see her from this angle; the bathroom is hidden behind me. But then she strolls into view, and *holy fuck*, my cock springs to attention like a goddamn soldier.

She's wearing this black lacy corset that barely covers her luscious tits, the fabric so sheer it's practically see-through. The corset stops at her hips, giving way to a pair of lacy black panties that hug her perfectly. Black thigh-high stockings and a garter belt complete the look, making my mouth water and my balls ache.

"Have a nice nap, sleeping beauty?" she teases, her lips curving into a wicked grin that infuriates and arouses me. "Or should I say, sleeping beast?"

I growl, torn between lust and fury. "What the hell do you think you're doing, Danica? Untie me. Now."

She taps her chin, pretending to think it over. "Hmm, let me see... Nope! Don't think I will. You see, I figured it was time for a little role reversal. How does it feel to be the one all tied up and at someone else's mercy, hmm?"

"This isn't funny, Angel," I snarl, tugging at my restraints. "When I get out of these—"

"You'll what?" she challenges, arching an eyebrow. "Spank me? Punish me? Ooh, I'm shaking in my stilettos."

Dani saunters closer, her hips swaying with each step. I can't take my eyes off her, drinking in every curve, every inch of exposed skin. It's taking every ounce of willpower not to lose my goddamn mind.

"You're playing with fire, woman. When I break free from these fucking ropes, I'm gonna turn that sweet ass of yours redder than a goddamn cherry."

I hate being powerless—too many memories of what that vicious bitch—the one who made me—did to me centuries ago. The feeling of being bound, helpless... it brings back shit I've spent lifetimes trying to forget.

Those memories are locked away deep where even Dani can't see them. She has no idea about the darkness in my past, and I want to keep it that way.

Dani pulling this shit has me seeing red, but at the same time, my cock is harder than fucking granite. It's a mindfuck of epic proportions.

She leans close, her lips ghosting over my ear, sending an involuntary shiver down my spine. "I think it's your turn to beg, Rhyland," she whispers, with challenge.

I force my eyes shut, trying to ground myself in the present. This is Dani—my mate, my angel—not that sadistic monster from my past.

When she nips my earlobe, I have to clench my jaw to keep from groaning. Fuck, she knows exactly which buttons to push and how to drive me absolutely wild. This dominant side of Dani is sexy as hell, but I'll be damned—

"Don't get it twisted, Angel," I growl, my voice dark and dangerous. "I don't fucking beg. Ever."

She pulls back, her eyes gleaming with mischief. "I highly doubt that babe," she purrs, trailing a finger down my chest. The light touch leaves a trail of fire in its wake. "I think you're gonna be begging me sooner than you think."

Goddammit. You have no idea what kind of beast you've just unleashed, baby.

I tug at the ropes again, harder this time, making the whole damn bed shake.

"Nice try, babe. But those are magically reinforced," Dani taunts, wiggling her fingers to show off her light magic. Fuck me, she's thought this through.

I grit my teeth, my jaw clenching so hard I'm surprised it doesn't crack. "Dani, I'm giving you one last chance to untie me. Or I swear to god, you won't be able to sit for a week when I'm done with you."

Deep down, I know my threats are empty. But fuck if I'm gonna let her think she can pull this shit without consequences.

She ignores my warning, climbing onto the bed with all the grace of a predatory cat. When she straddles my torso, my cock strains to reach her, desperate for the heat of her pussy. I groan, yanking at the ropes again, needing to touch her, to feel her skin under my hands.

Dani bends down, her tongue tracing the lines of my tattoos before zeroing in on my nipple. She tugs it between her teeth, then soothes the sting with her tongue. I can't help but moan, thrashing underneath her like a man possessed.

"Mmm... keep wiggling like that, and I'll come before I'm ready," she warns, her voice husky with desire.

I thrust my hips up, grinding my shaft against her lacey underwear, and she gasps. "Yeah? You want to come, baby? Too bad I'm tied the fuck up and can't touch you properly."

Dani smirks. "Oh, you can still make me come, and you will."

She stands above me, her feet on either side of my hips, and slowly, torturously, pulls her black lacy panties down. Then she moves up, positioning herself right above my face, her pussy mere inches from my mouth—my mouth waters. "I believe you never finished your dessert," she purrs, a wicked smile curving her lips. "And I hear licking the plate is customary."

I don't know what the fuck has gotten into her—maybe it's all the blood I gave her, or the denied orgasms, or my venom. Whatever it is, it's got me leaking on my stomach, my balls aching, and my cock harder than I've ever been in my fucking life.

She pushes her pussy closer to my lips, and the scent of her arousal hits me like a freight train. I can't help myself—I dive in, licking a long stripe up to her clit. She moans, her head falling back as she rides my face.

I groan into her, cursing and praising her in equal measure. My hands itch to touch her, to grab that perfect ass and pull her even closer. But all I can do is lie here, bound and at her mercy, as she uses my mouth for her pleasure.

And fuck me if it isn't the hottest thing I've ever experienced.

Dani grips my hair, using it as leverage as she rides my face with abandon. I can barely breathe, but fuck if I care. I work my tongue the way I know drives her wild, relishing every moan and whimper that falls from her lips. My cock throbs painfully, leaking precum at the sheer eroticism of the situation.

"Yeah, oh, fuck... just like that," Dani pants above me, her voice thick with pleasure. "I'm gonna come so hard on your face—you owe me orgasms, Rhyland."

All I can do is groan into her pussy as she grinds harder. I yank at the ropes again, desperate to touch her, to feel her. The denial only fuels my frustration, and I growl into her slick pussy.

It doesn't take long before Dani's crying out, her release flooding my mouth and coating my tongue. Her thighs clamp around my head, muffling her cries of ecstasy as she rides out her orgasm above me.

"Ohh...my god, Rhyland... fuck!" she shouts, her fingers tightening in my hair as she writhes and shakes. I swallow every drop of her sweet nectar, reveling in the taste of her pleasure.

Fuck, I've never been so turned on and frustrated, and pissed off in my life. Every nerve ending is buzzing, every muscle taut with the need to claim her—take back control. When I get out of these ropes, I'm going to bend her over and take her hard, teaching her exactly who's in charge.

"Oh, my god...I needed that." Dani shifts down my body and kisses me, our tongues tangling as she tastes herself on my tongue.

I jerk up to her closer, groaning into her mouth as I need her now more than ever. "Dani. Baby, untie me. Now."

She smirks, her eyes glittering with mischief. "Nope," she purrs, popping the 'p.' "I'm just getting started. Not until you beg, Rhyland."

I growl, tugging at the ropes. My body's still weak. Fuck, how much did she give me? "You must have lost your damn mind, baby," I snarl, my voice rough. "I. Don't. Beg."

I push down the darkness threatening to surface. This isn't about my fucked-up past—Dani has no clue what memories she's stirring up. She's just playing, being my feisty little angel, not trying to break me like that psychotic bitch did.

Dani sits up, her breasts brushing my chest as she straddles my waist. "We'll see," she teases, her eyes full of challenge.

She leans down, kissing my chest before trailing her hot tongue down to my abs, licking and nipping at each muscle and dip. I jump and grind up into her, my cock achingly hard and leaking like a fucking faucet.

"Hmm... someone is awfully eager," she purrs, nestling between my legs. "Let's see what we're working with here."

She grabs my cock, then she pauses, taking in the sight of my straining length. "Mmm...The Pleasure Pole—such a big *Viking Spear* you have." her voice all sexy and sultry.

Fuck, if that doesn't make my cock throb even harder, the head purpling and the vein pulsing, aching to feel her mouth wrapped around me again, her throat swallowing me down, taking it all deep down her throat.

"Put your mouth on it, Angel, and I'll show you a spear," I challenge, my voice rough with need. I'm practically vibrating with anticipation, my cock twitching and leaking in anticipation.

Instead, she surprises me by dipping her head even lower, taking my balls into her hot, wet mouth, her lips wrapping around one ball, then the other, her tongue swirling over the sensitive skin. I throw my head back and moan at the sensation, my hips bucking involuntarily. So damn worked up and unable to do anything but lie here and take what she gives me. She bathes my balls with her tongue, popping them out of her mouth every so often with a lewd, sucking sound that echoes in the room. The pleasure shoots straight to my cock, the sensation so intense it makes my toes curl.

Dani starts stroking my shaft with her free hand, her touch silky smooth as she glides up and down my length, working me like a pro. "Baby... if you don't either sit that sweet pussy down on my cock or wrap your lips around me, you're going to be sorry," I warn, my eyes darkening with the force of my need. "You have no idea what you're in for, Angel, and I won't be held responsible for your consequences."

She pops my balls out of her mouth with a wet, obscene sound, her lips glistening with her spit. "I'm willing to take that chance, babe. It's a rare sight to have you be the one squirming, and I'm enjoying this far too much to stop now."

Fucking. Hell. I'm so worked up I can barely think straight, and she's just sitting there, teasing me with that fucking smirk. I jolt my hips up, my cock aching for release, the head swollen and throbbing with need. "You've had your fun, now cut this shit out and untie me, Dani," I snarl, desperation bleeding into my voice.

She ignores my warning, taking me into her mouth inch by inch, her tongue swirling around the engorged head. I grit my teeth, watching as she attempts—and succeeds—to deep-throat me, my girth stretching her pretty little mouth.

"Ohh, fu... Dani... god damn, baby," I gasp, my hands curling into fists in my ropes as I fight to gain control. "Just like that...fuck."

She goes faster, taking me deeper, her lips stretched tight as she attempts to swallow me whole. Fuck, her mouth feels amazing, but it's not enough. I want more. I need to feel her throat constricting around me, choking on my length.

She rubs my balls with her free hand, her touch maddening as she sucks me off. I moan, my eyes rolling back in my head as pleasure zings through me, making my balls draw tight with need. Then her fingers skim lower, probing where no one has ever dared to venture.

I flinch and try to scramble away, my hips bucking. "What the fuck, Dani!" I growl, my eyes snapping open.

She pops off my cock, her lips red and swollen, drool and spit coating her lips and running down her throat. "What? Just testing the waters," she says, all calm like she's talking about the fucking weather. "There's a little backdoor button..." she wiggles her finger at my entrance. "Right..."

"I may be drugged and weak, but not enough for you to play in my ass," I snap, fixing her with a dark glare. I can feel a growl rumbling in my chest, a warning she'd do well to heed.

But Dani just hums. "How do you know you won't like it?" she teases, her hand inching closer again to my puckered hole. "You might find it's your new favorite thing, babe."

Fuck. Me.

I'm tied up, weak, and at Dani's mercy. I'm so fucking wound up I'm about to explode, and not in a friendly way. Dani rolls her eyes at my warning, and I swear, she will pay for that when I'm untied.

She takes me back down her throat, her finger still teasing my hole. I can't help but thrust up into her mouth, needing more, needing to feel her throat tightning around me. Dani moans, the vibrations shooting straight to my nuts. She starts circling my asshole with her finger, and it feels... fuck, it actually feels *good*. Sick, twisted, but good. Or maybe I'm so wound up that any touch drives me crazy.

"Fucking *Christ*, Dani," I grit out, my entire body tight as a bowstring. "Keep going."

She slows her mouth's rhythm, her lips dragging along my shaft as she keeps me on edge. If she doesn't speed up, I swear to god, I'm going to ram my cock down her throat. Her finger pushes inside me, just the tip, and I gasp as something inside me unfurls and lights up like a goddamn firework.

"Oh. I think I found something," Dani smirks, sounding way too damn pleased with herself. She keeps her finger gently pushing inside as she deepthroats my cock, stroking the magical spot she's found inside me. It feels incredible like my cock isn't the only thing on fire.

Fuck, I'm close, closer than I've ever been. "Ohhh... shiiiit...*fuck*, baby...I'm gonna come." I warn, my voice hoarse and desperate. "Fuck. *Please.*"

At that moment I know. I'm already cursing myself.

She pulls off my cock with a lewd, wet pop, the sound sending shivers racing down my spine. She slips her finger out of my ass, leaving me empty and aching, desperate for more. And then she just smiles at me, that infuriating, playful smirk that makes me want to wipe it off her face with my cock.

I clench my jaw, every muscle in my body coiled tight with the need to take control. She's pushing me, testing my limits, seeing how far she can take this before I snap. And fuck me, it's working.

This is payback. I know it. For all the teasing, all the denial I put her through tonight. But goddamnit, I'm done playing her little games. I'm done letting her call the fucking shots.

I know what I said, what I swore I'd never do. But fuck it all to hell, she's pushed me to the brink, and I can't take another second of this sweet torture.

"Oh my, did I hear that correctly?" She teases, batting her eyelashes with mock innocence. "I could've sworn I just heard the big, bad Viking *beg*. But that can't be right, can it? After all, you did say you don't beg, Mr. Alpha Male." She leans in close, her breath ghosting over my chest. "Or maybe... you just needed the right motivation?"

My patience shatters like goddamn glass. I yank at the ropes, every muscle in my body straining as I pour all my strength into breaking free. The restraints snap, the hooks tearing out of the headboard with a splintering crack. Wood explodes outward, the entire fucking headboard disintegrating under the force of my rage.

The Shadow's Grasp finally wearing off.

She's in fucking trouble now.

Dani's eyes widen in fear, her face paling. "Oh, shit," she breathes, scrambling for the bathroom like a bat out of hell.

But she's not getting away that easily. I move faster than her pretty little head can process, catching her mid-sprint and wrapping her up in my arms. I spin her around, the momentum carrying us until I have her pinned against the wall, trapped between the hard planes of my body and the unyielding surface behind her.

My hand finds her throat, gripping tight enough to hold her in place but not enough to hurt. Her caramel-gold eyes stare up at me, a delicious mix of fear and arousal swirling in their depths. She knows she pushed me too far, knows precisely what kind of punishment she's in for.

"Did you have your little fun, Angel?" I growl, my thumb rubbing over her pulse point, feeling her heart hammering beneath my palm. She swallows hard, her throat bobbing under my hand. "I fucking hope so, baby. Cause now you're in some deep shit."

DANICA

88

Well, shit. I did not see this coming. Apparently, Rhyland's supercharged vampire DNA bounces back faster than a rubber ball on steroids. Erik was out for the count for hours, but not my Viking.

Clearly, I didn't think this through.

I was so caught up in my "get even" scheme to realize I might just be poking the bear. The massive, really pissed-off bear.

And let's be honest, adding a finger in the booty hole was probably a big no-no for this alpha. Who knew alpha vampires were so touchy about impromptu butt exploration?

Mr. "I'm-too-alpha-for-ass-play" seemed to enjoy my little digital adventure more than he'd like to admit. If I hadn't pulled the plug (pun absolutely intended), he would've been shooting off like a hormone-crazed teenager in 0.2 seconds flat.

I guess I've discovered Rhyland's secret on/off switch. Who knew the key to bringing a thousand-year-old vampire to his knees was hidden in his own backyard? Talk about a plot twist!

Note to self: Maybe ask before going on a spelunking expedition in Rhyland's bat cave next time.

Now, the million-dollar question is: do I dare poke the bear (or, in this case, the vampire's ass) again? Or should I file this little tidbit away for a rainy day when I need to turn The Viking Vanguard into putty?

Next time, I'll bring a map and a headlamp. After all, there's gold in them thar hills!

I put on my best 'I'm not scared, you're scared' face and try to explain, "I was just trying to even the score, Rhyland. I won that bet, remember? That's how bets work. You know, you win some, you lose some, you get tied up and fingered some?"

Rhyland growls low in his chest, sounding like a pissed-off lion. "Yeah, well, remind me never to bet against you again, sweetheart." He bends down, his lips brushing my ear, hand still clamped around my neck like a sexy vise. "Because you play dirtier than a pig in mud. And I'm about to show you just how filthy I can get."

I almost smirk at that but think better of it. He's already madder than a wet hen, and who knows what he'll do to me. He releases my neck and steps back, but suddenly, I'm stuck to the wall like a fly on flypaper.

What in the...?

My corset is then ripped from my body (magically, might I add), leaving my girls out in the open, and my nipples harden.

It hits me like a ton of bricks—Rhyland's using his telekinesis on me. Something he's never done before, and it's scaring the ever-loving shit out of me. He could've Jedi mind-tricked me anytime he wanted, but he never has.

Until now.

Oh boy, I think I might have just opened Pandora's box with a crowbar and a stick of dynamite.

"You pushed me, Dani. Remember that. You asked for this," Rhyland grumbles as he stalks towards me, his eyes blazing with fury and desire.

"Rhyland...What're you doing...?"

"You think you're so clever, don't you? Turning the tables on me like that." He magically tightens a phantom hand around my throat. "Well, sweetheart, you've just opened a can of fucking whoop-ass. And I will ensure you feel every single consequence of your little game."

Shit.

I try to gulp around the tightening on my throat, it's so bizarre he's touching me without *touching* me.

"All is fair in love and war, baby," Rhyland says with a smirk—feeding me back my own words.

Our play on words.

I'm frozen in place, unable to move a muscle as he fists his hand in my hair, yanking my head back to force me to meet his gaze. "What the hell am I going to do with you, Angel?"

Fuck me hard like the hot Viking stud you are.

I open my mouth to reply, but before I can utter a word, his lips crash against mine in a bruising kiss. He plunders my mouth like a man possessed, his tongue thrusting against mine in a filthy dance that leaves me breathless. I moan into the kiss, my body melting against his as he consumes me.

Without warning, he spins me around, pressing me face-first against the wall. "I'm done waiting. I'm going to fuck this tight little cunt until it's milking my cock dry," he rasps, his hands gripping my hips hard enough to leave bruises. "You went too far, Dani."

Was it the drugging? The kinky rope action? Or maybe my adventurous finger exploration? Hard to pinpoint exactly what's got his Viking panties in a twist. Probably the unholy trifecta of all three. I mean, a girl's gotta get creative sometimes, right? Not my fault he's being such a drama queen about it.

I suck in a sharp breath as Rhyland lines up his Viking battering ram at my entrance. My body is shaking like a leaf, equal parts terrified and turned on. He starts to ease in, and holy mother of all that's holy, it's like trying to park a jumbo jet in a bicycle rack.

Inch by glorious inch, he works his way in until he's buried to the hilt, stretching me like I'm silly putty. "Oh, fuck," I whimper, my head flopping back onto his shoulder. He starts to move, slow and deep like he's trying to reach my tonsils from the other end.

I'm caught somewhere between "Is this what dying feels like?" and "Please, sir, may I have some more?" as Rhyland sets a rhythm that's slow, deep, and threatening to rearrange my internal organs.

My big mouth just can't help itself—

"Geez, is that all you've got? I thought Vikings were supposed to be tough," I tease, gasping for air, my knees about to give out.

Rhyland responds with a half-laugh, half-moan as he grips my hair at the base of my neck, tugging my head back—and picks up the pace, his hips slamming against mine with enough force to rattle the picture frames on the wall. "You and that damn, *mouth.*"

I can't help but cry out as he hits just the right spot. It's like he's got a GPS for my happy places. This back-and-forth between us, this constant game of one-upmanship? It's better than any workout routine. Who needs a gym when you've got a competitive streak a mile wide and a partner who's always up for a challenge?

Rhyland fucks into me with punishing thrusts, his fingers digging into my hips as he pulls me back to meet every brutal drive of his cock. The obscene slap of skin on skin fills the room, mingling with our moans and grunts of pleasure.

"Who's in control now, baby?" he snarls, his breath hot against my ear. "You like it when I fuck you like the naughty little angel you are?"

"Yes," I gasp, my voice hitching on a hard thrust. "Don't stop, Rhyland. Fuck, don't ever stop."

He chuckles darkly, the sound sending shivers racing down my spine. "Oh, I'm just getting started, sweetheart. By the time I'm done with you, you won't be able to walk for a week."

Rhyland's hands slide around to my front, groping my breasts with a rough possessiveness that sends heat rushing straight to my core. He pinches my nipples, rolling them between his fingers as he continues to piston into me from behind.

"Couldn't resist playing with fire, could you, Angel?" his voice a dark rumble that vibrates through my body. "You just had to go and stick that curious little finger in my ass. Well, sweetheart, you know what they say—turnabout is fair play."

Before I can even process his words, the world spins, and I find myself on the edge of the bed, thick leather cuffs encircling my wrists. He hooks them to the bars above the bed, leaving me stretched taught on my knees, entirely at his mercy.

I tug at the restraints, the leather biting into my skin in a way that only serves to heighten my arousal. *Where the hell did he even get these cuffs?* Probably pulled them out of his Viking ass along with that massive cock of his.

I guess I did ask for this, didn't I? Play stupid games—win stupid prizes. Or, in this case, win a one-way ticket to Spanksville, population: me.

I'm so turned on I can barely think straight, my body thrumming with a need so intense it borders on pain. I'm a livewire of sensation, every nerve ending screaming for his touch, his cock, his everything.

Rhyland steps back, admiring his handiwork with a smug grin that makes me want to slap him and ride him at the same time. "Now then," his voice a silken threat. "Let's see how you like having that tight little ass played with, shall we?"

Oh boy. I have a feeling I'm in for a wild ride. This Viking is about to pillage and plunder like it's 999 AD.

"First thing's first," Rhyland murmurs, circling me like a wolf about to devour his prey. I'm strung up like a piñata at a Viking birthday party, unable to move a muscle as he keeps me immobile with his telekinesis. "This ass needs a nice, red handprint, don't you think, Angel?"

I swallow hard, my throat dry. "Ye-yeah," I squeak, knowing this will be an "interesting" night.

He stands behind me, his chest on my back, his hand landing on my ass with a smack that echoes around the room. Thank God for soundproof walls—or, in this case, thank Lucian for having the foresight to invest in some quality noise dampening.

The sting of his palm against my skin is like fire and ice all at once, an explosion of sensation that has my nerves buzzing. "Ooh," I gasp, my head falling back on his shoulder.

"It's time to turn this ass cherry red, baby. You've been a very naughty girl."

His lips trail down my neck, nipping and sucking at my skin, my pussy clenching. He rubs my burning ass cheek, soothing the sting with one hand while the other comes down again, leaving another scorching handprint on my flesh. "Do you agree, baby?"

"Mmm-hmm," I moan, rolling my head back against his shoulder as he spanks me again. "Yeah, okay, I agree, I agree. You win, Rhy. Just... fuck!"

He chuckles, his breath hot against my skin. "Damn right, I win, baby. Now, let's see how much you can take before *you* start begging."

Rhyland's sexy hard body is like a damn furnace pressed against my back as he leans in close, his lips brushing my ear. "Where's that toy, Dani?" he rumbles, his voice a low, gravelly growl that sends goosebumps across my skin.

My nipples tighten at the thought of what's about to go down.

Fuck, I'm such a needy slut. "In my purse," I croak.

Rhyland moves so fast I swear I see skid marks in the air. One second, he's here; the next, he's downstairs, and before I can even blink, he's back, nuzzling my neck like an overgrown puppy.

My hair's doing its best impression of a tornado victim, whipped into a frenzy by his supersonic return. I half expect to find small birds and Dorothy's house tangled in there.

"Geez, Speed Racer," I quip, blowing the wind-blown strands out of my face. "Did you stop to grab a souvenir from every floor on the way back up? Or are you just showing off your vampire frequent flyer miles?"

He grins, the smug bastard. I swear, if cockiness were currency, Rhyland would be richer than Bezos and Musk combined.

"Just this souvenir..." he murmurs, hot breath against my skin. "Open wide," he demands, that damn sexy voice of his leaving no room for argument.

Hell, I'd do anything he says right now. I part my lips, taking in that smooth, silicone shape, my saliva coating it as his fingers tangle in my hair. "That's it, baby," he growls. I'm gagging, but goddamn, does it feel good. "Get it nice and wet for me."

My pussy clenches at the memory of how it felt inside me, the delicious vibrations that drove me to the brink of madness and back again.

When Rhyland is satisfied, he pulls the toy from my mouth, a thin string of saliva connecting it to my lips. He wastes no time working it inside me, the slick glide of silicone on sensitive flesh making me gasp and shudder.

"Breathe, Angel," he purrs, his velvety voice making me melt. God, he hasn't even turned that damn thing on, and I'm already squirming like a worm on a hook.

With the toy finally nestled back inside me, I tug at these damn cuffs, desperate to touch him, to feel him. But it's no use—my arms are screaming from this stretch.

He's dishing back precisely what I did to him—tied up and with no control.

"I'm gonna fuck this tight little ass and you're gonna scream my name like a goddess while I tear you apart," he vows, his hands gripping my cheeks, spreading me wide open for his wicked, wicked ways.

Oh god, I know exactly where this is going. My heart's racing like a damn hummingbird, and my nipples are diamond-hard at the thought. I can't hold back the moan that escapes my lips as Rhyland's tongue traces my asshole—his naughty, sinful tongue.

"Spread your legs, Angel, and stick that sweet ass out," he commands, his voice rough with desire.

My heart pounds as I obey, my legs trembling as I push my ass back, exposing myself to him, making myself vulnerable. The cuffs dig into my wrists, my arms stretched tight, giving just enough slack for this naughty position. The leather bites into my skin, sending a shiver racing down my spine as my body breaks out in goosebumps.

"Goddamn perfect," Rhyland growls, his big hands kneading my ass cheeks like the finest dough. I whimper at the rumble of approval in his voice, feeling cherished and desired, even as he prepares to wreck me. I'm right where he wants me, open and ready, and my pussy is dripping wet.

He buries his face between my cheeks, his tongue laving over my asshole in a way that has me keening and writhing against my bonds. Fuck, it feels so good. So dirty and wrong but so damn right. He licks and sucks and nibbles, worshipping my ass like a man possessed, like it's the most delicious thing he's ever tasted. My arousal builds with every passing second, my pussy clenching around the toy, my breath coming in short, sharp gasps. The feeling of his lips and tongue on my freshly waxed skin is almost too much to bear, the pleasure teetering on the edge of pain in the best possible way.

Rhyland spits on my asshole, the lewd sound making me clench and shiver. "You ready to get this ass fucking wrecked, baby?" he growls, the rumble of his voice reverberating through me. He punctuates the question with another long, slow lick. "You wanna be cute and try to toy with me? Play these little teasing games?" He slaps his hand hard against my sensitive inner thighs, right where my ass meets my pussy, and I yelp, my hips stuttering. "Lucky for you, your ass is mine now, and I plan on using it for my pleasure."

His words are filthy, degrading, and I fucking love it. I'm soaking wet, my body on fire with need, craving every depraved thing he wants to do to me.

"Then fucking wreck me, Rhyland."

Rhyland's answering growl is pure, primal savagery. His teeth sink into the tender flesh of my shoulder, biting down hard enough to break the skin. I can't help the cry that tears from my throat, my body arching into the exquisite mix of pain and pleasure.

It's a sensation I'll never tire of: the heady rush of his fangs piercing my flesh, the sweet sting of his bite, followed by the sensual pull of his mouth as he drinks from me. It's a claiming, a marking, a visceral reminder that I am his and his alone.

I can feel my blood trickling down my chest, a warm, wet trail that paints my skin crimson.

He soothes the sting with his tongue, his hands roaming over my body in a possessive caress. I know I'm in for the ride of my fucking life.

I can't help the low, desperate moan that spills from my lips as I feel my arousal dripping down my thighs, my body trembling with the force of my need. I'm so far gone, so lost in the haze of lust and desire...

I gasp as Rhyland nudges his way in, feeling like I'm being split in two by the world's most pleasurable baseball bat. Suddenly, the toy in me springs to life, and I yelp like a taser has zapped me.

When the hell did he get his phone?

"Oh my fucking fu—," I whimper, my voice high and needy. "Rhyland, please, for the love of god..."

"Such a filthy mouth on you, baby," he rumbles. "I want you dripping."

Sweet Jesus, I'm already soaked—my juices running down my thighs in a display that's anything but shy.

I snort despite my desperate state. "Any wetter, and we'll need to call Noah for his ark."

Rhyland, the sneaky devil, gathers my cum on his fingers, coating his cock and my ass with my essence. He positions himself again, that blunt head teasing me. "Beg for it, Dani," he rasps, his teeth scraping my ear. "Tell me how fucking much you want this cock. Plead for it."

I push back, desperate for more. "Please, for the love of all that's holy and unholy, move your Viking ass!" The burn and stretch of his thick dick—is heavenly.

Rhyland growls, his fingers digging into my hip. "You want this dick? Want me to fill you up, stretch you wide? Want it so bad you can't walk, think, or breathe?"

"No, I want you to recite the Declaration of Independence," I sass back. "Of course I want it, you big lug! Now move before I combust!"

I need to push back and show this Viking cock who's boss, but these damn cuffs and Rhyland's power have me trapped.

The slow slide of his cock, along with that damn toy, is pure, exquisite torture. I need more—deeper, faster. It's not enough to satisfy my craving.

Rhyland laughs, "Goddamn, someone is all worked up."

"Rhyland, please..."

He needs to get his ass in gear and fucking move like the thirsty bitch I am—

Rhyland sinks that last few inches in me—it's like fireworks behind my eyes. His hips slam into me with brutal force, sinking into my tight ass, the burn, the stretch, that final give of muscle—it's euphoric—I'm left gasping, shaking, clinging on for dear life.

"Yeah? Is this what you fucking need, dirty girl? Begging for my cock in this tight delicious ass like the filthy whore you are..."

I whimper, my eyes rolling back as he fills me. My ass is on fire, stretched to the max, and it's fucking glorious. Then, he turns up the toy, and holy hell, I'm assaulted by pleasure. The toy pulses and throbs, threatening to push me over the edge, and I can't stop the inhuman sounds from escaping my throat. It's too much, too intense, but God, it is so fucking good.

His hips are a blur. My ass bounces off his chiseled abs. The slapping of skin against skin echoes through the room as he claims me—owns me.

"Fuck, you feel so good, baby," he growls. "Love how your tight ass is clenching my cock. So fucking perfect, Dani. So goddamn tight."

I've never been big on the backdoor special—until Rhyland. My past experiences were either downright painful or just pissed me off. But with this man, it's like discovering a hidden, magical pleasure chamber. I swear I could become an anal addict for him.

That pain has now melted into pure pleasure. I'm teetering on the edge, my body wound so tightly that I'm sure I'll shatter from the force of my impending release.

I clench my inner muscles around him, squeezing his cock tight, and Rhyland curses, his hips stuttering as he tries to maintain his rhythm. "Fucking *Christ*, woman," he grits out, his fingers digging into my hips. "Give me what I want, Angel. Give me everything—drench me, Dani. I'm about to fucking explode."

His words are my undoing, the final push I need to send me hurtling over the edge. Rhyland senses it and quickly tugs the vibrator out with a pop—dropping it. He then circles my slick, swollen clit with his expert fingers.

"Rhyland! FUCK!" I come with a hoarse, ragged scream, my body convulsing around him as wave after wave of pleasure crashes over me, through me, threatening to sweep me away entirely.

It's like a goddamn supernova, an explosion of pleasure so intense it whites out my vision, steals the air from my lungs.

It's like nothing I've ever felt, a pleasure so intense it borders on pain, a release so powerful it leaves me boneless and trembling in its wake. Rhyland fucks me through it, his hips never faltering, his cock driving into my ass over and over again.

Rhyland's hand fists in my hair at the base of my skull, pulling my head back against his chest with raw intensity. "Breathe, baby. Breathe," he commands, his voice low and urgent.

Did I stop?

He taps my cheek, and I suck in a sharp, desperate breath, and the rush of oxygen only intensifies everything, pushing me further into a state of delirious pleasure.

"That's it. So fucking beautiful," he growls, punctuating each word with a thrust. "Fucking. Drench. Me."

He says it with each thrust of his hips, his cock hitting that spot deep in my ass.

I whimper, my release flooding me, hot liquid trickling down my thighs and soaking into the bed, leaving me boneless and breathless. Rhyland claims my mouth in a brutal kiss, all teeth and tongue.

"Such a good girl, Dani." He fucks me harder, faster. "I'm gonna fill this sweet ass up. Want that, baby? Want me painting your insides?"

Hell yes.

But I can only whimper in response, my body shaking and shuddering as he drives me closer and closer to another orgasm. But it's enough for Rhyland to push him over the precipice. With a final, brutal thrust, his cock pulses as he finds his release.

He lets out the *sexiest* throaty roar and holds me tight. His hand still fisted in my hair, the other arm wrapped around my waist, still stretching me tight, keeping me exposed. It's possessive and primal, sending a rush of heat through me.

Rhyland's hot cum floods my ass, triggering another mind-blowing orgasm. His fingers dive into my pussy, and I fucking explode, clamping down on him like a bear trap as I come with a scream that would wake the dead.

As the fireworks fade, my body goes limp. Rhyland, ever the gentleman (when he's not being a kinky bastard), releases my wrists and massages feeling back into my arms. I collapse against him, panting like I've run a marathon.

He scoops me up, and suddenly, I hear running water. Next thing I know, I'm being lowered into a warm bath that smells like a lavender field. Rhyland slides in behind me, his body a solid wall of muscle against my back.

"Rest, Angel. I got you," he murmurs.

I manage a weak thumbs up. "Mmmkay. Just... give me a sec to remember how to brain."

RHYLAND

89

I gather Dani's hair, twisting it into a messy bun atop her head. She's sprawled across my chest, her perfect tits on full display, golden globes rising out of the water with stiff, tempting peaks. Fuck, even after everything we've done, I still want her.

My hands glide over her soft skin, washing away the evidence of our wild fuck. I'm thorough, ensuring every inch of her is clean and soothed.

"Mmm... that feels good," she whispers, her voice heavy with exhaustion.

The warm water laps at our bodies as I check my angel over. She's drifting in and out, exhausted from our intense fucking. I need to make sure I didn't hurt her too badly—I fucking lost it after her little stunt, took her harder than I meant to. My possessive side got the best of me, and now I need to make sure she's okay.

"Rest, baby," I murmur, my hands kneading the tension from her muscles. "I've got you."

I carry Dani's limp form back to the bed, her body a warm weight against my chest. She's completely out, her mind and body overwhelmed by the potent mix of my blood, my venom, and the hours of relentless teasing I put her through.

She's a vision like this, all soft curves and smooth skin. I gently pull the hair tie out of her hair and tuck her under the covers, my fingers lingering on her flushed cheeks.

Goddamn, the balls on this woman. I'm still reeling from the shit she pulled tonight—fucking drugging me—tying me up to get her revenge. She had the nerve to tell me it was some new concoction she and Sable cooked up in their little science lab. A "secret weapon" for dealing with vampires, she said.

I hate to admit it, but she's not wrong. It's a clever move, even if I was on the receiving end this time. I can't help but smirk, a mix of pride and irritation. My little vixen, dishing out her own brand of chaos and not giving a single fuck about the consequences.

It hits me—she and I are two sides of the same coin. Both are stubborn as hell, and both are willing to go to extremes to get what we want. It's fucking infuriating and intoxicating all at once.

We are alike in so many ways.

The thought echoes in my mind, and I'm not sure if it thrills me or terrifies me. Maybe both.

But the way she folded and submitted to me only confirmed what I already knew about my naughty little minx. She's a fucking freak in the bedroom, a wanton goddess who craves the darkest, dirtiest pleasures imaginable. And I'm more than happy to oblige, to push her to the very limits of her desire and watch her shatter in my arms.

The memory of her screams, the way her body clenched and shuddered around me as I pounded into her, has my cock stirring back to life. I palm myself, groaning at the pressure. Fuck, I could go another round right now, bury myself in her sweet cunt and fuck her until she's hoarse from screaming my name.

Dani is sprawled limbs, akimbo, her hair a wild waterfall on the pillow. She looks like a fallen angel, debauched and ruined, and so fucking beautiful it makes my chest ache with possessiveness.

I slide in beside her, pulling her pliant body against mine. She molds to me instinctively, even in sleep, her skin warm and soft against my own. I bury my face in her hair, inhaling the scent of her, of us, letting it wash over me.

As I drift off, my mind replays the events of the night in vivid detail—the sights, the sounds, the sensations. It's a symphony of sin, a perverted lullaby that carries me off to sleep with my woman safe in my arms where she belongs.

My eyes snap open, heart racing as the nightmare fades. The crescent moon's still hanging in the dark sky—couldn't have been out more than an hour before that fucked-up memory clawed its way back. Tonight's little game stirred up shit I've spent centuries trying to bury, memories of *her*—that sadistic bitch who made me.

But she's gone. I made sure of it.

I turn, desperately seeking the warmth beside me, needing an anchor to the present.

Dani.

My angel, my salvation. She's all that matters now.

Her leg is draped over my waist, her head and arm resting on my chest, and her breath soft and even against my skin. I run my hand up her thigh, relishing the feel of her flawless skin and how she makes me ache with just a single touch.

I bury my face in her hair, inhaling her sweet scent—that unique mix of spice, honey, and desire that's all hers.

I was rough with her tonight, but fuck, did she have it coming. And if anything, I know she enjoyed that punishment more than I did. She knows exactly how to push my buttons and get a rise out of me, and I'm starting to think she enjoys my punishments more than she lets on.

She's perfect, absolutely fucking perfect, and she's mine.

Mine to protect, to possess, to cherish. And yeah, to punish when she needs it. Truth be told, she loves our little games of cat and mouse, the way I mete out my brand of rough justice for her bratty stunts. The fear, the excitement, the pure, raw need that sparks between us... It's a heady fucking drug, one we're both addicted to.

I won't give up our play, but perhaps I can devise other ways to get her attention to keep things fresh and exciting without pushing her too far.

Dani stirs, a soft moan escaping her lips as she snuggles closer, her hot cunt rubbing against my thigh. My cock twitches, hardening instantly at her touch, and I know I'm a goner. It's her fault—fucking hell, for being so goddamn irresistible.

I ease Dani onto her back, my body sliding between her thighs like it belongs there. Her tits catch the moonlight, perfect fucking globes begging for my attention. I can't resist. My mouth latches onto one nipple, then the other, teeth grazing and tongue swirling. She moans in her sleep, a soft, needy sound that goes straight to my cock.

I reach between us, brushing her silky petals, the wetness from our earlier activities still coating her sensitive skin. I groan as the smell of our joined arousal hits me, that musky, intoxicating scent that's purely us.

I position my cock at her entrance, feeling a jolt of pure, primal satisfaction as I sink into her heat. Closing my eyes, I rock gently into her, savoring the tight, wet clasp of her walls.

I start moving, slow and deep, savoring every inch of her. Dani stirs, those golden eyes blinking open to find me above her, already buried balls-deep inside her.

"Sorry to wake you, baby," I murmur, drinking in the sight of her sleep-mussed hair and flushed cheeks. "Just had to be inside you again—can never get enough of you."

Her lips curl into a smirk, that sass I love so much shining through even in her half-awake state. "Mmm, insatiable Viking," she purrs, arching into me. "Good thing I love being your personal midnight snack."

I crush my mouth to hers, fucking her with my tongue the same way I'm fucking her pussy. She moans into the kiss, the sound shooting straight to my balls.

Fuck, I'm in deep—head over heels for this incredible, infuriating woman. And the thought of losing her, of anyone taking her from me... It's enough to make my blood run cold.

But right now, with her wrapped around me, taking me so perfectly, nothing else matters. It's just us, lost in each other, exactly where we belong.

I lean back in my chair, Dani's perfect ass nestled in my lap, as we listen to this clusterfuck of the situation unfold. My hand rests possessively on her hip, fingers itching to slide under that tight tank top that's teasing me with just a hint of her cleavage.

Fuck, I can barely focus on the meeting with her body pressed against me like this.

Alaric, that stone-faced British prick who could cut glass with his accent, leans forward. "What the hell do we know about this bastard right now?"

Alaric's power is one of old—Blood Alchemy. A unique ability to transform the blood they consume into potent elixirs or potions, granting temporary enhancements or abilities to themselves or others. Handy trick, but it doesn't make him any less of a prick.

Brandon, the wolf sheriff Erik dragged in from New York, answers grimly. "Only that the asshole has the Soul Stone stolen from the Area Sixteen Cascade Command, Sheriff Liam Carter."

"So that's the sorry son of a bitch I nearly cooked alive," Emily says with a sly grin.

Vivienne, a redheaded vamp with a glare that could melt steel, arches a brow. "You're certain it was them, and they did, in fact, give him the stone?"

Vivienne, a descendant of Henry VIII, has the unique ability of Memory Harvesting. This ability allows her to extract and absorb specific memories from victims with a mere touch, allowing the vampire to relive moments or gain knowledge. It's useful but creepy as hell if you ask me.

Brandon nods, looking like he's just chugged a gallon of piss. "Yeah. Word has spread through all the packs like wildfire. The bastard's got his power back."

I tighten my grip on Dani, a low growl rumbling in my chest. Fuck. This is one hell of a mess we've landed in.

Lucian, ever the tactful fucker, chimes in with his usual charm. "Well, shit. I was hoping these dogs weren't stupid enough to just hand over their one bargaining chip to that fuckwad."

Brandon growls, a low rumble of warning that raises the hair on the back of my neck.

Lucian, grinning like the maniac he is, holds up his hands. "Sorry, buddy. No offense. You seem like a good dude. Maybe we can grab a drink later and swap some war stories. I've got a great one about a were-chihuahua and a vampire stripper..."

I roll my eyes, tuning out my brother's incessant fucking rambling. It's been a hell of a week, with Erik and Lucian dragging in every supernatural asshole they could find. Dani and Seraphina are turning Lucian's gym into their personal fight club, and Emily and Sable play supernatural telephone to rally the covens.

Now we've got Ayla, some witch with more power than sense, and Alaric and Vivienne, Lucian's UK cronies, joining our merry band of misfits.

It's a start.

Dani shifts in my lap, drawing my attention back to her. "What witch clans does he have in his back pocket right now?" she asks, her eyes narrow with concern.

Sable, ever the brains of our operation, consults her notes. "From what I have gathered, the Olympic Coven, Cedar Moon Coven, and Rainshadow Circle."

Ayla, with long dark hair and green eyes looking like she's stepped out of a goddamn Wiccan fashion magazine, leans forward. "I can speak to the other covens and see if they will listen to reason before joining forces with the wrong side."

Dani snorts, her fingers tracing teasing patterns on my arm that make me want to bend her over this fucking table. "Yeah, because witches are known for their reasonable nature and calm decision-making skills. No offense, Ayla."

I can't help but smirk as Dani's sass comes out to play, even with the world going to shit around us.

Emily's eyes narrow to slits, "I resent that, bitch. Just because some of us have a little more magical mojo than others doesn't mean we're all batshit crazy. I mean, have you met Rhyland? The dude's got 'anger management issues' written all over his broody forehead. In fucking neon."

What the actual fuck? What the hell did I do?

Lucian, the asshole, throws his head back and laughs like it's the funniest shit he's ever heard. I make a mental note to kick his ass later.

Dani laughs, unfazed by Emily's outburst. "Am I wrong, though? Come on, Em. When was the last time you made a decision that didn't involve setting something—or someone—on fire? Or ripping a certain someone through a damn vortex?"

Emily's face is a perfect picture of resentment, like someone just pissed in her cauldron. Sable's trying and failing miserably to hide her laughter.

Erik, the lucky bastard, stares at the ceiling with his arms folded, looking like he'd rather be elsewhere.

I feel you, brother.

"Oohh, burn... And here I thought witches were immune to fire." Lucian smirks. "Guess that's just another myth shattered, like the one about vampires being broody and sexless. Right, brother dearest?"

I shoot him a glare that would make Satan himself shit bricks, but the fucker just winks at me. I swear to god, I'm going to murder him in his sleep.

Brandon's eyes ping-pong between everyone like he is watching a supernatural tennis match, his face screaming 'WTF' louder than words ever could.

Alaric, looking like he's regretting every life choice that led him to this moment, asks, "Are you all always like this?"

In a moment of perfect, chaotic unity, we all chorus, "Yes!"

Vivienne rolls her eyes and lets out a breath that sounds like the last gasp of her patience.

Ayla tries to steer us back on track. "None was taken," she says, her voice calm despite the madhouse around her. "Witches usually don't get coerced—so, I find it extremely strange that even that many are working with him."

I run a hand down my face, wondering for the millionth time how this ragtag bunch of smart-asses and misfits is our best hope against Azrael.

Dani pipes up, her brilliant mind already working overtime. "He's got to be holding something over their heads, just like with the wolf packs," she muses, with sarcasm. "What, did he promise them all—unlimited magic and a pony?"

Lucian grins. "Oh, come on, Dani-girl. Don't sell the ponies short. I mean, who wouldn't want a magical, flying, rainbow-farting pony?" he snaps his finger quickly, pointing, "Ooh-ooh, better yet, what if it's Calimari or whatever and his gang with a dash of his unicorn glitter? Hell, I'd switch sides for that kind of equine awesomeness. Well, that and maybe a lifetime supply of tacos."

Dani rolls her eyes. "No, jackass. And it's *Calimero*, not whatever the hell you just said. There's no freaking way Azrael got through to Luminara. Use that brain of yours for once."

I lean forward—my patience wearing thin with Lucian's shit. "Enough with the bullshit, Lucian. Stop saying stupid shit with your goddamn fantasies."

Lucian, the insufferable prick, leans back in his chair, propping his feet on the table, ignoring us. "If Azrael is handing out magical ponies, I say we counter-offer with dragons. Don't we have to go to the fire realm?" He barely pauses for breath before continuing, "We need fire-breathing, scale-covered, bad-ass dragons. We'll be like the Mother of Dragons, but with less incest and more snarky one-liners. Who's with me?"

The room falls silent, everyone staring at Lucian. I resist the urge to fucking smack the shit out of him, reminding myself for the thousandth time why I both love and want to strangle my brother.

Fuck it.

With a mental shove, I send his chair skidding back. He lands on his ass with an undignified "Oomph!" drawing laughter from Emily and Sable. Dani tries to hide her giggles behind her hands.

Lucian picks himself up, grumbling as he rights his chair. "Real mature, bro," he mutters, shooting me a half-hearted glare.

I shrug, a smirk tugging at my lips. Sometimes, you gotta put the little punk in his place, even if it means getting a bit childish. Besides, it's worth it to see my Angel smile. Her laughter is damn near the best sound in the world.

Not missing a beat, "Oh sure, because nothing says 'we come in peace' like riding in on fire-breathing death machines." Dani quips. "Brilliant plan, Lucian. Maybe we can accessorize with some nuclear warheads while we're at it?"

"Alright, enough of this bullshit," I say. "We've got real fucking problems to solve. So unless anyone has some actual useful ideas, shut the fuck up, and let's focus."

Brandon, looking like he's about to pop a blood vessel, "I can tell you what it is. The wolves get off on his blood. It gives us power—and with power comes wars between the packs. I've never liked that shit, it's evil." He pauses, glancing at Erik. "No offense."

Erik merely shrugs. "It can be evil stuff in the wrong hands. So none taken, friend."

I resist the urge to slam my fist through the table. Of course, that's his secret weapon—feeding the wolves his blood, getting them hooked on that supernatural high. I know damn well what our blood does to other supernaturals—it's like a fucking adrenaline shot straight to the heart and twice as addictive.

I clench my jaw, my grip on Dani's hip tightening as the pieces fall into place.

Fucking Azrael—always playing dirty.

"I should've known that was his play to gain them. Bastard's turning them into his junkies."

Dani turns to face me, her eyes sparkling with that dangerous intelligence that never fails to get me hard. "So, what's the plan, big guy? We can't exactly set up a 12-step program for blood-addicted werewolves during a supernatural war."

"No, but we can cut off their supply. And believe me, Angel, withdrawal's a bitch."

Erik nods, his face an impassive mask. "Indeed. We must strategize carefully. Cutting off their access to Azrael's blood will weaken them but may also drive them to more desperate measures."

I lean back, my mind already racing with possibilities. This isn't going to be easy, but then again, nothing worth doing ever is. And taking down a power-hungry vampire with delusions of grandeur? That's definitely worth doing.

I nod, already formulating a plan. "Agreed. And we need to figure out what he's holding over the witches. No way they're joining his fucked-up crusade willingly."

As the others start discussing potential strategies, I pull Dani closer, burying my face in her hair. Her scent, mixed with the lingering sweat from her workout, grounds me and reminds me of exactly what I'm fighting for.

"I'll see what I can find out. Whatever it is, it can't be good." Ayla offers.

No shit.

Alaric, who's been quiet, finally speaks up. "Why isn't your mortal law or authorities doing anything about this?"

It's a fair fucking question. After all the work we've done to integrate into mortal society, you'd think they'd give a shit about a power-hungry vampire running amok.

Emily rolls her eyes, her fingers flying over her tablet as she speaks. "Oh, you know, just your typical mass cowardice," she drawls. "Turns out, when faced with a psychotic vampire with a power trip, our brave boys in blue suddenly develop a severe allergy to doing their jobs. It's all Azrael—they're too busy pissing their pants to actually, you know, enforce the law."

It's clear she's as fed up with this bullshit as the rest of us.

"I don't buy that for a second," Vivienne demands, looking ready to rip someone's throat out. "Someone should contact your local authorities and find out why they are not stepping in as they should be. There are special weapons put into place for this exact reason— In our country, this shit wouldn't fly regardless of how powerful one vampire is."

She's got a point. Mortals have devised various UV weapons to take us down if we ever get too powerful for their liking.

Lucian grins like a maniac. "Isn't it obvious? He's corrupted even them—I wouldn't put it past the fuckwad. Maybe he's offering them all-you-can-eat donuts. Or, you know, the slightly more sinister option of blackmail and mind control. But hey, who doesn't love a good conspiracy theory?"

I roll my eyes, but I can't deny that Lucian's got a point. Azrael's done this before, back when we busted him for his illegal blood and slave trading. The fucker's got no qualms about using his power, blood, and anything else to influence and corrupt anyone and everyone who gets in his way.

"Lucian's right," I growl, my fingers rubbing Dani's back. "We can't trust the mortal authorities on this one. Azrael's got his claws in too deep."

Dani twists in my lap, looking up at me with those big, golden eyes that never fail to make my heart skip a beat. "So what do we do? We can't exactly walk into the police station and ask if they're under the thrall of a psychotic vampire, can we?"

"No, but we can start digging. And believe me, Angel, if Azrael's left any trace of his meddling, we'll find it."

And when the dust settles? Well, let's just say I plan on being the last motherfucker standing.

Let the games begin, you blood-peddling bastard. I'm coming for you, and I'm bringing an army.

DANICA

90

"You're cheating, Dani!" Seraphina pouts, her usually sweet voice tinged with exasperation.

I laugh. "Oh, I'm sorry, I didn't realize we were playing by heavenly Little League rules. Should I ask the umpire for a ruling?"

We've been training since the ass-crack of dawn, on and off all day in Lucian's gym, our own little celestial dojo. It's our last session for the evening, before we call it a night.

Seraphina's been giving me the lowdown on the different angelic bloodlines. Apparently, I'm some sort of celestial mutt—part Warrior (thanks, Dad), with my fire, and part Time-Wielders. According to Seraphina, Time-Wielders can bend time, see the future, and control aging.

It's like being a superhero with multiple personality disorder.

On the other hand, Seraphina is from the Guardian line, which means she has mad skills in light manipulation, healing, and combat.

She also mentioned other freaky angel bloodlines, like astral projection and fear induction, because nothing screams "divine" like an out-of-body experience and the power to make people piss themselves.

"Dani, this is combat training, not time manipulation practice," Seraphina huffs, her halo practically steaming.

I snicker. "What, afraid you can't keep up with my mad skills? Don't worry, I'll put on some training wheels for you next time."

"Oh please," Seraphina scoffs, "I've been kicking butt since before your great-great-grandparents were in diapers."

"Yeah, yeah, you're practically a celestial fossil." Seraphina gives me a look that says she will kick my ass for calling her old.

Seraphina's glow-up? She's gone from heavenly wallflower to sassy queen bee in record time. After a few weeks of binge-watching trashy reality shows and hanging with us bad influences, she's a whole new angel.

And don't even get me started on the Lucian effect. That man is like the kinky Yoda to her horny Luke Skywalker. He's teaching her things that would make a nun blush. I'm pretty sure I saw her giving him a run for his money in the innuendo department the other day.

But the best part? Seeing her make herself at home here, like she's always been part of our little misfit family. She's claimed her spot on the couch, her favorite mug in the kitchen, and a special place in all our hearts. Watching her blossom and come into her own has been a highlight of this whole supernatural shitshow.

"Okay, okay," I concede, holding up my hands in mock surrender. "I'll try to keep the temporal trickery to a minimum. But if I accidentally pause mid-kick and face-plant, you'd better not laugh."

Seraphina's smile softens, her annoyance melting away. "Oh, Dani, you know I'd never laugh at you... for longer than five minutes, anyway."

"Gee, thanks," I snort, rolling my eyes. "You're a true friend, Sera." I grin, my light magic firing up in my hands. "Now, shall we continue this dance, or do you need a time-out, Granny?"

I'm in the middle of perfecting my angelic roundhouse kick when my phone starts belting out "Highway to Hell"—Damon's ringtone, naturally. I jog over to my stuff and pick up my phone while I towel off my sweat.

My little brother is supposed to grace us with his presence today, and I'm bouncing between excitement and nervousness like a ping-pong ball. Ten bucks says he's calling because he got lost and needs GPS coordinates to find his nose.

"I'm gonna take a shower," Seraphina calls out. "We'll resume our *fair* fight tomorrow, you temporal terror."

"Aw, don't be bitter, sweetie," I holler as the door shuts behind her. "Just remember, if you can't stand the heat, stay out of the angel's kitchen!"

I press the green button on my phone, fully prepared for brotherly chaos. "Hey, little demon," I drawl. "Let me guess, you took a wrong turn at Albuquerque and ended up in Narnia?"

Honestly, with Damon, I wouldn't even be surprised if he somehow stumbled into a magical wardrobe.

"Well, hello there, little firefly. Miss me?" The voice that slithers through the phone is like ice water down my spine, dark with malice and evil promises.

Azrael.

My fingers go numb, the phone nearly slipping from my suddenly clammy grip. My heart hammers against my ribcage like it's trying to escape, and I can taste copper on my tongue. The gym around me fades away, replaced by a suffocating darkness threatening to swallow me whole.

"Tsk, tsk, Dani dearest," he purrs, each syllable a venomous caress. "It seems we find ourselves in quite the predicament. I have a shiny new toy, and you... well, you have something I've been positively dying to get my hands on. How about we make a deal, hmm? A little quid pro quo between old friends?"

My breath comes in short, sharp gasps. The room spins, and I brace myself against the wall to avoid collapsing. Bile rises in my throat as images of what Azrael will do to Damon—flash through my mind like a horrific slideshow.

The realization hits me like a ton of bricks, stealing the air from my lungs. The last piece of the soul stone—that's what Azrael's after. It's the only thing that makes sense.

"What's the matter, sweetheart?" Azrael's voice oozes through the phone, with false concern, making my skin crawl. "Cat got your tongue?"

Anger surges through me, white-hot and blinding. "If you hurt him, I swear to God, Azrael—"

"You'll what, Dani?" he cuts me off, his tone mocking. "Kill me? We both know how well that's worked out for you. Why don't you quit playing the hero and embrace the pathetic, bleeding heart you've always been?"

I squeeze my eyes shut, a traitorous tear escaping and burning a path down my cheek. "What do you want?" I manage through gritted teeth. My jaw clenched so tight it aches.

"I think you know," Azrael chuckles, the sound grating against my nerves like nails on a chalkboard. "But since you're playing dumb, I'll spell it out for you. It starts with an 'S' and ends with a 'tone.' You've been such a good little puppy, fetching my toys for me."

His laughter echoes in my ear, and I fight the urge to retch. My legs give out, and I slide down the wall, collapsing to the floor in a boneless heap—Damon's face flashes—my baby brother is the only family I have left. If I give Azrael the stone, there's no telling what horrors he'll unleash. But if I don't...

"Fine," I whisper, my voice barely audible over my heart pounding. "But I need to know he's okay. Let me talk to him."

"Even better."

My phone buzzes. I accept the Facetime call with shaking hands, steeling myself for what I'm about to see. The image that fills the screen rips a silent scream from my throat, my hand flies to my mouth to stifle the sound.

Damon, my little brother, is tied to a chair, his face a mess of blood and bruises. His head lolls forward, his eyes barely open, and my heart shatters in my chest.

Azrael's face appears. His dark hair, black eyes, and twisted smile stretch his lips. "Tick-tock, Dani. What's it going to be?" He grabs Damon's matted hair, yanking his head back and shoving the phone in his face. "Say hello to your sister, Damon. She wants to make sure you're doing okay."

"D-Dani," Damon croaks, his voice weak and broken. "Don't. Stay awa—"

Azrael's hand connects with Damon's head in a sickening crack, and my brother's head snaps forward, hanging limply. Rage explodes inside me, a roaring inferno that consumes every other emotion.

"I'm going to fucking *kill* you, Azrael," I seethe, my voice shaking with the force of my anger.

"Idle threats, my dear," Azrael scoffs. "I'm giving you one last chance—the stone for your brother's life. I'm being more than generous here, but my patience is wearing thin. So, what's it going to be?"

"Fine," I spit, the word tasting like acid on my tongue. "Just tell me where. And I swear to God if you lay another finger on him—"

"Ah ah ah," Azrael tuts, wagging his finger at the screen. "No need for dramatics. Meet me *alone—DO NOT* bring that shitstain Viking with you, either. I'm feeling nostalgic, how about coming to your lovely parents' old place. You remember where that is, don't you?" His smile turns predatory, his black eyes glinting with malice. "Oh, that's right. You do. It's where my dogs tore your parents to shreds. Such a tragedy."

Pain lances through my chest, stealing my breath. Memories of that night flash before my eyes—the blood, my parents dead and shredded to a pulp—Azrael's so-called hellhounds. I blink back tears, refusing to let him see me break.

Damon tries to speak, but Azrael shoves something in his mouth, silencing him. Another punch and Damon's head snaps to the side, blood trickling from his split lip.

"Stop!" I beg, my voice cracking. "I said I'll meet you. Just... please. Don't hurt him."

"Good girl," Azrael purrs. "You have three hours. Don't be late, and no fucking portals—I don't trust you and that magic. Come alone, or he dies."

The screen goes black, and the phone slips from my numb fingers, clattering to the floor. Sobs wrack my body, tears streaming down my face. I can't lose Damon. I can't. But Azrael made it clear—I have to come alone. If I don't, he'll kill Damon, and then he'll come for everyone else I love.

I have to do this. Alone.

Rhyland's voice echoes in my mind, concern lacing his words. *"Baby? You okay? I feel your sadness."*

Shit. He can't know. I hastily wipe my tears, sniffing back my sobs. *"Yeah, I'm fine,"* I lie, my voice surprisingly steady. *"Seraphina just told me something that upset me. But I'm okay."*

"Okay," Rhyland replies, sounding uncertain. *"I'm in a meeting with the other vampires from the other countries. I'll be here another hour or so. Are you sure you're good?"*

Relief washes over me. Rhyland will be occupied. It's the perfect opportunity for me to slip away unnoticed.

"Yup," I chirp, forcing a cheerfulness I don't feel. *"You do you, boo. I'll see you after your meeting."*

I end the connection before he can sense the lie in my words. Taking a deep breath, I push myself to my feet, my legs shaking. I have three hours to save my brother, to face the monster who's haunted us for months.

And I'll be damned if I let Azrael win this time.

I race down to the vault beneath the mansion, my heart pounding in my ears. Lucian entrusted me with the code, a secret shared between us, a precaution against manipulation or compulsion.

My fingers tremble as I punch in the numbers, the soft beep of the lock disengaging and echoing in the stillness. I snatch the stone off the shelf; its weight heavy. It's almost laughable how something so small could cause so much chaos. I slam the vault door shut, the clang echoing in the empty room.

I race back upstairs, taking the steps two at a time. Jeans, black hoodie, hair up—the perfect "I'm definitely not about to do something incredibly stupid and dangerous" look. I creep back downstairs, my heart in my throat.

I pause at the sound of familiar voices. Rhyland, Erik, and Lucian are locked away in their council meeting, gathering allies for the war. But it's Emily, Sable, and Seraphina I need to worry about now.

I tiptoe past the living room, my heart doing a frantic tap dance in my throat, desperately hoping they won't spot me.

Ugh, this rescue mission would be much easier if I could just zap myself there like a budget Nightcrawler. But no, of course not—Azrael and his flair for the dramatic won't allow any handy dandy teleportation shenanigans. He's probably worried I'll pull some Avengers-level shit and portal in the entire celestial cavalry.

As if I'd risk putting a single hair on my brother's head in danger by provoking that snake's wrath.

So here I am, about to hit the road like a basic bitch instead of utilizing my stellar superpowers. Honestly, superheroes these days have it way too easy with all their fancy gadgets and modes of transport. Where's my suped-up, missile-launching, flight-capable motorcycle, huh?

The sound of laughter stops me dead in my tracks. I peek around the corner, spotting Emily, Seraphina, and Sable sprawled on the couch, eyes glued to the TV. I take a deep breath, steeling myself.

Just a few more steps, and I'm home free—

"Hey, girl!" Emily calls out, and I nearly jump out of my skin. "Get your ass over here, this episode is wild!"

"Oh, yes. We just saw Colin deflower Pen!" Seraphina says, blushing.

I squeeze my eyes shut, my mind racing. "Uh, thanks, but I think I'm gonna pass," I say, my voice wavering slightly. "I'm beat. Just gonna grab a sandwich and hit the hay."

Emily's eyes narrow, and I feel like she's staring straight into my soul. "You sure? You look like you've seen a ghost. Everything okay?"

Damn her and her freaky best friend intuition. "Yup, just tired," I lie, my smile feeling more like a grimace.

"Hold up," Sable chimes in, her pink hair in a messy bun, "wasn't Damon supposed to show up tonight?"

Fuck. Fuck. Fuck.

"Yeah, where is the little twerp?" Emily asks, her phone already in her hand. "I've been blowing up his phone, but he's not picking up."

A lie. I need a lie. Something believable. Something that won't raise suspicion.

My mind scrambles. "Oh, yeah...he called me earlier. Got held up at work. Said he'll be here tomorrow." The words taste like ash in my mouth.

Emily stares at me for a moment, and I'm sure she's going to call me out on my bullshit. But then she shrugs, turning back to the TV. "Alright, well, g'night. Get some rest, girl."

I let out a shaky breath, relief washing over me. "Will do. Night, guys." Seraphina and Sable echo back.

I practically sprint to the kitchen, snatching Lucian's car keys off the counter like my life depends on it. With fingers crossed that my backup plan will pan out, I dive into the cupboard, rummaging around like a madwoman. My hand closes around the vial and syringe, and I yank them out with all the urgency of a last-minute Hail Mary. I quickly load up the syringe, pulling the plunger back with a silent prayer that this shot in the dark hits its mark.

As I ease it open, the garage door creaks, and I wince at the sound. I slide into the driver's seat, my hands trembling as I turn the key in the ignition.

The gate looms ahead, and I curse under my breath as the guards step forward, their hands raised. "Sorry, ma'am, no one is allowed to leave without Mr. Edwards' permission. We haven't received any clearance."

Mr. Edwards? It takes me a second to remember Lucian's last name. *Shit.* "Yeah, Mr. Edwards is in a meeting and can't confirm that I need to leave. It's an emergency," I say, trying to keep my voice steady.

The guard reaches for his walkie-talkie. "If it's an emergency, you can't leave the premises alone. I'll need to confirm with Mr. Edwards."

Panic rises in my throat. "No!" I shout, startling the guard. "Sorry, it's just...um... not that kind of emergency. It's a, uh, girl thing, you know?" I give him a meaningful look, praying he catches my drift.

He stares at me, confusion written all over his face. I roll my eyes, my patience blown. "I'm on my period, dude!" I snap, throwing my hands up in exasperation. "I need to make a tampon run. Unless you want me to bleed all over Mr. Edwards' fancy leather seats, I suggest you let me through. Or you can explain why his car looks like a crime scene."

The guard's eyes widen, his face turning an impressive shade of red. He clears his throat, avoiding eye contact as he hurries to open the gate. "My apologies, ma'am. Please give Mr. Edwards my sincerest apologies."

I smirk as I peel out of the driveway, gravel spraying behind me. The road stretches out before me, dark and winding. My heart hammers in my chest, fear and determination warring inside me.

I glance at the dashboard clock, the glowing numbers seeming to mock me with their steady countdown. Two hours and forty-five minutes until my world either implodes or I somehow defy the odds stacked against me.

I quickly input my parent's address into the car dash GPS.

The route to my childhood home is burned into my memory, a trail of ghosts and nightmares that even now makes my stomach churn. The GPS gives me two hours and sixteen minutes to get there.

Leave it to Azrael to give me barely enough time to make it, the sadistic bastard. He's playing games, toying with me like a cat with a cornered mouse.

But this mouse has claws.

I grip the steering wheel until my knuckles turn white and slam the pedal to the floor. My jaw clenched so tight I'm amazed my teeth don't crack.

Azrael wants to dance? Fine. Let's fucking dance, you twisted son of a bitch.

This game ends tonight.

One way or another, it all ends tonight.

RHYLAND

91

I pace the room like a caged animal, my muscles coiled tight with tension as I listen to the others argue through the speaker.

Something's not right.

I can feel it in my fucking bones, a sickening sense of wrongness that seeps through our bond like poison. Dani's hiding something, lying through her goddamn teeth, and it's setting every instinct I have on high alert.

Lucian catches my eye from across the table, his expression grim. He feels it, too, that unsettling sense that something's not right. It still irks me that he can sense her through their shared blood bond, a constant reminder that he's tainted what's mine. But I can't focus on that shit right now.

We end the call abruptly, leaving the others to their tasks as I make a beeline for our room. I burst through the door, eyes scanning every inch of the space for any sign of her. But she's not here. The bed is empty, the sheets cold. I notice her clothes strewn across the floor, a trail leading to the closet. She's changed, switched out her usual attire for something else entirely.

I reach through the bond, my mind seeking hers, desperate for a connection. *"Dani, where the fuck are you? What's going on?"* I feel a flicker of her for a moment, a brief flash of her presence before I'm slammed out with a force that leaves me reeling.

What the hell?

She's never shut me out like this before, never blocked me so completely. I try again, pushing against the barrier with all my mental strength, but it's like slamming into a fucking black hole. I can't penetrate her mind—she's locked me out entirely.

I blame Lucian for that shit—teaching her all about mental fortitude. But she damn well isn't supposed to use it against me.

I growl in frustration, my hands fisting in my hair. Why is she doing this? What could possibly be so important that she'd cut me off and leave me in the dark like this?

A cold, sinking feeling settles in my gut. Whatever she's up to, whatever she's trying to hide... it's bad. Really fucking bad.

"Fuck," I growl, my heart pounding in my chest as I race downstairs. Emily, Seraphina, and Sable are lounging on the couch, their eyes widening as I storm into the room.

"Where's Dani?" I demand, my voice rough with panic.

They exchange a confused glance. Emily sits up straighter. "She said she was tired and went to bed," she says slowly, her brow furrowing.

My heart plummets to my fucking feet. I must look as wrecked as I feel because Emily's on her feet instantly, her eyes flashing in alarm. "She's not, is she?"

I shake my head, my jaw clenched so tight I feel my teeth grinding. "No. She's not."

Seraphina gasps, quickly standing.

"Damnit!" Emily snaps, her hands balling into fists. "I knew something was off. She couldn't have gotten far."

Lucian comes skidding into the living room, his expression thunderous. "My car is gone, and the guard at the gate said she needed to leave because it's that time of the month."

I feel like I've been sucker-punched, the air rushing out of my lungs in a whoosh. She's not on her period. I would know. I can always smell the change in her blood, the subtle shift in her scent. "She's not," I choke out, my voice strangled.

She lied. She fucking lied to me, to Emily, to the guards. What the hell is she doing? Where the fuck did she go?

Lucian has his phone out in a flash, his face a mask of fury. "You're fired, fuckface," he snarls into the receiver before hanging up with a vicious stab of his finger. He looks at me, his eyes blazing. "They know the rules. No one is to leave unless ok'd through me."

I run a hand through my hair, tugging at the strands until my scalp burns. "What happened?" I manage to grind out, my voice like gravel.

Emily shrugs. "Beats the hell out of me. She said Damon won't be here until tomorrow because he got caught up with work or some shit. But I know Dani. Something was off with her."

"Off?" Lucian scoffs, sarcastically. "Off is an understatement. Our little savior has flown the coop, and I'm betting it's not for a midnight snack run. We need to find her, like yesterday. Before she gets herself into some real deep shit."

My mind races, pieces clicking into place like a fucked-up puzzle. "My bet is something to do with her brother," I growl, my hands clenching into fists at my sides.

"She got a call from Damon just as I was leaving the gym," Seraphina starts, but then she trails off, her eyes wide as she shakes her head, hands flying up to cover her mouth. "No..."

Azrael. It's got to be it. I felt her sadness earlier, that faint twinge of melancholy through the bond. What if he called her? What if—?

"Check the vault!" I bark at Lucian, my voice sharp as a whip.

He doesn't argue, doesn't hesitate. He's gone in a blur of speed, leaving nothing but a gust of wind in his wake. He's back before I can sink to the floor, his face grim.

"Gone."

That one word hits me like a fucking freight train. No. She's taken the stone to bargain with her brother. I'd bet my goddamn life on it. Because I know Dani, I know the lengths she'll go to protect the people she loves. And if she's running off alone, lying to cover her tracks?

It means she's about to do something very, very stupid.

But where?

"Got her!" Lucian pipes up, his voice cutting through the tension like a fucking knife. "You can thank me later for installing GPS trackers on my cars," he snarks, waving his phone in the air like a goddamn trophy.

I'm off the floor in a heartbeat, my hand snatching the phone from his grip. "Where?" I demand, my eyes scanning the screen frantically.

"She's on the North 405 heading East," Lucian informs, his tone serious for once. I look closer at the map, my heart sinking as realization dawns. She's heading straight for Leavenworth— her parents' home.

"Get the car ready; we are leaving. Bring everyone!" I bark. This ends now. I'm not letting her face this asshole alone, not letting her make some fucking martyr play that could get her killed.

Lucian is out the door in a flash, his voice echoing back over his shoulder. "I call shotgun! And dibs on the first 'I told you so' when we find her!"

I ignore his jabs, my mind laser-focused on one thing and one thing only: getting to Dani before it's too late. I can feel her through the bond, a faint, flickering light that tells me she's still alive.

But for how long?

She can't be more than fifteen minutes ahead of us. We need to fucking move. Now.

I clench my fists, my nails biting into my palms hard enough to draw blood. Hold on, Angel. I'm coming for you. And when I find you, there'll be hell to pay for scaring the ever-loving shit out of me like this.

We all pile into Lucian's Cadillac Escalade SUV like a goddamn clown car. Emily and Brandon are crammed into the third-row seat, their faces grim. Erik, Alaric, and Vivienne are behind me, a wall of tense muscle and worry. Sable staying behind while Lucian's got Seraphina perched in his lap, his arms wrapped around her like a fucking seatbelt as I peel out of the property like a bat out of hell.

The engine roars as I push the pedal to the floor, the speedometer climbing higher and higher until the world outside is nothing but a blur. I weave through traffic like a maniac, cutting off cars and running red lights without a second thought.

There's only one thing on my mind, one singular focus that consumes me entirely: getting to Dani before it's too late.

DANICA

92

T he car stops, gravel spraying like shrapnel as I abruptly stop on the driveway.

Thirteen minutes.

That's all the time I have left to find Azrael and Damon before this twisted game reaches its climax.

During the entire drive here, Rhyland's been pounding on the walls of my mind, his fury and concern being a relentless battering ram. I've kept him locked out, shuttered away from the cold, hard truth. But when this is over—if I make it out alive—he won't let me hear the end of it.

Even Lucian attempted—he was trickier to keep locked out.

Not that I can blame him. I've gone completely batshit crazy on this one, flying solo straight into the viper's nest—exactly how Azrael wants it. Just me, the demented snake, and whatever sick scheme he has cooked up.

Well, two can play that game. I'm done being the mouse in this psycho's cat-and-mouse routine. Damon's life is on the line, and that line stops here. Azrael wants to tango? Let's dance, asshole.

I fire off a text to Damon's phone, my thumb hovering over the send button.

> Where the hell are you? I'm here.

The reply is instantaneous.

> Look at you, making it with time to spare. Bravo. Go to the clearing behind the house.

I tuck my phone and my secret weapon into my pocket and slam the car door behind me, the sound like a gunshot in the eerie stillness. Taking a deep breath, I break into a run, cutting through the woods and putting distance between myself and the innocent family living in the house that was once my home.

Do they know the horrors these walls have witnessed? The brutal slaughter of my parents, the night everything changed?

I push the thought aside, jaw clenched, and fists balled at my sides. Now's not the time for ghosts or what-ifs. Damon needs me, and nothing—not even the demons of my past—will stop me from getting to him.

The clearing looms ahead, the trees thinning to reveal a small open space bathed in moonlight. I slow to a cautious creep, straining to catch any sign of movement, any hint of the trap waiting to be sprung.

"Looking for someone?"

The voice comes from behind me, smooth as silk yet laced with venom. I whirl around, my heart leaping into my throat as I face the monster himself.

Azrael stands before me in the flesh, his handsome, dark features twisted into a cruel smirk. By his side, slumped on the ground and barely conscious, is Damon—bloodied, beaten, but alive.

"You're early," Azrael taunts, circling me like a shark. "I have to admit, I'm impressed. Though I shouldn't be surprised—you've always been a stubborn little bitch."

My fists clench until my nails bite into my palms, the pain grounding me amidst the roiling sea of rage that threatens to drown me. Damon could pay the price for one wrong move and one ill-timed retort.

Swallowing hard, I meet Azrael's gaze, my own eyes blazing with a promise of violence to come. "I'm here," I growl, each word precise and laced with venom to match his own. "Now let my brother go, you twisted fuck."

Azrael throws back his head and laughs, the sound like shards of broken glass grating against my nerves. "Now, now, Dani. Where would be the fun in that?"

He moves closer, his presence suffocating, oppressive. I hold my ground, refusing to be cowed by this demon-loving asshole and his sadistic games.

"The stone first," Azrael demands, holding out an expectant hand. "Then, and only then, will your dear brother walk free. Those are my terms."

Terms? As if I have a fucking choice in this matter. As if his twisted proposal is anything more than an ultimatum dressed up in pretty words.

But I know better than to argue. I see how this game is played.

So I slip my hand into my pocket and withdraw the final piece of the Soul Stone, its weight heavy in my palm. This small, unassuming object is the key to unfathomable power and, quite possibly, the end of everything.

I can hear its dark whispers—faintly.

With a steadying breath, I chuck the stone over to Azrael, watching it arc through the air in slow motion. He snatches it mid-air, his eyes glinting with a satisfaction that curdles my stomach.

"At last," he murmurs, stroking the stone like it's his long-lost love. "The power to reshape existence is finally mine."

I watch, horror-stricken, as Azrael slots the fragment into place with the others. The pieces click together like magnets, and the stone sits complete and ominous in his ring. The air around him seems to hum with newfound power.

Shadows engulf him as he seems to absorb the stone entirely. Dark eyes meet mine, a sinister smirk on his face.

My blood runs ice-cold as I absorb the full weight of his words. Just what depths of depravity is this monster capable of reaching?

Will that stone alone be enough to unleash Moretemis into our realm?

Before I can voice the question, Azrael turns his attention back to me, his smile all teeth and no warmth. "A deal's a deal, I suppose," he muses as if speaking more to himself than me. "Your brother, in exchange for the stone."

He snaps his fingers, and the black smoke binding Damon falls away like mist in the breeze. My brother crumples to the ground, unmoving, and panic claws at my throat.

"Damon!" I lunge forward, only to be brought up short by an invisible force slamming into my chest. I stagger back, gasping for air as Azrael regards me with cold amusement.

"Did I say he could leave?" He tsks softly, shaking his head in mock disap-pointment. "Now, Dani. You should know better than to think I'd make this easy for you."

The weight of his betrayal hits me like a physical blow, stealing my breath and my strength. Of course, he would never keep his word—this was all a ruse, a ploy to get what he wanted.

And like a fool, I played right into his hands—blinded by trying to save my brother.

"You son of a bitch," I snarl, fury burning away any lingering fear until all that remains is an inferno of rage. "I'll kill you for this, Azrael. I swear on everything holy, I will end you."

Azrael's cruel and mocking laughter rings out, smiling at the Soul Stone like a hard-won trophy. "Sure you will, *little angel,*" he purrs, the twisted endearment falling from his lips like poisoned honey. "I've always admired your spirit. It'll make breaking you all the more satisfying."

The words "little angel" make bile rise in my throat—that's Rhyland's cherished pet name for me, now tainted by Azrael's foul tongue—the audacity of this asshole to defile something so sacred with his venom.

Time seems to slow as Azrael stalks toward me, each measured step calculated for maximum impact. I brace myself, coiled tight as a serpent poised to strike.

I can't fire on him yet. Damon is too close.

My angelic fire simmers beneath the surface, my body a livewire thrumming with barely contained power. I clench my fists, fighting to keep the flames at bay—fear and rage are always their conduits.

"Ah, I see I've sparked something," Azrael taunts, his voice a dark caress that makes my skin crawl. "Can't have that now, can we?"

He lashes out with tendrils of shadow, whip-like coils that snake around my limbs and bind me against the rough bark of a towering oak. I grit my teeth, straining against the inky restraints as Azrael circles me.

Enough of this bullshit. I let the fire within me flare to life, a blinding corona of celestial flames that incinerates the shadows in a heartbeat. Azrael recoils with a hiss of displeasure as I crash to the ground, free once more.

Game on, you twisted son of a bitch.

I lash out with a barrage of fiery blasts, hurling searing spheres of holy fire at the demon's smug form. But Azrael is infuriatingly quick, dancing through the onslaught with unnatural grace, his laughter mocking me at every turn.

Switching tactics, I unleash a blinding torrent of light, casting shimmering tendrils of pure radiance that crackle through the air like a kaleidoscope of fireworks.

"Damon, move!" I shout, my voice strained with the effort of maintaining the onslaught.

My priority is getting him to safety, away from this monster's clutches. I glance at my brother, watching as he crawls inch by agonizing inch, his battered body fighting for survival with every ragged breath.

"Does it piss you off, Dani?" Azrael sneers, his voice seeming to come from everywhere at once as he slithers through the shadows. "That I've taken everything from you? Your mother..." He chuckles, low and cruel. "She was such a fiery thing, like you. She fought so hard to save herself...and the parasite growing in her womb."

White-hot rage surges through me at his taunts. My mother's life snuffed out before it could truly begin. Tears prick at the corners of my eyes, but I blink them back furiously, refusing to let him see me break.

"Does it piss you off that I survived?" I fire back. "Thought you could take an innocent baby—"

"Your pathetic adoptive parents," Azrael ignores me and continues, reveling in my anguish like a sadist savoring an exquisite vintage. "They were just sad, and they died so easily, didn't they?"

Flashes of that night assault me—Dad's twisted form, Mom's sightless eyes. I want to unleash the full force of my fury upon this fucker, to make him pay for every second of torment he's inflicted.

"You're a poor, sad, pathetic being, Dani," Azrael hisses, his shadowy form flickering in and out of existence all around me. "Always letting your feelings interfere with what dear old *daddy* tasked you with."

Anger flares inside me, a bright spark amidst the darkness, and I latch onto it with everything I have. It's all that's keeping me from shattering completely.

"Not everything, asshole," I snarl, tossing my hair over my shoulder with as much sass as I can muster while facing down the personification of evil itself. "If you think I'm some wilting wallflower just because I give a damn about people, you've got another thing coming."

As I look around, I square my shoulders, straightening to my full—albeit unimpressive—height.

Waiting.

"See, the way I figure it," I continue, unable to resist throwing a little extra vinegar in my tone, "being pathetic is more your shtick than mine. I mean, come on—groveling at the feet of your demonic sugar daddy, lapping up whatever crumbs of power he deigns to toss your way?" I shake my head in mock disappointment. "That's just sad, dude. Have you no sense of self-respect?"

Azrael materializes before me; his handsome features contort with rage, but I barrel on, undaunted. If I'm going down, I might as well go down swinging...and give him a few well-deserved verbal jabs in the process.

"But I guess that's what happens when you're a sniveling little bitch who can't cut it on his own merits," I taunt with a derisive snort. "You latch onto the first big bad who promises to make you a real boy, and next thing you know, you're his bitch doing all the dirty work while he sits on his throne getting his cloven hooves massaged."

The area grows very cold. My veins turn to ice. "Oh, my mistake then," he growls, the words laced with venom.

The shadows have now engulfed the clearing in an inky shroud. I reach for my time-warping abilities, grasping at the threads of reality and pulling them taut until the world around me slows to a crawl.

The manifested shadows drift like tendrils of smoke, their movements languid and ponderous in this dilated plane of existence. I zero in on the nearest wisp, channeling a concentrated beam of celestial light that lances through the gloom and strikes true.

The shadow recoils like a wounded serpent, Azrael's anguished roar echoing through the stillness as time snaps back into its natural flow with dizzying force. I'm flung backward by an unseen blow, the world spinning as I crash to the ground in a bone-jarring impact.

Dazed, I struggle to push myself upright, blinking away the stars that dance across my vision. But before I can fully regain my bearings, a blur of movement catches my eye.

Azrael is on Damon, his clawed hand wrapped around my brother's throat as he hauls his broken form into the air with sickening ease. Damon fights feebly, his struggles growing weaker by the heartbeat as Azrael's merciless grip tightens.

"Azrael, no!" The scream tears from my lungs, raw and primal. "Let him go!"

But my pleas fall on deaf ears. With a sickening crack that seems to reverberate through my very soul, Damon's neck snaps, his body going limp and crumpling to the ground in a boneless heap.

I can't breathe—can't think—can't process what I've just witnessed as the world narrows to a single, horrifying point—my baby brother, broken and still, his life snuffed out before my eyes.

"DAMON!!"

The scream rips from my throat, shredding my vocal cords until all that's left is a hoarse, anguished wail. Tears streak down my face, scalding and salty, as ragged sobs wrack my body with the force of a hurricane.

"I didn't say he would leave here alive, now did I?" Azrael seethes. "You should learn, Dani. Never to trust me or anything I say."

Damon is dead. Gone—ruthlessly ripped away from me by the same evil son of a bitch that stole my parents, my childhood, my innocence. Adrian, John. The list of people this piece of shit has taken from me never ends.

A part of me dies with Damon at this moment, the fragile threads of my sanity fraying until they're ready to snap completely. My mind teeters on the edge of a black abyss, threatening to shatter into a million jagged pieces.

What's the point anymore?

After everything I've sacrificed and endured, how much more can one person take before they simply...break? I've given my heart, soul, and humanity to serve a destiny I never asked for. And for what? More death? More unendurable agony?

I want to surrender, to let the darkness swallow me whole and find oblivion's cold embrace. Rhyland, Erik, Seraphina, Emily, Lucian...even they can't undo this loss, can't fill the void Damon's death has carved into my very being.

I've lost too much and witnessed too many horrors—felt too much pain.

He's taken everything from me that I hold dear.

Damon's sacrifice is the final straw that shatters what little remains of my spirit into a million jagged shards. As Azrael's shadow falls over me again, I wonder if the cold caress of oblivion would be a welcome reprieve from this endless cycle of torment.

I crawl to Damon's body, ultimately defeated. "D-Dam-on." I choke the words.

The Atherite stone—it has to work. it worked on Emily—

"You know," Azrael muses, his voice a dark caress that sets my skin crawling with disgust. "It's so easy to break you, weak humans. All it takes is playing on your bleeding heart and poof." He chuckles, the sound grating like nails on a chalkboard. "You're as useless as flies on shit."

I'm crying, sobbing uncontrollably as I crawl towards Damon's lifeless form, the rest of the world fading into a blur around me. Nothing else matters but reaching him, cradling what little remains of the brother I failed to protect.

I begin to focus on the power of the Atherite....

Azrael has other plans. With casual ease, he snatches me up, his fingers encircling my throat in a vice-like grip that steals my breath. I choke and gasp, clawing futilely at his unyielding grasp as my feet leave the ground, kicking uselessly.

Azrael's cold, soulless eyes lock onto mine, endless voids threatening to pull me into their depths. "No, I don't think I'll let you use that rock on your dear old brother," he sneers, with cruel amusement. "This is far too enjoyable—watching you fall apart."

His gaze sweeps over me with a hunger that makes my skin crawl. "But you can still be useful. Your blood—so delectable. Remember, I have every vampire under my command ready to hunt you down and drain you dry. Your little secret? It's out in the open now."

His lips twist into a vicious imitation of a smile. "I'm quite impressed you followed directions and didn't bring that Viking lapdog of yours. I wonder how he'd react if I took another bite? Do you think he'd mind sharing his precious pet? I'm dying to know what the sun feels like..."

Panic claws at my chest. Every vampire will be after me, my worst fears coming to life.

The memory of his fangs piercing my flesh, the searing agony and vile sense of violation, ignites a firestorm of hatred and terror that steals what little breath I have left. I shudder, my hands flying to claw at his wrist, desperate to break free from his merciless grip.

My angelic fire is no longer attainable as Azrael's shadows engulf me, suffocating me—I can't breathe. The whispering starts in my head.

"You're worthless."

"No one cares about you."

"You couldn't even save your family."

"What Kind of savior are you?"

"Your brother is dead because of you."

It's right. I couldn't save any of my family.

I close my eyes—I want to give in—give up.

His grip on my throat tightens.

But even as the darkness creeps in at the edges of my vision, that defiant spark inside me refuses to be extinguished. I glare at Azrael through the haze of tears and pain, baring my teeth in a savage snarl.

"I d-don't k-know," I rasp the words, tearing at my abused throat. "Why don't you f-fuck around and f-find out?"

Azrael's eyes glitter with dark amusement at my bravado, his lips quirking in a mocking semblance of a smile. "Such *fire*," he murmurs, leaning in until his face is inches from mine, near enough for me to feel his fetid breath on my skin. "I do so love it when you fight back, Dani. It makes the game so much more... invigorating."

His fingers tighten inexorably, cutting off what little air I have left. Black spots dance across my vision as I claw desperately at his hand, my nails scrabbling against unyielding stone. The world begins to fade, the edges of my consciousness fraying as the darkness closes in.

Azrael's putrid, scalding breath assaults my neck, his fangs glistening with venom and drool as he zeroes in for the kill. The stench of decay and malice rolling off him nearly makes me retch, his closeness a vile invasion that sets every nerve alight with revulsion and dread.

Just as I resign myself to oblivion's cold embrace, a roar of pure, unbridled fury shatters the night's stillness.

Rhyland.

DANICA

93

I slam into the ground as Rhyland collides with Azrael like a runaway train, the impact shaking the earth beneath me. I cough and splutter, my lungs screaming for air as I struggle to draw breath. Seraphina and Emily are beside me instantly, their hands reaching to steady me as I try to find my footing.

But I brush them off, my eyes scanning the clearing frantically for one thing and one thing only—Damon.

Where is he?

I crawl forward, my fingers clawing at the dirt and leaves, my vision blurred by a haze of tears and the black spots that dance at the edges of my vision. And then I see him, lying motionless just ahead, his broken body illuminated by the otherworldly flashes of light that split the sky.

"Damon..." I try to call, but the word emerges as a broken whisper, my vocal cords ravaged.

Behind me, the sounds of battle rage—the crack of splintering trees, the boom of thunder, the sizzle of magic in the air. But it's all distant, muffled, drowned out by the pounding of my heart in my ears as I drag myself towards my brother's still form.

I reach him at last, falling to my knees beside him, my hands shaking as I press them to his chest. I close my eyes, reaching deep within myself for that well of power, that spark of life that brought Emily back from the brink. I focus through the pain, the grief, the soul-shattering loss, pouring everything I have into the unmoving body beneath my hands.

But there's nothing.

No answering flicker of life, no surge of healing energy. Just a yawning void where my power should be.

"Dani!" Emily's scream pierces the haze of my concentration, but I ignore her, refusing to break the connection, to give up on the only family I have left.

It's not working.

No. Please. I beg silently, my heart shattering with every second that passes. Please, bring him back. Please don't do this to me. It's not fair. Why him? Why now?

I slam my fists against Damon's chest, desperation giving way to rage. "No! Damnit! You can't do this to me. It's not fair! WHY?!" I scream at the uncaring heavens, my voice raw and broken.

This stupid fucking stone is worthless!

"Seraphina!" I scream, my voice tearing from my throat. She's beside me instantly, her golden eyes wide with urgency.

"Help me. My stone... it's not working... you have to get it to work, please!" I beg, my hands trembling as I hold my lifeless brother.

Seraphina glances at the stone, then back to me, her eyes swimming with sadness I can't afford to see right now. I need her to fucking fix this. "Dani... I can't. It's too late. He's—"

"No." I shake my head violently, sobs ripping from my chest. Hot tears are cascading down my cheeks. "No, Seraphina. It's not too late—Help me!"

Tears spill down her face, her voice breaking, "Dani, listen to me. The stone chooses. It's not working because he's—"

Suddenly, I'm tackled and lifted off the ground, the world spinning as solid arms wrap around my waist. Out of the corner of my eye, I see flames erupting where I had been kneeling just moments before, the intense heat scorching my skin even from afar.

I glance back and see Seraphina, her wings encasing her like a cocoon, shielding her from the inferno.

Lucian looks down at me, Damon's lifeless body cradled in his other arm. "Dani, you need to wake the fuck up and get back in this. Look around."

I blink slowly, the fog of grief and desperation receding just enough for me to take in the scene unfolding before me. The clearing is swarming with witches and werewolves, their eyes glowing with unholy light as they circle us like predators sizing up their prey. And in the center of it all, Rhyland and Azrael are locked in a battle that shakes the very foundations of the earth, lightning splitting the sky and thunder rattling my bones.

My grief consumed me; I was so fixated on saving Damon that I missed the fucking apocalypse unfolding before my eyes. Azrael, the conniving bastard, must have had this army waiting in the wings all along.

I turn back to Lucian, my heart shattering anew as reality sets in. "But... my brother," I choke out, clinging to that last, desperate thread of hope. "I have to save him, Lucian."

Sorrow etches deep lines on Lucian's face. "I don't think you can save him, Princess," he says softly. "But you can help your man—he needs you. We all need you."

The words hit me like a physical blow. Lucian is right. I can't save my brother, but maybe I can still save everyone else.

With a shuddering breath, I force myself to my feet. I brush a strand of hair from Damon's pale, still face, my fingers lingering on his cool skin.

"I'm sorry," I whisper, the words catching in my throat. "I'm so sorry, Damon. I failed you. But I swear on everything, I will make this right. I will make that bastard pay for what he's done."

I turn to face the chaos around me, and the scene that greets my eyes is nothing short of apocalyptic.

Emily stands at the center of a firestorm, her hands outstretched as flames dance between her fingertips. With each gesture, gouts of flame erupt from the ground, incinerating anyone foolish enough to draw near. The scent of burning flesh and hair fills the air, mingling with acrid smoke.

Nearby, vampires hurl themselves at her, only to be repelled by a shimmering wall of energy. They crumple to the ground, writhing and clawing at their heads, shrieking in agony as blood pours from their eyes and ears.

Vivienne and Alaric move through the battlefield with lethal grace. Vivienne's silver blade flashes in the moonlight, each swing precise and devastating. A feral vampire lunges at her, and without breaking stride, she brings her blade up in a vicious arc. There's a sickening squelch as steel meets flesh, followed by a spray of dark arterial blood. The vampire's head separates from its body with a wet pop.

Beside her, Alaric fights with brutal efficiency. His massive hands close around a vampire's throat, squeezing until he tears the creature's head clean off its shoulders. A fountain of blood erupts from the stump of its neck, painting Alaric's chest in a grisly crimson sheen.

Erik moves like quicksilver through the battlefield, his sword flashing in the firelight. Each swing sends fountains of blood arcing through the air, painting the ground crimson. Severed limbs and heads litter the battlefield, the air filled with the wet, meaty sounds of tearing flesh and snapping bone.

Lucian and Seraphina leap into action, a whirlwind of power and precision. Seraphina moves with ethereal poise, her wings both shield and blade as she dispatches vampires with bursts of divine radiance. Beside her, Lucian is a force of nature, his hands rending undead flesh and bone like wet clay. In one fluid motion, he plunges his fist into a vampire's chest, ripping out the beast's heart and reducing it to a gory pulp in his grasp.

Brandon, mid-transformation, launches at another werewolf. The two beasts collide in midair, a tangle of fur and fangs. Brandon's jaws close around his opponent's throat, ripping out the jugular in a spray of crimson.

My stomach churns at the brutality, bile rising in my throat. The air is thick with the metallic tang of blood and the stench of death. Screams of agony mingle with bestial howls and the thunderous clash of supernatural forces.

Something shifts within me as I watch the people I love risk everything. The fear and grief crystallize into cold, hard resolve.

This ends now.

I will see Azrael fall whatever it takes, whatever price I have to pay for Damon, my mother, my parents, Adrian, and every life this monster has destroyed in his quest for power.

I clench my fists, feeling celestial energy building beneath my skin. As I throw myself into the fray, I silently vow that our side will be left standing when the dust settles.

No matter the cost.

I reach into my pocket, my fingers closing around the syringe. My eyes lock onto Rhyland and Azrael, two titans locked in a deadly dance of shadow and lightning.

I run, my feet pounding against the ground. I need an opening, a moment when Azrael's form solidifies from the shifting shadows. More than that, I need to tap into the same power I wielded in Aquaria. I need to stop time itself.

As I sprint towards my target, the battlefield becomes a deadly obstacle course. Fire rains around me, the heat searing my skin as I weave and dodge. Vampires and werewolves lunge at me from every side, their eyes glazed with bloodlust and feral rage.

A massive werewolf leaps into my path, its jaws snapping mere inches from my face. I drop into a slide, my momentum carrying me beneath the beast's underbelly.

I unleash a concentrated beam of holy light, the power surging through me like a river of molten gold. The effect is instantaneous and horrifying. The werewolf's underside splits open like overripe fruit, its innards spilling out in a steaming mass of gore. The stench of burning flesh and hair assaults my nostrils as the creature erupts into flames, its agonized whimpers lost in the din of battle.

I tuck and roll, springing back to my feet without missing a beat.

Two vampires materialize before me, their faces twisted into snarls of hunger and malice. I leap into the air, turning in a fluid arc as I call upon every ounce of my warrior training. I unleash twin beams of celestial light from my palms.

The vampires are engulfed in a blaze of pure, radiant energy. For a moment, they hang suspended, their bodies lit up like macabre lanterns. Then, with a sickening pop, they implode, their flesh and bone disintegrating into a fine mist of blood and ash.

I land in a crouch, the remains of my foes splattering against my skin in a warm, sticky spray. I swipe a hand across my face, smearing crimson streaks through the grime and sweat.

There's no time to be disgusted or process the horror of what I've just done. Rhyland and Azrael are still locked in their titanic struggle, the fate of everything hanging in the balance.

I push myself back to my feet and run, the syringe slick in my grip. As I draw closer, I can see the toll the battle takes on Rhyland and Azrael. Rhyland's shirt is in tatters, revealing angry red welts and deep gashes across his chest and arms. Azrael's once-immaculate suit is singed and torn, half his face a blistered, blackened mess.

I watch as Rhyland lands a devastating strike, his fist slamming into Azrael's jaw with a sickening crunch. The demon's head snaps back, black ichor spraying from his shattered teeth.

Rhyland can't use his telekinesis on this slippery fucker, as he keeps shifting through shadows. But Rhyland unleashes holy hell with lightning, landing a few brutal strikes. Azrael's face bears the scorched proof of Rhyland's power.

Azrael retaliates with a blast of pure, malevolent energy. The shadows coalesce into a writhing mass of tentacles and claws, lashing out at Rhyland.

I take a deep breath, reaching for that wellspring of power. The world around me slows, each moment stretching out into an eternity.

I push harder, pouring every ounce of my will into the effort. The energy builds until I feel like I might burst from its force.

And then, with a silent cry of triumph, I let it go.

The world stops. The battlefield, the forest, the very air itself—it all freezes in place, locked in a single, timeless moment. Rhyland and Azrael hover in mid-strike, their faces frozen in masks of rage and determination.

I move through the eerie stillness, my footsteps echoing in the unnatural silence. I approach Azrael from behind, my heart hammering against my ribs.

I raise the syringe, my hand trembling with fear and anticipation. I aim for the back of Azrael's neck, the needle poised over his pale, exposed flesh.

I steel myself, drawing in a deep, shuddering breath. And then, with a final, silent prayer, I plunge the needle deep into Azrael's flesh and push the plunger home.

I release my grip on time, and the world surges back into motion like a film reel suddenly kicked into high gear. The chaos of battle resumes in a dizzying blur of violence and sound.

Without hesitation, I unleash a torrent of celestial fire at Azrael's back. He whirls, surprise etched across his features for a fleeting moment before he shifts into shadow. But his form wavers, insubstantial as smoke, and he staggers like a drunkard.

I lock eyes with Rhyland, a silent message passing between us.

Shadows Grasp.

Understanding dawns in his gaze, quickly replaced by a cold, ruthless determination. He advances on Azrael with predatory grace, every muscle coiled and ready to strike.

Azrael collapses to his knees, black ichor oozing from his mouth. His flesh smokes and chars, the stench of burning sulfur filling the air. "What... what have you done?" he chokes out, his voice a wet, gurgling rasp.

Rhyland doesn't waste words. He plunges his fist into Azrael's chest with a snarl of pure hatred. The sound of rending flesh and cracking bone turns my stomach, but I can't look away. "This is for every goddamn thing you've done, you fucking bastard," he snarls, his face a mask of primal rage. "For Adrian, for Dani, for her whole fucking family. I hope you rot in the deepest pits of hell for all eternity, you worthless sack of shit!"

With a sickening, wet sound, Rhyland rips Azrael's heart from his chest. The organ pulses obscenely in his grasp, black blood oozing between his fingers. Azrael makes a horrific gurgling noise, his body convulsing before he topples over, his form turning to stone as the *true death* claims him at last.

Rhyland reaches down, tearing the ring from Azrael's lifeless hand and pocketing the Soul Stone. With a final, contemptuous spit on the piece of shit, he turns to face me.

His Nordic blue eyes are a storm of emotions—fear, regret, anger, and relief, all warring for dominance. I run to him, throwing myself into his arms with a sob. He catches me, crushing me to his chest so tightly I fear my ribs might crack. But I don't care. I bury my face in his neck, breathing him in as the tears fall unchecked.

Rhyland holds me; no words are needed as I pour my grief into his skin. The loss of Damon is a raw, gaping wound in my heart, the pain as fresh as the blood staining my hands.

Screams shatter our moment, a harsh reminder that the battle still rages around us. Rhyland sets me down, his expression grim. "This isn't over yet."

He blurs us back into the fray, and I waste no time unleashing hell on Azrael's remaining forces. White-hot fire explodes from my hands, scorching witches, vampires, and werewolves alike. The stench of burning flesh mingles with the coppery tang of blood, a nauseating cocktail that coats the back of my throat.

The battle seems to stretch for an eternity, each second marked by another life snuffed out, another enemy felled. It's not until Erik rips the heart from the last vampire, the creature's dying scream echoing across the clearing, that stillness finally descends.

Exhausted, I slump to the ground, my lungs burning with each ragged breath. Blood, soot, and gore paint my skin and clothes, the stench of death clinging to me like a second skin.

Through the haze of smoke and carnage, I see Rhyland approaching, his form battered but unbroken. He's drenched in blood, his clothes hanging in tattered ruins, but the set of his shoulders speaks of grim triumph.

Just as I allow myself to believe it's finally over, the sky splits open with a blinding flash of light—a swirling vortex of color slams into the earth directly on top of

Rhyland. The force of it sends shockwaves rippling through the ground, blasting me back—hard up against a tree.

I roll and try to catch my breath. My lungs scream as the wind is knocked out of me.

Rhyland struggles against the vortex's pull, the cosmic winds whipping at his hair and clothes. "Danica!" he shouts, his voice nearly lost in the roar of energy.

"Rhyland!" I scream, sprinting towards him with every ounce of strength I have left. Lucian and Erik blur past me, throwing themselves into the maelstrom in a desperate attempt to reach him.

Erik and Lucian are hurled backward by the sheer force of the vortex, their bodies smashing through trees as if they were twigs. They crash into the ground with the impact of a meteorite, leaving craters in the earth. They lie there, limp and unmoving, as if life itself had been knocked out of them.

With a final, desperate lunge, I hurl myself toward Rhyland. The wind tears at my hair, raging like a hurricane. My fingertips stretch out toward him, our hands almost touching. Then, with a deafening crack, the vortex vanishes, taking Rhyland with it.

Another blast rocks the open area like a shockwave, throwing me across the field—I hit the ground hard, the impact driving the air from my lungs for the second time. I can only lie here, stunned and disbelieving, as the reality of what just happened sinks in.

Rhyland is gone—vanished into the aether, stolen away by forces beyond my comprehension.

I hack and wheeze, my lungs desperately trying to remember how this whole 'breathing' thing works.

As I look up, my heart stops. Damon is walking towards me, his form silhouetted against the smoke-filled sky.

This can't be real. My mind must be playing tricks on me, conjuring up mirages in the aftermath of trauma.

"Damon?" My voice is barely a whisper.

Something's not right. As Damon draws closer, I see his eyes—they're red, the sclera shot through with crimson veins. It's like looking into the eyes of a stranger wearing my brother's face.

A sudden, desperate hope surges through me. Did the stone work? Did it some-how bring him back, even after I'd given up all hope?

I lurch forward, ignoring the screaming protest of my battered muscles and possibly broken ribs. Each step is agony, but I push through, driven by the need to reach him, to feel the solid warmth of his presence, and know this isn't just some cruel hallucination.

As I inch closer, a sinister transformation overtakes Damon's face. It starts with subtle shifts, his features contorting in a way that sends icy tendrils crawling up my spine. Then, in a heart-stopping instant, his visage warps into a grotesque, inhuman mask. Hunger and malice twist his expression into a snarling nightmare. Elongated fangs glint menacingly.

He's become the very thing he despises.

Damon's voice is a guttural growl. "I'm hungry."

In a blink, he's on top of me, moving with an inhuman speed and savagery that shatters reality. Searing agony explodes through my body as his fangs rip into my neck, tearing through flesh and sinew. A scream tears from my throat, primal and raw, echoing through the darkness.

The shadows creep closer, suffocating me, as a devastating realization slams into my consciousness with the force of a wrecking ball. Rhyland is gone, vanished into the ether, and the Soul Stone—that cursed, ancient relic—is clutched in his grasp. And here I am, staring down the barrel of my demise, about to be snuffed out by my own brother.

What have I done?

RHYLAND

94

I slam down hard on the floor, my body screaming in agony as I hit the ground with a sickening thud. My thoughts are whirring, my mind reeling as I try to process what the hell just happened. That vortex, that swirling maelstrom of light and energy…it felt like it was melting the flesh from my bones—the G-force was tearing me apart atom by fucking atom.

I retch, my stomach heaving as I puke up blood onto the gleaming surface beneath me. The coppery taste fills my mouth, and I wipe my arm across my lips, smearing crimson across my skin.

Slowly, painfully, I push myself to my feet, my eyes scanning my surroundings with growing confusion. This place… it's like nothing I've ever seen before. The walls are adorned with intricate, futuristic glyphs that seem to pulse with an otherworldly energy. A massive circular globe dominates the center of the room, its surface shimmering with a kaleidoscope of colors that hurts my eyes.

My mind flashes back to the fight, to the moment when Azrael fell at my feet, his life bleeding out onto the ground. The triumph I feel is so thick, so visceral, that I want to roar with it, to scream my victory to the heavens. The way I wielded the lightning, the way I cast it at that fucking bastard… it was unlike anything I've ever experienced.

His shadows were quick, dodging my assault with an almost beautiful fluidity. But when he materialized, when he finally showed his face… I was ready. I hit him with everything I had, my power crackling like a living thing. And when I ripped out his heart, when I felt it pulsing in my hand… fuck, it was glorious.

I look down at my hand, still slick with his blood and viscera. The sight should repulse me, should make me sick to my stomach. But all I feel is a dark, savage satisfaction.

My thoughts instantly return to Dani. The look of sheer panic on her face as the vortex swallowed me whole. I reach for her through the bond, desperate to feel her and know she's okay. But there's nothing—just a yawning emptiness where our connection used to be.

Is she feeling it, too? The ripped-out, hollowed-out feeling in her chest? The sense that a piece of her very soul has been torn away?

I clench my fists, my nails biting into my palms hard enough to draw blood. I have to get back to her. I have to find a way out of this fucking place and back to my mate. Back to the woman who holds my heart in her hands.

I look around at the alien landscape, at the strange, pulsing energy that seems to permeate every surface... I can't help but wonder if I'm already too late.

If I'm lost to her forever, trapped in a world that's not my own.

And the thought is enough to bring me to my knees, to make me want to howl with a despair so deep, so all-consuming, that it threatens to swallow me whole.

Tiny whispers begin to gnaw at my conscience—the siren call of the Soul Stone. I slam the door on them, barricading my mind against their insidious pull. I can't afford to lose focus, not now. Getting out of here alive is the only thing that matters.

I take a tentative step towards what appears to be a door, but its sheer scale makes me pause. It's fucking massive, towering over me like a colossus, and it looks like it's made of pure, unyielding steel. My eyes scan the surface, searching for a keypad, a handle, or anything that might give me a way to open it. But there's nothing—just a smooth, unbroken expanse of metal.

Suddenly, the door opens with a deep, resonant boom that echoes through the chamber. The two halves slide apart on some unseen mechanism, revealing a figure standing on the other side.

I stumble back, my heart hammering in my chest as I take in the sight of him. He's enormous, easily dwarfing me in both height and breadth. His armor is like nothing I've ever seen, all gleaming gold and intricate engravings that seem to shimmer with an inner light. He holds a massive staff, the metal as bright and polished as his armor.

He walks towards me with a measured, almost regal gait. His glowing pale green eyes are fixed on mine with an intensity that makes me want to look away. But I force myself to hold his gaze, to meet his stare with one of my own.

"Welcome to Asgard," he says, his voice deep and resonant. "We've been looking for you."

THE SEVEN REALMS

 1. Atheria. The Realm of Light and Creation. It is a realm of divine beauty and purity where celestial beings and creatures of light reside. It is a place of harmony and enlightenment, where the power of creation flows freely, shaping the fabric of existence.

 2. Aquaria. The Realm of Water. Aquaria is a vast world with vibrant marine life and mystical creatures, such as Merfolk, Skelkies, and Pirates. It is a realm of serenity and fluidity where the ebb and flow of tides hold great power.

 3. Luminara—The fae reigns supreme in the realm of Luminara, a world filled with enchanting beauty and mystical wonders. Luminara is a realm of ethereal forests, shimmering lakes, and glowing meadows, where the natural world is interwoven with magic and wonder.

 4. Mortalis—The Mortal Realm, where humanity resides with immortals and explores the boundaries of their existence. It has diverse landscapes, bustling cities, and uncharted territories. Humans navigate their everyday lives in Mortalis, unaware of the existence of other realms.

 5. Pyrothos—The Realm of Fire. Pyrothos is a land of perpetual flames and scorching heat, where volcanic landscapes and fiery mountains dominate. It is a realm of passion and intensity, where the essence of fire fuels the powers of its inhabitants. Pyrothos is home to powerful fire elementals, fire-breathing creatures, and ancient fire temples.

 6. Unbra—The Realm of Shadows. A world consumed by eternal darkness, where pure evil lurks, and creatures of nightmarish origins dwell. It is a realm shrouded in mystery and treachery, harboring ancient secrets and maleficent forces.

 7. Zephyria—Realm of Sky and Air— Zephyria is breathtaking, with endless skies and gentle breezes. No one knows what this realm is besides vast expanses of open air, where the wind guides the movement of everything.

THANK YOU

ey You, Yes You—The Amazing Reader Who Just Finished Book Three!

First off, high-fives, hugs, and a whole parade in your honor, because you? You're the real MVP here. Give yourself a round of applause for sticking with Dani and Rhyland through another chapter of their pulse-pounding, realm-hopping escapades.

Thank you from the bottom of my caffeine-fueled heart for diving back into the whirlwind world of the Crown of the Seven Realm series. Your support means the world to me and quite possibly to all seven realms (they're still counting votes on that one). These characters and their stories are my babies; you've just helped them grow.

Now, take a breath, grab a snack, and pat yourself on the back because you've survived the twists, turns, and cliffhangers (oh, the cliffhangers!). Your dedication to following our fearless (and sometimes fearsome) lovebirds on their journey is more appreciated than you know.

But hold onto your hats—or crowns—because this roller coaster isn't done yet. Get ready for Book Four, **DARK SKIES**, which is lurking just beyond the horizon, and it's packed with more realm-hopping shenanigans that'll test the limits of our fearless heroes.

Keep an eye out because Dani and Rhyland will be back before you can say "realm-hoping romance," and trust me, you won't want to miss the next leg of their journey. So, recharge your reading device, mark your calendars, follow me on social media to stay in the loop, and prepare your favorite reading nook. It's going to be a ride you'll never forget.

Until our paths cross again in the pages of Book Four, I'm sending loads of gratitude and the promise of more thrills, more heart, and yes, more swoon-worthy moments.

With all my thanks and anticipation,

A.L HAMPTON

Your Favorite Portal-Pushing Author, A.L. Hampton

ACKNOWLEDGMENTS

This book? Oh, it wouldn't even exist without some absolute legends! To my rockstar beta readers—**Kerry Taylor, Talia Harris, and Samantha Parisi**—you dove into those messy early drafts like pros, dishing out feedback gold while dragging me through those tough writing days. You're the true MVPs here!

And a massive shoutout to my fabulous ARC readers: Honestly, I couldn't have pulled this off without my amazing squad. Your faith in my wild storytelling fuels my creative engine like espresso on a Monday morning! Thanks for turning this dream into a reality as glamorous as a red carpet.

Special love to my friend and indie author cheerleader extraordinaire **Enola Henderson.** Your relentless support and promo hustle? Total game-changer! And to my friends and fam—thank you for tolerating my writerly obsessions and constant book chatter. Special thanks to my husband—your relentless cheerleading is basically my secret weapon.

A mega special thank you to **Talia!** Seriously, thanks for putting up with my shenanigans throughout this entire writing adventure. I lost count of how many late-night talks we had or how many times I begged you to read my latest ramblings—LOL! You're officially my hero!

To the fantasy community and my fellow indie authors: You all rock! Thanks for the inspiration and the warm welcome into this magical world.

And last, but certainly not least, to my fabulous readers: Your enthusiasm for the Crown of the Seven Realm Series is the cherry on top of this literary sundae. Thank you for every read, comment, and burst of excitement. You make this whole journey utterly worth it!

About the Author

Hi there! I'm A.L. Hampton, and like so many of you, I've been completely obsessed with books for as long as I can remember. There's nothing quite like getting completely lost in a story—you know that feeling when you look up and realize hours have passed? That's my happy place.

I'm absolutely head-over-heels for fantasy, urban fantasy, romantasy, and anything dark and paranormal. And yes, I'm totally here for the spice! After years of devouring every book I could get my hands on in these genres, I found myself thinking, "What if I combined all my favorite elements into one series?" That's how the Crown of the Seven Realms Series was born. I'm a total sucker for witty banter and characters that feel like real people— flawed, funny, and fierce. When I'm not busy torturing my characters, you'll find me gaming, or exploring the gorgeous Pacific Northwest with my patient husband and two spoiled dogs.

My background is a bit all over the place—I have an A.A. in Criminal Justice, a B.S. in Psychology, and an M.Ed. in Education. Turns out, studying human behavior comes in pretty handy when you're trying to write believable characters and relationships!

As a debut author, I'm beyond excited to share these stories with fellow book lovers.

Welcome to my world!
-A.L. Hampton

ALSO BY A.L. HAMPTON